BAEN BOOKS
BY JERRY POURNELLE

Fires of Freedom
Birth of Fire
Exile—and Glory

Oath of Fealty (with Larry Niven)

Fallen Angels (with Larry Niven & Michael Flynn)

The Prince (with S.M. Stirling)

LORD OF JANISSARIES

Jerry Pournelle
Roland J. Green

BAEN

LORD OF JANISSARIES

This is a work of fiction. All the characters and events portrayed in this book are fictional, and any resemblance to real people or incidents is purely coincidental.

A Baen Books Original

Baen Publishing Enterprises
P.O. Box 1403
Riverdale, NY 10471
www.baen.com

ISBN: 978-1-4767-8079-5

Cover art by Kurt Miller

First Baen Printing, September 2015

Distributed by Simon & Schuster
1230 Avenue of the Americas
New York, NY 10020

Library of Congress Cataloging-in-Publication Data

Pournelle, Jerry, 1933-
[Novels. Selections]
Lord of Janissaries / Jerry Pournelle and Roland J. Green.
    pages ; cm. -- (Baen ; 1)
ISBN 978-1-4767-8079-5 (softcover)
1. Imaginary wars and battles--Fiction. 2. Human-alien encounters--Fiction. 3. Life on other planets--Fiction. I. Green, Roland J. II. Pournelle, Jerry, 1933- Janissaries. III. Pournelle, Jerry, 1933- Clan and crown. IV. Pournelle, Jerry, 1933- Storms of victory. V. Title. VI. Title: Janissaries. VII. Title: Clan and crown. VIII. Title: Storms of victory.
PS3566.O815A6 2015
813'.54--dc23

                        2015025465

Printed in the United States of America

10 9 8 7 6 5 4 3 2

⊹⇒ CONTENTS ⇐⊹

Janissaries

Part One: Mercenaries 1
Part Two: Ship 37
Part Three: Tylara 63
Part Four: The Crossroads 89
Part Five: Tamaerthon 111
Part Six: War Leader 131
Part Seven: Scholars 163
Part Eight: Janissaries 189
Epilogue 214

Tran

A Political Glossary 219
Dramatis Personae 221

Clan and Crown 227

Part One: Thrones and Dominions 229
Part Two: If This Be Treason 275
Part Three: Angels and Ministers of Grace 327
Interlude: Luna 382
Part Four: Invaders 387
Part Five: Principalities and Powers 413
Part Six: Wanax and Warlord 461
Part Seven: Sky God 529

Storms of Victory 557

Part One: Searching 559
Interlude: Luna 629
Interlude: Gwen Tremaine's Diary 633
Part Two: Discoveries 637
Interlude: Gwen Tremaine's Diary 671
Part Three: Prophets 673
Interlude: D'jorr 629
Part Four: The Royal Sacrifice 734
Part Five: Affairs of Honor 765
Interlude: Luna 822
Part Six: Church and State 827
Maps 882

JANISSARIES

JERRY POURNELLE

To Tom Doherty

PART ONE
MERCENARIES

1

The mortar fire was nearer.

Rick Galloway heard the sharp *crump!* of at least five mortars. Then there was silence for a moment. It was just twilight, and twilight does not last in the tropics. Night came fast, and with it the sound of the African tropic highlands: birds, crickets, unidentifiable creatures calling each other in the sudden dark. A warm breeze rustled the dry grass on the hilltop.

There was a rattle of distant machine-gun fire. It sounded much too close.

"I think the roadblock has gone," Lieutenant Parsons said. His voice was surprisingly calm. "They will be here within the hour."

"Yeah." Captain Galloway swept his night glasses along the southern slope of the hill, down toward the crossroad where he had left Major Hendrix with the wounded. There was nothing to see. He turned carefully, letting the glasses sweep the perimeter of the hill that for the moment was his entire world. He saw nothing at all except the tiny remnant of his command. The men were digging in and had done a good job with the little they had.

"Where the hell are those choppers?" Galloway demanded. He felt sweat drip from his forehead despite the cooling breeze that sprang up after sundown. "Elliot."

"Sir." Sergeant Elliot was at the other end of the trench where Galloway stood. The trench had not been bunkered, but there was no time to construct better defenses for the command post.

"Can't you raise headquarters?" Galloway demanded.

"No, sir. Warner's trying." The big sergeant turned back to the radio.

"Perhaps we should let the men run for it," Parsons suggested. "Some may escape."

Rick shook his head. "What's to run to?" he asked.

Parsons shrugged. "We sell our lives to no purpose—"

"We're giving our employers another hour," Galloway said. His voice was as bitter as he felt, although he had tried to hide his feelings. "There's no point, André," Galloway said. "We don't speak the language, we're the wrong color, and we're surrounded. I expect half the troops have run anyway. They know the score. Elliot!"

"Sir."

"How many effectives do we have?"

"Maybe fifty, Captain."

"So there you are," Rick said. "About half the number we brought up this silly hill. The rest have run." He knew he was talking too much, saying too many words; but he was young and inexperienced, and afraid.

Parsons nodded in the darkness. He took a plastic bottle from his belt. "Wine?"

"Sure." Rick took the liter bottle and drank a couple of swallows of the cheap local wine. Parsons always carried a bottle. Rick was certain that "Parsons" wasn't the lieutenant's real name. Parsons spoke French and German and sometimes let slip a few words about Legion experience.

It hardly mattered. Rick wasn't a real captain, either. The operation was CIA, and the Agency had borrowed men from anywhere they could get them.

Galloway handed the bottle back to Parsons, who raised it in a mock toast. "Here's to us. There are damned few left."

"They're taking their own sweet time about coming," Rick said.

"Afraid of us." Parsons' voice was a mocking lilt in the dark.

"Sure," Galloway said. But they well might be, he thought. We've broken more than one Cuban mercenary outfit. With any help at all from the politicians who put us out here in Sainte Marie, we'd have won. At that it was a near thing. What was it Wellington said about Waterloo? A near-run thing—as near a thing as you'd ever hope to see. Well so was this, but the difference is it's us who lost it.

Officially they were volunteers, and received no direct support from the United States at all; but most of the men were veterans of the US Army, and the CIA had brought them in. The Cubans and Russians had made no secret at all of their aid to the other side.

"I got headquarters," Sergeant Elliot announced.

"*Mirabile dictu,*" Parsons muttered.

Rick crawled over to the radio. Perhaps prayers are answered after all, he thought. There was more automatic weapon fire from the south, and a mortar bomb dropped in fifty yards downhill. Rick estimated the enemy at less than a mile. It wouldn't be long now.

"Galloway here," he told the microphone. "Can you get us the hell out of here?"

"Negative."

The single word was a death sentence. Rick started to say that, then thought better of it. They knew. "Why not?"

"I'm sorry, Rick." Galloway recognized Colonel Blumfeld's voice. Blumfeld was one of the men who'd talked him into volunteering for this mission. "Washington has canceled all support. Highest level. I'd send the choppers anyway and to hell with my career, but I don't have any to send. They came and took them away."

"They?"

"Higher command." Blumfeld sounded unhappy. Rick thought he damned well ought to be unhappy. "Your orders are to surrender," Blumfeld said.

"Bat puckey. The Cubans will have us in a show trial as mercenaries," Rick said. "Then they'll shoot us."

"They say they won't."

"Sure. Colonel, are you sending me any support? Anything at all?"

"No."

"Then go to hell." Galloway handed the mike to Sergeant Elliot, then went back to where Parsons stood.

Parsons listened with a half-smile that barely showed in the starlight. Then he took out his wine bottle. "We had a good run," he said.

Rick reached for the bottle. "I'll drink to that."

"And now what?"

Rick shrugged. There were few choices. They were white men in a black country. Rick had always been quick to learn languages, but even he hadn't enough of the local patois to do more than buy groceries. They would be spotted easily wherever they went.

Major Jefferson had taken all the black troops on an infiltration raid. Rick hoped they'd escape, but without the black troops, there wasn't even the pretense of an integrated army. No blacks to speak and front for them. Rick wondered if that would matter. It might, depending on who captured them.

It was his first command, and very likely the only one he'd ever have. He wasn't experienced. He'd begun as a junior lieutenant, just out of ROTC from the state university, and his promotion to brevet captain was due to being in the right place and time; he knew better than to think it meant more.

Rick thought it didn't mean very much at all. Parsons was a career man, but the military wasn't Galloway's career. ROTC had been an easy way to pay for the college education he couldn't afford.

The other alternative was football. Rick was quick and wiry. Had he gone out for football, he could have got a scholarship, with all the other perquisites of a star. But he didn't like the game. It required too much commitment.

Instead, he had joined the track team and won his letter. Track didn't have the glamour of football; the football jocks got first choice of the girls. On the other hand, they often couldn't enjoy their opportunities because of injuries or training rules. Being a runner was definitely superior in Rick Galloway's view. He told himself that quite often. But track hadn't been important enough to the alumni; there weren't all those easy jobs available. ROTC had provided Rick's spending money.

When he graduated, Rick realized that he'd never committed himself to anything. He had neither joined a fraternity nor opposed them. He had few political opinions. He was a professional neutral, and he wasn't sure he liked the image.

A classmate, John Henry Carter, had been a career military man and had volunteered for the CIA operation in Africa. He had talked Rick into coming along; an adventure, something to do while he was young before he settled into a dull job and duller life. He'd known there was a possibility of being killed, but he'd never been seriously threatened in his life. He could outrun any danger.

Carter was the only black man Rick had ever known well, and the only friend he'd had in the outfit. Now Carter was off with Major Jefferson. Major Hendrix was missing a leg and had stayed behind to hold the roadblock south of them. Parsons and Galloway were the only officers left.

The plan had been for Galloway to take the hilltop and hold it until the helicopters came; then they could go back for the wounded. Rick hadn't liked the idea, but Hendrix made it an order. Someone had to hold the roadblock and someone else had to capture a landing area; Hendrix couldn't move, which left the hilltop to Galloway.

But Hendrix hadn't held the roadblock very long—and now there wouldn't be any helicopters.

And that's that, Rick thought. He had no choices left. For the first time, he couldn't even run . . .

Something caught his attention. Rick looked up. "What the hell?" He pointed toward the ink-black sky. A bright light moved among the stars. It seemed to come closer, and it made no sound at all. "Where did Labon get aircraft?" Rick demanded.

Parsons shrugged. "From the Cubans, I suppose—Rick, that is no aircraft."

He was right. The silent light moved closer, and in strange patterns like no airplane Rick had ever seen before. There was only the one light; it was impossible to make out the size or shape of the craft, but it blotted out stars. Too many stars. He realized with a shiver that it was *big*. It moved too fast and turned in weird patterns, and it moved in total silence. He felt the hair rising on the back of his neck.

It came lower, and a bright light stabbed down to illuminate the crest of the hill. There was enough light reflected upward to show what the tropical night had hidden.

"A goddamn flying saucer!" one of the troops shouted. There was a shot.

"Hold your fire!" Rick screamed.

Parsons looked at him curiously.

"That's nothing of Labon's. Why shoot at it? And—I'm not sure we *can* hurt it. . . ."

"It is landing," Parsons said.

"Of course." Rick felt an inane urge to giggle. Why not? he thought. We're defeated, surrounded, every one of us marked for a firing squad within the week, so why not flying saucers too? He felt lightheaded, and it was not just the wine. He was glad that he hadn't tried the local equivalent of pot.

Flying saucers weren't real. They weren't even science fiction. The girl he liked to think of as his mistress—he knew she'd have resented the label, and he'd never used it in her hearing, but he liked to think of himself as a man who'd once had a mistress—had been interested in science fiction, and had got Rick to read some of the classics; but neither she nor her friends "believed in" flying saucers.

The thing settled on the hilltop. It was very large, as big as a 707, and it wasn't precisely saucer-shaped, although seen edge on at a distance it might give that appearance. It was more like half a football sliced lengthwise, nearly flat at the bottom. It did nothing for a moment. Then a bright orange rectangle opened in the center of one side.

Sergeant Elliot caught up to him. Other troopers crawled into the CP trench. "What do we do, Captain?" Elliot demanded.

"Keep the men at their posts. There are still a thousand Cubans out there," Rick said. He studied the bright opening. Nothing happened. The only sounds were mutters from his own troops, and no one—or no *thing*—came out. "Take over," he told Parsons. "I'm going to have a look."

Parsons spread his hands in a wide gesture, a typical French shrug. "You are mad. But I will go with you—"

"No." Rick stared at the ship again. For a moment he felt rising hope. Could this be an experimental plane, something kept secret by the CIA and sent to get him out? The Agency had got them into this mess and would be embarrassed if they were captured. "Elliot, get headquarters."

"Can't, sir. Radio stopped working about the time we saw that thing."

"Flying saucer," someone muttered.

Rick had heard the stories. When people saw flying saucers, electrical gear stopped working. Ignition, radios, TV—anything electrical. But so what? He willed himself to believe that the Agency had sent this craft to rescue him. It made sense, even to risk a secret craft, in order to save the embarrassment of political trials and—

There was no point in just looking at it. He didn't want to go alone, but Parsons would have to remain in command, and Elliot would be needed to control the troops. He looked at the others who'd crawled into his CP. "Mason, come with me."

"Right." Mason was a corporal; a short, stocky man with a lot of self-confidence and a phlegmatic temperament. He'd do.

Rick slung his rifle and started forward. Mason carried his at the ready, walking just behind Rick. "I never believed in flying saucers," Mason said.

"Neither did I. Not sure I do now," Rick told him. "Could be the Agency coming for us."

"Yeah. Sure," Mason said.

Rick could guess how the man felt. Rick Galloway didn't believe it either. This was no illusion, no swamp gas. It wasn't the planet Venus or a weather balloon. This was a real ship which had silently landed on his hill, and it was too damned advanced to be anyone's secret weapon. Anyone with a fleet of ships like that could dictate terms to the whole world. The way it had come in, zipping along in silence and changing direction in random ways, it would be unstoppable by any missile or interceptor Rick had ever heard of.

He reached the lighted square. He could feel the troops behind staring at his back. The sounds of gunfire started up again off to the south, and probably half his troops had left their posts to come look at the ship. Others, though, were dug in, grimly waiting. They'd make the Cubans pay for the hill. But how long could they hold? Rick looked inside the ship.

The lighted square was a doorway into a small chamber about three meters on a side. There was no one inside, and there were few features to see except for what appeared to be sliding doors, closed, on three of the walls. The opening was less than two meters high, a bit low for Rick's six feet and a fraction. He stood outside looking in until he felt silly. Finally he shouted. "Anybody home?"

"Come in, Captain Galloway," a voice said. It was a perfectly ordinary male voice, nothing unearthly about it. "You have very little time, Captain. Come aboard."

"My God, maybe it is the Agency," Rick muttered. Whatever he'd expected, it hadn't been an ordinary human voice with an accent he couldn't place.

It spoke again. "You may leave your weapons outside. You will not need them, and they might tempt you to rash actions. If we wished you harm, Captain Galloway, you would be dead now."

That, Rick thought, was for sure. This thing—whatever it was—couldn't be worse than the Cubans. He unslung his rifle and laid it on the ground. Mason did the same, but threw him a significant look. Rick nodded. They both had knives, and Rick had his .45 automatic pistol under his jacket. He was certain that Mason had another.

The opening was inconveniently high off the ground, above waist level. "No gangplank for us," Rick told Mason. He put his hand on the sill. It felt like metal, but was slightly warm to the touch. "Here goes," he muttered, and vaulted in. Mason followed closely.

He had half-expected the opening to close once he was inside, but it did nothing. The doorway to his left slid open silently, revealing a short corridor. Rick gestured to Mason to follow and went down that. Another door slid open at the far end. The room beyond was very brightly lit.

He went in gingerly, feeling very much alone. Corporal Mason hadn't hesitated to lead an infantry attack on a Cuban tank two days before, and had himself crept up to it and blown off a tread with a satchel charge; he looked far more nervous now than when he went off to attack the tank. Rick wondered if he were as shaky as the corporal, tried to straighten up and get control of his face. It wouldn't do to let the troops see their officer shaken.

His eyes adjusted to the bright light. There were—beings—in the compartment. Three of them, and they were not human.

2

They were shaped like humans. They had two arms and two legs and two eyes, but the proportions were wrong. The shoulders were too high, almost as if they didn't have necks, and their heads rose from too-thick bodies. They wore clothing, coveralls of a shining metallic appearance, one dull grey, the other two in brighter colors that shimmered when they moved.

Their hands had only three fingers, but there were two thumbs—one on each side of a thick palm. They had no hair that Rick could see. Their lips were thin—far too thin to be human—and their mouths were too high on their strangely flat faces. Mouth too high, eyes too low, nose—not really a nose at all, Rick decided. Instead there was a fleshy snout-slit like a vertical second mouth. It rose until it almost reached the line joining the eyes.

It took an effort to look away from them and inspect the compartment. The room was nearly bare. All around the upper parts of the compartment there were screens, like TV sets but very thin. Some showed images: Rick's troops standing outside, Lieutenant Parsons and Sergeant Elliot talking and pointing, the machine-gun emplacements. The aliens seemed to have most of his defenses spotted, and their TV gave bright images although outside it was nearly pitch-dark.

The creatures sat at a long table placed crosswise to the door he had entered. It was too high—at least a foot higher than a table for humans would have been—and was transparent, but without the shimmer of glass, so that it was almost invisible. A small box with lights and colored squares rested on the table.

Rick had the impression of controls below some of the screens; at least there were flat plates about an inch square, some lit in bright colors, and others colored but dark. They might have been pushbuttons or touch-sensitive plates, but they might have been anything else. The room was as alien as the creatures.

Despite a strong desire to curl up in a corner and gibber, Rick studied the room carefully, trying to categorize and file the new information. He kept trying to convince himself this was a dream, but he knew better. Finally he was able to speak. "Hello."

When the aliens spoke, both the mouth and nose slits moved. "You have very little time, Captain Galloway," the grey-clad alien said. The voice was very matter-of-fact. It sounded masculine, but Rick reminded himself that he didn't know the creature's sex. Or, he thought, if they even *had* sexes. "Perhaps too little. We may have waited too long. We are here to rescue you and your men."

"Who the hell—"

"Later. There is no time."

Sure, Rick thought. Later. But the alien was right. The Cubans were approaching rapidly. He tried to organize his thoughts, but it was difficult to accept what he was doing, that he was talking with—things. The spokesman—man? No. Not a man. Not a spokesman, either, his mind gibbered. He had no concepts to use. Finally he found his voice. "What do you want with us?"

"For you to get your men aboard. Quickly, before you have none left." The alien spread its hands, palms down, in a gesture that meant nothing to Rick. The tone of its voice had not changed, but it was not difficult to guess that the alien was impatient. "As we have said before and doubtless must say many times again, if we wished you harm, you would be dead. What can we do to you that the Cubans will not accomplish within a few hours?"

The alien was obviously right, but that didn't make Rick feel much better. The "rescue" was not very appealing. "How do you know my name?" he demanded.

"From your radio. You have no more time for questions." This came from one of the creatures in bright coveralls. "You must act. Now."

"What about our weapons?"

"Bring them. Bring all of your equipment," Grey-coveralls said. "But quickly. When the Cubans are close enough to see us clearly, we must be gone. With or without you and your men."

"That's no choice at all, Cap'n," Corporal Mason said. "Better them than the Cubans." The trooper's voice was flat and without emotion.

"I'd thought of that," Rick said. He stood another moment in indecision, but he had made up his mind. "All right."

"Quickly," the alien urged.

"Sure. Come on, Mason—"

"You will leave him here," Grey-coveralls said. "As an earnest of your good intentions."

"Now, wait just a damned minute—"

"It's okay, Captain," Mason said. "I'm as safe here as out there."

"All right." Rick went back to the doorway. It opened for him. When he reached the entry chamber, another door opened on the side opposite the entrance to the chamber where the aliens sat. He saw a large empty compartment, more than fifty feet long and perhaps fifteen wide.

"Have the men go in there with their weapons," a voice said. It seemed to speak from the walls, but there was no sign of a speaker grille.

Rick jumped out of the ship and ran to his command post. Half the troops—perhaps more—had gathered there to stare at the ship. They stood clutching rifles and grenades for what comfort weapons could give.

"I did not entirely expect to see you again," Lieutenant Parsons said. "Welcome back."

"Thanks. We've got no time at all. Get the men aboard. Men, weapons, food, equipment, everything. Fast."

"But—" Sergeant Elliot was stammering. Rick had never seen the big sergeant confused before.

"That's a CIA ship," Rick said. He spoke loudly so that many of the troops could hear him. "Secret stuff. They've come to get us out, but they don't want the Cubans to see the ship, so we've got to load up quickly. Now move it."

"Sir!" Elliot ran over to the mortar emplacement, and some of the other troops gathered their gear and headed for the ship. Rick didn't know if he had fooled them or not, but the "CIA ship" explanation seemed the easiest and fastest way to handle the situation.

Parsons looked at him with raised eyebrows. His expression said clearly that he knew Rick was a liar. Then he shrugged and began urging the men onto the ship. Sergeant Elliot rounded up more.

Good troops, Rick thought. And each one had probably made the same decision: They *knew* what the Cubans could do. This was at least a chance.

The mortar team ran by with their tube, followed by others with the base and packs of mortar bombs. Men grabbed boxes and bandoliers of ammunition, stuffed their pockets with grenades. They were going aboard well armed.

Not, Rick thought, that it will do a hell of a lot of good. Weapons won't make us safer. But they do make us *feel* safer, and that's important.

"What is this nonsense?" Parsons demanded in a low voice. "You know that is not—"

"Can it. Hold onto the questions." Rick held up his hand and gestured toward the south. There was sporadic firing down there, some of it much closer than Hendrix could possibly be. The Cubans were mopping up the last pockets of resistance before coming up the hill. "Hendrix has had it," Rick said. "His last orders were to get as many men out as we could. Got a better way?"

"No. But—"

"But nothing. That ship won't wait, and we can't do anything for Hendrix and his people." Fear and a sense of guilt at abandoning their wounded made Rick speak more sharply than he had intended. "Shut up and get the men aboard. There's no time for talk."

André Parsons shrugged. "As you say. But there are questions you will answer."

"Don't I know it. Christ, André, don't argue. Just do it. Please."

"Very well." He went out to assist in dismounting the light machine-gun.

More troopers ran past. They carried packs, sleeping bags, helmets, ammo boxes, mess gear; the usual impedimentia of a marching army. They were not making much noise, and there was surprisingly little confusion.

Good troops, Rick thought. We did damned well, considering how little support we had. Not our fault we were beaten. For a collection of soldiers who had never served together before, we did damned well.

"That's the last," Elliot shouted.

Rick had been counting. "Only thirty-four went aboard."

Elliot looked ashamed. "I can't find any more, Captain."

They've run, Rick thought. Well, I can understand that. I thought of it myself. "Get aboard, then," he ordered. After Elliot climbed in, Rick followed. They were the last.

As soon as Rick cleared the entryway, the outer door slid closed. When he went through into the compartment with the troops, that entryway closed also. They were blocked off from the outside and from the control room—or whatever that room was, Rick thought. Mason was still in there with the aliens.

There was a loud musical tone, and a voice said, "Everyone will please sit on the floor. Quickly."

"Get down!" Rick shouted. "Hit the deck!" He sat heavily, just in time. There was a feeling of far too much weight, and some of the troops who hadn't obeyed quickly enough fell heavily. Loose equipment fell and rolled around the compartment.

There were sideways accelerations. The feeling of motion went on for a long time. Then it stopped and they had normal weight again.

"Medic!" someone shouted. One of the troopers was holding his wrist, broken in a fall to the deck. Sergeant McCleve went to the downed man. McCleve was an older trooper, a career soldier rumored to have graduated from a Mexican medical school and unable to obtain a license to practice in the United States due to heavy drinking. Rick didn't know, but McCleve had always seemed very competent.

The troops were all talking at once. Some swore, and one or two prayed. Others got up and roamed around the compartment. There was nothing to see.

They were in a large rectangular metal room, and very little more could be said about it. Rick couldn't even tell where the light came from; it was just there, and although there were multiple shadows, they were very faint.

"I think we got away," Rick shouted. "Let the Cubans figure that one out!"

There was a cheer that sounded artificial. Rick smiled grimly. He didn't feel much like cheering himself.

"Level with us, sir," Corporal Gengrich said. "How'd the CIA get a thing like this? And why the hell did they need us if they've got—" he waved expressively—"these?"

It was a good question, and Rick had no idea of how to answer.

"All in good time," Lieutenant Parsons said. "All in good time. Count your blessings."

"But—" Gengrich began.

"Shut up." Sergeant Elliot was nervous and fell back on military tradition as something familiar and understood. An officer had spoken, and that was that.

It won't last, Rick thought. Elliot had strong views about officers: he assumed they were competent, wanted them to be, *demanded* that they be. He knew that there were plenty of incompetents with bars and leaves, but he was proud enough of his Army that he'd kill himself trying to cover for them. But Rick suspected that Elliot would not hesitate to frag a bad officer for the honor of the corps.

There were more accelerations, this time not so violent. The ship was turning. Rick felt trapped, but he tried to keep his expression calm and unworried. He didn't know how successful he was at that, but he thought it was important that the troops think he was confident.

We are, he thought, thirty-six armed men and some heavy weapons, in a ship controlled by aliens—*aliens!* I don't have the faintest notion of where I am, where we're going, or what those creatures want with us.

He was certain they were in space. That decided one thing: they certainly didn't need any shooting. Not that there was anything to shoot at, but there were a lot of weapons available, and some might punch holes in the ship. The metal walls didn't seem too thick, and Rick had no idea of how strong they might be. Even supposing they could blow open a door and found air beyond it, and that they could go through the ship and kill or capture every alien in it—what then? They couldn't fly it; they couldn't land it; they couldn't even operate the food and water and air system.

And so far no one had threatened them.

✢ ✢ ✢

Two hours later they were all certain they were in space. There was a brief warning tone, and a voice said, "There will be a period of no-weight. Please secure all equipment and secure yourselves."

The only thing they could secure themselves to was a low bar a bit above waist height that ran around two sides of the compartment like the rails ballet dancers use for exercise. Rick managed to get most of the troops over to those walls. They tied lines to as much of the gear as they could. They were just finishing when there was another musical tone.

They had no weight at all. Loose objects drifted slowly. Several men looked sick, and one was. The vomit floated around in large pools. Other men turned green.

"Jesus, we got to get *out* of here!" one soldier yelled.

"Shut up!" Elliot didn't look too good himself. "Captain—"

He didn't finish the question. The ship went through more gyrations, none very severe. Then, slowly, everything drifting in the air began to settle toward the deck. They felt increasing weight, building up to what seemed almost—but not quite—normal again.

This time it was much harder to calm the troops. They hung onto their weapons and stared around the compartment looking for someone to fight, something they could do. Rick thought he could literally smell the fear in the compartment, and it was contagious. He felt like a caged animal.

"For God's sake, where are we going?" Gengrich demanded.

"The journey will last two more hours," the voice said. It spoke from nowhere at all.

"So they can listen to us," Parsons said. He lowered his voice to an undertone. "Are you certain there is nothing else you wish to tell me?"

"Not just now."

Parsons shrugged. "As you will. But I hope this does not last much more than a few hours. It will be difficult to control the men if it goes on much longer." He made a wry face. "It will be difficult to control me."

"Yeah," Rick said. He knew exactly how André Parsons felt.

✢ ✢ ✢

The voice's time estimate was accurate. Rick's watch said they had been aboard for four hours and five minutes when the warning tones sounded again and they were told to secure themselves.

This time they never had a period of no-weight, but the accelerations were short and sharp, in little spurts. There were periods of varying gravity between spurts. Finally they felt a slight impact, no more than they might have felt jumping from a chair to the floor. The accelerations ceased.

They didn't weigh enough. Nowhere near enough, and this was steady. Rick looked around in surprise, a wild suspicion coming to his mind. Some of the troops were muttering. Corporal Gengrich thoughtfully took a cartridge from his pocket and dropped it, watched it fall slowly.

About one-sixth gravity, Rick thought. There was no hiding that, and no hiding what it meant.

Gengrich shouted it first. "God Almighty, we're on the friggin' Moon!"

The troopers had little time to react to Gengrich. The compartment door opened, and Corporal Mason came in. His face looked like grey ashes, and he held his right arm against his chest. The compartment door remained open to the entry chamber, but all the other doors were closed.

"Mason—"

"Where the hell you been?"

"What's wrong, Art? What in hell did they do to you?"

The men were all shouting at once. Sergeant McCleve went over with his medical kit.

"At ease!" Rick shouted. Sergeant Elliot repeated the order more loudly. There were mutters, but the shouting stopped.

Rick joined Mason and McCleve. "What happened?"

"Jesus, Captain, we're on the Moon," Mason said. "The bastards brought us to the moon!"

"Yes," Rick said.

"I saw it all," Mason said. The troops crowded around to listen.

Rick nodded to himself. It was time the men found out what had happened. He thought he should have told them before.

"Those screen things," Mason was saying. "It was like TV. We lifted off, straight up, it seemed like, and the world kept getting further and further away until I could see all of it, just like on TV during a space mission."

"What happened to your arm?" McCleve asked. He slit Mason's

field-jacket sleeve and examined the wound. It looked like a neat round hole, thinner than a pencil, and it went through the jacket, the arm, and out the sleeve on the other side. There was no blood.

"They wouldn't talk to me," Mason said.

"Who?" "Who wouldn't talk?" the troops demanded. Elliot glared at them, but he didn't try to keep them quiet. He wanted to know too.

"Those critters," Mason said. "The—Captain, you saw 'em. I don't know what they are. Not men. Look something like men, but they're not."

Now there was a lot of excited babble. "Shut up," Rick said. "Let Mason tell his story."

"They wouldn't talk to me. We kept getting further and further away from the Earth, until I could see it—all of it—up to where I could see daylight and clouds over the ocean, just like on TV from Skylab. And they wouldn't talk. So I took out my pistol and pointed it at one— the one in the grey suit—and told him if he didn't tell me where we were going, I'd shoot him."

"Stupid," Lieutenant Parsons muttered.

"Yes, sir, it was stupid," Mason said. "The critter didn't do anything. Just waved his hand, kind of, and some kind of beam, like a laser beam, came out of the wall. Right out of the wall. I never saw any opening. Just this green light and it burned a hole right through. I dropped the gun and the critter came around and picked it up, and he said I should sit there and I should tell him if I needed medical attention—he talked that way, like a professor. Then he gave me a pill. I thought about it and then I took it, and after that it stopped hurting. And then we came on straight to the Moon. I saw us land. We're on the back side, Captain. The back side of the Moon. There's a big cave, and two other ships like this one."

When Mason stopped talking, the men began again. "You didn't tell us it was a goddamn flying saucer!" Gengrich shouted. His voice was hostile and accusing. "You said it was a CIA ship!"

"They were in a hurry," Rick said. "Would you rather be back on the hill waiting for the Cubans? Would any of you?"

They didn't know what to make of that. Nobody spoke of going back.

"We can always die," Rick said. "At least we can find out what these—people—want with us."

"Good advice." The voice came from everywhere and nowhere. "You will know very soon. The exit port will open and you will please carry all your equipment and weapons out of the ship. You will be told what to do after that. Please be careful. You are, as you have been told, on your planet's Moon. The air pressure will be lower than you are accustomed to, but there is more than enough air and oxygen for your species if you do nothing violent. Now please gather your equipment."

Rick felt totally drained of emotion. "Let's get with it," he said.

Elliot stood a moment in indecision, then evidently made up his mind. "Get that gear together. Move!" he shouted.

There was a cave beyond the door. Heavy material that looked like thick rubber sealed the door to the cave. The seal, which reminded Rick of the materials wet suits are made of, stretched for twenty meters or so into the cave. Beyond that the tunnel walls were made of rock, but shiny, as if it had been varnished. Rick felt it; the stuff was very hard, and he thought it had been sprayed on—probably to keep the air from leaking out through the rock walls.

When they had unloaded the ship, the entryway door closed, and they had no choice but to go down the tunnel. It went inward and down. They had no difficulty with equipment; everything weighed only a sixth of what it would on Earth, and one man could carry ten mortar bombs without great effort.

The tunnel was lighted, not with glowing walls as the ship had been, but with ordinary fluorescent lights. Rick examined one of the fixtures; it was stamped "Westinghouse." Common house wire ran from light to light.

As they went deeper into the cave, doors closed behind them. They seemed to be made from the same wet-suit material as the passage from the ship to the cave, and they appeared from the walls in a circle that closed together so tightly that it was difficult to see they weren't solid.

They reached the bottom of the ramp. Rick estimated that they had come nearly a kilometer. At the ramp's end was a big cavern, as large as a basketball gymnasium, and furniture. Rick saw tables, chairs, bookcases with books and magazines. Beds and army cots were clustered at one end of the area. A table held a coffee urn and bags of styrofoam cups, and a can of Yuban coffee stood next to the urn. On another table he saw loaves of bread of various American brands; jars of Jiffy peanut butter; cans of Campbell's soup. Paper plates and cheap plastic forks. Canned milk. Bricks of cheese; Vienna sausage; tins of sardines. There were no signs of fresh foods, meats or vegetables, but Rick was certain they wouldn't starve.

At the far end of the cavern was a TV set. It looked strange. Rick saw no maker's marks, unless some curious squiggles on a plate at the bottom meant something. It had no controls at all. A man's face looked out at them, and from the way his eyes and head moved, Rick thought the man was watching him.

Man. Rick stood staring at the TV. The face on the screen was human. He was certain of it.

"You are in charge?" The figure on the screen spoke without warning. The phrase wasn't precisely a question, but it did not sound positive either. The voice held a slight accent, but Rick was certain he had never heard anything like it before.

"As much as anyone is," Rick said.

"Then you are Captain Galloway. I must have information. First, is it true that you voluntarily boarded the ship that brought you here? There was no coercion from the *Shalnuksis*?"

"Shalnuksis?"

"The beings who brought you here. Were you forced to board their ship?"

"Not by them. There were some Cubans who didn't leave us many choices—"

"That is my second question." The man's expression did not change at all. Rick got closer to the set and examined the image carefully.

He saw a man who appeared to be in his forties. He wore a rust-colored upper garment that resembled a tunic, no buttons, a V-neck lined with blue and studded with decorations: a stylized comet and sunburst. The man's hair was short, and his complexion was darker than Rick's; about the same hue as an American Indian, but not quite so dark.

"Is it true that you would now be dead if the *Shalnuksi* ship had not taken you aboard?" the man asked.

"It's likely," Rick answered.

"One of your men was injured by the *Shalnuksis*. They have said they were merely defending themselves and did the least damage possible to the man. Is this true?"

"Yes—"

"Thank you. We regret that we do not have better accommodations. You are welcome to whatever you find there. You may eat now. We will have more to talk of later."

"Hey—damn it, what's going on?" Rick demanded. He was talking to a blank screen.

✢ ✢ ✢

They examined their prison. There was a hot plate and an electrical outlet on a long cord. The wire ran into the wall, and the hole it came out of was sealed with the wet-suit material. The hot plate had been made by General Electric. The coffeepot was Japanese, with Japanese labels. Everything in the compartment had come from Earth. Most had come from the United States, but there were articles from many other places. Some of the gear was new, much still in packing cases. Other equipment and stores had been used. There were radios and television sets, but they produced nothing beyond a few random hisses and howls.

After half an hour, they settled in to cook dinner. There was plenty to eat; soup and canned bacon and ham, canned vegetables, and pudding for dessert. André Parsons found a water tap—Kohler of Kohler—near the coffee urn. There was a drain beneath it. Other troops found cases of warm beer and several jugs of wine, enough so that everyone had a beer and a full cup of California red. There was plenty of coffee.

When they had eaten, they all felt better. The troops prowled about restlessly, but eventually began making themselves comfortable, using what was in their packs and whatever else they could find to bed down. Elliot pulled two of the single beds off to one side for Parsons and Rick Galloway. No one had eaten or slept for more than twenty-four hours, and soon most of the troops were sprawled onto beds and cots, or onto air mattresses on the floor.

The floor, Rick found, was uneven at the edges near the walls, but away from the walls it was artificially smooth and flat. It felt warm to the touch.

Rick sat with Parsons at a table near the TV set. They ate in silence. Finally Parsons said, "I see why you did not explain earlier."

"Yeah. Not that I could have," Rick said.

Parsons shrugged. "Five hours ago, I was prepared to be killed on that hilltop. Now I have eaten, I have a cup of wine and coffee to follow, and it is warm. No one is shooting me, and there is a comfortable bed. We have been lucky."

"Maybe."

"Have you thought of the implications of your television conversation?" André asked. "A human. A human who asks interesting questions. Are we volunteers? How was Corporal Mason injured? Would we be alive if we had not boarded the alien ship? All asked by a human in a voice of authority, as if he had every right to the answers."

Rick nodded. "I thought of that. It means somebody cares what happens to us. Maybe not a lot, but somebody cares. I keep hoping that's a good sign."

"It cannot be a bad one," André said.

"Dammit, you're calm enough—"

Parsons laughed. "I would have said the same of you. Rick, I am terrified, but it would do no good to let the men see that. Obviously you must feel the same way."

"Yeah. But I sure wish they'd let us know what they want with us."

"Perhaps nothing," Parsons said. He shrugged again in his expansive French manner. "Perhaps they rescued us for humanitarian reasons. Are we not worth it?" His smile was broad.

✛ ✛ ✛

"Captain! Cap'n, that TV's going again. They want you."

Rick struggled to wakefulness. His watch showed that he had slept five hours. It seemed longer, and he felt far better rested than he would have expected from five hours' sleep.

A dozen men were crowded around the TV. They were trying to talk to the man—as near as Rick could tell, it was the same one who had spoken to him before—but they had no success. It was only when Rick stood in front of the set that the man responded.

"It is time to discuss your situation," the screen figure said. "You will not require weapons. Leave them all, and any other large metal objects, and enter the doorway which will open in the wall behind this screen."

As he spoke a steel plate set in the wall swung away. A rubberlike airtight door stood behind it. "Alone, please," the screen said. "You will not be harmed."

"Maybe a couple of us ought to come anyway," Sergeant Elliot said.

"Thanks, Sarge, but I guess not," Rick said. "If they really want us dead, they'll let the air out of this compartment. And don't forget that. Elliot, for God's sake, don't let the troops do anything stupid while I'm gone."

"No, sir. But when will you be back?"

"I don't know."

"Cap'n, if you're not back in four hours, we can blow that door open—"

"No. Wake up Lieutenant Parsons and tell him he's in charge. I'll be back." Rick sounded a lot more confident than he felt as he went through the doorway. It closed behind him before the airtight in front of him dilated.

There was another corridor, and no one in sight. Rick followed that for a hundred meters until it bent sharply left, then led through two more rubberized pressure doors. He emerged in another cavern, one much smaller than the one he had left. It was well lighted, and there were at least a dozen of the TV screens of the kind he had seen in the ship and in the cavern.

There were both people and aliens in the cavern, perhaps a dozen of each. Several were studying the TV-like screens. An alien in grey coveralls, possibly the one who had spoken to him in the ship, came over to him.

The alien was six inches taller than Rick, but the extra height seemed to be all in the legs. The torso was not much longer than Rick's. The arms were longer than a human's, but not so much longer as were the legs. "There," the alien said. He indicated a door. "You would—do well—to be—careful—of what you say."

Rick nodded. "I understand." If this were the same alien, and Rick thought it was, it no longer spoke as easily and confidently as it had aboard the ship. Why? he wondered.

The door opened into an office. A desk faced the door. There were papers on the desk, along with two keyboards that Rick thought must connect to a computer. The desk held two of the flat TV screens, and there were other screens higher up. All were blank. The office had metallic square walls and floor and ceiling; a room built into the cavern. There was a rug on the floor which Rick thought was Persian; it had that pattern and look to it. There were other art objects that appeared to be from Earth: seascape paintings, a color photograph of the Golden Gate bridge, a Kalliroscope with its swirling shock-wave patterns.

The man he had seen on the TV screen sat behind the desk. The desk itself looked Danish modern and was probably from Earth. The man stood as Rick entered, but he did not offer to shake hands.

He was perhaps five feet ten, two inches shorter than Rick, and looked thoroughly human. He was a bit darker than Rick, face rounder, but he would not have attracted attention on any street in the United States or Europe. His expression was not unfriendly, but he looked harried, very busy and preoccupied.

The man spoke. It sounded to Rick more like the twittering of a bird than any human speech. "A parrot in a cageful of cats," Rick told André Parsons later. The alien answered in the same language, and the human nodded.

"Excuse me, Captain," he said. "Please be seated." He indicated chairs, both of aluminum and plastic, one a normal-height chair, the other like a highchair for an adult. "Doubtless you have many questions."

Now there's an understatement, Rick thought. "Yes. Beginning with, who are you?"

The man nodded, tight-lipped, again his expression more of impatience and mild annoyance than anything else. "You would find my name hard to pronounce. Try 'Agzaral,' which is close enough not to offend me. I am—you do not have the occupation. Think of me as a police inspector. It is close enough for our purposes. And do be seated."

Rick took the normal chair. The alien went to the highchair. It fitted perfectly. "And my—rescuer?" Rick asked. It was difficult to know how to speak. There were no referents, and Rick had no idea of what would offend either the human or the alien. Obviously he should avoid terms like "this critter" or "stretchy here", but what could he call the creature?

"His name translates as 'Goldsmith,' " Agzaral said. "Many *Shalnuksi* names derive from ancient occupations. That seems a nearly universal cultural trait among industrializing peoples. If you prefer his own language, it is 'Karreeel.' " The last was said with a twitter that Rick couldn't possibly pronounce.

"Pleased to meet you," Rick said. "An expression that we don't always mean, but given the way we met, I certainly do. Only—"

"Only you would like to know why he made the effort," Agzaral said. "I listened to part of your conversation with the other officer." He switched to the twitter-and-snarl language again and spoke briefly.

"We have need of you," Karreeel said. His facial slits flared briefly. "We have need of human soldiers, and we went to great expense and difficulty to locate you."

"But why us?" Rick demanded.

"Because you would not be missed," Agzaral said. "And you could be taken aboard his ship without anyone seeing it. There are severe regulations against allowing the ships to be seen."

"Flying saucers," Rick said. "But you *have* been seen—"

"*Some* have," Agzaral corrected. "Not Karreeel. The ships that have been seen were employed by students. Fortunately, none of those sightings can be proved." He sighed. It seemed to Rick a very human sigh. "It is my unpleasant task to investigate every instance in which a ship had been seen and reported."

"I see," Rick said. "And then what?"

"We have agents on Earth," Agzaral said. "They discredit the sighting reports."

"They've done a good job," Rick said. He remembered what he had thought of UFO stories, and the people who "believed in flying saucers." Brass-plated nuts. "The"—he hesitated at the unfamiliar word— "*Shalnuksis*—are studying us?"

Agzaral's lips curled in what Rick thought might be a thin smile. "No. Others study Earth. Including other humans. But the—" He paused. "I will not in future stop myself when I require a term that you will not quite understand. I will simply use the nearest equivalent. There is a High Commission which regulates trade with primitive worlds, particularly with Earth, and protects primitive peoples from crude exploitation. The Commission forbids trade or other intercourse with your planet."

"But why?" Rick demanded. He was surprised at how calm he felt. One part of his mind wanted him to scream and run in circles, flapping his arms, but instead he found it easy enough to sit calmly and politely conversing with a human who was not from Earth and an alien who resembled a stretched-out chimpanzee with a single nostril and no neck. It was all so completely ordinary; the conversational tones, the gestures—

Jerry Pournelle

"Your planet is in an interesting stage of development," Agzaral said. "Trade will not be allowed until it is decided what—until the studies are completed."

"What the hell do you want with *me*, then?" Rick demanded.

"I want nothing," Agzaral said. "You are, for me, a great annoyance. Karreeel has an offer which I believe you should consider."

"Shoot—uh, go ahead. What's the offer?"

"My—colleagues—and I are merchants. More correct would be 'merchant-adventurers,' " Karreeel said. When he spoke, he paused frequently, and Rick wondered if he had some kind of translating machine, so that he could think of what he wanted to say and get the English. There was no sign of wires or a hearing aid, but that wasn't decisive.

" 'Merchant-adventurers,' " Rick repeated. He couldn't help remembering that the Gentleman Adventurers of the Honourable East India Company had gone out and conquered India for England, and he wondered if the aliens had a similar fate in mind for Earth.

"Yes," said Karreeel. "We now have a need for human soldiers. The price of mercenaries has become—excessively high. We gambled that we could find soldiers here and yet not violate—Inspector—Agzaral's regulations. If you will agree, we will have succeeded."

"If we agree," Rick said.

Agzaral wagged his head in a manner that Rick thought strange; when he saw Rick's reaction, he checked himself and nodded. "You are under no compulsion to accept," he said. "When he has made his offer, I will tell you what alternatives are permitted for you."

"There is a planet, far from here," Karreeel said. "It has a primitive society, much more primitive than yours. The planet can support a highly valuable crop, one that cannot be grown easily anywhere else. We need assistance in getting those crops planted and harvested."

Rick shook his head. This didn't make sense. "Why don't you grow your own?"

The alien made a gesture with his left hand, and both his facial slits flared wide. "Why should one of us be condemned to live on a primitive world?"

"But we're not farmers—"

"We do not expect you to do any farming. There is a local population. Unfortunately, the planet is very primitive, in a state of—

feudalism. Our need is not farmers, but soldiers to impose a government which will wish to plant our required crops, harvest them, and deliver the harvest to us."

"And what makes you think we'll be interested in living on a primitive world?" Rick demanded.

"Your reward should be obvious. You will rule as you will, without interference. You will have wealth and power, and you will have only to see that our crops are grown. We will supply you with luxuries and comforts in trade."

"This sounds like a long-term project," Rick said.

"Of course," Karreeel said.

Before Agzaral spoke, Rick knew what he was going to say.

"The task will last your lifetime," Agzaral said. "Captain Galloway, surely it must be obvious to you that you and your men will never return to Earth."

4

"Just a damn minute!" Rick exploded. "You kidnap us, and then—"

"Rescued," Agzaral said. "I asked you about it. I have taken the trouble to check the story. It is obvious to me that you would be dead if Karreeel had not taken you aboard his ship. Do you dispute that?"

Rick felt the anger drain out to be replaced by fear. "No. I can't dispute that. But why can't we go home?"

"Because you would be believed," Agzaral said. "Too many witnesses. Karreeel planned on that, of course. By deliberately taking aboard such a large number, he made it certain that someone would take you seriously if you returned to Earth."

"You mentioned alternatives," Rick said.

Agzaral nodded. "You have few enough. None include going back to your own world. You would have to stay here, in that chamber where you are now, until transport could be arranged to another planet. Some of you could probably find positions as experimental subjects for the university. Others might—find different work. I do not know what would happen to the majority. The High Commission would have to decide. I would have to report that you have been offered employment and refused it. Humans unwilling to work do not always have a pleasant life on most of our worlds. And it may be several years before transport could be found—at least for all of you."

"That's not much choice at all."

"Or you may commit suicide," Agzaral said.

30

"That's even less." Rick touched the grenade through his pocket. It was a new variety; a small grenade not much larger than a golf ball, made mostly of plastic. It would explode into thousands of tiny fragments, surely enough to kill everyone in the room—including himself. It didn't seem a very useful weapon at the moment. "May I smoke?" he asked.

"I would prefer that you do not," Agzaral said.

"Okay. Look, how the hell do you expect thirty men to take over an entire planet?"

"Not an entire planet." Karreeel's tone didn't change; it remained matter-of-fact, calm, unworried. "Most of"—he twittered something incomprehensible—"is of no interest or value. Only one region will be worth controlling. Surely your men with firearms and other military equipment will have no difficulty dominating primitives with lances, bows, and swords?"

That seemed possible. Rick didn't care much for the idea. If the planet were that primitive in weapons, it would also be primitive in hygiene and medical science. Living there would not be much fun.

He wondered what it would be like to be on welfare in one of Agzaral's cultures. It hadn't sounded pleasant, but Agzaral was undoubtedly used to more luxuries than Rick was. But then there was that phrase "experimental subjects," and that didn't sound good at all.

There was another problem that would be even worse. "We're all men," Rick said. "And you'll be sending us to another planet for the rest of our lives—"

"Ah," Karreeel said. "I understand. Permit me to explain that there will be human females."

"You've kidnapped women?" Rick demanded.

"No. Providing a sufficient number might be difficult without—violating—the regulations. The planet—let us call it Paradise. That is a good name for a planet. Paradise is inhabited by humans."

"Bull puckey," said Rick.

There was silence for a moment. Rick wondered if he had offended the alien.

"It is quite true," Agzaral said. "There are humans in many parts of the galaxy."

"How?" Rick demanded.

Agzaral smiled thinly. "Don't your own scientists suggest that humans are not native to Earth?"

"I never heard of that theory being taken seriously. If people—humans—are spread all over the galaxy, how'd they get that way?"

"I doubt that you will ever find that out," Agzaral said. His voice had become very serious, with no trace of warmth at all. Then he shrugged. "There are no English translations of galactic history, and I have no time to give you lessons. For the moment, believe it."

Rick frowned. He wondered if it could be true. There were legends of early astronauts: Ezekiel and the wheel, cherubim, the biblical four-faced flying creatures; even the so-called evidence of commercial writers. Genesis could be interpreted as the transplantation of a very small number of people—the story said only two—onto a world where they hadn't evolved.

It was beyond Rick. He had never been a brilliant student. One reason he had worked in ROTC classes was that he had thought he might need the army for a job. The only subject he had consistently done well in was military history, and that hadn't promised a very good living.

Paradise. He smiled lopsidedly as he remembered a lump of uninhabitable ice had been named "Greenland" in the hopes of attracting suckers who might go there to settle. "Real people," he said. "*Homo sapiens.*"

"How sapient is debatable. Not merely for those on Paradise, but everywhere," Agzaral said. "But depend upon it; union with females there will be fertile."

Something else nagged at Rick. "You're a policeman," he said. "I get the idea that you're here to protect the people of Earth. All those regulations. Can't kidnap people who aren't going to die anyway. Yet you're sending us off to conquer this primitive place you call Paradise. Why aren't you concerned about the people there?"

Agzaral frowned. Rick wondered if he'd hit a sore spot. "Paradise—you may as well know the place's real name," Agzaral said. "In the dominant language it is called 'Tran.' Tran is not covered by the same regulations as Earth." He stopped and pressed his lips grimly together. "Besides, you can't do anything to the people there that they haven't been doing to themselves. You may save them much misery."

There was some mystery here, Rick thought. Agzaral's expression did not match his words. But what? "If it's that easy, why don't you do it yourselves?"

"We can't." Agzaral pointed to Karreeel. "Discoverers, colonizers, and developers have their rights, too. But when you arrive on Tran with your weapons, you might recall that the people there are as human as you or I. Captain Galloway, you must make a decision."

"How much time do I have?"

Agzaral looked to Karreeel.

"There is no vital hurry," the alien said. "Shall we say twenty-four hours?"

✢ ✢ ✢

Rick put the proposition to the troops. He wasn't surprised when there was a long silence, then babble. He knew how they felt; he'd wanted to babble himself when he left the interview with Karreeel and Agzaral.

Then a loud voice cut through the chatter. "Another planet? That's not possible."

Private Larry Warner, called "Professor" by the other troops, had a voice that could be heard in the middle of a battle. He was a college graduate, and Rick had no idea why the man had volunteered for the army, still less why he had volunteered a second time for a CIA operation. He argued with everyone: officers, noncoms, anyone who would listen. Only threats of severe punishment could shut him up. For all that, he was an educated man, and Rick had found his knowledge valuable in the past.

"Faster-than-light travel is impossible," Warner said. "We can't get to another star system—and there sure aren't any inhabited planets in the solar system. They must be lying to you."

"It seems a pointless deception," André Parsons said.

Sergeant Elliot had a simpler way. "Shut up, Warner."

"Where did the aliens come from?" Jack Campbell shouted. "Not this solar system. You said so yourself, Professor." Campbell was a college dropout who'd joined the army for lack of something better to do. He enjoyed teasing Warner. "Hey, I like it! Captain, I take it there'll be some changes in our status. Most of us can hope for something more than twenty years in the army and retirement—"

Rick shrugged. "I hadn't much thought about it, but I guess so. They talked like we could do pretty well what we wanted to."

"I have always fancied myself as a king," André Parsons said. "I see no reason why we cannot all become kings—or at least dukes and barons. Presuming we succeed, of course."

"We have to get out of here," someone shouted.

Babble broke out.

"Where to?"

"I've got a wife and two kids—I got to get back home!"

"Ten—hut!" Elliot's command quieted them for a moment.

Before they could speak again, Rick said, "We aren't going home. They made that clear, and I don't see any way to get there. They can let the pressure out of here anytime they want to. Anybody know how to breathe vacuum?"

"So what do we do, Captain?" Campbell asked.

"Stick together. Do what they want," Rick said. "Lieutenant Parsons is right. We can all get rich out of this. We can't go home, but we can be rich. If we stick together."

"Fight a whole planet?" Campbell asked.

"Not quite," Rick said. "But we could. We have the edge in weapons and tactics. There'll be a lot of people down there, though. A lot. If we don't stay together—well, when does anyone sleep?"

"First we need a new contract," Warner said. His voice had a smug quality that instantly irritated Rick. "A new contract. We can begin by electing a chairman—"

Sergeant Elliot looked as if he were having a stroke. "Elect! We got officers—"

"Who have no authority over us under the circumstances," Warner said. "Their commissions are from the United States, and we don't live there any longer. Why should we have to take orders from them?"

"Warner, one more goddamn word out of you and I'll break your neck." Elliot moved to stand near Private Warner.

"He has a point," André Parsons said. "Those who volunteer to go are also volunteering to accept Captain Galloway and myself as leaders." He turned to Rick and said, very formally, "Sir, I accept you as leader and captain of this expedition." Then he saluted.

Parsons had turned away from the troops, so that only Rick could see his face. His eyes showed sly amusement, and as Rick returned the salute, Parsons gave an exaggerated wink.

Rick had told Parsons that the aliens—and the human "police," who in some ways seemed as alien as the *Shalnuksis*—were probably listening to all their conversations; after that they were guarded, saying nothing they did not want their employers to hear. It made Rick lonelier than ever. He was losing Earth and everyone he knew, and he couldn't talk about it without risk of being overheard.

And yet, he thought, it might be fun. As Parsons had said, everyone at one time or another dreams of getting a chance to become a knight or baron or duke. Even a king. That didn't happen on Earth anymore, but it might happen to Rick Galloway on Paradise.

He had other fantasies. He knew enough of Earth's history to know of the mistakes made in going from the Middle Ages to an industrial society. He had seen pictures of Bombay and Calcutta. Perhaps, he told himself, he could help this new world avoid some of the mistakes. For Karreeel and his merchant-adventurers, this was a routine operation to make some money—or whatever passed for money in their culture— but for Rick it was a chance at adventure.

It was also inevitable, and he was uncomfortably aware that many of the arguments he used with himself and the men were born of necessity. They had no other choices.

✦ ✦ ✦

The first task was preparation. They would need supplies and equipment. Agzaral had told him that a reasonable amount of equipment could be obtained from Earth. He hadn't said what would be reasonable.

Rick set the troops to making lists. Weapons, ammunition, special equipment, communications, survival gear, medical supplies, soap; luxuries and conveniences that couldn't be manufactured on Tran even with all the help Rick and his people could supply. The lists became endless, and they began to cut them back.

They had very little information about Tran. Karreeel was certain there was no petroleum industry there, but neither knew nor cared whether there was petroleum at all: thus no internal-combustion gear. The other decision information was just as sketchy.

Rick asked the television set for an interview. Eventually Karreeel came on the screen.

"We need more data," Rick said. "How big is this planet? How much water? Are there hurricanes? How can I prepare when I don't know what to prepare *for*?"

"Your questions are reasonable. Unfortunately, we have not translated the data you require. That will be done later."

"Can you get the equipment I've asked for?"

"Some. Most."

"How?" Rick asked.

"It can be bought. Or stolen," Karreeel said. "I have little time for you. You will later meet someone who does. Until then, please do not annoy me further."

"Who is this—"

"A human. If you give me your list, I will see what can be obtained."

The screen went blank. Rick and André looked at each other. "They must have agents on Earth," Parsons said. "They spoke of purchases—"

"Yeah." Rick thought about that for a moment, then laughed. "Aliens among us. Agents of the Galactic Confederacy move about studying us. We read about it for years, and it's all true."

André Parsons laughed also, but neither of them thought it was really very funny.

PART TWO
SHIP

1

Gwen Tremaine was in love. Given that she was twenty years old and not at all unattractive, this shouldn't have been astonishing; but in point of fact she was more than astonished. She couldn't really believe it.

She had resigned herself to a lonely life. Not lonely in the sense of having no friends, although she had few enough; but she was convinced that she would never be in love, and even doubted whether anyone else ever had been. She had strongly suspected that all the poetic passages, all the lyric descriptions of how one felt when one was in love, had been invented by poets and writers who felt there ought to be such feelings but who had never experienced them.

Physical attraction she understood. She'd had several affairs and enjoyed them all. But what she couldn't seem to arouse, in herself or others, was whatever the poets felt when they spoke of love.

She had tried, and a few times she thought it was happening to her, but it never developed into anything more. The strong affection, the need for someone else's company that she saw in the few girls she got along with, sometimes she felt stirrings of it, but it never lasted. Generally what few stirrings she did experience happened after physical encounters, and usually hadn't lasted past the cold light of morning. For a while she had blamed her inability to fall in love on the men in her life, and indeed there was some justice in that. She'd been attracted to as thoroughgoing a collection of cynics, bounders, and just plain cads as it was possible for her to imagine. Even her friends said so. Not that it was so obvious when she met them. She didn't seek out the most popular boy in her high-school class, or lust after the jocks who could and did have every girl in the school. She was more likely to date the quiet ones with glasses who read a lot. Some had never had a date before her. Yet they invariably left her for her friends as soon as she'd built up their confidence to a level where they dared ask someone else for a date.

In truth, she scared hell out of everyone who tried to take her seriously. She was intelligent, she talked a lot, and she was interested in everything. She wrote for the school paper. She did so much extra classwork that she could get an A in any subject even if she turned in a blank final exam. She earned real money at such unfeminine activities as buying stale bread and reselling it to chicken farmers. In short, she was real competition for any boy she met, and the ones she liked were never secure enough to survive that threat.

When she was sixteen and a senior at John Marshall High, she met Fred Linker in the school library. Fred had never had a date in his life and was terrified of girls. Gwen was a bit cynical about men by that time, but she was enough of a product of her culture to wish she had someone to take her on dates. Fred seemed perfect. He wasn't at all bad looking, just shy. He liked to read and knew of works like *Silverlock* that she adored as soon as he told her about them. He was a good listener, and they shared many opinions. So she worked on him until he asked her out, and three dates later, he got the nerve to kiss her goodnight. He didn't know how to do that very well, but Gwen was a good teacher. She'd found books that told how.

Fred wanted to be a writer. He wrote constantly. Someday he'd sell a story. He was certain of it. He'd even sent a few off to magazines and got rejections slips.

Gwen read the magazines Fred liked, and three weeks later got a short story accepted in one of his favorites. She thought he'd be proud of her, and she knew she could show him how he could sell, too—it was only a matter of studying the editor's prejudices—but a week after that Fred took another girl to the sock hop. Later he sold three stories himself, but he never asked Gwen out again.

College hadn't been much different. Gwen's physical urges got stronger, and sometimes she was so lonely she'd read in an all-night restaurant rather than sit in her room; so lonely that she made resolutions about not competing with the next man she liked. She even tried to carry them out. It did no good. Even when she didn't actually do whatever her current boyfriend thought he was good at, eventually it would come out that she could if she wanted to.

Or maybe, she told herself as she dressed in her compulsively neat one-room apartment, maybe that's all wrong. Maybe they just didn't like me in the first place. God knows there must be *something* wrong with me.

I'm not ugly. She studied herself in the mirror. Too short, yes. Five foot two and eyes of blue sounds very good in songs, but in fact that's pretty short, and besides my eyes are more greenish-brown. Nose too pointed, face too angular, but there are plenty of girls with longer and pointier noses and they aren't ugly. And I've got all the right equipment. Not a *lot* of it, but in good proportion. I bounce all right if I go without a bra, and my hips aren't bony. I don't wear clothes well because I'm too thin, but I don't look too bad. Men don't turn away.

And everyone tells me I talk well. I'm bright and witty. They say it just after we meet, and just as they're walking out.

But this time it's different.

⊹ ⊹ ⊹

She dressed carefully. *This time for sure*, she thought. Things will happen tonight. She felt a delicious sensation of anticipation. Maybe this will last, she thought. Please. Let it last.

She grinned at her image in the mirror. To whom was she praying? Her image of the universe had room in it for a god, but not one who paid much attention to that kind of prayer. If prayer worked, there were a lot of people worse off than Gwen Tremaine praying their arses off. They didn't get what they wanted. Why should she?

But there was a chance. Les was different.

She'd met him in an all-night coffee shop near the university library. It had been quite late, and she was ready to go home. She was carrying a half-dozen books, and he'd seen the anthropology book. "That looks like a new one," he'd said. "I think I have not seen that one before. May I look?"

And then they'd got to talking. He was brilliant. She could tell that from the few things he said. But mostly he wanted her to talk. He liked listening to her—about everything, about *anything* she wanted to say.

He got her to tell him about growing up in Iowa, about moving to

California when she was fourteen, about high school and college and her unsuccessful love affairs, about her theories of history and physics and mathematics and especially anthropology and—

He liked her. He listened, and he liked her, and to Gwen that was devastating.

And she couldn't compete with him. Partly she couldn't because she didn't know what he did. He never said directly, but she had the impression that he was in advanced physics. Once he'd got her talking about the origin of the universe. She'd told him what she thought, and he scribbled some equations on a napkin. They meant nothing to her. He'd thrown the napkin away. She went back the next morning and retrieved it from the garbage behind the restaurant and went to the library. After spending all day working on them the equations still meant nothing to her. She couldn't even find many of the symbols.

Which meant he was a liar—only it didn't. Les didn't have to lie. He talked about himself only when she urged him to, and never to impress her. He'd already done that on the first night, when she found he'd read nearly every anthropology book ever written and understood all the major theories.

When she could get him to talk, she learned more in an hour with Les than she did in a month of classes.

For three weeks she had never seen him except in the coffee shop. He came in late, always after midnight, sometimes not until dawn. He drove a truck for spending money and had no fixed schedule; but he always came, and she was always waiting. They'd never discussed it, but she knew he came just to see her.

For three weeks they talked in the shop. He waved goodbye to her when it got so late she had to go home (or to morning classes).

Until yesterday. Yesterday he got up when she did, paid his check, and walked home with her. It seemed perfectly natural that he come in with her and that they go to bed together, and that he aroused her to flights of passion she had never supposed possible.

He stayed until noon.

And now he was coming back and wanted to take her somewhere. She dressed carefully. A skirt that didn't wrinkle. They didn't have to wrestle in a car—he was welcome in her bed—but who knows? she thought. She grinned at her image in the mirror. "Painted hussy," she told it.

The image grinned back. "We like it, don't we, ducks?"

"Damn straight," Gwen said. "Damn straight. Never thought I would—"

She laughed at herself, but she studied her small collection of jewelry and perfume just the same. What would he like?

"Independent. Liberated. And working my arse off to make him want me," she told the mirror.

"Hang on to this one," the image said.

"Right." If we can. Please. Let this be all right. Let this last.

✢ ✢ ✢

When the doorbell rang an hour after midnight, she ran to it, then caught herself. He knew she liked him, but she didn't want him to think she was *that* nuts over him. Still, she was a little breathless when she opened the door. Would he leap at her? Carry her to bed? She damned well wasn't going to resist—

He kissed her, but broke away quickly before that could lead to anything else. Then he grinned. "Later. We'll have a lot of time."

"Good."

"Go for a drive?" he asked.

"Sure. Where? Do I need a coat?"

"Actually, I had in mind a weekend trip. Can you pack a bag?"

She frowned. Was he *that* confident? But then he had reason to be. And why not? "I can get away," she said. "For a couple of days. but I ought to call my landlady and tell her—"

"Leave a note. It's late."

"What should I pack? Swimsuit? Ski clothes?"

"Do you like boats? Sailing?"

"I never went on one before. I don't get motion sick—I guess I've told you that."

"You have."

There it was. The tiny accent. "Just where did you grow up?" she asked.

"I thought you were the professional who'd guess from my speech patterns." He grinned.

It's a nice grin, she thought. A nice grin, on a nice face. She moved closer to him. "Wheedle, wheedle."

He pulled her against him and held her for a moment.

"You're just the right size," she said.

"How's that?"

She shrugged. "Big enough that I think of you as a big man, but not so big you tower over me. And not so big in other ways, if you know what I mean—"

He laughed. "We do seem compatible."

"Yes, I like that. I'll pack my sailing clothes," she said. "I won't be long."

✛ ✛ ✛

"I didn't know they kept boats in the mountains," Gwen said. "Just where are you taking me?"

It seemed a reasonable question. The road climbed steadily higher into the Angeles Mountains, directly away from the sea. At first she'd thought they were driving up the coast toward Santa Barbara, but he'd turned east.

The truck hummed along the road. It was a heavy Ford pickup, and the bed was crammed with odd shapes covered with a tarpaulin. That seemed strange too. Why a loaded truck for a weekend date? "Where are we going, Les?"

"Don't you trust me?"

"I—I don't know. I don't—Les please. Don't play head games with me."

"I don't want to, Gwen." His voice was very serious. "But I don't have much choice." He hesitated a moment. "You told me you want to learn. You like anthropology because you want to learn. To travel, see strange people and learn how they live—"

"Yes—"

"I can give you a chance to do that. Right now. But it's a long trip. Will you come with me?"

"Right now? Just like that? Not tell anyone—"

"Yes."

"Les, I can't—"

"Sure you can. You told me yourself, nobody cares what happens to you. Your mother's dead, and you haven't heard from your father in years. Sure you can. Who'll care? The people at the university? Landlady? Not really."

"But—right now? Just like that? Where do we go?"

"That's the part I can't tell you. A long voyage to exotic and distant lands. I can promise you that."

"With you."

"Yes. With me." He drove with both hands on the wheel, both eyes on the road; almost as if he were afraid of the truck. Now he let go to take her hand for a moment and squeeze it. "With me. I promise you that."

She thought about it. But it was all so strange. "What's in the truck? Your travel equipment? What—who are you? CIA?"

"What if I were?"

"I—wouldn't like that."

"Then I'm not," he said. "Let's see. Other question. The gear in the truck is for travel, but it is not mine. I get equipment for others. Get it and deliver it."

"But always at night—"

"Generally," he agreed.

"Les, where *are* we going? I thought Mexico for a moment, but we're going northeast. Where—"

"Can't tell you. But will you come with me?"

"If I don't?"

He let the truck slow. "I turn around and take you home."

"And then?"

"And then I leave. I have to go, Gwen. I'm sorry I haven't been able to tell you much, but I can't. I do want you to go with me, but you don't have much time to make up your mind."

"How long—how long will we be gone?"

"A long time. Years. But you'll see exotic places, faraway places, places you'll never see unless you come with me."

"I didn't pack very much," she said. "Not for being away that long. Will you buy me a grass skirt?"

The truck ran on for a second more. Then he stopped, turned, and kissed her. "I'm glad," he said. Then he started up. "We don't have a lot of time. They won't wait all night."

"Who won't?" she asked.

An hour later she knew.

2

Gwen was on the Moon. She had to keep telling herself that. She was on the Moon and talking to a TV set.

The face on the TV was human. Strange, but human, and after what Gwen had seen on the ship, any human face was a relief.

The man looked bored. "You have come voluntarily?" he asked.

An embarrassing question. Gwen was naked, except for a sheet that she wrapped around herself when she realized that the TV screen worked *both* ways. She sat on the edge of the bed to talk to the man in the rust-colored tunic who'd appeared on the screen. Les lay partly covered on the bed, and his expression was—worried? Why worried, she wondered.

"Yes, I came voluntarily," she said. "Les asked me to come. He said I would visit strange and exotic lands and—"

"You boarded voluntarily," the man said. "Will you be missed? Will your disappearance cause difficulties? Widespread search by the authorities?"

"I don't think so. I left a note for my landlady that said I was going for a weekend trip. She'll worry when I don't come back after that. She may call the police."

"They will probably assume you were murdered. That is no problem of mine." The screen went blank.

"That's over," Les said. He looked relieved.

Why relieved? And why had he been worried? There was a lot that Gwen didn't understand. But certainly she was glad she had come.

46

There were marvels enough, even here in the compartment. It was lavishly furnished, mostly with goods from Earth; but some of the furnishings were new and strange. There was the TV with its strange control box that could call up books and maps and all kinds of interesting material—the only problem was that she couldn't read a word of it. And there had been the aliens, and the experience of seeing Earth from space. Now she felt the low gravity of the Moon and could see the lunar surface on the TV screen. It was all frightening, but exciting, too.

"Who was that man?" she asked.

"A policeman," Les said.

"What would have happened if I had said you kidnapped me?"

"He probably would not have believed you. But if you had said the *Shalnuksis* had kidnapped you, there would have been trouble."

Gwen shuddered, but not in fear. It was all so marvelous. Aliens. Spaceships. And they were so nice to her. Les had given her clothes and jewelry—not that the gifts meant anything, but he had got them for her. He cared. She knew that. He cared.

"And you don't come from anywhere on Earth?" she asked. "I still can't believe that."

"It's true, though," he said. "My home is twenty light-years from here."

"How long have you been on Earth?"

"Four years. A bit more than that."

"But you speak English so well! No wonder I couldn't tell where you came from. How did you learn to speak English so well in four years?"

"It's a gift," he said. "I speak a number of human languages. Four from your planet."

"A number of human languages—Les, what do you do for these—for the aliens?"

"You can think of me as a civil servant," he said. "I pilot ships, make studies of primitives, buy equipment and see that it gets aboard ship—any number of activities that the traders or the confederacy need done."

"A civil servant."

"Sort of," Les told her. "That is, most humans work for the confederacy, but they sometimes rent us out to traders when the work involves other humans. Just now I'm doing some errands for the *Shalnuksis*."

"But why don't you go to Washington and tell them? Or someone? Why such secrecy?"

"Time enough for questions later," he said. "We will have a lot of time. For the moment, we are together, and we have a few hours before we go to the other ship."

"Another ship?"

"Yes. I'm supposed to take some people—human volunteers, soldiers—to another planet. I'll have to brief them on the way."

"Soldiers. Volunteers. You mean mercenaries." She made no attempt to disguise the contempt in her voice.

He laughed. "You don't like warriors? You ought to feel a bit sorry for these. They've got their work cut out. More than they know."

"Who will they fight? What are they going to be doing?"

"All in good time. You'll know more about them than you want to by the time we get to Tran. For now—" He reached for her.

For a moment she resisted, but she could feel his urgency.

Why resist? she thought. Why resent his need? A need for me. He cares. I can lose myself in him. And he keeps his promises.

He'd already showed her marvels beyond her imagination. What more would there be? She shuddered in anticipation.

✤ ✤ ✤

The screen came to life while the troops were cooking lunch. Rick Galloway went over carrying his new lists of equipment. There was a lot they needed, and they hadn't received much of what they'd asked for.

"No time," Agzaral said. "No time at all. Gather your equipment. You must leave this cavern immediately. There is a ship outside, and you must be aboard it with everything you propose to take with you. You have two hours." He seemed very excited. "You must hurry."

"Why? We can't go now. We don't have anything like the gear we asked for—"

"Some is aboard the ship. The rest may be supplied later. But hurry. Those who remain behind will not be happy with the consequences."

"Why?"

"You will learn," Agzaral said. "But you will not go at all if you do not board the ship now. Recall the alternatives I gave you. They have not changed."

"This is ridiculous," Rick said. "It makes no sense at all."

There was no reply. Agzaral continued to stare out from the screen.

At least, Rick thought, he doesn't look bored. Is that a good sign? It seems pretty frightening, actually.

"I cannot say I care for this," André Parsons said. "But I think of few alternatives." He turned to the screen. "Why should we trust you?"

"You would be surprised at how little that matters to me," Agzaral said. "But you will regret not having boarded the ship."

Parsons shrugged, then looked to Rick. "I think we should do it."

"Agreed," Rick said. "Load it up. Elliot, get them moving. We board ship."

"Move your equipment to the upper corridor," Agzaral said. "The ship will be ready to board shortly, and you should have all your possessions at the airlock."

They sweated the weapons and other equipment up the corridor. "Now get that other stuff," Rick ordered. "Clean out the cavern."

"Why?" Warner demanded. "What do we do with a gasoline lawnmower?"

"I don't know," Rick said. "But we'll never get another one. Now carry it up, Professor."

"Yes, *sir*," Warner said. "And the toaster, too?"

"Everything," Rick said. He picked up a coffee urn.

When they had all left the cavern, the entrance to it closed off.

✢ ✢ ✢

The ship stank. Although they couldn't see very much of the ship, it was obvious that it wasn't the same one they had come up in. The paint was stained and chipped in places. There were stains on the deck.

When they got the last of the equipment aboard, the entryway closed. There was no warning at all. Their weight increased. It was obvious that the ship was in motion. Rick estimated the acceleration at about twice the Moon's gravity.

After two hours, he began shouting. "What the hell's going on," he demanded. There was no one to talk to. The only TV screen was blank. It seemed silly to be shouting at empty air, but it was sillier not to do *something*.

Nothing happened. Some of the troops prowled the areas they

could reach. They found doorways that would open, and beyond them were latrines, storage compartments, another empty area. They found food in two other compartments.

The rest of the system was closed. There was no way into the rest of the ship.

"What the hell's going on?" Rick muttered.

André Parsons shrugged. "There is wine and whiskey in the storerooms. I suggest we have a drink."

"Is that all you think of?"

"No, but I think of nothing better to do at the moment."

More than fifty hours went by. They still had no word from anyone. They had been under acceleration the entire time. Rick worked out the distance, assuming two Lunar gravities. The answer seemed so unreasonable that he worked it again. Thirty-two million miles. A third of the distance from Earth to the Sun.

There was nothing on the TV. Warner began to complain that their employers had violated their contract. Rick privately agreed, but he saw no point in talking about it. If the *Shalnuksis* were listening, he didn't want them thinking in those terms. Finally Elliot shut Warner up.

A couple of troopers got roaring drunk, and Rick had to post guards at the door to the liquor compartment. The problem was— whom did he trust? Discipline was going to hell, and there wasn't much he could do about it.

Another forty hours went by.

✦ ✦ ✦

"TEN MINUTES." The voice sounded through their compartment. "You have ten minutes to prepare for no gravity. Ten minutes."

There was netting in the storerooms, and they put the loose equipment under that, but they kept their weapons. No one wanted ship's doors between them and their rifles.

The acceleration stopped, and they were in free fall, but not for long. The ship moved in short jerks. Then there was a deep tone— nothing like the warning tones they had heard from the speakers. This was a deep thrum that sounded through the whole ship, as if the ship itself were vibrating to the noise.

Rick's vision blurred. He could see, but not well, as if he were looking through heavy astigmatic lenses. The thrumming note got louder and increased in pitch. Then, gradually, the note died away and his vision returned. They began to feel weight again, more than before—almost a full Earth gravity.

The TV set came on. It showed Karreeel seated in his highchair. He looked almost comical, and some of the troops laughed nervously.

Then they crowded around shouting obscenities. There was no response. Instead, Karreeel began to speak in a flat monotone.

"I regret that this is a recorded message," the alien said. "Please listen carefully."

"Shut up," Rick ordered. The babble died, but he missed the first words.

". . . was unavoidable. You are now on your way to Tran, and you cannot regret your lack of proper equipment more than we do. Your success is important to us, and only great need forces us to send you with so little preparation." The alien spoke in a calm and detached manner, but Rick noticed that the mouth and nose slits flared more than they had during the interview in Agzaral's office.

"We will provide you with as much information as possible. The pilot of this vessel is of your species, and he has tapes of what we know of local conditions. He will translate the information and provide you with copies of the planetary surveys.

"You will be aboard the transport ship for approximately forty of your days. During that time the acceleration will be increased to that of Paradise to accustom you to the gravity you will find there.

"I regret that most of the information on local languages is very old, but doubtless you will learn those currently in use. You may need only one. We are interested in only a small area of the planet. You will also be given all the information required to plant and harvest the crops. The cultivation of the *surinomaz* is complex, and it is important that you follow instructions exactly. The harvest will be valuable to us, and thus to you. When next we visit Paradise, we will bring luxuries and necessities. You need have no concern, provided that you have grown what we require and are prepared to furnish it to us.

"Of course you must understand that if you have nothing to sell us, we will have nothing to sell to you.

"We wish you great success."

The screen went blank. Then a human face appeared.

The man was not as dark as Agzaral, and his eyes were lighter in color, but there was a faint resemblance to Agzaral even so. His voice had no accent at all. "You can call me 'Les,' " he said. "I'm the pilot. I'll try to answer questions."

"Take us back!" Warner shouted. "You have no right to change our contract! We enlisted under specified conditions and you have changed them. We quit!"

The pilot laughed. "You'll do it on Tran, then. I don't think anybody ever jumped ship in phase drive before, but you're welcome to try. Unfortunately, there's no known way you can report to us on what happens. Telepathy? Are you telepathic?"

"That's enough, Warner," Rick said. "Elliot, sit on him if that's what it takes."

"Sir." Sergeant Elliot grinned. This was the first thing he'd completely understood since they left the Moon, and he was eager to be useful.

"Equipment," Rick said. "We don't have what we need—we don't even know what we need."

"Yeah, that's too bad," Les said. "Karreeel is very sorry about that. You see, we got word that a shipload of government people had just come out of phase drive and was about to make a visit. That would have delayed your trip for months, maybe longer. Might have canceled it entirely. This ship is under charter to Karreeel's trading company, and you wouldn't believe what it would have cost to have it sit idle all that time."

"But—we don't know what to do when we get there," Rick protested.

"You'll get all the information you need," Les said. "Well, all we have, anyway. Look, this has all been done before. You'll manage."

"This is absurd," André Parsons said. "How do you expect us to establish control of an area and raise crops with almost no equipment and very little ammunition?"

"Don't know," the pilot said. "But you'd better try. Karreeel will keep his part of the bargain, but he won't trade with you if you've got nothing to trade."

"But it makes so little sense," Parsons said. "If they wish this crop, why send us with inadequate gear?"

"Well, it's too bad," Les said. "But his outfit can afford the loss. What they couldn't afford was the time they'd lose if you were still around when the Commission people arrived. You wouldn't have liked that much either. Hearings, committee meetings, more hearings, and all the time they'd insist they were interested only in what was best for you."

"Can't you explain some of this?" Rick asked. "Somehow you people don't act the way we always thought an interstellar civilization would—"

The pilot laughed. "I've read some of your speculations. Why did you think we'd be so different from you? Or that we'd treat Earth any different from the way the English treated India? Excuse me, I've got work to do. Among other things, I have to translate all this stuff."

"Can't a computer do that?" Rick asked.

"Yeah, but it's not as easy as you think. Have to set up the right programs for it. I'll be back." The screen went blank again.

André Parsons looked thoughtful. "What was it that the East India Company called native soldiers?"

"Sepoys," Rick said.

Parsons nodded. "Sepoys. Well, now we know our status."

3

The computer control system was complex, but eventually Gwen was able to use it for simple tasks, such as calling up pictures and documents. A good thing, too, she told herself. Otherwise she'd be bored to distraction.

Not with Les, of course. He was attentive and kind. He spent hours preparing dinners to be served in a romantic setting, with exotic music from a dozen worlds, wines and liqueurs from as many more, so that their evenings—and nights!—were more exciting than anything she could imagine.

But that was a few hours a day. You can spend only so much of your time being charmed. Or in bed, she told herself. Les had his work; he was translating documents for the mercenaries. That left her with mornings and afternoons (ship time, of course; since they had left the solar system there was nothing to be seen outside the ship—no star or sun to mark days or seasons) with nothing to do. Les wouldn't let her talk to the mercenaries; they weren't to know she was aboard. He insisted on that.

Which left her curious. Who were they? Why were they going to a primitive world called Tran?

When she first learned to use the computer's information-retrieval system, she could only look at pictures. The languages were a total mystery. The pictures were amazing enough; stars and nebulae, time-lapse photographs of multiple star systems with the stars so close they touched and sent streams of star-stuff spiraling off into the universe;

another time-lapse of a black hole devouring its companion, taken from close enough and with long enough time delay that she could actually see the real star diminish in size, torn into gases which spiraled down and down to vanish into a central nothing; and more. There were intriguing pictures of life on a hundred planets. She counted a dozen races. *Shalnuksis*, of course, and others; Centauroids. Octopoids. A race like humans, but obviously reptilian in ancestry. A world where humans—real humans—kept as seeming pets small winged reptiles looking for all the world like tiny dragons.

And it was frustrating because Les didn't want to answer questions. Not that he flatly refused, but he would put her off, ask what she thought of what she had seen, ask what it reminded her of, until the evening was over and once again she had done all the talking. His desire for knowledge about Earth was insatiable. He wanted to know everything, trivial or profound. No detail seemed unimportant.

An anthropologist studying her. But few anthropologists were so charming about it.

Eventually she found the file on Tran, the place where the mercenaries were going. She could read none of it, of course; but she had learned how to make the computer pronounce the words it displayed on the screen, and from that she learned the phonetic alphabet used by the Confederacy. She made very little progress learning that language. There were too many words referring to places and people and things and ideas that were thoroughly unfamiliar. This didn't surprise her. The real shock came when the computer showed her the languages of Tran.

She spent a day being certain. Then, in the evening, when they were together with a glass of amontillado ("One of Earth's finest products," Les had said. "Nothing to match it anywhere. Too bad regular trade with Earth isn't allowed."), she could stand it no longer.

"I was listening to Tran languages," she said.

He raised an eyebrow. "Nothing there to interest you."

"But there is! Les, I recognized some of the words! A lot of them. That language is based on an ancient Indo-European tongue! Some of the words are unchanged from Mycenaean Greek!"

"Astute of you to notice," he said. "I expect you're right."

"Les, you're teasing me. You know what this means. It means that there was an exchange of people—a lot of people, enough to bring languages with them—between Tran and Earth as far back as four thousand years."

"Other way," he said. "From Earth to Tran."

"I meant that. It's obvious that humans didn't evolve on Tran. It's only a colony. But why is it so primitive? Even relative to Earth. And Earth is primitive by your standards—Les, is *Earth* a colony?"

"No." He looked thoughtful. "Perhaps that's not the right answer. Perhaps you're right. Earth is a colony—"

"Les, you're not making sense. Did humanity evolve on Earth?"

"What do you think? You've read Darwin and Ardrey and Leakey. More sherry?"

"I don't want sherry, I want answers!"

He came over and filled her glass. "Don't be so serious," he said. "Now. You obviously think humanity is native to Earth. Tell me why."

An hour later, it was time for dinner. He still hadn't answered her questions.

✣ ✣ ✣

Dinner was exotic, as usual, but she wasn't interested in food.

"Hey. You're crying," he said. "What's the matter? You don't like *nastari*?"

"You treat me like a child."

"No. I treat you like an adult," he said. He was very serious.

"I—what do you mean?"

"You are an intelligent woman. You raise fascinating questions. Don't you want to find answers for yourself?"

"But you know, and I don't—"

"Do I?"

"You mean you don't know? You don't know where humanity evolved?"

"I don't even *know* that it did."

"But—" The enormity of what he'd said struck her. "But you—your culture—you've had space travel for four thousand years," she insisted. "If you don't know the answers, at least you have a lot more data! Give me some."

"I'm doing that. How much can you absorb in a few weeks?"

"Oh." She was silent for a long time.

"Gwen." His voice was very gentle, his expression very serious. "Gwen, accept it. All of it. Believe me, I care for you. And believe me when I say I'm trying to do what's best for both of us." He laughed. "My, aren't we serious. And the dessert will melt."

✢ ✢ ✢

Gradually she realized it: he was interested in what she thought. He wanted to know her ideas, and more than that, her reactions to what she was learning. But he was getting her talking to herself.

"What am I?" she asked her mirror. "Lover or laboratory animal? Anthropologist's informant, mistress, or—" She broke off. She'd been about to say "wife" and she didn't have any right even to *think* that.

And he did want to know. When she pointed out that some of the intelligent races she'd seen in pictures were identical to descriptions found in ancient mythology: centaurs, an aquatic race that might be mistaken for mermaids, a saurian race that might or might not have inspired the Minotaur legend—he not only listened, he insisted on having her describe and sketch the legendary creatures.

He also encouraged her to study Tran. She might think of something useful, something that would aid the mercenaries. "It would help a lot if you could," he said.

"Why?"

"If they succeed, they'll make a lot of money for the traders. Traders have influence with the Council. Won't hurt my career."

She stared in disbelief. "I—I thought I knew you better than that," she said. "Don't you care about the people on Tran? They're *human*. Don't you care?"

"Oddly enough, I do care," Les said. "Enough, in fact, to see if I can think of any way to help the mercenaries succeed with a minimum of slaughter. Because, you see, they really have to succeed—"

"Why?"

He ignored her question. "Can you think of anything that would help?"

"I don't know," Gwen said. "All the information I've seen is very old—"

"About six hundred years old," Les said. "No one's been there since, except for one fairly recent fly-by. We know they're still pretty primitive down there. No railroads, industries, paved roads. No technological civilization."

"But no one has landed for six hundred years?"

Les nodded.

"But I thought this crop was valuable—"

"It is. But there are some powerful reasons for the *Shalnuksis* to stay far away from Tran." He looked thoughtful for a moment. "It's best you know. Tran's not in the Council's data banks. Except for the *Shalnuksis* and a few humans who work for them, no one knows the planet exists."

He seemed very serious, and she knew he already regretted trusting her with even that much information. She wanted to tell him that he could trust her with anything, that she'd always be loyal to him no matter what he was doing. That thought shocked her because she'd never thought such a thing before. And was it even true? "What would happen if the—the Council found out?"

Les shook his head. "I don't know." He was silent for a moment.

She waited, hoping he'd trust her again, but instead he said, "But it wouldn't be good for me. The *Shalnuksis* would lose control. They'd never get their crop harvested."

"But without information, how can they expect a small group of mercenaries to get them anything?"

"Maybe they can't." There was definite worry in the pilot's voice. "But it is important. Have you any suggestions?"

"This doesn't make sense," Gwen said. "You say the crop is valuable, but they don't visit the source for hundreds of years—"

"Oh. Yes," Les said. "But you see, the real *surinomaz* won't grow under normal conditions on Tran. Just for a few years out of every six hundred. But for about five years, starting a couple years from now, it grows very well. The mercenaries could demand a pretty stiff price if they knew it." He sighed. "I guess the best thing will be to set them down near a small village in the right geographical region and hope they're intelligent enough to manage."

"They won't even know the languages—"

"They'll have to learn them."

"Why six hundred years?"

"Orbits," the pilot said. "Tran has two main suns. Both a little bigger and a little hotter than Sol. Planet's farther away from either of them, so it's not as warm. Reasonable climate, actually. But even with both suns, *surinomaz* won't grow properly. It's only a weed until the third sun comes close, but then for a short time it's the best stuff in the galaxy."

"But what is *surinomaz*?"

"Ever hear of Acapulco Gold?" the pilot asked.

"Marijuana—you mean drugs?"

"In a way. Look, back on Earth, you've just discovered endogenous morphiates. Know what I'm talking about? No? Well, it turns out that the brain manufactures its own painkillers and euphoric drugs. Chemicals similar to morphines. Enough of them in your system, and you have a natural high. *Surinomaz* makes the stuff, only by the barrelful. It has about the same effect on *Shalnuksis* as on humans, and they use it about the same way Americans use alcohol. And Tran Natural gets a premium price, like Talisker scotch, or the rarer wines."

Gwen stared at him.

"I see you don't approve," Les said. "Look, what is it to me if the *Shalnuksis* use drugs? Or to you?"

But there has to be more, she thought. There has to be. Or is it that I can't accept being in love with a drug dealer? "Isn't all this illegal?" Gwen asked.

Les shrugged. "The drug traffic isn't precisely legal, but no one really cares. Keeping Tran a secret—now, that's highly illegal."

"But the crop is important to you," Gwen said.

The pilot was very serious now. "More important than you can guess that the mercenaries succeed."

"Then you should stay and help them," she said.

"Can't. The ship's too valuable. And this trip has to be kept secret, which means the ship must return as quickly as possible—"

And then, as he always did, he changed the subject.

✦ ✦ ✦

The computer's files on Tran were sketchy. As nearly as Gwen could tell, the planet had never been visited except to obtain a harvest, and there had never been any systematic studies made. No one had been sufficiently curious. There were only groups of traders who had brought mercenary soldiers from Earth with instructions to seize a particular area and cultivate *surinomaz*, harvest it, and sell the product to ships that would come later.

That had begun in Indo-European times, as Gwen had deduced from the language. She was pleased to find confirmation in the computer's records. The first humans had been sent to Tran because a dominant life-form, centauroid (vaguely similar to the Greek centaur of legend, but the intelligent and unrelated centauroids she'd seen in other pictures far more so) and about as intelligent as a chimpanzee, could not be trained to do cultivation. She could not find out why humans had been chosen, or why, once they had decided on humans, they had brought a band of Achaean warriors and their slaves instead of planting a high-technology colony.

The original expedition had been expensive. In addition to the Achaeans, the *Shalnuksi* traders had brought a variety of Earth plants and animals, scattering seeds broadside on the planet and returning years later with more animals and insects. There had been no scientific rationale to what they had brought, no attempt at a balanced ecology. It was instant natural selection; adapt or die.

The records didn't say so, but Gwen wondered if one of the reasons that *surinomaz* had become increasingly difficult to cultivate might be the competition from Earth plants, animals, and insects. Tran's native life-forms used levoamino acids and dextro sugars, like Earth's, and thus competed for many of the same nutrients.

Tran's history and evolution was dominated by its suns. The two major suns together gave it at best only a bit more than ninety percent of what Earth receives from Sol; Tran was normally a cold world, with only the regions near the equator comfortable for humans. But then came the cyclic approach of the third star; for twenty years out of each six hundred, Tran received nearly twenty percent more sunlight, a combined total of ten percent more illumination than Earth ever got.

In those times of burning, ice caps melted. Weather became enormously variable, with cycles of drought and rainstorms alternating nearly everywhere. The higher latitudes, in normal times too cold for humans and resembling the Alaska tundra, were warmed and became temperate, experiencing a brief but glorious bloom of life.

The effects of the invader's passage were devastating to the human cultures. They never rose higher than an Iron Age feudalism. Gwen thought that curious and wanted to talk to Les about it, but she didn't feel very good and went to bed early.

The next morning she vomited her breakfast.

⁜ ⁜ ⁜

In a week she was certain. She went to find Les. He was seated at the control console dictating notes for the mercenaries. When she came in he looked up with a slight frown, annoyed that she'd disturbed him at work. "Yes?"

"I'm pregnant."

His face ran a gamut of emotions. Surprise, but then something else. It looked almost like horror. He said nothing for what seemed like an eternity. Then, his voice calm, he said, "We have reasonably complete medical robots aboard. I can ask the computer if they're up to an abortion."

"Damn you!" she shouted. "Damn you!"

"But—"

"What makes you think I want an abortion? I suppose this is an inconvenience to you. It—"

"Hush. There's more involved than you know."

He's serious, she thought. Deadly serious. Deadly. Now there's an appropriate word. "Les, I thought you might be pleased." Tears welled despite her effort to control them. Couldn't he understand?

"There's so much you don't know. Can't know," he said. "Gwen, we can't have a family life. Not as you think of family life—"

"You're already married. I should have known." She was alone again. Alone, and she couldn't go home.

His reaction startled her. He laughed. Then he said, "No. I'm not married." He stood and came toward her. She moved away. His face changed, the expression softening. "Gwen, it's going to be all right. You startled me, that's all. It will be all right. You'll see."

She wanted desperately to believe him. "Les, I love you—"

He moved closer. She was afraid, of him and of everything, but she didn't know what to do; and when he came to her, she clung to him in despair.

Two weeks passed. Les did not mention their future again. They entered Tran's star system, and Les busied himself finding a suitable place to land the mercenaries.

PART THREE
TYLARA

1

Tylara do Tamaerthon sat at the head of the great wooden council table beneath banners and armor taken in a hundred battles. Her blouse was fine silk, dyed a cornflower blue to match her eyes, but under it she wore mail. The dagger at her belt had jewels and a pommel carved to the likeness of a gull's head; a work of art, but the blade was made in Rustengo and was honed to a fine point. Her braided raven-black hair was crowned with a cap of hammered iron.

She was young and beautiful, and every man in the room felt her presence; despite her armor and the dagger at her waist, she seemed small and vulnerable, in need of protection.

Everyone seemed dwarfed in the great hall of Castle Dravan. Like all of the ancient castles of Tran, Dravan stood above caves of ice; there was a faint smell of ammonia in the council room as an acolyte opened a massive door far below them. Above ground, stone arches and great wooden beams stretched massively. Other rooms in the fortress sported rich tapestries and wood paneling, but here the bones and sinews of the castle showed nakedly. The only decorations were mementos of battles won.

There were many of those. Banners from places a hundred leagues and more distant gave mute testimony to the strength of Dravan and the skill of the Eqetas who had ruled here. Tylara looked up at them as if to draw strength down from the rafters.

It was her first meeting of the full council, and she had no real confidence in these westerners. They seemed so little like her husband!

And there were only two bheromen in attendance. The others were knights and merchants, a local priest of Hestia—this was a grain-producing region—and the inevitable priests of Yatar, two representatives of the yeomanry, a scattering of guildmasters. They called her Great Lady, and for the moment they respected her as Eqetassa of Chelm; but she was still a stranger who had never lived among them.

Her only real friends were the retinue she had brought from Tamaerthon, and they had no place in the council of this western land.

A messenger stood at the end of the table. What he read was full of flowery phrases and elaborate compliments, but his meaning was clear enough. She heard him out with impatience, then waved to have him led from the room. When he was gone, she looked down the length of the heavy wooden table. "Well, my lords? Wanax Sarakos makes us an offer. Have you advice?"

There was profound silence. Tylara smiled thinly. The silence was more eloquent than any speech could have been. Her bheromen wanted to accept the offer—or at least bargain with Sarakos while they still had something to bargain with. The yeomen and guildmasters—could they want Sarakos here also? Tylara looked at the impassive faces and read nothing. She knew too little of these people, and they were accustomed to hiding their thoughts from the great ones.

But if one of the bheromen spoke for accepting Sarakos, others would join. Or would they? These were her husband's people. Could they be so little like him? The memory of him stabbed at her, and she saw him as he had been: tanned, laughing, coming to her. She thrust the image from her mind before the tears came, for she had had this dream before, and it ended with reality—with Lamil cold and stiff in his bier.

She keenly felt her youth and inexperience. She was only twelve as they reckoned years here (in Tamaerthon they counted a child a year old at birth and added four more at age nine, so that she would be called seventeen there). She had lived far from these iron hills, and she did not know these people. It said much for her husband—and for the strength of his family—that they obeyed her at all.

"Captain Camithon," she said. "It seems no one wishes to speak. Perhaps you will advise me."

Camithon had served three generations of Eqetas of Chelm; his beard had greyed in that service, and his body was scarred with wounds. A long scar from a lance that had narrowly missed taking his eye ran diagonally across his cheek, giving him a somewhat ferocious appearance that he sometimes took advantage of in councils of war. He stood hunched over as if his very bones were tired, and as he stood he muttered about his estates which he had not visited in a year. But his voice was steady enough when he spoke. "The usurper marches with two thousand lances and a great train of foot," he said. "We have but a hundred lances, and we stand in Wanax Sarakos' way."

Tylara nodded gravely as she had seen her father do in clan meetings. Inwardly she wished to shout. Camithon was broadly proclaimed a splendid soldier and perhaps he was, but he could never come to the point until he had reviewed everything a dozen times and more.

She hid her impatience with good grace and thought no one noticed. She had learned endurance if not patience, and that would have to do.

"Dravan is strong," mused Camithon. He brushed his fingers against the scar on his cheek, as if to remind everyone that he had held Dravan in the battle that earned him his distinctive mark. "Our lady has seen to the granaries and magazines, and well done that was, too. This old castle has killed five armies—but it has never before been held with only a hundred lances, and it has never before been so thoroughly cut off from aid."

"As if there were any aid to send," one of the guildmasters muttered.

Camithon's sword rested on a map unrolled on the table. He lifted the weapon and used it as a pointer. "The Protector is here, ten days and more to the northwest with our Wanax Ganton. He has no more than a thousand lances, and the Protector cannot allow the young king to be penned up in any castle, no matter how strong. Thus he cannot come to our rescue himself, and I doubt he can spare any great strength."

Tylara wanted to shout. *I know all that*, her mind screamed. Outwardly she smiled and said, "You give us a hundred lances, but you have forgotten my Tamaerthan archers. I hope this usurper Sarakos makes that mistake. He won't make it twice."

There were murmurs of approval from behind her. Tylara's people could not sit at the council table, but she was attended by them; and the Tamaerthan yeomanry wasn't afraid to be heard in any council room. In their mountainous plateau by the sea, the clans did not live as peasants lived among the great lords and bheromen of the west.

She had a momentary twinge of homesickness. She longed for her high ridges, with the blue sea to the east, stark mountains rising from it to stand deep blue in dusklight and dawn. It would be so easy to go home. She had only to give up this castle to Sarakos and she could return as the wealthiest lady in Tamaerthon—or she could stay, with all her husband's lands restored. Sarakos would give her that, and the council would approve. She had only to say the words—

"A hundred lances and two hundred archers are still but five hundred fighting men," Camithon said. He spoke as if proud of his arithmetic. "Fewer, for not all our knights have squire and man-at-arms. And these walls, though strong, enclose a great area. We have no reserve. Every man is needed at his post. What happens when they tire?"

Now, she thought. Say it now. But she couldn't. She had sworn. And how could she host her husband's murderer in his own home? Receive Chelm as a telast of Sarakos? It was unthinkable.

Yet—how do else? If the chief captain had no stomach for a fight, there was no chance at all. She fingered her braids restlessly.

"Yet honor demands that we fight," Camithon said. He looked down the length of the council table. "Do any dare dispute that?"

Some may have wanted to, but none spoke.

"I have never been one to fight merely for honor," Camithon said. "I prefer to win. But we can do no good elsewhere, so if we fight, we must hold Dravan. We sit astride the only good road south. Until we are taken, Sarakos can take no great force in search of our young Wanax. We buy time for the Protector."

"Yatar knows what he'll do with it," Bheroman Trakon said. His voice was overly loud, nervous, yet Trakon was a good man who had stood by the old Wanax in his troubles, and had lost much for doing it.

"Unfair, my lord," Camithon protested. "The Protector is the greatest soldier of Drantos, and he has won before when all seemed darkest."

"And the Dayfather may produce a miracle," Trakon said. He did not turn to see the red face of Yanulf, Archpriest of Yatar. "Yet what else can we do? I trust Sarakos not at all. Of the bheromen who have gone over to him, more than half have lost all to his favorites."

"Which hasn't stopped dozens more from joining him anyway," the weavers' guildmaster muttered. "Half the bheromen—no, three parts of four—have welcomed Sarakos. We fight to no purpose."

"Do you counsel surrender?" Camithon demanded.

The portly guildmaster shrugged. "It would do no good. Sarakos has his own weavers, and they like not our competition. But it's a forlorn fight all the same."

"It is more than forlorn." Yanulf had stood silent and impassive thus far; now the priest drew himself to full height and spoke with contempt. "Fools. The Time approaches, and you babble of petty dynastic wars."

"Legends," Trakon said.

Yanulf smiled thinly. "Legends. Is it legend that the Demon grows in the night sky? Is it legend that the waters rise along the shore? That the lamils breed, and the madweed flourishes in your very fields? Is it legend that we sit in council hall with no fire burning, yet we are not cold?"

"A warm summer," Trakon said. "No more than that. The Firestealer has been banished from the vault of the sky and stands at zenith each midnight. Of course it is warm."

There were murmurs from the yeomanry and guildmasters. Yanulf's voice rose. "And in the Time of Burning," he intoned, "then shall the seas smoke and the lands melt as wax. The waters of ocean shall lap the mountains. Woe to them who have not prepared. Woe to the unbeliever." He laughed. "Woe to you, Bheroman. But Yatar will forgive you. My lady, this is not a time for war. It is a time to gather food, to fill the holy caves. Do you not smell the breath of the Preserver? When the Stormbringer approaches, Yatar takes care of his own; and his first sign is the breath of the Preserver."

"Aye," one of the yeomen muttered. "My nephew's an acolyte, and he says the ice has grown half a foot in the past forty-day. Grown, when the Firestealer stands overhead at midnight!"

"How long?" Tylara demanded. "How long until the Time?"

"The writings are not clear," Yanulf admitted. "The worst may not come for a dozen years. There will be other signs first. The Demon

Gods will visit and offer magic in exchange for *soma*. Strangers will come, with strange weapons and a strange language."

Trakon laughed.

Yanulf gave him a look of contempt. "It is written," he said. "Thus came the Christians, and thus came the Legions; and thus came *your* forefathers. It matters not whether you believe. Before the Firestealer plunges through the True Sun five times, these things will have come to pass."

"Plenty of time, then," Trakon said.

"Nay," Yanulf said. "When the signs are seen, all will seek refuge in the great castles. The petty wars you fight now will be forgotten as those who have built castles upon bare rock know their folly and bring their armies to strike. Soon, soon all will know that there is no safety beyond the caves of the Protectors."

Tylara let them talk, half-listening in case one said something new. There was little chance of that. The situation was simple enough, if you left out religion.

But dared she? The priesthood of Yatar was universal. Whatever local gods might hold this land or that, Yatar was everywhere that humans lived. In her own land were ice caves, deep beneath the rocks, and sacrifices of grain and meat were taken there to be preserved against the days of Burning, even though few believed in the tales carried by the priesthood. If the Time approached—a time of storms when no ship sailed, and the seas rose to lap at the foothills; when Tamaerthon itself became an island; when fire fell from the sky; a time when rains would not fall, and then deadly rains fell in torrents—

She had heard the tales. No one she knew believed them except for the priesthood. Yet everyone knew of them.

But there was time. Religion could wait. And for the rest the situation was simple enough. Wanax Loron had not been a good ruler, and three years before his death civil war had broken out. The bheromen who fought him had justice on their side. Even Chelm had wavered, closing the gates of Dravan against Wanax Loron when he sought refuge from the bheromen, yet never quite joining the revolt either. That had been under Lamil's father, before plague took him.

(Plague. The legends said that as the Demon Star approached, the plague ran through the land; and certainly the plague struck every year now, with more killed each time. . . .)

But Loron had hired mercenaries and had driven the bheromen back and back, until the great ones of the land had done the unpardonable thing and invited outside help. They had offered the crown of Drantos to Sarakos son of Toris, Sarakos in his own right one of the Five Wanaxxae, and son of Toris High Rexja of the Five.

Before the invasion began, Loron died; but Drantos was left with a boy king and depleted treasury. When the bheromen rallied to their new Wanax with one of their number as Protector, they were too late. Sarakos continued to press his claims. Twenty years before, the council of Drantos had arranged a royal marriage between Lana of Drantos, sister to Wanax Loron's father, and Toris Wanax High Rexja of the Five. It had been a brilliant diplomatic stroke, but now Sarakos could claim the throne of Drantos by blood, as the most legitimate adult claimant. A few minutes with a pillow would make him the only possible claimant.

And who could blame some of the bheromen for preferring Sarakos and peace to a boy king and war? Especially now, with the Demon growing visibly brighter in the night sky, and the priests of Yatar reading from their musty books and telling of the Time which would come. These were no times for a boy king. If only Lamil had joined Sarakos! He would be alive, and he—

"I say we fight." The accent was uncultured—the blacksmith at the foot of the table. "I have heard how they live in the Five. Better be dead for one such as me. Is my forge to be used to hammer slave collars for my friends?"

"Well said," Bheroman Trakon said. "Aye. Well said. For our honor, then. Yet—honor does not demand that we hold after all is lost. I say fight, and I will be on the walls; but when Sarakos brings up towers and siege engines, I say make the best bargain we can. For all of us."

"You may bargain, my lord," the blacksmith said. "But when the Demon stands high in the day sky, what do we folk do? Sarakos would like well enough to hold Castle Dravan for his people, but will he take my family into the cool of the donjon?"

"If he will not swear to that, then I make no bargain with him," Trakon said. "We of Chelm protect our own, even against the gods. But I think you fear too much the tales of the priesthood."

"When the Demon grows large and sky fire falls, you will regret those words," Yanulf said.

"We fight," Tylara said. "For the rest we must wait, but we fight. See to the defenses. And bring all who wish to come within the walls. Have the herds we cannot bring inside driven into the mountains. Leave nothing to sustain Sarakos. Nothing to eat. Hide all wealth. Cover and hide the very wells. Let Sarakos find our land unpleasant for his stay."

"It is evil to destroy food," Yanulf said. "Evil."

There was muttering from the low end of the table, but the peasantry could see it was necessary. One of the guild masters spoke for all the townsmen and crofters. "Do we make it hard enough, he may depart, leaving our own as our masters." He fingered his neck. "It will take a heavy collar to circle this. I cannot wish to carry such."

"See to it," Tylara repeated.

"Aye, Lady," Captain Camithon said. He paused until the bheromen were leaving, but had not gone so far that they could not hear him. "The young lord made no mistake in his choice. You're more of a man than half the bheromen of Drantos."

✣ ✣ ✣

The great hall was empty except for Tylara and her archer commander. Cadaric was almost as old as Captain Camithon. His skin was tanned by wind and sun until his cheeks were cracked like worn leather. He wore the jerkin and kilts of his own people; they had never cared for trousers. "You've made no mistake, Lady," he said. He seemed pleased. "We'll show these westerners what Tamaerthon shafts can do."

"Until we have shot them all," Tylara said. Now that the others were gone, she could slump in her chair. She seemed smaller and more vulnerable. She was afraid, and there was no need to hide that from Cadaric. He had known her from the day she was born, and had served her brother and her father before him. There was no one else within five hundred leagues whom she could trust completely. "I've brought you here to be killed in a strange land, old friend."

He shrugged. "And will that be worse than to be killed at home? I doubt not the Chooser can find me here as easily as in our mountains. When it is time to guest in his lodge, then guest you will. And yet," he mused, "and yet the Day father holds higher sway here. Do you think old One-eye has lost sight of this land? It would be pleasant to know."

"They say he sees the wide world," Tylara said. "Cadaric, I think they trust me not."

"They know you not. You are a young girl to them, and all they know is that their lad chose you. And because he did, they love you. Och, Lady, I know you mourn him."

And that was more than true. Tylara touched her cheeks, determined not to let the tears start again. A widow before she was properly a bride. It was the stuff the minstrels sang of.

Certainly Lamil had loved her. Eqeta of Chelm, one of the great counts of Drantos, he could have had his choice of a hundred ladies; but his ship had been wrecked on the rocky Tamaerthon coast, and after a summer (overly warm—could the priests be right?) he chose the daughter of a Tamaerthon chief. Tylara had no dowry, nothing to bring to the marriage—only two hundred archers, and a hundred of them free to leave after five years' service—but Lamil had chosen her above the great ones of his homeland.

She had loved to watch him; young and strong, calf muscles as hard as granite and standing out like thick cords from his slim legs. He browned to a deep copper in the sun. At night they ran on high ridges lit by the Firestealer. By day he laughed in the surf, climbed high on the ledges above the sea in search of young eagles. And he had laughed. Those were her favorite memories, of his laughter; laughing and swearing that he would have no other but her when she knew it could not be, laughing again at the furor he caused in rejecting the great ladies of Drantos and the Five.

And yet—it had been no silly match. Tylara brought nothing—and did not give anyone cause to fear an expanded county of Chelm. If no great lady caught the most eligible man in Drantos, then there were no jealousies. Yet she knew he had loved her.

She was married to him before he left Tamaerthon, but she was too young to go with him. The law required that the marriage be "consummated," and so it had been, but with a thick quilt between them in the wedding bed, and her father's dour henchmen standing by through the night.

And for a winter, while the Firestealer plunged through the True Sun, she had made ready to go to her new home, to join this strong and handsome young husband. She sang the winter through until her father pretended disgust that she could be so happy to leave. In spring, when shadows stood doubled at noon and the ice was thin, she sailed north with the yearly merchant fleet, too strong for pirates to molest. They sailed north, then west through the chain of islands and swamps, and then upriver. When they landed, she was so eager that she set out the same day. She drove so hard that her maidservants were exhausted and the archers muttered ribaldries.

They reached Castle Dravan only hours ahead of the news. Lamil had chosen to stand with the boy Wanax Ganton. There had been a great battle, and Lamil was dead. Most of his troops had died covering the retreat of the boy king and the Protector. Captain Camithon told her that the Eqeta had charged Sarakos and struck him on the helmet before the guards beat him from his saddle. A dozen men had held him while Sarakos personally delivered the death stroke.

"I mourn him," Tylara said, and there was ice in her voice. "Have your fletchers make true shafts, Cadaric. We will teach this Sarakos what plumage the Tamaerthon gull wears."

2

There were none but fighting men in the great hall of Castle Dravan. The council was not needed; and now Cadaric and three subcaptains of archers sat at the table among the knights and bheromen.

They all stood respectfully when Tylara entered. If the bheromen resented her archers sitting as equals to armored knights, they kept that to themselves. Their lady had shown how sharp her tongue could be during the few weeks that she'd been with them—and they had seen what those shafts could do. They waited until she was seated at the head of the table. Then all began to speak at once.

"Hold! Silence!" Bheroman Trakon pounded the table with a dagger hilt. "That's better." He smiled at her. "My lady."

She nodded her thanks. Trakon had been most attentive lately. His wife had died of the plague ten months ago. He was twice her age—but only that, and handsome enough. Certainly she could not remain a virgin ruler of this county forever. She would never find another like Lamil, and Trakon would do as well as another when her mourning period ended. But so soon, so soon—

"They come, Lady," Captain Camithon said. "Two days' march to the north."

"Two days if they're lucky," Trakon said. "They're so swollen with plunder, they're lucky to march two thousand paces an hour."

"But all of them?" Tylara asked.

"Aye, Lady," Cadaric said. He glared at the others, ready to resent any objection that a mere Tamaerthon archer would speak. But there was only silence. Trakon, Cadaric, and Camithon had seen the advancing enemy, and the others had not. "I counted five hundred banners in their vanguard alone."

"You scouted the land well?" Tylara asked.

"Aye, Lady," Cadaric said. "It's more than suitable. We could blunt them, aye and blood them as well, and not lose a handful were it done well."

More babble. Trakon pounded for order again. One of the knights shouted. "Blunt them? What madness is this?"

Tylara noted Trakon's grim smile. He had not been too proud to listen to Cadaric as they rode back from scouting. A good man, she thought.

"The passes are narrow," Tylara said. "The maps remind me of my home. In narrow passes one man is the worth of ten—"

"Narrow they are, but not that narrow," Captain Camithon said. He sounded hurt. Strategy was a matter for professionals, not for girls hardly old enough to bed lawfully. "Do we stand in the passes with our hundred lances, we would blood Sarakos, aye, but then his strength would ride over us. Then who would there be to defend Dravan?"

Trakon's grin widened. "Our lady does not propose a stand," he said.

"Then what in the twelfth name of Yatar are we talking about?" Camithon demanded.

Cadaric grinned. "It is plain that you in the west have not heard the tales of how Tamaerthon won freedom from Ta-Hakos and the other greedy ones about us," he said. "I propose to have a ballad sung for you. With my lady's permission?"

Tylara nodded, and before there could be any protest one of the younger archers began to sing.

There were mutterings at first, but the boy's voice was good. They listened in silence, not trying to hide their astonishment at this intrusion in a council of war. As the song went on, Camithon leaned forward eagerly and Bheroman Trakon began to grin broadly. Before the ballad ended, the knights and captains were huddled over the map. For the first time in weeks, there were shouts of laughter in the great hall.

✢　✢　✢

Tylara sat astride her horse. This in itself was shocking enough; but worse, she rode no gentle mare but a great stallion—a war-horse any knight would be proud to own. She sat atop a small knoll, surrounded by a dozen men-at-arms and as many archers.

This was the price she paid for coming herself to the battle. She had never got her people to agree to that—but she'd come anyway, and no one dared lay hands on her. One soldier, ordered by Trakon to seize her bridle and lead her back inside Castle Dravan, would bear the welt from her riding crop for weeks. She must see at least one blow struck against the man who had killed her husband.

Below were not only all her fighting men, but hundreds of peasants with brush hooks and axes. They were using these to cut the low scraggly wax-stalks from the hillside and carry them into the pass. For five hundred paces from the top of the pass to where it widened below, the narrow road was carpeted with the newly cut brush. More was piled high to either side.

Bheromen and knights and men-at-arms waited where the pass widened a hundred paces beyond the last brushpile. The armored knights sat on the ground, giving their mounts ease until they would be needed. A few polished mail and plate. Others threw dice.

About half the knights were mounted on horses. The others rode centaurs; not as reliable as horses, harder to tame, and more likely to bolt when threatened. Horses were far superior, but they were more costly. They had to be fed cultivated grains and hay; they could not live by grazing.

Priestly legend said that horses, like men, were brought to this place by evil gods. This did not seem reasonable, but like the other tales of ships in the sky, the story was universal. "Why else," the priests said, "must we labor so hard to eat, if the Dayfather intended us to live here?" They said that the stars were suns, and the wanderers other worlds, one of which was the true home of men. Whether or not the stories were true, men were more comfortable with horses than with centaurs, and she wished that more of her knights rode them.

Between the top of the pass and the broader area where her knights waited, the pass was quite narrow—no more than a hundred paces wide at one point. The hills rose steeply on either side. One of the peasants went up into that area with his brush hook. Before he could cut any of the upthrust stalks, a dozen voices halted him.

"Not here, you Dayfather-damned fool!" A guild journeyman ran up to show the brushcutter the proper place. It was important that there be no signs of activity on the hill above the narrow pass—

A horseman clattered over the top of the ridge. He drew his sword and waved it vigorously. "Enemy in sight," an officer muttered. Tylara nodded.

The knights and men-at-arms climbed to their feet, clumsy in their armor, and helped each other mount. This took time. The armor was heavy, and centaurs resented heavy burdens; although a few were so well trained that they assisted their riders. Before all were mounted, Tylara, from her vantage point, saw the leading elements of Sarakos' army.

The Wanax had deployed well. There were only fighting men in the van, and when the pass began to narrow, they fell into column in good order, not pushing each other or crowding together. Horsemen led; then a group mounted on centaurs; then more horsemen. They climbed the twisting road into the pass twenty abreast—a long column—lances high with banners fluttering in the chill morning wind.

The group behind was not so orderly. Carts drawn by mules and arrocks, crossbowmen mingled with spearmen, camp followers, cooks, prostitutes, and priests all mixed together.

A trumpet sounded, and Camithon's heavy cavalrymen trotted forward over the piled brush toward the top of the pass. They raised their banners. The brushcutters scrambled away behind them, down and onto the road, running back to Dravan, raising a thin cloud of dust as they ran.

Another trumpet sounded from the leaders of Sarakos' army, and the column halted. The group behind became even more disorganized as the marching horde piled onto one another. Trailing elements caught up and mingled with the leaders. Pity, Tylara thought. If the knights could get among that press for ten minutes, Wanax Sarakos would feel the losses. But the lead group was not disorganized, and it outnumbered her entire army.

Once again she felt doubts and fear, and she looked up into the vault of reddish-blue sky above, searching for a sign. But there was none. A cloudless cold day in the mountains; rare enough, the Dayfather showing himself in all his glory—but he showed no signs of favor. Would he care? Or would the ancient One-eye govern the day, choosing the most valiant to be slain, sending victory by whim?

There were more trumpets from Sarakos' column, and the vanguard knights spread across forty abreast. They moved forward at a walk, then at a trot. The lines rippled as lances fell into place, and the trumpet sounded once more. The trot became a canter as the charge swept forward.

"Now," Tylara prayed. "Now. In Yatar's name, NOW!"

Her own trumpets sounded. Her knights wheeled, and spurred their mounts ahead, trotting down the road toward Dravan, riding after the dust cloud raised by the retreating woodcutters.

Tylara muttered thanks to the Dayfather. That had been the first of the many things that could go wrong. If the knights would not run, if the sight of the enemy had brought them to a hopeless charge because it would be dishonorable to run—more than one battle had been lost through blind obedience to the dictates of a cavalier's honor. As this one might yet be.

"They flee! The cowards run!" The shouts rose from Sarakos' charging knights.

As her own knights rode away, there were tiny movements in the brush at the roadsides. Men hidden in holes beneath the brush thrust torches upward, then fled toward the sides of the pass. Thin wisps of smoke rose, here and there a flame. The waxy stalks caught fire quickly.

Her knights reached the wide place where they had waited earlier. They wheeled as one, facing the enemy. Their lances came down.

"The cowards hide behind fire!" someone shouted. "We will teach them!" The charging enemy came on harder, a hundred paces into the brush. Two hundred, and still they rode. Tylara held her breath.

When the leading elements were three hundred paces into the brush-strewn pass, a hundred paces beyond the top of the pass, her own trumpets sounded. There was a flash of movement on the hillsides above the pass. Bright kilts, dull leather, the dull shine of steel caps painted with earth colors. A moment before there wasn't a man to be seen. Now almost two hundred archers were standing behind shrubs, behind rocks, seemingly having risen from the very ground. They raised their bows, nocked arrows, and drew back to cheek and eye.

There were shouts from Sarakos' troops, but it was obvious to even the most stupid that there was no halting the charge. Safety lay ahead, through the screen of knights, out of the growing fire and away from the archers. The leading horsemen spurred harder.

Another pause. Then a shout from the hillside. "Let the grey gulls fly!"

The arrows flew with a deadly sound. In a moment the air was thick with them. Even as the first flight struck, another was on its way. Shafts the length of a tall man's arm and tipped with steel sped from bows drawn by men who'd used them since childhood. The second flight struck, and another arched out.

The slaughter was terrifying. The arrows pierced horses, saddles, even armor itself. Horses reared and bolted, crashed into each other, tripped and fell and stumbled over fallen horses. The centaurs screamed in rage and pain, their stubby arms flailing wildly, their half-hands frantically plucking at the arrows, their heads twisted to lick wounds. They seized their riders and tried to throw them off, or fell into the brush and rolled on their backs. Some plunged uphill off the road, to be shot down before they could climb far.

Still the arrows flew. The charge was broken into scattered groups, driblets of twos and threes and fours; not a solid wave of armored men with lances, but a disorganized horde fleeing past the archers, away from the growing fires, out into the broad area beyond—

To be struck by the countercharge of Tylara's knights. With a hundred paces to build momentum they struck the leading elements of Sarakos' forces, driving their enemy back toward the flames and the falling arrows, then wheeling away as yet another wave charged through to strike and turn. They too wheeled and joined their fellows; halted and dismounted.

Dismounted. One-eye Vothan had smiled on her, had not maddened her knights as he so easily might have done. They had obeyed orders. Most western knights wouldn't fight dismounted; the Eqetas of Chelm had trained these well.

They stood with leveled lances, poised just beyond the burning brushwood, an impenetrable wall on which Sarakos' men could break themselves again and again, but never get through. They could not have withstood a mounted charge by an organized group, but there was no danger of that. Sarakos' force milled about in the smoke and flame, galled by the ceaseless shower of arrows, held by the fire and the bodies of their own comrades. The dismounted line was more than able to kill the few who rode out of the smoke.

A brisk wind came up to whip the flames. They grew and flamed higher, until for five hundred paces the pass looked like the very Pit—a tangle of smoke and fire, shouting men, men unhorsed, dying horses, riderless centaurs maddened by fire and plunging into everyone. And through it all the Tamaerthon gulls flew with their deadly bite, flight after flight of the grey shafts.

The Sarakos trumpets sounded a frantic retreat, but for far too many there was no retreat possible.

The arrows did not come in flights now. The archers picked single targets, concentrating on men still mounted, bringing down their mounts to leave the armored men helpless in the burning brushwood. The pass filled with sounds of pain and terror.

Tylara sat her horse grimly, her mouth set in a hard line. I thought I would enjoy it, she thought. These are the men who killed my husband. I should enjoy their agony.

But she felt no joy at all, only sickness and horror which she must hide from her shouting escort, and the numbing realization that this was only the beginning. There would be far more, weeks more.

I hadn't known the horses would scream so, she thought. I expected to see men die, but I had not thought of the horses.

She continued to watch in sick fascination until she suddenly realized what she was doing. She had almost made a fatal mistake.

Sarakos was bringing up his own archers. Most were crossbowmen, or mounted archers with short bows they drew only to the chest; none were a match for her Tamaerthon clansmen, but two hundred cannot fight a thousand. It was time to go. She raised her hand and waved vigorously.

Her trumpets sounded in the pass. Cadaric waved acknowledgement and began sending his archers out; the forward ones first, then others, leapfrogging so that they kept a continuous fire onto the Sarakos troops piled up at the edge of the brushfire.

Another trumpet call. Nothing happened. Her knights stood at the pass. A few left the line, but they went only for their mounts, and when they were mounted they came back.

"Fools!" Tylara shouted. She spurred her horse down the knoll to where the knights and bheromen of Chelm stood. More mounted as she came, but they showed no signs of leaving.

"Ride!" she shouted. "Before the fires burn down and their whole army comes through! Ride, my lords. You've done well. One-eye

Vothan smiles on you. Sarakos will not soon forget this day. Now, in the name of the Dayfather, ride!"

Bheroman Trakon sat motionless. "The fire protects them no less than us. There was nothing behind their vanguard but foot. We have more work to do this day."

"Not true," Tylara shouted. "They were bringing up their horse archers even as I watched, and they have their crossbowmen. You will ride into their volleys, and the remnant will be charged by their cavalry."

Trakon didn't move.

"My lord," Tylara said. She tried to control the panic in her voice. "If you mean to die here today, I will stand with you. It will be no victory no matter how many we destroy, for we will have given Dravan to Sarakos. If we are caught here, anywhere but within the walls, we are finished.

"I would rather be killed with my husband's knights than ride to Dravan and live to see it fall to Sarakos. Is that your will?"

Trakon sat motionless for a moment, then shook his head as if to clear it of the morning fog. "You speak well, Lady. We have won no victory if we stay to be killed." He rose in his stirrups to shout orders. "Carry the dead and wounded away. Leave nothing for Sarakos. Let him believe that he has lost the quarter of his vanguard to ghosts, to achieve nothing." He turned and rode down the pass. After a moment, Tylara followed.

I follow, she thought. *It was my victory, but I follow.* She sighed, knowing what would be thought by everyone who saw.

✤ ✤ ✤

A week later, Sarakos reached Castle Dravan. The first attempt to storm the castle was repulsed; attack and defense might have been the opening steps in a ritual dance. The next move was also set; Sarakos dug in and erected pavilions and defenses around the castle.

There was no entry or exit from Dravan. Sarakos and his army waited for their siege train.

3

The siege towers rolled forward slowly. The armored heads of picks thrust out of them as if eager to attack the walls and gates of Dravan. Hundreds of men strained to push the monsters forward. Overseers shouted cadence. Boys poured melted fat on the axles. They would reach the walls by afternoon.

"It is time, Tylara," Trakon said. "Time and past time."

She looked helplessly at him, then at the others: Cadaric, his son Caradoc, and Yanulf. "Have I no other advice?" she asked.

"You know mine, Lady," Cadaric said. He clutched his bow. "There are no more shafts. As for me, as well to die; but it would be waste to no purpose."

Cadaric's son Caradoc opened his mouth to speak, but was silenced by his father's look. The young man looked down at the towers in hatred.

Yanulf nodded sagely. "What choice is there? In a day they will be inside, and it always fares ill with the populace when a place is taken by storm." He paused. "You need not stay, Lady. My place is with the acolytes in the caves of the Preserver, and we could find you a place there as well."

"No," Trakon said. "I will have a better bargain for her than that."

Yanulf bowed. "I will not wait, then." He turned to leave the battlements.

"I will send my son with you," Cadaric said. "Perhaps Yatar will aid him to return to Tamaerthon."

"And perhaps not," Yanulf said. "But it is well to have young men as apprentices." The old priest waved toward the armies below the walls. "Fools all. The Time approaches, and still men fight."

"But not for long," Tylara said. She turned to Trakon, but for a moment she could not find words. Finally she said, "Make a good bargain for our people."

"I will. It will be for the best."

Tylara stood at the battlements as Trakon went to the gate and hoisted the green branch of truce.

✛ ✛ ✛

Her ladies dressed her, and one of Sarakos' officers led her to the council chamber. She felt strangely light without mail and steel cap, and stranger still to be unarmed. Strangest of all was to see Sarakos in her place at the head of the table.

He looked young to be so powerful. He was a big man, but not fat; even his eyes showed strength. He was handsome, but she did not forget for a moment that this was the man who had killed her husband while others held him helpless.

His smile was not pleasant. "Welcome, Lady." He stared at her and she shuddered.

Sarakos was not alone in the room. Guards held Bheroman Trakon. His shirt was open; there was blood on his bare chest. "What is the meaning of this?" she demanded.

"You are all traitors," Sarakos said. "Traitors do not die easily, as you will learn." He motioned to the guards. "Take that carrion out and kill him with the rest."

Trakon shook off the guards and stood straight, although he winced to do it. "Is this how a Wanax keeps his promises?" he demanded. "You gave your word that the Lady Tylara and I—"

"Would marry," Sarakos said. "After the traitors were killed. And so shall you be. Joined forever." He turned and looked appreciatively at Tylara. "I can see why you wanted her. You may have to wait for her, but you will have her for all time when I am through." He waved dismissal to the guards.

For an hour, Castle Dravan sounded with the screams of the dying. Tylara was forced to stand at the window and watch as her soldiers were killed; some beheaded, the archers used as targets for Sarakos' crossbowmen, the officers flung from the castle battlements.

Then she was taken to Sarakos' bedchamber, and another kind of horror began.

She heard the massive door opening and whimpered, trying to draw her knees tighter to her chest. She kept her eyes closed. Which would it be: the crone with the whip or Sarakos himself? She remembered his parting words; "You have not pleased me. I would as soon have a corpse. But before you die, you will please me. You will beg for the chance."

"My lady."

The voice seemed different. Familiar, and youthful. It was not Sarakos—

"My lady. There is little time. You must come now."

She was afraid. Was it a trick? But the voice was urgent. She found the courage to open her eyes and turn her head, although she dared not hope.

She saw kilts—her own plaid—and looked higher. "Caradoc!" she cried. He reached for her and she let him help her stand. He gasped when he saw her back, and she leaned on him as he led her urgently out of the bedchamber. There were two dead men lying at her door.

The hour was early. They saw no one as they went down the back stairs to the large cistern below ground; then to the massive doorways that led still farther below; to the caves of the Protectors. The ammonia smell was strong. She hesitated, but Caradoc hustled her through and closed the doors behind. Two acolytes with torches came to help her now. Their faces showed disapproval of this invasion of their realm.

They went through darkened tunnels, turning until she was lost. Finally they came to a larger room lit with another torch. Yanulf was there.

"The guards were drunk," Caradoc said. "I killed four. No one else was awake."

"We must be gone before they are found," Yanulf said. The priest turned to the acolytes. "Fetch bladders."

They stared at him in horror.

"Do you think Yatar prefers his secrets to the torture of his friends?" Yanulf snapped. "This lady treated us well. She will not reveal what she sees, nor will Caradoc."

The acolytes hesitated a moment more, then left. When they came back, they carried inflated sheep's bladders.

Yanulf pointed to a door in the chamber. "We will go through there. You must breathe only from the bladders, and you must hold your breath as long as possible. The journey is steep, and we cannot pause to rest until we are through the tunnels and outside the door on the far side. It will be dark. Is this understood?"

Tylara stared at him in confusion. She wanted to lie down, to rest, to sleep, to forget the pain in her back and the terrible pain between her thighs. Pain filtered the memories, but not entirely. "There is no need," she said. "Give me your dagger, and—"

"Don't be a fool," Yanulf told her. "Do you think I have invited Sarakos to violate Yatar's house and just let you die?"

"I may carry Sarakos' child," she said. "I'd rather be dead."

"Time enough when you know. But it's unlikely," Yanulf said. He was thoughtful for a moment. "Very unlikely, even leaving out your virginity."

The priests of Yanulf were said to know when women could conceive.

"Alive there is hope of vengeance," Caradoc said. "For you and for my father. Until I see Sarakos gull-feathered, I will stay alive."

"Come." Yanulf handed her the bladder. "Before you use the bladder, breathe deeply. Many times." He demonstrated. "More." When he was satisfied, he motioned to the acolytes to open the heavy doors.

There were more doors beyond. These next were sealed with leather. Tylara felt the ammonia stinging her eyes, and even through the bladder she could smell the pungent odor when the last doors were opened.

Cold welled out of the caves. She took an acolyte's hand and let herself be led into darkness.

✧ ✧ ✧

There was no light at all. She felt the walls as they went through. There were shelves with baskets, and slabs of meat hanging below those. Between the shelves were slimy bulbous things, cold to the touch. Then there was ice.

They seemed to go on forever. The air in the bladder was stale, and her lungs ached so much that she nearly forgot her other pains. She was certain that she would faint from lack of breath, but at that moment they stopped. Light burst in from a door opened in front of them. They hurried through, past another door, and stood outside in the dying light of the night sun. To the east was the red of dawn.

There were horses. She felt herself lifted up behind Caradoc. She clung to him and they rode away. After a while, she fell asleep clinging to the archer. In her dreams, she had Sarakos flayed alive, and she smiled.

✣ ✣ ✣

The true sun was high overhead when at last they stopped at a crossroads.

"We must hurry on," Yanulf was saying.

"This horse must rest," Caradoc answered. "Carrying double has nearly foundered him." He reached up to help Tylara down, then led the horse to the watering trough that stood next to the stone heap. He bowed to the heap before allowing the horse to drink.

Tylara bowed as well. Crossroads were sacred to the Guide of the Dead. Then she turned to Yanulf. "Thank you."

"Thank him." He pointed at Caradoc.

"I have. But we would not have escaped if you had not—" she stopped herself.

"Broken my oath of secrecy?" Yanulf said. "Yes. Doubtless I will answer for that. But I spoke truly to the acolytes. Yatar cannot wish his secrets held at such a cost."

"Where are we going?" Tylara asked.

Caradoc answered from behind her. "This is the east road," he said. "Perhaps we will find the boy Wanax and the Protector. And if not—it leads home."

Home. She looked to the east, but Tamaerthon was more than a hundred leagues, across salt flats and pirate lands. "There's someone coming," she said. She pointed eastward. Two men and a woman were walking up the road. The woman wore strange-trousered clothing like the men.

PART FOUR
THE CROSSROADS

1

The planet below did not look like Earth. The polar icecaps were too large, and there was much more water, too little land. Despite the vast empty seas—because of them? Rick knew too little to guess—there were great deserts ringed by mountain ranges.

From high orbit there was no trace of man at all.

The pilot seemed to be afraid of them. He made them store all the ammunition for the rocket launchers and mortars in one locker and the guns in another. He made it clear that the two would be offloaded a considerable distance apart.

The last few hours had been continuous briefings with the pilot insisting that both Rick and André Parsons attend them all. They were told how to raise *surinomaz*, which had a complex ecology and even more complex harvest procedure; how to use the transceivers to communicate with the traders when they came for the harvest; endless details, and always an underlying note of warning that the people of Tran were human and deserved to be well treated.

The landing area had been chosen: far enough from the equator to have an endurable climate even after the rogue sun came close; far enough from the poles to be inhabited even during the centuries when the invader was far away; at high enough altitude to remain dry when the polar caps melted and raised the sea level a hundred meters. There were several areas that would do, and Rick had no way to know which was best. He had pleaded with the pilot to let them spend several days observing the planet before landing, but that request was refused. The pilot seemed to be in a frantic hurry. Rick wondered why, but there was no explanation.

They moved to a lower orbit, and the TV screen showed images of the country below: a few large cities, but mostly a land of villages and fields. Many of the villages and all the cities were dominated by massive castles. There were few roads.

Parsons wanted to land near a city, but Rick chose a village near a major road, fifteen kilometers from a castle. The orbital photographs showed an army encamped outside the castle and massive siege towers nearing completion.

"If there's a battle we may decide to join it," Rick said. "After we get some political intelligence."

"Nearer a city would be better," Parsons said. "And if you intend to take that castle, why land a day's march away?"

Rick again protested that they didn't know enough and should land a safe distance from conflict. Eventually Parsons stopped arguing.

They landed at dusk, just after the major sun had set but before the distant secondary was up. When the secondary sun fully rose, it would light the planet with a blaze like a thousand full moons, making the night as light as a heavily clouded day on Earth. When they landed, the tricky light— dusk from the sun, rays of dawn from the secondary— made weird images and shadows.

They offloaded the guns first, then the ammunition nearly a kilometer from their first touchdown spot. Rick was the last to leave. Before he could jump out, the hatch closed and the ship lifted.

"Stop! I'm still aboard!" he shouted.

"I know." The pilot's voice was impassive. The ship moved half a kilometer and settled to the ground. Rick heard the whine of machinery, but the hatch didn't open for several minutes. Then the voice said, "Now you can get out."

When he jumped to the ground, the ship lifted. Rick watched it rise into the clouds until it was gone. He hadn't really believed it would leave until then. He felt completely alone.

"It's really gone."

He fought a moment of terror as he realized the voice had been a woman's. He turned.

She was a tiny girl, not very pretty in the half-light. She was dressed in coveralls much like his own. "You're human," he said.

"You don't sound very sure of that."

"I'm not very sure of that."

"I'm human. My name is Gwen Tremaine, and I come from Santa Barbara."

"Santa Barbara. As in California? On Earth?"

"Yes." She tried to laugh, but she didn't succeed. "Oh, yes, I'm from Earth."

"We'd better get over to the others," Rick said. He moved closer to her and saw tears in her eyes. "Are you all right?"

"I'm scared as hell," she said.

"So am I. Uh—"

"I was the pilot's mistress," she said. "That's what you wanted to ask, wasn't it? I got pregnant and didn't want an abortion, so he put me out here." This time she managed a laugh. Rick thought it sounded horrible. "Pretty convenient. I asked him if this was the traditional way for flying-saucer pilots to get rid of excess baggage, but he didn't answer."

"Jesus!" Rick muttered. He led her through the scrub brush—it seemed a lot like the chaparral of the western United States, but there was a strange pungent odor to it—toward the distant lights where Parsons and the guns had been unloaded. He wanted to say something to comfort her, but he couldn't think of anything. God Almighty, he thought. She must be as alone as anyone has ever been. "Do you know anything about—about why we're here?"

"Probably more than you," she said. She walked beside him, but several steps away, as if repelled by him.

"If you know more than I do, I'd appreciate the information," he said.

"We've got plenty of time. Let me get used to the situation, will you? When he had me read up on Tran, he didn't tell me it was because he was leaving me here."

"When did he tell you—"

"That he was ditching me? About five minutes ago."

"That was—" He tried to think of something to say, but couldn't.

"A rotten thing to do?" she asked. "Sure was. You see, I thought I was in love with him." She walked on for a few steps. "Do I sound like you?" she asked.

"How?"

"Scared and trying to be calm about it when what you really want to do is run in circles flapping your arms."

"Do I sound that way?" Rick asked.

"Yes."

"I guess I do," he said.

✣ ✣ ✣

Parsons had assembled the troops on the hilltop. He seemed as surprised to see Rick as he was to see Gwen. "I thought they'd taken you on to wherever the saucer was going," Parsons said.

Rick didn't like the edge to Parsons' voice. He didn't much care for the way Parsons held the M-16 rifle, either. "They didn't," he said. "I guess he wanted an escort for Miss Tremaine." Rick explained who she was.

"I see. And now what do we do?"

"There are about a thousand things to do," Rick said. "When there's more light, we can go down to that village. The first thing is to start learning the local language. And figure out which side to take in that war we saw. Then—"

"There's one thing a bit more urgent," Parsons said.

"What's that?"

"I think it time we restructure the command," he said. The rifle swung around until it almost pointed at Rick.

"What the hell do you mean?"

"You are not an experienced officer," Parsons said. "An ROTC boy, with almost no combat experience. Under the circumstances, do you really feel qualified to lead?"

"As qualified as you—"

"No. This is my career. For you it was an accident," Parsons said.

"So you're taking over."

"Yes." Parsons shrugged. "If you like, I'll fight you for it."

"Isn't that a little barbaric?" Rick demanded.

Parsons smiled broadly. "Of course. We are on a barbarous planet. In fact, that is one major objection to you, Rick. You are unlikely to have the proper instincts for survival here. I have long noticed a regrettable tendency toward softheartedness in you. That was bad enough in Africa. Here it is likely to be fatal."

A circle of men had gathered around them. Rick looked at them. "Elliot—"

"Cap'n, I'm truly sorry. I thought about this a lot when Mr. Parsons first brought it up, back aboard ship. He's right. You just don't have the experience."

And he sounds really sorry about it, Rick thought. And probably is. One thing was certain. If Elliot and the NCOs accepted Parsons' takeover, there was nothing Rick could do about it. At best he'd cripple the command. They were all staring at him.

He had to say something, and quickly, before Parsons decided to shoot and be done with it. "Maybe you're right. André, you do have more experience than me. All right, you command." As he said it, he felt a wave of relief. Someone else could do the worrying.

"Glad you understand," Parsons said. "Sergeant Elliot, get our perimeter defense set up."

"Sir."

"And the rest of you clear out," Parsons said. He waited until the other troops were gone. "Rick, there is another problem. Surely you can understand that you can't stay with us."

"Why not?"

"You were in command. Some of the men would look to you every time I gave an order. It wouldn't work," Parsons said. His voice was low and urgent, almost pleading. "I ought to shoot you out of hand," he said. "That would be the intelligent thing to do."

"Bull crap. The troops wouldn't stand for it," Rick said.

"You see?" Parsons said. "Some of them do admire you. And there can be only one commander."

"So you're sending me off alone."

Parsons shrugged. "What else can I do? Look, I don't want to kill you. You can take your personal weapons—"

"Damn generous of you," Rick said.

"It *is* generous, and you know it. Also dangerous for me. Fair warning, Rick. I offered to fight you for the command. You refused, which was intelligent. But the next time I see you, I'll assume you've changed your mind. And I'll kill you, Rick. Make no mistake about that."

"You mean that, don't you, André?"

"Yes." He used his foot to indicate a backpack lying near them. "I've made you up a kit. A rifle. Two hundred rounds, which is more than your share of the ammunition. First-aid packet. A week's rations. You may keep your binoculars. You have your pistol, and I've included a box of cartridges for it. I haven't been ungenerous—"

"Damn you—"

"Please," Parsons protested. "Do not make me regret my generosity." He pointed. "The road is that way. Do not go toward the castle. Go east."

"I'm going with him." Gwen's voice was tightly controlled.

Parsons looked startled. Like Rick, he had forgotten that she was listening to them. "Surely you do not mean that," Parsons said.

"Surely I do," she said. She shook her head. "You're crazy. I've listened to both of you for weeks. Between the two of you, I'll take Galloway."

"Why?" Parsons asked.

"I just will. Or do you intend to keep me here?"

Parsons frowned deeply. "No, I suppose not. Very well. But get moving. I have a lot to do."

"You certainly do," Gwen said. Her voice was sugary sweet. "And you're less likely to manage it than you think. Let's go, Captain Galloway."

✢ ✢ ✢

Lower down, near the road, there were trees. They looked like gnarled evergreens, but the leaves were too broad, and like the chaparral they had a strange odor. Rick moved into the trees before he spoke.

"Are you out of your mind?" he asked.

"No." The girl's voice was strong, almost too loud.

"You didn't even act surprised . . ."

"I wasn't. I told you, I've been listening to both of you for weeks. Before we went up the hill I knew what was going to happen."

"You might have warned me—"

"To what purpose?" she asked. "There wasn't anything you could have done about it. He'd have beaten you in a fair fight, and you wouldn't shoot him without warning. Would you?"

"No. I guess not. So you knew they were going to mutiny. Did the pilot?"

"Yes. He predicted that you'd go your way and they'd go theirs."

"And you decided to come with me. Why?—careful, it's slippery here—" He put out his hand.

She moved away from him. "Let's get something straight," she said. "I've had one lover boy, and I don't need another."

"I wasn't—"

"No, I guess you weren't," she said. "But I did want to make it clear. And maybe that will give you some idea of why you. I get the impression that you're a little more human than some of those animals back there."

"They're not animals, they're soldiers. Pretty good ones. Gwen, this is silly, if you're scared of getting raped, you'd batter stay with Parsons. Not that I'm going to leap at you, but I'm not likely to live very long."

"Neither are they."

"What the hell do you mean by that?" Rick demanded.

"Nothing." She scrambled down the slope. "The road's down here," she said. "Which way?"

"Left."

"Away from the castle," she said. "See? At least you've got sense enough to walk away from a fight." She stopped to look intently at his face. "And don't get your macho image bent out of shape—I'm not calling you a coward."

"No, but you hit pretty close to home," Rick said.

"How's that?"

He told her how he had chosen track instead of football. "And don't tell me how sensible it was," he said. "I know it was sensible, but it bothers me."

2

The road was excellent. It reminded Rick of the old Roman roads he'd seen in Europe; cobblestones placed over enough rock fill to prevent settling. From the wear on the stones, the road had been there a long time, centuries at least. Unlike Roman roads, though, this one wound through the low hills and trees. Roman military roads had been unfailingly straight no matter what obstacles were in the way.

The trees and underbrush were strange, but they didn't seem particularly alien; no stranger than Africa had been when he first went there. There were no birds—at least he'd seen none—but twice he saw flying squirrels. At least, he thought, they look like the pictures of flying foxes in my old school books. I never saw a real one on Earth.

Gwen walked beside him, still keeping her distance.

"You decided to come with me. Do you have any—" Rick cut himself off and lowered his voice. "There's someone behind us," he said. They looked back to the last bend but saw nothing. Rick motioned Gwen off the road and into the trees. They took shelter in the underbrush. Rick held the rifle in readiness. Whoever was coming was making no attempt to be silent; footsteps clattered on the cobblestones.

Corporal Mason came around the bend. He stopped and looked ahead, then very carefully slung his rifle and held out his empty hands. "Cap'n," he called.

"In here," Rick said.

"Yes, sir. Figured you'd hear me comin'. Just didn't want to get shot."

Rick led Gwen back to the road. He slung his rifle, but made certain the strap on the shoulder-holstered pistol was released. "What brings you here?"

"About a dozen of us volunteered to come off with you, but Parsons and Elliot wouldn't let 'em. Elliot said it was all right for one of us, so we cut cards for it, and here I am."

"Flattering," Rick said. And, he thought, just possibly believable. It was also believable that Parsons had sent someone to finish him off. Parsons was a careful man.

Parsons might do that, but Mason wouldn't take that job. There were some who might, but not Mason. Rick suddenly realized that he was glad to see the plucky little corporal. At least he had one friend to watch his back in this strange place. "Welcome aboard," Rick said. "But you might want to explain—"

Mason spat in the dirt. "Parsons is a Foreign Legion type," he said. "The Legion uses up men. I've known some mercs who put in five with the Legion, and no thanks."

"Is Parsons likely to be looking for you as a deserter?" Rick asked.

"It's possible," Mason admitted. "It was Elliot said it was all right to take off, but maybe he didn't ask Parsons first."

"And probably didn't tell him later," Rick added. Another complication. "We'd better watch our backs."

"More reasons than one," Mason said. "There might be some others want out of Parsons' chickenshit outfit."

"Maybe we should wait and see," Gwen said. "But—" she looked thoughtful. "You wouldn't want too many."

"Why?"

She shook her head. "Woman's intuition—"

"Bat puckey. You've hinted a couple of times that you know things I don't. Isn't it time to let me in on the secret?"

"No. It's not time." Gwen was very serious.

"When will it be?"

"I don't know. But I do point out that as long as the men might run away to join you, you'll be a threat to Parsons."

"So I hide from him—"

"It's not that," she said. "Look, you won't kill him from ambush. But if he decides to kill you, you won't even know until he's done it. The only way you'll be safe from him is if he doesn't know where you are."

It made sense. It didn't sound very manly, but it made sense. Rick said so.

"There's another thing," she said.

"Yeah?"

"If the *Shalnuksi* traders learn where you are, they'll tell Parsons—"

"That's what really concerns you, isn't it?" Rick asked. "You don't want the Galactics to find you. Why?"

"Does it matter? You won't be trading with them. You can't possibly manage to grow those drugs alone—"

"Drugs?"

"I'll explain later. Rick, you won't be trading with them. It's certainly better for us if Parsons can't find us. All I'm suggesting is that we don't call attention to ourselves. Get out of this part of the country, and don't leave traces of where we've gone. Doesn't that make sense?"

"I suppose—"

"That's all I'm asking."

"It's enough. We don't even know where we're going. For that matter, we'll be out of rations soon enough. I saw what might have been a deer—"

"It probably was. There were a lot of Earth animals released here."

"Damn it, you're doing it again! What else do you know that might save our lives?"

She didn't answer.

✦ ✦ ✦

They rounded another bend. There was a crossroads marked by a small thatch-roofed shelter whose roof drained into a stone cistern and watering trough. The side road was dirt, heavily rutted with cart tracks and the prints of shod horses, but deserted at the moment.

Mason inspected the cistern. Leaves floated on top of the water. "We trust this stuff?" he asked.

"We'll have to eventually, and we'll want to start drinking local water while we're still pumped up with gamma globulins and the other shots we got—but I think we can wait a day or so until we've got a permanent base. Got purification tablets?"

"Yeah. I'll use them. Hand me your canteen."

They filled the canteens while Rick thought about their situation. The main road would have more traffic, but it would also be easier going. Not far down the side road he could see patches of water and mud.

"Horses comin'," Mason said. He pointed back the way they came.

"Off the road," Rick ordered. He led them into the trees beyond the crossroads.

There was a click as Mason released the safety on his H&K battle rifle. "They're slowin' down," he said softly.

"If they don't want trouble, we don't," Rick said. Two horses came into view. One carried an elderly man in yellow robes. There was a blue circle with a stylized thunderbolt across it sewn to the breast of the robe. The other horse was ridden double. The rider in front wore kilts and an iron cap, and carried a short sword slung at his left side. The other was cloaked and hooded. They stopped at the crossroads, and the other robed man swung down easily and led his mount to the watering trough, first pausing to bow to the stone heap.

The other two dismounted.

Gwen stared interestedly. "Notice the reverent gesture," she whispered. "Hermes. Guide of the Dead. He was originally a god of crossroads. Evidently he hasn't lost that function here."

The second rider threw back the hood and removed the cloak. Mason gave a nearly inaudible whistle. "That's a looker!" he whispered.

Rick gestured for silence. Mason was right. The girl was young—about twenty, Rick would guess, with long ravenblack hair. Even at this distance her eyes were startlingly blue. She had a classic Scandinavian shape to her face, and the woolen frock she wore would have brought a high price at Magnin's.

Only the kilted rider seemed armed, and Rick examined his weapons carefully. A leather case was fastened to the saddle; from its shape, it probably held a longbow. Otherwise there were no missile weapons. The man's sword was quite short. He also carried a dagger about the size of Rick's Gerber Mark II combat knife.

"This may be a good chance to talk to the locals," Rick said.

"They'll probably think we're horse thieves," Gwen warned.

"So we stay away from their horses. Mason, don't start anything unless there's no other choice. And keep an eye out back the way we came. Just in case."

"Sure."

"Not just for Parsons," Rick said. "The girl looks nervous, and they all keep looking back. And notice how lathered those horses are. They didn't stop because they wanted to. Okay, let's go make contact with the locals."

✢ ✢ ✢

The girl saw them first. She pointed and the younger man went toward his horse.

"Sling arms, Mason," Rick ordered. He spread his empty hands. "Gwen, can you tell them we're friends?"

"The last languages I was able to study from Tran were six hundred years old," she said. She raised her voice. "*Amici. Filos. Zevos.* No, dammit, that doesn't get through. Rick, bow to the stone heap. At least that will show we're religious."

"Right. You too, Mason. And keep your hands clear."

"Yes, sir."

Reverence to a stone heap. It did seem to have a beneficial effect. The others watched them warily, but they did nothing as Rick came closer.

The kilted warrior stared at Rick in frank curiosity. He eyed the slung rifle as if aware that it was a weapon. He seemed very interested in the scabbarded Mark II which hung hilt-down from Rick's suspender webbing.

The older robed man dipped water with a gourd and held it out to them.

Rick hesitated, thinking of the various amoebic life-forms that probably inhabited the unpurified water.

"He's a priest," Gwen said. "Blue sky and thunderbolt. Zeus? Jupiter?"

The priest nodded in comprehension. "Yatar."

"It really is," Gwen said. She seemed delighted. "Zeus Pater, the Sky-father. See, blue for the vault of the sky, and the thunderbolt—"

Rick let the priest hand him the gourd, gulped hard, and drank, hoping that when the inevitable happened it wouldn't be at an inconvenient time.

"You carrying wine, Mason?" he asked.

"Yes, sir."

"Hand it here."

Mason took the plastic liter flask from his belt. "Wine," Rick said. "Uh—vino."

The priest looked interested, and said something to his companions. They looked interested, too.

Rick tilted up the bottle and drank a swallow. It wasn't wine at all, but Scotch. Now what have I done? he thought. The others were gesturing toward the girl, and she held out her hand expectantly.

Rick handed her the bottle. "Strong. *Fuerte*. Not much. Uh—take it easy—"

The girl drank, looked startled, then drank again, slowly. She didn't seem shocked, which meant they must have some kind of distillation here. She said something which Rick took to be thanks.

"Cap'n, no wonder they wanted her to have a drink," Mason said. "The back of her dress is all bloody."

"Yeah? Have a look, Gwen—"

"If she'll let me," Gwen said. "Keep an eye on her boyfriend." She went over to the girl. "*Permiso?* Uh, medico."

She tapped herself on the breast. "Magister?"

"Magistro?" the girl said. She looked at Gwen with what seemed to be respect and stood still while Gwen tried to peel back the blouse. "Good Lord!" she muttered. "Rick, someone's abused this child badly."

Child, hell, Rick thought. "How?"

The girl reached up and unbuttoned the front of her dress and slipped it off her shoulders, leaving her back and breasts bare. Apparently they didn't believe in modesty here—at least not for the upper body. It was hard not to stare at the nearly perfect figure. She evidently didn't usually go without clothing, though; she had no tan at all.

She also had no objection to Rick looking at her, and he went over to examine her back. Someone had beaten her badly. Her back was a mass of bruises, and twice whatever had beaten her had flayed open the skin. It was going to scar. He took out his first-aid kit. "Know much about this?" he asked Gwen.

"No." She looked mildly ill.

"Better let me, then." He took out a swab. "Got to clean this and it's going to sting. Gwen, watch her boyfriend." He tapped himself on the chest. "Magistro," he said. "Medico." She winced when the swab touched the wound, but she didn't cry out. Rick painted it with Merthiolate and put a loose gauze bandage over the broken skin areas. "No tetanus inoculations," he warned. "Make sure you don't cut air off from the wounds. Better to risk aerobic infection. With all the horse crap on the roads, there's a high tetanus risk." He stepped away. "All right, you can cover yourself again." He gestured to show what he meant. "And have another drink. You earned it."

The girl smiled tentatively, then downed another slug of Scotch. She tapped herself on the chest. "Tylara do Tamaerthon, Eqetassa do Chelm."

"You get that, Gwen?" Rick asked.

"I think so. Eqetassa. That's right out of old Mycenae. If I'm not mistaken, she's a countess. If that's right, her name would be Tylara and she's from that place with the guttural sound."

"Tylara," Rick said. The girl nodded happily. He pointed to himself. "Rick Galloway, Captain of mercenaries." If long names indicated high rank, he didn't want to claim to be a peasant.

"Rick," Tylara said tentatively. She pointed to the robed priest. "Yanulf, sacerdos pu Yatar." The priest bowed. She pointed again. "Caradoc."

"Latin and Greek all mixed up with Mycenaean," Gwen said.

"Mykenae?" the priest asked. He pointed to them.

"No." Gwen shook her head. The priest frowned.

The kilted man took out a curry comb and began working on the horses. He glanced warily back at Rick and Mason from time to time, but didn't seem excessively suspicious.

An auspicious beginning, Rick thought. And that girl! Were all the women on this planet as lovely?

3

"Company comin', Cap'n," Mason called. "Lots of horses riding hard."

The others heard, too. Rick gestured toward the thickets by the road. There would be no room to hide the horses, though, and from the sounds, not enough time either. Tylara shouted something and Caradoc ran to his horse. He took down the leather case and withdrew a longbow, stringing it with an easy gesture that made Rick's muscles ache to watch.

A dozen horsemen rounded the bend two hundred meters away. The sight was like a blow. They were not all riding horses. Three of the beasts were centaurs. The riders wore mail armor, and white plumes streamed out from their helmets. The lead men carried lances, and they lowered them. Others drew sabers. They didn't act friendly at all.

Tylara shouted. Rick understood none of it, but he heard the word 'Sarakos' several times. She ran to Caradoc and drew his dagger, holding it as if she knew how to use it. Caradoc nocked an arrow. He thrust another into the dirt in front of him. There were only the two.

Two arrows, a short sword, and a dagger; but his new friends were obviously prepared to fight a dozen horsemen. Yanulf stood impassively by the cistern, his arms spread to the sky.

"What do we do?" Mason shouted.

Rick didn't answer for a moment. There would still be time to get into the trees. This wasn't his fight. From the uniforms, the approaching riders might be the local police. For that matter, he had no evidence that Yanulf wasn't a con man and Tylara his accomplice in the local equivalent of the badger game. He could be setting himself up as an outlaw. Probably was. And they could still run . . .

But dammit, he thought, I'm tired of running. You've got to choose sides sometimes. Why not now? "We fight," he said.

"Would you if she were a crone?" Gwen asked.

"Shut up. Mason, fire a couple of warning shots."

The H&K blasted at full automatic; a burst of fire that must have zinged over the heads of the approaching riders. They didn't slow.

Caradoc drew the arrow to his cheek and released it in a smooth motion. The lead rider took it full in the chest and fell from his horse.

And that's torn it, Rick thought. He raised the H&K and began to squeeze off rounds at semiautomatic fire.

⸶ ⸶ ⸶

When Tylara saw the strangers approaching, she first thought they might be from a local village despite their strange clothing; but moments later she knew better. They couldn't be locals, and she felt a twinge of fear. Who were they?

They were obviously wealthy. She didn't know what all the objects they carried or wore on their belts might be used for, but so much metal would be valuable. And all three spoke to each other as equals. She didn't know the words, but the tones made that clear.

"Evil gods," Yanulf muttered. "The Time approaches."

Caradoc glanced hastily at the stone heap, hoping for protection.

"Do your tales say how they will steal our souls?" Tylara asked. "They do not look like gods to me." Although, she thought but didn't say, the taller man was handsome enough to be, if not a god, at least from the tales of the heroes. "What have we to lose by their friendship?"

"Little," Yanulf admitted, and went to draw water to make the traditional gesture.

Their response had been surprising enough. Tylara was familiar with strong drink made by freezing wine and throwing away the ice, but she had never experienced anything like what she tasted when the man handed her his bottle.

The bottle itself was interesting, too. It was neither metal nor ceramic, and she had no experience with anything else. Then they had come closer, and examined her back, and the handsome one had done something that hurt at first but soon took the ache away. While he treated her she studied him close up. He was a warrior. The sheathed blade on his chest—what a strange place to carry it, but it looked handy enough, easily drawn, perhaps he had to fight often—was obvious. Less obvious was the weapon he wore slung over his shoulder. It resembled a crossbow, but there was no bow; and it was all metal.

He wore no armor that she could see. Only the one-piece garment that was jacket and trousers combined, mottled by dye to resemble the forest. His hat was a felt beret, and she had seen those before. The boots were green with black leather at the bottom, more like a peasant's boots than a warrior's. Then there were the bewildering things—all carefully crafted, all useful-appearing but totally mysterious—hanging from the straps over his shoulders and from his belt.

Rick. She caught that, but not the titles he named himself. And his companion—obviously a warrior and wealthy as well, certainly a knight, perhaps a bheroman—was named Mason. The girl called herself Gwen. Unreasonably, Tylara did not like her. She must belong to Rick, and Tylara knew there was no reason to resent that, but she did. One thing was clear enough. "These are no gods," she told Yanulf.

"Perhaps," the priest growled.

Old fool, she thought, but regretted that instantly; he had given up everything to save her. She had never heard of a priest of Yatar allowing anyone not a sworn acolyte in the lower caverns. Not even her husband's father had ever visited those caves below Dravan. Would Sarakos dare search there now?

The drink made her feel better. Much better, and she talked volubly with the strangers, almost forgetting the horror of the night before, until the one called Mason shouted warning and a dozen of Sarakos' hussars came toward them at the gallop.

She ran to take Caradoc's dagger, wondering what would have happened if she had asked—Rick—to lend her his own. Would he? With the dagger in hand, she felt little fear. They might kill her, but they could never take her back. And the strangers had taken their weapons from off their backs and held them like crossbows—

She was startled for the moment when Mason's weapon gave a crash like thunder, and even more startled when there was no effect. Caradoc's shaft killed its man, but no one fell to Mason's thunder. But then Rick raised his own weapon.

The result was unbelievable. Each time Rick's weapon spoke, a rider fell. Then Mason did the same. Caradoc stood with an arrow nocked but did not loose it. He watched in amazement, as Tylara did.

The fight was over before it had well begun. Men lay in the road, some dead, some groaning, while riderless horses and centaurs dashed past. Tylara had sense enough to grasp the reins of one of the horses, and Caradoc seized another. She saw that Rick did not seem to think of that, although Mason tried and failed. Why?

Caradoc handed her the reins of the horse he had caught and went out to give the fallen soldiers a final mercy. When he slit the throat of the first, though, Rick shouted, as if in horror. His companion said something, and the girl said more. Finally Rick turned his back. Did he hate Sarakos' troops, then? That much? And why? She would cheerfully let Sarakos die of green stinking fester, but his soldiers had not deserved such. Evidently Rick's companions convinced him, because he said nothing else; but it would be well to remember that he was a cold-hearted man, ruthless toward his enemies. But he was a man. Of that she was certain.

✣ ✣ ✣

"Leave him to his work, Cap'n," Mason was saying. "When in Rome and all that. Besides, if they're all dead, they won't be tellin' anyone who did 'em in."

Rick swallowed hard. In classical times it was normal to kill the wounded, even your own. It wasn't until Philip of Macedon that armies had hospital corpsmen. Philip gave a substantial reward to the corpsmen for each trooper they saved.

It bothered him that he hadn't captured any of the horses. They'd need them. Centaurs he could live without—they looked mean. He didn't know much about horses, either, but he'd rather ride than walk.

That problem was solved a few minutes later. After Caradoc (that name—wasn't there a Welsh king by that name? There was something wrong with Gwen's theory of language development here) had finished his grisly work among the wounded, he mounted his own horse and rode down the road, returning a few minutes later with four more he'd caught. He offered all of them to Rick.

Rick inspected the saddles. Wood, with leather trim, and rigid wooden stirrups. The horses were large and sturdy, and he suspected that they'd bring a high price on Earth. "Can you ride?" he asked Gwen.

"On Griffith Park bridle trails," she said. She eyed the horses nervously.

"We'll try to keep the pace down. Will our new friend get upset if we strip the dead? There's a lot of valuable equipment out there."

"I don't know."

"Me neither," Rick said. Homeric heroes always despoiled their dead enemies. Sometimes they even mutilated them. And they often made trophies out of any arms and armor they couldn't use. "Mason, go see what you can find," he said. "Swords. And if there's any armor that will fit either of us, get it, but strip the plumes off the helmets." He thought for a moment. "And don't touch the one the archer knocked down."

That seemed to be the right action. After Mason went through the dead, Caradoc did the same. He retrieved his arrow and stripped the man he'd killed, then went over Mason's leavings. He brought the loot over to the cistern and said something to Yanulf. The old priest indicated a sword, a breastplate, and a leather bag which Caradoc took over and piled reverently against the stone heap.

Aha. "Mason, take our stuff over to Yanulf."

The priest's selection from Mason's pile was considerably larger. "Wonder what the PC is," Rick said. "And who gets the loot."

"Redistribution system," Gwen said. "It's fairly common in some societies. The first people down the road will help themselves with Old Stone-heapy's blessings. Uh—don't like to say it, but it would be better if you carried the dead away from the road. That way they just vanished, and maybe no one will look too closely at what killed them."

"Covering our tracks?" Rick asked.

"Yes."

It made sense. Rick thought he was using that line a lot since he'd met Gwen. "Let's get at it, Mason. Maybe Caradoc will get the idea and help."

Caradoc did, but he obviously didn't understand. When they got the bodies stacked in the woods a hundred meters from the road, Rick made symbolic gestures and threw a few dirt clods over them. When Mason frowned a question, Rick said, "I'd rather he thought we have a screwy religion than leave him wondering why we're carrying bodies around."

They loaded their spare horse with loot, while Caradoc piled his own excess gear on the horse the priest had ridden. Then he rode off on a fresh horse and returned with two more. After a questioning glance at Rick, he gave the new mounts to Yanulf and Tylara. They mounted.

"Cap'n, they're waiting for us," Mason said.

"Yeah. Mount up." He swung into his own saddle and gave an experimental cluck. The horse moved slightly. It seemed very well trained and responded to the reins about as he had expected. "I'll lead yours at first," he told Gwen. "If you want me to."

"Please."

Rick edged his mount over until he was next to Tylara. "Where?" he said. "*Quo vadis? Donde?*" He pointed helplessly in all directions.

She frowned, then seemed to understand. She pointed down the road. "Tamaerthon."

"Your home?" Rick asked. He pointed to her, then the road. Tylara do Tamaerthon, she'd said. It must be. "You. Tamaerthon?"

She nodded vigorously, then swung her hands in a broad sweep to include the whole party. "Tamaerthon," she said, and she sounded quite determined about it.

PART FIVE
TAMAERTHON

Tylara had been away less than a year, but she had forgotten just how small her homeland was. The whole of Tamaerthon was no more than twice the extent her own lands of Chelm had been, and her father's holdings in The Garioch would have been thought suitable for a wealthy knight—almost too mean to support a bheroman. As for her father's great hall, it wasn't much larger than her council chamber in Castle Dravan, and indeed her father used it for council meetings, which usually—as now—were no more than a gathering of several of his henchmen.

That wasn't her only disappointment. Her reception was something less than enthusiastic. Her father had seen her leave as a great lady. He had sent more archers and more wealth than he could afford as her dowry.

Outside the council hall, the women of the village were keening the deaths of sons and lovers who had gone with their lady to die in a far land.

"I had thought ye might send me horses and knights," her father said. "And gold. But ye hae returned wi' no more than three men-at-arms and this priest."

"What choice had I? But I have come with more than men-at-arms." Tylara described the battle at the crossroads. "And twice more they fought when bandits and refugees would not leave us alone. Each time they left none alive." She described the weapons; the large ones like crossbows carried over the shoulder, and the smaller one-handed weapons they carried concealed beneath their jackets.

"But where do they come from?" her father demanded.

"From the stars," Yanulf said.

Drumold stared at the priest and back to his daughter. "Weapons of fire and thunder . . . then the old tales are true?"

"They are," Yanulf said. "You can see for yourself, the Demon Star grows larger each ten-day."

"Aye, I hae seen it at dawn when the night sun is low," Drumold agreed. "But the tales speak of evil gods." He glanced nervously toward the stone house where the newcomers were lodged. "Are these—"

"Not gods," Tylara said. "They are men. Men with great weapons, but men. For days they were sick nearly to death. The lady with them is ill yet."

"She carries a child," Yanulf said. "I do not know whose."

"Not gods," Drumold mused. "Men. And they befriended you. With such power as they have—" He grew thoughtful.

"That had occurred to me," Yanulf said. "When I saw the power of their weapons, I had thought to find the Lord Protector and the boy Wanax of Drantos. With the aid of these star men, we might have driven Sarakos from Drantos and returned the lady Tylara to her home."

"But they would no' aid you?" Drumold demanded.

"They could not," Yanulf said. "In the ten-day we sought the Protector's army, the Protector sought Sarakos. We heard the story from refugees three days after their armies met. The battle was thought to be equal at first, even though Sarakos had many more lances. But as the battle was fought, Sarakos smote his enemies with weapons of fire and thunder." The priest spread his hands. "Our friends are not the only men from the stars. More than a score, with weapons more terrible than any Rick carries, now are allied with Sarakos and hold Drantos for him."

"Rick was once of their company," Tylara said.

"Then why is he not with them?"

"She shrugged helplessly. "I do not know. I heard from the lady Gwen that Rick was once the commander of the star men. I know that he does not care to have them find him again."

"Then dare we keep him here?" Drumold demanded. "Is he a danger to our land?"

"He is our guest. He saved me from Sarakos once and twice from bandits," Tylara said.

Her father studied her face carefully. "Aye, and he has done more than that," he said. "When your mourning is done, will we see another stranger wed the daughter of the Mac Clallan Muir?"

Tylara had no answer to that. *I wish*, she thought, *I wish I knew. Whose child does Gwen carry? She does not act toward Rick as a woman does to her man, but the ways of the starmen are strange. I do not understand them. Especially I do not understand Rick, who likes well enough to be near me, but who has never touched me except to heal wounds. . . .*

And another memory. Rick's shouting rage when finally he understood what Sarakos had done to her. Almost, almost he had gone back to seek out Sarakos, but then Gwen spoke to him for a long time, and they rode on again.

But he did rage. He hates the man who harmed me.

"We hae our troubles here," Drumold was saying. "There was untimely rain, and the harvests will be poor. Wi'out the archers sent with you, we hae lost many of our pastures. Mac Clallan Muir does not stand so high as at the time you left, and when it is learned that my daughter can no longer send a thousand lances to my aid, it will go worse. Now you hae brought us guests who may draw the strength of Sarakos against us. Daughter, 'tis no' your fault, but this is not good."

He looked to his silent henchmen. They had no advice for him. Then he stared moodily into the fire. "But they are guests and they have my welcome, for what good it will be to them."

✣ ✣ ✣

"What's taking them so damned long?" Corporal Mason asked. "My stomach's growling. They could at least feed us."

"I expect that's what the debate is about," Gwen said. "Hospitality is taken very seriously in some cultures. If they feed us, they have to take us in and protect us from our enemies."

"Well, I wish they'd get on with it."

"Count your blessings," Rick told him. "At least there's a warm fire and we'll get a safe night's sleep." Which, he thought, was more than they'd had for weeks while they fled across Drantos, staying ahead of the occupation forces that Sarakos and his new allies sent out in waves. It had been a nightmare journey, with all three of them sick with classic cases of Montezuma's Revenge, knowing nothing of the language and customs . . .

"But we made it," he said aloud. "And without leaving tacks. So now what do we do?"

"Blend in," Gwen said. "Get established in the community."

"Sure." Rick pointed out the window. The scenery was lovely. The village stood on a flat alpine meadow high above the sea, ringed on three sides by snowcapped mountains. Except for the seacoast to the southeast, it might have been a scene from a picture postcard of Switzerland. "Beautiful," he said. "But I don't see a hell of a lot of cultivated land, and some of the fields I did see were gullied. No industry, and not much pasture land. Gwen, you've noticed more than I have, but it's obvious even to me that this is a warrior society. They probably get more of their food by raiding their flatland neighbors than they do by growing their own. There's only one way Mason and I can make a living here. Fortunately, it's a trade we know."

"Until we run out of cartridges," Mason said. "Which may not take long."

"So we get busy manufacturing muzzle-loaders," Rick said. "I've been trying to remember the formula for gunpowder. I think I've got it."

"Rick, you can't!" Gwen protested.

"Why not? You want them unspoiled? Think arrows are a cleaner way to go than gunshots?"

"It's not that," Gwen said. "God, I wish my head would stop aching. Rick, if you start using gunpowder weapons, you'll advertise our location as surely as if you sent Parsons a letter."

Mason growled low in his throat. "Cap'n, I don't know about you, but I'm sick of worrying about Lieutenant—ha, he's a general by now—about Parsons. You saw the country we came through gettin' here. With five hundred good men, we could hold those passes forever. To hell with bein' scared of Parsons and his crew. I just wish I could be sure he'd come."

"He's right," Rick said. "And he's not the only one tired of running scared."

"Have you stopped to think that the *Shalnuksis* may help Parsons?" Gwen said. "Probably will. Can you fight *them*? Not to mention that you're involving Tylara's father in a needless war with the most powerful force on this planet." She sniffed. "I'd thought better of you than that."

"What the hell do you want us to do?" Rick demanded.

"What we agreed. Leave as few traces of our presence as possible—at least until the *Shalnuksis* have done with their trading. Once they're gone, you'll only have Parsons to fight."

Once again, Rick thought. *Once again she makes sense. But why do I think she isn't telling me everything?*

2

The cave was cold and smelled of ammonia. Rick shivered as the old priest led him down winding corridors. "This is all secret," Yanulf said. "Although a secret better kept in the west than here. Still, secret enough."

"What is secret?" Rick asked. "Everyone knows there are caverns—"

"But not the size, or the location of the entrances, or how to enter them."

"Why show me?" Rick asked. He coughed from the ammonia fumes and the chill.

"They may believe you—they pay little heed to me," Yanulf said. "And I have learned this: that you starmen put your own meaning to what you see."

"This is all strange to me," Rick said. "What makes it so cold?"

Yanulf held the torch close to a bulbous slimy mass that covered one wall of the cavern. "The roots of the Protector. A plant. It is why I know the stories of the Demon Sun are true. In all my life I have never seen the Protector larger than a man's body. Recently it began to grow, and now grows daily. The growth began when the Demon Star was seen in the night sky, as the legends said it would."

"How does a plant make ice?" Rick wondered aloud. "There must be parts above ground—"

"Aye. It is very large. Thick leaves. In the west the castles are built above caverns, and the Protector climbs the walls and battlements. In this impoverished land they build few castles, and the plant grows on the rocks. You have seen it."

"Ah." He remembered a broad-leafed vine with thick stems and ugly white berries. "Scientists—uh, those whose task it is to study nature—in my home would pay much to see a plant like this." Sunlight to ammonia, and somehow the ammonia produced cold; the evolutionary advantage for such a plant on a planet in a triple-star system was obvious. "What is it you want me to see?"

"The size of the caverns and the barren storerooms. When the Time is upon us, the only safe refuge is in these caves. There will be no crops that year or the next, and poor ones for two more. So say the legends. Your drawings of the suns make me believe them."

"Which is surprising," Rick said. "You are a priest of Ius Pater, the Dayfather. Did you not think the stars are gods?"

"Can they not be?" Yanulf demanded. "You say yourself that they are older than worlds and burn forever."

And I'd best leave it at that, Rick thought. *I wonder why all the secrecy. Who are they hiding from?*

Yanulf opened a massive wooden door. The smell of ammonia was very strong, and Rick thought the torch dimmed. The priest held the torch high, and coughing, said, "You see. A few miserable offerings. There is meat and grain, aye, enough for a few ten-days, but not enough even for a single winter. How will these people live in the Time?"

The legends said that the approach of the third sun heralded evil times: fire, flood, famine, and typhoon. Those not prepared would die. They were mixed in with tales of the wars of gods, the appearance of fabulous monsters, and garbled stories whose point was the futility of dealing with the evil gods from the skies. It was hard to sort fact from fable, but Rick didn't doubt there would be hard times ahead. The whole climate would change.

They went deeper. The caverns were quite large, and some went far below ground level, back into the granite itself. Water trickled through some of the chambers. Others were choked with ice.

"It is said that Yatar demands sacrifices," Yanulf said. "These are stored away, to be cared for by the priests and acolytes. In some lands the storerooms are kept filled. But not here."

Eventually Yanulf led the way back out of the caves. Rick was surprised to see how far they'd traveled underground. "So it is in the other caverns of Tamaerthon," Yanulf said. "The priests and acolytes tell me that their storerooms are as barren as these."

"I'll take their word for it," Rick gasped. He walked faster toward the open air and sunlight.

✛ ✛ ✛

Drumold was horrified. "No harvests for two years? Then aye are we doomed. One year of poor harvest and we are starving before spring." For luck he spat into the log fire burning on the hearth of his council room.

"There should be a time of good harvest first," Rick said. "At least I hope so. I'm not much at climatology, but the legends say so, and it's not unreasonable."

"You know little of Tamaerthon," Drumold said. "In the best years we hae little enough land, and must take our chances in raids on the Empire. Nae, nae, the gods hate us, to let us be born in such times. I had hoped the legends false."

"But we have to do something," Tylara said. "You are Mac Clallan Muir. You have sworn to protect the clansmen."

"And I have!" Drumold thundered. "Are we not free of the Empire? Have the imperial slavemasters come to our mountains these ten years? Lass, I do what I can, but I am no magician, to grow crops in a stone quarry!"

"We can help," Gwen said. "We have ways of farming that may increase the yield—"

"Lassie, I tell you there is no land to farm," Drumold said moodily. "You hae seen that our best land is now split and cracked—"

"Yes." She spoke to Rick in English. "Heavy rains when they didn't expect them. Just showing them contour plowing will do a lot to stop the gullies—"

"In time to help?" Rick asked. "If we've got this figured right, they'll need to work their arses off starting next spring."

Drumold stared at them suspiciously. "I like it not when you speak so," he said.

"My apologies," Rick said. "Is there no land not plowed, then?"

Tylara laughed. "There's land enough in the Roman Empire. Fields left as parks for Caesar. Forests of game for Caesar. Herds for Caesar's gods. There's food and land there."

"A cruel joke," Drumold said. "There's food and land, aye. And legions to defend them, and the slavemarket for those who enter the Empire without Caesar's leave."

"Do you forget Rick's star weapons?" Tylara asked. She turned to Rick. "Your friends have taken all of Drantos with their weapons. Can we not do the same with the Empire?"

Dammit, I wish she wouldn't look at me that way, Rick thought. *I am not a god.* "I do not think so," he said. "Besides, there have to be better ways than fighting. Can't we parley with the current Caesar?"

Drumold and Tylara both laughed. "The only way Caesar wants to see any kin of mine is in chains," Drumold said. "We have little to sell to him save wool. What we get from Caesar we take with sword and bow."

If Caesar wouldn't parley, there might be another way to get his attention. "How strong is this Empire?" Rick asked.

"Bring the maps," Drumold shouted. He waited while a henchman unrolled parchments. "The Empire is no' so large as it was in my grandfather's day," he said. "But they hold the fertile lowlands, and the foothills, here and here. They keep a legion of four thousand mercenaries in this fortress." He indicated a point some twenty miles from where the foothills became steep mountains leading to Tamaerthon. "Within a ten-day they can have two more, and another ten-day an additional three."

And we've got about a hundred rounds for the rifles, Rick thought. "That's pretty heavy odds," he said carefully.

"The other starmen have taken all of Drantos," Tylara said. "Can you not do as well?"

"They needed the armies of Sarakos to do it." And I suspect Sarakos has reason to regret his bargain. He's not likely to be much more than a puppet for André Parsons. Serves him right.

Lowlands. In about five years, maybe less, that new Roman Empire was going to be under water—all but the high plateau that held Rome itself. And by that time the people of Tamaerthon would be starving. Except Mac Clallan Muir and his family. They wouldn't starve. According to Yanulf, the clan leaders and their children would—in theory, willingly—offer themselves as a propitiation to the gods. It came with the job of leader. In Drumold's grandfather's time, it had happened after three years of bad harvests, which was how Drumold's grandfather had got the position of high chief of Tamaerthon.

Damnation, there had to be something he could do. And he wasn't too likely to talk Tylara out of jumping off that cliff into the sea, either. That was one girl who was likely to take her duties seriously.

"You have raided the Empire in the past?"

"Aye," Drumold said.

"Tell me more of the Empire. How are the legions armed?"

"With lances and swords. How else?"

"Lances and swords—they're horsemen, then?"

Drumold seemed surprised. "Aye. Horses and centaurs. Mostly horses."

"Not footsoldiers." Rick described a classical Roman legionary: square shield, pilum, and *gladius hispanica.*

"There are no such anywhere I know of," Drumold said. "Ken ye any in your western lands, Priest?"

"No." Yanulf studied Rick's face. "What makes you think there might be?"

As near as he could figure it, the *Shalnuksis* had brought an expeditionary force from Earth in about 200 A.D., about the time of Septimius Severus. That had to be when the ancestors of these new Romans arrived. Severus still employed classical foot-marching legionaries, a bit degenerated from those of Caesar's time, but still the most effective infantry Earth would see until gunpowder. Evidently the same thing had happened to legions here as happened on Earth: they fell to heavy cavalry and lack of discipline. Now the heavy cavalry ruled everywhere that the terrain was suitable. This Rome was more like the Holy Roman Empire—aha! There would have been another expedition in about 800, the time of Charlemagne. This Rome must *be* the Holy Roman Empire. But he couldn't explain all that.

"One of the greatest kingdoms in our history was armed that way," he said. "Uh—what religion is the Empire?"

"They call themselves Christian," Yanulf said. "But the Christians of the southern lands say they are not."

"Yatar does not prosper in Rome, then?"

"No."

"Have they ice caverns? How did Rome survive the Time?" Rick asked.

Yanulf spread his hands. "They do not welcome visitors. Or rather, their slavemasters welcome them all too well. It is said that there are caverns in Rome, but who attends them I do not know. It is also said that there is a great library with many records of previous Times, but again this is not of my own knowledge."

Gwen had been listening with a growing look of amazement. "Rick, what are you thinking of?" she demanded.

That earned her a sharp look from Drumold, who wasn't used to having women speak up that way.

"North is barren," Rick said. "West is the salt marsh and west of that Parsons and Sarakos. South of us is mostly ocean. If we're going to get anything to store up for the Time, we'll have to take it from Rome."

"Man, are ye daft?" Drumold asked. "We raid the Empire, true, and done quickly, we often bring back cattle and horses. But we seldom escape punishment from the legions."

"He is not daft," Tylara protested. "He can—I have heard him speak of battles before. Of his victories over the Cubans—"

Yeah, I brag a lot when you're around, Rick thought. "What kind of punishment? What do the legions do?"

"Sometimes nothing," Drumold said. "But if we annoy them enough, they bring their army into the hills."

"And you fight them—"

"We try," Drumold said. "Aye, and we can win battles. But they come on, and we must take to the hills. They burn the villages and the crops and slaughter the flocks. Ofttimes we lose more than ever we gained. The Empire is a giant best left unawakened."

"But you have won battles against them," Rick said. "You must have, or they'd have simply occupied Tamaerthon and had done with it."

"Aye, we've beaten them in the passes," Drumold said. "In the passes, in the hills. But no one has ever beaten the legions on the plains. I think no one remembers the last time anyone tried."

So far it sounded a lot like the Scottish border country. Scotland remained free, but just barely. But there had been a time after Bannockburn when England feared Scotland . . . The rifles would probably win a single battle. The result wouldn't be anything more significant than looting a border province, but that could be the difference between life and death for Mac Clallan Muir. And for Tylara.

An organized raid, with a wagon train to carry out grain and a properly organized force to delay the legions while the wagons got into the passes. It was possible.

"How many men could you put into the field against the Empire?"

Rick asked. "For the biggest raid ever. Something to sing about for a hundred years."

Drumold frowned. "Not all the clans would respond to the summons," he said. "Perhaps three hundred lances. Two thousand archers. Another three thousand lads wi' swords. Perhaps a thousand more freedmen armed wi' whatever they can find. No more."

"And the nearest legion is four thousand strong," Rick mused.

"Four thousand legionaries," Drumold protested. "Wi' mail shirts, and good horses. Man, on level ground they'll ride us down."

Two thousand archers. Edward had four times that many at Crécy, but Edward faced the entire chivalry of France, at least thirty thousand men. Proportionally, Tamaerthon could field more troops against the Empire than Edward ever had.

But there was a vast difference. Archers alone could never face cavalry. Edward's main line at Crécy had been dismounted men-at-arms, fully armored knights. From what Rick had seen, Tamaerthon's three hundred lances would be at most five hundred men with no more than half of them armored. There was no way five hundred could form a shield for the archers. The legionary cavalry would sweep through. Once at close quarters, it would be all over for the archers.

Gunpowder? No. Even assuming Gwen was wrong about the possibility of the *Shalnuksis* helping Parsons, there just wasn't enough time. They'd need at least a thousand arquebuses and a ton of gunpowder. They'd need ring bayonets, too. It would take years. No. It wouldn't hurt to have some of the younger clan warriors start a systematic search for sulfur, just in case, but gunpowder wasn't the answer.

But there was another way. Heavy cavalry had been finished on Earth well before gunpowder put the final nails in their coffins. "Have any of your clansmen ever drilled with pikes?"

"Pikes?" Drumold asked.

"A long pole with a sharp metal point."

"Ye mean spears. We have spears."

"No, I mean pikes. How long are the spears you use? What formation do you fight in?"

That took a while. Eventually a henchman brought in a typical weapon. It was about six feet long, far too short to be any use against cavalry. The pikes used by the Swiss, and later by the *landsknechts*, had been eighteen feet long. As for formation, men who could afford no better weapon than a spear were peasants and didn't fight in any formation at all. They just went off to battle in droves and died in droves.

"How long can you keep the clansmen together without fighting?" Rick asked. "To drill." He had to explain the concept of training and drill. By now even Tylara was wondering about his sanity.

"The fields and herds would go to waste," Drumold protested. "And there's nae enough to feed such a horde in one place."

"There's food in the caverns."

"For the Time," Yanulf protested. "And not enough for that."

"Not enough for the Time," Rick agreed. "But enough to feed an army in training. What good will it do to keep what little we have? A properly trained army can beat the legions. We can march in—" he thought rapidly. There'd not be enough time for real training, and keeping the men too long without a battle would be disastrous for morale. "—in six ten-days."

"Harvest time," Drumold shouted. "Now I know ye're daft. You'd strip the land of the men at harvest time."

"You've said yourself it will be a poor harvest," Rick said. "Leave it for the women and children to gather."

"What do we eat for the winter?"

"It will be harvest season in the Empire, too. We take their crops. And they have to have granaries or they couldn't support regular troops in garrison. We'll have that grain, too."

"And you truly believe you can defeat a legion wi' your star weapons?" Drumold said.

No, I can't possibly. But they're not invincible—or wouldn't be if everybody didn't think they were. There's one way to fix that. "Sure. We've got other weapons you haven't even seen. But Mason and I can't do it alone. We'll need your lads properly trained and properly armed." Now's the time to back out, he thought. To hell with that. "If we're going to do it, late harvest season is the time."

" 'Tis a bold plan," Drumold said.

Tylara's brother had listened in silence. Now he stood. "I have lost comrades to the imperials," he said. "And I for one would like the chance to repay."

Tylara smiled happily. "It would be better to lose and die on the field than to starve in the Time," she said. "But with Rick's aid, we will not lose."

"You are crazy," Gwen said in English. "Stupid, bloodthirsty crazy—"

"Is it better if we all starve. Tamaerthon and the Empire alike? Do you have a better suggestion?"

"We don't have to stay here—"

"No," Rick said. "We don't *have* to. But I'm not running this time. I've given up running."

3

Drumold was arrayed as Mac Clallan Muir, High Chief of the Clans of The Garioch. His kilts were splendid, his armor covered over with silver badges. Gwen recognized some of the symbols: the horned bull of Crete splayed across a caldron; the ancient linked spiral found in virtually every Bronzè Age site in Europe and which Yanulf said represented order grown from primeval chaos; a dragon. There were others which she thought might be fabulous creatures—but after what she'd seen in the ship's data banks, she couldn't be sure.

Other clan chiefs were arrayed around Drumold, all dressed in their finery. Some of the bright-colored plaids might have come from the ancient Celtic tombs found in Dalmatia on Earth. The splendor of the chiefs contrasted strongly with the drab clothing of their warriors and the even drabber robes of the various priests.

Gwen could not keep track of all these. There were too many gods, and each had an order of priests. Some, like Yanulf, were full-time and consecrated; many of the minor gods, though, were served by men and women who had other tasks—artisans, landholders, ladies of households.

They all assisted at this ceremony. Reverently they opened a tomblike chamber cut into the granite cliff that towered above the alpine meadow; reverently they removed a stone box and opened it with great ceremony. Balquhain, Drumold's oldest son, took a battle-axe from the box.

The axe was double-headed and made of flint chipped to resemble bronze. Gwen felt tingles at her spine. This double-axe might have come from Earth four thousand years ago!

Drumold took the axe from his son and displayed it aloft. Then he went to a log altar erected in the center of the village green. A ram was tethered there. Drumold felled it with a single stroke of the axe.

He dipped the axe into the flowing blood. Two priests came forward with stone bowls of blazing pitch and bound them above the axe blade. Drumold brandished the fiery axe and chanted. Everyone present took up the cry.

Where had Gwen seen this before? Then she remembered. Scott's poem, when Roderick Dhu had summoned Clan Alpine. Roderick had sent a fiery cross through the hills, but that was in a nominally Christian land. Here they sent a stone axe with two fires. The ritual Scott described must have been more ancient than he knew.

A priest chanted curses to befall any clansman who failed to respond to the symbol, and a henchman took the axe and ran from the glen. The Garioch clans were summoned to war.

✛ ✛ ✛

The rogue star was visible for an hour after dawn, and there was dark for several hours each night. Tran's two suns drew closer together. Summer was gone.

"We ready, Cap'n?" Mason asked.

"No, but we're as ready as we'll ever be. These lads won't stay around much longer."

Mason nodded. "Yeah, they don't like drill much. But they're not that bad. Cap'n, did those battles you keep talking about really happen?"

"Most of them. I've mixed them up a little. Truthfully, I don't recall any time when there was a combined force of longbows and pikes, but pike and musket was a pretty standard mix for a hundred years." Rick grinned. "Besides, the stories cheer up the troops."

They could use cheering. Even with all of his tales of victory—by his account, he'd led half the successful armies of history—and the demonstrations of their magic weapons, most of his troops didn't really believe they could beat an imperial legion on fair ground. The priests, and the rogue star to confirm the priests' stories had scared enough of them into trying, but not many really believed they could win.

Rick wasn't sure himself.

The glen was curiously still. All summer it had rung with the sounds of hammers. A dozen smiths had been brought—some at swordpoint—to forge iron heads for pikes. The new saplings of an entire forest had gone into pikeshafts.

The hammers were still, and so were the shouts and curses of the drillmasters. Drill time was over. Now it was time to march.

⁜ ⁜ ⁜

Gwen was miserable. Her belly had swollen and she knew she was ugly. The midwives and even Yanulf himself had assured her that everything was normal, but they couldn't convince her. She had too vivid an imagination, and knew too well all the things that could go wrong even in a modern hospital. She'd had friends back on Earth who'd been ecstatic about natural childbirth—but she doubted that any of them had meant to be quite *this* natural about it.

Outside she could hear the sounds of the army assembling. They were about to march into the Empire, and there was nothing she could do about it.

She couldn't even run. On Rick's advice, Drumold had sealed the passes with armed parties of his clansmen. No one would leave Tamaerthon. Rick had made it plain that this especially meant Gwen Tremaine. He was certain that she knew more than she'd told him, and he was going to make sure she stayed with him.

There was a lot she could tell him, but Les had warned her against it. There was nothing he could do anyway. What could anyone do? Her original plan had been to find a hiding place, somewhere she could blend in and wait—

But she couldn't do that alone, and when she was honest with herself, she was ashamed of wanting to. These people were human, they weren't merely subjects of an anthropological study. And they faced starvation or worse. But she wished she had as much confidence in Rick as Tylara had. There was a scratching at her door. "Yes?" she called.

Caradoc came in. "We are leaving, Lady." He stood nervously at the door.

"Have you no one else to say farewells to?" she asked.

"No, Lady."

"I've told you a dozen times, my name is Gwen—"

"Aye." He hesitated. "Gwen. A lovely name. Will you wish me well?"

"Of course." She wasn't sure of what to say. This wasn't the first indication she'd had that Caradoc was interested in her—more than interested. She wondered why. She certainly wasn't pretty in her present condition, and as captain of one of the archery regiments, Caradoc could have his pick of a dozen girls.

But he seemed fascinated by Gwen and spent as much time with her as he could. He treated her like a goddess, and that was flattering—and he was a very attractive man.

She wanted to hate men. All of them. But she was lonely, and the need to have someone of her own was a physical ache. "Come back, Caradoc," she said. "Come back to me."

"I will." He hesitated, then came closer to her. "I will."

She took two steps forward into his open arms. She let him hold her, but she felt her distended belly pressing against him and she was afraid, afraid to care for anyone again, and she hated herself for wanting to.

PART SIX
WAR LEADER

1

Most of the outbuildings and slave quarters had been burned, but the villa still stood. Rick was surprised that it remained. Despite everything he could do, it was difficult to convince the camp followers that their purpose was to loot, not pillage and rapine. He had trouble enough keeping the army itself from breaking ranks and joining in, and only constant threats to abandon them thirty miles inside the imperial boundary stones kept them in line.

A hundred candles burned inside the villa, and most of his officer corps were getting drunk in the main hall. For that matter, there was plenty of wine in the smaller room where Rick assembled the senior commanders.

"They won't be fit for anything in the morning," Rick complained. "Listen to them out there."

"They'll be all right," Drumold said. " 'Tis their way of celebrating."

"They ought to be ashamed, not celebrating," Rick said.

"We won," Balquhain protested.

Tylara looked at her brother in contempt. "Won a fight you were not supposed to be in," she said. "Drove away the local militia and lost three men-at-arms doing it. Were you not told to wait for the army?"

"I do not run from a fight," Balquhain protested.

"The next time, you will," Rick said. "Or I'll send you back as escort for the wagon train."

"You'll not dare—"

"He dares," Drumold said. "We hae all sworn on oath to fight as Rick commands. We will keep that oath."

"I will ride with the scouts in the morning," Tylara said. "If you do not understand what Rick wants from you, I do."

Both Rick and Balquhain spoke at once. "There's no need for that—"

"There is," Tylara said. "The maps brought back today were wretched. You'll need better." She eyed Rick defiantly.

The problem was, she was right. Dozens of medieval armies were defeated because they hadn't an elementary notion of the terrain they operated in. Rick had laughed in contempt when he read how the crusade commanders hadn't even known where their own columns were, but now he was beginning to appreciate their problems. There were almost no maps, and nobody in his army thought a map was as important as any other weapon.

Nobody but Tylara. She'd had experience with maps in her western country, and she had a good eye for distance and detail. Her troops would obey her, too, which meant that a detachment she led would actually scout instead of stop at frequent intervals for loot. But dammit—

There wasn't a lot of choice. They were deep in the imperial province, and if they marched on without locating the local garrison, they'd all be killed. "Tylara will take the scouts tomorrow," Rick said. "Balquhain will stay with the heavy cavalry."

Balquhain opened his mouth to protest, but he saw his father's look and subsided.

"That's an important job," Rick said. "They'll take orders only from you or your father."

The heavy cavalrymen were a pain in the arse, and he'd be better off sending them home, but that was out of the question. The trouble was, all the armored men were aristocrats, and that meant they had silly notions about the obligation of the aristocracy to get out front and fight for their honor—which would mean that most of his officer corps would be slaughtered in the first five minutes of real combat, and that would demoralize the infantry. Somehow he'd have to keep his two hundred armored horsemen out of it until the pikes and arrows had settled the matter. "Drumold, I think you should entrust your banner to your son. We'll give the mailed knights the honor of protecting it."

Drumold nodded seriously, and Balquhain seemed satisfied. Tylara concealed a grin from her brother. Sometimes Rick thought she was the only one in the army who paid attention to his lectures on tactics.

✢ ✢ ✢

They marched in oblique order. The First Pike Regiment, a block of a thousand, was ahead and to the right. Behind and left of them was the First Archers, then the Second Pikes, his main body and two thousand strong. The Second Archers and Third Pikes, another thousand-man block, followed on the road. Rick kept the heavy cavalry force with him, just behind the First Pikes. That way he could keep an eye on them. If anyone was likely to do something stupid, it would be his armored ironheads.

The wagons and pack horses came last. They were escorted by a screen of mounted archers acting as MPs under Mason's command. It had taken some doing to convince Drumold and his subchiefs that carrying food *into* the Empire would be a good idea. There'd been shouting and sulking. By now Rick was getting very good at pretending rage. He shuddered at the alternative; the army would have to break up into foraging groups every time they wanted a meal.

Tylara's scouts fanned ahead of the column. Rick wished he could go with her, but he didn't dare. The troops looked more like an army than a mob, but they still thought they needed his magic star weapons to protect them. They had no real confidence in themselves, and that could just be fatal.

✢ ✢ ✢

Caius Marius Marselius, Caesar's Prefect of the Western Marches, was annoyed. He'd hoped to avoid trouble for two more years, after which he would retire to his estates near Rome and let someone else worry about the province. He was not surprised when a local militiaman reported an invasion of hill barbarians, but he was definitely annoyed.

He was also careful. The militia officer had seen only light cavalry, but he thought there might be a larger body of barbarians behind the cavalry screen. He'd been unable to get through to find out.

That was unusual enough to make Marselius take notice. Normally these tribesmen came in like a flood, looted whatever they could, and ran. They had not thought of security. Marselius wondered if a Roman officer had defected and was now leading the barbarians. He couldn't think of anyone, but it was possible.

"We'll have to go into the hills and teach them a lesson," he told his legates. "It's been ten years since we had an expedition beyond the borders. High time."

The senior legate looked at him curiously. Marselius smiled faintly. He knew what the man was thinking. Initiative was not encouraged in Caesar's prefects. An outstanding officer might be contemplating rebellion. Caesar needed no generals who commanded greater respect from their legions than Caesar held.

And perhaps the legate was right. Marselius knew he was no threat to Caesar. He wanted only to retire. But would Caesar believe that?

The Empire would fall to that kind of suspicion someday. Marselius was convinced of it. When prefects were afraid to carry out their plain duty—

"Whether we follow them to the hills or not, we will want to destroy these barbarians," he said. "Not merely defeat them, but kill so many that they will tremble at the very thought of Caesar. For this we will require the full legion. Send for the reservists, call up the local knights, and bring in the detachments from Caracorum and Malevenutum. We will strike when they are all assembled."

"That will give the barbarians time to gather loot. Many of the landholders will be ruined, and they will protest to Rome," the senior legate said.

"Let them. There are few patricians in the border hills. God's breath, must I live in perpetual fear of Caesar's wrath?"

The legate did not answer. He did not need to.

Four days later, Marselius listened to the reports with growing amazement. The barbarians had not stopped to loot the foothill country. They had marched straight into the province.

"By nightfall they will be at the villa of Patroclus Sempronius," the scout commander reported.

"So far?" This was ruin. Sempronius was a cousin of the empress. Worse, the considerable town of Sentinius was just beyond. Caesar would never, never forgive the prefect who allowed a Roman city to be sacked by barbarians. They would have to be stopped, and quickly.

"How many legionaries do we have?" he asked the legate.

"Three thousand, Prefect."

That would include all the regulars and a considerable number of the reservists under their local leaders. Marselius sighed with regret: he could remember when a full four thousand regulars were kept in the camps. Ten years of peace in this province had robbed it of half that number. Caesar didn't care to keep armies larger than necessary, for fear they would rebel.

"Three thousand should be more than enough," Marselius said.

The legate grinned agreement. "They are only barbarians. They have no armor and few horses. What can they do against our knights?"

"What indeed? Sound the trumpets. Before the True Sun sets, I want the legion between Sentinius and these tribesmen. We will attack them in the morning when two shadows show clearly."

✢ ✢ ✢

Rick sighed with relief when he saw Tylara return at the head of her cavalry. He still didn't like her going out on patrols, but had to admit that she was the most effective scout commander he had.

The villa where he stood was a good example. It was large and comfortable, and she'd not only waited for the advance guard before charging the thin screen of armed retainers defending the place, she'd also kept the troops from looting and burning it. Now it could be systematically stripped of its valuables. There were over a thousand bushels of wheat in the granary, and the barns held both wagons and horses to transport it.

He went down the broad steps to meet her, and helped her down from her horse. Not that she needed help, but he found he liked being close to her.

"I have seen the legion," she said. She spoke quietly, so that no one else heard.

"Where?"

"About thirty stadia."

The Romans used miles, a thousand paces of a legionary, but Tylara's people had stayed with the ancient Greek measure, about a quarter of a kilometer. "What were they doing?"

"They had dismounted and were pitching tents. I left five men to watch them. Two have crept close to the Roman camp. If the Romans begin to saddle their horses, they will bring word instantly."

I may just have fallen in love with you, Rick thought. *That is, if I didn't weeks ago*. He looked up at the suns. About an hour of daylight, and another three hours of dimmer but adequate light from the Firestealer.

"We'll fight them here," he said. "It's as good a place as any." There was a lake—not large, but big enough to stop heavy cavalry—five hundred meters to the south. It would do as an anchor for the right flank, and there was a game preserve, thickly wooded, a kilometer off to the left. Fifteen hundred meters was a pretty long line to hold with the number of troops he had, but it beat hell out of trying to form squares in open country.

"Pity they didn't come last night," Rick said. "We had a better position between those hills. But this will do fine. Let's find your father. We'll have to get the men into position while there's still light."

The preparations didn't take long. Rick had told them over and over the importance of bivouacking in a battle position, and eventually it had sunk in. He didn't have to adjust the fronts of the regiments at all.

The First Pikes were forward and to the left, at the edge of the woods, with a foam of armed camp followers stiffened with a few archers in the woods itself. The Second Pikes, his largest force, were two hundred meters behind and three hundred meters to the right of the First Pikes. The diagonal between was ditched, and stakes were set. Each stake was driven into the ground so that it slanted forward. They were set in a checkerboard pattern, three-foot intervals between stakes, so that the First Archers could move through the thicket. Behind them was Mason with his battle rifle.

Slightly behind and all the way over to the lake was the Third Pike Regiment. This left a gap directly in front of the villa of nearly eight hundred meters between the right edge of the Second and the left edge of the Third. He filled that with the remaining archers, and in front of them he had the troops dig ditches, drag up wagons and brush, and dig a random pattern of small hoof-catching holes.

"I want lanes between those obstacles," he told the engineer officer. Lanes would funnel the enemy for the archers and would also be a path for a cavalry counterattack if the moment came for one.

The engineers were a group of slaves liberated from looted farms. They'd been promised their freedom and a share of loot in exchange for their help. Rick's offer to pay them had surprised the slaves almost as much at it surprised his own troops. Some of them had even offered to enlist, but Rick refused. During the battle, they'd be locked in their barracks. He didn't need untrained and untrustworthy men wandering around at a crucial moment.

At dark Rick threw another screen of light cavalry forward to observe the enemy force. The other troops were allowed to fall out and make camp, leaving their weapons in place to mark their exact position on the battle line.

He rode around the encampment for an hour, stopping to talk with groups of clansmen around their watchfires. Julius Caesar had used a pickle to illustrate obscene jokes on the night before Pharsalia. How could you measure the morale value of a pickle? Rick settled for more conventional pep talk, emphasizing the surprise the Romans would get when the star weapons began knocking them off their horses.

Eventually it was done, and he could go into the villa for his own dinner. By then it was nearly midnight.

"There's one more order," he told a staff officer. "I'll hold you responsible for seeing that the cooks are up at dawn. I want hot porridge for every man in the outfit before the sun's an hour high."

✢ ✢ ✢

The man who until a few hours before had been master of the villa sat across the table and glowered at Rick and his officers.

"Caesar will have your head," he blustered.

Rick examined him curiously. The man was fat, about forty Earth years in Rick's estimation, and didn't look any more like a Roman than a heavy-cavalry brigade resembled a legion. Rick wondered which group of kidnapped expeditionaries had furnished his ancestry. That was one question it would do no good to ask.

"As Yatar wills," Rick said. "But you're likely to lose yours before Caesar knows of ours."

"I am cousin to Caesar," the man protested. "Caesar will ransom me."

"We'll see. At the moment I want information. How many troops will we be facing in the morning?"

"I am Spurius Patroclus Sempronius, and I do not betray Rome," the fat man said.

"Hah!" Balquhain stood and drew his dagger. "We'll see how he likes being sent to Caesar a piece at a time."

Sempronius turned slightly green, but he set his lips in a tight line.

"No need," Rick said gently. "My scouts have told me all I really need to know." He turned back to the prisoner. "Tell me this: what keeps the slaves from revolting? There were over a hundred here."

"Three hundred. Why should they revolt? They are well treated. And Caesar's legions would crucify them."

That or a variant on the theme was the answer to just about every question. Caesar's legions kept order and Caesar's officers collected taxes. Caesar's freedmen ran the post office, and Caesar's slaves kept the city sewers in repair.

"Is there no Senate?" Rick asked.

"Certainly. I am a senator of Rome."

"Curious. When does it meet?"

"When Caesar wills it, of course."

It turned out that Caesar willed it about once every five years. The meetings were brief and did nothing more than ratify Caesar's decisions and perhaps vote Caesar a new accolade. Compared to the Assembly, though, the Senate was nearly omnipotent: the Assembly met precisely once in each reign, to proclaim its acceptance of whatever new Caesar the army had elected. Otherwise the citizens had no part in government and wanted none; they were happy enough if Caesar would leave them alone. In exchange they got peace and order and protection from bandits like Rick.

Late Empire, Rick decided. The military was more like the time of Charlemagne, but the government was definitely from the Dominate period of the Roman Empire. The army kept the citizens from making trouble, the Praetorian regiments kept the rest of the army under control, and Caesar spent most of his time worrying about how to control the Praetorian guard.

Once Rick had Sempronius talking about politics, he was able to extract a little more information. The most important was that there was a town about twelve Roman miles away.

It had a granary, and the harvest had been good this year. Now all he had to do was get through the Roman legion guarding it.

+ + +

Tylara turned quickly at the sound of footsteps on the roof behind her.

"I thought I told all my officers to go to bed," Rick said.

"I couldn't sleep."

"Me neither." He came over to the parapet to stand beside her. The flat roof of the villa gave a good view of the watchfires spread out across the estate. Edward III had used a windmill as a command post at Crécy. This villa would be better.

"Do you truly believe we can win?" Tylara asked.

"Tomorrow? Yes. There's no reason why we shouldn't. We've got more troops, and we've got better weapons."

"I know you have few thunderbolts for your weapons," she said.

"Gwen must have told you," Rick said. Tylara nodded. "And yet you came with us, and you haven't told your father."

"For all my life I believed that the Empire had the best soldiers in the world," she said. "But now we will beat them, and it will not be because of the weapons."

"Weapons, organization—Tylara, nothing's ever certain in war, but if I wasn't pretty sure of the result, you wouldn't be here."

"How would you send me away?"

"If necessary, tied to a led horse," Rick said.

"Do you dislike me that much?"

"You know better. You *must* know better," he said. He moved closer to her. "I don't dislike you at all."

"But you have a woman—"

"Gwen? She's not my woman."

"Her child is not yours?"

"Yatar, no! What made you think that?"

"No one wanted to ask," Tylara said. "Then—there is no one else? No one you will return to?"

He put his hands on her shoulders. "The only girl I care about is you. Didn't you know?"

"I hoped." She hesitated. "Rick, I will always love Lamil. My husband—"

"And never anyone else?"

"I already love someone else."

Custom demanded a longer mourning period, but if Rick didn't care, she didn't. When he came to her, she did not resist.

2

He was awakened at dawn, as he'd ordered, but the cavalry screen reported no signs of movement in the Roman camp. Rick sent out another scouting force and tried to return to bed; after half an hour he knew it was no use and went out to see that the troops all had a hot breakfast. Wellington had insisted on hot meals the morning of Waterloo, and always believed the biscuit and "stirabout" had as much to do with his victory as anything else.

If the Romans attacked early, the sun would be in his archers' eyes. There wasn't anything he could do about that except worry.

The camp was deathly still. It wasn't the silence of professional soldiers confident in their abilities. There were sporadic murmurs, small jokes that normally would have brought belly laughs, speculations about various women, even some attempts to cheer, but each conversation died away to silence again.

"They're scared, Cap'n," Mason said. "I can feel it."

"Me too."

"It's the waitin'," Mason said. He squinted to the east. "Almost wish they'd come and get it over with, even if it'd be better with the sun higher."

"They'll be here soon enough. Walk around a lot. Look mean and be sure they see your rifle."

Mason grinned. "Won't show 'em the bandolier, though."

"This won't be our only battle," Rick warned. "Don't shoot yourself dry." He hesitated. "If everything comes apart, I'll try to get Tylara out.

The Romans will try to cut us off from the road back. If I can get to that first villa we sacked, I'll wait for you there as long as I can. You do the same."

"Right. I wouldn't worry so much, Cap'n."

"Don't you worry?"

"Don't get paid to worry. That's what officers are for."

✢ ✢ ✢

The true sun was half-high and the Firestealer three hands above the horizon when the scout messenger rode in. The legion was coming.

"All of them?" Rick asked. "How are they formed?"

"They are all together," the scout reported. "They come in two large groups. The one on their left is slightly ahead of the other one."

"And where is the lady Tylara?"

"As you commanded, she is retreating from them but keeping them in sight. She will send messengers if they divide their force."

"Excellent," Rick said. He turned to Drumold. "Sound the battle horns."

The Tamaerthon hill people were obviously of Celtic origin, and Rick had expected them to have bagpipes; but either their ancestors had been from a group that didn't use them, or the art had been lost during the centuries on Tran. Instead they employed a long, curled horn that looked something like a thin tuba. At Drumold's wave, these sounded, and the camp followers began the rattle of drums. The pikemen and archers ran to their weapons.

Rick climbed to the roof of the villa. It would be better for morale if he were with the ranks, but he couldn't afford courageous gestures. More than one battle had been lost because the commander didn't know what was happening to all his forces. The staff officers he'd chosen to keep with him didn't like being up there either, but he'd stressed the importance of communications until at least a few of them understood how vitally he'd need messengers whose orders would be obeyed.

His view to the east was partly obscured by low hills, but from the vantage point of the roof he could just see the scarlet and yellow pennants of his light cavalry. They had stopped at the brow of the hill and were looking at something beyond. He tried to pick out Tylara, but the distance was too great. He felt a momentary panic. Suppose she'd been caught by the Romans? But there was no point in worrying about that now.

The First Pikes were moving nicely into formation, a rectangle one hundred twenty-five men wide by eight deep. The Swiss had formed their pikemen into precise square blocks, but he had too broad a front to cover for that. As he watched, they grounded arms, acting nearly in unison. That way they wouldn't be exhausted when the combat began.

What looked like a forest of pikes came up just in front of him as the two thousand men of the Second presented pikes. The binoculars let him see individual troopers. They looked nervous. Well, so was he. Here came the archers to take their places among the checkerboard of sharpened stakes that marked their position. Their ranks were nowhere near as geometrical as the pikemen. They weren't supposed to be. If those heavy cavalrymen ever got among the archers to melee in hand-to-hand fighting, the battle would be over.

He shifted back to the horizon. His light cavalry were facing him now, and riding like hell. He raised the binoculars in time to see the first of the enemy come over the low hills twelve hundred meters away.

✢ ✢ ✢

The Romans trotted toward them like an armored flood. Tylara had no difficulty getting the light cavalry force to simulate panic. The problem would have been to hold them once the Roman horses broke into a trot. It looked as if nothing could stop that steel tide.

They rode hard, past the First and Second Pikes and down the cleared lanes leading to the villa. Their horses were lathered before they were inside their own lines.

Tylara had deliberately stayed in front, and now when she reined in, the others halted. Some of them might not have. One cavalry group—Rick called it a "platoon," a strange word—would go on south beyond the slave barracks to warn of any Roman attempt to circle the woods and attack from behind, but Rick had stressed the importance of halting first to demonstrate that they weren't *really* running away.

Once again she marveled at the details he thought of. Nothing seemed too trivial for him to worry about. Any good chieftain inspected his clan's weapons, but Rick looked at their boots and sleeping cloaks as well. Who would have thought of bringing spades? Or grindstones? Or of having special details to bring in wood for cooking fires? Without him they'd be lost. He was right to stay on the roof of the villa instead of the forefront of the clans. He wasn't afraid of battle, no matter what some of the young warriors said.

She dismounted at the villa steps. Just in front, her brother sat his horse with their father's banner, surrounded by their few armored cavalrymen. Tylara grinned to herself as she went up the stairs to the roof. These proud young men might protest that their place was at the forefront of the battle, but now that they'd seen the Romans, they didn't look so eager to charge out.

Rick was looking through his far-seeing glass. *Binoculars.* She'd have to remember that word. She went to the parapet to join him. His smile warmed her.

"How close did you get?" Rick asked.

"Longbow shot. They carry short bows, and we did not want to be closer."

"You're learning," Rick said. He muttered to himself in his strange language, then spoke in hers, but still more to himself than to her. "Lances and swords. No shields."

"Why have they halted?"

"Dressing ranks," Rick said. "But mostly they're hoping we'll break formation and come after them." He turned to a staff officer. "Go out to each regiment. Make certain the commanders understand that the Romans may charge and then act as if they're running away. They want us to scatter. If we take that bait, they'll cut us down. The first man I see breaking formation without orders, I'll shoot down from here."

"I had better take that message myself," Tylara said. "The clansmen will not like to hear it."

"They've heard it before, and I'll need you here. Get moving, Duhnhaig. And come back when you've told them."

The sept chief looked curiously to Tylara. She smiled thanks and gestured him on his way. "You speak roughly to important chiefs," she told Rick when Duhnhaig was gone.

"God dammit—no. Sorry. You're right. It's my fault if we lose no matter why. That's why I need you with me. I can handle the Romans—it's our own troops I have to worry about."

There was a blare of horns from the Roman ranks. They had formed into two massive blocks, each ten ranks deep, horsemen knee to knee, their lances with pennants held high. The trumpets blared again, but there was no movement.

They were answered by the drums of the clan women, and the shriller sound of Tamaerthon war-horns.

✢ ✢ ✢

Prefect Marselius cursed silently. He had hoped the barbarians would either charge him or break and run, and they weren't doing either. More and more he was certain that a Roman officer led them. He'd never heard of hill tribes standing in regular formation to wait for an attack.

Those blocks of spearmen looked remarkably steady, too. Over the centuries Rome had worked out tactics to deal with any situation. Standard practice when opposing standing spears was to come to extreme bow range and gall them with arrows until they charged, then cut them down with swords.

That wouldn't work here. He could see all too many archers formed behind those ditches and stakes, and he'd had experience with those hillmen's longbows. They outranged anything a horse archer could carry, and an exchange of archery fire would cost far more than it gained.

Standard tactics against archers was a charge with lance.

You rode as hard as you could and lost some men getting in among them; but once there, the battle was over. If they were mixed in with spearmen, as they often were, you did the same thing. If they'd planted stakes and other obstacles, several centuries would dismount and cut a path for the rest.

The tactical writers hadn't considered the situation of mixed blocks of archers and spears. Marselius had never heard of such a situation. But then he'd never heard of barbarians penetrating this deep and waiting for a battle, or of having cavalry screens that kept watch on him from camp to battlefield.

"The men grow restless," his senior legate said.

"Let them. Leave time for fear to grow among our enemies."

"We also tire the horses."

True enough. An armored man was a heavy burden, even for a warhorse. The longer they were saddled and still, the slower they'd be in the charge. "Sound trumpets," Marselius ordered. "Play false calls. Marching music."

The cornu blared out, to be answered from the barbarian camp by their own horns and drums. That, at least, was standard. The hillmen's women rattled tom-toms incessantly. It was said to be a form of supplication to their barbarous gods.

He reviewed the situation again, reconsidering his decision not to send any of his force around either the lake or the forest to fall on the tribesmen from behind. The morale effect of an attack from the rear was often devastating, but he suspected these barbarians wouldn't be shaken by it. Anyway, in that mass of irrigation ditches south of the villa, his cavalry would be worthless. It wasn't worth the cost of dividing his legion.

He could withdraw. Shadow the tribesmen, wait to catch them in the open. The legates would not care for that—it smacked of fear. And although in the open the barbarians would be the more easily defeated, more of them would also get away. No. They must be taught not to invade the Empire.

There was one other factor. The villa had not been burned. A bold stroke now would return it intact to Sempronius' family—perhaps even rescue the patrician alive. Instead of hatred there might be gratitude from Caesar's relative.

They must attack while the horses were still fresh. There was nothing to be gained by waiting. He stood in his stirrups. "Sound the calls for a charge with lance," he ordered.

The steel tide broke forward into a walk, then a trot. The lances came down in unison, and the armored horsemen poured toward them, spurring to a canter. Rick felt a final twinge of fear, swallowed hard, and gained control of his nerves.

They came in a single wave four ranks deep, riding almost knee to knee, their line stretching nearly from woods to lake. "They mean to roll right over us," Rick said. He wondered what he'd do if he were the enemy commander. A hard charge carried home? That would certainly be a more effective tactic than the French used at Crécy, where they'd come in small driblets of undisciplined feudal lords. These troops were a lot better than anything Philip had with him that August day.

They were almost within extreme archery range. Rick could be certain of the exact line because he'd had it marked with stakes. The archers lifted their bows and drew back. One or two released arrows. Rick hoped their noncoms got their names. The time of release had been carefully calculated: assume heavy cavalry moves at fifteen miles an hour, and time the flight of an arrow to longest range—

"Let the gulls fly!" someone called. The arrows flocked upward in a volley, arced high, and fell among the charging horsemen.

The effect was instantaneous. The lines in front of the archers lost their geometric precision and dissolved into a wave of rearing wounded horses. There were screams as horses and men felt the bite of the iron-tipped shafts.

English longbowmen could get off a flight every ten seconds. The

Tamaerthon archers were just about as good. As the Roman cavalrymen—Rick still couldn't bring himself to call a formation of armored men on horseback a "legion"— covered the final two hundred fifty yards, the Tamaerthon gulls flew three more times. Then the archers skipped back among their stakes and fired at point-blank range.

What struck the archer's line wasn't an orderly formation at all. The horsemen were moving too fast to stop when they saw the angled stakes, and tried to guide their mounts around them, but the horses got in each others' way, while wounded and riderless mounts dashed randomly among them.

Meanwhile, the First Pikes had taken the initial shock—only there wasn't one. The first rank of pikemen knelt and held their weapons butt grounded, angled at the eyes of the horses. The next three ranks held theirs high, points outthrust over the heads of the kneeling first rank. They presented a wall of pointed steel, and the horses wouldn't stand it. They swerved about, or halted, some with a shock that dismounted their riders. Not a single lance struck home among the pikemen.

"This would be the time for a charge," Rick muttered. "But I can't. They're not disciplined enough to stay in formation."

The first line of Romans dismounted to attack the pikes with swords. They were braver than their horses, and several got in among the pikemen, although most were thrust down by the heavy points. The few who managed to close slaughtered several of the front rank, but the rear files thrust forward to strike them down. The pikemen shouted triumph, and the cheer ran down the ranks.

It was all happening at once, and far too fast for anything Rick could do to influence the battle. The battle on Rick's left wing was nearly over before the Roman horse could reach the much larger block of archers and pikemen close under the villa.

As the leading wave of Roman cavalry approached the broad face of the Second Pike Regiment, the horses shied away from the steady wall of points edging to their left so that they clumped in front of the archers. The wagons and downed trees and other obstacles concentrated the enemy ever tighter as each horseman tried to go down one of the cleared lanes.

The grey gulls flew down the cleared lanes to strike down horses and riders alike. The charge came on, deeper into the pocket. The line of archers here was much thinner than that between First and Second Pikes; it had to be because there was three times the front to cover. The arrows flew less thickly, and the comparative safety of that front, compared to the solid wall of pikepoints, drew more and more of the steel-armored Romans like a magnet.

Those stopped by ditches and trees dismounted and continued forward shouting war cries.

"Now!" Tylara shouted. "Use your star weapons! Now!"

"Not yet." Rick watched the situation develop. The Romans on foot were dangerous. Their armor partly protected them from arrows. But they were also much slower, and the archers had more opportunities to shoot. The Roman wave came forward ponderously, past the wagons, around the abatis of felled trees, around and over the ditches, onward toward the archers who now had no protection but their stakes. The archers fell back involuntarily, back again—

To be stopped by backing against the heavy cavalry and Drumold's banner. They held for a moment, resolutely firing another volley of arrows point-blank at the Romans among the stakes that had been their final defense line.

"Now," Rick said. He shouted to a mounted messenger below. "Now!" He ran for the stairs, shouting for his orderlies and his messengers. It was time to get into the battle.

✛ ✛ ✛

Tylara watched the opening charge of the terrible Romans without fear. She had confidence in Rick, if not in her clansmen. When she saw the Roman wave break against archers and pikemen alike, she was certain they had won.

But the Romans pressed on. When they dismounted to charge headlong toward the archers and her father's banner behind the archery line, Tylara took fear again. Did Rick not understand that if that banner fell, half the clansmen would try to save themselves any way they could? Why did not Rick kill them with his thunder weapons?

He seemed to have forgotten that he was armed. He was far more concerned with shouting orders to messengers. Now he ran for the stairs. Tylara followed, wondering.

The din of battle filled her ears. She heard Rick shout again, but she could not understand him. Just below, not thirty yards from the steps of the villa, there was desperate fighting, with the Romans marching forward into the hail of arrows. The archers retreated, still in an orderly line, but here and there a man broke and ran—

The Romans had to be stopped. Her light-cavalry escort stood near the villa. It would not be much use against armored men, even armored men on foot. But her brother's heavier-armed men might be thrown in now—Rick was running there, and his orderly was holding a horse for him. Was Rick going to lead them himself against the Romans?

That was Rick's affair. The light cavalry was hers. She shouted to them to dismount and led them forward to stiffen the retreating line of archers. The archers let them through gladly, and she rushed forward swinging her battle-axe. She knew she was not skilled with it, but the only way to be certain the others would attack was to lead them herself.

A Roman thrust at her with his lance. She parried with the axe, stepped inside his reach, brought the axe around to cleave at him. It struck his helmet but did not cut through, and while the man was staggered by the blow, an archer ran forward and struck the Roman again with the mallet used to place stakes. The armored man fell.

Other Romans advanced. Many of the archers had no more arrows, and although a few drew swords and stood resolutely, others melted back. They would all run soon—

The Roman line halted. There were screams and shouts, and the Romans faced about, bewildered—

The Third Pike Regiment had faced left and charged the Romans. They formed an irresistible battering ram of steel points, and they pressed onward, catching the Romans from the side and from behind.

There were more shouts. The rear ranks of Second Pikes had also joined the battle, wheeling to form a block thirty men square and bearing down on the Romans, mounted and dismounted alike.

Now the Romans thought of nothing but retreat. Those still on horseback tried to get back out through the narrow lanes between the ditches, while those afoot tried desperately both to catch their horses and avoid the pikes coming from either side. Another volley of arrows fired point-blank struck among the Romans caught in the pocket.

They were still dangerous. A Roman charged at Tylara and she swung her axe furiously, missing him but causing him to flinch away.

Then the pikemen came on again, and the Roman threw down his sword and fell at her knees.

Tylara turned from the battle to look for Rick, just in time to see him lead the heavy cavalry off to the right.

✢ ✢ ✢

Rick shouted orders as he ran. "Third Pikes to face left and charge." He saw that messenger off and called to another. "Second battalion of Second Pikes form square, face right, and charge." *Now I hope to God all that drilling we did during the summer has an effect. We've got them! By God, we've got them.*

There was one weak point. When Third Pikes moved into the battle, they'd leave a gap between them and the lake, while what used to be their front would become their fully exposed right flank. A charge there or through the gap would be disastrous.

It wasn't likely. The Romans hadn't kept back a reserve. Poor tactics. It was always worthwhile keeping a reserve.

Without reserves you couldn't exploit the enemy's mistakes, and victory generally went to the side that made the fewest errors—

He found his horse and threw himself into the saddle, waving to the heavy cavalrymen to follow. He cursed when he saw Drumold and his son leading. He didn't want the banner exposed. But then he saw why. The others hadn't moved, but now reluctantly followed their chief and banner. Of course. They wanted to get in on the fight, and here Rick was leading them away from it. Drumold had worked a miracle in holding them as it was.

Okay, the banner came too. Now he didn't dare commit this reserve until he was certain of victory. He wished he could see what was happening out in front of First Pikes. That charge had shattered them, and it would take damned good work to re-form for another—but the Romans had shown they were steady, and he had no right to assume their commander was a fool.

They rounded the right—now the rear—of Third Pikes, shouting battle cries to reassure the infantry. He didn't want them panicked by hearing strange hoofbeats behind them.

Out in front, things were quiet for a moment. The right wing of the Roman army had pulled back and was milling around. There'd be a little more time before they could get into any formation for another charge.

First Pikes were standing at ease, looking curiously back toward the main battle. Balquhain raised the clan banner high. A cheer ran up and down the ranks.

The archers linking First and Second had returned to their stakes, and a few more were out in front of them stripping bodies and making sure what they stripped were bodies. There didn't seem to be any way to stop that.

Inside the pocket, the slaughter continued. The escape lanes were piled with bodies, and some enterprising officer of the Second had pushed a knot of pikemen into each one. The pikemen stood behind heaps of dead and faced the villa, preventing anyone from escaping. The Romans inside that caldron were pressed so close together that they couldn't use their weapons. They'd be tiring now, too. That was the trouble with armor. The protection it provided came at a high cost.

Ha. The Roman right wing had got itself into formation. Rick used the binoculars to pick out their commander's scarlet cloak and gold bracelets. The man stood in his stirrups to study the battle. It was obvious that he didn't know where to charge. The best place—Third Pike's flank—was covered by Rick's heavy cavalrymen; hit Third and the Romans would expose *their* flank to a cavalry charge. Meanwhile the Roman commander was losing half his army down in the pocket.

Aha. He was going to have another go at the junction between Second Pikes and the archers linking First and Second. If they got through there, they'd cut Rick's forces in two, and they'd have an excellent chance to crush his main force as well as relieve the pressure on the troops caught in the caldron. It was good tactics, but stupid. If they couldn't break the archers with their first charge, why think they could do it now when the horses were getting winded?

But what else could he do? Pouring men into the caldron would be worse than useless. What would I do if—

"We stand like cowards!" Dughuilas, chief of the largest of the subclans, drew his sword. "I will not have it said that I watched this battle without taking part."

Oh, God dammit. That's all I need. "Hold!" Rick shouted. Half the cavalrymen had drawn weapons, and even Drumold was looking anxious. "We protect our men here. If we leave this place, the Romans will strike—"

No good. They weren't listening. Rick drew his Mark IV .45 automatic and aimed it just past Dughuilas' left ear. He fired.

The clan leader winced. At four feet, the muzzle blast would be enough to take off hide. "Another step forward and I strike you from the saddle," Rick said. "You and any other who desert."

"Desert? We want to fight!" someone shouted. "You'll get the chance to fight. Hah! They're going to try

it." He pointed. The Roman line swept forward again, this time in a thick column, aimed like an arrow between First and Second Pikes.

Again three flights of arrows struck among them before they could reach the stakes. This time they pressed forward, heedless of losses, walking the horses into the staked area now hastily abandoned by the archers—

It was the last of the Roman reserve. Rick spurred forward, riding hard toward the First Pike Regiment. He had no thought that the others would follow him, and they didn't; they made straight for the Romans. Well, that would be all right now. The important thing was to get First Pikes to face right oblique rear and charge. They'd finish the Romans a lot more thoroughly than these ironheads.

But at least the chiefs would get a chance to fight.

They do, I don't, Rick thought. *Not that I particularly want to. But this battle's all over except the cleaning up, and I haven't fired a shot.*

Then he grinned when he remembered that he had fired exactly once.

4

The battle was ended. Wherever Rick went, the men raised cheers. Tamaerthon casualties were light, and the Romans were totally defeated. The triumph was complete.

But then he felt the elation drain away with the adrenaline that had sustained him. In the military history books, the battle ends with the victory. The chesspieces are swept into the box, and all is quiet.

But there was no quiet. There were the screams of pain, from horses and men, mingled with the shouts of triumph and joy from the victors. An archer sat stupidly as he watched the blood flow from an arm severed above the elbow. A Roman warrior writhed in pain as pikemen stripped off his armor and cursed him for bleeding on their loot. And everywhere the horses and centaurs screamed and shied away from blood.

The centaurs were the worst. Worse, somehow, than the dying humans, far worse than the horses. The beasts tried to use their ill-developed hands to pluck out arrows or stop the flow of blood. They were not intelligent enough to understand what had happened (in a million years, would they have evolved good hands and high intelligence?), but they were sentient enough to be aware. Like dogs, they howled and whimpered and begged their human masters for help that couldn't be given. *Thank God*, Rick thought; *thank God the Romans used few of them.*

And thank God this is done. With luck we won't have to do it again. I can be through with war. The battles in Africa weren't so bad. The helicopters came and took the wounded away. You didn't have to look at what you'd done.

He had no more time to brood. There were a million details to attend to at once. Stop the slaughter and let the Romans surrender: the aristocratic airs of Rick's heavy cavalrymen helped there. It was beneath their dignity to kill an enemy who couldn't defend himself. Some of them were even intelligent enough to realize that if your enemies thought they'd be killed anyway, they'd fight on after the battle was lost.

Slaves directed by Mason and his MPs stripped the dead and disarmed the captured. That couldn't be trusted to the clan warriors. And Rick had to convince the chiefs, and they had to convince the archers and pikemen, that the loot would be divided fairly. The idea that a battle was won by all and all should share in the spoils was new to the hillmen.

Cavalry screens had to be sent to keep contact with the Romans who had escaped and to watch for any new Roman units. Arrows had to be recovered from the battlefield and distributed. Midwives and priests had to examine the wounded. Prisoners with deep punctures in chest or abdomen had to be killed mercifully—there wasn't anything else you could do for them. Other kinds of wounds had to be cauterized, or washed and bound up—thank God they hadn't come up with the insane theory of bleeding a wounded man!

And that's something I can do now, Rick thought. *I can teach medical science. I don't know much, but I can teach the germ theory of disease, and aseptic practices, and get some of the acolytes interested in anatomy and dissection. But how do we develop penicillin? Maybe we can't. Sulfa drugs? I don't know anything about them, either. No technology. No chemistry theory, no experimentalists, no scientific method. No surgeons, and I don't know enough, but I can make a start. I can teach them how to learn, and maybe one day a perforated gut won't be a death sentence.*

Grooms and camp followers had to be sent to collect the captured horses. Let the centaurs go—those not mortally wounded. The hill clans weren't used to them and wouldn't keep them. Send more MPs to see that no one stole horses or ran away with loot. And total up the butcher's bill.

Medieval armies left that to heralds. After Agincourt the French heralds had inspected the battlefield and worked with the English heralds to collect the names of the dead and captured. That useful organization hadn't developed on Tran. Rick had tried to foresee the problems of victory and organize for them, but even so he had to be everywhere at once.

And everywhere he went, men stopped what they were doing to cheer him. He could feel pride in that. He'd won the battle, and it was worth winning. Without the grain, the hill tribes were doomed. And the cheers were important, too, if he were to have any control over them. Men want to cheer a commander who wins victories for them. But he wished they'd get on with the work and let him hide in the villa. It was a splendid victory, but he didn't want to see the battlefield any longer.

✢ ✢ ✢

Tylara came into the villa leading a prisoner. "I have found the Roman commander," she said.

He'd been stripped of his armor and gold bracelets, but she'd let him keep his red cloak. Even with that, it was difficult for Rick to recognize him as the haughty officer he'd seen organizing the final charge.

Rick invited him to sit and sent for wine. The Roman seemed surprised. He studied Rick's face carefully and listened to his speech, then shook his head. "You are no Roman."

"Of course not," Rick said.

"I had thought these bar—these hillmen must have been led by an officer trained by Rome."

Rick smiled faintly. In a way, that was true, but hardly the way this man thought. "Lord Rick Galloway, war chief of the host of Tamaerthon," Rick said. *Pretentious*, he thought. Pretentious, but necessary. Perhaps he could use this man.

Words cost very little. "I have long admired Roman ways," Rick said. "Your men fought well, as did you."

"Ah. I am Caius Marius Marselius, Prefect of the Western Marches."

"Prefect. In the Rome I knew, a prefect was both military and civil governor. Is that your office?"

"Yes." A gillie brought goblets of wine, and the Roman officer drank thirstily. "Thank you," he said to Rick.

Rick studied the Roman officer. *Head bloody but unbowed*, he thought. A proud man holding his head up after defeat. But he knows he's beaten, and maybe he's sensible.

"You can prevent a great slaughter," Rick said. "We have come for grain and loot. Now that we've beaten your legion, there is nothing to prevent us from sacking the town of Sentinius. I would rather not do that. If you will arrange for the wealth of the town and the contents of the granaries to be loaded on wagons and brought to me, only officers to inspect the granary will enter the city. If you do not, we will take the town by storm, and there will be no controlling the men and the camp followers."

The Roman's eyes narrowed. "You ask for tribute from Caesar?"

Damn. Of course he'll see it that way. "No. I demand what is mine by conquest. I will have all of the grain and much of the wealth. That is certain. The only uncertainty is whether or not the people of Sentinius and the city itself will survive the experience. Do you truly believe the citizens can oppose me now that their legion is destroyed?"

The Roman officer pursed his lips in thought. He took a deep breath and said, "No. The citizens would be killed to no purpose. How am I to arrange this?"

"You will be free to go. My cavalry will watch the city gates. If by sunset tomorrow there are no wagons of grain, then we will do as we will with Sentinius." Rick paused. Might as well sweeten the pot. "In addition, I will release your soldiers and whatever equipment we cannot carry with us the day we cross Caesar's borders to return to our mountains." Rick shrugged. "What use are they to me? We are not foolish enough to wait for a ransom which would likely be escorted by five legions."

Marselius seemed puzzled. "Now I am certain that you are not a barbarian," he said. "Who are you?"

"That is no concern of yours."

"Perhaps not. What assurance have I that you will not sack the city no matter what we do?"

"You have the word of a Tamaerthon lord," Tylara said coldly.

"I have seen you shouting at your officers to make them spare captives," Marselius said. "You are no barbarian." He seemed to take comfort from that. "Very well, I agree. But may I ask, why this concern with grain? In the past, the hill tribes have raided for other wealth—"

"I remind you that I also demand some of the more usual loot," Rick said. "Small valuables. Trinkets. Goblets. Cloak pins and ornaments. Jewelry. I do not doubt that your citizens will keep their most valuable objects, but make certain that they send out enough gaudy luxuries to please my clansmen. As to why we are concerned with grain, if you care to return—as my guest—after the loot is transferred, I will tell you. It is a story worth knowing."

✤ ✤ ✤

The last of the wagons rolled westward. They were an impressive sight; over a thousand wagons loaded with wheat and barley and oats and a grain that Rick had never seen before which grew on a plant resembling a giant sunflower, and produced a seed that more resembled rice than anything else. Other wagons were loaded with onions, spinach and other vegetables needed for winter nutrition. Fifty were loaded with heavy valuables—furniture and bolts of cloth and iron implements. The light-weight loot—rings and ornaments and personal arms—had been distributed to the army. Interspersed with the wagons were flocks and herds driven by camp followers and liberated slaves.

An impressive sight. Drumold had never seen its like. Everyone was certain there was food enough for all, enough to last through two winters—And they were utterly wrong.

✤ ✤ ✤

Columns of pikemen and archers guarded the wagon train, and the light-cavalry screens were well out to the flanks and forward to warn of any Roman attempt to recapture the loot of Sentinius. Rick took a position among Mason's mounted archers in the rear guard.

He shifted uncomfortably in the saddle, not caring for the weight of the Roman mail he wore. It itched. He'd rather do without armor, but that wasn't possible. He needed the armor and a personal bodyguard of freedmen loyal to no clan chief—and Mason at his back whenever possible. That wasn't because he was worried about the enemy; the problem was that he might be assassinated by his own officers.

The army was loyal enough. He'd won a complete victory with trivial casualties: a score of pikemen killed when the Romans managed to close with the first rank, another score of archers and pikemen cut down in the desperate fighting that closed the day, and nearly thirty heavy cavalrymen who hadn't sense enough to let the pikemen and archers do the work and had to go riding in to fight in personal combat with the defeated Roman heavies. Most of the armored men were related, and the survivors blamed Rick for their losses; if he had led the armored charge himself instead of riding to bring the pikemen in, they would not have lost sons and brothers . . .

They also resented losing the opportunity to sack a Roman city.

"Let them," he'd told Tylara and Drumold. "If we turn those lads loose in Sentinius, they won't be fit to fight for a ten-day. We'd be helpless against any kind of Roman attack. Don't forget that a full thousand Romans got away—more than enough to kill us all if we scatter. I would rather stay in a strong position and let the Romans bring the loot to us."

"We have defeated the Roman legion," Balquhain said. "They can bring in no other for a ten-day. The chiefs know this, and they say that we can use that time to loot the province. There would be much wealth."

"To what purpose?" Rick demanded. "We have taken more grain and loot than we have wagons to carry it in. It will take a ten-day and more to transport what we have back to the passes, and we will be fortunate to get it all into The Garioch before the snows begin. Seizing more wouldn't help us, only harm the Romans—and when the Demon Sun is closest, we may have need of them as friends."

"Caesar will never befriend us," Drumold said.

"Perhaps not, but only a fool gives his enemies reason to hate him, and I am no fool."

"No one says you are," Balquhain protested.

"Then let them do this my way, as they have sworn." *And let me go back to the hills without a useless battle. I don't suppose it's possible to live the rest of my life without another fight like this. It takes a quart of wheat to feed a full-grown man for a day. The fifty thousand bushels of wheat we've taken can't possibly last us two winters. But there's no more to do this year, and for that I'm grateful. Glory's a heady drink, but the bar bill's damned high.*

The chiefs had accepted the decision, but they had another complaint, too. Rick had distributed the loot among the soldiers rather than giving it to the chiefs to parcel out. They felt he was trying to undermine their authority.

They were right. He'd bought the loyalty of the common soldiers and noncoms, but incurred the hatred of many of the officers. The result was that he had to wear armor and endure the itch. Considering what he'd got for it, Rick thought the price worth paying.

✛ ✛ ✛

The cavalry escorted the Roman prefect into the camp on the third night of the march. Freshly shaved and in clean clothing, he looked very different from the last time Rick had seen him—but he'd wisely refrained from wearing jewelry. His sword had been bound into its scabbard so that it couldn't be drawn, but they had let him keep it.

"I had not thought to see you again," Rick said. "I had even thought those troops you've kept ten miles south of me might be planning an attack."

"If your information is that good, you also know I have fewer than two thousand men," Marselius said. "I have come to see if you will honor your word and release my legionaries. Also I wished to hear this curious story you said it would be worth much to know."

"Then you will not be disappointed," Rick said. "But will Caesar not have your head? Surely he will say you have not done all you could to punish us for invading his realm."

"Caesar will have my head no matter what I do," Marselius said. "He will not deal lightly with a prefect who allowed barbarians—your pardon, but that is what he will consider you—to escape unharmed with the loot of a Roman city." He shrugged and lifted a goblet of wine in salute. "But Rome will not be well served by wasting the balance of my troops. Your cavalry scouts would give ample warning of my approach, and if we could not face your longbows and longer spears before, how can we now? I have never seen weapons like those spears. You call them pikes?"

"Yes."

"An interesting weapon," Marselius said. "I have not read of its like. Although there are stories of a time when Romans fought on foot and carried throwing spears, the records say nothing of these pikes." The Roman governor eyed Rick curiously. "In our earlier meeting, you spoke of 'the Rome you knew,' as if you were not certain it was the same as our Rome. Do you know of Roman history, then?"

"More than you know," Rick said. "Rome was once a nation of free men. Its citizens were its army, and a Roman citizen did not bow to any man."

"Are you then a Republican?" Marselius asked.

"You know of the Republic?" Rick asked.

"There are tales. In books, mostly. Caesar does not encourage

Romans to read those books, but I have seen copies. Livius, and Claudius Nero Caesar, and—"

"The history written by the Emperor Claudius! It survives here?"

"Yes—"

"I would pay nearly anything for a copy," Rick said.

"It is written in an ancient language few can read—"

"I have an officer who reads Latin." *I'd forgotten where I am*, Rick thought. A treasure like that. On Earth, Claudius' histories were lost centuries ago. I wonder what other lost documents they have in this new Rome. "Do you know that the Emperor Claudius lived on another world?" Rick asked. "That your city of Rome is but a copy, and there stands on another world lit by another sun the original city of the Tiber?"

"How do you know of this?" Marselius demanded. "I have always suspected, but the priests say it is not true, for God created but one world and anoints but one true king, who is Caesar—" he hesitated. "Christ came but once, and to but one world. The priests are certain of it. But I have never been certain that world was ours."

"It was not," Rick said. He wondered how much he should tell the prefect. If the Romans immediately began intensive farming of all their land, they could store up enough food to save part of their population. Otherwise nearly all would die.

There was no point in telling him about starships and the *Shalnuksis*. That still left a lot. "I come from a land far to the south and so far west that one could sail for weeks before reaching it," Rick said. "There we have many old documents, and there we know that the stories of the worlds are true. If you wish a sign, look to the skies. The Demon Star comes close, and soon there will be fire and flood and famine in the land."

The Roman's eyes narrowed. "I have heard such tales," he said. "And I have heard another, that you come from farther away than the other side of the world."

Now who's been talking? Rick spread his hands. "The old legends are true," he said. "As to the other story, I do not gainsay it, but I make no such claim. Now listen and I will tell you of the times to come. They are times to make brave men fear."

PART SEVEN
SCHOLARS

Snow lay deep in the passes of Tamaerthon. Rick could hear the winds from the north scream past the walls of his lodge.

There were no palaces in Tamaerthon. Drumold's lodge home, over a hundred feet long and half that wide, with walls of earth and stone ten feet thick, was the largest structure the hill country boasted. When the army returned from the raid on the Empire, the tribesmen built a lodge for Rick within the stone fortress circle and close by Drumold's. It was nearly as large as the chief's, which meant that the great hall was nearly impossible to heat, and Rick spent most of his time in the smaller room he had built to use as an office. It had whitewashed walls he could write on with charcoal.

He had intended to work there, but he found that very difficult. There was no glass. The best they had for windows was thin, oiled parchment; there was no good light even in daytime. He began to understand why the Northmen had slept late and spent their evenings at drinking bouts and listening to bards recite. What else could they do?

He desperately needed to plan for spring, but that was difficult. No one in Tar Tageral was skilled at making parchment, and the ink was terrible. He could make notes by scrawling on the whitewashed walls with charcoal, or using his ballpoint pen to write on a precious page of his notebook. But when pen and notebook were gone, there would be no others.

At first he'd thought it would be easy to bring technology to Tran.

Now he knew better. He had to concentrate on tools; in fact, tools to make tools, and often that meant going back to first principles. Wire, for example. He knew that ancient jewelers had made small quantities of wire by painstakingly hammering it. About the time gunpowder was invented, the Venetians discovered the art of drawing wire through holes in an iron plate. The craftsman sat on a swing powered by a water wheel and seized the wire with tongs, letting his weight on the swing aid the work. But how thick a plate? How do you drill holes in iron? And where do you get the copper bar stock to make wire from?

And steel. Knowing that steel was iron with just the right amount of carbon was all very well, but how much is the right amount? And how do you experiment if you can't operate a forge and you don't want the smiths to think you a fool?

There were dozens of similar problems, and they gave him a headache. For relaxation, he invented the English custom of tea parties. Of course they didn't have tea here, but they had a plant whose boiled leaves made a caffeine drink. Rick was getting used to the somewhat bitter flavor—and teatime was a good way to spend an afternoon. He was drunk in the evenings more often than he liked.

Sometimes he would invite twenty or thirty people; sometimes none but Gwen, if she cared to join him. He was not unhappy if she chose to stay in her rooms at the far end of the great hall from his "office." She had grown increasingly moody and uncommunicative as her time approached, and her gloom and that of the weather in combination were more than enough to depress him.

But each afternoon he would have tea in his great hall. Any diversion was welcome.

✠　✠　✠

Corporal Mason brushed snow from his sheepskin greatcoat and dashed for the hearth fire. He warmed his hands thankfully before turning to the others. "Cap'n, its *cold* out there," he said.

Tylara laughed. "This is a mild winter. The Firestealer has plunged into the True Sun, but the ice in the middle of the lochs is barely thick enough to walk on."

"Thank God I wasn't here for a bad winter," Mason said.

"Each winter will be milder," Gwen said. "And each summer hotter." She clutched her teacup close to her swollen belly and stared into the fire.

"Aye," Tylara said. "The Demon Star is visible a full hour after sunrise, though both suns are in the sky."

"I've lost track of how many Earth days we've been here," Gwen said. She patted her swollen belly. "About eight months, obviously. We've missed Christmas."

"It's probably local Christmastide for the Romans," Rick said. "Or is it? I don't remember when the Catholic Church officially adopted Winterset as the day for Christmas. Anyway, we can have our own."

"We'll have to share," Gwen said. "Yanulf is making preparations for his own ceremony . . . I suppose to ensure that spring will come."

"No," Tylara said. "We have long known that spring will come whether we coax the Firestealer out of the True Sun or no. But should we not give thanks for the signs that winter will end?"

Mason shivered exaggeratedly. "God knows that's something to be thankful for," he said. He took a seat near the fire. "Be glad when spring's here."

"Not half as much as I will," Rick said. He grinned at Tylara.

Her answering smile was warm. "We always celebrate the return of spring. This year will be double joyful."

"Even for your father?" Rick teased.

She laughed. "It is only his way, to complain that the dowry will impoverish him. He will drink as much at our wedding as any three others."

Rick looked curiously at Gwen. Caradoc, who had been invaluable during the battle and now was commander of the archer company that was Rick's personal guard, was often in Rick's great hall. Usually he had business there, but sometimes what he wanted to discuss was trivial. He always managed to say a few words to Gwen before he left.

Would the spring ceremony be a double wedding? Officially, Gwen was the widow of an Earth soldier; the story provided an acceptable explanation of her condition. Only peasant women had illegitimate children. Since no one knew precisely when by local time Gwen's husband had been "killed," it was decided that her period of mourning would end at the same time as Tylara's.

"Spring's a long time away," Rick said. "Too long. For now, let's have an old-fashioned Christmas. No turkey here, but we can have a goose—"

A distant trumpet sounded.

"That's the lads down in the lower village," Mason said. "Reckon I'd better go see what it's about."

"You don't have to go out in that cold," Rick said. "That wasn't an alarm—"

"It's all right, Cap'n," Mason said. "I'm glad of something useful to do. I've been getting cabin fever." He got up and put on his heavy coat. The wind blew flurries of snow into the great hall when he went out.

✣ ✣ ✣

The letter was on thick parchment. It was brought to Rick in his office.

The Roman had spoken the same language as Tylara, and she had told Rick that there was one universal tongue from the Five Kingdoms to Rustengo. But the letter was written in Latin—Rick could read enough of it to know that. He sent for Gwen and handed her the parchment. "Can you read that?"

"Just barely. I had three years in high school." She sat near the fire and read laboriously.

" 'From Caius Marius Marselius, onetime Prefect of the West, to Lord Rick, war leader of the tribes of Tamaerthon, greetings. Peace be with you and your house. This letter is sent by the hands of Lucius, my freedman and friend, who brings you—' I think that's 'gifts'—'and a message which I hope—' I don't know that verb. It's future tense. From the content I'd guess it was 'will heed.' Anyway. He says, 'Lucius has power to speak for me.' It's signed with a lot of flourishes." She handed Rick the parchment.

He looked at it curiously. "No way to tell if it's genuine. But I suppose it is. Who'd fake it?" He nodded to his freedman attendant, a young NCO who'd escaped from a Roman slave barracks and fled to the hills. "Send their leader in, and see that the others are given food and drink and a fire. They are my guests."

"Sir!" Jamiy stamped to attention, did an aboutface, and left the room.

Gwen giggled. Rick looked wryly at her.

"Well, it's funny, that's all," she said.

"I tend to agree," Rick said. "Blame Mason. He's the one who's been teaching them military manners—mostly learned from watching old British Army movies, I think. It amuses him." And he thought, it's not really so funny. There's a point to military ceremonial. Under the circumstances, I'm not so sure Mason's wrong. We'll probably have to fight again. Even if I manage to wriggle out of it, I'll need disciplined forces.

The visitor was wrapped in woolen clothing so that only his nose and eyes showed. When he took off his scarves—three of them, counting the one wrapped around his face—and the hooded cloak and the thick gloves, Rick saw that he was quite elderly and very thin. His beard and long hair were nearly white, and he had almost no teeth.

Dentistry, Rick thought. Have to invent that from scratch. Thank God my teeth are in good shape, but that won't last. If I live long enough, I'll lose them all. Dentistry's another benefit of civilization you take for granted until you haven't got it.

"Were you able to read my master's letter?" the elderly man asked.

"Yes. What is your message?"

"Do you object if I sit? My bones are old, and the cold has made them brittle."

"Please do." Rick indicated a chair near the fireplace. "The matter must be urgent, to bring you here at Winterset."

Lucius sat heavily and huddled forward for warmth. "It is that. But first—" He reached down to a leather case he carried and took out a thick roll of parchment. He held that near the fire to warm it until it would unroll slightly, then held it out to Rick. "Marselius thought you might prize this," he said.

Rick took it curiously. The letters were handprinted in a block form and easily recognized. He read slowly. "Ego Tiberius Claudius Drusus Nero Germanicus—" He broke off, staring. "Is this truly a copy of the great history by the Emperor Claudius?"

"To the best of my knowledge," Lucius said. "I have no reason to doubt it. You are pleased with the gift, then?"

"I am indeed," Rick said. He frowned. What was this going to cost? "I am pleased that Marselius remembered my interest."

"He has written down every word you spoke," Lucius said. "I know, for he dictated them to me."

"May I see?" Gwen asked.

Rick was reluctant to let the parchment scroll out of his hands. He knew that was silly. He couldn't read it, and he'd need her help. He gave it to Gwen and watched to see that she didn't damage it, but she held it as tenderly as she might hold a baby.

"There are other documents," Lucius said. "One seems to be the story of how a group of soldiers came to this world from another."

"Where are these documents?" Rick demanded.

"Prefect Marselius has them," Lucius said. "They, too, could be gifts for you."

"Your friend is generous," Rick said.

"What does he want in exchange?" Gwen asked.

Rick frowned at her, but Lucius didn't seem upset. "Your friendship," Lucius said. "And an alliance."

"Alliance?"

"Perhaps I should begin with what has happened since you left." Lucius shifted in his chair.

"Jamiy," Rick shouted. "Tea, please."

"Sir."

"So what has happened?" Rick asked.

"The legions of the western provinces have proclaimed Marselius as Caesar," Lucius said. "I see this does not surprise you, and indeed it was inevitable if Marselius did not wish to be recalled to Rome and executed. The soldiers you released from captivity had no more pleasant expectation, and Marselius was popular with the other troops as well— and they could see the Demon Star. They have heard the tales. We all have. They believed Marselius when he told them what he had learned from you of the times of trouble to come. Few of the province, citizen or soldier, believe that our present Caesar will know what to do—or indeed care.

"Naturally, Marselius first sent for his family. His son and grandchildren were on the family estate near Rome. I was tutor to the household, as I have been for thirty years. For the past year, I have been working in the libraries of the friends of Marselius and his son. The letter that ordered young Publius—I call him young Publius, although he is a man older than you, my lord—the letter that ordered young Publius to join his father also instructed me to take many documents including that history by Claudius." Lucius sighed. "I fear we have betrayed many trusts, but Marselius assures me that the parchments will be replaced for all those who survive the coming times."

Jamiy brought in a pot of tea and three stone cups. As he put the tray down, Rick studied Gwen. She didn't seem overjoyed by the news of the documents. Rick wished he could think of a good reason to have her leave. I could simply order her out, he thought. *I don't have to be polite to anyone—well, except Tylara and her father. What is she hiding from me?* "Jamiy."

"Sir."

"Tell Major Mason that our new guests have brought important documents, and that I would like him to see that they are given to no one but me. No matter who might ask for them, they come to me and no one else. Is this understood?"

"Sir." Jamiy stamped to attention.

"Excellent. Dismissed. Lucius, your story is fascinating. But has Marselius a chance? Will not Caesar bring the other legions against him?"

"Certainly he will try," Lucius said. "But neither Caesar nor the army likes winter campaigns. They will wait for spring. By spring Marselius will have a surprise for Caesar." He grinned toothlessly. "Marselius has freed many slaves, and is training them to make and use those long spears you call 'pikes.' He has studied your methods well, and is also training crossbowmen since only your hill clans use the longbow."

"A surprise for Caesar indeed—"

"A surprise for you," Gwen said. "What advantage will you have now?"

"You need none," Lucius said. "Marselius offers alliance with you."

"A trap to get you back onto the plains," Gwen said.

Rick switched to English to say, "Gwen, teach your grandmother to suck eggs. And please stop interrupting. I want to know everything I can about the situation, and you are not helping."

"I'm sorry," she said. "I—I seem to be scared all the time lately. I don't want—I'll shut up, Rick. And I am sorry."

"We know that you have no reason to trust Marselius," Lucius said. "But he does not expect you to send your soldiers to help him. What he wishes is assurance that you will not raid the western provinces. We will pay you well for that. Marselius intends to plant many of the parklands and game preserves in grain. He will build storage places in the high hills. We will keep much, but there will be enough to send you more than you could take by raiding the Empire."

"Do you have caves to store it in?" Gwen asked.

"Few, Lady." Lucius looked thoughtful. "The older documents all stress the importance of caves as the only safe place when the fire and the deadly rains fall. There are caves in the northern hills, and others near Rome. Perhaps we can take those. But there is no chance at all if we must fight your hill tribes as well."

It can work, Rick thought. *For that matter, I could do more. Once Marselius is involved in a civil war, I could join him. The army would follow me, and with allies in the Empire, I could take Rome itself. A civilized place, with real potential. Who could stop me?* "And he went forth conquering, and to conquer."

William took all of England with less going for him, and the English were better for it. Well, better in the long run. They didn't see it that way at the time. "So stark a man," the chronicles say of him. "So very stern was he, and hot, that no man durst do anything against his will." But even his enemies said that a man could cross England with his bosom full of gold. I could govern better than Caesar . . .

No, I'm no conqueror, and the face of battle is not a lovely sight. I'd rather be a teacher—and we don't have to fight anymore. "It is not my decision alone," Rick said. "But I will counsel Drumold to accept this offer. And to make another. There is land in the hills below our mountains. The Romans do little with it because they have better. Yet we have crofters with no land at all, and our best is no better than those hills. Let us work that land in peace, and it may be that we will have gifts for Marselius in exchange for the gifts he offers."

"Rick, you can't turn down tribute," Gwen said in English.

"I don't intend to," Rick answered. "But trade's a lot more stabilizing than tribute." He turned to Lucius. "There will be many details, but I believe we can agree. With the Demon Star coming near, there will be slaughter and death enough. We need not add more."

2

Rick used charcoal to add another equation to the list on his whitewashed wall. He wished he had been a better physics student. He couldn't remember the basic equations of harmonic motion, and he wasn't sure he had derived them correctly. "Newton was one smart cookie," he muttered to himself.

The wall was covered with equations and notes and memoranda. One whole section listed things urgently needed, such as paper, and better lamps, and an adequate supply of pens and ink—all of which would be needed so that he could copy out a table of logarithms from his pocket calculator before its batteries failed. Another held the best data he had been able to obtain on crop yields. Next to that were diagrams of plow designs and crop-rotation schemes.

There were endless details. The work would never be finished; but it was more satisfying work than building the army had been. The raid had bought time, but now he could do something lasting. Tamaerthon could become a center of learning, a place whose security rested on something more solid than military power. If only he had decent light to work by . . .

When he heard the knock at his door, he turned with relief. The work was satisfying, but conversation was a welcome diversion.

Caradoc stood uncertainly in the doorway. "Come in," Rick invited. "There's good wine in the flask on the table."

"Thank you." Caradoc poured a cup of wine and looked curiously at Rick's charcoaled equations and the diagrams of the Tran system.

Rick knew that Gwen had been teaching Caradoc to read, and the archer commander had shown a lot of interest in Rick's work in the past. Today, though, he said nothing.

Rick frowned. "Some problem, Captain? Speak up, man."

"I am concerned for the lady Gwen," Caradoc said. "She sits and stares at the fire, and wants no one with her. It cannot be good that she wishes always to be alone."

"Don't let her be. Stay with her."

"Lord, I try, but she has an evil temper."

"That she does." Lately she had taken to throwing things. Rick had long since given up trying to talk to her. He looked at his chalked calendar. Tylara had grown increasingly moody as well. Certainly the long winter had a lot to do with that, but she seemed to be brooding over something else as well—something she wouldn't discuss. I'm surrounded by unhappy women, he thought. Just when things are going so well.

Whatever Tylara's problem, though, there was a simple explanation for Gwen's moods. "Her time comes near," Rick said. "I do not have personal experience, but I am told that all women are hateful for their last days before a child is born. Especially a first child."

And, he thought, *it would be particularly tough for Gwen*. She didn't even know when the baby would come. The local day on Tran was slightly more than twenty-one hours long, and the gestation period seemed to have stabilized at two hunred ninety local days, as opposed to two hunred seventy on Earth; but would that be true for Gwen? No one knew. Straight mathematics; multiply two hunred seventy by twenty-four and divide by twenty-one, and you'd get three hundred days. How much of human physiology responded to hours passed, and how much to the day-night cycle? And was Earth's moon involved? Women's menstrual cycles seemed to coincide with Luna, but Tran's double moons were small and much closer than Earth's. Did they have an influence?

"You care for Gwen, don't you?" Rick asked.

"Yes, Lord. And before the raid, I believed she cared for me. Now I do not know."

"She mourns her husband," Rick said. "But you are right. She is too much alone. I'll speak with her about it."

✣ ✣ ✣

"Your boyfriend's worried about you," Rick said.

Gwen sat close to the fire. She looked up without smiling. "Oh, leave me alone!"

"For God's sake, Gwen, snap out of it!"

"Why?"

"Do you think your problems are unique?" Rick demanded.

"Yes."

"Okay, I put my foot in it that time," Rick said. "Look, I've talked with the midwives. And Yanulf. They think everything's normal—"

"The medical experts," Gwen sneered.

"Well, they've delivered a lot of babies," Rick said.

"Sure. And lost a lot of mothers. Rick, I'm scared out of my mind!"

"Sure you are," Rick said. "Mind if I sit down?"

"Suit yourself."

"Thanks. Look, I've probably started a population explosion here, but I've taught them the beginnings of the germ theory of disease," Rick said.

"You couldn't have. I've tried," Gwen said.

"You didn't go about it the right way. I told them diseases were caused by little tiny devils, and that blessed soap and boiled holy water would drive them away. They can accept that." He looked thoughtful. "You know, I may be right about a population explosion. It happened that way on Earth."

Before the end of the nineteenth century, women often died of "childbed fever." But then came Ignaz Semmelweis with his theory that childbed fever was caused by physicians' dirty hands. His colleagues forced him to resign for saying it was their fault, but though he ended his days in a madhouse eventually enough of them believed him— after that most women lived to raise their children and have more. "There's no way we won't change things here," Rick said. "It isn't easy, but I'm trying to look ahead. Maybe we can avoid some of the problems we had on Earth."

"Maybe we can't."

"Look, dammit, snap out of it," Rick said. "You're working yourself into a depression. Keep it up and you'll get to me, too."

"I'm sorry," Gwen said. "I really am. But it all seems so futile."

"Why? Because we can't go home? We can make a home here," Rick said. "And—dammit, Gwen, we're more useful here than we ever were back on Earth. There wasn't much chance that anything we'd do there would change history, but we can here. We've already changed political history. We've got peace with the Empire and land to farm. Even if Marselius loses, we can hold those border hills for long enough to get in a harvest. With the new plows I've got the smiths working on, we'll triple the yields. We've helped these people already, and there's a lot more we can do!

"Sure, I've got an ambiguous status. The bards are trying to make up ballads about the raid, and they keep running into the fact that I never fought anybody. They can't figure out if I'm a war leader or a mere wizard. But whatever I am, everyone wants to learn from us.

"Gwen, we can start a university! Well, we start with grade school. But we can found a learning center that will *really* change this world. Look at what we can teach! Just the idea of scientific method and experimental science will bring on a revolution. And mathematics. We're not genius level, but we know more about geometry and algebra than was known on Earth through most of history. Medicine. Dental hygiene. Physics. Even electricity. I'm not up to transistors, but I can make batteries and vacuum tubes and—what the hell's the matter with you? You look like you've seen a ghost."

"Rick, for God's sake—you haven't built radios, have you?"

"Not yet. I'm still having trouble getting wire. But—"

"Don't! Please, please don't." Her voice held genuine panic.

"I see," Rick said. He stood and went to her, then took both her hands in his. "Don't you think it's time you told me about it?" he asked. "For God's sake, Gwen, what did Les tell you, and why can't you tell me?"

Tears welled in her eyes. "We're safe now," she said. "Just don't change anything. Oh, Rick, I'm scared—"

"I know you are. But I don't know why. Gwen, please. Please tell me."

She buried her face in her hands and wouldn't talk anymore.

✢ ✢ ✢

Three days later a messenger arrived from the west. Drumold summoned his counselors to his great hall to hear the news.

The messenger was a young clansman who was proud of his mission. He said greetings to Drumold, then spoke to Tylara. "Six days ago there came to Ta-Kartos a dozen lords and knights of Drantos. They had traveled in great haste and could go no farther. One lord asked if the lady Tylara lived. All were overjoyed to learn you are safe in your father's hall. They then asked my chief to send a messenger to you, and I left that night. They asked me to greet you as Great Lady, Eqetassa of Chelm, and to say they regret they cannot come to you. They beg you to come to them."

"Eqetassa of Chelm? But I have been driven from that land," Tylara said. "Who are they?"

For answer the messenger held out a signet ring.

"Camithon? But I saw him die," Tylara said. "He was thrown from the battlements."

"A trick to bring you to them," Drumold muttered. "Sarakos hates you yet."

The messenger looked pained. "Do you say that Clan Ebolos aids enemies of Mac Clallan Muir?" he demanded.

"No, no," Drumold protested. "But I do not understand what they want of my daughter."

"Nor I," the messenger said. "But Calad my chief listened long to their story. Then he bade me speak these words: 'I have learned that which is of great importance to all the clans of Tamaerthon. I beg that Mac Clallan Muir and the Lady Eqetassa come to Ta-Kartos with all haste.' "

"In this winter?" Drumold demanded. "Nay, it will wait until the snow is gone from the passes."

"My chief says not."

"Father, you may wait," Tylara said. "But I have never heard that Calad is easily alarmed, or that he does not know how deep the snow lies in the passes. As for me—do you return now?" she asked the messenger.

"As soon as I am dismissed," he said.

"Then tell your chief that the dowager Eqetassa of Chelm will arrive as quickly as she is able."

"Tylara, is this wise?" Rick asked.

"What has wisdom to do with it? Sarakos may sit in my council hall, but they are my people yet."

Damnation, Rick thought. *Of course she'll go.* "I'll get things ready," he said. "We can leave in the morning."

"I had hoped you would come with me," Tylara said. For the first time in several days, she smiled at him.

Drumold sighed. "Tell Calad your chief that Mac Clallan Muir will join him within a ten-day, and that the Lady Eqetassa will accompany him."

✦ ✦ ✦

Ta-Kartos was at the western edge of the mountainous highlands that formed Tamaerthon, and over the centuries had been built into a strongly walled town. After five days' travel across the frozen lochs, Rick was glad to reach the somber fortress.

Calad, chief of Clan Ebolos, was nominally subordinate to Drumold as Mac Clallan Muir, but that was a point no one wanted to stress too hard. When Drumold's party was invited into Calad's council hall, Drumold was content to take a place opposite Calad and leave the question of which end of the table was head and which foot for someone else to worry over.

Besides Calad and his advisors there were half a dozen knights and bheromen of Drantos. Before they could be presented, Tylara ran up to their leader—an elderly soldier whose craggy face held a long ugly scar. "Camithon!" she cried. "I could not believe, even though I hold your ring and heard them describe you. I saw you thrown from the battlements of Castle Dravan."

"Nay, Lady, I was not thrown. Before they could do that, I broke free of them and jumped. Would I not know the places where the moat is closest to the walls? Once away from Dravan, I had aid from the countryside until I could join Protector Dorion and the young Wanax. . . . You must not know, then: I am Lord Protector of Drantos."

"Protector—"

"Aye. Dorion was killed in the battle with Sarakos. To say this is to say little. He was torn to shreds by thunder weapons. Aye, at my side, and we nearly a league from the battle."

"Mortars," Rick said.

Camithon looked at him curiously.

"Lord Rick is our war leader. He knows of these weapons," Drumold explained.

"Where is the Wanax Ganton?" Tylara asked.

"The lad has caught the fever," Camithon said. "He rests in this castle." The elderly soldier paused. "We have come as beggars," he said.

"To beg Tamaerthon aid against Sarakos. Yet, in truth, we come as more than beggars. We bring news I think you will not find unwelcome."

"It had best be welcome news," Drumold growled. "I am nearly frozen. What news have you that could not wait for you to come to us?"

"Hear him out," Calad said. "I did not lightly send for you. Protector, tell Mac Clallan Muir of the war in Drantos."

"After Castle Dravan fell, I fled to the army of the Protector Dorion," Camithon said. "We caught Sarakos in an unfavorable situation and thought to destroy him in a great battle. I do not know who would have won that day, but suddenly our knights were cut down like wheat before the scythe. Sarakos had made alliance with men from the stars who hold evil weapons." He paused to study Drumold's expression. "You say nothing to this?"

"We know already," Drumold said.

"Strange," Camithon mused. "Yet this makes the telling easier. After Sarakos and his allies had beaten us, we fled to the mountains where we thought to fight on. Sarakos made our task the easier, for his armies ravaged the land. He turned out every bheroman in Drantos to replace them with his favorites. They so enslaved the commons that all, great and humble, were ready to join us. We fought no great battles—we knew we could not win such. But we harassed the land, burned the crops, killed his messengers, struck down his new knights and bheromen when they took possession of their villages. Sarakos has known no peace in Drantos. Many of his horses have starved or been eaten. Even so, many of his soldiers are dead of hunger and the plague, and many more have fled. He will lose more before spring, for the snows have closed the road to the Five Kingdoms, and we have destroyed the harvests in Drantos.

"It was after winter came that we heard of your great victory over the Roman legions. I have once before seen what Tamaerthon archers can do in battle, and it came to me that with the forces I hold and can gather, and with the aid of some thousands of your archers, we can drive Sarakos from Drantos and restore the lady Tylara to her dower lands. This I have come to ask."

Drumold leaned close to Rick. "What think you of this?"

"Lord Camithon," Rick said, "have you forgotten the starmen and their weapons?"

"No," Camithon said. "This is the welcome news I bring. The starmen have divided. Many have fled from Sarakos. Fewer than a dozen remain. Surely a dozen men will not frighten you who have bested the Romans."

"How do you know the starmenhave divided?" Rick demanded.

Camithon smiled grimly. "I have brought a present for Mac Clallan Muir and his daughter." He turned to an officer. "Bring in the prisoner."

The officer left and returned moments later with a man dressed in peasant woolen trousers and thick jacket. He had a scraggly beard that hadn't been shaved or trimmed for weeks, and his hands were shackled together with iron bracelets riveted to a foot-long chain.

He stood sullenly, looking defiantly at the council table, until he saw Rick. He stared a moment, then shouted, "Captain! For God's sake, Captain, help me!"

It was Private Warner.

✦ ✦ ✦

Despite the blazing fire, Rick's quarters were cold. *And not just the chilly air*, Rick thought. He could feel the chill radiating from where Tylara sat by the hearth.

"I had thought you would be pleased," she said. "Are not your enemies my enemies? Sarakos can be killed, and I can rid myself of this burning hatred for him—"

"We don't know that," Rick said. "Tylara—Tylara, every time I think of what Sarakos did to you, I get sick. I hate him as much as you do. I love you!"

"You do not seem to."

"More than you know," Rick said. "It is my wish to make Tamaerthon strong without endless war. Should we risk all that for revenge?"

Before she could answer, there was a knock at the door. "Come in," Rick called with relief.

Warner had been shaved and given better clothes. He was almost pathetically grateful when Jamiy brought him in. "Thank God you're here, Captain. Thank God—"

"Have a seat," Rick invited. "Jamiy, pour him a cup of wine."

Warner sat gratefully. He chugged the wine, and Rick poured his cup full again. "Take it easy," he said. "Before you get drunk, I want to know your story." He laughed. "You know, it wasn't a week ago I was wishing I had you around. I was trying to derive some of Newton's equations. Think you can remember college physics?"

"Yes, sir," Warner said. "Uh—ballistics?"

"Maybe," Rick said. "But mostly just general science." He switched to the local Tran dialect. "Warner, this is the lady Tylara. We'd both like to hear your story."

"Yes, sir. But could I have some more wine first?" Warner drank eagerly. "Where should I begin?"

"We know Parsons made an alliance with Sarakos," Rick said. "And that you helped him win the battle against the Drantos army. What happened after that?"

"At first it was pretty good," Warner said. "Captain, I can tell this better in English."

"Go ahead. I'll translate for Tylara."

"Yes, sir. Well, like I said, at first it was pretty good. We'd won, and we owned the country. Parsons gave each one of us a couple of local girls. It was a little funny owning slaves, but that's the way things are here. We had women and jewels and lots of good food and pretty good wine, and it was like Parsons said it would be. We lived like kings. Even out in the field we had servants. We took over the best houses for quarters, and we didn't have to fight much—just when the locals ran into something they couldn't handle. Then we'd come up with the machine guns and the mortars.

"Everything was fine for a couple of months, but then it all came apart. Guerilla war. Captain, it was like Vietnam, only worse, because we didn't have any choppers or trucks or anything. We had to ride horses, and by the time we got anywhere, the charlies had gone off into the hills. We weren't safe anywhere outside castles. Ride through the woods and you never knew but what an arrow or a crossbow bolt would kill you.

"It just never stopped, and it didn't look like it was ever going to get any better, either. Those people hated us, and we couldn't kill *all* of them. And it got kind of hungry, too, even for us—and we had more to eat than the poor bastards with us. And Parsons! He got so mean, you couldn't get near him. Claimed it was all our fault—we weren't disciplined enough—but he'd fix that. So one day a bunch of us got fed up and rode off."

"How many?" Rick asked.

"Twenty-two," Warner said. "Gengrich and I organized it. We went south, to the city-state territory. We needed some way to make a living, so we arranged to hire out to the city republic of Kleistinos. They fed us and our wives—most of us brought one or both of the girls we'd been living with—and we didn't have to fight, either. Come spring we were supposed to escort a big caravan south, and that sure sounded like easier work than what Parsons had us doing."

"So how did you end up here?"

Warner looked sheepish. "I got drunk, passed out in a tavern, and woke up with those handcuff things. The local tavernkeeper sold me to the Drantos rebels."

"I see. Excuse me, I'd better tell Tylara what's going on." Rick summarized Warner's story.

"They are not rebels," Tylara said coldly when Rick finished. "They are fighting for their homes against bandits."

"Yes, Lady," Warner said. "If you say so—"

"She *did* say so," Rick said. He changed to English to say, "I'd be very careful, were I you. She's got a sharp temper and a sharper dagger." He poured himself a cup of wine. "What weapons did Gengrich take with him?"

"One of the mortars," Warner said. "And our rifles and pistols, of course."

"So André has one mortar and the recoilless. How many mortar bombs?"

"I'd guess a dozen," Warner said.

"The starmen are greatly weakened," Tylara said. "And Sarakos has lost much of his army."

"They're not as strong as they were," Warner agreed. "Captain, are you planning on fighting them?"

"I don't know."

Tylara looked at him coldly.

"Sweetheart, you don't understand," Rick said. "They think because we handled the Romans so easily, Parsons can't be that tough. They just don't know. One mortar shell in the right place, and I don't have a pike regiment, I have a disorganized mob. And Yatar knows what machine-guns would do to my archers—"

Tylara got up and went to the door. "Jamiy," she said. She pointed to Warner. "Take him to his quarters."

"He's to be well treated, but he is not to escape," Rick said. "Warner, I really am glad to see you. If we all survive, you're going to be a professor in the only university on Tran."

"I'd like that," Warner said. "It's got to be better than fighting for a living."

Rick waited until Jamiy and Warner had left, then turned to Tylara with a sigh. "All right, darling. Let's have it out."

3

Her cold look changed to one of unhappiness. "I do not like to quarrel with you," she said.

"God knows I don't enjoy it much either—"

"Please. Let me finish. All winter my father and I have waited for you to speak formally to him of our future."

"I was waiting to be sure you wanted me to," Rick said. "And I wasn't sure when would be the right time—"

"I had hoped you wanted me."

"I do. God knows I do. I love you," Rick said.

"As I love you. More than you know. Our customs are not yours. Never in our memory has a woman married before she was avenged, yet—yet I was willing to do so. Rick, your ways are strange. You are not like my husband was. You are a warrior, but you do not wish to fight. I have seen men insult you, and yet you did nothing, though lesser words demand blood—"

"Is that what you want? Should I collect heads?" The Tamaerthon clansmen no longer kept the heads of their enemies as trophies, but there were many legends of heroes who had.

"Hush," she said. "No. You should not. I have come to understand that although killing gives you no pleasure, you are no weakling. And I have seen you in the great battle, and again when you have spoken of the school you wish to build. I know which pleases you more. I have heard you tell of the things you wish to teach, and how this will help everyone—the clans of Tamaerthon and all the others on this world.

There is much about you I do not understand, but there is much I do know, and I have come to love you. Not as I loved Lamil. That was nearly unendurable—no, do not look away, and do not be sad. I was no more eager for my wedding night with Lamil than I am to have you possess me. Between us there is more than Lamil and I ever had. Lamil was handsome, but he was frivolous. He had no daemon driving him as you do. Nor did I, then, but I have since learned what duty is, and no less a daemon rides me now. You and I, we may belong to each other, but we also have ambition. Not for wealth, but for something greater."

He came to her and put his hands on her shoulders. "Then why are we standing like this—"

She removed his hands gently and stepped away. Her face held concern and sadness. "Please. This must be said. Rick, when I believed Sarakos secure in Drantos, I swallowed my hatred for him though it burned like fire. I had thought you must feel the same, that the man who, who—*gods!* that a man who had done that to me should live!"

"You can't know," Rick said. "God, sweetheart, you can't know—"

"I dream of flaying him," Tylara said. "Yet, because of what we believe you will do for Tamaerthon—aye, for all the world—I have lived with the knowledge that Sarakos would never be punished. As did my father and my brother. We agreed—you are important to Tamaerthon, and we have no hold on you. There is no reason for you to stay in Tamaerthon—none save what I hope you feel for me—yet we need you. And so I have not died trying to avenge myself. As much as I hate Sarakos, I have grown to love you more. Once I lived only to kill him. Now I have you."

"But now you want me to kill Sarakos for you."

"Now it is possible," she said.

"No. What's changed?" Rick asked. "André Parsons has fewer men, but he still has more than enough weapons to destroy us, and without the pikemen, Tamaerthon is doomed. Do you trust Marselius? I do as long as he is afraid of my pike regiments, but not longer. And we may yet have to fight Caesar if Marselius fails."

"Are you certain nothing has changed, my husband-to-be?" Tylara asked. "The starmen are divided. Sarakos has lost half his army. Is this nothing?"

"Is it enough?"

Jerry Pournelle

"I do not know. These are things you know," Tylara said. "But this I do know. Chelm is mine. Lamil left no other heir. You have heard how it fares with the people there. They die. There is endless war. The Time approaches. Do I not have a duty to them? And do you not have a greater one?"

"Me? I've never been there—"

"You brought the starmen here," Tylara said. "Now they are as wolves in the land. Have you no responsibility for this?" Tears welled in her eyes. "My love. My father feels as I do. If you truly believe that nothing can be done to rid the land of these evil men, then we will send Camithon on his way without aid. But I beg you, think on it."

She would have to say that. My responsibility. I brought them here. I didn't want to, and I—what the hell's the point in quibbling? I brought them. But dammit—"My university will be more important than you know," Rick said. "We can change this world. Should we risk all that merely to kill Sarakos?"

"My love, I know there is no other like you," Tylara said. There was no banter in her voice at all. "But can not the lady Gwen and the man Warner teach much of what you could?"

There went my last argument, Rick thought. *Oh, dammit.* "Yes. They can," he said. *God help me, she's right. And nobody else can stop Parsons and Sarakos. Can I? Sarakos is no problem. His medium and heavy cavalry don't sound as effective as the Roman heavy troopers, and my pikemen have a lot more confidence now. But I still need massed formations, and Parsons has the mortar and at least a dozen riflemen— more than enough to scatter the pikes for Sarakos' heavies—*

Skirmishing archers could take Parsons, if we could get him on a decent killing ground. But he's too damn smart to be caught that way. He'll always have enough local cavalry with him to keep the archers at a distance. So how to get the Earth troops separated from the rest of the army—

"You have a plan," she said. "I have seen that look before."

"Something Warner said. Tylara, even if everything works properly, a lot of people are going to be killed—"

"More than will die if we do nothing?"

"No. Not nearly so many." He sighed and took her in his arms. "I could have had my pick of a hundred women," he said. "I could *have* a hundred women. So of course I have to be in love with you." He kissed her. They stood close for a long time.

Then she pushed him gently away. "In spring," she said. "And for now—we must send food for Camithon's army before he loses more men and beasts to hunger."

"Yes." And a thousand other details. Summon the western clansmen and start drilling them in the new tactics. More pikes and arrows. Baggage and grain carts. Politics. Keeping the clans working together was hard enough; now they'd have Protector Camithon and the boy king to worry about as well.

And more details yet. Patrols to seal the passes and keep secret as long as possible the fact that Tamaerthon was arming for war. A second iron curtain so that when spies inevitably found that the clans were mobilizing they still wouldn't be able to report that they were drilling with pikes. And inside that the greatest secret of all.

"Why do you smile?" Tylara asked.

"It would take long to explain," Rick said. How could he tell her he'd thought of calling his inner circle "The Manhattan Project"? But of course he couldn't use that name. It would signal Parsons as clearly as would a report that someone in Tamaerthon was gathering tons of manure and sulfur.

They'd need a secure area to leach saltpeter from manure.

His scholarship wasn't good enough to make sulfa drugs or penicillin, but something simple like that would be no problem at all. Saltpeter seventy-five percent, charcoal fifteen percent, sulfur ten percent: fifteen to three to two, a formula tested in war's caldron for centuries. And they'd need a gristmill with no metal parts in which to grind it.

And there'd be a thousand more details. The business of war. They sing ballads about heroes, but the details are what win campaigns.

Or lose them.

PART EIGHT
JANISSARIES

1

Gwen's delivery had been difficult. The baby was large and she was small. She was many hours in difficult labor, and afterwards was laid up for weeks. She remembered few details. One vividly stayed in her mind: the moment when Yanulf laid her baby on her breast. That couldn't have been more than a few seconds after the boy was born.

She didn't remember telling Yanulf that the boy was to be called "Les," but she didn't regret that. Someday she'd be able to tell Les of his father and give him the message the pilot had left for his child.

It took a long time to regain strength. For weeks she could only nurse her son once a day. Fortunately two other children had been born a few days before Les, both to robust clanswomen with milk to spare. Later Gwen wondered if this had not been the origin of the ancient custom of godparents; without other women's aid, Les would have died.

Gradually she became aware of life outside her lodge. At first she took little interest beyond a feeling of bitterness that Rick and Mason had not returned from Ta-Kartos and had not allowed Caradoc to return either. She had one letter from Rick, telling her that the university could begin the next summer, if the peace with Marselius held. She was delighted. Everything seemed to be going well.

Then she found that many of the young men were gone. All of the officers and noncoms of Rick's new model army had been summoned to Tar Kartos, as were the smiths. When she tried to find out why, she learned nothing. None of the women knew why their men had been sent to the western mountains. A few thought there would be another raid when the ice had melted in the lochs and passes, but no one was certain. There was no way to find out. For the first time since she'd come to Tran, Gwen was afraid that she'd lost control of the situation.

The suns stood at an angle of thirty degrees and the snows had melted in the lower passes before Yanulf was allowed to visit Ta-Kartos. He returned to tell her in great secrecy that Rick planned war to restore Chelm to Tylara.

"Aye, Lady," he said. "They tell me I will be able to return to Castle Dravan before Midsummer's Day. Even as we speak, the fiery axe runs through The Garioch."

Gwen was horrified. This was the ruin of all her plans. "But—this is madness! He makes war on the starmen?"

"Aye. No one knows what the lord Rick intends, but it is said that he has a plan to destroy both the starmen and Sarakos. I do know that he has every cart in the land carrying manure to a place near Tar Kartos where he has built a water mill."

Manure. "And he also gathers brimstone?"

Yanulf looked surprised. "Aye. Manure and brimstone. But I do not know what magic he can make with those."

"I do," Gwen said. Gunpowder. "Every cart in the land" was probably an exaggeration, but it still meant that Rick was making a lot of black powder. Why had he decided on war, black powder against machine-guns? "Yanulf, I must speak with him," Gwen said.

"It would not be wise," the priest answered. "You have yet to regain your strength. Besides the army marches as soon as the clans reach Tar Hastigar. You might not arrive before the war begins."

"Then it will be even more important that I speak with him."

"Your fear shows clearly," Yanulf said. "Do you not believe that the lord Rick will be able to defeat the starmen? Drumold believes so—"

"I do not know," Gwen said. What can Rick be planning? He doesn't take foolish chances. He must believe he can do it. And if he does— "But there is much that he must know before he goes to battle. We must go to him."

Yanulf studied her carefully. "This is important to you."

"It is important to everyone on this world," Gwen said. "On this world, and on other worlds as well."

"Can you not send him a message?"

"None that he would believe," Gwen said. "Nor dare I tell anyone what must be said. It would be more unwise to write it. No, I must go myself, and quickly."

"I believe you," Yanulf said. "I will arrange what I can. But we will not travel swiftly, my lady, for you would not survive a swift journey. And we will require nursemaids for your child, and soldiers to escort you. This will take time."

"We have so little time," Gwen said.

"I will do what I can."

✣ ✣ ✣

"It would be better if we waited," Camithon said. "The spring rains are barely over, and the mud will be thick. We will not be able to travel swiftly."

There were murmurs of assent from around the council table. Rick was pleased to see that Drumold and Balquhain said nothing, but waited for Rick to speak. "Neither will Sarakos," Rick said. "But more than that: we will not have sufficient food to wait longer and still carry supplies with us. Mason has trained the new troops well."

"I'd like more time with them," Mason said. "But I think they'll be steady enough."

"Thus we gain little by delay," Rick said. He pointed to the map on the council table. "At noon on the day after tomorrow we march. We'll take the direct route along the road. At dawn tomorrow I want the scouts out ahead to make certain that news of our passage does not get to Drantos ahead of us. Now there are other details." He unrolled several parchments, and bowed to the boy seated at the end of the table.

"Majesty, these are decrees," Rick said. "The most important proclaims a general amnesty for all acts prior to this spring and guarantees that each man will inherit from his father. When we reach the borders of Drantos, these will be sent throughout the land as quickly as possible."

"You ask me to forgive the traitors who rose against my father," the boy said. His voice rose. "Never!"

"You must," Rick said patiently. "How else can we arouse the countryside against Sarakos? Think upon it, Majesty. Would you rather sit on your father's throne, or look at your kingdom from exile?"

"If every man inherits from his father," Calad said, "how do you propose to reward our clansmen and allies?"

"Sarakos has created vacant places enough," Rick said. "Lands without heirs, for those who would be bheromen of Drantos rather than clansmen of Tamaerthon. One of these documents gives Mac Clallan Muir the right to dispose of the ownerless lands in two counties. Another gives the lady Tylara the same rights within Chelm."

"My lord," the boy said, "the price of your aid comes high."

Rick said nothing. After a moment, Camithon said, "It is not so high as might be. We came to Tamaerthon as beggars, and we leave with hopes of victory. Sign, lad. You will not see a better bargain."

Rick took the parchments to the end of the table. In the past weeks he had come to like the young king. The boy was intelligent enough to bow to the inevitable.

"What are these other parchments?" Ganton asked.

"One is a treaty of alliance between Tamaerthon and Drantos," Rick said. "It contains provision for the Roman Empire to join the alliance if Caesar wishes." And getting both Camithon and Drumold to agree to that had taken many nights of arguing; nights that Rick would rather have spent planning the battle. Eventually the growing Demon Star had convinced them more than any arguments Rick could make. When the invading star got closer, the lands to the south would be too hot to live in. They could expect hordes of refugees, an influx they couldn't possibly accept. And the refugees would come armed—a wandering of the tribes such as had happened in Julius Caesar's time. It would take a strong alliance to force them to settle elsewhere.

"Another document states that you will live in the household of the lady Tylara during your minority," Rick said.

Ganton smiled. "Oh, I'd like that. She's nice," he said. He looked up at Camithon. "Since the Lord Protector agrees, we consent," he said formally. He took the pen and scrawled his name on each parchment.

One less thing to worry about, Rick thought. *At least we've made a start on the mess I'll face after we win.*

If we win.

✦ ✦ ✦

Gwen arrived at Tar Kartos to find the fortress town nearly empty except for Caradoc and a company of mounted archers.

"The lord Rick received the message that you were coming," he said. "He could not wait, but asked me to remain to greet you. He left this for you." The archer commander handed her a parchment.

Gwen unrolled it. "Gwen," it said. "I've already had Camithon send marching orders to the holdout forces in Drantos. This operation takes careful timing, and I've got to move now if we're going to link up with them. I can't wait for you.

"If you're still in a hurry to talk to me, Caradoc will escort you. You'll be taking your chances. I intend to make a fight of it as soon as I can, so you might be coming into a battle. I think we'll win, but nothing's certain in war.

"My advice is to stay in Tamaerthon. Even if we lose, they're unlikely to annihilate us. There'll be enough force left to hold Tamaerthon no matter what. The university is more important than the war. I've sent Larry Warner back to The Garioch. He wasn't much of a soldier, but he ought to be pretty good as a professor. If I don't come back, you'll have all of my share of the plunder from the raid, and that ought to be enough to get a school going.

"I almost left orders to have them keep you in Tar Kartos, but I'm just scared enough of what you know that I want to leave that choice up to you. I hope you decide to stay." The parchment was unsigned.

She looked up to Caradoc. "How long will it take to catch up to them?"

"They left nine days ago," he said. "And they intended hard marching. We can travel faster than they, but I doubt we will reach them in much less than a ten-day."

Just possible, she thought. *Yes. I may get him to call off this war before it's too late.*

I may not get there in time, either. "I will come with you as soon as I have arranged quarters here for the nursemaids and my baby," Gwen said. "We must find Rick before he battles the starmen."

✢ ✢ ✢

They reached the rear guard of Rick's force seven days later. It took another day to pass through to the front. The countryside was wooded and hilly, and the single road was clogged with baggage carts and camp followers. Toward evening they reached an area where the countryside opened out and the road ran through broad fields. The army had deployed in battle array across a front three miles wide. Before they could reach the forward edge of the front, they were stopped at a roadblock. Despite Gwen's shouts and Caradoc's rank, they were firmly escorted back to a headquarters pavilion a kilometer behind the lines.

The headquarters was occupied by orderlies and staff officers. Messengers came and went in obvious preparation for a major battle on the next day. No one seemed to know why Rick had taken the light cavalry and several heavily laden wagons three kilometers farther up the road to the only village in the area.

Just before evening, Gwen heard shouting and then saw several groups of heavy cavalrymen ride northwest up the road. The sun was setting when she heard them returning. They were followed by the mounted archers at full gallop and, a few minutes later, by Rick and his personal guardsmen.

He paused to send messengers off with orders, then came into the pavilion. Gwen would not have recognized him if she hadn't heard him talking. He was dressed in chain mail and the scarlet cloak Marselius had sent as a gift. His helmet was the typical bullet shape with nasal guard worn by heavy cavalrymen, and he wore steel shoes and greaves rather than boots. As he came in, Jamiy helped him remove his helmet and gorget, but he kept the rest of the armor on. He sat at the table across from Gwen. "They told me you were here," he said. "If you'll excuse my saying it, you couldn't have come at a worse time."

"Why?"

"Because I've a battle to plan," he said. "Before dawn tomorrow, which means there are a million details tonight. If you've got something to say, Gwen, make it quick. I want you a good way toward Tamaerthon before the fighting starts."

"Your concern touches me."

"What's that supposed to mean? You could have stayed in Tar Kartos. I wish you had. I don't intend to lose tomorrow, but if I do, I'm counting on you to start the university. I still think that's the most important thing we can do for this planet."

"The most important thing you can do is to call off this war," Gwen said.

"Are you ready to tell me the truth at last?" Rick asked. "That calls for a celebration." He turned to the door. "Jamiy, a flask of wine, please. And ask the lady Tylara to join us when she arrives."

"Sir. I think I hear her patrol coming now."

"Good. All right, Gwen, why is this so important, and why haven't you told me before?"

"It wasn't my secret," Gwen said. "Why couldn't you leave things alone? Everything was going so well. We had a perfect place to hide, and enough to eat. Parsons would grow those stupid drugs—"

"That's debatable," Rick said.

She looked up in alarm. "Why?"

"Parsons and Sarakos don't have much of a hold on this country. They'll be doing well to feed their army, much less grow a couple of thousand acres of madweed." He shrugged. "It doesn't matter anyway. With any luck, Parsons and Sarakos will both be dead by morning."

"How?"

Rick grinned without humor. "I selected this place pretty carefully. Took real timing to reach it just about the time that Parsons would. We've got a nice muddy field out there—better suited to my infantry than Sarakos' cavalry. Ideal for a battle. Of course there are other places like that, but this one has a special feature. There's only one village for thirty kilometers up the road ahead."

"I don't understand—"

"Swampy fields. One village. We held it last night and most of today, but we let Sarakos chase us out of it this afternoon. We had to run fast. Didn't get a chance to burn it down. Warner says Parsons and his people don't like sleeping in fields. Guess where they'll make their headquarters tonight—"

"What are you planning?" Gwen demanded.

Rick looked at his watch. "The hardest part was the fusing," he said. "Took me weeks to come up with a slow match that burned reliably, and I still can't time it too close. Making twelve barrels of gunpowder wasn't so difficult, and it was no trick at all to bury it in the village. An hour or so before dawn, André Parsons is going to get one hell of a surprise."

"You're going to kill them all? And destroy all their equipment?"

"I certainly hope so. I wish there were another way, but I can't think of one. I can't even parley with them. If André knows he's fighting me and not just locals, he'll be a lot more suspicious. Were in hell is that wine?" He shouted for his orderly.

"You don't look very pleased," he said. "I thought you lived in terror that Parsons would find us and report to the *Shalnuksis*. Now you won't have to worry."

"Oh, boy!" she said. "And I was trying to be careful. I didn't expect you to be able to win—"

"Thanks for the confidence."

"Rick, this isn't a game! If you win—when you win—will you be able to grow the *surinomaz* for the aliens?"

What is this? Rick wondered. He had noticed her alarm when he told her Parsons might not be able to grow the crops for the aliens. Now this.

Could I manage it? Probably. I've got enough allies, and I can talk Camithon and the king into it provided we can import enough grain. But I can think of at least one damn good reason not to deal with the aliens at all. Why is she worried about surinomaz*? And how can I make her tell me what she knows?*

He shrugged. "Without the equipment Parsons has? Not easily. Madweed isn't a popular crop here, and taking that much good land out of grain cultivation wouldn't be simple. But Gwen, I've been listening to those legends about the dangers of dealing with the sky gods."

Jamiy came in with wine and pewter cups. "The lady Tylara has returned safely," he said. "She will come when she has spoken with her brother." The orderly hesitated. "I do not think she was pleased to learn that the lady Gwen is here."

Rick laughed. "I don't expect she was," he said. "Thank you." He filled the cups. "Look, what's got you scared?"

"I don't even know where to begin."

"Maybe I can suggest something," Rick said. "I've given this a bit of thought, too. Try this. The rogue sun comes at six-hundred-year intervals, and that's the only time the *Shalnuksis* have any interest in Tran. That's roughly 1400 A.D., 800 A.D., 200 A.D., 400 B.C., 1000 B.C., and 1600 B.C. The languages are Indo-European and you've several times mentioned similarities to Mycenae and Crete. That's 1600 B.C. or a little later; the rogue's period isn't a full six hundred years. All right so far?"

She nodded. "It's the earliest I'm sure of. Archaeologists on Earth have violent arguments about the languages of the Mediterranean in that time period—"

"They'd love to know what we know," Rick said. "All right. The 1000 B.C. expedition blends in with that. Maybe that's when they brought the Celts. Then or 400 B.C. There's no question about 200 A.D.—that's Imperial Rome about the time of Septimius Severus, and we've even got Lucius' parchments. Then about the time of Charlemagne they brought in a group, and there's plenty of evidence for that. Charlemagne was crowned Holy Roman Emperor on Christmas Day in 800 A.D., and they must have picked up some of his heavy cavalrymen not long before. That brings us to 1400 or so. There's not one single trace of that visit. Why not?"

Gwen didn't say anything. Rick leaned forward to throw a block of peat onto the small hearth fire.

"We know they didn't skip that time," Rick said. "You told me you'd studied Tran languages of six hundred years ago. But nobody knows anything about longbow tactics, so they couldn't have brought English or Scots or Welsh. Maybe French. The French didn't learn anything from Crécy. Only nobody ever heard of the Swiss pike, either. Nobody knows how to make plate armor, but they were using it in Europe in 1400. So who did they bring? There's no sign of mixed races. No Orientals or blacks or Indians.

"And 1400 is well into the age of gunpowder, but they never heard of it here. Is that reasonable? And it's not just weapons. Magna Carta in 1215. Nobody ever heard of it. Thomas Aquinas, Roger Bacon, Malatesta, all thirteenth century. By 1400 a whole slew of geniuses had lived, and nobody's ever heard of them. Not even Lucius, who's spent his life digging in old documents; or Yanulf, who's got epic poems so old there's even a version of Homer. The 1400 expedition vanished without a trace.

"What happened, Gwen? Did somebody kill the lot of them?"

She looked up unhappily. "Les thought so. For about the same reasons you just gave. Why hasn't there been any progress on Tran? You can't blame it *all* on the unstable climate," she said. "But he didn't know. There weren't any records in the computer."

"But that was why you didn't want electricity. Or anything else. You weren't all that worried about Parsons, it's the *Shalnuksis* who've got you scared."

"Of course. But if Parsons knew where we were, he'd tell them." She took a deep breath. "Rick, have you guessed the rest of it? Secret caves. Fire from the sky. And those epic poems about the bad luck that comes from dealing with the evil sky gods. They bring wondrous gifts but take them back again. Fire will fall from the sky, and the only safe place is in deep caves. And there's another I don't think you heard—about a taboo place where nothing grows, and a lake with a glass bottom—"

Rick nodded gravely. "They don't do things by halves, do they? Atom bombs—"

"I don't *know*. But even without knowing about Yanulf's epics, Les thought it likely. That's why he wanted me to run away. Hide as far from Parsons as possible."

"And why you didn't warn me that Parsons was going to mutiny," Rick said. "So you'd have someone to go with."

"Yes. Rick, I'm sorry."

"Sure. But I don't understand why you didn't tell me all this before."

"Because I didn't know what you'd do. Rick, I'm sorry I've kept you in the dark, but after all, we've done pretty well. We have a safe refuge, enough to eat, a place for a university—I thought of starting one before you did, but it seemed better to let it be your idea. Everything was going fine. Why should I complicate matters by telling you about problems you couldn't do anything about? And I was afraid you'd want to warn Parsons. After all, they were once your men—"

"I probably would have. I'd do it now if I weren't about to kill them anyway." He drained his wine cup and cursed. "If I'd known before, maybe this war wouldn't have to be. André can't have any love for Sarakos."

"You still don't understand," Gwen said. "You have to warn him now. Rick, no matter who wins tomorrow, we've got to be certain the victor has enough power to be *sure* of growing *surinomaz*."

"The hell we do. You've just told me that dealing with the *Shalnuksis* isn't very smart. So we just vanish. Hide in the caves when they show up. Let them whistle for their drugs."

"It's not that simple," Gwen said. "Rick, you said your university would be important to the people of Tran. You seemed to care."

"Sure, I'd like to accomplish something worthwhile," Rick said.

"That *surinomaz* crop is more important than your university," Gwen said. "And to far more people than just those on Tran. It's important to the whole human race."

2

Rick refilled his wine cup. "I think you'd better explain that last statement," he said carefully. "You've told me often enough that this *surinomaz* crop isn't worth *that* much to the *Shalnuksis*. How can it be important to the whole human race?"

"It's a long story," Gwen said.

Rick looked at his watch. "We've got between four and six hours before the gunpowder blows. That ought to be long enough. Only this time tell me the whole story. I'm tired of trying to operate in the dark."

"You haven't done too badly," Gwen said. "All right. If the *Shalnuksis* send a ship and find out there's not been a harvest and won't ever be one, they won't send another. But if they think there'll be good harvests, they'll arrange for ships to come every year the crop will be good. Eventually they'll have to send Les."

"Jesus Christ. Gwen, are you still in love with that SOB?"

"I don't know. Sometimes I am. Not that it matters." She spoke defiantly. "Don't look at me like that. I know what you're thinking, and it's wrong. Rick, he didn't just throw me out. I could have gone with him."

"Why didn't you?"

"Because they wouldn't have let our baby live."

"They? Who? And why not?"

"The Confederacy. They breed their human servants. Even if they'd let my baby be born, they wouldn't have let me raise it. All their human children grow up in a school."

"Gwen, what the hell are you talking about? Breed humans?"

"For loyalty," Gwen said. "But sometimes they breed in 'wild' humans from Earth to give the strain initiative. Les had a wild grandmother, and they won't allow more wild genes in his line. Rick, I know it sounds fantastic."

"Fantastic. That's a good word," Rick said. "How long has this been going on?"

"At least five thousand years."

Five thousand years. "And you believe that?"

"Yes. Everything I saw in the ship's data banks is consistent with it. And look how long they've been coming to Tran."

"But five thousand years? Gwen, all that time, and they've never made an official visit to any government on Earth. All that time they've been dealing with us without contact—"

"They can't and they won't," Gwen said. "They don't allow barbarians in their Confederacy. They have a stable union of nearly a hundred races. Most of those never did have periods of unlimited growth. When they run into an aggressively unstable race, there's usually a war. They've exterminated some races they decided were hopelessly barbaric. As a result, they've achieved what human philosophers always wanted but no one really believes we'll ever have: universal peace and order and stability."

"If they're so damned peace-loving, why have they kept raiding Tran? Why drop atom bombs on their last expedition?"

"The *Shalnuksis* aren't peace-loving," Gwen said. "They just don't have any choices in the matter. They're a long-lived race, and Tran is a—Les called it a family business. The *Shalnuksis* don't want Tran industrialized, and the Confederacy doesn't know about Tran."

"There was a police inspector. Agzaral. He knew all about it," Rick said.

"Agzaral and some of the other humans know. They're keeping it secret from their government."

Why wouldn't there be corruption in a bureaucracy five thousand years old? "And your friend Les is helping them keep it a secret?"

"Yes." Gwen fought tears. "Rick, it's not what you think. It's so hard to explain! Have you ever heard of janissaries?"

"Sure. Slave soldiers of the Ottoman Empire. Administrators, too. They pretty well ran the empire for the Turks. Taken in childhood as tribute from Christian subjects and brought up in schools, lived in barracks and forbidden to marry—God almighty! Gwen, what are you driving at?"

"What you've guessed. Humans aren't members of the Confederacy, but human soldiers and policemen and administrators like Inspector Agzaral enforce the Confederacy policies. That's why Earth has a special status—not taken into the Confederacy and not interfered with. They need a strain of wild humans to mix in with their tame janissaries."

"Slave soldiers. Bred for loyalty, and raised in creches—Gwen, do you believe all this?"

"Yes. Why would Les make it up? Why would he say he was a slave?" she demanded. "He was crying when he told me. He said he felt like a dog attacking his master, like a traitor—"

"If they're that loyal, why *was* he betraying them? All because of you?"

"No. Oh, maybe partly," Gwen said. "But that's not the real reason. Rick, he said it was important that the Confederacy never learn about Tran because—he said the Confederacy's governing council is worried, now that humans on Earth are going into space. Some of the Council wants to knock Earth back to the Stone Age. Agzaral thinks that may have happened once already. Don't you see, the humans are being torn apart! They're bred for loyalty to the Confederacy, but they're humans, too. They don't know what to do or who to trust."

"Does this council truly expect human soldiers to bomb Earth?" Rick asked.

"The Confederacy Council doesn't know who to trust either," Gwen said. "But there are humans who argue it's the best thing. That wild humans simply can't be allowed to get loose with their crazy ideas about unlimited growth and continuous progress. They've enforced the peace for thousands of years, and that's more important to them than a planet they've never lived on. But other humans want to save Earth. The Council doesn't know what to do, and neither do Agzaral and his people.

"Some of the janissaries—I may as well call them that," she said. "Some of the janissaries want the Confederacy to force Earth into membership. It would mean that the Confederacy Council would interfere in Earth's government. Humans would have to accept the

Council's policies. Stability. Limited growth. The end of what we think of as progress."

"I see," Rick said. "They call it 'stability.' But there's another word for a society that hasn't changed in thousands of years. Stagnant. Or decadent."

"That's almost exactly what Les said. His group wants to do more than just save Earth from destruction. They want—Rick, it sounds trite, but they want humanity left free."

"But where does Tran come in?" Rick asked.

"If they do bomb Earth, or even if they just make Earth into another decadent member of the Confederacy, humans on Tran will still be free. With any luck, one of Agzaral's people—probably Les himself—will be sent here to collect the drugs. Only this time he won't be leaving on such short notice. They can bring translations of their textbooks. Scientific equipment. And they've got the kind of bureaucracy you'd expect after five thousand years of stasis. Agzaral thinks they might even be able to lose a ship in the recordkeeping and send it here after the *Shalnuksis* have gone away."

"Except that the *Shalnuksis* will be doing their best to kill off anyone who could help Tran progress beyond the Iron Age—"

"Yes. They will. They'll almost certainly bomb the groups they've been trading with. But they might trust that mission to Les or one of his friends. They don't like long journeys to out-of-the-way places. That's one chance, anyway. And another is to hide. They won't kill everyone on Tran. They can't afford to, because they'll want to do some more drug trading six hundred years from now."

Rick shook his head. "They've got the stars. Why do they traffic in drugs?"

"You don't understand real decadence," Gwen said. "Who are the heavy drug users on Earth? It's not the poor and downtrodden who have big parties with bowls of cocaine."

"And I suppose the *Shalnuksis* make a lot of—what? Money? Do they have money? Anyway, the drug trade profits them."

"It must," Gwen said. "But I wonder if they do it for profits at all. It must be a game to them. Excitement." She thought for a moment. "Take the Mafia as an example. Surely the top dons are fabulously rich already. They could retire, go legitimate, but they don't. It must be like that for the *Shalnuksis*."

"So if we don't grow the drugs, your friends won't have any legitimate reason to come here."

"Yes. And the first ship here may bomb the planet before we've had time to prepare—"

"And this is why you were hiding?"

"Yes. It was all we could think of to do. Les didn't have much time to talk to me. He was afraid the ship was bugged. He had to whisper everything to me in bed. He didn't want to leave me here, but I wouldn't let his damned machine abort my baby, and there wasn't another choice. He told me to run away and hide and stay a long way away from where they'd be growing *surinomaz*. When we heard Parsons plotting to throw you out, we thought I'd have a better chance if I stayed with you. Les even told me to marry you. Maybe I would have, too, if you hadn't met your raven-haired beauty."

Rick didn't know what to say to that. Would he have found Gwen attractive if he hadn't met Tylara? It hardly mattered, and it was too late to worry about, anyway.

It was too late to worry about anything. He looked at his watch. Five and a half hours at most. And a battle to be fought in the morning. The battle didn't seem so important now. What was? Assume what Gwen said was true. What should he do about it?

"I wish you'd told me earlier," Rick said. "This makes—it makes everything we've done rather trivial."

"Not really. You've done rather well."

"I've survived. Look, we don't need André's military equipment. I presume that you've got communications gear. You'd have to, if you expect Les to find you again."

She nodded. "I have a transceiver. He told me when to listen, and not to answer unless I hear a certain code phrase."

"So. I guess I can grow the damned crops for the *Shalnuksis*. Maybe we can even work it so they don't kill too many people with their bloody bombs. Tylara says the caves under Castle Dravan are even deeper than those in The Garioch. But it's pure dumb luck we can do what's needed because you wouldn't tell me enough to let me make an intelligent plan."

"I wish I had," Gwen said. "But I didn't really trust your abilities. We—Les and I—thought Parsons was right: that you were too inexperienced, that Parsons would have a much better chance.

"But Rick, it wasn't blind luck. Sure, all you were working for was survival, but you're an ethical man. I don't think it's luck at all. Ethical actions may be the best survival tactics after all. I wish I'd acted that way. Instead I trusted Parsons, knowing he'd use brutal tactics—and he failed completely. I wish we'd warned you about the mutiny and told you everything we knew."

"So do I."

He thought about what she'd said. Had he acted ethically? Not always. He had tried, and that had to count for something.

Ethics as the best survival policy, even without complete information? He wasn't sure he could accept that as a general proposition, even though it had worked here and now and this time. The most you could say for sure is that if you did the ethical thing and you did survive, you'd have an easier time living with yourself.

Which, he thought, brings up another point. He sighed and turned toward the door. "Jamiy."

"Sir." The orderly came into the pavilion.

"We took one of Sarakos' officers prisoner this afternoon," Rick said. "Bring him to me, and bring me parchment, pen, and ink."

"Yes, sir."

"Why do you want him?" Gwen asked.

"Ethics. You said that the most practical action is the ethical one. I'm not sure I believe that, but I am sure I've got no business sitting here waiting for a bomb to go off under a dozen men I brought to this planet."

Her eyes widened. "What are you going to do?"

"What I should have done in the first place," Rick said. "I'm going to send a letter to André Parsons and offer to parley."

3

"Man, are ye daft?" Drumold demanded. "We hae won, and you would throw it away." He looked sideways at Rick. "I had thought you loyal—"

"They are his countrymen," Tylara said. "As is Gwen. We are not."

"You know better," Rick said angrily. "Aye. They are my countrymen. I brought them here, as Tylara reminded me. And if bringing them made me responsible to the people they oppressed am I less responsible to my own men?" And then, bitterly: "You are in no danger. Dughuilas never tires of saying that I have never fought in a battle. You do not need me."

"If you are offended by Dughuilas' words, I will have his head brought to you," Drumold said. "Och, talk sense. You know full well your value to us. As do we. Wi'out your direction we fight as we did before you came, as a mob. 'Tis your craft that bested the Romans. If we have not often enough told you that we know your value, I tell you now. Do not be offended by hasty words spoken wi'out thought. I do not doubt your loyalty, and well can I understand that you wish to save your countrymen. But think of the risk!"

"I have," Rick said. "It's mostly to me. I've planned the battle for you. The catapults and ballista are in place, and their officers know how to use them as well as I do. You know what weapons Parsons has—if they survive. I have not told him of the gunpowder buried beneath the village, and it's likely he'll go back there if our talk fails to convince him."

"I do not care for this at all," Drumold said.

"Nor I." Tylara pointed to Gwen. "What has she said to take away your senses?"

"I didn't want him to do this!" Gwen protested.

"It would take too long to explain," Rick said. "But I tell you this. If I am killed tonight or tomorrow, the only way you'll live through the Time is to listen to Gwen and do as she tells you." He looked at his watch. "It's time to go. I told Parsons I'd meet him and Elliot and one other on the road midway between the lines. Mason—"

"No sir."

"Eh?"

"I said, 'No, sir.' This is a volunteer job, Cap'n, and I'm not volunteering."

"I see. Maybe that's wise of you. All right, I'll go alone."

"I do not think I should permit you to go at all." Drumold said.

"I doubt you can stop me," Rick said. He held his hand near the holstered Mark IV .45. "I don't doubt you could kill me, but that seems a strange way to save my life."

Drumold stood aside.

"That's all then," Rick said. "I'll be back in an hour."

✢ ✢ ✢

All was quiet at the forward outpost. Rick stared out into the darkness. Tran's outer moon gave very little light, and he could see nothing on the road ahead. He heard footsteps behind him and turned to see Mason.

"I'd feel better if you were coming along," Rick said. "But you're right. You're needed more here. If I don't come back, take charge of the catapults. A dozen of them firing grenades ought to knock out Parsons' machine-gun."

"Yeah. Maybe. Cap'n, I'd like it a lot if you didn't do this, but I know you have to. I don't believe you can talk sense to Parsons, but I hope I'm wrong. He's got some pretty good men with him. Elliot, McCleve, Campbell—"

"That's the way I see it," Rick said. "Okay, here I go."

He was startled by another voice behind him. "Wait," Tylara said. "I am coming with you."

Like hell you are. He stopped and turned. "No."

"Yes. You have said there is no danger to you. If there is none to you, there is less to me."

"You won't even understand what we're saying," Rick protested. "We will speak in English—"

"Yet I am going," Tylara said. "Do you think I wish to live twice widowed but not yet a bride?" She smiled softly. "And I give you the same reply you gave my father. You cannot stop me without killing me, and that is a strange way to protect my life."

Oh, bloody hell. And she means it, too. "All right. Let's go."

⚜ ⚜ ⚜

There were footsteps on the road ahead. Rick halted. "André?" he called.

"Yes. Hello, Rick."

There was no mistaking that bantering voice. "Who's with you?"

"Sergeant Elliot and Corporal Bisso," Parsons said.

"Let me hear them."

"It's us, Captain," Elliot's voice called from the darkness. "Nobody else."

"And who is with you?" Parsons asked.

"Tylara do Tamaerthon," Tylara replied.

Now where did she learn enough English to know when to answer? Rick wondered. Mason?

"You have brought a woman?" Parsons asked.

"Sure, André. This is a flag-of-truce meeting. I didn't think I needed bodyguards."

The low laughter came back. "Still naïve, my young friend. Well, this time you were correct. I have brought no more than you have heard. Do we now stand and shout in the darkness?"

"No. There's a hill about a hundred yards to the left. It's bare on top. We'll go up there and sit. I've brought a dark lantern."

"So have I. Well, let us get to it, then."

They reached the top of the knoll together. Rick pulled back the dark shutter from his candle lantern. He could see Parsons grin as he sat down.

"I must say I am completely surprised," Parsons said. "I suppose I should have suspected when I heard that hill tribesmen had won a great victory over the Roman legions, but I did not." He took a flask from his belt. "Wine?"

"Later—"

Parsons' laugh was a low, mocking sound. "Ah. Me first." He tilted up the flask and drank. "Are you certain you will not join me?"

"I have my own," Rick said. "I was about to offer you some. Share mine?"

"Perhaps it is better if we each keep our own," Parsons said. "That way there is no suspicion." His voice hardened and took on a more serious note. "Why have you asked me to meet you? Do you wish to surrender your army?"

"No. I came to tell you things you don't know. First thing: have you listened to the local legends? About caves, and fire from the sky?"

"No."

"I thought not. But you do know about the caves."

"I know there are caves beneath many of the castles," Parsons said. "They are important in the local religions. My friend Sarakos was very unhappy that he could think of no way to enter those under one of his castles. He would like me to help him cope with the ammonia, but I have better things to do."

"You'd better learn about the caves," Rick said. "That's one reason I wanted to talk to you. If I lose this battle tomorrow—"

Parsons laughed.

"I said 'if,' and I meant 'if,'" Rick said. "We'll get to that later. But if you win, you'll need to know about the caves. You'll need them for fallout shelters."

"I fear you make little sense—"

"Listen." Rick told him of his deductions about the fate of the 1400 expedition, and Gwen's suspicions. He was careful to be certain that Elliot heard the story as well as Parsons.

"Interesting. I do thank you," Parsons said. He sounded very thoughtful.

"Of course that may not matter to you," Rick said. "I understand you won't be able to raise the *surinomaz* for the *Shalnuksis*." He laughed. "You said I didn't have enough experience to accomplish the mission, but I seem to have a bigger and better army than you do. And there's no guerrilla war where I live. So who's so damned efficient now?"

"That is unkind of you," Parsons said.

"My apologies. But you see, that *surinomaz* crop is more important than you know. A lot more."

"How do you know this?"

"Gwen. Remember her? The pilot's girlfriend. She found out a lot

about the people who brought us here. There's a lot going on up there."
He pointed to the bright stars and their strange constellations.

"You have not told me why this *surinomaz* is important."

"I don't know that I can trust you," Rick said. "It involves a lot of people. Including some back on Earth. But assume I'm lying. It's still important to *you*. Without that crop, you won't be getting any juicy trade goods from the *Shalnuksis*. In fact, André, just what *are* you accomplishing with your superior skills and experience?"

"Is there any point to this conversation?" Parsons demanded.

"Certainly. I hope to persuade you to join us," Rick said.

Parsons laughed.

"Why not?" Rick asked. "Together we can grow those crops and trade with the *Shalnuksis*. We might even be able to capture a starship and get the hell off this planet! If we work together.

"Or we can go on fighting, and no matter who wins we both lose. You aren't going to grow that crop. Sarakos can't even feed his army! The people here will never stop fighting as long as he's here. But you must know already that we've been welcomed as liberators. My alliance is with the legitimate king, and I've got most of the nobility as well. I can get crops planted and harvested. You can't.

"Come over to our side, and you'll have an honored place. Wealth and influence, and you won't have to fight all the time. We both win. Fight me, and we both lose."

"So," Parsons said. "You are persuasive, if over confident. And yet I wonder. I have been thinking since I received your letter, what is it that you can do? Gunpowder? Muskets? I think you have not had enough time. Hand grenades? Undoubtedly, and catapult bombs as well. Tell me, what range do you get with them?"

"Enough. And I have a lot of them," Rick said. "André, for God's sake, let's end this damned war here and now. Can't you see it's better if we work together?"

"I see that you are the cause of my troubles," Parsons said. "The guerrilla war—"

"That was spontaneous," Rick said.

"I do not believe you. Without you the resistance will collapse, and in the morning we will destroy this barbarous army of yours." He smiled thinly. "What makes you think I will share power with you and your hill clans?"

"You share with Sarakos—"

"For the moment. I need him. But that will not be forever."

"André, you've gone crazy," Rick said. "What do you want?"

"What I said I wanted before we left the Moon," Parsons said. "To be a king. And I do not think you can offer that. Rick, you are a fool. Without you, your cause collapses. I will have your army as well as my own." His hand darted under his jacket.

It seemed to Rick that everything moved in slow motion. Parsons' hand reached his pistol, and Rick threw himself violently aside, his hand scrabbling for his own weapon.

Then there was a shout. "No! Dammit, no!" Elliot's shout startled Parsons so that he fumbled his draw, but Rick was still too slow. He had the .45 in his hand, and the safety off, but before he could swing it around to point at Parsons, André's own weapon was lining up with Rick's head—

There were three shots very close up. Rick's ears rang with the muzzle blast. He heard shouting, but it was incomprehensible through the ringing in his ears. Gradually he realized that he was still alive, and that he felt no shock or pain.

André Parsons fell heavily. His face held a look of total surprise. "My honorable young friend—" he gasped. Whatever else he was going to say never got out.

"Take it easy," Sergeant Elliot was saying in the Tran dialect. "We surrender." Elliot held his empty hands high, and after a moment Bisso did the same.

"What happened?" Rick asked. "Who—"

"I tried to stop him myself," Elliot said. "I already made one mistake about you, Captain. I didn't want to let Colonel Parsons make another. But he was too fast. I didn't even draw. It was your girlfriend there." He pointed to Tylara. She sat motionless, still holding Mason's pistol in both hands in the approved military grip. One of the baggy sleeves of her cloak was charred, and wisps of smoke rose from where she had shot through it.

✢ ✢ ✢

Mason came up the hill moments later. "You all right?" he asked.

"Yes—" Rick's ears still rang. Tylara had been no more than a foot behind him when she fired. His head was clearing, but it seemed to be a long time doing it. Tylara seemed dazed as well. And now here was Mason. "Where did you come from?" Rick demanded.

"Out there," Mason said. "I did a little scouting in case Parsons brought a sniper. Nobody around just at the moment, but after those shots there will be. We'd better get going. How you doing, Sarge?"

"Just what is going on?" Rick asked.

"Hell, Cap'n, I wasn't going to let you come out here by yourself," Mason said. "Figured I'd be more use out where they couldn't see me. Only you had to pick a place I couldn't get close enough to! Good thing Tylara thought of borrowing my pistol. She's been taking lessons dry-firing that thing for weeks now. Cap'n, we really had better get going."

"All right." He got up and felt himself swaying until Elliot steadied him with a hand on his shoulder. "Tylara—"

She got up slowly. She kept the pistol in her hand, but she was careful not to point it at anyone. "I had not known," she said softly. "I did not intend to—shoot—but once."

"They'll do that," Mason said. "Come on, I hear people comin' from both directions. You move out—I'll hang back and discourage visitors." He patted the H&K battle rifle affectionately.

"What now, Elliot?" Rick asked.

"We'll accept your offer," Elliot said. "If it's still open."

"It's open," Rick said. "But it won't be for long." He looked at his watch. "You have no more than two hours to get back to the village and bring any men who want to come. Bisso will stay with me."

"Yes, sir," Elliot said. "Two hours." He stood awkwardly for a moment, obviously fumbling for words. "I'm not much for apologies," he said. "I thought I was doing the right thing back when we first landed. Now—"

"You don't have to apologize," Rick said. "Just get back with the men. Leave equipment if you have to, but bring the men and what you can carry. Two hours."

"Yes, sir. Two hours."

Forty minutes after Elliot brought a dozen men and the light machine-gun to Rick's pavilion, the gunpowder exploded.

EPILOGUE

Tylara looked down from the battlements of Castle Dravan with satisfaction. The last remnants of Sarakos' siege works had been removed, leveled over. They were gone without trace. Dravan stood strong again.

It would need to be. Sarakos was dead—had that been his body in the silken robes? The gunpowder bomb had obliterated the face. Whoever that was, Sarakos had died; and with neither king nor starmen to lead them, his armies had dissolved at a touch from Rick's pikemen and archers. Drantos was free, but there were rumors of war from the north, and more than rumors of invasions from displaced tribes to the south.

The Demon Star stood brightly above the horizon, visible even at high noon. She thought she could already feel its warmth. The Time was coming, and there were myriads of details for the attention of the Eqeta and Eqetassa of Chelm. She turned away from the battlements to where Rick and Gwen stood, and she smiled faintly. Rick was sending Gwen away. She need no longer fear what her husband might feel for his countrywoman.

✣ ✣ ✣

"They can't expect a crop for another year," Gwen said. "The invader star won't be bright enough. Are you sure you won't need me here?"

Rick shook his head. "I'll manage. Tylara doesn't like having you around anyway—"

214

"I've noticed."

"But the main thing is to start the university as soon as possible. You'll have Warner and Campbell, and I'll send you McCleve as soon as he's finished his work on a tetanus inoculation."

The medical sergeant had already developed a smallpox vaccination, and was teaching anatomy to some of Yanulf's acolytes. That knowledge would soon be spread too far for the *Shalnuksis* to eradicate even with atom bombs.

"I wish you didn't have to stay here," Gwen said. "Not—Tylara has nothing to be jealous of. But there's so much to do."

"I'll come by for visits," Rick said. "I want to keep an eye on Marselius. He's keeping the peace so far, but you never know. I confess I envy you. A tranquil university life looks pretty tempting compared to what we'll have to do here."

More detail. Fields to be cleared for the *surinomaz*. Careful planning of the cultivation area so that the population could quickly take refuge in caves. The caves to be stocked with food, and more fields to be plowed with the newly designed plowshares. And always the threat of wars—

Tylara came to join them. Rick took her hand and stood close to her. Living with her was like having a dozen wives: one moment she could command armies, but in the next she would be shy and seem helpless. At the moment she wore armor and looked very much the warrior aristocrat.

They'd been married two months, and he understood her less now than he had when they first met. There was only one certainty: he couldn't imagine living without her.

Well, one other certainty. Gwen's leaving couldn't hurt. The Chinese ideograph for "trouble" was a stick drawing of two women under one roof, and the last months had shown the truth of that.

"Before you go, there's something I've been meaning to ask you," Rick said to Gwen. "You might not want to tell me. You once mentioned that Les had a message for his child. I'd like to hear it."

"All right," Gwen said. "It wasn't long. He said he wanted his child to know this much: that his father believes that the human race has a greater destiny than to be the slave soldiers of a so-called civilization preening itself over remaining unchanged for five thousand years." She looked up at the Demon Star. "I hope he was right."

"Damned right he was," Rick said. "Even if Les can't come back with his textbooks and a ship. All we need is time, and we'll have that. We'll have six hundred years. It didn't take Earth half that long to go from the steam engine to the space shuttle. We'll do it in a generation because we start with more."

Gwen nodded agreement. "A lot more. And we know starships are possible."

"Yes. That does help. You go start your university, and I'll deal with the *Shalnuksis*. One way or another, your child will inherit the stars."

"Our children," Tylara said.

TRAN

JERRY POURNELLE
ROLAND J. GREEN

A POLITICAL GLOSSARY

THE GALACTICS

The Galactic Confederation is a loose federation of non-human races, governing Earth's region of the spiral arm of our Galaxy. Its member races include the *Shalnuksis*, the *Ader'at'eel*, the *Fusttael*, and the Finsit'tuvii. The *Council* is the supreme governing body of the Confederation; the *High Commission* is a subordinate body, in charge of relations with non-member races, particularly humans.

TRAN

The Five Kingdoms is a confederation of northern kingdoms (including Ta-Meltemos, Ta-Lataos, and Ta-Kartos) under a High Rexja.

Drantos is an independent kingdom under its own Wanax, although it has been claimed by both Rome and the Five Kingdoms. *Chelm* is part of Drantos.

Rome is a (self-proclaimed) empire, descended from Romans of the time of Septimius Severus (c. 200 A.D.) brought to Tran by the *Shalnuksis*.

The City-States are an array of independent cities lying south of Drantos and south-west of Rome. Their most prominent members are *Vis* and *Rustengo*.

The Sunlands is the general term for everything south of the City-States.

The Westmen are nomadic horse barbarians from beyond the High Plains, ultimately descended from Scythians.

⊹⇌ DRAMATIS PERSONAE ⇌⊹

THE GALACTICS

Inspector Agzaral—Confederation High Commission law enforcement officer.

Jehna Sae Leern—Courier for the Ader'at'eel.

Karreeel—*Shalnuksi* merchant, in the Tran trade.

Les—Human pilot in *Shalnuksi* service; Gwen Tremaine's husband.

Wilno—Retired Confederate naval officer, classmate of Agzaral.

THE STARMEN

Private Jack Beazeley—Mason's right-hand man.

Sergeant Harold Bisso—Elliot's right-hand man.

Private Alexander Boyd—Gengrich's chief of staff.

Sergeant Willian Campbell—Professor of Engineering at the University.

Private Lance Clavell—Rick Galloway's ambassador to Nikeis.

Sergeant Major Rafael Elliot—Top kick of the mercs; Provost of the University.

Rick Galloway—Captain, U.S.A.; Colonel of Mercenaries, Eqeta of Chelm, Captain General of Drantos, War Leader of Tamaerthon.

Corporal Arnold Gengrich—Leader of mutinous mercs; Lord of Zyphron.

Private Alan MacAllister—Expert sniper.

Sergeant John McCleve—Medic; Professor of Medicine at the University.

Major Art Mason—Rick's right-hand man; Marshal of the Captain General's Household.

Sergeant Ben Murphy—Bheroman of Westrook.

Private First Class Arkos Passavopolous—"The Great Ark"; machine-gunner.

Private Lafferty Reznick—Murphy's partner.

Corporal Mortimer Schultz—Master of Foot in Rustengo.

Gwen Tremaine—Rector of the University.

Corporal Jerzy Walinski—Balloon crewman.

Warrant Officer Larry Warner—Chancellor of the University.

THE ALLIANCE

Ajacias—Bheroman of Drantos, in the Sutmarg.

Apelles, son of Lykon—Priest of Yatar.

Balquhain—Drumold's son and heir.

Camithon—Lord Protector to Ganton until the young Wanax reaches his majority.

Corgarff—Subchief to Dughuilas.

Caradoc—A lord of Clan Tamaerthan; rescuer of Tylara from Sarakos in *Janissaries*.

Drumold—Mac Clallan Muir; Tylara's father.

Dughuilas—Chief of Clan Calder.

Enipses—Bheroman of Drantos.

Ganton, son of Loron—Wanax of Drantos.

Hilaskos—Bheroman of Drantos.

Mad Bear—Chief of the exiled Silver Wolves clan of the Westmen (the Horse People).

Maev, merchant's daughter—Handfasted to Apelles.

Monira—Leader of the war-trained Children of Vothan.

Morrone, son of Morron—Companion to the Wanax Ganton.

Pinir, son of the smith—Master Gunner in the Royal Artillery of Drantos.

Rudhrig—Eqeta of Harms.

Lady Siobhan—Art Mason's fiancée and Gwen Tremaine's office manager.

Teuthras—Colonel of First Tamaerthan Hussars.

Traskon, son of Trakon—Bheroman of Drantos.

Tylara do Tamaerthon—Rick Galloway's wife; Eqetassa of Chelm and Justiciar of Drantos.

Yanulf—Highpriest of Yatar and Chancellor of Drantos.

THE ROMANS

Flaminius Caesar—Emperor of Rome.

Titus Frugi—Commander of Flaminius' legions against the rebellion.

Titus Licinius Frugi—Legate, commanding the Fourth Legion.

Lucius—Freedman and confidant to Marselius.

Gaius Marius Marselius—Former Prefect of the Western Marches; later Emperor.

Octavia Marselia—Publius' daughter.

Archbishop Polycarp—Founder of the movement for the united worship of Yatar and Christ.

Publius—Marselius' son and heir.

Marcus Julius Vinicianus—Exiled Roman nobleman and chief spy for Gengrich.

THE ENEMIES

Prince Akkilas—High Rexja Toris' sole surviving legitimate son.

Issardos—High Chancellor of the Five Kingdoms.

Matthias—Highpriest of Vothan.

Phrados the Prophet—Religious fanatic opposed to the united worship of Yatar and Christ.

Crown Prince Strymon—Heir to Ta-Meltemos.

Prince Teodoros—Strymon's younger brother.

Toris—High Rexja of the Five Kingdoms.

Volauf—Captain General to Matthais.

Walking Stone—Paramount war chief of the Westmen.

BOOK I
CLAN AND CROWN

PART ONE
THRONES AND DOMINIONS

1

The rocket sputtered for a moment, then rose swiftly above the worn cobblestone courtyard of the old fortress. It hissed upwards in a column of fire, trailing golden sparks and a faint smell of brimstone as it climbed until, without warning, it burst loudly into a shower of silver. The crowd gasped in wonder.

High above the courtyard, two richly dressed boys about fifteen Earth years in age clapped their hands in wonder. They huddled together in a window cut in the wall of the keep thirty meters above the gawking populace. One of the boys shouted aloud when the rocket burst above Castle Edron.

"Quiet! The Protector will hear us," the other boy said. "He'll make us join the others."

"He is nowhere about, Majesty."

"Ah." Nothing like those rockets had ever been seen on the whole planet of Tran. Even kings should be able to gawk at them without losing status.

But, Ganton thought, kings must think first of their dignity, and for the opinions of the nobility. No monarch ever needed his lords' good opinions more than I do. Another rocket arced across the darkening sky. This one trailed blue sparks. "Oh—look!" he cried. The True Sun had long set, but the Firestealer was high enough to cast baleful shadows and light the summer sky above the fortress capital of Drantos.

Ganton shouted again as yet another rocket burst. Ganton son of

231

Loron, Wanax of Drantos, he might be; but he was also nine years old, fifteen according to the reckoning of the starman Lord Rick; and the rockets were fun to watch. "Perhaps we could make weapons from those," Ganton said. "Do you think so?"

"The lord Rick says he will," Morrone answered.

He speaks in those tones, Ganton thought. *They all do, when they speak of Lord Rick. They never sound that way when the talk is about me. They rebelled against my father. The wonder is that I lived this long. It is no time to be Wanax, but I have no choice of times.*

More rockets flashed upward from the palace courtyard. Each sent down silver and gold showers. One burst with a loud sound.

"Was it like that?" Morrone asked.

"Louder," Ganton answered. "Much louder." He had no need to ask what Morrone meant. "It was just a year ago."

"A whole army," Morrone said. "All killed in an instant—"

"No. Only their leaders were killed. We yet had a battle to win. Not that it was difficult, with the Wanax Sarakos dead, and all the starmen kneeling to Lord Rick. But the armies of Sarakos were defeated by good Drantos warriors, not star weapons."

Morrone nodded, but Ganton thought his companion didn't really believe it. Sarakos had conquered nearly the whole of the Kingdom of Drantos. Until the great battle, Sarakos held the entire County of Chelm and most lands of the other great lords. His writ ran everywhere except into the hills where Ganton had hidden with the Lord Protector and the remnants of the loyalist forces. Sarakos had defeated the best Ganton had, had killed the first Lord Protector. Then the starman Lord Rick had come with the wild clansmen who obeyed his wife's father, and in one day, one grand battle—

More rockets flashed upward. "You spend firepowder with both hands," Morrone said.

Ganton shrugged. "It is no small thing, the birth of the lady Isobel as heiress to the greatest lord of Drantos. Besides, the firepowder was given to me by Lord Rick himself. Come, can't I show my pleasure at the honor he does me, to have his child born in my capital?" *And without my leave, although I would have given it cheerfully—*

He felt Morrone draw away, and wondered if his friend were angry. Ganton had few enough friends, and almost none his own age; soon, he supposed, Morrone too would treat him as Wanax rather than friend. All too soon. And that would be right and proper, but it would be lonely as well—

"There," Morrone said. He pointed to the horizon to the south. "I can just see it. The Demon Sun."

Ganton shuddered slightly and hoped that Morrone wouldn't notice. Only a star, the starmen had said. A star that wandered close to Tran every six hundred years. Not a demon at all, only a star.

"It might as well be a demon," Morrone said, as if reading his thoughts. "The Demon Sun comes, and we live in the Time . . ." His voice lost its banter, and took on the singsong notes of a priest. "The Time draws near, when oceans will rise. Storms shall rage, and gods will come from the skies to offer gifts. Woe to those who trade with gods, for after the gods depart there shall be smoke and fire and destruction—" Morrone broke off as suddenly as he had begun. "There's someone coming." He pointed. "On the south road. There, just below the Demon Sun."

Ganton stared into the dusky light. One of the Earthmen had told him that the Firestealer was as bright as a hundred full Moons, but the words meant little to Ganton. He was willing to believe that a place called Earth was the home of humanity, but the thought held little impact for him. Tran was home enough.

The light of the Firestealer was more than bright enough to see by, but it made for tricky light, and cast strange shadows. But—yes, there was a large party riding up to the south gate of the town. "Merchants, I'd say," Ganton muttered.

"Doubtless. From the southern cities, by their clothes. What would they be doing here?"

"Come to make obeisance to me," Ganton said. He chuckled.

"It may be," Morrone said. He sounded very serious.

Ganton laughed aloud. "The southern cities would sooner give up their gods than their councils and assemblies and meeting halls. What could they possibly gain?"

"Lord Rick's protection," Morrone said.

And once again that tone, Ganton thought.

"Caravan ho!" The guard's challenge faintly reached their high perch.

"They're too late," Morrone said. "The gates are locked for the night. But surely they know that . . ."

Someone in the caravan shouted to the sentries. Ganton couldn't hear what was said, but it seemed to cause a stir. "Officer of the day!" the sentry shouted.

Ganton frowned in puzzlement and looked at his friend. "What do you see?" he asked. "Who could cause such excitement?"

Morrone shook his head. "I can't make it out."

"The starmen have tools to see with," Ganton said. "They call them—*binoculars.*" He said the unfamiliar word gingerly. "Binoculars."

"You should have them," Morrone said.

Ganton shrugged. "Whose? They are the personal equipment of the starmen, and there are no more than a dozen of those—*binoculars*—in all this world of Tran. How should I have them?"

"You are Wanax!" Morrone said. "These starmen are not great lords. The lord Rick himself is no more than Eqeta of Chelm. Aye, and that only through his wife's first husband. Ach. The Eqetassa Tylara no more deserves that title than I do. Less, for I was cousin to the last Eqeta, and she no more than his unbedded wife."

Ganton stared in amazement. He had heard complaints before, but none so open. "Yet when you speak of the lord Rick," Ganton said. "Your voice. You speak of him as you would of—of Yatar."

"Your pardon, Majesty. I spoke in haste—"

"You will not do this to me!" Ganton shouted. "Finish what you have begun. What is this you say? If you have complaints against the lord Rick, say them now. Speak to me as friend—"

"I say no more than do hundreds of your loyal nobility," Morrone said. "We respect the lord Rick, and we would follow him—but we fear his upstart family. We fear they will bring their kilted barbarians to Drantos by scores—"

"I would they would bring tens of scores of their archers," Ganton said.

"Perhaps. But when they loose their gullfeathered arrows—who will wear the grey Tamaerthon plumage? Your enemies or your friends?" His voice fell. "Majesty. Ganton, my friend. I know it must be hard—"

"Hard," Ganton said. "Hard indeed. Even the Protector fears the lord Rick and the star weapons. As he should. You were not there, but I was there, when the other starman, Parsons, the renegade, made common cause with Sarakos, and turned those weapons on my armies.

Men, horses, all destroyed, and the sounds of thunder everywhere. No one safe. My Captain-General died at my side, and we five furlongs from the battle!

"But it will change," Ganton said. "I will not be in leading strings forever. Listen."

There were more shouts below. Then a rumble. "The gates," Morrone said. "They open the gates, even at this late hour! Who?"

"We must go see," Ganton said. "Race you—" He leaped from the window seat and was down half a flight of steps before Morrone could follow.

They raced down the stairs, shouting and laughing.

✦ ✦ ✦

The Lord Protector was waiting for them at the second landing. His scarred, weatherbeaten face and the plain broadsword hung on his belt contrasted sharply with the rich blue and scarlet court attire and jeweled chain of office. He was obviously far more at home in the saddle than the throne room.

Ganton caught himself in mid-stride and drew himself to full height, trying to walk carefully and correctly, hoping that Camithon hadn't seen him running—

"Sire," Camithon began.

By Yatar, I'm for it now, Ganton thought.

"Sire, you should not have absented yourself for so long," the Protector said. "You do little honor to the lord and lady of Chelm, after they have so honored your house by bringing forth their first child here."

Once more, Ganton thought. *Tell me once more how honored I am, and I will scream curses on your ancestors*—"My house is honored indeed. But perhaps there were practical reasons as well? If the lady Tylara bore her child in Chelm, her clansmen in Tamaerthon would be slighted—and if in Tamaerthon, would not the knights and bheromen of Chelm know insult? My house was a convenience to them. And to the realm, of course. To the realm."

Camithon frowned, and the great scar across his face grew dark. For a moment Ganton was afraid. The old warrior was perfectly capable of bending his sovereign over his knee—although, Ganton reassured himself, never in public.

"It's true enough," Ganton insisted.

Camithon nodded. "Aye. Yatar's own truth. But there is such a thing as the right words at the wrong time."

"I heard a disturbance," Ganton said. "I came to see—"

"Aye. A starman. Come to see Lord Rick. With a gift."

"Oh."

Camithon didn't have to explain the significance of that.

✢ ✢ ✢

The walls were thick stone crowned with battlements. The gates were set in massive porticos, and made of heavy wood studded with large iron knobs. The small mounted party was barely through when the gates crashed shut, and they heard the locking bar, a log nearly as big around as a telephone pole, fall into place. Ben Murphy rode on in silence for a moment, then turned to his companion. "Guess it's too late for second thoughts now," he said in English.

In contrast to Murphy, the other man was mounted on a centaur. It didn't look much like the classical centaurs; the upper torso was more apelike than human, while the body itself resembled a moose as much as it did a horse. Its rider looked around through half-closed eyes. "I reckon we could get out of here," he said. He reached forward to stroke the centaur's back. "Dobbin and me've been through a bit on this stupid planet. Don't reckon we'd let these city types stop us."

"Naw," Murphy said. "We'd never make it."

"Hell we couldn't." Lafe Reznick patted the H&K battle rifle slung over his shoulder. "Say the word, Ben, and I'll hold 'em off while you break out the one-oh-six."

Murphy snorted. "And what'll you bet they don't have crosshairs on us right now?" He pointed up to the high tower of the castle that dominated the town. A skyrocket rose from the tower's base as he pointed.

"You really think the captain would do that?" Reznick demanded.

Murphy shrugged. "Maybe not. But what about Mason? Or Elliot?"

"Yeah. I forgot about Sergeant Major Elliot," Reznick said. "Guess they all went over when Captain Galloway shot Colonel Parsons. And Elliot's just the man to see we don't get away." He squinted up toward the castle. "Up there—or hell, maybe right over in one of those doorways with a submachine-gun."

"He wouldn't even need that," Murphy said. "With those goddamn

Tamaerthon archers of his, Christ, they could have us stuck over with gullfeathers 'fore you could unsling that H&K."

"You do think of the cheerfullest things."

"You say what?" One of the riders drew level with Murphy and threw back her hood. She was quite pretty, and much younger than the two soldiers. "You have afraid?" she asked.

"Naw, I'm not afraid," Reznick said. " 'Course not, honey. I wouldn't bring you here if I was afraid."

"I hear afraid," she said. "The mounts know we afraid."

"Just nervous in the service," Murphy said. "To your place, if you please, Lady . . ."

The girl started to say something, but checked herself. She halted to let Murphy and Reznick draw ahead and the three other women catch up to her. Then she began to chatter to them, speaking the native language far too swiftly for Murphy to understand her words.

Murphy and Reznick rode on in silence until they reached the castle gates, which seemed at least as massive as the town portals had been. As they approached, the gates swung open.

"Expectin' us," Murphy said. "Well, here we go." He stood in his stirrups and turned to the group behind him. "No weapons," he said, grinning to himself. I don't speak this local stuff too bad, he thought. Bettern' Honeypie speaks English. "No matter what happens, keep your hands off your weapons. You have seen our star weapons. These gentry will be watching us, and their captain has weapons to overpower any you have seen us use."

The women nodded solemnly. The five merchant adventurers behind them looked around uneasily.

"They could get us bloody well killed," Murphy said. "Tell them wives of yours I mean it."

"I already did," Reznick said. "Christ, Ben, there's times I can't believe any of this."

"I know what you mean." He shook his head wryly. "Fightin' in Africa, 'bout to be finished by the Cubans and we get picked up by a goddamn flyin' saucer. And even then it don't make sense. This whole planet, none of it makes sense."

"Except to Captain Galloway."

"Yeah. I guess."

"Hell, Ben, it was you said we ought to come here . . ."

"You agreed," Murphy reminded him. "I didn't twist your arm." He grinned. "Anyway, I still think it was best. That paper the Cap'n sent us, it said he really did understand things here. He knows why there's people here, and what those saucer critters want, and—"

"And you can believe as much of it as you want to," Reznick said. He paused a moment, then matched Murphy's grin. "And we both sure as hell want to believe a lot of it."

"Yeah. Let's go." He led the way through the open gates.

The courtyard behind the gates smelled of burned gunpowder. It was packed with people. Archers in kilts held them back to make a lane that Murphy's party could ride through. "Like MPs," Murphy said.

"Big deal." Reznick squinted upwards. "Don't look now, but there's a sniper up in the tower over the gate."

"Yeah, I spotted him. Don't matter. There's a dozen of those archer types on the wall up there, too. There's sure as hell only one way to play this now."

The wall ahead of them was taller than the first, and the gateway through it was so narrow they had to go single file. The gate itself was a long mazelike corridor, with two twists barely wide enough for their mounts. Then they came out into an inner court, empty except for half a dozen richly dressed courtiers.

"Welcome," one called. "In the name of Wanax Ganton, welcome to Castle Edron. I am Parilios, Chamberlain to Wanax Ganton and servant to the Lord Protector, in whose name I bid you welcome yet again."

"Sounds good so far," Murphy said. "Uh—we have come at the invitation of the lord Rick, Eqeta of Chelm, Great Captain General of the Forces of Drantos, Colonel of Mercenaries . . ." He gave the last title in English. "We are Benjamin Murphy do Dirstval and Lafferty Reznick do Bathis, Merchant Traders of the Sun Lands."

"The lord Rick is here and awaits you eagerly," the chamberlain said. "He has been foretold of your coming. He bade me say that his food will be no more than filling for his belly, and his drink no more than moisture for the tongue, until he has spoken with you at last."

"Fat chance the captain ever said that," Murphy said *sotto voce*. "Bid the Wanax, and the Lord Protector, and Lord Rick a thousand thanks in our names, and tell him that we came in haste to his summons."

There was more ceremony before they were invited to dismount.

Eventually they were led into an antechamber. A cheerful fire blazed at one end of the room, and there was a table laid out with wine and food. Washbasins stood on a sideboard. "I will leave you to refresh yourselves," their escort said. He turned a pair of identical sand glasses, and took one with him. "I will return when this is done." The chamberlain bowed and left them.

The women began to chatter, but Murphy made a sharp gesture, and they fell quiet. He eyed the glass. "About twenty minutes. We going to take the women in with us?"

"Why not?" Reznick demanded.

Murphy shrugged. "This is royalist country," he said. "Not like the south where we were. And the girls aren't exactly out of the nobility—"

"Dirdre and Marva are now," Reznick said. "Married me, didn't they? That makes them as good as anybody."

"Okay if you say so. Wonder where the bloody plumbing is?"

"Through there, I'd say," Reznick said. He walked over to a small curtained doorway and looked inside. "Yep. Looks to me like it hangs out over the town. Shall we go relieve ourselves on the commoners?"

✢ ✢ ✢

"Cap'n?"

Rick Galloway turned from the window as one of the skyrockets burst in crimson. "Yes?"

"Two things," Art Mason said. "Lady Tylara says you're supposed to be downstairs enjoying the fireworks—"

"Hell, I know that," Rick said. He lifted a crystal goblet and tossed off the full cup of wine it held. "Three days we've been on display. Tylara likes all the fuss." He grinned slightly. "Isobel really is a beautiful little thing. I guess Tylara's earned all this glory. But why she wants it is beyond me." He poured another drink.

Mason shrugged. "I never claimed to understand women."

"What was the other thing?"

"Murphy's here."

"Murphy?"

"Private Ben Murphy," Mason said. "Along with Lafe Reznick. Two of the troops that ran away south with Warner and Gengrich. They just showed up at the gate, dressed up like rich southern merchants

and attended by some women and bullyboys. Murphy told the officer
of the guard that he's got a present for the Eqeta of Chelm, the great
Captain-General of the Host of Drantos—"

"Humph."

"Hell, he's layin' it on thicker'n glue, Cap'n. But I think you'll like the
present. It's all wrapped up in silk and gold cloth, but it's about yay
long and maybe this big around—"

"The recoilless!"

"Could be," Mason said. "It just could be. Anyway, he's downstairs
in the entry hall. I checked with Elliot and we had the chamberlain
give him wine and some chow, and I figured I'd better get you before
that Camithon gets at him."

"Yes. Good thinking. I'll come." He started toward the door.

"Not without we dress you proper," Mason protested. "Wait, Cap'n.
I'll help you into your armor."

"I do not need armor."

"Hell you don't," Mason said. "Cap'n, now dammit I mean it, don't
you go down there without your mail shirt. Here, take the pistol off.
That's it. Now duck—" Despite Rick's protests, Mason eased him into
a shirt woven of tiny metal rings.

"Damn thing's too heavy," Rick said.

"Wasn't heavy it wouldn't do much good," Mason said. "Here, lift
your arm—" Deftly he buckled Rick's pistol and combat knife under
his captain's left arm. "Now you look proper."

"And feel like an idiot."

"No, sir." Mason was emphatic. "You gotta be practical."

I've been practical all my life, Rick thought. I do the sensible,
practical thing, and I feel like a coward half the time.

Mason saw Rick's expression. "Cap'n, you don't know what Murphy
wants. I grant you, he probably didn't come to make trouble. Not
coming inside the gates like that. But Christ, Cap'n, this whole place is
about to explode. Ambassadors from both Roman outfits. That
diplomat from the Five Kingdoms, he's nothing more than a spy—hell,
they're still technically at war with us! Not to mention our own nobles.
Wasn't an hour ago I had to disarm two of those barons, Dragomer
and Kilantis—"

"Who?"

"Couple of the barons who went over to Sarakos," Mason said.

"Took advantage of the amnesty after we beat Sarakos. They come from the north central hills."

"Yeah. I remember," Rick said. "Hard to blame them for going over, being that close to the Five Kingdoms and all. Why disarm them?"

"Fighting over something. I didn't bother to find out what. Just got their dirks."

"They drew steel in the palace?"

"Yeah."

"Where was Wanax Ganton?"

"Up watching the fireworks," Mason said. "Hell, Cap'n, if they'd drawn weapons while the kid or the old geezer was there I'd've done a lot more then disarm them, you know that."

"Yeah. Sorry. All right, let's go." He led the way to the thick nail-studded door and pulled. It opened slowly. It ought to, Rick thought. The damn thing must weigh five hundred pounds in this gravity. One heavy mother. There were men outside the door. Rick nodded to Jamiy, his orderly, and the brace of Guardsmen. Then he turned to the fourth man who stood stiffly aloof from the others. "Captain Caradoc."

"My lord." Caradoc was dressed in bright-colored kilts. He wore a jewel-handled dirk at his waist. A bow and quiver hung over his shoulder. He was no older than Rick. Caradoc bowed deeply, and waited until Rick returned the greeting before straightening.

"It's good to see you again," Rick said. "How went your journey?"

"Well enough, my lord. I had fast horses and Yatar's favor."

"I'm pleased to hear it." Rick put as much warmth in his voice as he could. More than once Caradoc had saved Rick—and his family. Caradoc was really Tylara's man, henchman of her father, son of one of her father's subchiefs. Loyal men high in the Tamaerthon clan system were rare . . .

"We'll go down to audience hall," Mason said. One of the guards went ahead at a trot. The second walked ahead of Rick. Mason walked alongside Rick, with Jamiy and Caradoc following.

All this rigmarole just to go downstairs, Rick thought. *Places of honor and all. And yet there really* are *damned few I can trust to walk behind me with weapons.*

They went down a narrow stone stairway to a broad hall hung with tapestries, then along that to an arched entry into a much larger chamber.

Rick had just gotten inside when he heard a gravelly voice call,

"Make way. Make way for the Wanax of Drantos." A party came through another entrance. First two men-at-arms. Then the King's Companion, Morrone, a lordling Rick found a bit pretentious. Next came Camithon, the scar-faced Lord Protector.

"Who ranks who?" Mason asked in English.

"I'll have to think," Rick said. It was a hell of a complex question. As Protector, Camithon ranked everyone except the king. On the other hand, before he became Lord Protector he'd been Tylara's general, and he held most of his lands as a mere bheroman in her service. If that wasn't complex enough, Rick and Tylara were technically host and hostess here, since Wanax Ganton had generously offered his palace to Tylara during her confinement and delivery. Which made Camithon guardian to Rick's honored guest—

"My lord," Camithon growled. He bowed slightly. Rick bowed in return, then bowed even deeper to Ganton as the boy came in.

"Majesty," Rick said. "I trust you have enjoyed the celebrations."

"We have," Ganton said. He looked around at the minor nobility and others who had come into the hall.

The boy's all right, Rick thought. *Got a pretty level head. And he listens to Tylara. Then there's the rest of these. Half of 'em want to make me a god, and the other half want to put a knife in my ribs.* "Majesty, I would ask a favor," Rick said. "The use of your hall to receive these starmen."

"This is your house," Ganton said ritually. "I wear no crowns while you and your lady are here. I would ask that you allow me the pleasure of watching you receive your friends."

"Certainly, sire. And my thanks."

One end of the room was dominated by a throne on a high dais. Below that was a lower dais with less elaborate chairs. Yanulf, chief priest of Yatar Dayfather, was already there. So was Sigrim, high priest of Vothan One-eye, Chooser of the Slain. They did not rise when Rick came to the dais. As he took his seat on the lower platform there was a stir at the door. Tylara had arrived.

She looks pale, Rick thought. She's still so damn beautiful it almost hurts to look at here, though. Her raven black hair shone as always, and her eyes were startlingly blue. There wasn't much to show that she'd been through a difficult labor, forty hours in the house of Yatar. Rick shuddered at the memory. If he'd lost her—

He couldn't follow that thought. "Sweetheart," he said in English. Then more formally for the court, "My lady. Will you join me?"

"Thank you." Her voice was like ice, and there was winter in her smile as she sat beside Rick.

Christ. I didn't send for her, Rick thought. *I should have, but I just forgot. But*—"I am pleased that you were able to join us. When you did not come I worried." And that ought to make her wonder. "Chamberlain, summon our guests if you please."

"You sent for me?" Tylara demanded.

"Benjamin Murphy do Dirstval and Lafe Reznick do Bathis, Star Lords and Merchant Traders of the Sun Lands," the chamberlain announced.

"Ah," Rick said to himself as Murphy came in. I remember him now. Belfast Irishman. Made a bundle playing poker until most of the others wouldn't play with him. Nobody thought he was cheating. Just good. Good man with the light machine-gun, too.

He couldn't recall very much about Reznick, except that he always teamed with Murphy.

Murphy and Reznick came to the dais, followed by two women and four men, obviously armed servants. The men carried something heavy and bulky wrapped in silk and cloth of gold. They reached the dais and looked at Rick in mild confusion. Then Murphy stamped to attention and saluted.

Automatically Rick returned the salute. Then he laughed. "You're supposed to bow or kneel or something," he said in English. He heard a strangled grunt from Tylara as she suppressed a laugh. "Welcome to my house." Rick changed to the local dialect and raised his voice. "It is good that we meet again. Your other friends among the starmen will welcome you also."

"Yeah, well, I'm happy to be signing up with you again, Captain," Murphy said. "And I've brought you something—"

"Yes. I'm damned glad to get the recoilless back. That is the one-oh-six, isn't it?"

"Sure is." Murphy turned and gestured. His companions unwrapped the tube. Another took the cover off the tripod stand, and clapped the barrel onto it.

"You've trained them to use it?" Rick asked.

"Not really, sir," Reznick said. "But they *have* seen us use the thing."

"Yes. We'll continue this in private," Rick said. "Meanwhile, there's a ceremony. We'll coach you." He motioned to Murphy to kneel, and said in the local language, "We will accept you to our service. Do you offer me service, of your free will, according to the customs and uses of this land?"

"We do," Murphy and Reznick said in unison.

"Then your enemies shall be my enemies, and who wrongs you wrongs me," Rick said. He held out his hands. "Place your hands between mine. There. Now repeat after the chamberlain . . ."

✢ ✢ ✢

"Thank Ghu that's over," Rick said.

"Who is Ghu?" Tylara asked seriously.

"Uh—a local deity back on Earth. Probably no jurisdiction here." He watched Murphy and Reznick leave the audience hall, and felt an overpowering urge to go with them. *Fat chance*, he thought. *Now that the fireworks are over we have to go show Isobel off to every goddam bheroman and knight in the joint, and get the king's blessing and*—"You needn't smirk about it," Rick said.

"Your desire is obvious," Tylara said. "It will do you no harm to be patient. Tonight you must be with me."

"Yeah." It *was* important. Tonight's ceremonies were supposed to be fun, but they would also mark his formal acknowledgement of Isobel's paternity. Until he did that, she was officially no more than a little bastard.

And Isobel was the most beautiful little thing he'd ever seen, and he certainly wanted everyone to know she was his—which still seemed like a miracle—but Lord, Lord, those lords were dull. . . .

2

"What now?" Reznick asked.

"The first thing I want is a drink," Ben Murphy said. They were led through corridors, then up stairs, then down a flight. "And I think I'm lost. Ho, guide there, where are our companions?"

"Your ladies have been shown to their chambers. You are wanted in the orderly room." The trooper who led them obviously spoke no English; but they had no difficulty recognizing the last two words.

Reznick laughed. "Just like the real army." They followed their guides until eventually they were led to a stone doorway guarded by two kilted archers. Murphy nudged his companion. "More of those MPs. Okay, let's go in . . ."

"Hats off in the orderly room," a voice said in English.

"Bat puckey," Murphy muttered, but he took off his hat. He stared at the heavily bearded man who'd spoken. The man stared back, grim-faced. "Who—Warner? Larry Warner?"

"Sure is." Warner grinned broadly. "Here to welcome the geeks bearing gifts. How are you, Ben? Lafe? You're looking good. New beards and everything."

"Warner, for God's sake, we thought the locals took you off to sell you."

"They did. Sold me to Lord Rick."

"You look pretty rich," Reznick said. "For a slave."

"I'm no slave," Warner said. "Fact is, I've got the softest duty there is. Here, have a drink." He poured generous dollops into silver cups. "Go on, drink up."

"Yeah—" Murphy drank. "Holy Mother, Larry, what is that stuff?"

"Potent, eh? You bet your arse it's potent. That's McCleve's work. Can you imagine him doing without a still?"

"No. What's the old lush doing now?"

"He's Professor of Medicine at the University of Tran."

"The which at what?"

"Professor of Medicine. At the University. Of Tran."

"Tran's the name of the whole goddamn planet," Reznick protested.

"Right on," Warner said. "And now it's got a university. Come Murphy, surely you've been hearin' of the University?"

"Oh, crap," Reznick said.

"Yeah," Murphy agreed. "One of the best things about staying down south was not having to listen to your crazy accents—Hey, what are you doing?" Warner had gone to the door and was gesturing to the guards outside.

"Sending for the MPs," Warner said. "You man, get the Corporal of the Guard."

"What for, because we didn't like your stupid accent?"

"No, you'll see, it's nothing to worry about. A detail somebody forgot to attend to. Anyway, about the University. About half-teaching and half-research. McCleve teaches the acolytes of Yatar about sanitation and cleanliness. I teach math. Campbell does engineering. Even the Captain takes a stint at teaching. But mostly we've got teams of students and acolytes doing research. Soap. Substitutes for penicillin. Grinding microscope lenses. Figuring out how to make nitric acid. All kinds of stuff. And history, too."

"Professor," Murphy said. "We used to call you 'Professor' back in Africa."

"Now it's for real," Warner said.

"So just where do you fit in?" Reznick demanded.

"Think of me as a kind of warrant officer," Warner said. "That'll be close enough. Ah. Here're the guards. Corporal, these star lords have not had their weapons peace bonded."

"Yes, sir." The guardsman gestured, and two of his troopers used thick line to tie Murphy's sword into its scabbard. They finished with an elaborate knot. Then the corporal took out a thin copper dish of red wax. He melted the wax over the lamp on the orderly room table and sealed the knot with a flat lens-shaped stone. Then they began working on Reznick's weapon.

"What the hell's this for?" Reznick demanded.

"Orders," Warner said. "Here, have another drink, and I'll tell you things." He waited until the locals had finished their business and left. "Officially, this whole palace is under the king's peace," Warner said. "No challenges can be issued here. In fact, though, there's lots of nobles with the hereditary right to fight their enemies even on palace grounds. But they can't challenge one of you to immediate combat since you've got your weapons bonded." Warner shrugged. "Protects you and the locals both . . ."

"What about—" Murphy cut himself off.

"Pistols?" Warner asked. "You'll turn those in here and now. Uh— I got to search you, too."

"You and which army?" Murphy demanded.

Warner shrugged. "Thought you'd rather have me do it than Mason," he said. "But if you'd rather deal with Mason. Or Sergeant Major Elliot—"

"No way," Murphy said. "I'll sit still for it. Here." He took out a .45 Colt Mark IV automatic and laid it on the desk. "My combat knife too?"

"No, you keep that for your own protection. I expect you'll get your pistol back in a couple of days, too, after you've learned a little about life here." He eyed Reznick suspiciously. "Lafe, I expect you've got a hideout gun somewhere. Let me give you some good advice. Be damned careful whom you kill, self-defense or not. The clan system is really strong here. You kill one guy and you got a hundred relatives after your blood. Not to mention the Captain if you knocked off one of the people he needs." Warner wrote out a receipt for the firearm. "Now you, Lafe."

"Yeah, yeah," Reznick said. He laid his .45 on the table. "Okay, what now?"

"Now I take you to the party," Warner said. "And try to brief you on all the stuff that's going on. Not that you'll understand it. I don't understand it myself, and I've been around a year." He paused. "Why'd you come in, anyway?"

"Seemed like a good idea," Murphy said. "It's getting messy down south. Sea raiders. Big wagon trains coming north, lots of weapons and bringing their whole families and damned well going to find a place to live. Looks like things are *really* bad a thousand miles south of us. Famine, war, plague—you name it."

Warner nodded. "We'd heard some of it. 'The Time approaches, when the seas shall rise.' "

"They have, too," Reznick said. "About half of Rustengo's docks are awash, and the harbor area is salt swamp."

"It'll get worse," Warner promised. "Still, you guys had a good setup. Got titles and everything." He chuckled. "I don't remember Dirstval giving out city knighthoods to mercenaries."

Ben Murphy chuckled. "Yeah, but I like the ring of it. 'Benjamin Murphy do Dirstval' sounds better'n Private Murphy, CIA . . .'"

"So why'd you give up all that?"

"Did we? You told that MP we were 'star lords.' I heard you."

"Well, it's a little complicated," Warner said. "Far as the locals are concerned, you're important merchant traders from the south. That's near enough to noble, up here. But I'd act real respectful to Sergeant Major, was I you. And Art Mason's an officer now."

"Suits us," Reznick said. "We want to get along here."

Murphy nodded agreement. "Yeah. It's pretty bad down south, Larry. Damn all, it's getting worse, and nobody down there is going to watch our backs. We had each other, and Lafe's wives, and nothing." He stopped for a second, then went on. "Used to be, I had a wife. Nomads killed her. Lafe and I hunted the bastards for a ten-day. Hell with that. Anyway, one day the pistols will run dry. Or somebody'll catch us and torture us for our secrets. You heard the fables, about what they do to the Little People here?"

Warner nodded. "Grim fairy tales indeed."

"So when we heard Colonel Parsons had bought it, and the rest of the troops was doing all right and there wasn't even any war to fight—well, I figure Cap'n Galloway will take care of us. He always tried when we was back home."

✦ ✦ ✦

They stood on the balcony behind the musicians and looked down at the grand hall with its kaleidoscope of colors. The granite walls had been hung with tapestries and rich colors, but the place still had a fortresslike look to it. Nearly everything on Tran did.

The musicians seemed in good form. Someone had brought up

wineskins, and clay goblets were going around freely. Every few minutes someone raised a toast to the Infanta Isobel, and everyone had another drink. The music seemed mostly strings and drums, with little of the thin reedy wails that Murphy had become used to in the south. Most of the music was incomprehensible, but sometimes they struck up tunes Murphy recognized. "The Girl I left Behind Me," the drinking song from *Student Prince*, "Garry Owens". . .

Murphy estimated three hundred people were crammed into a hall built for half that many, and all were wearing their best clothes, which meant the most colorful.

"There's a hell of a lot of those MPs out there," Reznick said. "Who are they?"

"Well, technically they're guardsmen to Mac Clallan Muir," Warner said.

"Mac which?"

"Mac Clallan Muir. Look, Captain Galloway—there he is, recognize him?—Captain Galloway married the lady Tylara do Tamaerthon, widow and dowager countess—well the local title is Eqetassa, but that's pretty well countess—of Chelm. That made the Captain Eqeta. Lady Tylara's father is an old clan chief named Drumold. Tamaerthon has a goofy system of titles that *nobody* understands, but Mac Clallan Muir is Drumold's most important one. He made his son-in-law his war chief."

"War chief," Reznick said. "Of what?"

"In theory, of all of Tamaerthon," Warner said. "In practice, Captain Galloway's war leader of all the clans that'll take orders from Drumold. That's most of 'em, but not all. There. That's Drumold over there." He pointed to a man in bright kilts studded with silver pins. He wore a dozen gold bracelets, and several gaudy necklaces. Warner noticed Murphy's grin. "Yeah, I think so too, but you better never say nothin' he can hear. Old bastard'll split your liver in a second, and don't think the Captain would do much about it, either.

"Anyway, back to the MPs. As war chief of the clans, Captain Galloway was entitled to a bodyguard. What he did was have Art Mason recruit a whole mess of 'em, lots more than anybody expected, and use 'em for military police. Not just young nobles, either. Kids from different clans. Even clanless ones, and freed slaves—"

"So now the only clan they've got is Captain Galloway," Murphy said.

"Yeah. Exactly," Warner said. "Smart of you."

"Just like us," Reznick said. "But where do we fit in?"

"Sort of like a headquarters company," Warner said. "First thing is you'll probably be posted back to the University and told to write down everything you remember. *Everything*. Then there's the traveling schools. You'll learn about them. Main thing to remember is that Captain Galloway's *our* boss and we're all right if we don't forget it."

"But these MP types. Excuse me, but this is Drantos. Tamaerthon isn't even a part of this kingdom, is it?"

"No. But remember they're supposed to be Captain Galloway's bodyguards, and he's the host this ten-day. Outside the palace Art's MPs wouldn't have any jurisdiction 'cause we're not in Tamaerthon, but Lord Rick—that's what they call the captain here—theoretically put them under the command of the Lord Protector. That one."

He pointed to a big scar-faced man with a perpetual scowl. "So they're keeping order in the kingdom as well as in this palace," Warner finished.

"And Corporal Mason takes orders from that Protector guy?"

"Major Mason. Sure he does," Warner said. "Sure."

"Christ, this is worse than the south," Reznick muttered.

Warner laughed. "Just getting started, Lafe. See those two? There, and on the other side of the room—"

"Yeah?"

"Romans. The one on the right is ambassador of the Emperor Flaminius—"

"And the other one from Marselius," Murphy finished. "Yeah. We've got a lot to tell the Captain about that situation."

"Oh? Like what?"

Murphy looked thoughtful. "Larry, not that we don't trust you, but the only thing we got left to deal is information. How about I tell the Captain, and he tells you?"

Warner chuckled. "You're learning, Ben. You're learning. Shall we go downstairs and join the party? Your ladies and friends will be along in a minute. Try to stay sober, and for God's sake don't insult anybody."

3

Rick's head was bursting. Hangover remedies didn't work any better on Tran than on Earth. Not as well. There was precious little aspirin on Tran, and a lot more fusel oils in the liquor.

"Two hours and I'm for the Grand Council," Rick said. "Holy Yatar, my head is killing me—"

"You earned it," Tylara said. "I thought you had determined to drink all the wine in Edros."

Close to right, Rick thought. I don't do that too often, but last night—Oh, well. What's really irritating her is that I was too drunk to pay attention to her after the party. "You will come to Grand Council, of course."

"Of course," she said. "Shall I accompany you now?"

"I think no," Rick said. "I think I'll get more information if I talk to them in English."

"As you will."

"Dammit, I'm not keeping secrets from you." He went to put his hands on her shoulders, but she seemed to draw away from him. "All right. I'll see you in Council." He left the bedroom hoping that she would call him back, but she said nothing.

✢ ✢ ✢

He went downstairs to the stone chamber he'd had fitted out as a situation room, a copy of his offices in Tamaerthon. There were maps painted on three walls; the fourth was blank white, with charcoal nearby to write with. A big wooden slab table filled the room's center.

Benches surrounded it; benches weren't comfortable, and that made for short meetings. In contrast, Rick's chair at the head of the table had been specially carved for him, with padded seat and thick arm rests. If need be he could outsit those who argued with him in this room—

"Ten-shun!" Elliot commanded as Rick came in. The troopers around the table stamped to their feet. Murphy and Reznick seemed a bit surprised, but they didn't object. Rick said nothing until he had taken his place at the table's head and sat down. Then he nodded. "At ease," Elliot said.

"Thought we left that crap behind with Parsons," Murphy muttered.

"That'll do," Sergeant Major Elliot said sharply. He didn't like people who talked back to officers. Elliot's idea of perfection was an officer who knew his place commanding troopers who knew theirs. Of course the sergeant major was indispensable under any such scheme . . .

"Two reasons for this meeting," Rick said. "To find out what you know about the southern situation, and to bring you up to speed about the mission here. I'll start off."

Only where? he wondered. There's so damned much they don't know. So damned much *I* don't know. Humpty Dumpty told Alice to begin at the beginning and go through to the end. Then stop. But if I do that I'll be here all day.

"First, the basic mission hasn't changed," Rick said. "We're here to grow crops for the *Shalnuksis*, and if we don't grow their damned *surinomaz* they won't trade with us, meaning no more modern conveniences. So we've no choices there."

"Captain, are you sure those—those saucer things are coming back?" Murphy asked.

"Not entirely," Rick said. "But they told us they were, and they left communications gear. The pilot told Gwen Tremaine that the *surinomaz* crop was important, both to him and the *Shalnuksis*." And he left *her* a transceiver. Left her pregnant, too. So now she's got a year-old kid with no father within light-years.

"The trouble is," Rick said, "that *surinomaz* isn't easy to grow. The locals call it 'madweed' and they hate the stuff."

"Uh—"

"Yes, Warner?"

"Captain, just 'fore I left the University, we got reports about witch women and shamans who used madweed for a useful drug."

"We'll want to check that out. Bring it up in the Science Council meeting." Another meeting, after the Grand Council. All I do the whole day through is sit in meetings—"

"Yes, sir."

"Anyway. We need a lot of the stuff, and people don't want to grow it. Land's limited. With that rogue star coming close the growing seasons will be longer, and we can get more food out of each acre—but somebody's got to feed the people who grow madweed for us. For years. We'll want at least four years of bumper crops of the junk.

"So that's one problem. We need peace, only that rogue star is playing merry Hobb with the whole planet. I saw your reports, Murphy. Migrations. Wandering tribes in the south. I'm not surprised—fact is, it's going to get worse. What's the chances of holding off the migrations at the borders of the city-states?"

"Not much, sir," Murphy said. "If we could have done it, I would have, rather than come up here."

Rick nodded. It's like a ball of snakes, he thought. "What if I sent a big force? Twenty mercs and a couple of thousand local warriors?"

Murphy shrugged. "I don't think that would work very well," he said. "First thing, the city-states might not let your troops through without a fight. But even if you made some kind of alliance with them, there's not much for a defensible border down there."

"That was my impression," Rick said. He pointed to one of the maps on the wall. "But it also looks as if eventually there'll be impassable swamps to the south, after the Demon Star melts enough ice to get the seas up forty or fifty feet. Until then we'll just have to do the best we can. Now what do you hear of the Roman situation?"

"Stand-off," Murphy said. He turned to Reznick and got a nod of confirmation. "At first Marselius was winning. Had new tactics that I reckon he learned from you. But now old Flaminius has recruited some new legions and called out his reserves, and he's holding his own."

"Okay. I'll want all you know about that. Order of battle, force levels, anything you've got." Rick glanced at his watch. "You've got about an hour. Tell me."

✢ ✢ ✢

Drumold drew himself to his full height, resplendent in bright kilts and golden bracelets. There was no doubt that he spoke not as Rick's father-in-law, but as Mac Clallan Muir, Grand Chief of the Clans of Tamaerthon.

His words echoed through the council chamber. "Man, are ye altogether daft?"

Rick tried to smile. It wasn't easy. The echoing voice hurt his head. For a moment he wondered just how many wars had begun because some king or general had come hung over to an important council meeting. Tylara's father had his rituals, and this was one of them; but there were plenty in the Grand Council who didn't know Drumold. For that matter there were plenty who did, and who might make political capital out of even the appearance of a quarrel between Rick and Drumold. "No more so than yesterday, I think. And today I am better informed."

"Och, perhaps I spoke in haste," Drumold said.

Lord, do I sound that grim? Rick wondered. He looked to Tylara, but her look was no help this time. Often she could interpret the impact Rick was making; despite her youth she'd had a lot more experience leading these hotheaded people than Rick had, and she'd presided over her own Councils before Rick ever met her.

"Yet," Drumold was saying, "let us think clearly what we want, and how best to get it. So long as Marselius and Flaminius make war, they cannot send one legionary against us. Let them make peace—or let one side win—and where are we? Rome has long claimed the whole of Tamaerthon. Och, aye, there was a time when they claimed Drantos, indeed all this world of Tran. And will Marselius be such a friend and ally once he is undoubted Caesar and has no need of us?

"My Lord Rick, you propose to make an end to this war, even spend our blood and treasure to do it! I say you have not been well advised, and I understand it not."

There were loud murmurs, but no more than Rick had expected, given the number of people packed into the room: so many that the table, the largest in all of Drantos, could not hold them, so that many of the lesser mobility, as well as commoners, sat in chairs set in rows stretching all the way to the far wall.

The table itself held too many for a sensible meeting. The young Wanax Ganton, nominally in charge but delegating that to Rick; the

Lord Protector Camithon, scarred face glaring at anyone who opposed him or forgot the least courtesy due the king; three of the five great counts of Drantos, four counting Rick and Tylara. Like William-and-Mary, Rick thought. Rick-and-Tylara, a two-headed monster to rule Chelm. Some of the wealthier bheromen and knights. Guildmasters. All to represent the Kingdom of Drantos.

Then the priesthoods. Old Yanulf, splendid in blue robes, scowling because the Council bickered instead of getting on with preparations for the Time. Sigrim, high priest of Vothan One-eye, Chooser of the Slain, a warrior god everyone feared and few loved. Florali, the elderly lady—Rick though of her as a vestal virgin although she was a widow—to represent Hestia, the Good Goddess of grain.

The composition of the Council came from long tradition. Men had died contesting the right to sit in Council. Reducing its size was nearly impossible. King, lords, commons, and priestly orders together made up the Great Council of Drantos, an unwieldy structure at best; but there were lots more at today's meeting. Drantos was allied with Tamaerthon. Some of the Tamaerthan clansmen put it more bluntly. Tamaerthan warriors, led by Lord Rick, had only the year before saved Drantos from occupation by Sarakos, Heir Apparent of the Five Kingdoms, and despite the relative sizes of the two lands many clansmen thought Tamaerthon was and ought to be the senior partner. Certainly Tamaerthan chiefs and warriors must sit in the Grand Council. Consequently, one side of the table was filled by kilted hill tribesmen, scarcely thought more than barbarians by the great ones of Drantos—but they kept those thoughts to themselves.

Usually.

" 'Tis far to our interest to end these wars." The voice rose shrilly from Rick's left. Morron, father of the King's Companion and Eqeta of the south-central region of Drantos. "Our trade is ruined by this war," Morron said. "Each side takes its tolls, and all profit is lost to finance their wars. The sooner the issue is settled, the better for Drantos."

"Hah!" Drumold shouted. "So we have the truth of it. Tamaerthon is to be sold for the benefit of Drantos."

"Enough!" Rick shouted. He pounded the table again. "Enough, I say!" His hand went to his pistol. The babble ceased. Once, weeks before, Rick had fired a round into the ceiling as a means of shutting off debate. "Drumold, my old friend, you wrong me."

The old chieftain looked hurt, then thoughtful. "Aye," he said reluctantly. "I spoke in haste. Yet I cannot retract this much: it is not in our interest that the Romans make peace among themselves."

"Do not be so certain. True, while Roman fights Roman they cannot attack us—but they cannot defend themselves, either. Of the eleven legions in Rome before the civil war began, scarcely six remain in condition to fight."

"Och, and who will invade Rome?" This came from Dughuilas, Chief of Clan Calder. "Unless we do, divided as they are . . ."

"The High Rexja, for one," Tylara said.

Dughuilas and Drumold stared at her. Women did not speak at Council in Tamaerthon.

"He will want to avenge his son Sarakos," Tylara continued. "If we fight the Romans, the Five Kingdoms will be in Drantos within five ten-days. If we do not—will not Rexja Toris eye the Roman lands with greed? He has bheromen and knights, even sons of Wanaxxae who hoped for lands in Drantos. How shall they be rewarded, now that the Five hold no sway here?"

"Such a one as Sarakos deserves no revenge," Drumold muttered. Balquhain, his oldest son, pounded the table in agreement.

"Do you think you know that better than I?" Tylara demanded.

The room fell silent. Everyone had heard that Tylara had been tortured—some even whispered *raped*—by Sarakos, but no one expected her to mention it.

Rick took advantage of the silence. "We cannot fight Rome, for if we march east then Toris will lead the armies of the Five Kingdoms into Drantos."

"Then strike the Five," someone said. "Now, before they prepare."

"Leaving a divided Rome behind us?" Rick asked. "When we can't be certain of the friendship of *either* faction?"

"We have aided Marselius," Tylara said. "He sends us gifts."

"Aye. We sent him aid after we bested him in battle," Drumold said. "He is a proud man and his legionaries are prouder. They will not forget how the clans stood against them—and won."

"Another good reason for alliance," Rick said. "And how sure are you that Flaminius will not win while we flounder about in the north? It is certain enough that Flaminius bears nought but malice toward

Tamaerthon. Let Flaminius win, and we will be as grain between the upper and nether millstones."

And about now, Rick thought, is when someone's going to think of the master stroke of dissolving the alliance and letting Tamaerthon float off on its own. There, Dragomer is about to speak—

"This is madness." The voice thundered from immediately to Rick's left. Yanulf, Archpriest of Yatar, stood defiantly, his arms thrown out wide. "The Time approaches. And in the Time of Burning, then shall the seas smoke and the lands melt as wax. The waters of ocean shall lap the mountains. Woe to those who have not prepared. Woe to the unbelievers.

"And how have we prepared?" he demanded. "The starmen have come, exactly as prophecy foretold; they themselves tell us of The Time. We bicker among ourselves and make talk of petty wars, when the ice caves are empty of stores. I say it is time we fill the caves with grain and meat against the Time, and cease this talk of 'interests.' There are no interests more important than preparation for The Time."

"Well said," someone shouted. The guildsmen stamped their feet in approval.

"Well said indeed," Rick agreed. "And another thing is certain: as the Demon Star comes closer, the lands to the south will be hurt first. Their people will stream north looking for places of refuge. That has already begun. The city-states of the south can scarce defend themselves; they will not seek to halt these migrations."

"We can hold the borders to the south," Dughuilas said.

"Perhaps," Rick agreed. "But what of the southeast? What of the river valleys there?"

"Roman land," Drumold muttered. "Under Roman truce from time out of mind—"

"Roman until city-state mercenaries take it," Tylara said. "Aye, take it and open the roads for those coming from the south. They will want soon enough to have the wanderers leave their lands."

There was silence again while the council members studied the great map Rick had caused to be drawn on one wall of the chamber. The Drantos contingent saw it first. The river valley with its roads pointed like a dagger at the heart of Drantos—but it equally threatened the western border of Tamaerthon.

"It could be," Dragomer said. "The cities have produced good soldiers."

"Mercenaries," Dughuilas said. His voice was filled with scorn. "No match for the chivalry of Tamaerthon."

"They have been a match for better cavalry than yours," Dragomer said.

Not the wisest thing he could have said, Rick thought. Dughuilas was chief of a large clan, and led a powerful faction of the Tamaerthan upper classes; and Dragomer was one of the Drantos lords who'd invited city-states mercenaries into Drantos in their revolt against young Ganton's father.

"I remind you of the King's Peace," Camithon said. "Answer gently, Eqeta Dragomer."

"I need not answer at all," Dragomer said. "Were the cities to find one leader—"

"They have not done so in memory." A new voice. Corgarff, a subchief. "Nor do I fear they will do so now. Not so much as to send my sons to die in a Roman fight, to save lands for Rome. Unless—" He paused for a long moment, until he had everyone's attention. "Unless this Star Lord Gengrich, who leads the starmen lords in the south may yet come to lead all the cities? Perhaps the Lord Rick can tell us more of this man who once followed him."

I'll have his blood, Rick thought. I'll—

"Careful," Tylara said. She kept her voice low. "He is Dughuilas' man, and Dughuilas has good reason to wish you ill."

"That is not well said." Camithon was very much Lord Protector when he spoke. "The Lord Parsons rebelled against the lord Rick. The lord Gengrich deserted the cause of the lord Parsons, and by both our laws and the laws of the starmen remains in rebellion. How is the Lord Rick guilty of blood shed by rebels against his rule?"

But I am, Rick thought. *I brought them here, and I let them get away from me. And now they're like wolves among sheep.*

"They are rebels, but the Lord Rick has done little to capture them," Corgarff said. He didn't sound comfortable.

He's only following orders, Rick thought. Dughuilas' orders. *Fairly crude way to embarrass me.*

"He has done more than you," Yanulf said. "And by Yatar's blessing, the lord Rick prevailed against the lord Parsons." He glanced at Sigrim.

"And the next day Vothan One-eye was pleased to smile upon our armies.

"But enough of this. Our talk does nothing. My lords, the Demon Star rises even as we speak! The ice forms thick in the caves. Yatar sends us the means of life, but we must grasp them. We must make sacrifice. We *must*."

"Indeed," Rick said.

"The stories of previous Times are clear," Yanulf continued. "Those whose castles stand on bare rock will learn their folly, and seek the caves of Yatar. There will be wars enough then.

"And then shall the gods come from the skies to trade; and from that trade shall come good and evil. And fire shall fall from the skies, and men shall smoke and burn as faggots, and their sores shall not heal. The only safety is the caves of Yatar and his Preserver."

"How can we grow the grains we need while our young men stand in arms?" Camithon demanded.

"Let the Star Lords protect us," shouted a guildsman. "They have power. Let them use it."

"Aye, we hold great power," Rick said. "Enough to turn the tide of battle, once, twice, several times. But I think not enough for the troubles that come."

There was a long pause, as everyone considered what Rick had said. "If the starmen cannot defend us, and we cannot defend ourselves—" "March north." "No, march east." "Plant crops and trust to Yatar . . ." The babble rose in pitch.

"Your advice, Lord Rick?" Ganton spoke carefully and clearly, his boyish voice penetrating the noise. The room fell silent. "We would welcome your advice."

"Majesty, I would send an embassy to Marselius. A strong Rome has ever been important for the safety of Drantos. It is doubly important now. The Roman civil war must end, and Marselius owes us much already; while Flaminius owes us nought but hate.

"To see that Tamaerthon does not suffer from this, I say send Mac Clallan Muir himself as ambassador. Assisted by the Eqeta Morron and the Lady Gwen, and such others as I and the Lord Camithon shall agree to."

Camithon looked thoughtful, then turned to Drumold. "My lord. Will you seek truce between the Romans, and alliance?"

Drumold looked thoughtful. "Alliance with Rome. 'Tis a strange thought. Strange indeed. And yet—I will not oppose it. Aye. The Lord Rick is convincing. There is danger in a strong Rome, but there is more in a divided Rome during these times."

There were murmurs of approval.

It doesn't look like anyone saw it was a setup, Rick thought. Which is just as well. Machine politics, medieval style . . .

"Then let it be done," Camithon said.

"Go with the blessings of Yatar Skyfather," Yanulf said. "Go swiftly, before The Time comes on us and we all perish."

4

"How is your head?"

"Better," Rick said. "I wasn't sure you were speaking to me."

"You are my husband. How can I not speak to you?"

"Come off it," Rick said wearily. "What's wrong, anyway?"

"Nothing is wrong."

Sure. I can believe as much of that as I want. "I love you—"

"And I you."

"Do you?"

"Certainly." She seemed about to say something else, but instead she turned away. "The meeting begins soon, and I must see to Isobel. I will be there when you begin."

"Look, Gwen means nothing to me! But I have to see her. She's the only one who might know what the *Shalnuksis* are going to do. And she asked to see me alone. Don't you understand? We need her. The whole country needs her."

"Certainly I understand," Tylara said. "You told her that her child would have the stars."

"It was a way of speaking," Rick said. "Our children will have no less opportunity."

Her smile was wintry.

"For the stars, or here on Tran," Rick insisted. "You need have no jealousy of Gwen Tremaine!"

"I have none."

"You damned well don't act that way! And now you're angry, and I'm sorry."

"Have I reason to be angry?"

"Tylara, please. I don't need this," Rick said. "And I must speak to Gwen."

"I understand perfectly." She strode from the room.

Women, Rick thought. Is she determined to drive me away from her?

✢ ✢ ✢

He brooded all the way down the stone corridors to the guest suite. He paused at the door, then knocked.

"Enter."

Gwen Tremaine was standing at the window. Yellow light streamed through light brown hair, showed up green eyes. She was very short; "five-foot-two," the song said, and that was about right. She wore a spectacular blue gown, cut in a style more Parisian than anything fashionable on Tran. It was made of some kind of blue silk that shone in the evening sunlight. She continued to stare out into the gathering dusk as Rick came in.

"A penny for your thoughts," he said in English.

She laughed. "There aren't any pennies here. But I'll tell you anyway. I was trying to decide which made me sadder, that Earth is out there somewhere, or that my baby's father is there—"

"You do miss him, then?"

She shook her head slowly. "Rick, I don't know. Sometimes I want him so bad I could die. And sometimes I just want to kill him." She turned away from the window. "I was in love with him, you know. I could say I was kidnapped, but I wasn't. I got on that damned flying saucer of my own free will because the man I loved asked me to."

"And left you here when you got pregnant."

"Yes." She went over to the small table and sat down in one of the wooden chairs. "Wine? Yes, let's both have some."

"The real question is did Les mean it when he said he'd come back?"

"Yes. That's the real question." She drank the full glass of wine and poured another. "He said he'd come back—but Rick, have you ever thought that maybe he intended all along to dump me here? That he never did tell me the truth about anything? Sure, I got pregnant and wouldn't let his damn machine do an abortion, but maybe that was just a good excuse to get rid of me. Maybe he was tired of me anyway."

"You didn't think that last time we talked." Rick took the chair across from her and lifted his own wine glass. "Cheers."

"Cheers. No. Last time we talked I was sure he loved me. Next time maybe I will be, too. But just now—just now I'm not sure."

"Okay. But he did give you the transceiver. And he told you about the rebellion among the human troops of the Confederation—"

"It's not a rebellion," Gwen said. "More a—a dissent. And—Rick, have you told anyone about this? Anyone at all?"

"No."

"Not even Tylara?"

"Not even Tylara. I won't tell any locals. Or any of the troops, either. Not unless I have to—if you and I are both killed, someone here has to know. Warner, maybe."

"Yes, I've thought of that too. But don't tell him yet."

"I won't. Next subject. You know more than me about what the *Shalnuksis* will do. Had any more thoughts?"

"Some. Over there—that wooden chest. It has maps, areas I think might be best for raising *surinomaz*. One good area would be along the western border of the Roman Empire."

"Which we don't own. Oh—have you heard about the Council this morning? I'd like you to be on the delegation to Rome."

She nodded. "Another journey. More time away from my son."

"Take him with you—"

"Into a civil war? Don't be silly. But you're right, I have to go. I can inspect the potential cropland on the way. Meanwhile, we want to begin growing madweed on our side of the border. We won't get a full crop this year, but we ought to start experimental plots now. Get some experience with the stuff. It's tricky, Rick. The ecology is all bound up with some little mammals that are something like rats. They swarm into the fields and die, and when they rot they fertilize the plants. They also stink to the throne of God."

"Not to mention necrotic products—"

She nodded agreement. "I'd think those fields get pretty unhealthy. Which is one reason the peasants don't want to grow madweed. You've got your work cut out to make them do it."

"Convicts. Criminals—"

"I suppose. And when you're done with them, when the madweed fields have killed most of them, the *Shalnuksis* will finish the job for you."

"When?"

She shrugged. "I don't know. Certainly they'll want to trade with us as long as we have *surinomaz*, but after that—you have as much evidence as I do. I think they'll try to find out which is our center of culture, and destroy it."

Rick nodded thoughtfully. Certainly there was plenty of evidence. Every six hundred years, when *surinomaz* grew well under the influence of the Demon Star, the *Shalnuksis* came to Tran with a fresh crop of Earth mercenaries. Roman legionaries, Celtish warriors, Franks. And every time, when the aliens had got all they wanted, they tried to exterminate their agents. The legends told over and over of *skyfire*, and everyone knew where there were fields of glass . . .

"So we'll want to be sure we don't build anything modern-looking."

"That may not be good enough. Rick, there were Tran languages in the computer on Les' ship. They talk to locals. They'll ask questions, and I think our University will be the first target."

"I thought of that too," Rick agreed. "Which is why I'm not putting much into brick and mortar. By the time your boyfriend starts dropping atom bombs on us, all the important people will be long gone to the caves. Meanwhile the traveling teams go teaching science to every villager in Drantos. And—Gwen, this is all crazy! A galactic civil war over Earth—"

"I told you, it's not a civil war. Just a disagreement among the leaders of the Confederate Council," Gwen said. "And I think it's crazy too, but—" She pointed out the window.

"Yeah." Crazy or not, they are here, on Tran. It wasn't Earth. Given that one undoubted fact, what couldn't they believe? "Look, your friend Les is the best chance we'll ever have for getting off this planet. And he told you he'd come for you—"

"If he could. Yes."

"And you believe him."

"I remember I did when he told me," she said. "I don't know about now. What difference does it make? He *is* our only chance."

"And what about the rest of us?"

"Rick, I don't know."

"Yeah." But it wasn't likely that Les would give a damn about the mercenaries. He might care for Gwen and their child. That might even be likely. But there was no reason at all for him to worry about a bunch of mercs. "Gwen, why did you want to see me alone?"

"Your wife doesn't like me. I don't much care for her, either."

"She's jealous. She thinks I'm your baby's father. Or that I could have been, anyway. Your wanting to see me alone didn't help the situation."

"It didn't hurt it, either."

"No, I expect you're right. Not much would."

"And I just wanted the chance to speak English and talk without having to worry about what I say. Rick, it gets pretty bad up there in Tamaerthon. Always on guard so that I don't give away something—"

"And you're not on guard with me. You're not keeping any more secrets?"

"No, of course not."

You sure as hell did, Rick thought. For damned near too long. So how can I trust you now? "So. How are things at the University? Any trouble?"

"No. And of course I have the pistol you gave me—"

Another point of contention with Tylara. She thought she should have had André Parsons' .45 Colt. But Tylara had plenty of experience protecting herself on Tran, and Gwen had none—

"Do you like my dress?" she asked.

"Yes. I was just admiring it."

"It's called *garta* cloth. Larry Warner got it. Rick, it's a *very* close weave."

"So?"

"So we could make a hot-air balloon from it."

"You're kidding. Hot damn, of course! Observation balloons! They used them in the Civil War, and the Franco-Prussian War, and—can you really sew the seams tight enough?"

"Yes. We've tested a small model, and Larry made glue from horses' hooves. It will really work. The only problem is the cloth. It comes from the south. We don't have enough, because the trade routes are in a mess. It's very expensive—"

"Sure looks it. Warner got that lot?"

She nodded.

"And gave some to you?"

"He had the dress made for me," Gwen said.

"Why?"

"None of your business-"

"The devil it's not," Rick said.

"Captain Galloway, I have not asked you to be my protector. I don't ask now."

"Sure, Gwen. I thought Caradoc was sweet on you."

"He likes me—"

"Seems to me you encouraged him, back when you were pregnant."

"I might have—"

"And now Warner. Gwen, I need both of them. You play them off against each other, and you'll get one killed sure as hell!"

"No, that won't happen."

And there's not a lot I can do anyway. Keep them apart? Nonsense. Warner and Gwen are needed at the University, and Caradoc goes there to see her whenever he gets the chance, and how do I stop him?

"There's more news," she said.

"All right. What?"

"I know of a village where they make drugs out of *surinomaz*."

"Somebody else mentioned that. Warner?"

"Probably. Anyway, there is such a place. One of the traveling medicine-show teams came in with the news."

"Which one?"

"Doesn't matter. The merc with the outfit was Beazeley, but it was an acolyte, Salanos, who had wits enough to come tell me."

"That could be important. If there's some local use for the stuff it might be easier to get people to grow it."

"Yes. I'll check that out, shall I?"

"Please. And the balloon—that's a great idea. It could be decisive in the Roman civil war. Observation of the enemy, command and control of our own forces, artillery spotting—Gwen, it could really be the winning factor."

"Thank you."

"You don't look too happy—"

"Should I be? More battles—"

"They'll be fought anyway," Rick said. "And people will starve no matter what we do, too. But at least we can save some of them, this time, and we can get civilization spread so far across this planet that the *Shalnuksis* and their goddam *skyfire* can't root it out—"

"We can try," Gwen said.

5

Tylara stared at the roughly whitewashed door of the farmhouse. The one-eyed image of Vothan stared back. She waited until she heard a faint click and saw movement behind the one eye.

"Who seeks entry to the house of the Wolf?" a voice demanded.

"Tylara do Tamaerthon, Eqetassa of Chelm."

"Enter, Lady," said a rough voice, followed by the sound of a lock turning.

Tylara stepped into the house, stamped the mud off her riding boots, then glared at the man who'd let her in. "What are your orders about tending the door, Bartolf?"

The man turned the color of a winter sunset. He swallowed. "To recognize all who come, and let them enter with hands open and empty."

"Did you ask me to open my hands?"

"No, but—"

"But *nothing*. I might have been a spy disguised as the Lady Tylara. If I had been—" Her right hand darted into the full left sleeve of her riding tunic. Then she raised it. As the sleeve fell back, it exposed her husband's Gerber Mark II combat knife. She'd borrowed it for just this sort of demonstration.

"You'd have been dead from that mistake, Bartolf."

"Perhaps, Lady Tylara," he said. "But an enemy in your place wouldn't have lived enough longer to do hurt or learn much." He raised his voice. "Bennok! The berries are ripe."

The tapestry on the opposite wall of the antechamber rippled, then rose as a dark-haired, pimple-faced youth slipped through a waist-high opening it had concealed. He held a small crossbow, the sort noblewomen used for shooting birds and rabbits. Not enough, thought Tylara, then saw that the thin point of the quarrel was barbed and glistening with something green and sticky.

"Poison?" she asked. "And the point has been made small enough to enter ringmail."

Bartolf nodded. "That was Monira's idea. The rest was all his." He reached down to tousle the boy's hair. The boy carefully sidestepped out of reach.

"That was a very good idea, Bennok," said Tylara. "Are there others who keep watch?"

"Oh yes, Lady. With the poison on the quarrel, any of us can do the work. So we all take turns."

"Very good." She reached into her purse and pulled out a silver piece. "This is for your good work."

Bennok didn't reach for the silver. "Will there be one for all the others, Lady? I can't take it unless there is."

Tylara tried not to sound as confused as she felt. "I think there will be silver for all of you."

"Oh thank you, Lady. Now maybe we can buy those longbows ourselves if Bartolf goes on saying he won't give them to us." He darted back under the tapestry and vanished.

Bartolf was red-faced again. "I'm sorry, Lady Tylara. I should have told you. They've all eleven of them sworn an oath to be as brothers and sisters and have all their wealth in common. The only things they'll call their own are weapons and clothing."

"And Monira was the leader in this, I'll wager?" said Tylara, smiling to show that she wasn't offended.

Bartolf returned her smile uncertainly. "She spoke for them all when they told us. I don't know if that was her idea, though."

"And you don't think you ever will?"

"No. They are good at keeping even the secrets we don't want them to keep."

Someday that might make trouble. Now it proved to Tylara that her idea was succeeding beyond anything she'd expected.

Thoughts sometimes took on a life of their own. This one was born in bitter sleeplessness during the early days of pregnancy. She lay awake, unable to sleep, unable to stop torturing herself with restless thoughts—

She was certain that Rick had not fathered Gwen's child, but her mind would not let go of the matter. Let her think of stars and star weapons, and it would end with that question. That night it began simply enough, when Rick musingly told her that the starfolk would come and it might be useful to capture one of their ships.

Tylara could scarcely conceive of a starship. She never expected to see one. Yet certainly something had brought Rick and the others to Tran. All the priesthoods agreed that mankind had not been created here. If humanity came from another world, then there must be ships to travel between the worlds.

And Rick wanted one. He wanted one badly.

If he had a ship, would he leave her?

Or would he first teach everyone on Tran the secrets of star weapons and starships, as he said he would do? It scarcely mattered. There was no way to capture a starship. Rick had laughed at his own idea. His star weapons would be useless.

And Tylara lay pondering stars and starships and weapons and children—There were no dangerous weapons. Only dangerous men— and women, and children. If the starmen were all like Rick, reluctant to kill, sentimental, fastidious to the point of squeamishness . . .

How *would* you take a ship of the sky-folk? You would certainly need to surprise them, so they would not be able to use their fire weapons.

But suppose, suppose half a dozen children could get aboard such a ship. Not ordinary children. Children well trained, dedicated, fanatic followers devoted to service . . . Then at a signal they pulled out knives and fell on the crew. That would be surprise indeed. No one thinks that an eight-year-old girl can be dangerous, unless she is a trained warrior, and maybe not even then. The *Shalnuksis*, according to both Rick and Gwen, would not be sending trained warriors. They would send merchants, easily surprised and once surprised easily killed.

But you would need to have the children trained and ready long before the skyfolk came. And they would have to be kept a secret from *everyone* until then. There were those on Tran who might warn the skyfolk if they could. Lady Gwen could be one of those. And Rick surely would not approve of this. Why should he know?

So began the Houses of the Children of Vothan, for boys and girls up to the age of ten who'd been orphaned in the wars. There were plenty of those, enough to fill many more than the seven Houses everyone knew about.

In those seven Houses orphans were fed, clothed, sheltered, and taught trades. Some learned to be midwives, seamstresses, carpenters, shepherds, smiths. Some learned new skills, such as the wire-making or distilling. In one House the boys were destined to become acolytes of Yatar, the girls to serve the hearth goddess Hestia. There was a House near Rick's precious University.

And there was an eighth House. Six boys and five girls, from six to nine, picked for quick wits, strong muscles, and keen eyes and ears, brought here to learn one thing and one thing only—how to kill. Some of them had good reasons to learn, others just had talent. All had been doing well at their lessons, the last time she visited them, six ten-days before her confinement.

Bartolf led her through the door from the antechamber into the main room of the house. As she stepped into the room she heard a thump, a squeal like a piglet's, and the rasp of a knife blade.

"Aiiii, lass!" shouted a wheezing male voice. "Have ye learned nothing about holding a knife? That one—it'ud stick between his ribs, even the rope round his neck canna save ye then! Fast in, faster out, that's the way it must be."

Tylara stepped out into the room. In one corner a man-sized dummy lay on the floor. One boy lay under its head and upper body, gripping a rope drawn tightly around its neck. On top of it lay the girl Monira, her knife thrust up to the hilt in its chest. As Tylara approached, Monira sprang up, bowed quickly, then helped her companion crawl out from under the dummy.

"Are you hurt, Haddo?"

"No, Monira. Only my breath knocked out." He also bowed to Tylara, then walked off with Monira as if both Tylara and their teachers had become invisible.

"My regrets, Lady," said the teacher with a shrug. "Sometimes she gets taken so that she forgets everything. Mostly, though, she's a joy to watch. Ah, if I'd had a girl like her when I—" He broke off abruptly as he remembered to whom he was talking.

The teacher's name was Chai, and he had reason to be cautious in talking about his past. He was a former thief who'd taken advantage of the wars to practice his skills, and in due time came before the Eqetassa's justice. Unlike most common thieves, he had real skills. He could even read and write. And he'd once been a priest of Yatar. A spoiled priest, but admitted to the mysteries . . .

That was the morning that Tylara decided to establish the Houses; and Chai, his name and appearance changed, became one of the Masters . . .

Tylara watched Monira and Haddo sit down cross-legged in a corner and wipe each other's faces with damp clothes. Monira was beginning to have a woman's body, but she would never be beautiful even with her thick fair hair. A troop of Sarakos' cavalry had taken care of that. At least nothing showed when she was dressed, except her broken nose and the scars on her chin and one ear.

Tylara had been through a similar ordeal, at Sarakos' own hands, and she also would bear scars both inside and out for the rest of her life. Compared with what Monira had survived, though, Tylara knew her own experience was a child's game. No great wonder that Monira sometimes saw one of those men instead of the training dummy.

In another corner of the room stood the third teacher, Rathiemay, wearing knight's armor. He was showing three of the Children how to attack an armored man.

"—get him to bow his head, if he's wearing a helmet like this. That will leave a patch exposed at the back of the neck. Yes, that's it," he added, as one of the Children prodded it with a blunted dagger. "A good hard thrust right there. If he's not dead at once he's easy to finish off." He saw Tylara and straightened up. "Good day, my lady."

"Good day, Lord Rathiemay. How are they doing?"

"No one could wish for better pupils, my lady. They seem to have been born with steel in their hands." His face was bright with his smile, reminding Tylara oddly of her husband's expression when he spoke of the University or some other great scheme for bringing hope and life to Tran. She remembered how he'd looked the first time she came, sour and grumbling over being a knight sent to teach commoner children how to strike down his brothers in arms. To be sure, he was grateful that the Eqetassa had given him this chance to restore his fortunes, but still . . . Now he looked almost like a father teaching the children of his own body the family trade.

"Where are the other Children?"

"Out in the woods, learning tree-climbing," said Chai.

"Without a teacher?"

"Na, na, Lady. They're learning from Alanis. His father was a woodsman, there's no sort of tree he can't climb. It's a mizzling grey sort of day, so no one's likely to be seeing them."

Tylara pulled eleven silver coins out of her purse and handed them to Bartolf. "For the Children. I hear they want some new bows."

"Aye, but they've also spoken about some sandfish buskins for the tree-climbing. We'll have to let them decide."

"You let *them*—choose what they'll buy?"

"Oh, not everything, Lady. Only the things likely to be life or death for them. Why not? Does a carpenter let a butcher choose his mallets for him?"

Tylara thanked the man, drew the hood of her cloak over her head, and was outside in the rain without remembering quite how she got there. What had she done? The Children of Vothan were no weapon to lie quietly in a scabbard until she choose to draw it. They were a sword with a life and a will of its own, which might choose its own moment to be drawn and drink blood.

Whose?

A dangerous experiment. Was it best ended now, while she had control? Or—

Or might there be uses for this weapon? Used well, used now, before the skyfolk came . . .

Tylara grew more hopeful as she walked back to her horse. By the time she was in the saddle and returning to where she'd left her escort, she knew the Children of Vothan would not be a weapon only for a single battle. The skyfolk were not the only enemies to her and her house.

PART TWO
IF THIS BE TREASON . . .

6

Corgarff knew that he was out of favor with Dughuilas when his clan chief did not invite him to sit or offer him a drink. He stood in front of the table facing Dughuilas and another man he didn't know, until he felt like a small boy waiting to be whipped by his father. The only light in the cellar came from two candles on the table, throwing strange twisted shadows on the cobweb-shrouded brick of the walls.

"That was not well done, what you said at the Grand Council," said Dughuilas.

"I thought it the best thing to say at the time. And indeed, is it not possible that the Lord of Chelm thinks too much of his countrymen still?"

"Whether he does or not is no concern of yours," said Dughuilas. "You thought poorly, and spoke worse. If you wish to sit longer on the Council with me, you will need to think better or speak less."

"I will do neither unless I know why you are so tender toward the Lord Rick so suddenly," said Corgarff. "Was it not he who spoke harshly to you and did all but smite you with the open hand the day we fought the Romans? Was it not he who made fighting men out of plowboys and swineherds? Is it not he—?"

"He has done all this and more," said the second man. He wore a hooded cloak, and kept the hood drawn over his head so that his face stayed shadowed.

But his accent was not that of the Tamaerthan upper classes. Nor yet that of the Drantos nobility. Who, then? Corgarff thought it would be dangerous to ask—and probably death to know.

"And speak more softly," the man continued. "We cannot trust the tavernkeeper if he thinks he has anything worth selling." Dughuilas put a hand on his dagger but the other shook his head. "In time, perhaps, but not now on the mere chance that he might have heard something useful. If we kill too many rats, the wolves will escape."

"If the Lord Rick is a wolf, what harm to oppose him in Council?" Corgarff demanded. "And he will send our sons to die in Roman wars for Roman causes. Rome, whose slavemasters have tormented us these centuries—"

Dughuilas held up his hands to gesture for silence. "Spare me. I can make the speech better than you."

"The Lord Rick will be strong as long as he and the Lady Tylara keep their wits," said the second man. "We can do nothing to change this. Indeed, we should not. Your friend who thinks so well of the Lady Tylara would not have any injury done to her or her blood. Without your friend, much we hope can not be done."

"You should not have said that," said Dughuilas sourly. "You have given this rattle-jaw knowledge I had not intended he should have."

"If you have plans for Corgarff which you are not telling, expect little from me," said the second man. His voice was so even it was impossible to tell if he was angry or not. "I think you need my friendship as much as we both need—our friend's."

Who could he be, that he could speak to the chieftain in that manner? But if he was not angry, Corgarff was. He almost forgot to lower his voice. "Lord Dughuilas, I have perhaps spoken unwisely. Yet you speak as though I were a traitor. Were you not my sworn chief, I would have your blood for this."

"I did not wish to call you traitor, for indeed you are no such," said Dughuilas smoothly. "Forgive me those words, and I will forgive you for yours."

Corgarff took his hand from the knife hilt.

"Sit. Sit and join us." Dughuilas poured wine and lifted his own glass in salute. "Drink, clansman."

"Aye. Thank you, my chieftain." Two mysteries here. This man, this conspirator; and beyond him a mysterious ally. Hah! thought Corgarff. That one I can guess. Probably the Lady Tylara's brother, Balquhain. A hothead, the darling of old Drumold's age, bound to become Mac Clallan Muir in time . . . Certainly no other noble of Tamaerthon was as likely to wish to uphold the old rights of the warriors without injuring the Lady Tylara.

"The Lord Rick has brought victories," Dughuilas' companion said. "Victory over Rome—"

"A mockery," Dughuilas said. "What matters victory at the price of all we hold dear? Lord Rick makes knights of crofters and peasants. They obey their chiefs not at all."

"It will become worse," the second man said. "It is this 'University' that spawns your troubles. It is from there that these dangerous ideas come. This place is important to Lord Rick. Harm that, and he will know of the anger of the knights."

"If we wish to injure the University, I can give some aid," said Corgarff. "A smith's boy from my land works there. I have heard that his father has not long to live, and he fears his mother and sister will want. Only a little gold could buy him, I think."

"Is he fit for any work we might give him?"

"As fit as anyone of such blood can be."

"The Lord Rick would not have said that," said the second man.

"Hang the Lord Rick!" snarled Dughuilas.

"As Yatar wills," said the second man quietly. "But I think he is more likely to hang us, if we cannot use whatever tools come our way."

Dughuilas nodded sourly. "Och, aye. But a man of the old blood must keep watch on this peasant lad. You, Corgarff."

"Aye, Chieftain." He paused a moment. "Perhaps there is a way. One hears that the University prepares a new machine. They say it will fly through the air! That men may fly as gulls!"

"Och!" Dughuilas stared in wonder. "Can this be true? Then woe to our enemies, when warriors can fly—"

"And when they do, your order is finished. What need of knights then?" Dughuilas' companion asked.

"Och. Aye, it is so," Dughuilas said. "The Lord Rick will raise up peasants, while the men of blood fall. This must not be."

Corgarff nodded grimly. "I had not thought—but it is true enough. Already the University is guarded by the sons of crofters. Even freedmen. Freedmen with arms! But hear. In the past, when a new machine is prepared, the University is open to all who wish to come and watch. The Lord Rick does not seem to care who learns his secrets."

"He is a fool," said Dughuilas.

"One wonders," said the second man. "Perhaps he plays a game too deep for our understanding. Surely we *would* be fools if we did not reckon on that."

"Fools we are not," Dughuilas said. "And our cause is just. Lord Rick would destroy all we ever lived for. It is our right to oppose him. Let us destroy this University, and all its arts, forever and aye. Swear it!"

The three stood. "We swear," they said in unison. Then they raised their glasses, drained them, and dashed them to the floor.

⁜ ⁜ ⁜

The University was located in a town at the northwestern border of Tamaerthon. The place had been noted for its medicinal springs, and had long boasted a small temple of Yatar where acolytes came for training; a natural place for a center of learning, but open and vulnerable.

Rick had the town's defenses repaired, and now a proper city wall was under construction. There were also a mortar and a light machine gun. It wasn't likely that the University would fall to an enemy.

Larry Warner locked the armory door and returned the salutes of the archers who stood outside it. He was going to his quarters when he heard a call for the proctor on duty. Warner immediately changed his plans and headed for the gate area. He arrived to see a small caravan ride up.

"Who comes?" a local guardsman called.

"Sergeant Major Elliot."

Holy shit, that's who it was all right. With a pretty big crew, too. Damn, Warner thought. With Gwen Tremaine gone off on embassy duty, Warner had been senior man present. He rather liked being in charge. Now here was Elliot. Crap.

"Let the Sergeant Major in," Warner commanded. Maybe I ought to keep him out—that's too silly to think about. What do I do, set up as some kind of king here? Stupid. "And ask him to join me in my quarters after he has been shown to the Visiting Officers' Quarters."

⁜ ⁜ ⁜

"Ho, Sarge, what brings you here?"

"Cap'n sent me down south," Elliot said. "Buyin' some of that *garta* cloth you like. Brought you a whole mess of it."

"Hey. That's all right." Rick Galloway had been pleased with the balloon idea when Warner described it back at Castle Edron. The problem had been the cloth, which could only come from the south, and Warner had been afraid he would be sent there to buy some. Instead, Rick sent Warner and the two new troopers back to the University, where for two ten-days Warner had enjoyed being in charge . . ."Have to get to work on the balloon, then."

Elliot nodded in agreement. "I brought orders on that. Cap'n wants a test model in a ten-day."

"Can't do it."

"You can try!"

"Sarge, I'll do my goddamn best, but nobody is going to sew up that thing in a ten-day! You got any idea how *big* that sucker is?"

"No—"

"It's *big*. Take that from me. Uh—Sarge, why are you here?"

"Captain's orders. I'm the new Provost for the University."

"You?"

"Yeah. Show you the written orders tomorrow."

"Shit. And where do I fit in?"

"Hell, Professor, I treat you like a civilian. You're my boss—so long as it's not a military situation. Comes a military situation, you're back in uniform. Like a weekend warrior. It's all in the orders."

"Oh." That's not bad. Not bad at all. Makes good sense. Elliot was Parsons' man. Killed a lot of Drantos soldiers while he was working for Parsons. Must be a ton of nobles who'd like to even the score for their relatives. Blood-feuds and all that. Makes sense to get Sergeant Major Elliot out of Drantos, and God knows the University's important enough.

"I'm also supposed to help you with the bookkeeping," Elliot said. "For the travellin' medicine shows." He frowned heavily. "Do those things do any good, Professor?"

"Sure. Look, we send out a merc and couple of local warriors and some junior priests of Yatar. They go out and make maps and get a resource survey. That's worth it all alone—Sarge, the maps here are really something else! Most of 'em have their own country bigger'n the Roman Empire, for crissake!

"But there's more to it. They go to the towns and teach hygiene. Germ theory of disease. Antiseptic practices."

"Does it work?"

"Yeah, sometimes," Warner said. "And sometimes not, I guess. Sometimes we get the old 'what was good enough for Granny' routine—"

"So you convert Granny," Elliot said.

"Right-o. Or we try to." He drank another glass of wine. "Sarge, I had a thought. The captain likes you around him. Is he going to base his Roman expedition out of here?"

"He may have to."

"Crap."

"You don't like that?"

"Don't like this place mixed up with war," Warner said. "Yeah, I know how that sounds, coming from me, but it's true."

"Funny, I agree with you," Elliot said. "More to the point, I think the captain does too. But what else has he got? Anyplace else is controlled by the local lords—Larry, why do the lords hate Captain Galloway so much?"

"I would too," Warner said. "Lord Rick comes in and makes his pikemen and archers more effective than the knights, pretty soon the troops are going to wonder what it is the heavy cavalrymen do that makes them so important. It's a good question, too."

"How bad is it?"

"Bad enough that Captain Galloway had better wear armor any time he's got Tamaerthan lords around," Warner said. "Bad enough that you and I ought to keep lookin' over our shoulders, too."

"Yeah. All right, I'll do just that. Hey, have you got a drink? It's hot work, riding up those hill paths."

"Sure." Warner clapped his hands and a girl about eighteen years old came in. "Sara. Cold beer, please. Thank you—"

"She's a looker."

"Want to borrow her?"

"Hooker?"

"Naw, slave," Warner said. "Yeah, I know, the captain doesn't approve of slavery. I liberated her, Sarge, but she won't leave. Where would she go? One day a freedman will marry her, I expect, but meanwhile she works here and she likes working for starmen—"

"Well, Larry, I don't have anybody to clean up for me—"

"I'll send her over to help until you get something permanent set up. One thing, be polite to her. I always am—ah. Thank you, Sara."

She set down two large tankards and curtsied. They drank. "Good beer," Elliot said. "Soft duty up here."

"You wouldn't say that if you'd seen me today," Warner said. "Working on fuels for the balloon. Hot air's all right, but I think I can figure a way to make hydrogen for the next one. If I can make a good sizing for the cloth to seal it so it'll hold hydrogen."

"Hydrogen. What's the matter, Professor, afraid you'll run out of hot air after the first one?"

"Ho-ho. Anyway, now that the cloth's here I can really get to work. Have any trouble?"

"I don't ever have trouble, Professor."

"Yeah." Actually, Warner thought, that must have been a hell of an expedition. Mercs, locals, Tamaerthan archers, pack animals for the trade goods, more pack animals for the fodder—taking a zoo like that over muddy roads and through the hills couldn't have been much of a picnic.

"Usual market for this stuff is Rome," Elliot said. "So we got it at a good price."

"Where? Rustengo?"

"Found a whole warehouse full about a hundred klicks north of there. With the roads to Rome closed off they were grateful for the chance to sell."

"Hmm. And the Romans really like the stuff—"

"That's what I hear."

"Maybe a good bargaining point for Miss Gwen. I think we'll send a messenger tomorrow to tell her."

"All right by me. I got a few other items of interest."

"Good. Seriously, did you run into any trouble?"

Elliot grinned. "Nothing I can't handle, Professor. Some bandits in the hills outside Viys. About two hundred."

"That's damned near an army, around here."

"We unlimbered the H&Ks," Elliot said. "No sweat." He seemed pleased at the memory. "Didn't have to use too many rounds, either. After that, nobody wanted to give us any gas. Word spread pretty fast."

"Yeah. No sign of Gengrich?"

"No. He could have been trouble."

Larry Warner nodded. "I hear he's set up as a pirate king. One of these days we may have to deal with him. More beer?"

"Sure. And don't forget to tell that girl I want to borrow her. You're right about Gengrich, they're scared of him down there. But they're scared of everything. The whole south's talking about the Roman situation. Half of 'em want the Romans to keep on fighting each other. Long as that war goes, the Roman frontier posts aren't manned, and the southerners have a place to send the refugees that keep streaming in.

"Then there's the others, who mutter about the lost trade, and how things are going to hell. And all the priests of Yatar are out soapboxin' about The Time, and how they better store up food against the years of famine—"

"They're right there," Warner said. "One reason for this University. We're as much an agricultural research station as anything else. And there's our traveling road shows—"

"Right. Captain said I was to help you get those organized." Elliot stretched elaborately. "Larry, things look pretty good, considerin' where the Cubans had us."

"Sure," Warner said.

"Relax. Captain Galloway knows what he's doing."

"I hope so," Warner said. "Damn, I hope so."

⁜ ⁜ ⁜

Rick put down the report from Sergeant Elliot and nodded in satisfaction. Tylara came and took it from the table. She puzzled over each word.

"I'll read it to you if you like," Rick said.

"I'll ask you to do so. Later," she said. She went on reading.

"Your English is getting very good," Rick said. "I'm proud of you."

"Thank you." She went on poring over the parchment, her finger resting at each word. Finally she looked up. "You have promised mediation in the Roman Wars," she said. "You had Elliot make that promise in our names."

"Yes."

"You did not consult me about this, yet the promise is as Eqeta of Chelm—"

"Dammit, I don't have to consult you! I am the Eqeta of Chelm!"

"So much for your fine promises," she said. "We rule as equals. But you are perhaps more equal than I."

"I am also Captain-General of Drantos, War Chief of Tamaerthon, and Colonel of Mercenaries," Rick said. "Posts I had *before* I married you. Do you tell me everything you do?"

"The important things. Must we quarrel?"

"That's what I was going to ask."

"Then let us not. I was going to say that I approve of your stratagem in the south. It brought us the cloth at a lower price, and there is no way for them to know if you keep the promise. Soon no one on Tran will be teaching you anything about bargaining."

In spite of Tylara's heart-stopping smile, Rick wasn't entirely sure those words were a compliment. He frowned. "I intend to keep the promise and try to negotiate a peace, if we can't give Marselius a victory."

She stared at him. "That is impossible. How can there be peace in Rome after three seasons of war?"

"Not easily, I admit," said Rick. "But if Marselius issues the proclamation I'm about to suggest, the chances will be better. He should announce that he will punish no man for any act done in obedience to a proclaimed Caesar. I've already proposed to the ambassador that Flaminius do the same. A mutual pardon for everything done during the war." They did that during the Wars of the Roses, when the English Parliament formally legislated that no man could commit treason by obeying a crowned king. If they hadn't, there wouldn't have been a Yorkist or Lancastrian left.

"Marselius might agree. He might even keep such an agreement. Not Flaminius. The man is a fool. Otherwise he wouldn't have pushed Marselius into rebellion at all."

"Perhaps Flaminius wouldn't agree, by himself. But can he go against all of his commanders? They're losing soldiers, sons, estates. Some of them must be wiser than he is about what needs to be done to prepare for The Time. If they no longer need fear for their lives, who knows what advice they might give? I don't."

"It is still a pardon for treason. Do we want anyone to make the lot of the rebel so much easier?"

"There are different kinds of rebels, it seems to me. Marselius with his legions is not the same as a mountain bandit with a dozen ragged followers."

"Not in your eyes, at least. I hope that this does not mean that all starmen take their oaths as lightly as Colonel Parsons did."

Rick sighed. When she got this sharp-tongued, he could either change the subject or be sure of a fight. It wasn't worth having a fight now. He would have to lead her gradually if at all toward his own position on how to treat rebels. There were going to be many of them, as The Time approached. The Time itself would kill enough people on Tran. If being generous with pardons could reduce the toll of life and property from the rebellions, wasn't it at least worth trying?

It wouldn't be Tylara's way, of course. For her or any other Tran dynast, the rule for rebels had been, whenever possible, "Hang first and ask questions afterward." One more thing to be changed. If possible.

✦ ✦ ✦

The charts on his office wall grew more detailed, and he collected chests of papers.

Item. It had been the warmest spring in living memory. Some farmers, heeding the priests of Yatar, planted early, and found their crops growing high. Others waited. All chanced heavy rains and hail. The entire pattern of Tran agriculture was changing.

Rick's survey teams went through the land, teaching and gathering data.

According to the reports, they did more data gathering than teaching; but they had accomplished the first agricultural survey in Tran history. What crops here? What last year? Are you using the new plows introduced by the University? What fertilizers?

Those using the new plows were able to get their seeds in so fast they were heard to talk of being able to get a second crop before winter. Those who'd used the new plows the year before talked even louder. With more fodder during the winter, their draft animals were stronger than usual.

Rick gathered all the information and reduced it to statistics. The raw data sheets went up to the University. Slowly his database grew.

He also dictated letters. One letter went to Gwen; that one he wrote himself. Except for Tylara no Tran native could read English, so that for sending messages to Gwen and the mercs it was better than code. That was worth the inconvenience of writing for yourself.

Find out if Marselius can send us a dozen or so trained clerks and scribes who can write well and teach things like basic filing procedures. It may be, of course, that the Roman civil service of the time of Septimius Severus has vanished, but I rather think something very like it must have survived. Else how could they have kept even this much of an Empire together for so long? And I am told the Roman "scribes" are said to know magic. Probably simple scientific training. Whatever it is, we can use it.

Which would set Gwen hunting bureaucrats among the Roman rebels. The priesthood of Yatar would be another problem. If Rick could forge a Roman alliance, would the priests cooperate? The Romans were Christians who persecuted Yatar and Vothan One-eye as pagan gods. Lord, Rick thought. What must I do? I *need* the hierarchy of Yatar, to spread science through the land. And will the Christians cooperate?

The priests of Yatar were the key to survival. They must have a strong organization, or the temples couldn't have survived the Rogue Star and the nuclear bombardments, not once but at least three times. With the cooperation of Yanulf and the priesthood much could be accomplished; without it, Rick was in trouble.

It was ironic, his going to all this trouble to re-invent bureaucracy. However, the whole idea looked different here on Tran, where information that could save thousands of lives might be lost because there *wasn't* a policy of writing up three copies of everything.

Rick put down the pen and held his head in his hands. More than ever he felt the pressure. "Every time I want to do anything, I first have to do two other things, one of which is impossible," he shouted. "Tiger by the tail, hell! I've got two tigers, and I've got to get them together so I can ride them. One foot on each!"

There was no one to hear him but the walls of his office, and they made no answer. Rick sighed and lifted his pen again. He had to write Warner at the University . . .

7

The chair creaked under the weight of Caius Marius Marselius, onetime Prefect of the Western Marches, now Caesar by right of conquest and proclamation of the legions. It was not a title he had sought, but once the proclamation was made it was one he had to win—or be killed for. Not just him. His son as well. All his house. Flaminius would leave none alive.

And when Marselius marched in triumph to Rome? What of the house of Flaminius? Time to think of that when it happened.

Outside they were lighting the streetlamps. Marselius could see them go on, one by one, down at the base of the hill where his villa stood. Benevenutum was a large city, third largest in the empire, and in many ways as pleasant as Rome; but it wasn't Rome, and an emperor who did not hold Rome was only a rebel.

Marselius bent forward to squint at the parchment he held. The late-afternoon light was fast failing. His freedman Lucius wrote with a firm hand, but it seemed harder to read lately.

Well, neither of them was getting any younger. His own eyes were not what they used to be. He summoned a servant to bring lamps, then he waited until the man went out before spreading the letter again. Not that he did not trust his servants, but this was too important. The confidential report on the embassy coming to him from the Lord and Lady of Chelm and the Kingdom of Drantos, written by the one man he trusted entirely . . .

—Drumold, father to the Eqetassa Tylara, would seem a typical barbarian chieftain. However, he is very intelligent and entirely trusted by the Lord Rick. He has made enemies among the clan chiefs of his own land in his loyalty to the Eqeta, which hints of a kind of courage most uncommon among barbarians. They are often brave in battle, but seldom understand and still more seldom show the higher civic virtues.

Lucius, Lucius, my old friend, thought Marselius. You spent too long as tutor to my son Publius. Now you *will* lecture, whether it is needed or not. Or perhaps you are rambling as old men often do. Well, before the snow comes again we shall both be so high in the world that everyone will listen to us for as long as we want, or else we shall be forever silent.

The Lady Gwen Tremaine is of the starfolk, but knows much history and reads Latin well. She is said to be very intelligent but is certainly young for the place she holds in the embassy. It is said that she owes this to having been Lord Rick's mistress, after the death of her husband.

The Guardsmen of Chelm—

Marselius skimmed the description of the embassy's escort until he found mention of star weapons. Good. They were bringing one which used the firepowder. Too many of his officers were skeptical about the star weapons and badly needed a demonstration, his own son among them. He himself would not mind learning more about these new war machines, so that if the alliance came about he would be able to plan the battles properly.

Certainly he would not need that many more ordinary soldiers. He had two full good legions of his own and a third which was neither so full or so good, plus enough cohorts of foot archers and pikemen to make up two more legions if that honorable title could ever again be allowed to foot soldiers. Then there were the light horse and foot scouts recruited locally. No lack of men.

Except—if Lord Rick did send a strong force as well as star weapons, it would release more of his own men for local defense. The reservists in the legions whose homes were close to the boundary between the two Caesars would fight better if they knew their own homes were safe. More militiamen would come forward. And there were the borders to the south to be held. He could use what Rick might send—and it was never good to let a man know that he could buy your friendship cheaply. No, Lord Rick would have to be ready to send an army to Rome if he ever wanted an army from Rome.

Marselius got up to pace back and forth in front of the great map on the wall. Mentally he shifted a cohort here, sent a tribune to raise more militia there. Everything would of course be discussed at length in the council of war he must hold before the embassy came, but he wanted his own ideas fully prepared before then. The older he grew, the more necessary it was to appear infallible and the harder it was to do so.

✢ ✢ ✢

Gwen Tremaine stretched luxuriously and let herself slide down into the hot water until only her face was above the surface. The tiled tank wasn't *quite* large enough for a swimming pool, but otherwise it was living up to everything the name "Roman bath" implied. It was the first really adequate bath she'd had since Les dumped her on Tran.

It had surprised her, how much more important the little things of civilization seemed when you didn't have them. Sometimes they loomed larger than the big ones. She knew that if she got a cavity the tooth would have to come out, with no anaesthetic except ethanol. She knew that if she had another baby and needed a Caesarian, she would probably die, and the baby hadn't a much better chance. She could accept these dangers, at least intellectually.

Hot baths were another matter. You missed them every morning and every night and every time you got sweaty or dirty. It was the same way with Vivaldi concertos, cold beer, Chicken Kiev, pantyhose—

"Lady Gwen?" said a small voice from right above her head.

Gwen controlled a foolish impulse to plunge out of sight. Instead she sat up, crossing her arms over her breasts. "Yes?"

"My name is Octavia. I've been sent to help you with your bath."

Which was no surprise. She'd rather expected someone waiting for her when she went in to take her bath. If Marselius was going to do her the courtesy of letting her bathe alone, he would certainly not leave out things like servants, towels, and scented oil.

"Thank you, Octavia." Gwen ducked under to get the last of the soap out of her hair, then climbed out of the bath. Octavia clapped her hands, and two older girls came in with deliciously warmed towels. When they wrapped her in a robe of fine wool, Gwen felt she had found civilization at last. Eventually the others were dismissed, and Gwen was alone with Octavia.

Who was she? While the others had dried her body and combed her hair, Gwen examined the girl minutely. Octavia looked to be about twelve or thirteen, and was already at least two inches taller than Gwen. With her big bones she'd grow even more. She was red-haired, but apart from that her strong, rather plain features had a lot in common with Marselius'.

And although her manners were impeccable, she spoke to the servants in a voice which made her requests orders to be obeyed. Gwen looked down at the hem of the girl's robe. It was embroidered with an elaborate pattern done in gold thread and what looked like pieces of blue enamel or seashells.

When the others had left, Gwen said, "You're kin to Marselius Caesar, aren't you?"

The girl dropped the towel and blushed as red as her hair. She didn't seem to know which way to look, other than not at Gwen. Finally she said, with an admirable effort to control her voice, "Are you a witch?"

"No. You just look like Marselius, and your gown doesn't look like a servant's clothing."

Octavia looked down at the hem but couldn't blush any brighter. "Grandfather will be angry with me for not changing my gown. It's the sort of thing he never forgets himself. I suppose you learned to notice it too, when you were a soldier."

"I'm not a real soldier," said Gwen. "My husband was. After he was killed they needed someone to read all sorts of books for information about our enemies. I was going to have a baby, so they wanted to help me and gave me the job." Gwen had told that story so often that she almost believed it herself. She smiled. "Don't imagine me in armor and a plumed helmet, waving a sword at the head of my troops."

"If we had your kind of soldier in Rome, I could be one too," said Octavia. "I like to read. In fact, my father says I spend too much time with the books."

Impulsively Gwen hugged the girl. She stiffened but didn't draw away. "I'm sorry. It's just that you sound like me when I was your age. My father said the same thing about me."

Fortunately she'd been able to do other thing besides read, and get straight As, like sell stale bread to chicken farmers and other things which made money. Also, she'd never been short of boyfriends, although none of them stayed around for more than three dates after they realized how much brighter she was. Octavia wasn't going to be able to do much except read her books until she was old enough to be married off. That wouldn't be long. Caesar's family must marry, and quickly, to cement alliances . . .

"Are you a spy?" Gwen asked.

Octavia giggled. "Yes, but it's not what you think." She paused, then said impulsively, "Lady Gwen, if you promise not to tell anybody what I say, I'll tell you why I'm here."

What an offer! Gwen didn't hesitate a moment. "By Yatar Skyfather and Hestia I swear I will never tell anybody what you say except the Lord Rick, and then only if he needs to know. I can't break my oath to him, you see. Is there anything else I should swear by?"

"No." Octavia looked thoughtful. "You must tell me sometime of Yatar, and I'll tell you about Christ." Then she really smiled for the first time. "You see, my father Publius wants to sleep with you. So my grandfather asked me to be in your company a lot. That way my father will be unable to get you alone. He would be ashamed to ask you to go to bed with him while I was around."

"I should hope so!" said Gwen indignantly. Then she laughed. The idea of this likable twelve-year-old girl as a chaperon to Gwen Tremaine was impossible to take with a straight face. If Octavia only knew how Gwen had lived—

Except—if it really did save her from having to either refuse Publius or submit to him, there was nothing funny about it. She hadn't heard that Publius was a Don Juan, but she had heard that he was arrogant and hot-tempered. That sort of man often disliked being turned down, enough to make trouble for the woman. Refusing him could be trouble.

And some day Publius would be Caesar, if Rick's plans worked, and they probably would.

Actually, the offer was flattering. Caesar's heir must have his choice of women. And there were advantages to being Caesar's lover . . . but not on a planet with no contraception except the rhythm method and very little obstetrical knowledge! If she'd wanted a man in her bed, she could have had Caradoc for a husband a year ago. Or Larry Warner, who was kind and gentle and intelligent and a very good partner in managing the University. Or—

"How does your father know he would find me attractive?" Gwen asked.

"He saw your arrival. When your party was greeted by my grandfather's officers, my father was among the guardsmen. He often does that."

"I see." So. Intelligent, if devious. At least Publius knew the value of information. "I'm flattered," she said. "But I'm still really in mourning for my husband. Sometimes it's hard to believe he's dead. You know they never found his body?" Another story she'd told so many times that she had to fight not to believe it herself.

"That must make it worse, doesn't it?"

"Yes." Something could be made of this girl. Caesar's granddaughter. "Have you brothers?" Gwen asked, although she was certain she'd heard—

"No. I'm my father's only child. To his great disappointment." She lowered her voice. "He doesn't even have illegitimate children. Not since he was ill—"

Mumps, probably, Gwen thought. "That makes you an important girl." It also removes one chief reason for refusing an offer by Publius. We'll play that one as it lies—

"They say I will be. If Grandfather can capture Rome, then some day my husband will be Caesar." Octavia looked very serious. "I don't think I'll have much to say about who that is, either. Did you choose your husband?"

"Yes. Where I'm from women always choose their own." And it doesn't seem to work any better than arranged marriages, either. "Octavia, you must swear an oath to me, one like I swore to you. You must not talk about anything I tell you, except with your grandfather and your father. Then we can be friends."

"Do I have to tell my father? Grandfather doesn't tell him a lot of things he thinks he should know. I've heard Father cursing about that."

So Marselius did not entirely trust his own son and presumptive heir. That was information worth a good deal—so much so that Gwen almost felt guilty about making friends with the girl. She was so obviously lonely, desperate for intelligent company where she didn't have to hide her talents, that—

The next moment Octavia made matters worse. "I'm glad we're going to be friends, Lady Gwen. It will be a lot easier to keep my father away from you, if you know what I'm doing. I told my grandfather that, but he didn't seem to understand what I was talking about."

"He has a lot on his mind," said Gwen absently. And even when he didn't, Marselius Caesar didn't seem like the sort of man to listen to his granddaughter's complaints.

She needs a friend, Gwen thought. And I can be that to her. Our cause is her cause, and she may some day come to see that. And she needs a teacher, someone to tell her of the changes coming to Tran. If—*when* her grandfather becomes undisputed Caesar, Octavia will hold power enough. Power during The Time, power for two generations after. In Rome, the best organized nation on Tran. I will deceive her as little as I can, but I have no real choice. This opportunity—

"By Saints Matthew, Mark, Luke, and John, and by Holy Mary, I swear that I shall say nothing of what the Lady Gwen tells me, except to my grandfather Marselius Caesar," said Octavia. "And him only if he asks me."

"Good," said Gwen, in a normal tone. She was tired of whispering. She dropped her robe on the couch and started pulling on her clothes. "And you can tell me of Christ," she said.

After all, Gwen thought, I was raised Christian. If I have a religion, that's it. If I let the Romans convert me—I'll have to ask Rick about that. It might be useful.

✢ ✢ ✢

Marselius Caesar's chair creaked not quite in rhythm with his pen. This letter to Lucius could not be trusted to any scribe. If he could have sent it by a bird of the air or a starman's flying machine he would have done so.

—would have seen their way clear to aiding us anyway, certainly the utter folly of Flaminius the Dotard hastened matters. He not only refused to permit the embassy to enter his claimed land, he even refused to offer them safe conduct. When the Lord Drumold heard this last, his anger was frightful.

In fact, the clan chief had nearly provoked a fight with Flaminius' patrol by the language he used about their Caesar, his habits, and all his ancestors back to the founding of Rome.

So we will have the aid of the Lord Rick, in whatever amount we may need. I still hope we will not need any. Flaminius may not be his own master; that evil message may have come from senators and officers who fear to lose everything if he submits himself to me. It is to be hoped that these men will listen to reason after we issue a proclamation of a general pardon. I do not think the Senate will delay long in issuing it, although there is some opposition.

He started to add, "including Publius," then decided against it. Lucius had known Publius since the boy was six; he could fill in that sort of detail for himself.

Much honor is also due to the Lady Gwen. She has done good work, particularly in choosing the scribes and clerks we are sending to Drantos under the treaty. The Westerners' asking for them helped convince many of the Senate that we were not dealing with barbarians, much as the firepowder weapons helped convince the army. The Lady Gwen showed so much knowledge of scribes' work that one wonders how a woman of equestrian rank came by it.

She has also become a good friend to the Lady Octavia. This I welcome. Except for yourself, none of Octavia's teachers have been worthy of her. As she will be of an age for betrothal within no more than a year and a half, this has caused some concern.

Another sign of age—worrying about your grandchildren's fitness for marriage.

Back to what he knew best.

What we can ask for from the Westerners, is likely to be more than we need. However, we can ask for two legions of foot, one of pikes and one of archers. There will also be a force of horsemen equal to another legion, including mounted archers. We will have firepowder weapons, and the starmen will bring all of their star weapons which are fit for a long campaign.

I hope there will be no need of a long campaign. With such strength, we can stand up to Flaminius in a pitched battle with a good hope of winning it. One such victory would be enough to give us Rome, before men and wealth which will be needed for The Time is destroyed.

Let us pray for the favor of Christ and the aid of St. Michael.

To Lucius, Freedman of this house,

Friend to Caesar,

Honor and Farewell.

Caius Marius Marselius Caesar.

Larry Warner looked up at the balloon swaying overhead and decided that it was about as inflated as it would ever be. He nodded to the man standing beside him.

"Okay, Murphy."

Ben Murphy raised both hands. "Let go the top rope! Second crew, heave away!"

Five men at the foot of one fifty-foot pole let go of the first line and stepped back. At the foot of the second pole on the opposite side of the hot-air balloon, five more men started pulling. The rope slipped through a ring at the top of the first pole, then a loop at the top of the balloon, sixty feet above the ground. Finally it slipped through the ring at the top of the last pole and fell on top of the men pulling it. From the way they were laughing and cursing, Warner didn't think anyone was hurt.

He folded his arms on his chest, hoping for Murphy to give the next order on his own. Ben would be taking the First Balloon Squadron (one balloon and about forty men) on campaign against Flaminius Caesar in another three or four ten-days. It would have been simpler for Warner to go himself, but Captain Rick's orders were strict: nobody from the University faculty into combat. Murphy and Reznick tossed for it, and Reznick won. Or had Murphy? Warner knew better than to ask.

It didn't matter much anyway. Larry Warner was happy not to be shot at. Besides, he'd been first up, the first aeronaut anywhere on Tran!

That had impressed everyone, including all the girls and even Gwen Tremaine. There were rewards to be gained from heroism—

But all in all, the life of a University professor was better. Especially in this University, where the faculty was in full control.

The balloon swayed a little more with the overhead rope gone, but the men on the ground lines had it firmly under control. The overhead rope strung between the poles had held it up while the hot air from the fire under the launching platform flowed up the inflation tube underneath and filled the balloon. Warner had figured that one out himself, and was quite proud of his invention.

"Draw the neck rope!" shouted Murphy. A team of men pulled on the rope which tightened the neck of the tube hanging down from the balloon. Now the balloon looked like a gigantic mushroom with a large misshapen head and a very short stem. Warner checked his gear and walked toward the platform. Murphy could finish the job on his own now, except for the last order to "Let go."

"Cover the fire!" The men who'd tightened the tube pulled a brass plate over the hole in the platform. Warner climbed up onto the platform as the men wrestled the observation basket on to the brass plate. When the balloon rose, it had to lift the observation basket and crew straight up. Dragging was a real danger at launch and landing times, which was why the balloon needed such a large ground crew.

But the benefits! "Your turn next, Ben," Warner called.

"Right. Sure you don't want me this time?"

"No, I'd better check things out." Not that Murphy couldn't do it, but that would be bad for Warner's image. And there was the new telegraph system, a thin wire stretching from the balloon along the tether; the only Morse operators in the University were Larry Warner and two of his crewmen, and they didn't speak English . . .

Warner checked the observation basket and its gear even more carefully than he'd checked his own. Today was supposed to be an endurance test, to see how long the balloon could stay up with extra ballast and fuel in place of a second man. There were extra bricks of the resin-coated straw they used for fuel when aloft tied to the netting above the basket. If sparks from the brass firepot in the floor of the basket reached them, they could be cut loose before they set the reed basket itself afire. Around the rim of the basket were hung sandbags for ballast and two skins of drinking water.

All improvised, all Warner's inventions. Well, with a little help from the others, but not much. And he'd got it all done before Gwen came back from Benevenutum.

Everything seemed to be all right. Some of the men in the squadron believed that Warner was a wizard and the balloon was his familiar spirit, which would tell him of any negligence on their part in preparing it for the flight. He was supposed to discourage superstitions, and he would—eventually. Just now it was handy for them to think that. It was a long way down if anything went wrong.

Warner climbed into the basket and braced himself, legs spread wide and the fingers of one hand twined in the netting. The men on the ropes slacked off a little and the balloon lifted a few inches clear of the platform. Warner grinned. He had a lot of excuses for taking this flight, but one he didn't admit was simple enough. He liked it. The nearest thing to flying . . .

Except for the length, this flight should be almost routine. It looked like there might be too much wind up high, but here in the lee of Ben Hakon he should be safe enough. Idly he wondered who the hill had been named for.

The men who'd moved the basket and handled the overhead ropes now took their places on the handles of the winch. If Campbell had been allowed to make gears for the winch, it wouldn't have needed twelve or fifteen men. However, that was another of Captain Rick's orders—"I don't want it perfect, I want it Thursday!" So the winch needed a dozen men on the handles when the balloon was full, and the balloon itself had no ripcord or top vent. It rose or fell with the air inside it and the sheer strength of the men on the winch.

That, though, was the Mark I, and his crews were already at work on Mark II. They might have it finished by the time Murphy took it to battle.

He made one last check. "Looking good," he called. "Let it play out some." Murphy nodded. The balloon rose about three feet above the platform, before the winch crew caught it. It *was* crude, but as long as it was the only balloon on the planet, who cared?

Warner took a deep breath and began to sing as the winch crew let the balloon rise. He'd sung on the first ascent, to keep his teeth from chattering from sheer blue funk. Some of his crew thought it was a hymn to Yatar Skyfather, and now they expected him to sing every time the balloon went up. He wondered what Murphy would do. Oh, well.

> *Off we go, into the wild blue yonder,*
> *Flying high, into the sun. . . .*

As the platform dropped away below him, he saw Gwen standing by one of the poles, trying not to laugh. Was it the song, or his singing?

✢ ✢ ✢

Therrit had planned to do his work while the balloon was still rising. Lord Corgarff had said this would do the most damage. However, Lord Corgarff didn't know how many men were around the winch while the balloon was going up. Therrit did not trust Lord Corgarff to pay the promised gold to his family if he was caught before he could even do the work.

So Therrit stood well back, until the balloon looked no larger than his fist held out in front of his nose. Then the men on the winch pushed a long wooden rod in under the drum, to stop its turning. The rod could be put in place and then pulled out again quickly, without anyone having to reach in under the drum and risk getting their hands broken.

More than half the drum was still covered with rope when the balloon stopped rising. Therrit realized that if he could pull out the rod, the balloon would probably start rising again, just as Lord Corgarff wanted. It would be harder to make pulling the rod out look like an accident, but if there was enough smoke no one would see him, and they would never know. The crewmen thought the balloon could talk, but Therrit knew better. Warner had told him many times.

It was too bad that Professor Warner had to die. He was a gentle master, considerate of his servants. But Warner had no gold to keep Therrit's sisters from starving. They could enter Warner's service, but the Star Lords had no understanding of what was fit for the daughters of yeomen and what work was fit only for slaves or freedwomen. He might—he might loan Therrit's sister to the Lord Elliot, as he did with his own Sara!

No. The only safety for his family was the protection of his clan. Lord Corgarff would not order this without the consent of Chief Dughuilas, and Dughuilas could protect anyone!

Therrit waited a little longer, until he saw the lady Gwen walking back to her tent. Corgarff did not seem to care if the lady was hurt or not, but Therrit did not want to make war on women, particularly this one. She treated the sons and daughters of yeomen as if they were the children of knights.

Therrit waited so long that he became aware that Corgarff was looking at him, rather than up at the balloon like everyone else. The lord's patience must be running out. Therrit walked cautiously toward the platform, pulling a brick of *skyfire* out of his pouch. It looked like any other brick from the outside, but it was only a thin layer of straw and resin pasted over a leather lining. The leather was filled with firepowder and other things to make smoke. Therrit walked until he was within easy range of the banked-up fire under the platform. Then he tossed the brick underhanded on to the coals.

The firepowder made all the smoke he'd expected, also a noise like the time when lightning struck his father's barn and a smell like the hot spring behind the University. Everybody except Therrit was caught by surprise. All those near the platform scrambled up, and a few ran. Therrit threw in a second brick, there was more noise and smoke, and it looked like everyone was running.

He couldn't wait to see better. He ran up to the platform, drawing his knife as he did so. Having gone this far, he had to be ready to cut the rope if everything else failed.

The locking rod came out at the second pull. He saw the winch handles begin to move and jumped aside. The winch rattled, the handles whirled fast enough to break a careless man's bones, and the rope on the drum shrank. Therrit pulled away the bronze lid over the firehole, cursing as it scorched his fingers, and tossed in the last two bricks. The noises made the platform shake and the winch creak, and the smoke came up so thickly that Therrit could barely see or breathe. Choking and holding the rod out in front of him like a blind man's stick, he groped his way to the edge of the platform and jumped down to the ground.

✛ ✛ ✛

Warner knew something was wrong when he saw the smoke swallow the platform and winch and heard the explosions. He didn't know what until the balloon suddenly started rising. Even then he was more interested than frightened. The winch getting out of control was something he'd lived through before, for a couple of minutes at least. The Balloon Squadron was a pretty good outfit, considering that he was the only man in it who'd ever heard of balloons six ten-days ago.

Then he saw the men scattering from around the winch, and more smoke billowing up. He hoped whatever was wrong didn't wreck the winch completely.

The balloon jerked sideways, like a mouse batted by a playful cat. Warner shouted heartfelt obscenities. Then he had to cling to the basket and the netting with both hands and both feet, wishing he was a monkey with a tail he could use as well.

He'd risen out of the lee of Ben Hakon into the wind. From the way the grass on the hilltop was moving, the wind must be blowing half a gale. He swore again. He should have sent somebody up to the hilltop to test the wind, or carried more ballast so that the balloon wouldn't rise—

The balloon jerked again. Now Warner felt more like a fish being played by a fisherman. A cold spray drenched him as one of the water bags burst. That would make the balloon even lighter, which right now was the last thing he needed. More jerks and Warner heard the frame of the basket creak and ropes part in the netting. If this went on much longer, the basket would rack itself apart and leave him—

Suddenly the balloon was rising again. Warner froze in the netting until it stopped for a moment, then peered over the edge. The rope was loose and someone was clinging to the free end. As Warner watched, the man dropped to the ground and lay there. The balloon shot up again. The basket still swayed ominously, but with the rope loose the strain on it was less. Warner slipped down inside the basket and wished he could sing. Right now, Yatar Skyfather really needed propitiating! His mouth was so dry that he couldn't have sung a note with a gun pointed at him.

✢ ✢ ✢

Therrit was slipping away from the platform when the rope came loose. His heart was pounding like a drum and he was sure that everyone was looking at him and fingering their swords.

He still stopped to watch Murphy's frantic chase after the loose end of the rope. He cheered when the star lord caught it, and groaned when he lost his grip and fell.

Murphy lay like the dead.

"You did it!" screamed a voice almost in Therrit's ear. "I saw you! Traitor!"

Therrit whirled to see Lord Corgarff coming at him with a drawn sword. He looked wildly around, his universe crumbling. His laird, his chief, accusing him! "No, Lord! Lord, you owe me protection!"

"I am chief to no traitors!" Corgarff screamed.

Therrit cursed. There was no place to run. Even so he hesitated to raise weapons against his lord—but it was that or die here. And who then to watch over his sisters?

He'd sheathed his dagger and Corgarff attacked so fast there was no time to draw it. He was still holding the locking rod from the winch. He swung frantically and the heavy rod smashed into Corgarff's sword arm. He howled and his weapon went flying.

Therrit didn't bother to pick it up. Men had heard Corgarff and were running toward him. It would be hopeless to fight. Yet—where could he run?

Was there no one to protect him? Warner might, but the Professor was high in the balloon, a dead man. Murphy? The star lord lay on the grass. He would be no help. Then who?

The Lady Gwen might protect him. Run, then, run to her and clasp her knees to beg for mercy for his family. He was a lost man, but the Lady Gwen might spare his sisters—

⁜ ⁜ ⁜

Gwen ran to the entrance of her tent when she heard the explosions. She was in time to see the balloon shoot up and break loose and Murphy's heroic try at catching it. She sent one of the guardsmen off to bring Sergeant McCleve for the injured man and another to get Sergeant Elliot. He was going to be needed, if only to make her feel that she knew what she was doing until she really did. Then she turned back into the tent, to dismiss her scribe and pull on her cloak.

Thus there was only one guardsman on duty outside the tent when Therrit ran up and threw himself at Gwen's feet. The guardsman tried to pull him away but he clutched her knees. "Lady, Lady, save me! Lord Corgarff wants my blood, but I only followed him for gold. My family will starve if they do not—"

"Wait!" said Gwen. His babbling was making it impossible for her to think. "Lord Corgarff paid you to let the balloon go?"

"Yes."

"Now he wants to silence you permanently."

"Yes. If you save me, I will tell—"

"There's that damned dung-spawned traitor now!" came from outside the tent. Gwen jumped back and nearly fell as the man clutched her skirt.

"Let go, you fool!"

"Lord Corgarff, the Lady Gwen has—" began the guardsman.

"The Lady Gwen will not protect a traitor, unless the High Rexja's bought her too!"

"You cannot pass, Lord—ahhhggghhh!" and the sound of steel into flesh and against bone.

The guardsman's fidelity to his oath bought the fugitive the time to crawl under the table, the scribe the time to crawl out of the tent, and Gwen the time to pull out her pistol. She could barely hold the .45 with two hands, but she had it aimed at the door when Corgarff charged through.

The sight of a star weapon in a woman's hands stopped him for a moment. "Lady Gwen, put that away. You have drawn it in the cause of an evil—"

"I heard what you think, Corgarff," she said. After she was sure her hands and her voice would stay steady, she went on, "I will protect this man until he has told me everything—"

Corgarff's cry was an animal's. Fortunately his first slash was wild. His sword hacked into the tent pole. He was raising it for a cut at Gwen's head when Elliot's voice came from outside.

"Freeze, you son of a bitch!"

In desperation Corgarff whirled to slash at Elliot. Sergeant Major Elliot laughed as he jumped back out of range.

"Don't kill him!" Gwen shouted.

"No problem." Elliot's Colt blasted twice and Corgarff screamed as the slugs ploughed into his thigh and leg. He took a step forward, then started to fall. Elliot slammed the pistol alongside his head to make sure he went down all the way.

"Is it over?" Gwen asked.

"So far," Elliot said. " 'Cept we might lose this one." He raised his voice. "Send for the corpsmen!"

Gwen held the tent pole to keep from falling, Elliot caught her before she brought the tent down on top of them, then led her to a chair and checked her pistol. "Miss Tremaine, you really ought to practice more with that. You had the safety on. He'd have run you through before you could fire a shot."

"Really?" Gwen started to laugh at the silliness of her own remark, then caught herself before she lost control. "Get McCleve and more guardsmen. Make sure nobody we don't know gets near these two until we've talked to them. I mean *nobody*, Sergeant Major."

Elliot automatically snapped to attention. He knew when an officer was speaking. "Yes, ma'am."

"Thank you. And we'll want messengers to go to the Garioch and Drantos." She swallowed. "Is there anything I've left out?"

"Not that I know of, ma'am." He bent over Corgarff. "But this one's going to need first aid, or he'll bleed to death before McCleve gets here. Those forty-fives tear a man up some."

"All right. You stand guard. No one comes in, Sergeant. I'll try to help him."

What lay under Corgarff's bloody clothing was as bad as Gwen expected. Somehow she managed to go to work on it. After a while she found it was no harder than cutting up onions and green peppers for a homemade pizza. Maybe she was finally adapting to living in the Middle Ages. She'd have to, or spend half her time in her room and the other half being sick to her stomach.

9

This is it, Larry Warner thought. Jesus Christ. Come all the way here on a mucking flying saucer, and get killed in a hot-air balloon. Jesus H. Christ.

The balloon continued to rise. The air inside was cooling, so that it had lost part of its lift, but the balloon's slightly flattened shape gave additional lift from the updrafts. Warner huddled in the bottom of the basket while he worked this out. Eventually he got up the nerve to look over the edge at the ground below.

It was hard to judge his ground speed. He tried to estimate distances between farms as he passed over them, timing his passage with his watch as he swept across the valley below. It was difficult because there were few roads, and nothing was square. Tran was a planet of horse—and centaur—carts, not automobiles.

After several attempts he got the same result twice. He was probably doing about thirty-five miles an hour, much faster than the best any rescue party could do. If he stayed up no more than an hour, he'd be nearly a day's ride from the University. The only hope he had for quick rescue was to come down on top of someone friendly—which wasn't very likely, because he had no control over altitude.

He could rise—a little—by dropping ballast, but as for bringing the balloon down before the hot air cooled and it lost lift—well, that was what rip panels were for, in balloons back on Earth. In theory, he could climb up the netting and slash at the cloth with a knife, to let out some of the hot air. One look at all the empty air between him and the ground cured him of the notion. He wasn't that desperate yet.

The best course looked to be letting the balloon cool naturally. He could slow its fall if necessary by dropping ballast, rather than by lighting up the fire. Meanwhile he would pull up the rope and make a big loop in the end. He hoped he remembered enough of his Boy Scout knot-tying to make one which would hold. That would give people on the ground a better hold on the rope.

Then—wait until he passed low enough over a village for the rope to reach the ground. Throw the rope out, shout to the people, and hope they understand what he was saying. It would still take luck, but not as much as bringing the balloon down by himself. It was going to take luck to live through this. He'd have to be *very* lucky to save the balloon for the campaign.

Moving cautiously, with one hand always gripping the rigging, Warner made a complete scan around the balloon. When he looked to the north-northwest, he let out a yell which would have scared any seagulls within a half a mile. Then he took the names of most of Tran's gods in vain.

He'd completely forgotten about the Labyrinth Range, a tangle of jagged peaks and dense thickets at the head of the Saronic Gulf. They got their name because few who tried finding a path through them ever got out the other side. Sensible people preferred to go around either end of the range.

Warner wouldn't have any choice. The range was a good seventy miles from end to end, and there was no way at all to steer a free balloon. He would have to go over.

How high? One task of the University was mapping Tran; they were the only geodetic survey the planet had. He'd sent a team of locals out with a crude transit to measure mountain heights—

And if he remembered right, the Labyrinth Range was three thousand meters high.

Nine thousand feet. More than that. A lot higher than he was just now. Twice as high, maybe.

Would it be better to try to land? No. Not in this wind. Neither he nor the balloon would live through the experience. I'll just have to go over, he thought. Be still, my heart—

'Tain't funny, another part of him said, but he ignored that. Better to laugh, and not think about it.

He looked down once more to be sure, and decided. The ground was already rising into the foothills of the Labyrinths. He'd have to get up to ten thousand feet and stay there for at least an hour. The Labyrinths were thirty miles across at their widest point. If he came down anywhere inside them, he'd freeze or starve to death before they found him, if anyone could be persuaded to go looking, and assuming he was lucky enough to survive landing on a glacier . . .

Get the rope up first. Can't dump that. Need it. Have to come down on the other side.

Which is the Pirate Lands, more or less claimed by Rome but in practice abandoned to anyone who wanted to live there. They weren't worth the troops it would take to garrison them. And beyond there are salt marshes, far too wide to cross. It's the Pirate Lands or nothing . . .

So. First things first. Get a fire going, then pull up the rope. He took three fire bricks from the rigging and stuffed them into the fire pot. His Zippo was filled with naphtha, and hard to light, but eventually it burned, and once he had flame the bricks caught nicely. The resin in the bricks was extracted from something the natives called volcano-bush. It grew in patches in the forests to the south. People said that in late summer, when the bushes were full of resin, lightning striking a patch could make it go up like a bomb, acres at a time. In winter and spring the bush wasn't as resin-loaded, but there was still plenty to provide fuel for the balloon's firepot.

He had to lay on six more bricks before the balloon was rising fast enough to suit him. He was sure he'd overdone it. There was undoubtedly a long lag between making heat and getting lift. But the mountains were coming closer and closer, and it was better to be too high than too low.

The fire blazed hotter and hotter. Soon he had to flatten himself against the side of the basket to keep from being scorched. He hoped the firepot wouldn't crack or the basket catch fire.

At least there seemed to be plenty of wind over the Labyrinths. He saw a plume of snow trailing from one peak in his path. Unfortunately that peak was also still above him. He threw on another brick, then counted what was left of his fuel supply. About half-gone. Better try dumping ballast for a change. There was also the second water bag, but everything he'd been taught said that drinking water is the *last* thing to go.

He dropped two sandbags, then the mountains were on him.

✢ ✢ ✢

The balloon came closer to the range; then, suddenly, it began to rise, plummeting higher and swifter than Warner had ever seen.

"Updrafts!" he shouted. Of course there'd be an updraft on the windward side of the mountains. It lifted him so fast that his nose began to bleed, and his ears hurt dreadfully until he could make them pop. Even the fillings in his teeth hurt.

By noon he'd left the Labyrinths behind him, after crossing them with several thousand feet to spare. Now the problem was cold. He'd been dressed for a summer day in Tamaerthon, and the temperature up here was well below freezing. The thinner air of Tran meant the temperature dropped off faster with height. It also meant that his present altitude was the equivalent of the tops of the Alps or Rockies on Earth, high enough to make breathing hard.

"Hoo-hah," he shouted. "Mucking bastards. Join the army and see the world, they said. Hell, they said *the* world. Didn't say dogmeat about any *other* worlds. Recruiting officers. They *always* lie to you—"

There was a terrible temptation to *do something*, but he was just rational enough to know he was suffering from oxygen starvation. Better to sit still and rage at the world. Presently he began to sing "The Friggin' Falcon."

✢ ✢ ✢

When the balloon descended to a lower altitude, Warner could think again. This time he had few choices. His fire bricks were nearly gone, and if he didn't come down here, he'd be into the salt marshes.

The cold dry air at high altitude had left him thirsty. He pulled the plug on the water bag and drank until he was clear-headed and hungry. He munched a piece of dried meat from his ration pouch and composed a mental memo, suggesting that the next *Shalnuksi* ship be asked to bring a few parachutes for the Balloon Squadron.

Now that his fingers were thawed out, he could tie a large bowline in the end of the rope. He was just in time. The balloon sank so rapidly that he knew that something would break if he hit the ground this hard. The last brick went into the fire and the last of the ballast went overboard. Then he threw the loop over the side. The ground below was forested now. If he could lasso a treetop he could pull himself down, and have something to tell Elliot besides. The sergeant could use a lariat as well as an assault rifle! He'd even roped a centaur on a bet.

Warner wasn't Elliot, but then the treetops weren't centaurs. They stayed put, and eventually Warner got lucky. The loop caught a branch and went tight. By now the balloon had lost so much lift that Warner's muscles were enough to pull it down into the trees. The minute the basket was at the level of a good stout branch, Warner grabbed it with both hands and swung himself into the tree.

The branch promptly bent under his weight, letting him dangle until he lost his grip and dropped to the branch below. It bounced him like a ping-pong ball on to the next branch, and that one let him slide down on to the ground, a drop of ten feet onto leaves and needles. Warner hit with a paratrooper's five-point roll.

The first thing he did when he got his breath back was kneel and kiss the solid ground. The second thing he did was look up.

Four bearded men looked back at him. They wore homespun breeches and leather shirts. Two carried crossbows, one a spear, and one an axe. None of them looked ready to use the weapons, but none of them looked particularly friendly either.

Warner knelt and kissed the ground again, then stood up, holding his hands out to show he bore no weapons. After a moment the man with the bushiest beard laid down his crossbow, knelt, and also kissed the ground. The others followed him. Then they all stood up. The leader pointed upward at the balloon now draped over the treetops, then at Warner. Warner nodded. The leader made what Warner recognized as one of the signs against evil spirits, then raised his crossbow.

Warner shook his head sharply. They probably thought the balloon was a monster which had carried him off. "No," he said aloud. "Do not hurt it." He hoped they'd understand him. Most of Tran spoke dialects of the same language, but some of the dialects were pretty far apart.

"It—is yours?" asked the leader.

So he wouldn't have to conduct the discussion in sign language. "Yes. It is my skybeast. A wizard who is my enemy cast an evil spell on it, so that it fell from the sky. I must stay with you for some days, until I can call other wizards to my aid. They will come, take off the evil spell, and reward you well if you help me."

He looked sternly at them. "They will also punish you if you do not treat me well. The beast will see everything which happens among you, and tell the other wizards."

"You have nothing to fear," said the leader. "We are of Two Springs village, we live by law." He fumbled in his pouch and brought out a cake of what looked like ground-up nuts. Warner ate half of it. There were nut shells as well as meats in the cake, but that didn't matter. They had fed him, and that made him their guest. More than unknown wizards would punish them now if they harmed him.

He turned back to the balloon, raised his arms, and recited a few Army regulations in English. Then he smiled at the men. "The beast has seen what you did, and is glad. Now let us go to your village."

"Your beast will be safe?" said one of the men.

"It will be now that it is on the ground," said Warner. Right now the last thing he wanted to do was straw-boss a gang of Pirate Land villagers into lowering his balloon from the top of a fifty-foot tree. He wanted a drink, a meal, and a girl, and not to have to think about balloons for a while.

10

"You're wearing a new perfume?" said Warner, toying with his glass. Gwen smiled and picked up the wine jug to refill it.

"Yes. Marselius Caesar sent it. He said it was a gift from the Lady Octavia."

"How is she?"

"She is well, but unhappy that I won't be coming with the army."

"I'm glad you're not going."

"I'm not," she said tartly. Warner covered himself by taking a sip from his glass and mopping his plate with a piece of bread.

It was frustrating. She'd obviously laid on this dinner and put on the blue gown to welcome him. She looked good, she smelled good, and he was damned sure she'd feel good if he got close enough. So far though, that blue gown might have been armor plate.

Then she giggled.

"Yes?" he prompted.

"I was thinking about that girl, the one on the second night."

Warner was puzzled for a moment. "Oh, you mean the one who was afraid the skybeast could see us."

"Yes. Did she really think it would tell tales to the other wizards?"

"I don't think it was the other wizards she was worried about. I think she was afraid the Great Balloon God was going to tell her husband."

"Oh." She giggled again.

He wondered what had gotten into Gwen, other than more wine

than usual. She was curious about everything he'd done in Two Springs village, including the girls he'd bedded. You'd have thought she'd be jealous of that.

"You know, I think I should have seen this before," she said. "The people really think a balloon is magical. Even some of the people around the University, who can see that it's a machine. Out in the villages, if someone comes in a balloon, they'll think he's a wizard. They'll listen to what he says! We can start teaching them all the things they won't learn otherwise!"

Warner stared. It made a weird kind of sense. If the teaching squads went out with a balloon, they'd get a lot more attention. People wouldn't sit around waiting for Old MacDonald or the village granny to try the star knowledge. It might not even have to be a man-carrying balloon, either. That would save a lot of cloth and—

"The *surinomaz* processing!" Gwen looked ready to jump out of her chair. "We can start in that village where the mid-wives know how to make *surinomaz* into a medicine. If they'll teach the wizards what they know, we can prove that the *surinomaz* is useful. People will start *wanting* to grow it. Larry, you may have just saved a whole planet!"

Warner got up and went around the table. "Gwen, you're as smart as you are beautiful. You thought of what to do with the balloons. I just went along for the ride, so to speak."

She stood up and kissed him on the cheek. "Larry, you're a lot braver than you think you are."

Warner put his arms around her and bent to kiss her lips. For a moment he thought she would turn away. Then her face came up and their lips met. Hers trembled, then opened. He tightened his grip. Small fireworks started to go off in various parts of his body.

He held her closely, then let his hands wander downwards.

"Don't."

"Don't what?"

She sighed. "Maybe I mean 'do.' It's been a long time. But just for the moment, I'd like to be held, and not have to think about what happens next."

"Suits me." He held her, and they stood that way for a while.

This could be damn serious, Warner thought. She's one hell of a girl. Nobody like her. And we've done pretty well, running this place. Is it time Larry Warner settled down?

To what? Fidelity? She'd want that. More'n the local girls would. Monogamy, too. And she knows I'm no damned wizard. But it wouldn't be so bad, and besides, it doesn't't have to be decided now. Nobody's said anything about forever, just tonight . . .

He bent to kiss her again.

Crash! Wood slammed against stone and metal rang.

"Dog!"

An angry voice made more echoes in the room. Something struck Larry Warner's head. A hard blow, that left a ringing in his ears. Gwen screamed.

Warner fell to the floor as if unconscious. The instant he was down he snap-rolled under the table, then rolled again to get behind it. As he stood he drew his Walther .380 automatic, wishing it were the .45 hanging by the door with his jacket. The Walther would just have to do. By the time he was back on his feet he had spread his legs and was holding the piece in both hands, his eye sighting down the barrel at the kilted figure in the room—

"Larry! No!" Gwen shouted. "No!" She dashed across the room and into Warner's line of fire.

He'd almost squeezed off the round! He jerked the piece upwards to point at the ceiling, and from pure rage and frustration he fired. The shot sounded very loud in the enclosed room.

"Larry!" Gwen screamed again. Then she saw where the pistol was pointed.

"Move!" Warner commanded. "No son of a bitch comes bustin' in on me! I'll blow the bastard away—" He stopped shouting as he realized who the intruder was. "Caradoc?"

The archer captain had been in command of the search party that found Warner. He'd stayed behind to see that the balloon was safely loaded on the pack animals. And, Warner realized, he'd not only finished that task in record time, he must have ridden like hell to get here. Why? To see Gwen. And maybe he was jealous of Warner, too.

Now he stood there defiantly. "If you have honor, you will allow me a weapon," Caradoc said. "You may have your star weapons, and I my bow . . ."

Warner laughed. "*You* talk about honor, Boy Scout. Not me. I fight for pay. And you're dead."

"Larry, you can't." Gwen wasn't shouting any longer.

"Why not?"

"Captain Galloway will have you shot, that's why."

"I need no woman to argue for my life!" Caradoc shouted.

"You need something you haven't got," Warner said. "You also need to explain how you got in here."

"Miss Tremaine!" The shout came from the hall.

"Jesus, that's Elliot," Warner said. He raised his voice. "In here, Sergeant Major."

Elliot came in. His .45 was cocked and ready. He looked at Warner, then at Caradoc. "Okay, Professor, what's happening?"

"Nothing," Gwen said. "It's nothing at all. Please leave."

"Not friggin' likely."

"It's okay, Sarge," Warner said. "We were showin' Captain Caradoc a couple of moves, and maybe it got out of hand. I let a round go into the ceiling."

Elliot looked suspiciously at them. "Sure that's all?"

"Yeah."

"It's all right," Gwen said.

"Okay, if you say so." He snapped on the safety and holstered his pistol. "If you say so."

Warner waited until Elliot was gone before he spoke again. "I'm still waiting to know how you got in here, Captain," he said finally. "Past the guards. My guards. They weren't supposed to let anyone in here, not anyone at all. But I guess I know, don't I? You had them betray their trust. You being their commander and all, you could do that. So now you just tell me why I shouldn't have them and you both up on charges?"

For the first time Caradoc looked worried. "There is no reason," he said finally. "You are correct. But the men are not at fault."

"Larry—"

"Yes, my lady?"

"Larry, don't do that. He—had a right to think he could come here."

"I see."

"I have said it already," Caradoc said. "I will not listen more to—"

He's going to try it, Warner thought. He'll come for me. He's one of those, one of the berserker types and he'll dive for the gun. When he does, it'll be chancy. A .380 just isn't that much slug. No fancy shooting, just empty the damn piece into him and take my chances after that. Should work.

But damn all, I don't really want to kill him—

Abruptly Warner put the pistol in his pocket.

"What are you doing?" Caradoc demanded. "Have you discovered honor, or—"

"Main thing is, I'm unarmed," Warner said. "And you, my friend, aren't going to try unarmed combat with me. You've seen me practicing."

Caradoc fingered his sword. "Get a weapon. Any weapon," he said. "It may be said that Caradoc son of Cadaric is a fool. It will never be said that he slew an unarmed man."

"Nobody's going to be slain," Warner said. "Gwen, would you please leave us?" He changed to English. "I got some talking to do with Muscles here."

"You're sure it's all right?"

"Yeah, no problems now."

"I want promises from both of you. That you won't fight," she said. She looked thoroughly miserable.

"Sure," Warner said.

"I swear I will not draw weapons against this man except on a field of honor with all due ceremony," Caradoc said.

"Good enough for me," Warner said. He eyed Caradoc thoughtfully. *I didn't promise I wouldn't draw weapons if he gets physical.* "Gwen?"

"Oh, all right." She paused in the door. "I—I'm really sorry."

"Have a seat," Warner said. He indicated the table. "There's wine and glasses. Have some."

"You make free with the lady's table. As if—as if it is *your* table."

"No," Warner said. "That is not the way of it. But understand that the Lady Gwen and I are from the same lands. I have known her for many years. I know she would wish us to make ourselves comfortable."

Caradoc went to the table and sat. He waited until Warner had poured for both of them, then drained his glass in one gulp. "It is not finished," he said finally.

"Maybe it is," Warner said.

"You have sometimes acted as a friend," Caradoc said. He stared moodily into his empty wine glass. "And I think I have been a fool."

"We all are, sometimes," Warner said.

Caradoc took in a deep breath. "Lord Warner," he said formally. "What is the Lady Gwen to you?"

"Why is that your business?"

"Perhaps it is not. And yet—If she has been more than a friend, without you promising a lawful marriage, I will have your blood. No, hear me out," he said, raising a hand as Warner opened his mouth to reply.

"I know that if I kill you, the Lord Eqeta Rick will have my head. You are worth ten of me, in his plans for facing The Time. Perhaps he is even right to value you so highly.

"I do know this, however. No lord can ask me to stand by like a capon, while you play the cock with Gwen. I love her. If she does not love me, then let her say so and she can be free to bed any man she wishes. Until she speaks her mind, beware of my sword."

Warner nodded. Nobly said, he thought. Corny, but noble. Larry me lad, you didn't think it through. Old Musclebound here isn't just a rival for a quick roll in the hay. He wants to marry the girl.

Come to that, you were thinking about it too—

That was when she was right here, and we were about to go in there.

He means it all. He'll challenge me if he thinks I've wronged her. And what the hell, I might not win. He's good with a sword, and better with that bow. Warner shuddered at the thought of a belly wound. And suppose I win? Captain Galloway would have my hide. And Caradoc's got relatives and they'll all want my blood. He's sure as hell got more relatives than I have rounds. Sooner or later one of them will get me. Unless Captain Rick buys off Caradoc's family. He might do that, and then lock me in some castle tower and let me have a girl once in a while if I'm a good little wizard . . .

What was it Samuel Johnson said about sex? "The expense is damnable, the position is ridiculous, and the pleasure is fleeting." Yep. Just now I can sympathize.

"You've no horns from me," Warner said. "My word on it."

The look of relief on Caradoc's face made Warner glad he'd said it. Hell, Gwen was all right, but there were other girls, and Jesus, the archer seems like he's really in love with her.

Warner poured more wine for both of them. "Caradoc, I like Gwen. I like her a lot. She's smart and pretty and I can talk about a lot of things with her I can't talk about with anyone else. I don't love her. She doesn't love me. If there is anyone she loves besides her dead husband, it's you." He hoped that wasn't laying it on too thick.

"Nothing has happened between us that you need to worry about.

Nothing will, either. If you get her to marry you, I'll dance at the wedding and take your kids up in my balloon."

Caradoc's face twisted. He was trying to talk, but nothing happened.

"You mean that—" Caradoc said finally.

"Sure do."

"But—" Caradoc sighed. "And yet it is too late."

"Why in the name of Yatar's pissoir is it too late?"

"I have betrayed my trust—"

"Not by me," Warner said. "If anybody has you on charges for that, it'll be the lady." He laughed. "Go to her, you Yatar-damned idiot!"

✧ ✧ ✧

Gwen sat in the chair by her bed, her face buried in her hands. She felt frightened, ashamed, and guilty all at once, and she wasn't sure which was the worst.

She'd done wrong by her own standards, never mind those of Tran. She'd as good as played the tease with Larry Warner, and that was something she always tried not to do. Usually she succeeded too, particularly when she liked the man as much as she did Larry. She'd hurt Caradoc even worse, and more stupidly. She'd *never* played off one man against another. Nobody deserved that, not even some of the real turkeys she'd met the summer she worked as a secretary. Certainly Caradoc didn't.

So much for her own standards. She'd done an even worse job by the standards of Tran, and right now they were what really counted. A woman was a wife, daughter, or mother of some man on this planet. She could also be a widow for a while, but her time for that was running out. Even if it wasn't, being a widow didn't give her the right to play around after a respectable man had made an offer of honorable marriage. Noblewomen here had more rights than she'd expected, but this wasn't one of them.

If she went on this way, she would soon be considered to have lost her rank. She would no longer have a chance for an honorable marriage. Instead, she'd be getting one proposition after another, none of them honorable. If she accepted, she'd be hardly better than a common prostitute. If she refused, she'd need Rick's protection from the angry man, and Tylara might not let him give it.

I could retreat. Be something like an abbess of the University.

The thought almost made her laugh. She wasn't likely to take any vows of celibacy, or even pretend to have. And without that, the University might be wrecked and her own life would certainly be miserable.

So would Caradoc, the man who loved her.

Well, ducks, said the voice in her mind. It's like this. You can't be your own woman here.

Tell me something I don't know.

All right, but if you can't be your own woman, what about being the woman of the best man around?

Can I get him?

There was a knock on her door.

Maybe you've got him, she thought. She knew what she'd say if that were him—

Caradoc came in, kicked the door shut, and promptly knelt. Everything she'd planned to say went right out of her mind. For a man to kneel to a woman was to place himself totally at her mercy. He would listen to any insult from her, carry out any command, abandon kin or honor or life itself at her word. He was giving her absolute power over him, trusting that she would not abuse it.

He started to talk when she wound her fingers into his hair. She didn't remember most of what he said, because she was trying too hard not to cry. All she remembered was a phrase about "my kin are beginning to wonder where my wits have gone."

"Caradoc," she said, and repeated it until he looked up.

"Yes, my lady."

"No lady. Just Gwen." She took a deep breath. "Caradoc, you know they never found my husband's body, after the battle where he was killed."

"Yes."

"That is why I have not felt free to take another husband. I have not been sure that he was dead."

"But—more than a year?"

"Caradoc, he was—so full of life. Like you. If you died but no one found your body, how long would your kin go on wondering about you?"

He smiled for the first time. "Quite a while, I think. Particularly my aunt, who is sure I am doomed for hanging."

"It is the same for my husband. I have not until now been ready to think of another man."

The smile faded. "But—now?"

"I am ready."

Then she did cry. Fortunately Caradoc was there, with his arms around her and a shoulder for her to cry on, even if it was clothed in muddy sweat-fouled wool. Being in his arms felt so comfortable that before long she knew that if he led her to the bed she would go happily.

"No."

"No what?"

"No, I shall not ask for my betrothal rights tonight, or until I return from the war."

"But—you might not return."

"All the more reason for us to sleep apart until we know my fate. You are the mother of one child who will never see his father. Do you want to be the mother of a second?"

He was right, of course. But—"The priests of Yatar are said to know—"

"I will let no priest tell me when I may bed my wife!" He kissed her. "It will be enough to ride against Flaminius as your betrothed husband. My kin will swear to guard you if I do not return, or I will know why!"

Ah. This alliance made sense, more than any other. There was no man on Tran to whom Tylara owed more. While Gwen was unmarried Tylara could object to Rick working at the University; but Tylara do Tamaerthon wouldn't risk offending the man who'd rescued her from Sarakos.

Even if Caradoc were killed—no. I won't think of that.

And Les? Your baby's father?

But Les was a long way off, and Caradoc was here; and Gwen had been lonely a long time. Too long. She drew in a deep breath. "Very well. I accept it as you wish."

"Good. Now you can help me take a bath. Either that, or put me in the cellar so that my stink will kill the rats!"

11

Dughuilas dropped a handful of coins on the table without counting them, drew his cloak over his shoulders, and stepped out into the second-floor hallway. He did not look back. The girl was hardly worth it, and certainly not worth more than a fraction of the price the mistress of the house asked.

There must be something to be said for her, of course. Otherwise she wouldn't have been whoring long enough to have a maid of her own. The maid was a little blonde who would have been lovely but for her broken nose. Probably a war orphan, and Dughuilas suspected she'd have been more interesting than her mistress. However, old Echenia wouldn't let such things go on in her house, and that was an end to it.

Dughuilas tasted sour bile. The war would begin in less than a ten-day, and it was wrong. Far wiser to let the Romans tear each other like hungry stoats in a cage. Why couldn't Drumold understand that? Fascinated by the warlock son-in-law, the upstart.

And I must follow him! A coward, who has never proved himself in battle. Even in the Roman battle—yes, yes a great victory for the Lord Rick—even there he avoided combat. He raced for the pikemen rather than falling upon the Romans like a man!

Dughuilas shuddered at that memory. The Lord Rick shamed him before a whole army, firing his star weapon to startle Dughuilas and nearly bringing him off his horse. He'd felt fear—real fear—and of Rick, a man whose blood would turn to water if he ever got within sword's reach of a proper battle. He ruled from Tylara's bed, not from the saddle, and what sort of chief was that for a man to follow?

At least they'd had a scare at the University over the sky-machine! Whatever Corgarff might have said under torture, it shouldn't be enough to allow a trial of Dughuilas before the other clan chiefs. At worst, he could demand right of trial by combat against his accuser, and since that would be Lord Rick or perhaps Drumold, neither of them his match—

Something struck Dughuilas hard in the side of the neck. It hurt like a rat bite, and when he put his hand up to the pain he felt blood trickling and the tip of a dart. Some child's prank with a crossbow. Curse Madam Echenia, she couldn't keep order in her own house! She'd get no more custom from him or his clansmen.

He took another downward step, but unaccountably his foot came down on empty air. He fell forward, swallowing a shout and throwing his arms out to break his fall. He didn't want anyone to see his clumsiness.

Pain shot up his arms and he didn't quite protect his head. He tasted blood where a broken tooth had gashed his tongue, but somehow it didn't hurt as much as he'd expected. In fact, nothing felt quite normal any more. His tongue seemed thick and swollen, filling his mouth. Now he tried to shout, but only a croak came out.

Poison.

Poison on the dart.

The High Rexja's men, a plot to ruin Tamaerthon! He had to live, to warn Drumold before it was too late—or could it be—

He couldn't finish the thought. He rolled over to draw his dagger, but fell heavily on his back, his arms unwilling to obey. Above him the light from the candle on the stair landing shone on blonde hair. Another shape bent over him, and hands fumbled at his purse and sword. Dimly, as if from the bottom of a well, he heard leather tear and thongs snap.

Then a small hand in a glove clamped down over his mouth. He tried to bite, got a mouthful of leather, felt his stomach heave. Something cold struck him in the eye and he floated away on the pain until it and everything else ended.

✣ ✣ ✣

"The dagger in the eye went straight into Dughuilas' brain," said

Tylara. "Instant death. His killers took his purse, sword, and boots. They must have been well away before anyone found the body."

"Is it known who did it?" asked Rick, as his head popped out from the fur chamber robe. The messenger with the news of Dughuilas' death had arrived as he and Tylara were getting ready for bed.

"The maid to one of the women of the house has disappeared," said Tylara. "She may have been working with the killers, or she may have been slain as well. She was only a half-grown girl, so she could hardly have done the work herself.

"Beyond that, who knows? We know that both the High Rexja and Flaminius have spies among us. Dughuilas was a champion and clan leader, a bannerman. But more like, it was some enemy. He had enough, and all knew how he spent his nights before going to war."

She says the right words, but she does not seem upset, Rick thought. One of our officers dead . . . a man I never liked. "He was an important leader, and his clan will demand blood," Rick said. "A proven captain in war—"

Tylara stared. "A proven captain in the kind of war we used to fight! The kind of war which would have destroyed us a year ago. For the kind of war you have taught us, the fewer like Dughuilas we have, the better."

"Perhaps, up to a point. But I cannot be everywhere at once—"

"The more reason for not having Dughuilas in any of the places where you are not."

"Are you then glad that he is dead?" Rick demanded.

"I am not as unhappy as you seem to be. Why, I cannot understand. He was no friend to you or your cause."

Ah, but you do understand, my love. Don't you? "He was yet a brave man. A proven leader, a man of courage . . . and if we seem to care little for finding the killers, people may wonder why. You say Dughuilas had enemies. This is true. He also had fellow clansmen, who will be at my back on campaign."

"The guardsmen can keep watch."

"How many of Clan Calder can we afford to kill?"

"None. But I doubt we must kill any. Dughuilas' killers will be found."

"And if they are not?" Rick asked.

She shrugged. "It is in the hands of Yatar." She wriggled into the bed and pulled the covers about her. The bed was large, so that there remained a little distance between her and Rick. "Vothan One-eye has done us no ill turn by this."

"Exactly what everyone will be saying. He was our enemy, and he is dead. It is not much of a secret that Dughuilas is suspected of planning the balloon accident."

"It is also not much of a secret that Dughuilas has been the leader in half of what the knights and bheromen have done against you. Do you care so little for your plans that you will fret over the death of one of their worst enemies?"

"I do not. But there are honorable and dishonorable ways—"

She looked ready to spit on the floor, or even in his face. "You are not the only judge of honor here. I also have to judge what honor demands, for us and for our plans and for our children. Have you forgotten that? Or was André Parsons perhaps right? Are you too soft toward enemies to live long among us?"

"Enough!" Rick leaped from the bed. "I will go to my rooms. I have never laid hands on you, but by Christ—" He stalked toward the door, then stopped and turned. "I've lived longer here than Parsons," he said. "But then perhaps this is because I'm a coward. Go on, you can say that. Everyone else has."

He fumbled with the bolts of the heavy door. Can't even make a decent exit, he thought. Crap.

"My love." She stood next to him, and her face held grief. "My love. Forgive me." He gently gathered her into his arms and held her while she cried into the fur of his robe. Her hair had its old silky springiness back, now that she'd completely recovered from Isobel's birth.

"Forgive me, my love," she said finally. "Nor I, nor anyone doubts your courage or your honor. Only you. You have doubts enough for all of us, foolish doubts, for you are the bravest men I have ever known."

"Not likely—"

"Enough for me, then. Now come to bed. How can we let a man like Dughuilas ruin our last nights together? Come to bed, my love . . ."

✦ ✦ ✦

Later, after they had made love, he woke and lay sleepless. In a few days he would lead an army to war. Vothan One-eye would be loose in the land again. And how many soldiers have told themselves that what they do is right? All of them?

Now I've got to fight, and if I'm killed, will any of my plans be carried out? I think I'm indispensable. Necessary. Have to stay alive or no one will. Easy thing to talk yourself into. Easiest thing in the world.

Reasonable. Makes sense. Hah! The man who wondered if he was a coward because he had gone out for track instead of football in college still lurked inside the Eqeta of Chelm. Not very far inside, at times like these.

I can change what they think. I can prove myself. If I don't—

Dundee. John Graham of Claverhouse, Viscount Dundee, the only man since the Bruce to unite the Highlanders; the man who might have kept Scotland independent of England and the Stuarts on its throne. He'd known he was indispensable. So had the chiefs.

But at Killiecrankie, Dundee personally led the army. "Once," he promised his allies. "Once only. But until they know I am worthy to lead them, I cannot lead them where we must go."

And he'd fallen at Killiecrankie, ending the Highlander cause . . .

I have to win their respect. How, I don't know. But I have to do something . . . with Dughuilas dead by assassins it's even more necessary. Reasons of state. And I have to live with myself as well.

Tylara stirred slightly, and he covered her bare arm, resisting an impulse to waken her and lose himself in her. Then he stared at the ceiling again.

PART THREE
ANGELS AND MINISTERS OF GRACE

12

"Pass in review!"

Drums thundered and pipes skirled as the massed forces of Rick's army marched across the parade ground.

"Eyes—RIGHT!"

The First Pike Regiment marched past, their pikes held aslant, the regimental banner dipped in homage to Rick and the others on the reviewing stand. The banner held three battle streamers; one, Sentinius, might be an embarrassment under the circumstances, but most of Rick's units had been there and were proud of it.

Rick glanced to his right where Publius stood at attention, but gained no clue as to what the Roman was thinking. Publius was an enigma; his manners were perfect when in public with Rick, but spies said he was given to cursing the barbarians whenever there was the slightest reason. He was also interested in women, and his success as a Don Juan impressed even the lustiest of Tamaerthan lords.

And what, Rick wondered, must Bishop Arrhenius think of his Emperor-to-be? The Roman Christian Church seemed considerably less preoccupied with chastity than did its counterpart on Earth, but even so there *was* the Sixth Commandment . . . More to the point, though, what did His Lordship think of all these pagan allies? Whatever he thought, he said nothing. He stood next to Publius, splendid in his cope and mitre; and if he longed to go make converts among Rick's army, he showed no signs of it.

Second Pikes marched past, then Third and Fourth. They kept their lines straight enough, although they were not expert at parade ground formations. Rick wondered again what impression he was making on the Roman officers. His army was hardly uniform; it seemed that no two men wore the same equipment. Some had breastplates, some mail byrnies. Some had Roman helmets, others had modified captured Roman equipment until it was hardly recognizable; some men wore leather jerkins and no armor at all. None had a lot; the pikes were supposed to be lightly armed, able to march hard and fast, then fight for a long time. Rick knew their value; but would these haughty Roman officers understand?

"Present—Arms! Eyes—RIGHT!" Battalion guide—on banners rose high, then snapped downward to the salute. There was another thunder of drums, then fifty pipers; and finally the archers.

Rick saw Publius nod sagely as they went by. They were impressive enough even to look at, their long bows held at high port, and over their backs quivers filled with grey gullfeathered arrows a clothyard long, tipped with a deadly bodkin point that would penetrate armor at short ranges, and kill a horse at two hundred paces and more. There were never enough archers; it took years to train them, years spent at the archery butts when you might be doing something more lucrative. Many wealthy enough to become archers would not; they considered themselves part of the chivalry of Tamaerthon, and learned to ride and fight with lance, usually neglecting the art of the bow. Most of the archers were sons of yeomen and freeholders, the closest thing to a middle class Tamaerthon had.

The archers wore kilts of bright colors, and colored shirts, and many had jewelry, particularly bracelets. They'd fared well in Rick's previous battles, and being lightly armed and mobile they'd been able to get extra loot despite Rick's orders about sharing the booty.

Even the Romans appreciated their value; although Rick suspected that Publius did not understand the value of combined arms, cavalry, pikes, and archers fighting together as a unit, each covering the others' weaknesses.

Behind the archers came Tamaerthon's knights. They were impressive enough in their haughty ways, but they were not as well mounted as Drantos knights and bheromen—certainly not as well as the Roman heavy cavalry, the splendid cataphracti who'd once dominated most of this continent. Their armor wasn't as good, either;

the chivalry of Tamaerthon couldn't really take its place in the main battle line. With training they could make good scouts. He'd organized about three hundred of them into a Hussar Regiment. The rest had too much pride for that.

"You have brought mostly Tamaerthan troops," Publius said. "I see few enough of the chivalry of Drantos."

"True, my lord," Rick said. "I saw little need for more heavy cavalry. Your legions should suffice for that. Instead, the Lord Protector chose to send auxiliary troops. Light infantry and cavalry. And foragers, and wagons, and siege engineers. We will have trouble enough feeding this army as it is; why add to that trouble?"

Publius frowned. "It is the cataphracti who decide battles," he said. "Others can be useful, but the art of war consists of having heavy cavalry in the right place and using them well."

So far it does, Rick thought. I hope to change that . . . "Aye, my lord. But the chivalry of Drantos can hardly match your legionaries. It would seem a worthless exercise to bring them when we have more need of wagons and transport."

And I can just hear Drumold grinding his teeth at that one, Rick thought. He knows his cavalrymen are no match for Romans, not even one-on-one—certainly not in unit engagements.

"You honor us," Publius said. "But—I see few enough soldiers here—"

Fewer than these defeated one of your legions, Rick thought. And did it in their first battle. Now they've got pride, and they *know* they can stand up to a Roman charge . . .

The Tamaerthan Hussars trotted by. Their nominal colonel-in-chief was Tylara; today they were led by Teuthras, one of her cousins. Tylara, after many protests, had seen the necessity of having someone completely trustworthy to hold Castle Dravan, their home. Rick sent her with most of the mercenaries, their ammunition, and weapons; the weapons were under guard of Tamaerthan Mounted Archers, and there were equal numbers of loyal Drantos and Tamaerthan troops with her. Rick had no real doubts that the dozen mercs he sent with her would remain loyal—but there was no point in tempting them.

Behind the light cavalry came engineers with siege engines, including portable ballistae and catapulta—and wagonloads of their ammunition, clay pots filled with gunpowder and potshard shrapnel.

And finally the mercs: Sergeant Major Elliot, Corporal Bisso, and a dozen troopers in camouflage coveralls and web belts, carrying rifles and grenades.

"We have brought enough, I think," Rick told Publius. "Those men alone can win any battle we might fight. Each holds a thousand men's lives in his hand."

"This is still not all of Flaminius' army."

"If you saw a thousand of your men die, suddenly and violently, for no reason you could see, while the enemy was yet a mile away, would that not be decisive?" Rick asked gently.

Publius shuddered. "Indeed."

And you're wondering how much of that to believe, aren't you? Well, you'll find out soon enough.

✢   ✢   ✢

They were five days march into territory claimed by Flaminius. There had been no battles; only an endless series of minor crises, decisions to be made, looters to be punished—

"We come as liberators and allies, not as thieves and enemies!" Rick had thundered to his army; but if the military police weren't watching, the soldiers would take anything they could carry. Chickens, pigs, sheep, cattle; it didn't matter, if it were edible they'd soon have it.

At least they weren't setting fire to things; and after Rick hanged two men, the rapes stopped. Of course there were the ambiguous cases, where the girl's relatives claimed rape while the trooper claimed seduction; those had to be settled as they came up, generally in favor of the trooper if he had half a story. "Nobody ever got raped in an upper bunk," Rick remembered as a judgement of an American military court; if the girl didn't appear abused, the same principles applied here.

They rode on. Toward evening, Corporal Mason came in, followed by a score of his Mounted-Archer MPs. "More trouble, Captain," he said in English.

"How?" Rick asked warily.

"Clan Calder types. They're still talking."

Dughuilas' clan. Rick could guess what they were saying. That the forces of Tamaerthon were led by a coward, a man who'd struck their clan chief in battle, but had never faced an enemy man to man.

"Anyone in particular?" Rick asked.

"No sir. I kept an eye on Dwyfyd, but it don't seem to be him."

Dwyfyd was Dughuilas' eldest son; now he had the name Dughuilas as well, although not everyone used it yet. They would, eventually; for the moment there was talk about this twenty-year-old who'd inherited the leadership of one of the largest clans. He was a good friend to Tylara's brother Balquhain, which might help, and then again might not.

"No suggestions as to who killed Chief Dughuilas?" Rick asked.

Mason shook his head. "Most reckon that a man who goes to whorehouses often enough is eventually gonna get something he didn't want."

"Too right."

"Here come the Hussars," Mason said. "I'll go—"

"No, stick around for the report."

"Okay, if you say so."

The light cavalry officers rode in. Today the force had been headed by Balquhain, Teuthras, and Drumold himself.

"Hail, Mac Clallan Muir," Rick said formally.

"Hail, son-in-law."

"Any sign of Marselius?"

"None. Nothing but enemies. Enough of those. Skirmishers, raiders, light cavalrymen—"

"We drove them off easily enough," Balquhain said.

"At the cost of seven troopers," Drumold said. "That was no' well done, boy."

"I am no boy," Balquhain protested. "And since what hour has Mac Clallan Muir counseled retreat when we have not yet fought? We drove them away, and we killed nearly a score. A small victory—but it was victory."

"Headstrong, headstrong," Drumold said. "Lad, lad, do you not yet realize, the important thing is to win the battle. Not these tiny fights that are no more than tournaments! They do us nae good at all. Is this not so, Lord Rick?"

"We need all the light cavalrymen we have," Rick said slowly. "And we need information more than small victories . . ."

"It is no surprise that *you* would say that," a young officer said.

"Tethryn!" Drumold said sharply.

Tethryn. Dwyfyd's youngest brother, another young lordling of Clan Calder.

"That was not well said," Balquhain said. "The Lord Rick has strange ways, but he wins victories . . ."

"Men who fight *win* victories," Tethryn said. "Wizards have other ways." He wheeled and rode away.

✢　✢　✢

Rick rode with Drumold back to his camp after they had supper with Publius. They rode in silence for a while through a light drizzle. Drumold had sent their guards a few lengths away so they could talk without being overheard, but then he said nothing for a long time.

Finally he drew closer. "Did my daughter put some new worm in your guts, Rick? Or is it the old one eating at you?"

"The old one. They're all certain I'm a coward. I have to show them. But how?"

"You've no need, lad. We know—"

"You, perhaps." And perhaps not. "Not the others. I've got to do something. But I can't get within twenty stadia of the fighting!"

"You'll no' be so far from the battle when we meet Flaminius."

"By then it could be too late."

The older man flicked something invisible from his horse's mane. "I think it is eating you more than usual," he said. "Doubtless the affair of Dughuilas has provoked more talk than usual, and you hear it. Or— has my daughter been at you? If so, thrash her. I'll no' say a word against you or let one be said."

Rick sighed. "And how long before Tylara repaid me with usury? It is no light thing, to lay hands on your daughter."

"Aye. I have cause to know," Drumold said pensively. "Lad, you are concerned about more than this."

"Yes. We received word from Marselius today. He marches from the north—on the east side of the River Pydnae. We have yet to reach that river. If Flaminius can cut us off—"

"Perhaps it will be that Marselius will come upon him first."

"That, too, concerns me. Mostly, though, we're getting deeper and deeper into the Empire—I'd not want to face the whole of Flaminius' strength unaided."

"Nor I. Even with your star weapons."

"They might be enough. They might not be." Rick sighed. "Converging columns is a tricky enough war plan when you have good communications. It can be disaster without. We're inviting defeat in detail—"

"A phrase I know not," Drumold said.

"Military strategic term. If you can divide your enemy into small forces and fight them one at a time—"

"Ah."

"And that's what we invite," Rick said.

"Do you think Marselius has played us false?" Drumold demanded.

"No. He has no reason to. And we have his son hostage, too." Rick laughed. "Actually, nothing has gone wrong, my old friend. We are well within the time limits we set."

"And yet you fash yourself—"

"Yes."

"I see." Drumold rode in silence for a few moments. "You wish to find Flaminius' army, and Marselius. And you wish to force a crossing of this river." Drumold looked thoughtful, then grinned. "I think I shall wake up with a fever tomorrow morning."

"A fever?"

"Aye. A light fever, of the sort which keeps me from riding with the scouts. I shall stay back with the main body, to do what you have done here. *You* can lead the scouts in my place, and no one will spend a moment wondering why."

With any luck at all, there'd be at least one good fight with Flaminius' patrols. The Emperor couldn't simply go on giving ground forever. There might be a stiff fight at the river . . .

I'll be at the head of the army, Rick thought. For a few days, anyway. Lead from in front. Yeah.

Idiot. You'll get yourself killed, and there's no one able to extract your forces out of this trap. Nobody but you. And without this army, Tamaerthon is finished. The imperial slave masters will be in the Garioch. Your friends, relatives, sold into slavery because you had to prove yourself. You're brave enough, now stop trying to—

Shut up! You talked me into track because it was sensible. All my life I've done what's sensible. This time I'm going to lead my troops to battle, and that's that!

Only—there's Tylara to think of. She'll find out, and ask why I've risked myself when I didn't have to.

"And if my daughter says aye about it, send her to me," Drumold said. "She may now be so great a lady that she will say aught to her husband—but let us see what she says to her father, who remembers her a naked babe making puddles in his lap."

13

Rain fell lightly all through the day. The cavalry troopers didn't want to ride out in that. After all, the Roman cavalry wouldn't be out either.

Their reluctance was mostly for show, Rick found. And they were flattered that Lord Rick, the Commander-in-Chief, was riding with them. But the rain continued, so that he could hardly see the men to either side of him, and they made no contact with the enemy.

And the next day, messengers arrived at dawn. Marselius was indeed across the River Pydnae, marching south through the low hills to the east of the river. Directly ahead of Rick lay more hills and thin forests, good territory for battle. North and east, though, were swamps; if the two armies were to link up, they'd have to do so east of the river.

Where was Flaminius? His generals could read maps as well as Rick . . .

"Mount up!" Rick ordered. "We ride hard for the bridge. I want a mixed force of pikes and archers across that river before nightfall."

✧ ✧ ✧

The sky was grey with low-hanging clouds. The horses picked their way cautiously over muddy patches as the scouts rode out across fields to either side of the hard-packed dirt road. Rick led two hundred Hussars, plus Caradoc with twenty guardsmen and Elliot with two other mercs.

They'd covered about seven kilometers when a guardsman from the point squad rode back.

"Fresh dung, my lord. Horses, with a few centaurs."

"Hmm. How shod?"

"Iron shod," the scout reported.

That meant cavalry. Roman farmers didn't usually bother. Time to mark up a map. One thing about this campaign, he had decent maps, done by Roman scribes. The enemy might surprise him, but the terrain wouldn't—at least not too much. The scale of the maps did leave something to be desired: the little clearing ahead wasn't marked. Not far beyond was the river, with its convenient bridge. Not far to go at all—

Rick rode to the center of the clearing, then reined and held up his hand for a halt. The well-used dirt road ran across the clearing and into the woods on the other side.

He'd just got out the map—

"Ho! Look out, goddammit!" someone shouted from behind him. There were three pistol shots, close together, then the shouts of his troops mingled with Roman battle cries.

Rick stuffed the map hurriedly into his saddle bag and stood in his stirrups to look back along the dirt track they'd followed. Men in Roman helmets darkened with mud were darting out of the trees, their swords flashing among the scouts. One of the mercs was down, and two more were firing from horseback, wasting ammunition.

The Roman troopers slashed at the horses with their swords, while archers farther back in the woods let fly at the riders. There were more shots from the mercs, but the Romans were mixed well with Rick's troops and there weren't clear targets.

"Cease fire!" he shouted in English. "Elliot! Get out here in the clear! Dismount and set up weapons. Prepare to receive cavalry! They're sure to be coming."

Switch languages again. "Caradoc! You and your guardsmen, stay with Elliot! Guard their weapons!" Now for his Tamaerthan scouts. "Hussars move out this way! Follow me!" He rode toward the other edge of the clearing.

I've got to get my people disengaged, get some kind of order into this, get them out of the tangle with the ambushers. Elliot can take care of them after that. Dammit, those Romans were good!

They'd almost reached the other edge of the clearing when the woods on both sides of the pathway sprouted archers and the air came alive with arrows.

Too damn late, Rick thought. *We're tangled up with them again.*

We've got to buy Elliot and the guards enough time to set up. "Charge!" he ordered. "Forward!" He spurred toward the enemy.

Arrows whistled in. Rick's armor turned the two which hit him, but a third hit his horse in the shoulder. It jumped and squealed, but the arrow wasn't in deep enough to be a major wound. Rick raised his M-16 and squeezed off five rounds. He thought he hit three men. Then he was at the clearing's edge.

He slung the rifle across his saddle horn and drew his saber. In among the trees the sword was as good a weapon as a firearm. He slashed at one man, striking him at the shoulder, then he was past and into the woods.

He had time to notice that the woods stank. Most of the trees were lower and bushier than Earth trees would be; but mixed in with them were what could only be European scrub oak.

He bore to the right. The road would be there, and more of his scouts were forcing their way along the track. Behind him a trumpet sounded; the high pitch of a Tamaerthan horn, not the low rumble of Roman signals. Someone had ordered recall of the point group. Who? It was the right move. Rick should have given the order himself, but he was separated from his staff. He heard men behind him. His, he hoped.

There were crashing sounds, and someone rode up behind and to his left. Rick turned, sword raised.

"Hold, my lord!"

It was Jamiy, his orderly, holding his round target to protect Rick. Just then they burst through to a second clearing; the patch of woods between this clearing and the one where they'd been attacked couldn't be more than fifty yards thick.

Shouts and screams erupted ahead. The guardsmen of the point squad came pounding back down the path into the clearing. Hard on their heels was a mass of mounted Romans. As Rick and Jamiy rode into the clearing, the point troopers rallied to them, while from behind another dozen men who'd been following Jamiy came into clear territory.

The Romans ahead weren't the splendid legionary cataphracti; these were more lightly armored, with round shields, looking more like traditional Roman cavalry of the older days. They were scattered from chasing the point men; and Rick's troopers were lining up in a passable formation—

An organized charge will always carry against disorganized force. Which dry lecturer had he heard say that, light years away and a lifetime ago? But it was probably true. And there was Rick's trumpeter—

"Make ready to charge!" he ordered. He unslung his rifle and began a slow deliberate aimed fire, chopping down anyone in the Roman group who looked like an officer. He hit five men. The rest were still coming. Lord, what soldiers!

"Sound the charge!" Rick ordered. "Forward!"

His light cavalry moved ahead in a passable line, sweeping toward the more numerous but scattered Romans. Rick held the rifle uncertainly. It would be better if he halted and fired but that wouldn't do at all, not now with his troops at his back. Better to sling it again and use saber and pistol.

They struck the Romans, cut down more leaders, and were swept into the thick of the action. More and more of Rick's troops were coming from behind him, while extra supplies of Romans kept bursting into the clearing. Rick quickly lost track of what was happening to anyone except himself. This wasn't a battle; it was a series of small-unit actions, two- and three-man engagements moving as rapidly as horses and centaurs could carry them.

And it was getting out of hand. There'd be no point to fighting his way to the river unless he had enough troops to force a passage. "Rally back to the first clearing!" Rick ordered. "We must see to the star weapons! Sound 'Follow me!'" He turned to ride back toward the woods, followed by what was left of his troops—how many? He had no idea at all. More than a hundred, he thought. The trumpet sang behind him as he rode.

They reached the edge of the clearing just as a fresh wave of Romans burst through from the other side. Rick had no chance to count them, but it looked like a lot, enough to spread all across the clearing and still have depth to the formation. Enough to be a serious threat to Rick's whole command—

And behind that first wave of light cavalry the orange light of the True Sun glinted on silver links! Cataphracti, regular legionaries. Except for star weapons there wasn't a thing in Rick's cavalry command that could stand up to them.

Well, I've found Flaminius' army, he thought. Now all I have to do is live to get back and report it. Run like hell!

✠ ✠ ✠

They reached the first clearing. Elliot had that situation under control; he'd set up a fire base in the clearing's center, and was shepherding wounded and stragglers into its protection. There were still archers in the woods, and Elliot's position was within extreme bowshot; but an engagement between a scope-sighted rifle fired by a man lying prone, and a bow used by a man who had to expose himself to shoot, wasn't really a contest. The Romans would soon run out of archers.

"More troops coming!" Rick announced. "Heavies. We'll want to blunt their charge and get the hell out of here!"

"Yes, sir!" Elliot answered. "Better get down—"

Too late for that, Rick thought. The rest of his Hussars were entering the clearing in headlong retreat. There were more of them than Rick had expected, a least a hundred. They'd come part way across when the Romans came through the trees.

"Caradoc!" Rick shouted. "Send four men back to Drumold! Have him bring up the rest of the cavalry on the double. We've found the enemy's main army." Caradoc said something that might be an acknowledgement.

Rick fired six rounds into the advancing Romans. Three riders went down and a fourth was thrown as his horse stumbled over one of the bodies. Rick wished he had the H&K instead of an M-16. The lighter bullet would punch through armor just as well if it hit squarely, but could more easily be deflected if it didn't.

Then the retreating Hussars swept past and the Romans were nearly on him. Rick spurred forward; better to be moving than a standing target. A Roman soldier came at him with lance, but Rick swerved, firing at him as they closed; he missed, but the noise startled the trooper so that he raised the lance point. Then a Roman with an officer's breastplate was straight ahead, lance lowered and ready to skewer Rick in the saddle. Rick flattened himself on the horse's neck. The lance dipped, too far. The point drove into the side of Rick's horse a moment before the two mounts crashed together. Rick's horse started to topple. He hurled himself out of the saddle, trying to leap clear of the falling horse.

The thrashing animal missed him by a yard. Rick fell heavily on the M-16. He rolled off it to find the action hopelessly jammed with mud. He scrabbled at his pistol; his hand was numb from the fall, and his thumb swollen so that he had to use both hands to get the safety off. He shot the Roman officer at point blank range, letting the heavy .45 slug batter through the man's armor. Another Roman mounted on a centaur was charging toward him; there was no clear shot at the man. Rick aimed at the center of the centaur's body and fired twice.

The animal screamed, a nearly human sound, its stumpy arms and badly formed hands tearing at the wound. The Roman screamed also, in rage and something more, horror and sorrow. He jumped to the ground and charged at Rick, his sword held high. Rick fired, once, twice, before the Roman staggered; the force of his charge carried him to Rick, and the sword swept down. It never hit. Suddenly there was a round shield held in front of Rick; Jamiy stood left flank rear, his sword bloodied from some previous action.

"Thanks," Rick grunted.

His orderly didn't answer.

✢ ✢ ✢

The Romans charged once more, to be cut down by fire from Elliot and his mercs. Even Roman discipline wasn't good enough to get them to charge again, and they withdrew toward the woods.

Rick's charge had carried him almost to the clearing edge; a Roman horseman swept past, and Rick shot him out of the saddle. The horse stopped in its tracks, within easy reach. Rick quickly holstered his pistol and gripped the reins, ready to mount. He got one foot in the stirrup before the horse had time to react.

Then more shouts. The guardsmen had swept forward to rescue their leader. Rick's new mount panicked and reared, throwing Rick forward. He landed sprawled across the saddle like a bag of grain, and the horse bolted forward into the woods.

He was among the Romans. One of their troopers slashed at his head. The sword glanced off his helmet. Rick struggled to get back into the saddle and draw his pistol, but he knew he would be too late. There'd be no Jamiy to take this blow. His orderly was back there, down, maybe dead, maybe not, but Rick was alone except for two guardsmen and a Tamaerthan officer who lay in a tangled pile just ahead.

The Roman moved in for the kill. Stupid, Rick thought. This is what you get, trying to lead the goddam army yourself. You get dead, and who leads now?

Then the Tamaerthan clan officer who lay at his feet lurched upward, barely able to stand. He staggered between the two horses, and his rising shoulder caught the Roman's second downcut. The clansman stabbed at the Roman's horse.

"Tethryn!" Rick shouted.

The Roman's horse jumped as Tethryn's knife entered his belly. The Roman trooper had to grab for the reins, and his next sword cut was spoiled. Rick managed to get astride his mount and get out his .45. There was one shot left in the magazine. Rick held the pistol to within a foot of the Roman's chest and fired. The man screamed and fell backward, and Rick's horse bolted again. This time it plunged out of the woods into the clearing, galloping across and up the narrow road toward the second clearing, as Rick tried frantically to secure his pistol before he dropped it.

The second clearing was empty except for dead and wounded. Rick's runaway mount carried him across at a slowing gallop; by the time they were to the other side, Rick had managed to holster his pistol and get the reins in both hands. The horse was tiring fast; it shouldn't be long before he could control it—

Except that he was being carried into unknown territory toward the Roman army.

14

The forest beyond the second clearing was only a thin screen of trees along the bank of the narrow, swift-flowing River Pydnae. Rick's horse was tiring fast before he reached the river. When they reached the bank, the animal was more or less under control.

A dozen guardsmen, led by Caradoc, trotted up behind. "Are you well, my lord?" Caradoc called.

"Well enough now," Rick said. "Except for them." He pointed.

Not quite three hundred meters off to his left was a bridge, a wooden roadway on stone piers. Between him and the bridge stood more than two hundred mounted Roman cataphracti. Their officer, easily recognized by his scarlet cape, was pointing at Rick, but the troops were not moving. Possibly afraid of star weapons?

Nonsense. Their mission was to control the bridge. But there weren't any troops visible on the other side, which meant—

"Caradoc, get your fastest messengers riding back to the main army. I want the whole Tamaerthan army here as soon as possible. They're to keep in formations, but I need them fast."

"Pikes too?" Caradoc asked.

"Especially the Pikes. Have another messenger go to Publius and ask him for as many *alae* of heavy cavalry as he can send. Tell him the main bridge over the Pydnae is intact, if we can just get enough troops across to hold it."

Caradoc turned to ride back and find messengers.

Rick and the Roman officer faced each other at three hundred yards. The Roman still did nothing.

Trying to make up his mind, Rick thought. Wonder how old he is? His ambush worked perfectly, but his outfit was shattered by weapons he can't understand. He ought to be terrified, but there he is, defending that bridge, trying to decide whether his best move is to stay there or attack me. He can't know who won back there in the clearing, or how many troops are left on either side. But he does know where his main army is—

Suddenly the Roman officer made his decision. About half the Romans formed up and came toward Rick at the trot. A hundred of them, against his dozen; impossible odds, even with a new magazine in his pistol. "Let's get out of here," Rick called. He pointed back toward the trees.

The guardsmen wheeled, and they rode back the way they'd come. About half the Romans took out bows and let fly; the rest came on at a fast trot, lances lowered; and now Rick's horse was under control, but exhausted, impossible to get moving at anything more than a fast walk. Rick swore and dug in his spurs. He wasn't going to make it to the woods in time. He drew his Colt, cursing as he worked the safety with his swollen thumb.

A flight of arrows whizzed past, then another. He felt wasp-sting pains as a couple of points just got through his armor, and felt his horse shudder. This time he got out of the saddle before the horse started to go down, but still he landed clumsily. A worse pain than the arrows shot through one ankle. He lurched to his feet and tried to sight on the Roman commander. Good luck, Tylara—

Elliot rode out of the woods at a canter, leading a spare horse. At the same time arrows and bullets flew from behind several trees. Four Romans went down, but others kept on coming. Elliot unslung his H&K and emptied a magazine at full automatic. This time the effect was obvious. The Roman point was scattered, with a dozen horses wounded. They plunged and reared, leaving the Roman force in disarray. The officer shouted something, and they wheeled to fall back to the bridge.

✦ ✦ ✦

Elliot rode up with the spare mount. "Need a lift, Captain?"

"Damn straight." Rick mounted and rode into the trees. Finally he had time to stop and survey the situation. Nothing broken. Maybe. His ankle hurt like hell, and his thumb throbbed like fury, but he didn't have time for them just now. "Thanks, Sarge."

"Nothing to it," Elliot said.

"Yeah. Sarge, have you got that one-oh-six with you?"

"Yes, sir." He pointed; Bisso was about fifty yards away with the weapon. "Want me to drop the bridge?"

"Christ, no! We need that bridge. No, what I have in mind is blowing open a path for some of our troops to get across. Do that and we've got the Romans trapped."

"Yeah. Why don't they retreat?"

"I don't know. But I can guess. They don't want to go tell Flaminius Caesar that they retreated from a bunch of barbarians. They're probably supposed to hold this side of the bridge so Flaminius can get his army across."

"You think his army is near?" Elliot asked.

"Looks like it. Why else would there be both scouts and legionaries? I think we've run into their vanguard, and that officer there knows it. So he's waiting for reinforcements he's pretty sure to get."

Elliot looked thoughtful. "Be hard to hold too many more with just the troops we have here."

"I know. I've sent for the whole army. First thing, I'll need to borrow your H&K. Fine. Now, let's see if we can get across that bridge."

✦ ✦ ✦

Elliot dismounted and shouted orders. Bisso and his companion moved to the edge of the woods and set up the one-oh-six on its tripod. The Romans, meanwhile, did nothing.

"What the hell?" Bisso asked.

"Still don't want to retreat," Rick said. "Not from barbarians. But that last clip spooked 'em enough they don't want to charge, either—set up the light machine gun over here."

Elliot fussed with the machine-gun sights, then bent over the one-oh-six recoilless rifle. "Clear everyone from behind," he said. "All of you—get! Move, dammit. Okay, Captain, ready when you are."

Rick faced his dismounted guardsmen. "Stand easy. When that gun goes off, it will be damned noisy. The mounts won't like it, so hold them. When you hear the charge, ride like hell for the bridge. We'll go right over. Don't stop to fight. Just get over that bridge. Okay, Sergeant Major, stay ready. We'll wait as long as we can. I'd like to have some reinforcements."

"Sir."

Only we can't wait too long, Rick thought. The rest of Flaminius' army will be coming up too. Or that detachment will decide to retreat across the bridge and we'll really be for it. I ought to go now—

Yeah. Now, before you lose your bloody nerve and won't be able to do it. Who the hell do you think you are, Napoleon at the Bridge of Lodi?

While Elliot was making sure of his sights, a dozen guards archers came up on foot, with a fresh supply of arrows and a message from Caradoc. The ambush in the rear was defeated, and new troops had come in from the main force. There were a lot of Romans scattered in among the forests, but they'd ceased to exist as an organized force.

The main army was coming, but it would be an hour or more before any infantry could arrive. Drumold and the Tamaerthan heavies ought to be along sooner. There was as yet no reply from the Romans.

And Rick thought he could see dust rising far down the road across the river. Flaminius? Or imagination? Whatever, it was time.

"Guardsmen, mount up! Elliot, stand ready to fire!"

"Sir." He bent over the sights.

"Mind your mounts!" Rick called. "Shoot!"

"Fire in the hole!" Elliot shouted. The recoilless blasted leaves off trees in a triangle behind it. Horses reared.

The shell exploded among the Romans just at the bridge. Horses reared and plunged, and one whole section of Roman cavalry bolted away. A number of Romans were down.

"Got the range first shot," Elliot said proudly.

The Roman troops milled in disorganization. Their officer shouted at them.

"Fire!" Elliot shouted.

This time the round struck near the Roman officer. More of their cavalry went down.

"Ride!" Rick ordered. "Sound the charge."

Trumpets blared, and they were riding forward at the gallop. There was no time to shoot at anyone, and nothing to shoot at either. Rick had drawn his saber; he held it point forward as he rode hunkered down to the horse's neck. He hoped someone was behind him.

He galloped onto the bridge, then across it. Some of the bridge planking was missing; his horse barely jumped across one gap. Then he was at the other side. He turned to the right and brought the horse up sharply.

Twenty guardsmen had followed and were on the bridge. Jamiy, his sword arm bound to his chest, was in their lead, mounted on the centaur he favored. He shouted at the beast and it turned to stand next to Rick.

"Dismount!" Rick commanded. "Dismount and hold the bridge!"

The Roman saw his danger now, and was trying to rally his troops to charge across. A score made for the bridge approach, then fell as Elliot's light machine-gun stuttered. Rick unslung the H&K and waited; two Romans made it onto the bridge. He shot them off it, feeling ashamed as he did.

The Roman officer rallied his troops and drew up in column formation fifty yards from the bridge. There was more rifle fire from the woods, and some Romans dropped. By now Rick's guardsmen were also dismounted and had unlimbered their bows.

"You haven't a chance!" Rick shouted. "Surrender in honor!"

The Roman officer stood in his stirrups and waved forward. The Roman line charged. Lances dipped in unison as they thundered toward the bridge—

Elliot's machine-gun stuttered again. Rick added to the fire with his H&K. He found he had trouble seeing. There was a mist in his eyes. Lord God, what troops! He aimed low, at the mounts, hoping not to kill any more of the Romans.

The charge was broken, but still a half-dozen Roman troopers managed to get to the bridge. They rode on, and now there was nothing for it but to shoot them down in a hail of arrows and bullets.

The other Romans withdrew. Their officer was down, lying half-under his mount.

A dozen Tamaerthan heavy cavalry burst from the woods. Drumold's banner led the way. More of the chivalry of Tamaerthon followed. They charged toward the Romans.

"No!" Rick screamed. He struggled to get onto his mount. "You! Ischerald! You're in charge. Hold on here. Jamiy, follow me!" Rick spurred back across the bridge.

They reached the other side. "See to their officer," Rick shouted to Jamiy. "Get an acolyte of Yatar. Instantly, damn you! He's too good a man to die like that!"

He rode slantwise until he was between Drumold and the Romans.

Then he led the Tamaerthan troopers forward. The Romans rode away until their remnant was brought to bay, the river bank at their backs. A few stripped off armor and dove in. They vanished in the swift, muddy water, and Rick couldn't see what happened to them.

Probably doomed, he thought. One of the more unpleasant life forms on Tran was the hydra, a fresh-water squidlike mollusk that could grow to twenty feet in length. The big hydras preferred clear, slow-moving water, but there were smaller forms in nearly all deep streams. One forded Tran rivers with care.

The remaining Romans sat their horses defiantly. There were no more than fifty left, and now they faced fifty Tamaerthan heavies and twice that many guardsmen. Still they stood proudly.

Rick reined up a hundred yards from the Romans.

Drumold rode up. "I came as soon as possible."

"Thank you. We must get reinforcements over the bridge. We've got to hold the other side."

"That may no' be so easy," Drumold said. "As I topped the rise yonder I saw the flash of armor. Perhaps twenty stadia away. Legionaries, I think."

"All the more reason to hold the bridge," Rick said. He thought for a moment. "We'll need to ride out and show ourselves to the Romans, before they get close enough to see how few we have across the river. That should stop them for the day. Can you get your chaps to let themselves be seen and then retreat back here?"

"Aye, although they will not be pleased to do so. But they will do it—Rick, we have already been told of your charge for the bridge. And earlier, in the clearing. No man will call you coward now."

Yeah. I knew that. And I've killed a lot of good men to make it happen. Ah, hell.

"And what do we do here?" Drumold asked. He pointed at the Romans.

"I go to speak with them."

"And if they shoot you down?"

"Then you're in command." Rick rode forward alone, his hands spread out empty. When he was fifty yards from the Roman line he held his hand up, palm forward. "Hail, soldiers of Rome."

There was a long pause. Finally a Roman soldier rode forward. "Hail, barbarian."

"Lay down your arms," Rick shouted. "You have fought honorably, against star weapons and great odds. Now accept honor and take quarter."

"From whose hand?" the Roman demanded.

"In the name of Marselius Caesar," Rick replied. "You will have heard of his amnesty for all who follow an enthroned Caesar. This I too swear. I am Rick Galloway, Colonel of Mercenaries, Eqeta of Chelm, War Leader of Tamaerthon, War Lord of Drantos, Ally and Friend to Marselius Caesar."

The Roman seemed to think that one over.

"Archers!" Drumold shouted from behind him. "Prepare the gulls."

A group of guardsmen dismounted. They drew their long bows from bowcases.

"You know what Tamaerthan archers can do," Rick shouted. "You will die to no purpose. How can it serve Rome to have her finest soldiers slaughtered? Lay down your arms."

"Way! Way there!" someone called from behind.

A group of guardsmen and acolytes of Yatar came out toward Rick. They carried the Roman officer in a blanket.

"Your tribune lives," Rick shouted. "We tend his wounds. He bids you lay down your arms."

The Roman decurion looked back at his companions. Then slowly he rode forward. A few yards away he halted, drew his sword, and dismounted. Silently he came forward and presented it hilt first. Then he knelt in submission.

✛ ✛ ✛

Drumold led the Tamaerthan heavy cavalry across the bridge and down the road, as guardsmen collected the Roman weapons. Half an hour later, the first blocks of pikemen arrived. Rick sent them across the bridge to secure their foothold on the other side.

And now there was nothing to do but wait. And hurt. His clothes were stuck to him with blood from the arrow wounds, his ankle was starting to swell, and his thumb and whole right hand were already swollen. He'd forgotten to take off his ring; they would have to cut that off, and soon, too, or he'd lose the finger. There were other bumps and bruises he felt now that the adrenalin was no longer flowing.

But we won, he thought. " 'Twas a famous victory . . ."

✛ ✛ ✛

Caradoc rode up with the rest of the Guard.

"You'll be personally responsible for the Roman prisoners," Rick said. "I have promised them safety. They keep all their property except weapons, and they're to be well treated. All of them. And guarded by enough troops that they won't *try* to escape. I don't want one single one of them harmed. Is this understood?"

"Yes, Lord," Caradoc said.

And there aren't a hell of a lot of people I can give that order to and be sure it will be carried out.

"Can you come now?" Caradoc asked. "There is a man you must see."

Rick sighed wearily. "Is it urgent?"

"Very urgent, lord. It is Tethryn."

"He lives?"

"For the moment. The priests did not think he should be moved, but he was determined to speak to you, and has come." Caradoc paused for a moment. "I think it makes little difference whether we move him or not."

"I'll come," Rick said. "I owe him my life."

Tethryn lay on a horse litter at the edge of the clearing. His brother Dwyfyd bent over him. They look so much alike, Rick thought. Alike, and young and—Dwyfyd's eyes were wet with tears.

"Lord Rick." The dying boy's voice was almost inaudible.

"Hail, my friend and companion—"

"Thank you."

"You must rest."

"There is no time, Lord. Vothan One-eye has chosen me to guest in his hall this day. But I hope—you will not believe you see only enemies—in Clan Calder now. Some—some of the lesser chiefs . . ."

"Some of them would rather I did, so they can continue to plot against me?"

The boy was silent so long that Rick thought he'd fainted or died. Then he nodded. "Aye. Couldn't let you die—to make them happy. Not—when—they lied. My father was wrong. You are—no coward."

Tethryn's eyes closed, and Rick moved away to leave Dwyfyd alone with his brother.

Damn. Hell and damn. The kid wasn't eighteen yet.

⊹ ⊹ ⊹

"It is done?" Rick asked.

Dwyfyd nodded silently.

"He was a brave companion," Rick said. "He will have no minor place in Vothan's hall."

"Lord—"

"Yes?"

"May—may I ask a boon in Tethryn's name?"

"Yes."

Dwyfyd didn't hesitate. "Corgarff's life, Lord."

"Why?"

"He is my clansman. And—there are reasons."

Aha. So you know that your father was involved in the plot against the balloon. Probably ordered Corgarff's part in it. And you want to make that up.

"You do him no great service," Rick said. "He will be a cripple—"

"None the less, I owe him. And his family."

And you've probably paid off that crofter's family, too. "Clan Calder has a worthy chief," Rick said. "Caradoc, have messengers ride swiftly. Carry my orders to Lady Gwen that Corgarff is to be pardoned. Tell her that a writ will come soon. She is to stay the headsman's axe."

"Aye," Caradoc said.

And you don't approve. But you'll send the fastest man anyway, won't you? There's real loyalty. If there's time to save Corgarff, you'll save him, though you'd rather watch him die.

Pity we don't have working radios. A couple of sets would make a lot of difference. Semaphore? Heliograph? Telegraph towers? We could put those up. Have to think about it. Certainly we could link key points to share messages within a few hours . . .

And there were a thousand other details, and meetings to hold tonight, now that he'd located the edges of at least one legion. Battles to plan and kingdoms to govern and he hadn't even planted the first stick of *surinomaz* and Lord how every joint and muscle ached!

But some problems were solved. They held the bridge. There would be no difficulty in linking up with Marselius—indeed, Flaminius might be caught between them. He'd have to fight.

And there were political victories. Clan Calder an ally. Or at least its chief is. The Romans I killed today haven't died to no purpose.

There'll be fewer knives aimed at my back, and the longer I live the more I can do on this world—

How many get the chance to change the destiny of a whole world? I've been given that chance. Every man who died today will save hundreds over the next few years.

He told himself this as he swung up into the saddle. He would go on telling himself this, until perhaps someday he would believe it. And through it all, he could still hear the small voice in his mind which said, "Rick Galloway, are you *sure* you're not a coward?"

15

The monotonous beat of the kettledrums ceased. Second Pike Regiment spread forward to stand guard, while Third Pike began construction of a temporary camp. Roman engineers supervised as the pikemen, assisted by archers, drove stakes and dug ditches.

"Bloody waste of effort," someone muttered behind Rick. One of the Tamaerthan knights.

"It will not be *your* effort wasted," said another knight. Dwyfyd, Rick thought. Better, though, to pretend he hadn't heard at all.

At least none of the knights was arguing that they ought to dismount and take their ease while the foot soldiers built their camp.

"Aye. We hae learned from the Romans to sleep well at night, knowing we will no be surprised. And that, my lords, is no small thing."

Drumold, of course, Rick thought. But the voice seemed to come from a very long way away. Suddenly he swayed in the saddle—

⁜ ⁜ ⁜

"My lord."

Rick didn't want to open his eyes. There was a hot smell. Lamp oil. Why would they be burning lamps in the afternoon? He opened one eye. Yellow light. Brown walls. He tried to sit up.

"Stay easy, my lord."

His eyes focussed at last. A young acolyte of Yatar. And Rick was on a cot, in his own tent. It was late enough that lamps were lit.

"Is he awake?" Drumold's voice came from outside.

"Yes, Lord. I will go for the priest."

"Do that." Drumold came in to sit next to Rick. "Are ye well, lad?"

"Certainly." He tried to sit up, but his head felt light. "I don't understand what happened—"

"Hah. You're battered and torn, lost blood from three wounds. Your thumb's the size of a gull's head and your ankle larger than his body. Withall, you sit a horse all day and you wonder you faint? Rest, lad."

"Can't," Rick said. "Where is Publius?"

"Camped nearby. All is well, Rick."

"Is there word from Marselius?"

Drumold hesitated.

"There is, then."

"Aye. But—"

"Drumold, we have a battle to plan!"

"It will wait a day."

It won't, Rick wanted to say; but instead he let his head fall back on the pillow.

☩ ☩ ☩

He awakened the next morning to the sounds of trumpets and shouting men. He tried to leap from his cot, but his ankle wouldn't hold him. Then Mason was there to help him back to bed.

"What—"

"It's nothin' to be worried about, Cap'n. Some bigwig from Marselius' army, with a legion for escort."

"A legion? That's Marselius himself!"

"Likely it is," Mason said.

"I have to go meet him—"

"How?" Mason asked. "You can't hardly stand long enough to dress yourself."

"Damn it, I can't greet Caesar from my bed! Get my robes!"

"Robes, hell," Mason said. "You go out, you wear armor. And you eat some hot soup first."

Soup. That sounded good. But armor? Yes. Not for the reason Mason thought. Not assassination; but it would be fitting to greet Marselius Caesar in armor. Marselius would be wearing his best, no question about that. "All right, help me get on my mail. The shiny set."

"How about this?" Mason asked. "Arrived an hour ago."

It was a new set of armor, featuring the breastplate fancied by

Roman officers. Bronze oak leaves—no, by God, those were gold!—were soldered to the shoulders. There was a shirt with mail sleeves to go under it. The links were silvered, and the finest Rick had ever seen.

"Fancy enough," Mason said.

"A king's ransom," Rick said. "From Marselius?"

"No, sir. From Publius. In honor of your taking the bridge."

"I will be dipped in—" Publius? That ass?

The armor fit perfectly. Which of Rick's people had Publius got his measurements from? It hardly mattered. And certainly this was the right thing to wear . . .

✣ ✣ ✣

"Hail, Caesar," Rick said.

"Hail, friend and ally." Marselius smiled and came closer to clasp Rick's hand and shoulder. It was a genuine embrace, making Rick wince. "Your pardon—"

"It's nothing." But he was glad for the armor.

Both armies stood in ranks in the bright light of the True Sun, watching their commanders greet each other. Wine was poured, and Rick and Marselius drank, then exchanged goblets and drank again. "Silly ritual," Marselius said. "But I suppose necessary—shall we go inside, while Publius and Drumold carry on?"

"Yes." He followed the Roman into the command tent. Maps were already spread on the table.

There was a man seated by the table. Two of Marselius' personal guards stood next to him.

"I think you did not meet Aulus Sempronius," Marselius said. "He was the tribune commanding Flaminius' troops at the bridge."

"Hail," Rick said. "I am pleased to see that you live."

"I understand that was your doing. Thank you."

"You will recover, then?"

He didn't look good. His left leg was stretched stiffly before him. It was bound in leather splints. His left arm was also bound to his chest.

"I do not know," Sempronius said. "Your—" He struggled with the word. Finally he said it. "—*priests* say I will. Our healers are less certain. Your rituals are strange but they seem efficient—"

Marselius looked worried. "My Lord Bishop will arrive in a moment," he warned. "Does it go well, son of my oldest friend?"

"You call him friend even now?"

"Certainly. Because your father sees his duty to serve Flaminius makes his friendship no less valuable. More."

"Ah." Aulus Sempronius was silent for a moment. "I do not think your son shares this view. Left to him, I would be in the hands of the *quaestionairii*."

"Never," Rick said. "You surrendered to me. Who harms you answers to me!"

"By what right do you speak thus to Caesar?"

Publius had come in. Rick turned slowly. What I'd like to say, you pompous little bastard, is by right of the magazine in this Colt. But that won't work too well—

"By the right that any honorable man holds. By the rights of honor," Marselius said. "Hail, Publius."

"Hail, father. Hail, Lord Rick."

"Have you no more to say to our ally?" Marselius demanded.

Publius nodded, his lips pressed tightly together. Then, in a rush, he said, "I ask pardon. I should not have spoken as I did."

"Why hasn't he attacked?" Publius demanded. He turned to Aulus Sempronius. "Why?"

"I cannot answer—"

"Aulus," Marselius said. "Aulus, I have granted full pardon and amnesty to all who will accept. There were no conditions, and there will be none. But—will you not submit to me as Caesar? Will you not aid me in ending this war? How can it harm Rome, that this war end?"

Aulus frowned. "And yet—Ah. How can it matter? He has no need of battle," Aulus said. "As you must know."

Rick nodded. "I thought that the bridge too lightly guarded. We were intended to cross."

"Your spies have served you well," Aulus said bitterly.

"No. It should have been obvious there were too few troops to hold it long," Rick said. "Only you fought so well I did not understand until now. And when we march for Rome—"

"He will let you go forward. Then we retake the bridges, and hold you to this side of the river until you starve. May I have wine? Thank you. It deadens the pain."

"It is not good for you," Rick said.

"More witchcraft of Yatar?" Deliberately he poured another goblet of wine and drank it off. "Soon you will lose your army to desertion." Aulus laughed sharply. "If we do not lose ours first."

"You have many deserters?" Rick asked.

"As must you."

"We've seen few enough of yours," Rick said. He looked to Publius. "Have they come to you?"

"They do not go to Marselius Caesar," Aulus said. "They go home, to protect their families from bandits and slave revolts, and the legends of—of—"

"Of The Time," Rick said softly. "So you know of that also."

Aulus nodded, and drank again, his third large cup. "Our bishops say that God will punish this world."

That's one way to look at it. I wonder how many deserters Publius has had. None we caught, but we weren't really looking for them.

"So Flaminius will not attack," Marselius said.

"Caesar, he will not," Aulus Sempronius said. "But say not Flaminius, who is not here."

"Who commands?"

"Titus Licinius Frugi."

"Gah," Publius said.

"I feared as much," Marselius said. "My best legate. He was with me at Sentinius."

At Sentinius. "Then he will find my pikes and archers no surprise," Rick said.

"None," Aulus said.

And he knows my secret. The secret of any hedgehog formation. If you don't attack it—how can we take the battle to cavalry? We can't even *catch* their cavalry. And if they wait until we're in line of march and sweep in—

"Then we march on Rome," Marselius said. "If he refuses battle, so do we."

"Except that the further we go—"

"The more recruits we will have," Publius said. "We come closer to our home estates. And to lands which know Flaminius the Dotard all too well."

"He will burn the crops," Rick said.

"How can he?" Marselius demanded. "His own troops won't let him. Nor will Flaminius. Nor will the Church. He *can't* burn himself out. No. We march on, and when he attacks, we've got him."

Or he's got us, Rick thought, but there was no point in saying that. How did it go?

> *On foot shuld all Scottis weire,*
> *By hyll and mosse themselffs to reare.*
> *Let wood for walls be bow and spear,*
> *That enemies do them na dare.*
> *In strait places gar keep all store,*
> *And byrmen ye planeland them before,*
> *Then shall they pass away in haist,*
> *What that they find na thing but waist.*
> *With wiles and waykings in the night,*
> *And meikill noyse maid on hyte,*
> *Them shall ye turnen with great affrai,*
> *As they were chassit with sword away.*
> *This is the counsel and intent*
> *Of gud King Robert's testiment.*

But Flaminius couldn't possibly have heard of Robert the Bruce. Or could he?

✣ ✣ ✣

Two days march were two days of agony for Rick. His ankle remained swollen, so that he could not stand in the stirrups. He recalled the ancient joke, a cavalry manual: *Forty Miles in the Saddle,* by Major Assburns. It took on new meaning with each mile.

But I can't lead from a wagon, he thought. Though I'm going to have to, if this keeps up.

They marched onward into Flaminius' territory; and the deeper they went, the hungrier they were. Despite Marselius' certainties, the land *had* been laid waste; there was little or nothing to eat. All food and stores had been carried away, and the fields burned.

They grew weaker in other ways, too. For every recruit they collected, they had to leave two men behind as garrison. They had, when they began, three legions of cataphracti, two veteran and one militia, and two cohorts of Roman pikemen, nowhere near the standards of Rick's veterans. Now one of the legions was under strength, and there was only one cohort of Roman pikes.

They had also begun with three cohorts of *cohortes equitatae*, a mixed force of two light-armed infantrymen for each light cavalryman. The infantrymen ran alongside the cavalry, supporting themselves by holding the horse's mane so that they could keep up. An excellent idea in theory; Rick wondered how well trained they were. However good, there were only two cohorts of those now; the third was left to guard the crossing of the River Pydnae.

The whole Roman army wasn't much larger than Rick's force; while Flaminius was said to have five legions, three of them veterans, as well as numerous militia and auxiliaries.

"My lord."

Rick looked up to see one of his cavalry officers. "Yes?"

"Five stadia ahead, Lord. There is a villa. It will not open its gates to us."

Rick frowned. "Yes?"

"My Lord, Balquhain wished to batter down the gates, but Lord Drumold sent me to find you. Lord, the villa is defended only by women and loyal slaves. Balquhain told them to surrender or they would be given to the soldiers. They slammed the gates in his face. Then Lords Drumold and Caradoc came."

"I see. Go and tell Drumold I'll be there as soon as I can." He looked back down the road. Art Mason and Jamiy were close behind. Jamiy's arm was bound in a tight sling against his chest. Wearily Rick waved them forward and spurred his horse to a fast trot. The result was agony.

And I can't tell anyone what my problem is. . . .

✣ ✣ ✣

"Surrender in the name of Marselius Caesar," Rick shouted.

"My lady says that she will never open her gates to barbarians."

Was that an intentional pun? The double meaning was obvious, but it certainly wasn't intended to be humorous. And undoubtedly it expressed the deepest fears of the matron who guarded that villa.

"We need Tylara here," Rick said.

Drumold nodded. "Aye. You see now why I sent for you."

"Yes. There's little honor in victory over women. But a damn good chance of an incident worth more to Flaminius than a new legion."

"So I have told my son," Drumold muttered.

Balquhain bowed his head. "Aye. I see that now. I was a fool."

First damn sign of wisdom I've seen from you, Rick thought. But no time for that now. "Mason, bring up the one-oh-six."

"You have a plan?" Balquhain asked.

"Yes. You're part of it." Part of it now, anyway. "Listen . . ."

"Fire in the hole!" Reznick shouted. The one-oh-six recoilless blasted fire; the shell smashed against the stout gates of the villa.

The instant the larger weapon fired, Rick and Mason fired concussion grenades from the grenade launchers on their H&K rifles. The grenades went over the wall to explode inside the courtyard beyond.

At that same moment, Balquhain, Caradoc, and ten other picked guardsmen rode to the gate. They flung themselves off their mounts. The gates sagged on their hinges; four men hit them at once, and the topmost hinge of one gave way. They scrambled into the villa.

Rick rode up behind them, and painfully climbed inside the ruined gate. "My ladies!" he shouted. "You see we have broached your defense. Yet only officers stand in your courtyard. My army stays outside. You will not be harmed. Come out, in the name of Marselius Caesar—"

Caradoc and two guardsmen brought over prisoners from the outer wall; two young men, obviously slaves, and another, no more than ten. The boy struggled, but could not move in Caradoc's grip.

The villa door opened, and a woman about thirty-five ran out. "Rutillius!" she screamed.

Rick nodded in satisfaction. That's one victory I can be proud of. Why can't they all be like that?

✦ ✦ ✦

It was late in the day, and Rick made camp at the villa. Only his officers were permitted inside; and before they entered, Rick asked formal permission from the mistress of the household.

"You will be paid for what we consume," Rick told her. "We are allies to a lawful Caesar, not conquerors."

She shrugged and gave a bitter laugh. "There's little enough to consume."

Her name was Aemelia, and her husband, Marcus Trebius, was an officer in Flaminius' army. She didn't know if he was alive or dead; but three days before, Titus Frugi's soldiers had stripped her villa of every able-bodied slave and freedman. They had also taken nearly all her food, and burned what was left.

"You seem to bear little love for Flaminius," Rick said.

"I have little."

"Then why did you not surrender to Marselius?"

"You are not Marselius," she said.

"Ah. My barbarians—"

She blushed. "We were told—told that it would be far better to fall into the hands of Publius than among the barbarians."

"Ah. Meaning—"

"That Publius asks," she said. "But I wronged you. I—thank you. For saving my son. For sparing my home." She came and stood near him. "Welcome, to my home and hearth . . ."

✢ ✢ ✢

"Captain . . ."

What the hell? Aemelia moved next to him in the dark. She was tense with fear.

"Captain."

The voice was Mason's. Out in the hall. Quickly Rick rose and went through the connecting door to the other room. He pulled on a robe and opened the door. "Here. What is it?"

"Messenger, Captain. From Marselius. Said it was too important to wait until morning."

"I'll come—"

"Armor, Captain. I'll help you—"

"Give me five minutes," Rick said wearily. "Then come help." And just how close a friend to Tylara *are* you?

✢ ✢ ✢

Lucius, Marselius' trusted freedman, stood in the library of the villa. Drumold, Elliot, Balquhain, Caradoc, and a dozen other officers waited with him.

"Hail, Lord Rick."

"Hail, Lucius. You bring a message from Caesar. It must be that you have found Flaminius' main army."

"Yes. No more than forty stadia. Some march toward us. Their light cavalry are everywhere—"

Rick bent over the maps. "Good territory for it. They'll be trying to circle past us, get some behind and some ahead. With more troops strung along this ridge above our line of march."

And worse than that. There were a number of parallel roads here, and Marselius' army was split into columns, divided into three main forces: Rick's on the left, Marselius himself in the center, and Publius on the right. With luck, Flaminius could hit one of the flanking columns and punish it before Marselius could come to its rescue. Or circle behind them and harass from the rear. Or—

"It is clear that we must know what Flaminius is doing," Rick said. He turned to his officers. "Send out the Hussars. But in a body, to patrol and return. Not to fight. They're our eyes, and we'll need them."

"I'll go myself," Drumold said. "Now?"

"Yes," Rick said. "Elliot, get the troops on alert, but keep them in camp. Until we know what Flaminius is doing it's silly to do anything—"

"And yet we have no choice but to continue," Lucius said quietly. "Or soon we will have no grain for the horses."

"Yeah," Rick said. He tasted sour bile. Horses eat a *lot*. Cavalry horses eat more than that. Stay here a week, and they'd have no striking force at all.

"Caesar demands that we march tomorrow," Lucius said. "I have brought his plan of battle."

✢ ✢ ✢

The battle plan was no plan at all. March ahead and trust to God. Not that Rick knew of anything better.

"There is one more message," Lucius said. "I have waited until we are alone to give it."

Rick poured two goblets of wine. "Yes?"

"Your officer, Tethryn, shall have the Untipped Spear."

"Ah." So the Romans of Tran had preserved that ancient Imperial honor. "Dwyfyd will be pleased to add that to his brother's tomb carvings."

"Publius wanted instead to give money."

"He had a reason?"

"Ah. He said to his father, 'If I were as close to the purple as you, I would not waste Roman honors on the dead barbarians.' " Lucius smiled. "Caesar replied, 'If I did not honor my friends, I would not be as close to the purple as I am.' "

"And what happens if Caesar falls in battle?"

Lucius shrugged. "Publius is not evil, Lord. He is a strange lad. Well educated. Perhaps I was too strict. I do not know. But—well, we can pray to the saints that Marselius lives to be enthroned. I am unlikely to outlive him. And Publius may yet grow to a stature worthy of Rome."

✢ ✢ ✢

The cavalry returned an hour past full light.

"We found nothing," Drumold said. He pointed to the map spread on Rick's field desk. "So far as I can tell, we went to this spur of the ridge."

"A good ten stadia past where you should have been ambushed."

"Aye—"

"Meaning there will be an ambush there when the full army marches up that road," Rick said. "You can be sure of it."

"So what shall we do?" Balquhain demanded.

"What would you do?" Rick asked.

Balquhain spread his hands. "I know not, truly. Time was, and no so long ago, I would ride that road thinking myself safe. Now—now I see the danger, but I know little what to do about it."

Nor I, Rick thought. He was about to say that—

"My lord!" Jamiy burst in. "Lord, the Captain of the Guard sends word. New forces coming from the west."

"New forces?"

"Drantos soldiers, Lord. Royal Guardsmen."

"What the de'il?" Drumold demanded. "Why? Could aught be— no, no, I will not think such things."

Nor I, Rick thought. Lord God. And last night I betrayed her. Could this be Tylara coming? Or has something happened to her?

Or—I'm a damned fool.

✢ ✢ ✢

Camithon stood at the door. His head was bowed, and the old soldier actually stammered. "Lord—lord, I knew not how to prevent him. Aye, our young Wanax has grown—"

"And so you came with him."

"Aye," Camithon said. "What was my duty? I am a soldier. I know well enough that I am 'Protector' of young Ganton, not of the Realm, which I know not how to govern. And as our Wanax conceived this mad notion while the Lady Tylara was no more than a day's ride from the capital, I sent messengers to inform her that she should remain as Justiciar of Drantos, while I escort the Wanax. What else could I do, Lord? For he *would* come. To prevent him I must lay violent hands upon him—and I cannot believe his nobility and guardsmen would allow that. Must I then begin civil war?"

"No. Where is the king?"

"Ah—the servants are erecting his tent, and he is at his ablutions— in truth he hides until I bring him word of how you receive his visit. I think he fears you somewhat."

"He cannot overly fear me, or he would not be here. What forces have you brought?"

"A hundred lances, lord."

Three hundred heavy cavalrymen. Probably more; each lance was led by a knight, and many of them would have brought squires as well as men at arms. Picked men, no doubt. Man for man as good as Romans. Possibly better. But not disciplined; a hundred Roman Cataphracti would be more than a match for these three hundred.

But they were heavy cavalry, trained to fight in ranks three deep and cover a three-meter front. They could hold a third of a kilometer, at least for a while.

"And servants, and fifty porters leading a hundred pack animals," Camithon continued.

"Rations? How long can you live without forage?"

Camithon shrugged. "A day? There was little enough forage in the wake of this army!"

Rick nodded. Well, that was another four hundred mouths to feed. Plus horses, who'd need grain and hay. There'd be no centaurs among picked Drantos troops.

One more damn thing to worry about.

"This is primarily a Tamaerthan expedition," Rick said. "And it is my command. This is understood?"

"Aye, Lord. By me and by His Majesty."

"Good. Then have the courtesy to inform the Wanax that when His Majesty is finished with his ablutions, the Commander-in-Chief would like to see him."

16

Titus Licinius Frugi reined in his horse and resisted the impulse to stand in the stirrups. His officers were watching; they should not see him appear uneasy.

They were among a thin wood at the top of a long ridge that lay parallel to his enemy's line of march. They could see most of Marselius' force from here: the center, with Marselius himself, lay on Frugi's left, ready to march up the military road to Rome.

On that side Frugi had four legions to face Marselius. More than enough to sweep Marselius from the field—but that would be wasteful of men. Frontal assaults always were.

But if he could bring a legion around the ridge to take Marselius from behind—

Marselius had entrusted his left wing to barbarians. To Frugi's right, at the bottom of the ridge, was a secondary road in a thin strip of cleared level ground perfect for his heavy cavalry. The barbarians, separated from Marselius by the ridge, would march into that.

He pointed to the road. "How far up it did they come?" he asked.

"There." One of his staff officers pointed down the slope.

"That far. Excellent." If the barbarians had scouted that distance last night, they would surely do so again now that they were marching . . .

First would come the barbarian light cavalry. They'd be no match for Cataphracti; drive them back, back upon their own marching columns—and charge on, using the fleeing enemy as a screen.

And if the enemy came on without sending scouts ahead? Even better. The road ran between the forest and a stream. The barbarians would have to march close to the trees; close enough that their archers would have little time for their deadly volleys as his hidden troops burst out. Let his legionaries get among the archers, and the barbarian army was his. Kill the archers! The pikemen were not of themselves dangerous. Horse archers could shoot them down—provided that they were not in turn shot down by those bright-kilted fiends with their long, gullfeathered arrows that could outrange his best by half again.

He shuddered at the memory of the disaster at Sentinius. Not again! Never again would he send Cataphracti charging at the pikes while the grey gulls flew in thick flights . . .

From his ridge he could see all the way back to the river. Most of it was fertile farmland, but there were scattered orchards, patches of forest, and low rolling hills to block his view.

A horseman rode up behind him. "It is a splendid view. A pity to spoil it with the ugliness of war."

"Yes, my Lord Bishop." And how much of that did my Lord Bishop Polycarp believe? Possibly all of it. To the best of Frugi's knowledge, Polycarp was a good man—despite having the favor of Flaminius.

Marselius, my old friend. Were you right to revolt? Has Flaminius the Scholar brought us to that? But civil war is always the worst of disasters, the worst of evils. Better a dozen bad emperors than an endless series of wars for the purple. Once, Rome ruled from the sea to the West Escarpment, to the borders of the Five Kingdoms. Aye, even the High Rexja sent gifts to Caesar. Then came a year when three Caesars claimed the throne at once.

"But will not the trees and hills there prove troublesome?" the bishop asked. "They will hide your enemy."

"They serve to block Marselius' view as well, Your Grace."

"And that is important?"

"All important, Your Grace. If we but knew where *all* of Marselius' forces were, we would have them. We could win a bloodless—well, nearly bloodless—victory."

"How is this?"

Have I better things to do than give lessons in tactics to a servant of the Prince of Peace? No. Not for an hour. Perhaps longer. "If we know where each is, we can concentrate all our force against a small part of theirs. Break through their line, sweep about their flanks, come from behind. Their soldiers like this war no more than we. Given the chance, they will come to us rather than die for Marselius."

"Will you give them quarter, then?"

"Yes."

"Yet Caesar has ordered—"

"I know what Caesar has ordered, Your Grace. And I know what I must do. I will send the remnants of Marselius' force to the frontier posts." *If there are any remnants. I have six legions. Two that Marselius doesn't know about. Enough force to roll right over, smash my way—* "I will give them quarter if I can."

"And your are certain of winning?"

"I am, Your Grace. We have six legions plus the foot. Even counting the barbarians as a legion, Marselius has but four."

"So you have half again his strength."

"More, your Grace. With forces matched this evenly, it is as the square of the two. Say thirty-six to sixteen. As if we had double his force. But that would be for a frontal assault. I think we can do better when Marselius advances. He always was a rash leader."

Polycarp looked at him sharply. "Be certain of victory. Then go with God. For Rome can little enough afford the loss of her knights, when the barbarians pound at our gates, and the star our ancestors called Beelzebub hangs higher each day. But—will not Marselius simply remain where he is? Why should he place his head in your snare?"

"He has little choice, Your Grace. There is very nearly nothing to eat where he is encamped." Flaminius Caesar had rightly forbidden him to strip *all* of the lands along Marselius' line of march; but he had allowed him this valley. A raven crossing that land would need to carry rations.

Marselius and the barbarians carried rations, of course. Grain and fodder for the horses, too. But never enough, not for that army. Marselius would have to fight, on ground chosen by Frugi. And Marselius would lose.

✣ ✣ ✣

An hour passed. Trumpets sounded from the west. Marselius was on the march. But the barbarians were deploying as if for battle. They hadn't moved up the road. Not even their light cavalry.

Then there were shouts from his troops. A staff officer rode up jabbering.

"What? Speak up, man!"

The officer pointed.

Two miles away, a brightly colored object trailing black smoke rose in the sky. A wind carried it toward him. When he strained his eyes, he thought he could see a thin line connecting it to the ground. Smoke rose from the place it was tethered.

"What?" Frugi asked. "Surely it is nothing to fear." But he felt fear, all the same. Fear and terror of the unknown. Star weapons . . .

Star weapons were only weapons, he told himself. Like bows, with long-ranging arrows. Like ballistae that shoot far. But as bows need arrows, the star weapons need—need something I don't have a word for. But something. And their supplies are limited.

Another staff officer rode up. A *frumentarius*. Why was he so excited?

"*Balloon*," the intelligence officer stammered.

Titus Frugi frowned in puzzlement.

"We heard of them from the Pirate Lands, Proconsul," the officer said. "But we paid no heed. Until now."

"What are you jabbering about?"

"*Balloon*," he said. "See, it drifts toward us on the wind. And it is higher than we can shoot. Look closely, Proconsul."

Titus Frugi looked, and saw disaster. There were men in the basket hanging below the balloon. They were pointing at the troops hidden in ambush.

✦ ✦ ✦

The semaphore flags waved. An acolyte of Yatar stared at the basket beneath the balloon and called out letters. Another wrote the message.

"S-T-A-F-F BREAK O-N BREAK Y-O-N-D-E-R BREAK R-I-D-G-E BREAK STOP."

"We have found the enemy's staff officers, Lord," the scribe said.

Rick hid a thin smile of amusement. These lads were so proud of being among the very few who could read that they forgot that anyone else could. "Thank you." He turned to Mason. "Think it's worth dropping a couple on the ridge?"

Mason shrugged. "Sure."

"We'll wait a bit more, though," Rick said. "Ah. Murphy's located an ambush force. Just about where I'd figured from the map. But it's nice to have it confirmed. Dismounted. They'll be out of action for a while—"

Gradually he gathered details as the semaphore flags wagged and waved. Two legions poised here. Another there, masked by an orchard. Two more in reserve. Hah. Titus Frugi had more force than Marselius had suspected. Must have drained everything, every trooper he could raise—

"Caradoc!" Rick shouted. "Get me messengers to ride to Marselius. Win this battle and by Yatar we've won the whole bloody war!"

✣ ✣ ✣

"It was you who said it would be disaster," Bishop Polycarp reminded him.

And it damned well is, too, Titus Frugi thought. But how can I avoid a battle? I can't even disengage! By now Marselius knows every formation I have, how many, where they are—

Is he wise enough to divine which troops I can trust and which I can't? Which I can allow to wander through the trees, and which must stay under the eyes of their centurions? (And one legion whose centurions weren't trustworthy; that whole legion had to be watched by another.)

"What would you have me do, Your Grace?"

Polycarp shook his head slowly. "Avoid slaughter. If you must fight—fight barbarians. Do not let Roman armies kill each other while the heathens remain!"

Good advice, old man. But I've fought those barbarians. You haven't. Still, I suppose there's nothing for it.

It had looked so simple. Until that thing rose in the sky. And now—now everything he did would be reported to Marselius. While he had no information at all on where his enemies marched.

Disaster. Strange how small a thing can bring disaster. And how little you expect it.

✣ ✣ ✣

Presently the enemy strategy was clear. Marselius' right wing advanced, slowly, through the croplands and orchards, while the barbarian left wing stayed behind. With his army split by the ridge, Frugi couldn't simply sweep Marselius from the field; and how could he break past the barbarians and fall on Marselius from behind now that his ambush was discovered?

"They are only foot soldiers," one of the legates said. "Barbarians at that. How can they withstand a charge of legionary horse?"

"I have described Sentinius to you," Frugi said wearily. "And then they had no *balloon*." The evil thing hung in the sky directly to the west. It must somehow communicate with the ground, because Marselius deployed against the legion Frugi had hidden in the orchards; and when the legion withdrew, Marselius closed his ranks again.

"It is held to the ground by that rope," the *frumentarius* said. "Cut the rope and it must drift free. This has happened before."

"How do you know this?"

"We heard this from spies," the intelligence officer said. "But we did not believe them."

"So." Frugi pointed to where the end of the balloon's tether lay. "We need go only there—"

"Where there are few barbarians," the legate said.

That was true enough. There were no more than a hundred to guard the balloon's tether. But—"Few indeed," Frugi said. "Now consider this. Their whole formation is like a funnel, with only emptiness at the bottom. With nothing where they keep their *balloon*. As if they cannot believe we know it to be vulnerable. Or that we do not know its value. Tell me, Legate: would Caius Marius Marselius know the value of a *balloon?*"

"He would, Proconsul."

"Then can we not assume that the barbarians who possess it must know?"

"We can—"

"Then we must assume they will protect it. With their star weapons, perhaps. With *something*. No. I will not send a legion down those lanes to chase a lure." Frugi studied the battle ground again. "But— perhaps—"

"Yes, Proconsul?"

"Their left flank. Spearmen. Supported by archers, but the archers are further in. There is a gap between their spearmen and the woods. I would suppose their horse waits there, just beyond where we can see, hidden by those woods. But—their horse is no match for a legion; and we have horse archers in plenty. These barbarians have never seen *our* archery. Perhaps, Valerius, it is time they learned."

"It will be my pleasure to teach them," the legate said.

"Do so. Recall the Eleventh from hiding in the trees and remount them. Take them and the Eighth. Deploy the Eighth against the barbarian cavalry which will surely be hidden on your right. Bring the Eleventh to archery range and shoot down those spearmen. Shoot enough and they will run. When you have broken through their line, ride behind the enemy. Ignore the *balloon* and whatever protects it. Sweep behind the barbarian force and fall upon Marselius in the center. As you do, I will send the other legions in a general charge. We will crush Marselius."

His enthusiasm was infectious, and the legate was caught up with it. "Hail, Titus Frugi!" he shouted away as he rode away. When he was gone, Frugi's smile vanished. Go with God, Valerius, Frugi thought. As for me, I am afraid.

⁜   ⁜   ⁜

"I still think it's stupid," Art Mason said. "Hell, Cap'n let *me* go—"

"No. You and Elliot are needed here. Just see that Frugi doesn't break through anywhere. And look out for the king."

"Ye're daft," Drumold said. "But I hae long ceased to vex myself wi' thoughts of controlling you. Still, what will you accomplish?"

"Possibly nothing," Rick said. "But you exaggerate the danger. There is none to me, and little to anyone else. You do not have the game 'chess' here, do you?"

"Not by that name," Drumold said.

"No matter. It is a war game. There are many ways to win, but only one way to win quickly without great slaughter. Let's go." Rick waved his group forward: Reznick, Bisso, and two other mercs, plus a half-dozen guardsmen. The mercenaries wore kilts and bright tabards, and their battle rifles were wrapped in cloth bowcases. From a distance they looked like any Tamaerthan light cavalry.

They rode southeast, toward Marselius' legions. When they were close to the base of the ridge, they dismounted and turned the horses over to two guardsmen. Rick led the others into the thin scrub that covered the ridge.

"Okay," he said. "This is as good a place as any."

The mercenaries shed their kilts and pulled on camouflage coveralls. The guardsmen also abandoned bright colors and put on drab kilts and leather helmets. When they were dressed, Rick led them up the ridge.

Halfway up they paused in a wooded draw. Rick took out his

binoculars, while Reznick shook out signal flags and waved them. Rick focussed in on the balloon, "Okay, they've seen us," he said. He watched the flag man. " 'L-E-G-I-O-N-S A-T-T-A-C-K-I-N-G L-E-F-T W-I-N-G.' Get the rest of that signal and acknowledge. I want a look over that way."

He couldn't see. The brush was too thick and the draw too deep. Then he heard distant thunder. The recoilless, and possibly grenades.

"Murphy says First Pikes are holding," Reznick reported. "No change otherwise."

"Nobody above us on the slopes?"

"Not until we reach the top."

"Okay. Let's move." They climbed up the draw.

When they were nearly at the top of the ridge, they took more signals from Murphy in the balloon. Rick nodded and waved Reznick forward.

Reznick screwed the sound suppressor on his nine-millimeter Ingram submachine gun. He moved carefully up the draw, guided by Murphy's directions, until he was near a small thicket. The Ingram made no more noise than the loud tearing of cloth as he fired an entire clip into the bushes. Then he reloaded and went to inspect his work.

After a few moments Rick heard a low whistle. He waved the others forward.

Twice more Reznick took the silenced Ingram forward. Then they were at the top of the ridge.

"Move!" Rick ordered. "Up. Go like hell!"

They dashed over onto the level ground on top. Rick was panting, and his legs felt like lead. My arse aches, too, he thought. Hell, a man with piles didn't ought to be doing this! A Roman trooper stood just in front of him. Rick fired twice with his .45 and the Roman went down. Then there were two more Roman soldiers. One held his shield forward and raised his sword—

Rick shot through the shield. Reznick fired from behind him and three more Romans went down. There were a dozen more dismounted Roman troopers. Reznick and Bisso fired at full automatic, short bursts, slow, methodical fire; the Romans collapsed in heaps. Then they faced five mounted Roman officers.

"Surrender!" Rick shouted. When one of the Romans wheeled, Rick shot his horse. The animal screamed in pain. "Kill the horses!" Rick shouted.

Bisso's battle rifle thundered. Then it was joined by two more. As the horses began to buck and plunge, a Roman in a scarlet cape leaped free and drew his sword.

"Hail, Titus Frugi!" Rick called. "Why throw you life away to no purpose? I have come to speak with you."

Frugi licked his lips and looked around. One of his officers was struggling to free himself from a fallen horse. Bishop Polycarp's animal had not yet been killed; His Grace sat with his hands raised as if in blessing. His other three officers were taken, struck down and seized by these grim men; and his bodyguards lay in heaps.

"Set up over there," Rick shouted. Bisso and the other two mercs laid out their battle rifles. "Anything comes over that lip, kill it." He turned to the Roman commander. "Now, Proconsul, let us talk."

"Who are you, barbarian?"

Hah, Rick thought. The way he asks that, it's a good thing I came myself. "Rick Galloway, Colonel of Mercenaries, War Lord of Tamaerthon—and friend to Marselius Caesar, who sends you greetings. Only two days ago I heard Marselius himself praise your courage and honor. And your good sense—however, you must not run away, Proconsul. And while I permit you to hold that sword for the moment, you must eventually put it down."

"While I hold it—"

"While you hold it you can kill yourself," Rick said.

"That, Titus Frugi, is forbidden," Bishop Polycarp warned.

"My Lord Bishop," Rick said. "I had hoped to include Your Grace in our meeting. Can you not prevail upon the Proconsul to lay down that sword?"

Titus Frugi looked around helplessly. His officers were taken or dead. The strangers looked perfectly capable of dealing with any rescue attempt—not that there was any sizable force nearby anyway. He stood shaking with rage and frustration, then threw down the weapon with a curse. "Speak, barbarian," he said. "I have little choice but to listen."

17

"Here they come." Art Mason raised his rifle.

The two legions of cataphracti moved in formation, certain of themselves, riding proudly. The lead formation deployed, ready to ride through the chivalry of Tamaerthon to Drumold's banner lifted high above them.

The Roman trumpets sounded. Lances came down in unison. The Romans moved forward. At a walk. A trot—

"Now," Mason said.

The light machine-gun opened up in sharp, staccato bursts. Then the recoilless. The center of the Roman line went down; the troopers behind crashed into them, and the orderly line dissolved into confusion. The rear ranks crowded against each other.

"Fire in the hole!" Elliot shouted. The recoilless blasted again. More Romans fell. Their charge was broken before it had ever begun.

Tamaerthan and Drantos horse alike surged forward into the confusion. The Roman forces were bunched together, so that only the outer troops could use their weapons. The Allied cavalry, heavy and light alike, could dart in, strike, and dash back to the charge again.

The other Roman legion reined in about a hundred yards from the pikemen and took out their bows.

Mason turned to his trumpeter and nodded. Shrill notes sounded, and two hundred Tamaerthan longbowmen ran out of the trees where they'd hidden.

"Let the grey gulls fly!" Caradoc ordered. The first flight of arrows fell upon the Romans from behind.

The trumpets sounded again, followed by the thutter of drums and the squeal of pipes. First Pike Regiment surged forward at double time. They flowed across the ground toward the Romans.

Mason dismounted and opened the bipod of his H&K battle rifle. He lay on the ground and fired randomly into the Roman formation until the pikemen closed. The Romans found themselves in a desperate engagement.

✟ ✟ ✟

"I had not known," Titus Frugi said. He raised Rick's *binoculars* again and stared at the scene below, then cursed. "Who ever saw foot soldiers attack cavalry?" It was an event totally outside his experience; the surprise was as complete as if the pikemen had risen into the air.

First the star weapons. The Eighth Legion's charge was thoroughly broken before they ever engaged the enemy. Now they were trapped, forced back against the Eleventh which was in desperate straits, archers behind it and those spear men in front. Could Valerius withdraw? Would he? He searched for a sign of his subordinate, hardly able to hold the binoculars still. What other marvels did these starmen have?

"You see," Rick said gently. "Two legions could not break my pikes. Not when they have the aid of star weapons. As you must know." He waved to indicate the dead and dying heaped around them. "Your bodyguards fared no better. What use is this slaughter? How will Rome survive if all her soldiers are dead?"

"And you?" Polycarp asked. "What do you gain from this?"

"I am a friend of Marselius Caesar," Rick said. "When Rome's borders are safely held by my friends, Tamaerthon and Drantos are safe. These are perilous times, Your Grace. More perilous than even you can know. We all need friends."

"Indeed."

"Even Rome," Rick said. "Perhaps Rome most of all."

On the field below the slaughter continued. Now the Romans were trying to withdraw, as the deadly Tamaerthan gulls flew again and again.

"Two legions," Bishop Polycarp said. "Two legions destroyed, and you have not yet met Marselius."

Not destroyed. Not yet. Disorganized, useless as fighting instruments until reformed. Doomed, unless they withdrew. But not yet destroyed . . ."What would you have me do, Your Grace?" Titus Frugi asked.

"You yourself said it was disaster," Polycarp said. He pointed to the balloon. "Will it not continue? Today your forces retreat with what Valerius can save. Tomorrow the barbarians advance. With *that*, watching, always watching. Wherever we go, it follows." He shuddered. "And I say nothing of the fire and thunder weapons."

"I ask again. What would you have me do, Your Grace?"

"End this madness."

"How?"

"One of our trumpeters survives," Rick said. "Sound the retreat."

"So that your cavalry can pursue."

"What of that?" Rick asked. "Will any be saved if they stand and fight? Where will Valerius take those legions?"

"Along the road, to hold the ford."

"Then send one of these," Rick said. He indicated the captured officers. "Have Valerius take his legions to the next crossroad and make camp. You and I will meanwhile go to speak with Marselius Caesar." Suddenly Rick's calm detachment snapped. "For God's sake, stop this slaughter," he shouted. "Haven't we had enough?"

"More than enough," Polycarp said. "More than enough."

Titus Frugi ground his teeth together. Then, grimly, grudging every word, he spoke to his trumpeter. "Sound the general retreat," he ordered.

✢ ✢ ✢

"Forward, lads!" Drumold shouted. "Up the road! Forward!"

"For Drantos! Forward!"

The young king was right alongside the Tamaerthan leader. No way to stop them, Mason thought. It even makes sense. If we can get any sizable force around the ridge and behind the Roman main body, we've won the day. The same plan Titus Frugi had, only he couldn't carry it off. As long as there's no ambush.

Not sure we can do it. The Tamaerthan cavalry aren't that good, and there aren't that many of them, even with those Drantos troops. Either way, best send a couple of mercs to look out for Ganton—

"Sir!" The young rider was nearly as out of breath as his horse. An acolyte of Yatar.

"Yes, lad?"

"Orders from the *balloon*. Halt at the ford. The Romans are going to surrender."

So, Mason thought. Captain's done it again. Now all I have to do is convince Drumold and the kid. He spurred his horse forward.

✛ ✛ ✛

Drumold paced around and around the table in the largest room of the villa. "Och," he said. "I canna say I care for the situation. The Romans have their forces intact. All their forces, and all Flaminius' forces. While we are here, in their midst, without rations—"

"Which they're sending—"

Drumold cut off Rick's protest. "Which they *say* they are sending. But we have none yet. And I do not think they will let *their* troops— nor their horses!—starve to feed us."

"Your fears are groundless," Rick said. "They will send food. And why do you fear the Romans?"

"Iron," Camithon said.

"Iron?" Drumold asked.

"Iron," the Protector repeated. "Iron makes Rome what she is. They have much, we have little."

"That's a pretty sharp observation, Cap'n," Elliot said. "Like those mills I've seen. They've got millponds behind dams, and overshot wheels with gear trains. They can run on less water than any mill I saw in Drantos."

Or in Tamaerthon, Rick thought. Which means they can run during more of the year. "Iron mines and good mills—I suppose they use them to drive bellows?"

Elliot nodded. "Saw just that about five klicks from here. Regular foundry."

"Which means when the Romans discover gunpowder—and they will—they'll have the means to make guns. Lots of them," Rick mused. One more headache. Add gunpowder and guns to Roman discipline and recordkeeping and they'll own this end of Tran.

Which might be no bad thing—although Drumold and Tylara weren't likely to see it that way.

"If Tamaerthon is threatened, how long before Drantos falls?" Ganton asked.

Smart lad, Rick thought. Ganton seemed more sure of himself, now that he'd led troops in a battle. It hadn't been much of a battle, nor had

Ganton played a large part in it, but he'd been at the head of his guards, right alongside Drumold and Balquhain.

"What should we do, then?" Rick demanded.

"What we should have done before," Drumold said. "Take hostages. Think, lad. They have here the whole strength of Tamaerthon and Wanax Ganton to boot. Surely Publius has thought of this. And 'tis Publius who will remain, while Marselius marches on to Rome."

"Without us," Camithon added. "Without us."

"You yourself refused his offer to take us to Rome," Rick protested.

"And what of that?" Drumold demanded. "Should we put our heads deeper in a noose? Protector Camithon did well to refuse such a dangerous offer."

"And you genuinely fear for our lives?"

Drumold shrugged. "Perhaps not now. But later—when Publius realizes that he holds all the strength of Rome? What will happen to Tamaerthon then? Aye, and to Drantos as well. You ask it yourself, lad—what happens when the Romans have star weapons for themselves? We can no conquer Rome. We can no destroy the Romans. We can take hostages. Take them, lad. Now. While we yet can."

"Is that your advice also?" Rick asked Camithon.

"Aye."

"Elliot?"

Sergeant Major Elliot shrugged. "You know these people better than I do, sir. But I'd feel some better if we could be *sure* we'll get home—and after, who knows what they might do? How can it hurt?"

"Majesty?"

Ganton shrugged. "I must heed the advice of those wiser than I."

Rick sighed. "It's no substitute for a policy," he said. "Even if it is traditional. But I dine tonight with Marselius, and I'll see what I can do."

✢ ✢ ✢

There were only Rick, Marselius, and Lucius at the dinner; Publius had to see to the ordering of the troops and the final surrender of Frugi's camp.

Rick waited until the dinner was finished and they had both had wine. "Some of my officers are concerned," he said.

Marselius frowned. "About what?" he demanded.

"Loot, for one thing."

"Ah. There was little fighting, thus few fallen enemies to despoil." Marselius shrugged. "I will see to it. There should be ample gold in Titus Frugi's camp. I will arrange a donative to our gallant allies."

"Thank you. There is another concern."

Marselius looked puzzled. "Of what? The victory could not be more complete. With few casualties on either side. A brilliant stroke—"

"Which increased the size of your army," Rick said. "But leaves us in desolate territory, dependent on rations we do not have."

"Food is coming," Marselius protested. "Wagonloads of grain. The first arrive tomorrow." He drained a goblet of wine. "What are you saying?"

"That some of my soldiers are afraid they'll never leave Roman territory alive," Rick said. "And Drumold fears that the strength of Rome may be sent against Tamaerthon, now that Rome has no civil strife. My apologies, Caesar, for being so blunt."

"Better to be blunt," Lucius said. "Tell me, Caesar, would you not be, ah, concerned, also, were you in his situation?"

"I suppose I might," Marselius said. "And what do you suggest I do?"

"Drumold wants hostages," Rick said.

"And you?"

"I want only to return to my University. There is much more I must do before The Time—"

"But you do not protest. You prefer to take hostages."

Rick said nothing.

Marselius frowned. "Then you do not trust me—"

"Nonsense," Lucius said. "Caesar, are you under the illusion that you are immortal?"

Marselius looked thoughtful. "I think I see an answer," he said at last. "My granddaughter has asked me to visit the Lady Gwen. Now I shall let her. Lucius, ride to Benevenutum, and inform Octavia that it is my desire that she continue her studies in Tamaerthon. Choose suitable companions and servants to join her—but she is to meet the Lord Rick's forces and accompany them on their return. It is fitting that she be escorted by our allies." He turned to Rick. "Will that be satisfactory?"

"Certainly."

For a few moments the room seemed cold; then Lucius smiled broadly. "It is a scheme that has merit. May I join her, after we have taken Rome?" The old man sighed. "I have often dreamed of retiring to some center of learning. I would appreciate the opportunity to see this place. And the Lady Octavia will be very pleased."

"You will always be welcome," Rick said. "Caesar, this is inspired. The Lady Octavia can learn much to aid Rome during The Time; and not even the most suspicious will believe that you or your son would endanger her."

And beyond that, Rick thought. Beyond that, she'll meet young Ganton—and who knows what might come of that. It's time Ganton got a systematic education. Golden years and all that—he can't object to being a student prince for a while. Where he'll be with Octavia. Gwen says she's intelligent and attractive, and Ganton's young. . . .

"An excellent plan," Rick said again.

INTERLUDE: LUNA

 18

Earth, blue and fragile and lovely, swirling storms and shining seas, filled one wall of the office. Les had seen half a hundred planets, and none were lovelier.

I suppose it could depend on your viewpoint, he thought. Humanity came from there. A lot longer ago than most of them suspect. But home is always the nicest place . . .

Stupid thought. I haven't got a home.

Les stood in the doorway a moment longer, then entered the office. The room was panelled in wood, with a Kashdan carpet and luxurious furniture; but Les noticed little of that. Despite the opulence, the office was dominated by the Earth.

The colors swirled gently. Earth wasn't really visible from that office, but a real-time holographic display was trivial among the honors and privileges earned by the man Rick Galloway had known as Inspector Agzaral.

Even so, neither Agzaral nor any other human had earned the right to do what Agzaral did next. He opened his desk drawer and took out a small electronic device. After inspecting it carefully, he nodded to Les. "Hail, slave," Agzaral said.

"I greet you, Important Slave," Les replied formally. He fell silent as Agzaral adjusted the electronic gear. After a moment, Les could hear faint voices: his and Agzaral's, speaking meaningless pleasantries in the official Confederation Standard tongue for civil servants.

Agzaral nodded in satisfaction and leaned back in his chair. "That should be sufficient," he said. "Sit down. Have some sherry. I regret that the shipment of Praither's Amontillado has been delayed, but Hawker's is a substitute I have found acceptable. Did you have a pleasant journey?"

Les waited as Agzaral poured sherry into a crystal glass, then solemnly tasted it. "Excellent," he said. He glanced at his hands. No tremble. Voice all right. Emotions nicely under control. It was difficult to deceive Agzaral, but not impossible. "Pleasant enough trip going," he said. "Dull coming back."

Agzaral smiled faintly. "Ah. You found it pleasant to learn that the woman was pregnant?"

"How the hell—?"

"Gently," Agzaral cautioned. "That goblet would be difficult to replace. There is no cause for alarm. Our employers do not know. Your efforts to deceive the recorders were entirely successful with regard to the *Shalnuksis*. But tell me, did you really expect to deceive *me*?"

"I'd hoped to."

"Unwise," Agzaral said. "Most unwise. You would do far better to trust me."

"Trust you? How the hell can I trust you when I don't even know what side you're on?"

Agzaral spread his hands wide and let them drop to his lap. "Side? You would seriously have me choose a faction? Now, when the alternatives are still forming? Try not to be too great an ass, my friend.

"And don't protest. When it comes to politics, you are an ass. I can admire your courage. Your skill with languages. Your prowess as a pilot, and—Yes. I envy your success with women. You even seem to understand some of Earth's political quarrels. But when it comes to the important skills, the ability to know the High Commission and the Council—" He shrugged. "You're an ass."

"At least I take a stand. I'm not a damned trimmer like you—"

Agzaral laughed. "Some day one of your stands will be against a wall. As to being a trimmer, is it unwise to have every faction think I am its agent?"

"When they find out—"

"If," Agzaral said. "And think upon it, my fellow slave. If *you* do not know which faction I truly favor, then *they* cannot know either." He chuckled again. "So. You have taken a stand. Tell me where."

"Well—"

"Come, come, a simple question. Which faction do you favor? Who is its leader? Which race champions your position?"

"All right, so I don't know," Les said. "But I know this. I'm for leaving Earth alone. And Tran, too. Leave them develop by themselves."

Agzaral nodded. "The position taken by many of the more powerful Ader'at'eel. Unfortunately not all of them. They are joined by the Enlightenment Party of the Finsit'tuvii. But I fear that coalition is not the most powerful faction."

"Is that true?" Les demanded. "The Ader'at'eel want Earth and Tran left alone?"

"Substantially. Of course they don't know that Tran exists. But four of the Five Families do indeed support that position."

"Then—?"

"But then there are the Fusttael," Agzaral continued smoothly. "Their opposition is formidable. They hold no overpowering advantage, but they have the most strength at the moment."

"And what do they want?" Les demanded.

"They want to destroy Earth . . ."

"Destroy the Earth!"

"More or less."

More or less. He looked at the holograph again. A beautiful planet, filled with humans. Wild humans, not slaves of the millennia-old Confederation. Humans who would soon burst into space, find their way to the stars—who were about to come uninvited into Confederate territory.

More or less meant more. Bomb Earth civilization back to the Stone Age, and trust there'd be enough humans left for breeding stock. They only needed enough wild genes to temper the corps of slave soldiers. Enough to improve the breed of Janissaries . . .

"What does the Navy think of this?" Les demanded. "Or your service?"

"The opinions of slaves do not matter—"

"Come off it."

"But certainly the Navy has divided opinions," Agzaral said smoothly. "It is likely that some ships would refuse to take part in the necessary operations. But—enough would obey the orders."

"We can't let that happen!"

Agzaral spread his hands. "How do we prevent it? But I agree, it would be regrettable. And there is the third alternative."

Sure, Les thought. Human membership in the Confederation. Forced membership, imposed now while the Earth was helpless. A junior membership, with Earth controlled by the High Commission. Peace, unity, and—stagnation. A static society. Stasis for a thousand years. Still, it had to be preferable to bombardment and destruction . . .

"The balance of the Ader'at'eel would bring Earth into the Confederacy now," Agzaral said. "But enough of this. Your report. Will they be able to grow *surinomaz?*"

"Possibly," Les said. "Of course there will be the mutiny. It will be settled by now."

"Yes. With what outcome?"

"Either of the mercenary leaders should be competent with those weapons against that population."

"Ah. So the survey ship will not be wasted."

"I think not. And the soldiers will want resupply. Ammunition, soap, penicillin—"

"You understand their needs," Agzaral said. "I will send you to Earth to procure for them. I recall that you enjoy that work."

"I'll do it, but I want to pilot the ship that goes back to Tran."

"To what purpose?" Agzaral asked.

"Why do you ask? I'm a pilot. I know Tran exists. Not too many pilots do. I'd think you'd want me to."

"It's reasonable," Agzaral said. "You will not be able to take the first ship, however. One leaves immediately. Piloted by *Shalnuksis.* Tran is not too far off their course, and they want to see for themselves how Tran has revived since their last series of visits."

"Last time they went there, they bombed out half the civilization. What will they do this time?"

"On this journey, nothing—"

"That's not what I meant," Les said.

"I know. But I have no better answer."

Les nodded in submission. "Is their first ship carrying supplies?"

"A few. Whatever we had. The mercenary leader Galloway had made suggestions before they departed, you may recall. We used his list. Some of what they wanted was easily obtained. For the rest—your task, now."

"All right. Provided I get to go back myself."

"Why are you so anxious to go back?"

"Does it matter?"

"It might." Agzaral was silent, obviously waiting for Les to speak, but Les said nothing. "Very well. I took the trouble to look up your ancestry," Agzaral said finally. "Rather a lot of wild human strain." He paused. "They'll never allow the child to live if they learn of it."

"How will they learn?" Les demanded.

"Gently." Agzaral glanced at a timer on his desk. "We do not have much longer to speak freely. Let us not waste these minutes. They will not learn from me. But I must know what you intend." He pointed to the Earth. "You have lived long among wild humans. In some ways you act like them. Many wild humans mate for life. This seems unnatural to me, but I know they do it. Is this your intent?"

Les didn't answer.

"I must know."

"I don't know," Les said. "I've thought of it. Live on Tran, with Gwen and my children. Doesn't that tempt you?"

"Earth would tempt me more. But it is not so attractive that I would forsake what I have. Consider. The girl and the child may both be dead."

"You think that hasn't haunted me ever since I let her go planetside?"

"Yet she seemed competent enough," Agzaral mused. "I expect she has survived. She may, however, have found another mate."

"Yeah. I thought of that, too."

"What will you do in that case?"

"I don't know that, either."

Agzaral nodded in sympathy. "Certainly your interest in Tran would be much abated?"

"Yes. But I have to find out."

Agzaral looked at the hologram for long enough that Les saw movement in Earth's clouds. Then spoke decisively. "You will have that chance," Agzaral said. "I hope the knowledge pleases you."

PART FOUR
INVADERS

19

Autumn had come. Despite his charcoal brazier Apelles felt the chill damp of the stone chamber high in the tower of Castle Armagh. The Firestealer crept toward the True Sun, and now both were in the sky together; the days grew short. Evening came and lamps had to be lit, but still there was work to be done.

Armagh was three hundred stadia east of Castle Dravan, and nowhere near as comfortable; once again Apelles marvelled that Lord Rick would move so much of his household to this godless place. Truly there was no accounting for the ways of the starmen! Even so, Apelles was content, now that he was a consecrated priest of Yatar. The room's present discomforts were small compared to those he'd endured as an acolyte. He was more concerned about his pen, which was made of soft iron and had a blunt point that scratched the paper.

Despite the scratchy pen, Apelles worked steadily. He was careful not to make a blot. A blotted sheet had to go back to the pulp vats, and there was never enough paper no matter how hard the acolytes labored. It took time to pound logs to pulp, shred rags, then soak and stir and matt the resulting brew until it yielded thick sheets to be rolled out on sieves. It took even more time for the paper to dry satisfactorily. Then it had to be coated with a wash of clay and dried again. Making paper was no easy work; Apelles knew, because it had not been long since he had done it—until he had learned to read and write.

He had learned his new work from Roman scribes, and he was proud of his knowledge. Work carefully, record everything; that was the way to control a nation. The power that he held was great, real power, power easily abused had he been so inclined; but he was a sworn priest of Yatar, a shepherd, not a wolf.

He wrote steadily, and finally his desk was clear. He leaned back in his chair and smiled in satisfaction at his files. Truly they held power! Here, the manpower lists; names and locations of officers of the Army of Drantos, those on active duty and on leave, fit for service and on the invalid list. Over there were duties and taxes owed and paid; equipment issued; every detail. Some day he'd have the entire Army in his files, and then let the bheromen try to shirk their sworn duty to the crown!

He nodded soberly at that thought. Yatar save the Wanax! Some bheromen and knights resented young Ganton's stay at the University, but Apelles knew the value of education, which gave even young swineherds the power of writing . . .

In another file were the names of every field in the Cumac region of County Chelm. Who owned them. Who worked them, and whether villein or free, and for what service or rent. What was planted, and what seed, and what fertilizer for what yield. Endless rows of words and numbers, carefully arranged.

And in yet another file, the names of all the acolytes and deacons and priests and archpriests, those who would be promoted and those who would serve out their lives as laborers in Yatar's fields and caves and monasteries . . .

The caves were not in his files. Their locations, and what stores they held, and how thick the ice and ice plant; these were state secrets, and those files were kept by archpriest Yanulf himself. Apelles had seen them, once; he'd have to be content with that.

And here—

The magic box made squawking noises. Apelles stared dumbfounded. One of his duties was to guard that box and listen for messages; but he'd had little regard for that task. Privately he would have expected Yatar himself to appear before a small box like that could speak to him.

But it *was* speaking. First in the local Tran dialect, but wretchedly. "Ait, are there anyone there?" it demanded.

Then in other languages Apelles didn't know, but always demanding, insistent.

When he shouted for a messenger there was real fear in his voice.

✢ ✢ ✢

The voice on the transceiver was thick and sibilant with trillings and drawn-out vowels. Rick was certain he was speaking to one of the *Shalnuksis*. He had only seen the aliens on three brief occasions, all more than two Earth years in the past, but he had no trouble recalling them: humanoid, two arms and two legs, but with the wrong proportions. Shoulders too high, necks short or nonexistent. Short torso but long arms and legs. Three fingers and two opposed thumbs, thin lips surrounding a mouth too high in the face. Fleshy snout-slit instead of a true nose, almost like a vertical second mouth rising to eye level . . .

The alien spoke in bursts. They'd done that before, Rick recalled; although not always. When they'd made set speeches the words flowed smoothly; it was when they engaged in spontaneous conversation that they hesitated.

The transceiver was a simple device: a rectangular sealed box, with a grill on one face. Below the grill was a colored square. There were no other controls, not even an on/off button.

He touched the control square. "Galloway here," he said.

"Ah," the alien voice answered. "Captain Galloway."

"Is this Karreeel?" Rick asked. The name Karreeel translated to "Goldsmith," Inspector Agzaral had said. Karreeel had seemed to be in command of the *Shalnuksi* who'd hired him. At least he'd done most of the talking.

"Karreeel is not here," the voice said. "I am Paarirre. Captain Galloway, are you in control of your men?"

"Yes."

"And where is Mr. Parsons?"

"Dead," Rick said.

"Ah. And you have—gained political mastery of a—suitable region?"

"Yes. We hold the area around this castle, and we are preparing to plant it all in *surinomaz*."

There was a period of silence while the aliens digested this information. Then: "Excellent. We have brought goods for you. Where do you prefer that we land them?"

"North and east of this castle there is a high plateau," Rick said.

"We see it."

Aha, Rick thought. They know where we are. He nodded significantly to Mason, who solemnly responded. "It is a large plateau. You may leave the goods at the southern edge."

"We will choose our own place on the—plateau."

"As you will. I prefer that you land at night, so that you are seen by as few inhabitants as possible. They have frightening legends about sky gods."

"We may—discuss—this later. For now, tell us: how large a territory do you control?"

"How should I describe it?"

"We understand all your—common units of measure. Use those."

Rick looked at Mason and shrugged. Best be somewhat truthful, he thought. Enough to show good faith. But don't give them enough information to help pick targets for *Shalnuksi* bombs. "I hold the land for a hundred kilometers around this castle," he said. "And I have an agreement with the neighboring kingdoms."

There was another pause. "*Surinomaz* requires much cultivation. Those who work its fields must be fed."

"I know. I can trade for food. But I must have more ammunition before I can take a larger territory. How did your troops do this in the past? You must have helped them directly."

There was another pause. "That is not your concern. Can you secure sufficient territory?" the alien voice demanded.

"Certainly. I have that now."

"Very well. This night, when it is fully dark, will be—convenient to us. Come to the—plateau."

"I can't get there that quickly," Rick said. And since you know where I am, you must know I can't get there by tonight.

"You need not come at all."

"I have three kilos of partially refined *surinomaz* sap," Rick said. "If you care to have it."

There was another pause. "The crop this—year—will not be of high—quality. Still, it may be worth taking. When you come to collect the goods we have brought, bring the *surinomaz* and the transceiver. Do not bring heavy weapons. We will be watching as you approach. Farewell."

"Tells us one thing," Art Mason said. He followed Rick out of the chamber, enclosing the transceiver, and shut the door, just in case the push-to-talk switch wasn't the only way the device could operate.

"What's that?" Rick asked.

"They're scared of our heavy weapons. We can hurt their ships."

"Seems reasonable," Rick agreed. Les, the human pilot of the ship that had brought them to Tran, had acted the same way, insisting that the ammunition and the recoilless and mortars be kept separate when they unloaded. "I wonder what they've brought us? Whatever it is, we'd better get ready to ride."

✠ ✠ ✠

The escort was saddled and waiting. Beazeley and Davis, with Art Mason. Six Royal Drantos Guardsmen, and a dozen Tamaerthan mounted archers with Caradoc. A string of pack mules.

Tylara nodded in satisfaction. "It says much for our rule. You go to bring as great a treasure as this kingdom has ever known, yet you feel safe with no more than a dozen lances."

Never thought of it that way, but I guess she's right. "We should return in two days," he said. "Sure you don't want me to leave Caradoc with you?"

"There is no need. The lands are quiet. I have more fear for you."

"Nothing will happen." Not this time, anyway. He held her close for a moment.

✠ ✠ ✠

The trail was wide enough for two abreast, and presently Rick found himself beside his captain of archers. Caradoc was singing. The words were in the Old Speech, but the tune seemed familiar to Rick. After a moment, Caradoc turned to Rick and grinned. "An air from our wedding dances," he said proudly.

"Ah," Rick said. And aha. A song from the Top Fifty a couple of years ago. Gwen must have put new words to it.

"With your consent, I would return to the University for the winter, Lord," Caradoc said.

"Certainly. I'd intended for you to be with your wife."

"I thank you." Caradoc grinned again. "It is doubly important now."

"Aha?"

"Yes. As I left, my lady told me she believes that we have been blessed by Hestia."

"Congratulations." And I really ought to cheer, Rick thought. This should make life with Tylara a bit easier . . .

✢ ✢ ✢

There were a dozen cartons of cigarettes; a case of penicillin; ten bottles of Bufferin and four of vitamins; some needles and thread and sewing supplies including an ancient foot-powered sewing machine; baling wire and pliers, which Mason eagerly seized; a carton of paperback mysteries; and a box of random supplies with items as disparate as nutcrackers and soap. The rest was ammunition: cartridges for both the H&K and M-16 battle rifles, .45s and nine millimeter for the pistols and the submachine guns, grenades, mortar bombs, and fifty rounds for the recoilless.

Tylara looked at the supplies with satisfaction. "Now they have come. Are they likely to come again this season?"

"They said not," Rick answered. "They won't be here for a long time, possibly a full Tran year. They'll probably come next fall, when we have a full crop of *surinomaz*."

"Then I wish to return to Castle Dravan."

"Need we go there?" Rick asked. "There is little to attack us from the west."

"I hear tales of Westmen in the High Cumac," Tylara said. "More have been seen this fall than in the previous twenty years."

The Westmen were nomads who generally stayed on the high desert above the enormous fault known as the Westscarp. "If more come, Margilos should warn us," Rick said.

Tylara snorted contempt. In times long past, Margilos had paid tribute to the Five Kingdoms. Now it was in theory an independent city state famous for breeding centaurs. "I doubt they would," Tylara said. "They're half-nomad themselves. Unless one believes the old tales."

Rick looked helpless. Tylara giggled. "It is said the men of Margilos have centaur blood, and there is much debate whether the first was begotten by a man on a centaur mare, or did a lady of Drantos enjoy the favor of a centaur stallion." They laughed, then she said urgently. "It is not a joke one makes when men of Margilos are present. They are quick to anger, and when enraged they feel no pain. Like the centaurs they breed."

"I'll remember. But surely you're not worried about Westmen?"

"No."

"Then it might be better to stay here. We can't be *sure* the *Shalnuksis* won't come again until next year—and I don't want them to know we value Castle Dravan. They may find out, of course. But why help choose targets for their *skyfire*?"

"I do not disagree," Tylara said. "Yet the risk is worthwhile. Armagh is no comfortable place to winter. I would be in Dravan before the thaws, and travel in winter is difficult."

Something in her voice made him turn to look at her. She smiled and patted her belly.

"You too?" Rick demanded.

She frowned.

"Gwen is also pregnant. Caradoc just told me."

"Ah." Tylara laughed. "That is one child of Gwen's who will cost me no sleep." Then she came into his arms. "This time it will be a boy. I know it. And our son should be born in his own castle."

20

A hot wind blew down from the high escarpment. The day was already a scorcher, although it was only spring here in the foothill country. There ought still to have been a nip in the air. The hot air provided less lift for the balloon, too.

"She looks ready to me, Murph," said Corporal Walinski. "What about you?"

Ben Murphy looked at the twelve-foot balloon. It was already straining at the ropes held by the two archers. He tossed one more fuel brick into the firebasket underneath it, then gripped the main rope in both large hands. For a moment he glanced back into the wagon bed where Lafe Reznick was napping, but Lafe was still asleep. Or pretending to be. "Ready to lift," Murphy reported.

"Let go on the hold-downs!" shouted Walinski. The two archers let go and stepped back, while the balloon rose freely into the afternoon air. Murphy let the rope run through the blocks mounted on the wagon until the hundred-foot mark passed, then snubbed it around the cleat by the driver's seat. The balloon was now high enough to be visible from the next village, but low enough to be controllable.

"Think she'll stay up long enough?" Walinski asked.

"Yeah, if we give the pitch fast," Murphy said. "We're getting good at the spiel. Sure is hot, though."

"Compressive heating," Walinski said.

"Which?" And where in hell did Ski learn words like that?

"They called it compressive heating back in Los Angeles," Walinski said. "A special wind, a Santa Ana. Hotter'n hell, even in winter. And dry. Real dry. That's what this is, I think. Comes down off those high deserts. As it comes down lower it compresses, just like the Santa Ana in L.A."

"Well, it sure makes it hot enough," Murphy said. Winter had been wet in Drantos. Lots of snow in the east, and not so much in the west. And nowhere near as cold as the locals expected, meaning the whole damn planet was heating up right on schedule as the rogue star came closer.

Murphy pulled off his jacket and pulled his wizard's robe out from under the seat. "Hey Lafe, better wake up. Duty time."

Reznick sat up sleepily. "Anything special about this village, Ski?"

"Not that I've heard."

"Same here," Murphy said. "The standard routine." He could damned near do that in his sleep by now. Take the wagon in. Use the balloon to get everybody's attention, and show the wizards' mighty power, then bring it down. Demonstrate magic, and let the deacons and acolytes of Yatar show the local clergy about sanitation. Make holy water by literally boiling the hell out of it! Ask about madweed. Do the crop survey—what was planted and how it grew. Tell 'em about the new plows, and show the blacksmith how to make one. Have Lafe put on his weapons show, a demonstration of star weapons so they'd know what they'd face if they ever revolted against their rightful lord the Eqeta of Chelm. And—

"Some new orders came by messenger this morning while you both was still in the sack," Walinski said. "Find out about the Westmen."

✛ ✛ ✛

"More been spotted?" Reznick asked.

"They didn't *tell* me nothing. Just orders."

Murphy sighed. If he'd been awake, he could have questioned the messenger. Fat chance Ski would ever think of doing that. Ski could fight, but he wasn't much for questions. Wasn't much for brains, for that matter. But he had seniority over Ben Murphy, because he'd stayed with Parsons and came over to Captain Galloway with Elliot. He hadn't gone south and set up on his own.

Can't win 'em all, Murphy thought. And Ski don't give me much trouble, 'cept when he's drunk, and at least he knows it when he is. I've had worse bosses.

He could remember better bosses, too. His luck had been strange, these past few years. Strange, but better than it used to be. There'd been a time when he had no luck at all. It was because of that time that he was on Tran, ten light-years from home, calling himself Ben Murphy and playing wizard to the heathen, instead of following his father's trade under the name his father gave him. Now at least things weren't all running against him.

He pulled on his robe, then picked up his assault rifle and kept watch while Walinski and Reznick put on their wizard suits. Walinski's was by far the fanciest, since he was supposed to be the master wizard and Murphy and Reznick his journeymen, with the acolytes of Yatar to help them.

Walinski had just finished dressing when Agikon, the senior acolyte, shouted an alarm and pointed upward. The balloon was wobbling alarmingly on the end of the rope.

"Wind?" Murphy called.

"Wind, hell!" Ski shouted. "Look!"

A flight of arrows leaped out of the woods to the left of the road. Two hit, and the balloon wobbled again.

Walinski unslung his battle rifle.

"What's to shoot?" Murphy demanded. "Probably some local kids. I'm surprised nobody took a shot at it before."

"Maybe. That was good shootin'," Ski said.

"Uh." Come to that, it *was* good shooting. About as good as Tamaerthan archers, and they were the best on Tran. "Ski, I don't like this. Let's laager the wagons out in the open field. Just in case."

"Well—"

Murphy didn't wait. He turned his wagon sharply and stood up, bringing his hands together over his head. He repeated the signal, then whipped up the horses. Lafe Reznick looked puzzled for a moment, then jumped down and ran back to the next wagon to urge its driver along.

"Gonna feel stupid," Ski muttered. "But we hafta patch the balloon anyway."

That was for sure. The balloon was losing altitude fast. Murphy looked back. The other carts were following, closing up as Ben sent his in a circular track. He was halfway into the field, the laager not yet formed, when he hit a patch of mud. The wagon stuck fast.

"Holy shit, that's all we needed," Ski said. "We'll have to patch the balloon just to lift us out of the mud." He looked at Murphy. *What did you get us into now?*

Murphy swore. He was about to jump down from the cart when a flight of arrows fell around them. Walinski screamed and reeled against the cart with an arrow sticking out of his face. One of the acolytes fell with an arrow in his chest. The horses were untouched.

There was another flight of arrows. The Drantos Guards archers yelled and brought up their crossbows. Walinski was screaming his head off, clawing at the arrow in his face. He'd dropped his rifle. Murphy threw himself down into the wagon box and peeked over the edge, his rifle ready.

"What the hell do we do?" Reznick shouted.

"How the hell should I know?" Ben answered. There weren't any targets. Murphy squinted, estimating the distance to the trees. Two hundred meters, near enough. He whistled. "That was a long bow shot!" he shouted. "Even for Tamaerthans!"

"Damn straight!" Reznick answered.

Murphy thought about the implications. One of Captain Galloway's high cards were those Tamaerthan archers. Used in connection with other troops they could be devastating, because they outranged everyone else. Drantos crossbows could carry about as far as Tamaerthan longbows, but they were slow to load, and nobody in Drantos really believed in long-range archery. Tamaerthan archers loved long-distance shooting. But those weren't Tamaerthan troopers out there, so who were they?

More arrows fell. By now everyone was behind a wagon or under cover, and nobody else was hit. Curious, Murphy thought. The horses and oxen pulling the carts hadn't been touched. Not even Reznick's centaur. Dobbin was cowering behind Lafe's wagon, whimpering the way the animals did when something threatened them and they couldn't fight or run away.

About my own situation. Can't fight and can't run. Things were quiet now, but—"It's a horse raid," Ben called.

"Yeah, that's what I figure," Lafe answered. "Somebody wants them beasts alive."

Murphy strained to see into the forest, but there was nothing visible. "Hell, maybe we ought to let 'em have 'em."

"Not Dobbin, they don't."

"Probably don't want him. Just want the horses and oxen. Probably too smart to want a centaur," Murphy said.

"Now you lay off," Reznick said. "But we better do something here. Want me to look at Ski?"

"Yeah, in a minute. You stay down just now, first things first. Move them carts!" Murphy shouted. "Go around me! Laager those damn wagons!" Just because the lead wagon couldn't move didn't mean they couldn't make a wagon laager. Murphy nodded in satisfaction. Agikon had caught on, and was bringing up the other carts. At least they'd have some cover—

A dozen light cavalrymen burst from the woods. They rode crouched low against their mounts, most of their bodies invisible behind their horses. They didn't look like anyone Murphy had ever seen.

"Westmen!" one of the acolytes shouted.

✢ ✢ ✢

Murphy snapped down the battle rifle's bipod and rested the legs on the wagon seat. Ski was still screaming, but Murphy put that out of his mind along with everything else except his sight picture. Aim for the rider, but low enough to hit the mount if you miss. Get the good sight picture. Squeeze off a round—

The first rider fell. Ben shifted targets. On the second shot both horse and rider went down. The rider leaped free, but Lafe Reznick's burst took him in the chest. Ben looked up long enough to wave thanks.

Shift aim again. Keep it smooth. Another down. Three shots for the fourth. *Don't rush it!* Concentrate. New sight picture—

The nearest enemy was no more than twenty meters away when Murphy shot him off his horse. Then, suddenly, the Westmen were riding back toward the woods. Murphy picked off one more rider, and a last one seemed to fall out of the saddle in sheer surprise.

Then there weren't any more targets. One of the downed riders tried to get up, but a crossbowman took care of him. Two more Westmen rode from the woods and grabbed a loose horse while Murphy was changing magazines. Then things were still.

Not quite, though. Walinski was still yelling his head off. One of the acolytes was trying to hold him while another looked at the arrow piercing from near his left eye down across the cheek to come out at the neck. It was a bloody mess, but it hadn't hit a major artery or Ski wouldn't be able to yell.

"Lafe! Go look after Ski," Murphy yelled. "But be ready to cover me. Agikon!"

"My lord!"

"Take Lord Walinski's rifle. Keep watch on the trees."

"Aye, Lord."

The acolyte handled the H&K with confidence. Captain Galloway didn't encourage training locals to use star weapons, but out here in the marches you needed all the help you could get.

"The rest of you stand guard! I won't be long." I hope. Going out in the open is probably stupid, Murphy thought. But I'd best see what I'm up against, and maybe get some information the captain can use.

Murphy knelt by the six dead men while Agikon watched the forest. The closest man had a bronze sword, a thing he'd seen only in shrines to Vothan farther north and east. It was long enough to be used from horseback, and had gold wire wound around the hilt.

The rest of the men were armed with short spears or light lances, and long wicked hornbacked compound bows, almost too big to use from horseback, only they sure could. They also had knives. Most had no armor, but one was wearing a mail shirt obviously made in Drantos. They didn't have much clothing, breechcloths and a rough wool cloak, but just about every one of them had something of gold: an armlet, or a brooch, or just gold wire wound loosely around his neck.

They were all muscle and bone, and it looked as if they hadn't had enough to eat for a long time.

So these were the Westmen. Not many ever saw them. They lived in the unexplored high plains beyond the Westscarp, and few who'd entered their territory ever returned. Not that there was anything to go up there for.

The last man lay too near the trees, and he could just lie there. Ben Murphy wasn't about to get that close. But as Murphy turned away, the man leaped to his feet. He started to run toward him, but after a step he fell again. Ben whirled and leveled the rifle—

"Mercy, I beg you!" the man shouted. "I am not one of—one of the Horse People!"

"What the hell?"

"Mercy!" He stretched out on the ground, reaching toward Ben, crawling painfully toward him. "Mercy!" he screamed again.

Think fast, Ben. Maybe a trick. But—He went over to him. The man was bald, no better dressed than the Westmen—and he had no weapons at all.

"Who the hell are you?" Ben demanded.

"A priest of Vothan! Take me to your wagons, before the Horse People come to kill me!"

"Maybe. What were you doing with the Westmen?" Murphy demanded.

"I was a priest of Vothan, at a shrine outside Margilos." The man spoke haltingly, with good grammar but hesitating sometimes. "A fool of a merchant from the—south wanted a guide, to lead him to the—the Westmen, that he might trade for gold. The chief priest thought that a good thing, and ordered me to go, for I had been to the top of the Scarp in my ordeal. But when we went again, the Horse People sacrificed the merchant to Pirin the Thunderer and made me a slave."

"So what the hell are you doing here?" Murphy demanded.

"The chief of the Red Rocks thought I brought him war luck, and now all the Horse People are coming down from the Westscarp. Above, all is heat and drying streams and death."

"Holy shit," Murphy said. "They're *all* coming down?"

"Those who can," the priest said. "So they brought me with them, slave and translator. I thought you evil wizards until I saw the blue robes of Yatar among you. Then I threw myself from the saddle and lay on the ground in hopes the Red Rocks would believe me dead. But I think my leg is broken."

A cool customer, Murphy thought. And a damned lucky find, a man who's been up there with them horse archers for years. "Okay, Baldy, let's get you to the wagons." And away from them trees, which give me the willies. "Here, get up, lean on me. You'll have to hobble."

It was slow going. When they were halfway to the wagons, Lafe Reznick came out to help. "What did you find?" he asked.

"Priest of Vothan the Westmen kept as a slave. Could be valuable to the captain—"

Suddenly Agikon was shouting, and before Murphy could see why, the acolyte fired five rounds, semi-automatic but so fast it sounded like full rock 'n' roll. A horse screamed. "Lords, the Westmen!" Agikon shouted.

There were a dozen of the light cavalry coming across the field at a gallop. Some had spears held low like lances. The others carried short javelins ready to throw.

They seemed awfully close. People were yelling all around, and it was hard to concentrate. Wish I had a grenade, Murphy thought.

"Don't leave me!" the old priest shouted.

"Get him movin'," Reznick said. He unslung his rifle and knelt. "Go on, Ben, go like hell."

Murphy helped the priest toward the wagons. It was like a nightmare, the kind where no matter what happens you can't move fast enough. He glanced back over his shoulder. More Westmen, maybe twenty of them, riding like hell straight toward the laager. "Let's go, let's go," Murphy said. He pulled the old man along, heedless of the priest's gasp of pain. As they reached the laager he heard Reznick's H&K chatter at full auto.

Murphy handed the priest to an acolyte. "Take care of him!" He ran back into the field. Reznick was changing magazines. He slammed the actuating lever home and fired again. The Westmen were galloping toward him, getting too close.

"Run like hell, Lafe! I'll cover you!" Murphy shouted.

"Right!" Reznick turned and ran toward the wagons. Three of the onrushing horsemen let fly with arrows. Lafe stumbled and fell. He got up, not running as fast. The horsemen were getting closer and closer to him. Murphy fired over his partner's head, full automatic, but the horsemen kept coming. Reznick stumbled again. "Ben, Ben, look after my wives—"

He tried to get to his feet, but there were two arrows in his back. Murphy tried to ignore him, concentrate on shooting, cut down the horsemen before they could reach Lafe, but they kept coming, and one was getting closer and closer and his lance came down, and Murphy shot him four times but the lance came on anyway. Reznick turned in time to see it coming. He tried to dodge, but it hit him full in the chest.

"You mucking bastards!" Murphy slammed a new magazine into his rifle. Agikon came up behind him with three of the archers and they fired another volley. There were only three Westmen left, but they kept coming until Murphy shot them all down.

⁜ ⁜ ⁜

Lafe Reznick was already dead when Murphy knelt beside him. Ben looked up at the sky, then muttered prayers he hadn't remembered since he left home. He felt something snuffle against his neck and turned. It was Dobbin. The centaur must have broken his tether when he saw Reznick fall.

The centaur bent down and sniffed at the blood on Reznick's chest and face. His half-formed hands patted Lafe's clothing clumsily, as if trying to tidy it. Then he reared, threw back his head, and let out a long, wailing scream. It reminded Murphy chillingly of the legends of the banshee.

21

Ben Murphy screamed curses to the sky. Then he went back to the laager. Dobbin could do as much for Lafe now as anyone. Scratch one man who'd do to ride the river with. The hell with that.

Two archers were holding Walinski. Lafe had worked on getting the arrow out, but he hadn't finished the job. First things first, Murphy thought. Methodically he gave orders. Collect all the enemy's weapons and gear. Retrieve the balloon. Lighten the bogged-down wagon. And keep guard, there might be more out there. When the archers and acolytes started on all that, he had time to deal with Ski.

"It's going to hurt," Ben said. "I got to cut it out of there."

Walinski screamed something.

Ah, quit your bitching, Murphy thought. Why couldn't it have been you? No, that's not fair. Hell. He found a bottle of McCleve's best tucked into Lafe's gear, and brought it over to Ski. "Drink it!" he shouted. "Take a good slug. Right. Another. Now I'll have one, gimme."

He took a drink from the bottle, then added a teaspoon of fine powder. It was made from madweed, and the old woman from the last village had sworn by it. Untested drug, Murphy thought. Probably the wrong thing to do, but what choices have I got? "Here, Ski, have another couple of slugs."

While Walinski drank, Murphy heated an iron rod in the wagon's balloon firepot. When it was red-hot he took it and went back to Ski. "Gimme the bottle—"

He handed the bottle to an acolyte and took a deep breath. Well,

405

here goes—He used his combat knife to slice quickly down the shaft of the arrow, cutting open the tunnel it had made. Ski screamed again, and blood poured out. Too much blood. Murphy drew the heated iron rod along the wound. There was a smell of burning meat.

Probably the wrong thing, Ben thought. God knows I've made a hell of a scar. But it's got to be open. Too much risk of tetanus, and maybe the Westmen poison their arrows. Got to be open and cleaned out and got to stop the bleeding.

He used a Johnson & Johnson sterile dressing to cover the wound. There were a dozen in the first-aid kit, and when would there ever be more? And the bottle of peroxide was small, it would all be used treating Ski and the wounded archer.

Ben Murphy felt a long way from home.

The village was about a klick away, and nobody had come out to help them. Murphy gave Walinski the rest of the bottle, and supervised getting the wagon train going again. They'd have to go in without the balloon, one wizard dead and another wounded; if they were going to impress the locals at all, they'd need all their gear. And a story. And meanwhile, somebody had to get word back to Captain Galloway.

The hardest part was getting Lafe's body. Dobbin stood guard, ready to fight anyone approaching.

"We could kill it," Agikon said; but when he saw Ben's face, he shrank away in fear. "Forgive me, Lord."

Murphy didn't answer. He tried talking to the centaur in soothing tones. "This is me. I've ridden you a dozen times. I'll take you back to Lafe's wives, but you got to let me have Lafe. Come on, Dobbin, it's all right—"

Eventually he whimpered and stood aside, letting Ben and Agikon put Lafe's body in the wagon. Murphy covered his partner with wizard's robes.

The village was called Irakla, and like all high plains settlements it had a wall. This far west it wouldn't really be as much for defense against men as against a native beast called the gunkel, an omnivorous rodent the size of a dog, with an elongated body like a weasel, a scaly hairless tail, and armor plates something like an armadillo. It had sharp claws, big teeth, and a stink spray that wasn't as bad as a skunk but more than enough to keep humans away from it. Unfortunately, the gunkel was perpetually hungry, stupid, and fearless, and it thought humans built houses to store food for it to eat.

The wall had been supplemented by a hastily dug ditch. There was also a watch tower. The gates were shut, and there were no animals in the fields. The watch tower was manned, and through chinks in the wicker areas of the wall Murphy could see the glint of helmets and spear points.

Murphy had put the robed acolytes in the lead wagon, and the gates opened quickly when they came near. A squad of villagers carrying spears and scythes came out to cover their entrance. One elderly man came to Murphy. He pointed to the wizard robes. "Where is your sky-beast?" he demanded.

Aha, they've heard of our traveling magic show. "The Westmen slew the sky-beast with arrows," Murphy said. "And they have killed others, and wounded the master wizard."

"An evil day. I am Panar, chief of this village. You are welcome here, Lords, but I fear the Westmen will destroy us all."

Murphy patted his battle rifle. "Though there are many Westmen, still we have our magic," he said. "The Westmen slew two of us and wounded my master, but we have killed all of the Westmen we have seen."

The caravan moved into the village. There was only one street, and the wagon train nearly filled it. The gates were hastily shut again.

Most of the population crowded around them. A couple of pretty girls caught Murphy's eye. Were they interested in having a child with sky-wizard blood? A lot of village girls were, which was one reason Murphy hadn't married again. Not like Lafe, who was happy enough with two wives, and what would they do now? They weren't noble, except that Lafe made the locals accept them, and—

The chief came back from seeing the gate closed. "Lord, Bheroman Harkon sent messages three days ago, warning us of Westmen in strong bands. He was leading his knights against them, and summoned the men of our village. Thus we have few fighting men, and could not come to your aid when we heard the battle nearby. Forgive us, Lord."

Murphy waved his hands in a blessing sign he'd seen old Yanulf use. "No problem," he said in English. "You are forgiven, and indeed had you tried to aid us you would all have been killed. How many lances does Bheroman Harkon lead?"

"Lord, I do not know how far he proclaimed the ban," Panar said. "I would guess no more than fifty."

Murphy nodded. No point in scaring people, but he could guess what would happen if the average Drantos heavy-cavalry leader ran into a sizable band of Westmen. Those hornbacked bows would be punching his men at arms out of their saddles before they knew there was an enemy near them. The next Drantos bheroman would probably face Westmen armored with the spoils from Harkon's army.

"Has anyone told the Lord Eqeta?" Murphy demanded.

"Lord, I do not know."

So it comes down to how smart Harkon is, and there's no way I'm going to find that out from this group.

"Lord, will you stay and protect us with your magic?" Panar asked. Some of the others crowded close to hear Murphy's answer.

The first levy of young men went to Harkon. There's me, and there's the secondary levy, not one whole hell of a lot to hold this place with if I've got to face any number of those Westmen. But what the hell, you knew the job was dangerous when you took it, Fred . . .

"I will stay," Murphy said. "But we must send messages to the Lord Eqeta. That is more important than our lives."

He'd expected opposition to that, but the village chief nodded sagely. "If the Lord Eqeta knows, we may yet be saved," he said. He looked thoughtful, started to turn away, and finally turned back. "There are two young men here who have won many races. Their horses are very good."

Obviously the right troops to take a message, but what was Panar looking so nervous about? Hah. "I will not inform Lord Harkon that you did not send your best men," Murphy said. "It is well for us that you did not." He pointed to the wagon's shadows. "When there is but one shadow, have them come to me. We will send them when it is dark. Meantime I will write a message for Lord Rick."

"Ah."

He's impressed, Murphy thought. Because I know Lord Rick, or because I can write? Don't matter much. "Before then I must tend to the wounded, and all your women must watch, as must you and your village deacon." This place would be too small to have a real priest.

"We will show them the healing magic revealed by Yatar to High Priest Yanulf. For now, have them boil water."

"Aye, Lord." Panar left to give orders.

Murphy was alone with Lafe's body. Bloody hell, he thought. I'm not as young as I used to be. He looked over to the wagon where Ski lay in a drunken stupor, and envied him. There was a lot of the powdered extract of madweed in the medicine chest . . .

Batshit, Murphy thought. Not that again. I took that trip back on Earth.

Why not, though? You ain't going to live through this anyway, might as well go out happy—

That's not happy, that's dead already, and shut up, he told himself. Christ, Lafe, why you? You got me off the stuff. And into Africa. Damn this goddamn planet, first Sindy and then Lafe—

You found Sindy here, and you had a good year. Do you wish you'd never married her?

No. But damn all, Ski looks happy. And it's sure going to be tough without Lafe. Nobody to watch my back. Nobody I trust now, except maybe the captain. Sure nobody else. Don't trust Warner, Lafe said. And not Gengrich either. Lafe had been right about Gengrich. Maybe not the professor, maybe Warner would do, but Lafe had been right, don't trust anybody you don't have to. They'd smuggled the one-oh-six away from Parsons without letting anybody else know. "Keep a couple of aces," Lafe used to say. "Can't hurt." Hadn't hurt, either, and a fat friggin' lot of good that does Lafe now. Jesus, God, are you up there? He was a good man. Please, somebody, remember that.

An ugly column of smoke rose against the sky. One of the village women saw it and began to wail. Must be another village, Murphy thought. He called for Panar and pointed out the smoke to him.

"Aye, Lord, Katos lies in that direction."

Christ, what do I do now? I'm too damned tired to think. "What other villages are there near here?"

"Four within one day's ride, Lord. Five, counting Katos."

"Forget Katos. Send to the others. Do not send your best messengers. Have all the people come here. They should bring their flocks and beasts and everything they have, food and fodder, and come here quickly where I can defend them with sky weapons."

"There is not room inside the wall for half of them!"

"Well, we build a new wall, and a ditch." That would keep the cattle from straying and the Westmen from riding up to the walls. They weren't likely to be dangerous on foot. Except for those long-ranging arrows. But I've got three rifles, and maybe Ski'll be able to fight.

"Building a wall will take many hands from the crops," said the chief.

Jeez, the soul of a bureaucrat. "How many crops will you harvest if the Westmen burn you out and kill you all?"

Panar shrugged. "What matter, if Lord Harkon does the same?"

"The hell with Harkon. I speak with the voice of the Lord Eqeta."

The old chief spat into the dirt, then squinted into Murphy's face. He said nothing.

"Look, dammit!" Murphy said. He patted his rifle, then opened his wizard robe to reveal his pistol and combat webbing. "Watch!" He drew the pistol and fired at a gourd in a nearby market stall. Everyone turned to stare at the sound, so he blew another gourd away while they were watching. "There. That is small magic." He patted the rifle again. "And this is big magic."

The chief nodded. "I have heard. You are a sky god."

"Not a god, but I know the sky magic."

"You know the Lord Eqeta, who is a sky god," Panar said. "And that is enough. You will tell the Lord Harkon?"

"I will."

"The messengers will go now."

"Good."

The chief left, and Murphy sat down in the wagon. A couple of village kids looked shyly at him, then dodged back into their home behind the market stall. A girl about sixteen walked by, carefully not looking at him, but she'd changed into her best clothes.

My people, Murphy thought. He laughed at himself, but even as he did he thought of what he could teach the villagers about self-defense. Pikes and spears. Stand your ground against cavalry. Discipline and trust the man next to you, and you're as good as any cavalry.

He realized he was taking on a lot of responsibilities. The villagers would be grateful, but their lord wouldn't much care for his giving military training to the peasants. But if that kept Ben Murphy alive long enough to get a message back, that ought to square things with Captain Galloway.

What of Lady Tylara? What if the local lord didn't like his villagers taking matters into their own hands this way?

Ben laughed again. Too bad for Bheroman Harkon. The pike regiments had already taught peasants they could do things for themselves. Murphy wasn't doing anything new. Besides, he was the great-grandson of a man who'd been hanged for shooting a landlord's agent, and he wasn't inclined to be very tender about landlords' feelings.

PART FIVE

PRINCIPALITIES AND POWERS

22

Escorted by eight Royal Guardsmen on each side, the roasted stag marched up the aisle between the banqueting tables. Halfway to the high table, it stopped and bowed to Wanax Ganton. The two men under the draperies hanging from the platter were excellent puppeteers; the stag seemed alive, although, much to his host's surprise, Ganton had personally speared it in yesterday's hunt.

Lord Ajacias beamed when Ganton acknowledged the stag's obeisance. His daughter Lady Cara also saw that Ganton approved, and giggled. "Is that not marvelous, Majesty? Hakour our chef has been a good and faithful servant for many years, but he has never given us such a meal as this."

For the tenth time, Ganton wished that the Lady Cara seated beside him was instead the Lady Octavia Caesar. Octavia did not try to gain his favor. She did not always agree with him. Quite the contrary. She also did not giggle. And though her ankles were not so slim as the Lady Cara's, Caesar's granddaughter had by far the best clothing on Tran, and wore her gowns and robes with a grace and dignity that suited—

His thoughts were shattered by the metallic click of a star weapon made ready to fire. "HALT! WHO IS THERE?" the Lord Mason thundered in a voice like Yatar passing judgement. He came forward from his place at the end of the table, his rifle leveled at the stag, the small knife—*bayonet*, that was the word—pointed at the animal's throat.

"The stag!" The response was given by Hanzar, Guards Officer of the Day. The other guards, splendid in their new clothing—*uniforms*, Lord Rick called them—presented their weapons.

"What stag?" Mason demanded.

"Wanax Ganton's stag!"

"Then pass, friend!" Mason acknowledged. "Make way for Wanax Ganton's stag!"

Then from within the stag a loud voice shouted. "Long live Wanax Ganton!" Lord Rick himself leaped from his place to repeat the cry, and all the banqueters, two hundred and more, stood and joined the cheering.

Ganton threw back his head to laugh with the others, but inwardly he could hear Lucius speaking in his ancient dry voice. "And in the midst of the triumph, at the time of a conqueror's greatest glory, there rides in his chariot the lowest-born slave of the Empire, who never ceases to say, 'Remember Caesar, thou art but a mortal man.' The cheers of a throng are easily gained. Honor is more elusive." He could hear the old man, and see Octavia nodding agreement—and also hear the Lady Cara giggle.

The stag was brought forward to the salutes of the starmen and the Guards. Their—*uniforms*—green shirts and trousers, green jackets, black boots and black belts with sheathed daggers, silver badges on their black berets, made them look remarkably like the starmen in the dim light. Lord Ajacias had done his best with candles and torches, but a hall large enough for two hundred was far too large to be lighted properly.

Now the guards, the starmen, and picked men from Lord Rick's Mounted Archers and Hussars all came forward, presented their weapons, and crashed them against the floor while the stag and its table passed between their lines on its way to the sand pit between the banqueting tables. The men who'd animated the stag came out from beneath the draperies, and they were also in the uniform of the Royal Guards. All presented their weapons, then saluted in the starman's manner. "Permission to withdraw?" Hanzar shouted.

There was a long pause. Ganton realized that Lord Rick was staring at him. "Permission granted!" Ganton called, and guards and starmen and Tamaerthans all retired in a complex drill, halting in pairs and clashing weapons as others passed between them, twirling weapons as they knelt on one knee, then rising with more flourishes. They left the hall to the thunder of applause.

✠   ✠   ✠

Morrone appeared from somewhere. He held a knife as long as an archer's sword. As King's Companion, it was his duty to carve and taste the first portion of all meat brought to the high table. Ganton had always thought his friend graceful, but now he looked just a bit awkward and unrehearsed after the performance of those soldiers.

But first Yanulf. The archpriest rose from his place opposite Ganton, and spread his arms wide. "Yatar, Great Skyfather, we thy servants give thee praise and thanks . . ."

"Majesty?"

His host was trying to get his attention. Ganton acknowledged him with a nod.

"Majesty, the weapon carried by the starman who challenged the stag—was this the same weapon they showed this afternoon?" He shuddered. "Is it safe that such weapons be brought into my hall?"

"Star weapons are safe while starmen are loyal," Ganton said.

"And are they loyal, Majesty?"

"You saw," Ganton said.

"Aye, Majesty. I saw disciplined men perform well what they have learned."

"And—"

"I say no more—"

"I command you, speak what you think."

"I saw them loyal to the starmen," Ajacias said. "I saw them cheer my Wanax. But I have not seen them obey the anointed of Yatar."

". . . and we thank Thee for the abundant rains of spring and the mildness of the winter," Yanulf was saying. "And we beg Thy aid, that Thou might intercede with Hestia and all Thy great family, that our seed might not rot in the ground, but flourish and multiply, and our harvest be great that we may offer great sacrifice to Thee. And as The Time approaches, incline the hearts of our lawful rulers to know and do Thy will . . ."

"You demand a demonstration?" Ganton asked. "They have come with me—"

"Majesty, I demand nothing!" Ajacias protested. "I spoke only when commanded! Forgive me!"

"There is nothing to forgive—"

". . . and let it be Thy will to aid us. Arise, Lord, hasten to aid us, for our need is great . . ."

"—and perhaps you have been of more service than you know," Ganton said.

One good thing about Yanulf. Lady Cara was silenced. She wouldn't giggle while the Primate of Drantos invoked the blessings of Yatar. Indeed, she stared as if hypnotized—and yet she probably wouldn't be able to remember a word that Yanulf has said. While Octavia would have been eager to talk, to discuss Yanulf's sermon and compare Yatar to the Roman Jehovah and his son Jesus Christ, to ponder the vision of Bishop Polycarp that the Christ was in fact the Son of Yatar, that Yatar and Jehovah were One—

"—the Time of Testing cometh upon us. Woe to that man who fails to prepare. Woe to him, great lord or villein, who has not done the will of Yatar and laid by goods for The Time . . ."

"I am told that smiths to the south have learned to make star weapons of their own."

Ganton pretended not to have heard. Ajacias would learn of the new weapons in due season. For now there was not enough firepowder in the realm to stoke all the *guns* for more than a few blasts. There was a shortage of ingredients, especially saltpeter. Ganton had learned how to make firepowder, but not how to extract saltpeter from dungheaps. He wondered if he should not have paid more attention to that day's lecture. But a Wanax was no mechanic!

"And so we invoke Thy aid." Yanulf's prayer ended. Morrone attacked the stag as if it were his blood foe, and then tasted the slice he carved and pronounced it good. And now, finally, the cooks' apprentices could come out and carve the beast and all could get down to the serious business of eating.

But Ganton couldn't forget the idea he'd had while Ajacias was questioning him. There was one way to show all that the starmen were loyal to the Crown. If only Lord Rick would agree! But for now, there was dinner, and the giggles of Lady Cara . . .

✢ ✢ ✢

The Royal Guardsmen began a sword dance, complex beyond belief, with elements of Tamaerthan dancing mixed with something very like a polka. Their razor-sharp sabers flashed in the candlelight, earning the king's applause.

Rick Galloway watched with approval as young Ganton refused another cup of wine and asked for water instead. The king's request probably shocked the steward, but it meant Ganton would have a clear head. He was going to need it to fend off Ajacia's questions.

"Boy's learnin' the king business," Art Mason said as he took his place beside Rick. "And damn good thing you made 'em put these tables up."

They were seated behind and to the left of the high table, in a place near an entrance. Rick had insisted that every entrance in the hall be blocked by a table with mercs and Royal Guardsmen, and to hell with protocol. "Yeah?" Rick prompted.

"You been listenin' to that Ajacias?" Mason asked. "Every question, everything he says, he tries to stir up trouble. That business about making star weapons to use with firepowder, he's really trying to talk the kid into something. And when he's not stirring up trouble or fishing for classified information, he tells how it's time to make peace with the Five Kingdoms."

"You think he's a traitor?"

"Hell, Cap'n, you thought so or we wouldn't be here." Mason grinned. "I thought you was nuts, wanting to honor a guy that might be plotting against us, but I see it makes sense." He pointed to the candles at every pillar. "Candles and new livery for the servants. Just those must have cost him a fortune."

Rick returned the grin and poured wine. "We needed to come north anyway," Rick said. "We had to stay somewhere. Why not with Ajacias? Anyway, it seemed like a good idea at the time." A good idea, but not mine, he thought. But nobody on Tran is going to know that. Except maybe Gwen. Who else ever read about Queen Elizabeth I, and her answer to plots?

Silly plots, like Babington's, she could leave to Walsingham and his secret police, who needed a spectacular success every now and then. More serious situations, involving persons of wealth and stature and importance, she took care of herself: her method was to visit them. As Parkinson, Rick's favorite historian, had put it, they could hardly plot while she was there, and they were financially ruined by the time she left. Her visit to Euston Hall in 1578 rendered the Rockwoods harmless for at least a decade . . .

And Lord Ajacias, a bheroman in the vital Sutmarg region bordering the Five Kingdoms, was far too important to accuse without evidence—or to be allowed to get away with treason.

"Anyway, we got him on trading with the enemy," Mason said.

Rick nodded. Mason's patrols had intercepted a pack train of hides and fine wine just as it reached the border. Not only did the hides have Ajacias' brand, but the idiot had written a letter to the Wanax of Ta-Meltemos inquiring about the last shipment and detailing what special payments were wanted. "Hang onto the smugglers," Rick said. "We might not want to accuse Ajacias. Not Just yet, anyway—"

"Right." Mason waved expansively. "He's sure not going to hire many troopers this year. Not after two weeks of this."

"Yeah, but you know, he doesn't seem to mind. Really acts like he's being honored to have the Wanax here."

"Well, sure, he'd like his daughter to be Wanaxxae."

"Fat chance," Rick said. "What else did your patrols turn up?"

"Confirmation," Mason said. "Just like you thought, they're raising armies in the Five Kingdoms. Just how big and what for I can't tell. Too many cavalry screens. But they're mobilizing. Funny thing, not so much cavalry as stores. Like they're expecting a siege."

Rick shrugged. "The Time—"

"Sure, but they're increasing the garrison, too," Mason said. "Least I think so, but it's hard to find out anything for certain."

"One more problem," Rick said. He turned as his orderly came up behind him. "Yes, Jamiy?"

"A message, Lord. From the Lady Tylara."

"Ah. Give it to me. Wait, I'll move away from the table. Impolite to read while the Wanax is eating his dinner. Mason, if you don't mind I'd rather you stayed here to watch out for the Wanax." Rick got up from the hard bench with relief. The guards started a new dance as Rick retreated to the corridor behind the banqueting hall.

He broke the wax seals and unfolded the letter, noting that it was paper, not parchment. Fairly good quality paper, too; the University's mills had got the knack of it now, so there were few ink runs mixed with her painstakingly written words. As he held the parchment close to the beeswax candles, he wondered how far the University's research into illuminating gas had gone.

To the Lord Rick, Eqeta of Chelm, War Lord of Tamaerthon, Captain General of the Hosts of Drantos, Beloved of Yatar, from Lady Tylara, Eqetassa of Chelm and Justiciar of Drantos,

Greetings!

My beloved, your children and heirs are safe and well, and I trust this finds you the same. I am also well, though I miss you greatly and wish only for our reunion.

Rick nodded and smiled to himself. Leave it to Tylara to put things in that order. Titles. Health of the children. And only then the really important news, that she was all right.

The feud with the Mac Naile has proven more troublesome than I like. It is well that I have come, for this may yet become a challenge to Mac Clallan Muir. Aye, and there is worse, for there is murmur among the lesser clans that much booty may be found at your University. Thus must I strengthen its defenses, yet do so from afar so that it will not seem that Mac Clallan Muir holds sway in this place which you insist must remain above all clans and crowns.

And you're doing the right thing even though you don't agree with me about the University, Rick thought. Thank God I met you, Tylara. I'd better come up there now. It makes sense, it's not just that I want to see you, my love—

My father sends his greetings, and his thanks that you have sent Makail his first grandson to visit him. Though he has not said so, you may be certain that he is even more grateful for my escort.

Eight mercs, Caradoc with two hundred Mounted Archers, and a hundred lances of Chelm chivalry. Tylara had been sure they would be more than enough to persuade the recalcitrant Mac Naile.

And though that dispute is I think soon ended, there are rumors of others, and it seemed to me that there must be a source of this strife. Thus I spoke with Corgarff, reminding him of your generosity in sparing his life, and of the loyalty of his sons, and of the devotion his new chief holds to you. In this way I persuaded him to tell what he knows of the

Dughuilas affair. What he told me has earned him a visit by the headsman—

Oh, Lord! Rick thought. What—

—but mindful of your wishes, I have given him a second pardon, which will assuredly be his last.

As you suspected, there was indeed a plot, with Dughuilas, and a highly placed henchman to Mac Clallan Muir, to the end that only the highborn would command, and all your work would be undone. Corgarff will not name my father's traitor henchman, but says again and again that he knows not the name, only that he was assured that none of the conspirators bore ill will toward my father or myself, nor indeed toward you, but only toward the changes you make. As you are fond of saying, you may believe as much of that as you will; for my part I do believe it, or rather that Corgarff believes it.

And there was yet one more conspirator, one that Corgarff actually met, but the man was hooded and the light dim, so that Corgarff would not know him, aye though he met him again. From his speech he seemed not of the Drantos nobles, yet certainly he was not of Tamaerthon, yet indeed he was a man of parts and gentle speech and ways. When I put it to Corgarff that the man was likely a priest, Corgarff seemed surprised, then agreed it was possible. You must speak with Yanulf and ask him to see to the loyalty of his archpriests, for there may be one who bears us ill will. The danger is small, now that his instruments are taken, but treason must never be allowed to pass unpunished.

If there be time I will enclose more, telling you of my love, and of our children, for Lady Isobel ceases not to ask for her father, and is quite put out that you do not place her in her bed each night as was your custom. And I would have you do the same with me, each night aye and each day as well. . . .

"My lord," Jamiy said. "If you have a moment."
"Eh?" Rick looked up from Tylara's letter. He'd been staring at it for

a long time. His eyes felt the strain from the dim light, and he blinked several times. "What is it?"

"Carlga the smith and Fnor the master miller would speak with you."

"How much did they bribe you?"

"A silver each, Lord."

"Ah." Quite a tidy sum. "Their business must be important. Bring them."

Jamiy grinned and pocketed the money. Sometimes Lord Rick demanded a share of the bribes paid to get his attention.

The miller and smith were in their finest clothing, with leather purses and jeweled peace-bonded daggers hanging from their belts. Men of substance, Rick thought.

They stammered a bit, but their manners were good, and they were obviously accustomed to speaking to the nobility. Rick learned that the smith employed five journeymen and a dozen apprentices, while the miller was a town councillor. Even so, they had difficulty coming to the point.

"And the demonstration with the stag was indeed marvelous," Fnor was saying. "The Royal Guardsmen in particular. Is there aught they cannot do?"

"We have sons," Carlga said. "The miller and I both. They would gladly serve in the guard."

"And our hearts would be gladdened to see them so honored," Fnor added.

Aha. The point at last. Rick said nothing, and the silence dragged on. Can't ask them direct what bribe they're offering, Rick thought. How long do I have to wait?

"Indeed, my heart would be so gladdened," Fnor said at last, "that I would build a new mill. Beside my present mill, for there is ample water, more than ample now with the greater rains. I would build a wheel of the sort that your clerks describe, of the kind that the Romans have. Carlga will bring his forge to that mill, so that the wheel might drive his bellows and work trip hammers in the new manner. All this at our expense, and a year's products of the mill and forge to the guards."

Generous offer indeed, Rick thought. But a year's products be damned, what's needed is a real hammer mill here where transportation's hard to come by. There's coal, and iron ore, and this is a damned good place for a foundry. Long way from any likely targets, too. Not likely to be bombed out.

"Your forge is fired with wood?" Rick asked.

"Aye, Lord. I have heard of using blackrock, but I have never seen a forge like that. We tried once, but without success."

"There will not be many years before burning wood to make metal and glass will be forbidden," Rick said. "As wood grows more scarce, you must learn to use blackrock."

"Where may we learn?" Carlga asked.

"The traveling clerks will know, but there is a better way. Have you a son to follow in your trade? Excellent. Send him a year to the University near Tar Kartos in Tamaerthon. There he will learn to use the blackrock, and much else."

"We would also learn the arts of making the—*guns*—which use firepowder," Fnor added. "Master smith Carlga makes strong iron."

"Not all strong iron is strong enough," Rick said. "The art of making *guns* is not so easily acquired." Especially not here in a border county ruled by a possible traitor. "Nor can I promise your sons, nor any man, a place in the guards.

"Yet you need not look so downcast," Rick continued. "The guards are sworn as brothers, and will accept among them none who have not earned their place, and who will not take the same oath to Vothan."

The men sobered at the mention of Vothan. Like his Earth counterpart, Old One-eye was more feared than loved. "But I can promise this," Rick added quickly. "Let them present themselves to Lord Mason before the Wanax departs, and if they please him, we will take them with us; and if they work hard—" Dammit, what I want to say is apply themselves, but that sounds stupid in the local language— "If they will work and give their attention to the task before them, I doubt not they can earn a place in the guards." And take the first step toward ennobling their families . . .

"So. Since I cannot grant what you asked, I cannot accept what you offer. Yet I wish the mill and forge to be built, and to that end I will loan half the cost from the Captain-General's purse. You will repay the debt in iron, and the first fruits of the forge belong to the crown."

"Generous, lord," Fnor said. "You deserve your reputation. And we will send our sons to the Lord Mason in the morning. Thank you, Lord."

✦ ✦ ✦

Ganton sat cross-legged on the great bed, cradling a cup of wine in his lap and looking around the comfortable tapestry-hung room. It was, of course, Lord Ajacia's bedchamber. Idly Ganton wondered where Ajacias was sleeping, and who he had displaced, and who that one had caused to move.

Morrone was hovering at the foot of the bed, casting an occasional glance at the door. "Oh, go to whatever girl you've asked," Ganton said irritably. "I can undress myself."

Morrone grinned. "Thank you, sire. But it would be best if I did my duty first."

"Then do it. Lord Rick received a message tonight. They brought it during dinner, and he went out to read it. My guess is that it came from the lady Tylara, else why would they not wait until morning, or at least until dinner was finished?"

"Yes, sir?"

"If from Tylara, then it may have come from the University," Ganton said. "I would know if it did."

"Aha. Majesty, had there been letters for you, they would have been brought by now."

"Perhaps."

"Surely."

"Then Octavia has chosen not to write to me."

"You cannot be certain. Indeed, you do not know the message was from Lady Tylara, and certainly you do not know that it was sent from the University. Can you doubt that the Lady Octavia would take any opportunity to write to you? I cannot."

"Ah. You believe then that she does not dislike me?"

Morrone shrugged. "What matter her likes and dislikes? I believe that she is intelligent. As to you—you brood too much. I am certain that my lady of the evening has a friend—"

"But are you certain your lady mother did not play the Eqeta false with a panderer from the stews of Rustengo?"

Morrone laughed again. As indeed, Ganton thought, he must, for if there were any hint that I was serious—I should watch my tongue, even alone with my only friend.

Then Morrone's laugh died and his voice became very serious. "Are *you* certain that you are not getting yourself into more of a coil about the Lady Octavia than she deserves?"

"And why do you reckon her deserts?" There was a hint of danger in Ganton's voice.

"Majesty, it is my duty to advise you."

Yes. It is, Ganton thought. And indeed, you were one of the few who supported me when I thought to bring the Lady Octavia north on this tour. But I did not, through the advice of the Lord and Lady of Chelm, and Chancellor Yanulf, and Camithon—

"Advice! I hear nothing but advice, from my first visit to the jakes in the morning until you blow out the last candle at night! Only Yatar could listen to so much advice!"

"Yatar does not need advice," Morrone reminded him. "You do. Or you have said you do. You are of age now, and the time has passed when I could speak to you as once I did, but I will, once more. Ganton, my friend, if ever you wish my silence, you have only to say so, and I will remain your friend yet."

"Ach, not you also!" Ganton shouted. "They all say that! All, all, they threaten to withdraw their counsel, and though they do not always say so, it is in their minds, that my father lost his throne through failure to listen to his advisors. And yes, yes, that is true enough, but much of what I hear is senseless! Yet must I listen, and smile, lest someone with more power than wits be mortally offended! Surely there is more to being Wanax than this?"

Morrone made a wry face. "I offered one of the rewards of majesty, and you made free to insult my mother for reply." He grinned to show he wasn't offended. "And there is little chance that Lady Octavia would ever know, though why you remain so tender for the feelings of Lord Rick's hostage to the Roman alliance I will never know."

"Is she no more than that?"

"How can she be else?"

"If Lord Rick and Chancellor Yanulf think of nothing but hostages, why have they not gathered in the children of Publius' dead sister?"

Morrone shrugged again. "The discussion grows serious. Will you have more wine?"

"Yes."

Morrone poured and brought the goblets to the bed. "Caesar's other grandchildren are not important because they cannot be offered in marriage. Not when the eldest is five. While the Lady Octavia is ripe enough. Majesty, think you that I oppose your suit?"

"Of course not." Morrone had more than once been messenger when the University authorities tried to keep Ganton and Octavia apart.

"For indeed, were she queen, the way might lie open to more than ever we dream," Morrone said. "Rome itself." He stepped back and raised his hand in the Roman manner, and there was no mockery in his voice at all as he said, "Hail, Caesar."

"Only if—only if Lord Rick permits it," Ganton said.

Morrone nodded. "Aye, for the moment the starmen hold power over us. But they will not forever mock the anointed of Yatar!"

That phrase, and the way Morrone said it, reminded Ganton of something, someone else who'd said that in just that way, but the wine and the venison and the lateness of the hour overcame him before he could remember who it had been.

23

The morning ritual was the same here as at the palace. Rick dressed, put on armor, and with Mason beside him came out for his first appointments. His personal guards waited for him in the corridor. Today they were commanded by Padraic, the under-captain of the Mounted Archers. Four guardsmen walked ahead, then Rick and Mason, followed by Jamiy and Padraic.

Mason hadn't much cared to have a new man armed and behind his captain, but he hadn't any choice. Caradoc went with Tylara to the Garioch, and somebody had to be Mason's second-in-command of the MPs. Padraic, son of a Drantos lord and a Tamaerthan mother, knew the customs of both lands, and had been loyal since the archers were formed. There wouldn't be anyone better . . . which didn't stop Art Mason from worrying.

Rick had no trouble reading his companion's mind. Mason worried a lot about loyalties. At least, Rick thought, he understands why we've got to expand the leadership, bring in locals and govern by Tran customs and law, and not just be a flock of wolves here. Mason understands. And Gwen. I think Elliot and Warner. The rest—well, the rest of them saw what happened when Parsons tried taking over by force, but I'm not sure how well they learned the lesson. And how loyal are they? To me, to anyone?

They reached the chamber set aside for them by their host. Beazeley and four locals stood guard outside.

"All secure?" Mason asked.

Beazeley grinned. "Yes, sir, all secure *now*."

"Eh?"

"Found two different listening places," Beazeley said. "Alcove behind a tapestry, about like you'd expect. But something different." He opened the door and led the way inside a stone chamber about twenty-five feet square. "Behind that tapestry, there, by the window. That was one. And see that picture there? Back of that's a corridor. Real secret passage."

"Who was in there?" Mason demanded.

"Unarmed clerk types," Beazeley said. "Real anxious to prove they were unarmed, too."

Rick nodded. "I expect they would be. Have you secured that corridor, then?"

"Yes, sir. I put two MPs at each end of it. Nobody to go in without your permission. Rest of the room's clean, as far as I can tell." Beazeley laughed. "I didn't look too hard for electronics."

"No. Thank you," Rick said. "All right, we'll deal with Lord Ajacias later. Meanwhile, Art, go escort the king, please. And I expect we'll need wine, and a pot of that stuff that passes for tea. Morrone will have to see to that."

"Yes, sir," Mason said. "Okay, Jack, let's go."

Rick paced around the room. It held a carved slab table, two side tables, three comfortable chairs, some benches, and a solid-looking cabinet that probably unfolded into a writing desk. On a whim Rick went to it and opened it. There were no dwarves inside, but it did have goose quills, parchment, and ink.

"Make way," someone called outside. The door opened, and Mason stood aside to let Wanax Ganton enter. Lord Morrone followed him in.

"Welcome, Majesty," Rick said.

"Thank you."

Morrone gestured, and servants brought in wine and a silver service of the local equivalent of tea. It was bitter stuff, but it did have caffeine. If only the *Shalnuksis* would bring a few pounds of real coffee—

"Thank you," Ganton told Morrone. His voice held dismissal, and Morrone left Rick and Ganton alone in the room.

"Your Companion was not overly pleased to leave us," Rick said.

"Nor your soldiers."

"Shall we sit?" Rick asked.

"Thank you." Ganton took one of the chairs.

"Wine or tea?" Rick asked.

"Wine, but it is not right that you—"

"I have no fear for my dignity," Rick said. He poured a goblet of wine and a large mug of tea and brought them to the table. *The boy's nervous*, Rick thought.

"I think we have not been alone since I came of age," Ganton said. He smiled thinly. "Nor do my advisors approve now."

Why would they? The last thing any public official needs is to find out his sovereign is cutting deals the civil service doesn't know about. "It is good to see you. You look well."

"Thank you. As do you." He looked nervously around.

"The room is safe, Majesty," Rick said. "My soldiers personally removed the scribes Lord Ajacias had set to listen to us, and now they guard the passageway behind that picture."

"I see. Is that not a treason?"

"Only if you wish to be."

"But the law—"

Ganton seemed very serious, and Rick suppressed a chuckle. "Majesty, law and justice may be served when there has been a crime that harms someone. Here there has been no harm, and thus the matter of treason may be left to expediency and advantage."

"Do you see advantage in accusing Ajacias?"

"Not at present," Rick said. "He seems popular with his knights and villeins. Who would replace him?"

"My question exactly," Ganton said. "Then that is settled."

There was a long awkward silence.

"Lord Rick," Ganton said. "The banquet last night was splendid. The guards, and the star warriors, all were magnificent—"

"But?" Rick prompted.

"But there were questions. Some asked—some asked if the starmen were truly loyal to me," Ganton said with a rush. "And though I assure them they are, though I assure them you are loyal, though I believe this with all my heart, still will there be doubts."

Rick frowned. *Just what was eating the kid?* "I will not remind you of the proofs we have already given," Rick said. "You must know them all."

"Aye," Ganton said. "And yet still are there doubts! But—it came to me at the banquet. There is a way. If you could—if you could give me a star weapon. A small magic, not the large. The weapon the Lady Tylara used to kill Lord Parsons. And binoculars," Ganton continued. "A different kind of magic. Together they would show—they would show that you do not fear to have your Wanax armed in your presence!"

"Um," Rick said. Oh, boy! The trouble is, it's not unreasonable. Not the way he looks at it, not the way his council will see it.

"I can pay," Ganton said. "I would not expect you to take the personal equipment of one of your warriors, but perhaps one would sell for much gold?"

Hell's bells, there's half a dozen would sell every goddamn thing they've got if Mason and Elliot didn't hold equipment checks every ten-day, Rick thought. And I'm not sure some of 'em haven't sold gear already. We never did have a complete inventory of personal weapons and equipment.

"This is no small request," Rick said.

"I know."

"By God, I think you do know," Rick said. "But let's be certain. You ask that I place my life—that of any of my soldiers—in your hands. Not just in law, but in plain fact. Wait—I would not interrupt lightly. I know that I have already done this, and deliberately. I do not keep a large bodyguard, I travel with the court rather than stay in my stronghold of Dravan. But what I know may not be so plain to my soldiers. You ask that I show them that I trust you with their lives."

"Aye. A great favor to ask, yet one I think necessary, if I am truly to be Wanax of Drantos."

No question about that. Which means you've given me a decision to make. And you know that, too. Meanwhile, we're making changes everywhere. Triphammers and water mills. Paper and ink. Deep plows. Fertilizer.

"It is not a decision lightly to be made," Rick said. "I must take counsel."

"But you will consider the matter?"

"I will—"

"Captain!" Mason's voice came from beyond the door.

What the hell? "With your permission, Majesty?"

"I confess as much curiosity as you, my lord."

"Come in, Mason."

Art Mason came in quickly. Morrone followed before anyone could stop him. "Messengers, Cap'n," Mason said in English. "From Murphy, up on the plateau. Peasant boys. They brought a parchment, but they've already told everybody in the castle. Horse archers from the high desert, Westmen. They attacked the wizard train. Killed Lafe Reznick and wounded Ski, chopped up a couple of villages, killed the local borderer baron. Everybody in the castle knows."

✢ ✢ ✢

Mason spoke too fast in the star language, and Ganton could catch only a few words. Outside he could hear people shouting in the courtyard, and someone ran through the corridors.

"Lord Rick—"

Lord Rick didn't seem to hear. He took a parchment from Lord Mason and spread it out on the table. Ganton stood and moved closer to Rick. Neither Rick nor Mason objected, so he looked over Rick's shoulder, and made a firm vow to spend more time at his English lessons when he went back to the University. *If* he went back, and that seemed more and more an impossible thought.

Westmen. The word was a literal translation of the Tran term, and it leaped at him from the page. The Westmen had come to the southwest high plains. They'd come in strength, and had slain a bheroman and his knights, and—

Lord Rick looked up to see Ganton trying to read. For a moment he hesitated, then handed the letter to Mason. "Read it to us," he ordered. "Translate as you go."

"Uh, Cap'n—"

"Please."

"Yes, sir." Mason cleared his throat and began to read.

The news was worse than Ganton had imagined. Hundreds of Westmen, mounted archers, every bit as skilled as the dreaded Tamaerthan archers. There—there was nothing on Tran to match them! Nothing but star weapons. How many did the Westmen number? In the Tales of The Time there were stories of fierce monsters from the west, tens of thousands of demons mounted on horses that ate human flesh. Could they be Westmen?

—I regret to report that Private Lafferty Reznick was killed in action. I would put him up for the Legion of Merit if I could. He saved my ass, and more important he saved Baldy, this Priest of Vothan who lived with the Westmen for ten years and more, so I got good intelligence on the Westmen. If I get a chance before I have to send this off I'll put down some of what he told me, but the most important is, there's drought up there in their desert. They're all coming down. Not so many right now, not more than a few hundred, but they'll all come down sooner or later. God knows how many that is, but it's a lot.

Corporal Jerzy Walinski has been severely wounded, and is not yet returned to duty, but is expected to recover. Four knights, three esquires, and nine men-at-arms with full armor, plus twenty-five farm boys of the local militia, are all that have come back from Baron Harkon's force. I keep hoping there'll be more, but I don't think there will be. There's no sign of the baron.

A star lord dead, another wounded, and of a bheroman's forces not one of ten alive!

Ski can't travel, and I don't have enough troops to fight my way back to Castle Dravan. So I holed up here, and we're digging in. I hope to God this gets through, Captain, because if it don't, we've had it and no mistake. I can hold on for a while. This is no strategic hamlet, but I know a few tricks, and the villagers are willing to fight if somebody shows them how. Which is me, I guess, because there's nobody else to do it, and I just hope that ammo holds out.

So I hope you can send me some help before it's too late. I know you got troubles of your own, but you got to get here pretty quick if you want to see us alive. If you don't make it, I'll try to wreck the H&Ks before they get me.

Yours very respectfully,
Benjamin Murphy do Dirstval,
Onetime Private, U.S.A.

Mason finished reading and handed the parchment to Rick.

"We must send aid," Ganton said. "And quickly."

Lord Mason and Lord Rick were looking at each other. They didn't seem to hear.

Other parchments lay on the table. Maps, and a sketch of one of the Westmen. Ganton also noted the bow, longer and thicker than the horse bows of Drantos or the Five Kingdoms, or even of the Romans.

"Your Lord Murphy seems a wise captain," Ganton said. "I would honor him. With your permission. And a grant to the wives—" he could make himself say it now, although the idea had grated on him while Reznick was alive. "—to the wives of the Lord Reznick. Only upon your advice, my lord."

He had not forgotten. One of his first acts upon coming of age was a grant of land to Protector Camithon—which earned him the cold scorn of Lady Tylara. Not that she objected to honors given Camithon, who was, after all, her general; but he was *her* general now that he was no longer Protector. Her advice and consent had not been asked, and that she was slow to forgive.

Lord Rick said nothing.

"Forgive us, Majesty," Mason said. "We can—we can talk about that later."

"Aye." Ganton went to the side table. Before Morrone could interfere, he poured three goblets of wine and brought them to the center table. "My lords," he said, and set the goblets down. "To the memory of Lord Reznick."

They drank, and Rick looked up woodenly. "He came a long way to die."

"Aye," Ganton said. "Yet the Chooser will find a man, however far he travels. But he will have an honored place in Vothan's Hall, I think."

"Yeah." Rick looked thoughtful. "Art, what can we send Murphy?"

"Not a hell of a lot. You know what's mobilized."

"You'll have to go. He needs some quick reinforcements. Ammunition, and a mobile force." Rick strode quickly to the door and opened it. "Jamiy!"

"Sir!"

"Alert Captain Padraic. The Mounted Archers will prepare to move out. Combat gear and rations."

"Sir!" Rick's orderly ran off down the corridor.

I wish I were obeyed as Lord Rick is, Ganton thought. And command as he does. He took no advice, no counsel. He needed none.

"Your pardon, Majesty," Rick said, as if suddenly realizing that Ganton was in the room. "It is best we act quickly. Have I permission to alert your guards? We should return to Armagh, and quickly."

"Armagh, my lord?" Ganton asked "Not Dravan?" Lord Rick's Castle Dravan was certainly the proper place to organize the defense of the High Cumac. One of the castle's functions was to guard the passes up the Littlescarp.

"Aye, sire," Rick said. "But first there must be a Council of the Realm, and meetings with our allies of Tamaerthon and Rome. And I must see to the growing of *surinomaz* and other affairs at Armagh, which is as easy to reach from the University as your capital of Edron. Thus I suggest you send word to summon the council to Armagh."

"It is hardly convenient," Morrone said. "Nor comfortable—"

"Murphy's not very comfortable out there facin' those Westmen," Mason muttered.

"Let us hear no more of comfort!" Ganton said. "My Lord Morrone, it is my will that the Council of Drantos be summoned to Armagh, to meet within the ten-day. See to it."

Morrone was about to reply, but Ganton's look silenced him. "Aye, Majesty. Immediately."

Ganton wanted to leap and shout. He felt as he had the first time he had seen the sea, or bedded a woman. This was power, of the kind Lord Rick held, real power . . .

"So that is done," Ganton said. "Another thing, Lord Rick. Harkon's stronghold. Westrook. A strong place, I have heard. With Lord Harkon dead, someone must hold it. Perhaps Lord Murphy should go there."

"That makes sense," Mason said.

"We don't know the roads," Rick said. "Not enough information to make a decision."

"Yeah, but it stands to reason a castle's easier to hold than a village," Mason said. "When we get back to Dravan, we can send up some of those new bombards, and gunpowder. Who'll be in charge up there, now that the regular baron's had it?"

They speak to me as a companion, Ganton thought. Not as a boy, not as a king, but as a fellow warrior! They listen, and consider, and ask—"I believe Bheroman Harkon has a son not yet of age."

"Maybe Murph could take over that place," Mason said. "He's pretty sharp, Cap'n."

"We'll see," Rick said. "Time enough when we get him some ammo and find out what the score is." Someone had refilled his goblet. He drained it and set it down. "So now we have Westmen."

"Yeah," Mason said. "The Time's coming. Weather's gone crazy. Gotta raise madweed. Feuds in Tamaerthon. Clansmen eyeing the University's wealth. Riots and migrations in the south. The Five Kingdoms raising new armies. God knows what for. So we get to deal with Westmen. Why not?"

Rick joined Mason in laughter. Mason fetched the wine jug and poured the last into their three glasses. Ganton had never seen the starmen act this way before. This is what it is to be a man, he thought. To do what must be done, and know that you will, and that your companions will not fail you.

And I am here with them, but can I do what I must? Can I do what they expect of me?

Again they raised their glasses. "Why the hell not?" Rick said, and again they laughed, and Ganton drank with them, while inside he was afraid.

24

They rode hard through foothills covered with thorny scrub. Just before midday, the stark battlements of Castle Armagh loomed up ahead. Ganton spurred his horse and rode up alongside Rick. "Not the most comfortable of places, but yet a welcome sight," he said.

"Aye, Majesty." Forty miles in the saddle. Major Assburns. Not a joke to tell the king, but bloody hell my arse is sore!

"Your County is peaceful," Ganton said. "I had half-thought so small a party might meet up with robbers."

"It could have been," Rick acknowledged. The party they'd taken to visit Lord Ajacias in the Sutmarg had been enormous: guards, Mounted Archers, Yanulf's train of scribes and priests and acolytes, musicians, courtiers . . . The intention had been to eat up Ajacias' substance, and they'd done that. There were only ten in the group riding to Armagh. The others had been sent back to the capital, or up the Littlescarp to aid Murphy, or, like Yanulf, followed at a more leisurely pace.

"Perhaps messengers already await us at Armagh," Ganton suggested. "From the University."

"Possible," Rick conceded.

"By Yatar, I like this!" Ganton shouted. "To ride hard, all day and half the night! To eat venison roasted over a campfire, and sleep in furs on the ground—hardships, but we do this as friends, without advisors, without endless ceremony. I have not felt so alive since—since I led men to battle!"

"It can be a good feeling." Until the battle's over, and you have to look at the butcher's bill.

"I wish we had gone with the Lord Mason," Ganton said.

Rick shifted uncomfortably in the saddle. "If the Lord Mason and the Guard cannot relieve the Lord Murphy, we two would be of little use."

Ganton nodded seriously. "Aye. We must needs send an army, and only you and I can arrange that, so we are needed here. I know this, but it galls me to send my friends where I cannot go."

"Me too, sire. But it's part of leadership, to learn to be sensible. The semaphore will tell us when Mason gets back to Castle Dravan and is on his way here. Meantime, we have plenty to do."

"Aye." Ganton stood in his stirrups and turned. "Hanzar!" he shouted. "Ride ahead and tell them the Wanax of Drantos comes to guest with the Eqeta of Chelm."

Rick shifted his weight again. At least one of his problems was about to solve itself. In an hour he'd get a hot bath, and there was still half a tube of Preparation H . . .

⁜ ⁜ ⁜

Sergeant Chester Walbrook came out of the low doorway followed by two guardsmen. Their backs were bent under the load of heavy crates wrapped in mylar sheeting. Walbrook sent the guards ahead with acolyte torchbearers, then ticked off entries in his notebook. Finally he nodded to Rick. "That's the lot of it, sir."

Rick turned to the blue robed priest. "You may seal the caves."

Apelles motioned to his acolytes.

Rick suppressed a grin. Somebody's got to work. Who should it be, me? Not that I won't get my chance, with Mason coming in tomorrow. And the Grand Council of Drantos to meet in another ten-day. First things first, get this ammunition off to Castle Dravan. It'll be needed.

The door was heavy wood with heavily greased thick ironwork, set firmly into carved stone lintels deep in the bowels of Castle Armagh. "This is fine work," Rick said. "I have not seen its like in Drantos."

Apelles nodded. "I too was impressed, Lord, and wished to have another like it, but alas, when I inquired, I found that is not to be. The mason was from the southern Roman provinces, the lands south of Tamaerthon where Roman law is weak. He had got a Roman matron with child, but fled before he could be brought before the magistrates. How he came here I know not, but so I was told."

"And now?"

Apelles shook his head sadly. "He had learned nothing, for he bedded the daughter of the local village chief. Her father and brothers killed him."

Sergeant Walbrook chuckled. "It happens. Too bad, though. That's a good storage place for the ammunition." He eyed Apelles, then changed to English. "Captain, are you sure you want these locals to guard our ammo?"

"You have a better plan? Want to sit guard over it yourself?"

"No, sir—"

"It would be soft duty, but I can't spare troops for that," Rick said. "And the rest of this place is theirs anyway." He turned to Apelles. "We can go now."

Apelles motioned to the acolytes. Two carried torches and led the way uphill. The rest fell in behind Rick, Walbrook, and Apelles. Mason would have a fit, Rick thought.

The acolytes led the way up, then turned sharply left and down again. The smell of ammonia, always present in the caves, grew stronger. The trail narrowed. It was still a full yard wide, but seemed narrower because to their left was a sheer drop into black nothingness too deep for Rick's flashlight to illuminate.

Across the ten-yard gap was a rock wall covered with a bulbous slimy mass hung over with icicles and ammonia droplets. There was a slight wind through the cave, enough to bring in fresh air; otherwise they would not have been able to breath because of the ammonia.

"Hard to believe that damn iceplant reaches all the way up to the surface," Walbrook said. "I reckon we're three hundred feet down."

"Yeah, the root system is amazing," Rick agreed. "I'm even more amazed at how it makes ice." The local name for the plant was "The Protector." It was sacred to Yatar; legend had it that the nearer the rogue star came to Tran, the more efficient the icemaking capabilities of the Protector. That was interesting enough that Rick had asked for weekly measurements, but so far the data were insufficient for any real conclusions.

The acolytes hurried them through this area. The entrance and main corridor of the cave were far too large to be kept secret, but somewhere nearby the cave branched into a labyrinth of ammonia-filled passages that only Yatar's servants could enter. Grain and meat were stored there in the ice, gifts to Yatar—gifts to be returned from Yatar to his people during the worst seasons of the Time.

"We have not guarded weapons before," Apelles said. He paused a moment as if making up his mind. "And I am told it would be more fitting that those consecrated to Vothan One-eye guard your weapons."

"I have heard this also," Rick said. Not least from the Vothan priesthood. "But the servants of Yatar have always held the Caves of the Protector, and have distributed the gifts of Yatar fairly and with honor. How should I change what has always served the people and the god alike?"

Apelles bowed to acknowledge the compliment.

Sharp lad, Rick thought. Get my opinion now, while nobody's listening. Next he'll try to get me to say it in public. He's learning his bureaucratic skills—and I can't even complain, since we brought in Roman scribes to *teach* them how to set up a bureaucracy.

Christ, I hate paperwork! But we can't live without it. It takes a quart of wheat every day to feed a man. A bushel of oats to feed a war horse. The food has to come from somewhere. Food, wagons, weapons, ammunition—all the details of keeping an army in the field, and then there's food for all the peasants growing madweed. We're getting very dependent on this bureaucracy, which means the priests of Yatar. So long as Yanulf is in charge of the Yatar cult in Drantos, that's all right. But he won't live forever . . .

As they reached the cave entrance, a junior acolyte ran up to them. "Master Apelles," he shouted. "Master, you are to tell the Lord Rick that the Lady Tylara has arrived."

✣ ✣ ✣

Tylara was lovely. She ran toward him, but before she could reach him they were intercepted by a tiny dark-haired bombshell. "Daddy!" she screamed. Rick scooped Isobel up and held her high, while she laughed, and her hounds bared their canine teeth and growled that anyone, even the master, would so treat their charge.

"She's grown so," Rick said.

"They do, Lord," Erinia the nursemaid said. She sniffed, her comment on men who let their children grow up without them.

"And the boy?" Rick asked.

"He sleeps, Lord," Erinia said. "As well, after a ride like today's." She spoke with a thick Tamaerthan accent, and her manners were of the clans, not the households of Drantos. There would be no point in asking her to fetch the boy; she'd let him see his son when he woke, and not before.

There was no talking with Tylara, either, not while Isobel was there. She clutched at Rick and laughed, and when he put her down she held his legs.

So little time, Rick thought. So damned little time to spend with them, and so much to do.

✤ ✤ ✤

"How could I not come?" Tylara said when they were alone at last. "Dravan is our home, and these Westmen menace it. Should I then stay in Tamaerthon?"

Rick laughed. "I hoped you would come." He went to her.

She returned his kisses, then pushed his hands firmly away. "Later. First we talk alone. Then with the Wanax. And then we bathe." She kissed him again. "It will no be so long . . ."

"Long enough." He went back to the writing table where her last letters lay. "The University," he said. "You say it may not be safe."

She shrugged. "The minor clans and lawless ones see much wealth and few soldiers in a town bordered by wild hills and lochs. They dream of more booty taken in hours than they will see in their lives. Can you blame them for those dreams?"

"Maybe not, but we can't let it happen. Is it safe there?"

"For the moment. Until Mac Clallan Muir must withdraw his men. Rick, that may not be so long, unless you have gold and grain to send. If they are to feed their children, the dunnhie wassails must go and work their lands. My father cannot forever keep them as guardsmen, and he cannot send other clans whose chiefs have no love for this place where crofters are taught to defeat warriors."

"I know. I suppose the first thing is to send some Drantos troops to help keep watch. Only I'd want to send Chelm soldiers, and we'll need them all against the Westmen. I'll need Caradoc and his archers in the west, too."

"Strip away Caradoc's archers, and your University will no last the season," Tylara said. "Your starmen will needs be alert all the time, and even so there are few enough of them to face a thousand hillmen."

"The University must survive, Tylara."

She had been ready to reply more sharply, but something in his voice made her say merely, "At the expense of our lands?"

"At all expense. Tylara, every six hundred years this planet, all of it, all its peoples, are knocked back into a dark age. That has to stop. Has to, and the University is the only way."

"Then we must find ways to protect our University," she said. "It too will be part of our children's rightful inheritance. We must preserve Chelm as well—and I doubt not that I have for a husband the only man alive who can do all that."

✣ ✣ ✣

The rooms were perfect duplicates of Rick's office suite in Castle Dravan: small office with writing desk, larger conference room with slab table and sideboards with wine cruets. The walls either had maps painted on them, or were smooth-surfaced and whitewashed for writing. A charcoal brazier stood in one corner, and a rack for cloaks and weapons in another. Apelles had even duplicated the carvings on the chairs . . .

"Within a ten-day we meet with the Grand Council," Rick said. "And before that, we'll meet with Lucius and Octavia and Drumold. But you're *my* council."

Tylara nodded agreement from her place at the other end of the table. Between them sat Elliot, Gwen, Warner, and Art Mason. "This is not the Council of Chelm," Tylara said. "Nor any lawful group. Yet—"

She didn't finish the sentence. She didn't have to. This was a meeting of the starmen who held the power of gods. For a moment she seemed very vulnerable.

"I think you'll like Octavia," Gwen said. "That is, if you can get Ganton to spare her for a couple of hours." They all grinned at that; they'd hardly seen her since she arrived with Gwen and Warner.

First came reports. University research projects. The quest for movable type—

"—but I wouldn't print any books yet," Gwen concluded.

"Why not?" Rick asked.

"Because the *Shalnuksis* can't possibly misunderstand their significance," Gwen said. "They'd *know* they were faced with a major outbreak of technology. God knows what they'd do."

"They may know anyway," Rick said.

"Also, do you want to just throw all these changes at Tran?" Gwen asked. "You're going to lose control of the situation anyway—"

Rick saw Tylara's frown.

"—and some changes are more unsettling than others."

"I'll think about it. Meanwhile, keep working on it," Rick said. He sighed heavily. "We haven't a lot of time. Next order of business. Elliot, you were with Parsons. He tried to run things by force. I've used a different policy. What do the men think of my way, now that Parsons is dead?"

"Cap'n, I was dead wrong about you, and I've said so," Elliot said.

"I'm not after an apology, Sergeant Major. I want an assessment of the situation."

"Sir." He looked at the ceiling for a moment. "Colonel Parsons had not yet attempted to plant *surinomaz*, but it's reasonable to suppose he'd have done no better at that than he did in holding the land," Elliot said. "While he was in command, we lost Corporal Hartford to guerrilla activity. Five more troopers were severely wounded. A total of twenty-three successfully deserted.

"Since you took command, Private Reznick has been killed in action, and three others have been severely wounded, all in battles. There have been no losses to guerrillas. Ten former deserters, eleven counting Mr. Mason, have returned to duty, and nobody has run off. Troop morale is high. We have over six hundred acres in *surinomaz*, and I guess there's no revolt brewing out there even if the peasants aren't too happy about growing the stuff." He shrugged. "On the evidence, your way works."

"And the men realize that?"

"Most," Elliot said. "All that count."

Meaning there are things you aren't telling me, Rick thought. But no point to that now. "The key to 'my way' has been to cooperate with the legitimate rulers here."

"You have done more than this. You have become one of us," Tylara said.

"The point is, I've tried to regularize our positions. One key to that is Wanax Ganton. Another has been the triple alliance of Drantos, Tamaerthon, and Rome."

"I would place your friendship with Yanulf and the Priesthood of Yatar at equal importance," Tylara said. "Especially as The Time approaches. Husband, no one has more admiration for you than I. I also know that you do not recite your accomplishments to gather praise from us. What is it you wish to say?"

"I have a policy question," Rick said. "But I wanted everybody to look at it from the right direction. The question is—what do we do about Ganton?"

"What should we do?" Gwen asked. "I mean, what are the choices?"

"You've watched him with Octavia. That's the first question, do we encourage this match? Beyond that. Do we want him to be Caesar?"

"Does he want to be?" Gwen asked. "Not that it would be automatic. The position isn't really hereditary."

"True," Rick said. "Look, here's the situation. The Westmen are coming down off their plains. Lots of them. They're pretty good troops. Probably can't take castles—" he looked to Mason for confirmation.

"Not by storm," Mason said. "Not stone ones, anyway. But they can wipe up anything else. Murphy had the best ditch, logs, and earth system I've seen on this planet, and he wouldn't have been able to hold much longer—would have lost already if it hadn't been for the battle rifles."

"So what'd you do with him?" Warner asked.

"He's set up in that castle Harkon used to have," Mason said. "With a lot of peasants to guard. He'll be okay until the food runs out."

"So we can hold castles, but not the land," Warner said. "So how do we feed those people?"

"Going to be worse than that," Mason said. "Below the Littlescarp things are too wet. Up on the high plains, that hot wind that comes down from the desert is drying things out."

"Probably the source of some of our rain," Warner mused.

"Could be," Mason said. "But for sure it won't do the crops much good. I don't know what the climate's going to be like, but up in the high plains it's been the driest spring anyone can remember."

Gwen was studying the map on the far wall. "Could we abandon the high plains?"

"It is my land," Tylara said. "Mine and Rick's."

"It's nobody's land if there's nothing to eat," Rick said.

"Captain, you have to hold it anyway," Mason said. "Otherwise the

Westmen will ride right across to the Littlescarp and come down into Drantos proper. I'd rather fight them up there where they don't have so much room to spread out."

"The legends are relatively clear," Gwen said. "The Westmen swept all the way to the gates of Rome during one of the times of turmoil. Possibly the last one."

"So we'll have to stop them. Only who commands?" Rick asked. "Me?"

"You can't," Elliot said. "The *Shalnuksis* are coming, and you've got to deal with them. And somebody's got to keep the *surinomaz* crop growing—"

"There's the University situation, too," Gwen said. "It really is getting serious."

"Tylara told me," Rick said.

"Yes, the minor clans see much booty and little danger," Tylara said.

"Which makes for sticky diplomacy with Mac Clallan Muir, and you'll be personally needed," Gwen said.

"More than that, Captain," Elliot said. "If you send a sizable army up into drought country, the logistics are going to get sticky. With Apelles and his clerks to help I can probably handle most of the administration, but somebody's got to enforce our decrees. There's nobody except you to stand up to the barons."

"Can Caradoc command?" Warner asked.

"I suppose he must go," Gwen said.

"Yes, he'll be needed out there, but he can't be commander," Rick said. "He hasn't enough rank yet. We can groom him for promotion after this. But it'll be a long campaign."

"Then you certainly cannot go," Gwen said.

"Yeah," Rick said. "But more than one empire has come apart because it couldn't solve the problem of nomad light cavalry. We've got better armor and equipment, but Murphy says there'll be a *lot* of Westmen. It'll take discipline to beat them."

"For a long war that requires discipline, count not on Drantos warriors," Tylara said. "Even those of Chelm."

"That's the problem. The Westmen won't fight until they've got an advantage. We can win every ten-day and get nowhere, but any defeat can be disaster," Rick said. At Manzikert the Byzantines won the day but at dusk became scattered. They were cut up in detail. After that

Alp Arslan's Turks ravaged Asia Minor so thoroughly that when the Crusaders went through a generation later they found brambles growing in what had once been thriving cities.

"If you want disciplined troops, you need Romans," Gwen said. "You could ask Caesar for a legion or two. Oh—of course! There are only two men in Drantos who could command Romans. You and young Ganton. And if he leads Roman soldiers in a successful battle, then he really is eligible to become Caesar."

Tylara looked at Gwen in surprise, then nodded agreement. "So this is what you meant when you began. When you asked what we are to do with Wanax Ganton." She shook her head slowly. "To ask such a question is high treason—my lord, you have been with Ganton these past four ten-days. You must know better than we what we must do. As you always do."

"I don't *know*," Rick said. "But I don't see we've much choice. Can we put together a disciplined force without Romans?"

"Only if you lead it," Tylara said. The others nodded agreement.

"So we need Romans. Can anyone command except the Wanax?"

"Only Publius," Tylara said. "He might command both Romans and our bheromen." Rick winced, and Tylara nodded agreement. "Aye, he is quarrelsome and likes not 'barbarians.' And I think he will like even less this conceit of Ganton as Caesar."

"There's an understatement," Gwen said. "But you won't get Publius to come west anyway. He's got all he can do as Marselius' proconsul."

"I agree," Tylara said. "But though Romans will obey their officers, the bheromen will not follow Roman legates. And we cannot trust the defense of our western lands to Romans alone."

"What's the rest of it, Captain?" Warner asked. "You obviously thought this far already." Elliot gave Larry Warner a sour look, but still nodded agreement.

"First thing, if we've got Roman armies in the west, we want Dravan held by somebody trustworthy, which means Tylara."

There were murmurs of agreement.

They all agree. Why not? They won't be separated from their families. Well, Caradoc will. And Reznick's kids won't ever see him again. We didn't even ask them. Rick lifted a small bag onto the table. "These are Reznick's personal effects," he said. "Some of the stuff goes to his wives."

"What'll happen to them?" Warner asked.

"Dirdre wants to take the kids and go stay with Murphy," Rick said. He shrugged. "She thinks the kids will do better with their father's partner. There's nothing left for her back south, and she's not happy here."

"That's Honeypie," Warner said. "What about Marva?"

"She has no plans."

"They don't have any status here in Drantos," Gwen said. "Both would be welcome at the University, where it's not so important—"

"We'll ask Marva. Dirdre's pretty well decided," Rick said. He opened the bag. "The point is, most of his personal gear goes to Dirdre and Marva, but *we* decide who gets star weapons." He took out a .45 Colt automatic and opened the action. "Unless somebody objects, this goes to Tylara. She'll need it."

Rick hadn't expected any objections, and there weren't any. He slid it down the table. Mason caught it and handed it on to Tylara. She let it rest on the table in front of her.

"Lafe had another personal weapon," Rick said. "This Browning automatic. I think we ought to give it to Ganton." He worked the action a couple of times. "Nice piece. Elliot, do you think the troops will object?"

"I was just wondering about that, Captain," Elliot said. "No, I don't think so. It makes sense, the way you've got things set up. We can probably outdraw him anyway . . ."

"There is perhaps a better way," Tylara said. "Have the ladies Dirdre and Marva give it to Wanax Ganton in the name of Lord Murphy. If he accepts it before the Council it will settle the question of their nobility—and by inference, that of all the consorts of starmen."

"He's sure not going to refuse," Rick said. "You don't mind this wholesale elevation of commoners?"

Tylara laughed. "What was I, except the daughter of Mac Clallan Muir, until I married the Eqeta of Chelm? Of all on Tran, I am least likely to object to giving widows their rights."

"All right. That's two problems done. One more. The University. I'll send some Drantos troops up—maybe their officers can become students. But I'm also going to ask Marselius for a cohort of Romans."

Everyone looked at Tylara. She spread her hands. "I like not legions coming west, and I like this no more. Romans in Tamaerthon! But I see the need, and I believe my father and my brother will also. But there may be trouble with the other clans."

"Maybe some of them would like to volunteer for the war," Mason said. "Come west with Caradoc."

"Why would they go?" Warner asked.

"Loot." Mason reached into his pocket and came out with a length of intricately plaited golden wire. "The Westmen carry everything they own, and most have some gold."

"That is well conceived," Tylara said. "It may be that no small number of landless ones will come." She laughed. "I think they will cause no problem in Chelm!"

They'd sure as hell better not, Rick thought.

"Might even settle some of them up there," Mason said. "There's lots of good land gone to ruin. Be more by the time the Westmen get done. Not much rain this year, but it's good land even so. Parts are a lot like Tamaerthon."

"That takes care of some of the hotheads," Warner said. "But what we really need is to unify Tamaerthon under Mac Clallan Muir."

"It will not be," Tylara said. "There is too much jealousy. Lord Rick has brought a crown to the clans, but he cannot give it to my father. Nor can he take it himself."

"Not and work with Ganton," Elliot agreed.

Another problem, Rick thought. Like a ticking time bomb. Cross that one when we come to it. "We are agreed, then?" he asked. "Then I'll send for the others." One meeting done, two to go.

⊰ 25 ⊱

The field stank, and from within it came strange sounds: snarls, wild birdsongs unlike any Rick had heard elsewhere, mysterious rustlings of leaves.

"I would go no closer, Lord," Apelles said. The blue-robed priest gestured expansively. "This hill is safe, but closer the wild things might reach us. Lamils, grickirrer, even the birds. When they have been long within the madweed, they fear nothing, and even a scratch can be death."

"Necrotic products," Rick said. He took out his binoculars and examined the field of madweed. It seemed ringed with small rotting corpses; the lamils, which ate madweed pods and died in frenetic convulsions. ODd on joy, one of the mercs said. The stench was overpowering even here, fifty meters from the field.

In front of him were hundreds of acres of madweed, the largest patch anyone in living memory had ever seen. Keeping that patch growing took work; left to itself, madweed grew until choked out by a tough, thorny vine that acted much like a predator, living on the decay of madweed and lamil alike until it produced a tangle of poisonous madweed and thorny vines impenetrable to anything larger than a rabbit. One of the major tasks of Tran farmers was to root out the madweed and destroy it with fire while being careful not to breathe the smoke.

Here they were required to grow it, and they didn't like the job. That was obvious: from Rick's hill he could see a dozen mounted men-at-arms watching the field, and he knew there were more nearby.

Rick scanned the field. Peasants wearing leather leggings and aprons and thick leather gloves moved carefully with machetes. They trimmed pathways through the plants. Behind the machete wielders came women and children with hoes to chop out the vines and other weeds. Behind each group of women and children were adolescents armed with spears. Despite the thick leather armor they moved carefully and alertly.

Rick dismounted and moved toward the field. Apelles reluctantly followed.

"Must we get so close?"

"Yes." *The whole damned country is in an uproar over this stuff. I can at least see it up close.* Rick contemplated the nearest plant. Three stems formed a triangle nearly ten feet on a side, and rose over six feet high. The ground inside and around the triangle was thickly overgrown with spotted, scaly creeper. There were two dead lamils inside the triangular mass. Another animal, about the size of an Earth rabbit and very much alive, peered at them from the tangled edge of the madweed plant. Its face wore an expression of complete stupidity, almost a cartoon of idiocy. One of Rick's troops had dubbed it "dumbbunny"; it wasn't hard to see why.

"Careful," Apelles whispered. He held his staff like a spear pointed toward the animal. "Back away, slowly."

The young priest was very serious. Rick slowly drew his pistol and slipped off the safety as he followed instructions. After a moment the dumbbunny wriggled out of sight into the creeper.

"The leaves are not yet strong and the seed pods not yet developed," Apelles said. "I doubt that the grickirrer would have attacked us. But one does not know, and when they are mad from chewing the pods, they fear nothing. Of those bitten by them, one of three dies in agony."

Rabies? Rick wondered. *No Pasteur treatment here, and McCleve didn't know how to develop it.* "Pretty hard on the harvest workers," Rick said.

Apelles nodded.

"Who are they?" Rick asked.

"Some are convicts promised a full pardon after two seasons," the priest said. "Others are landless, who have been promised fields of their own. And slaves purchasing their freedom."

"It can't be much fun."

"No, Lord. And even with leather greaves and leather aprons, we will lose some. That is why we need cavalry, to prevent them from running away."

"Be certain they know they'll be rewarded," Rick said. They reached their horses, and Rick mounted. "Give them plenty to eat. Tell them their families will be cared for if they are killed. And see that our promises are kept."

"Aye, Lord," Apelles said. "We do this already."

"Yeah." Rick reined in and looked back over the fields. We reward them, but it still takes cavalry to keep them working, and I damned well don't blame them.

He rode back to the castle at a gallop.

✛ ✛ ✛

Mad Bear of the Silver Wolf clan kept the old custom this morning. He rose well before dawn, when the Child of Fire and the Death Wind Bringer were still in the sky. They gave more than enough light to let him find the highest place near the camp. He climbed to the top of the rise, and there raised his lance to the east, west, south, and finally north from whence came cooling winds and gentle rains. Then he kept watch until dawn.

He had not done this since before the Warriors' Meeting of the Silver Wolves judged that the clan should move east, into the Green Lands. If human enemies came, the four warriors who watched by night would be enough to give warning. If other enemies came, no warning or battle would save his people.

And perhaps there would be no demons. Certainly there could be none from the west, where the Death Wind already blew. Not even a demon could live in a land where no man could travel longer than his waterskins would last.

Now the families who had chosen him leader were camped farther east. They had not yet gone down through the Mouth of Rocks and into the Green Lands themselves, but the grass was no longer a brittle brown stubble underfoot. The horses could carry their riders when needed, and the babies no longer wailed all the day at their mother's dry breasts until they died. It might even be possible to take old Timusha along some days' journey farther instead of leaving her to die. She had great wisdom. Something she knew might save all of Mad Bear's people until they reached the Green Lands.

So Mad Bear walked out under the night sky and kept vigil. He hoped it would prove a wise use of the strength he would need for the fighting that awaited them in the Green Lands.

He was thirsty by the time the sun rose. He'd been much thirstier in days past, and compared to the ordeal of his initiation, this thirst was nothing. He watched as the Father Sun gave color back to the plains and drove away the Child and the Bringer and all the lesser stars. A light breeze puffed against his bare chest, bringing the scent of horses and dung fires and the sounds of the camp waking to the day. For a band which numbered no more than three hands of tents and thrice as many mounts, they made much noise. They would have to make less in the Green Lands, where they would have enemies again.

After the horses were led out to graze, Mad Bear saw Hinuta climbing up to him. He would not have admitted it to anyone save the Father Sun, but he was glad to see that Hinuta carried a waterskin.

"What news?" he asked, after drinking.

"A rider has come from the camp of the Two Waters, a half-day north of us. He bears a message from their High Chief. Will we ride with him as far as the Mouth of Rocks? If we ride well together that far, he will let us go on with him until we reach the other Silver Wolves."

"He is generous. Or has he too few warriors of his own?"

"I think it is not weakness. If he lacks men to defend his women and horses, why let those not his clansmen in among them? That is turning the wolf among the newborn colts."

"True." The people who followed Mad Bear had been chosen to be the last of the Silver Wolves to leave the clan's ancient grounds. Someone had to do this, to perform the last sacrifices to the Sky Father and the Warrior, and see that the shrines were left clean and safe from defilement. The lot fell on Mad Bear and his people, and they called themselves honored, until they finished their work and learned that the rest of their clansmen were ten days' march ahead of them. Try as they might, they hadn't closed the gap.

"It would also be admitting our weakness, to shelter under the wing of another clan," said Mad Bear.

"If they do not know of our weakness, they are more stupid than the ranwang." Hinuta drew his sword and sat down to work on the leather wrappings of the hilt. It was one of only five swords among the warriors who followed Mad Bear, won by Hinuta's father from a Green Lands warrior many years ago. Hinuta took good care of it, although he could not use it with much skill. It would have been dishonorable to question his right to his father's gift. Also, he was a good-natured, generous man, who would share his last mouthful of water or sack of grain with those in need.

Mad Bear thrust his lance point-first into the ground and prayed for the Earth to strengthen it. Then he walked slow circles around it. It was certain that they would not overtake their own clan before they reached the Green Lands. They might even have to travel for some days in the Green Lands themselves before they saw another Silver Wolf. And they were only a hand of hands of warriors.

In the Green Lands, it was said, the warriors lived in stone houses, hard to set on fire. When they rode out to battle, all of them carried swords or long lances, and wore iron shirts to cover their bodies. They were not cunning in war, so it was not hard to force them to fight against odds. Unless you could do that, however, they were very hard to kill. And each stone house might hold several hands of warriors, and there were many stone houses in the Green Land.

It was still possible that the chief of Two Waters meant treachery. But it did not seem likely, as long as the rest of the Silver Wolves were far out of his reach, ready to take vengeance. It was very certain that the Green Lands did not seem a good place for a small band to wander alone. At least they should have a strong friend close at their backs.

"We will ride with the Two Waters," Mad Bear said finally. "Or at least we will, as long as no warrior of ours has an unjudged blood-feud with any warrior of theirs."

"The Two Waters people have long memories," said Hinuta. "You should ask old Timusha. She will know."

That seemed good advice, but when they got back to camp they found the women keening around the tent where Timusha lay dead; she had never awakened. Mad Bear felt uneasy. To have her die as he was coming to ask her advice and wisdom seemed an evil omen.

He would keep watch all tonight, with the point of his lance propped under his chin to prick his flesh if he so much as nodded. Perhaps Timusha's death was a punishment for his not watching according to custom. He would also give her a horse sacrifice beside her grave, although she was a woman and not a warrior. He had been ready to listen to her as though she were a warrior, so perhaps it could be said that made her one.

✣ ✣ ✣

The head of the column had vanished over the hills to the west before the rear guard left Castle Armagh. Within an hour the road was obscured by dust, and from the castle tower Rick and Gwen saw only occasional glints of sunlight on a helmet or pike—or caliver barrel. As the last troops left the castle, the semaphore towers linking Armagh with Dravan came alive, warning the garrisons ahead to be ready for the main army.

For a while they had been able to see the flash of red at the column's fore: Caradoc's Roman cloak, a gift from Publius Caesar. With it had come other gifts for Caradoc: a new back-and-breastplate from Drumold, and Tylara's gift, a magnificent black gelding fit for a knight or greater. Mounted on his new charger and dressed in his finest, he looked every bit the warrior commander, and his troops liked that. Rick anticipated no problems promoting him after this campaign, and he looked forward to it. He could use another trustworthy general.

Rick watched the Mounted Archers until they rounded the flank of a hill and vanished. Below in the castle courtyard, sergeants' voices rasped. "Line up and keep your eyes front, you lamils! Now it's back to work!"

The newly raised Second Company of the Guards was about to march out for archery practice. So far they seemed to be shaping up fairly well. Certainly the cadre sent from Mason's First Company was working hard enough! They had incentive, of course—the better they did, the more secure their promotions. When rank meant not only honor but a better chance for yourself and your family to live through The Time, you worked hard to hold on to it.

It had been hard to persuade some of the veterans that there was honor in staying behind to train new troopers. They all wanted to go out with the column. Rick shook his head and turned back to watching the road.

After Caradoc and his personal guard came more troops, mostly Romans under their legate Titus Frugi. Tylara had been surprised at Caesar's choice of commanders, but Rick thought it made excellent sense. Frugi was a good general; and he couldn't possibly be tempted to revolt when at the head of a single legion stationed deep within the territory of Marselius' most powerful friends.

Finally, nearly a mile behind the column's point riders, rode Wanax Ganton with Camithon, Tylara and her children, and Lady Octavia. Perhaps because the ladies were traveling with him, it had not been difficult to persuade Ganton to take a safe place in the middle of the column rather than be at its front. "Roman generals do not risk their troops by acts of foolish bravado," Rick had said, and perhaps that had also stung the young king.

"He'll do," Rick said aloud.

Gwen had put down the binoculars now that Caradoc was out of sight. She looked very attractive in her skirt cut off just below the tops of her boots. It would have been thought scandalously short, except that she'd started a new fashion; now half the young women of Drantos had whacked off their skirts. "Who'll do?" she asked.

"Ganton."

"I think you're right," Gwen said. "He seems sensible enough." She giggled. "Handsome, too, but I feel sorry for his lady friend just now. I hope he doesn't get over-amorous for a few weeks—not until he's willing to take that pistol off! I'm sure he'd wear it to bed."

"I can't imagine that Octavia is sleeping with him," Rick said.

"Not yet," Gwen agreed. "But don't make book for the summer. She likes him. Sure, he's a good catch, and the throne of Drantos is probably safer than anything Caesar's relatives can expect just now. But Rick, she really likes him."

"Interesting. He's pretty thoroughly smitten too. Can it be we jaded old dynastic manipulators have made a love match?"

"I hope so," Gwen said seriously. She sighed. "Or do we believe in love matches anymore?"

"What's that supposed to mean?"

"Nothing. You've got Tylara—would you stay with her if she were a peasant's daughter?"

"Gwen, I hated seeing her ride off today!" And my children—

"That's not what I asked. You know damned well you wouldn't have married her if she hadn't been important," Gwen said. "Love and marriage. Or marriage and then love. Or just marriage. Any of them seems to work, doesn't it?"

The middle of the column vanished over the crown of a far hill.

Just as they disappeared, Rick thought he made out long dark hair tossing in the wind, and a wave of her hand. He closed up the binoculars. "I thought you were in love with Caradoc."

"What's love?" she asked. "I respect him. I care for him, and he protects me. Sometimes from myself."

The shadows were getting long. Rick led the way down from the tower. It stood above his apartments. An oil lamp had been lighted at his table, and a large pitcher of wine stood next to it. "Dinner in an hour or so," Rick said. "Glass of wine first?"

"Sure."

He poured and handed her a goblet. "I really thought you were in love with Caradoc."

"Oh, let it alone, Rick. I am, I guess. But—well it's not really the same. I wouldn't—I wouldn't get on a flying saucer for Caradoc. But he isn't going to ask me, either. And what about you? Don't you sometimes get enough of your raven-haired contessa's dynastic ambitions?"

"Come on, she's wonderful! Who else could I trust to hold the strongest castle on Tran?"

"So do you keep her for love or advantage? You needn't answer. Just as I don't have to answer you." She sipped the wine. "This is quite good."

"Yeah, it turns out Sergeant Lewin used to live in the California wine country. He's been giving them tips."

She sipped again. "Rick, when will they come?"

"Who?"

"The *Shalnuksis*."

"I've got skywatchers looking for satellites from Tamaerthon to Dravan—you've got as good an idea as I have, Gwen."

"Mostly I'm reminding you of something. Distilling. Hammer mills. Printing presses. If they see real changes on Tran, they'll do a *lot* to wipe them out."

Rick sat heavily. "Yeah, I know. But we have to do *something* for these people! Gwen, I was out there in the *surinomaz* fields last week. Week. Hah. We don't even have weeks. But I was out there, listening politely while Apelles told me about the cavalry patrols that herd the peasants back to work—have you seen *surinomaz*? I'd imagine working in that stuff is as close to hell as you can get. And I'm making people do it!"

"Rick, you've no choice—"

"Like hell I don't. I could run. Vanish somewhere."

"That wouldn't be very smart," Gwen said. "In the first place, you wouldn't like it much, hiding out. But suppose you did. Are you mad enough to suppose that one of your men wouldn't try growing *surinomaz*? Or that any of them would be gentler than you? Do you really think anyone *cares* what happens to peasants?"

"You do."

"Maybe a little," she said.

"I think that's the worst of it," Rick said. "Nobody really gives a damn. Even Tylara thinks I'm crazy, worrying about people who aren't clansmen—"

"It's going to get worse, too," Gwen said. "And you're avoiding the subject, which is how far can you go in making changes before the *Shalnuksis* bomb you out."

"Yeah, but look, if we disperse knowledge far enough, the *Shalnuksis* won't dare try to destroy everything. They'd have to drop enough bombs to make the planet uninhabitable, and that would ruin their little drug racket. They can't risk that . . ."

"Can't they?" She shrugged. "Rick, I don't know. Les may have known, but he didn't tell me that much. I do know the *Shalnuksis* are afraid of wild humans. Another thing, suppose what we do—"

Her look of fear was contagious. Rick automatically lowered his voice. "Suppose what?"

"That what we do gets back to the Confederacy. That they find out Tran exists. Then it wouldn't be *Shalnuksi* businessmen we'd have to deal with. It might be somebody who thinks this whole planet is a cancer!"

"Christ almighty! But how would they know?"

She laughed. "A hundred ways. The *Shalnuksis* tell them. They send a human pilot and *he* tells them. Inspector Agzaral decides to make a new deal. Rick, I don't *know*, I can only make guesses from what Les told me."

"Yeah. But—Gwen, I don't know either, but I do know I've got to do *something*!"

"To assuage your conscience," she said. "You're forcing the peasants to work the fields, so you need a higher cause to justify it."

"I—yeah, I guess that is it," Rick said.

"So why are you ashamed of being ethical?" Gwen asked. "For that matter, you *have* a higher cause. The University, for example. Rick, did you ever read a book called *Connections*?"

"I saw several of the TV episodes."

"Well, I wish we had that book," Gwen said. "But I can remember some of it. How glass-making led to a shortage of wood, and that made coal valuable, and coal mining needed pumps, and that resulted in the steam engine. And acetylene, and illuminating gas, and coal tar—Rick, we've already changed life on Tran, it's just that you can't see the changes from orbit. Unless you've studied Earth history, you wouldn't see them no matter how closely you looked. There are a hundred students who *think* now. Maybe not well, but they ask questions, they wonder *why* things happen, and they know the difference between chemistry and alchemy. We'll send them all over the planet."

"That's your work."

"No, it's yours," Gwen said. "I know who keeps the University going. If it survives—"

"Your University has to survive," Rick said.

"Ours. And I want it to, but we can't be sure."

"How will they know?"

"They're not above capturing and interrogating you," Gwen said. "Not at all."

"I know. But I'm not going near them without mini-grenades. Their detectors don't seem to find them—didn't on the Moon, anyway. Pull the pin on one of those and they'll have to scrape the walls."

She looked at him thoughtfully. "You'd do it, too. Will the others?"

"Elliot will, I think."

"What if they take a local?"

"They might do that. But most of the *Shalnuksis* are *lazy*, Gwen. You didn't know the local languages when you landed. How much time will they put in learning? And most locals don't know about the University, and the ones that do don't know where it is—how many can even read a map?"

"I hope you're right," she said. She got up and paced around the room. "You—don't even mind," she said. "You *like* for me to know things you don't."

"Sure—"

"It's not sure at all," Gwen said. "All my life men said they wanted me to be smart, but when I showed I could do something better than they could, they left me." She stood at the window and watched the darkening sky. "You're not like that. Why?"

"Too much to do, I guess." He got up and joined her at the window, knowing what would happen next, not wanting it to happen but unable to stop himself.

She turned toward him. "It wasn't fair, you know."

"What wasn't?" he asked.

"Meeting Tylara just after we were put on this planet. Les— expected us to say together. I think we would have, if we'd had a chance. If we hadn't met her so soon."

"And?" He put his hand on her shoulders.

"I have to go back to the University tomorrow."

She moved closer to him, and after that they didn't talk at all.

✢ ✢ ✢

He woke startled and sat bolt upright. Gwen was on the other side of the room, fully dressed. "Hello," she said.

"Where are you going?"

"To dinner, of course." She came over to sit on the edge of the bed. "We're both crazy, you know that? Caradoc would kill you. He'd *have* to try. And Tylara would have me boiled over a slow fire."

Rick shuddered. "Sorry. That image is just a bit too graphic. She might do it."

"Adds a little spice, doesn't it? Stolen fruit's the sweetest and all that."

"Gwen—"

"No," she said. "I do *not* want to talk about it. Rick, we're not in love, but we'll always be a bit special to each other, and in this crazy place maybe that's all we can ask for. And now I'm going down to supper, and after a decent interval you'll come join me, and we'll just plain forget this happened."

"Do you want to forget?"

"No," she said. "No, my very dear."

"Would you get aboard a flying saucer for me?"

"I don't have to say." She jumped away from him before he could catch her. "See you at supper."

PART SIX
WANAX AND WARLORD

26

Tylara do Tamaerthon, Eqetassa of Chelm and Justiciar of Drantos, looked about the great hall of Castle Dravan with feelings of satisfaction. This was home as it should be, lacking only her husband. Her guards stood like statues along the far wall. The floors were newly scrubbed, the tapestries newly cleaned. Her well-trained servants were carrying away the remains of an excellent meal and had brought in flagons of the new wine. There was nothing to apologize for.

Not that Wanax Ganton noticed. He had eyes only for the Lady Octavia, and might have eaten straw from filthy plates for all he knew. Soon enough he would leave the table, to find some excuse to be alone with the Roman girl. Tylara smiled faintly. Octavia knew what she was doing. Or she'd better. She seemed genuinely to care for the young Wanax.

And he for her. Tylara fingered the Colt at her waist. *I believe he would give his binoculars for her, though possibly not the Browning pistol,* she thought. *Rick wished me to encourage this match, but in truth I have little enough to do.*

Caradoc, with the young Roman officer Geminius, sat across from Wanax Ganton. The archer seemed nervous. Was it because he was at table with his superiors? Tylara didn't think so. There was too much of Tamaerthon in Caradoc son of Cadaric; he wouldn't be awed by royalty—especially royalty not officially present. Someone had told Ganton of a strange custom, *incognito* Rick had called it, whereby a Wanax might travel as an eqeta, or even a bheroman, and be treated as such, even though everyone knew he was *really* the Wanax. It seemed strange, but Ganton had insisted, and it seemed to work. Tylara doubted that Caradoc was much agitated by the Count of the North.

And Caradoc certainly isn't afraid of *me*, she thought. We grew up together. If my first husband hadn't been shipwrecked in the Garioch, our friendship might have become something more than that. How little I knew, how few my ambitions as daughter of Mac Clallan Muir! I might easily have wed the son of my father's henchman . . .

A sudden thought struck her. Caradoc was one of two living men who had seen her naked. No, five if she counted the priests of Yatar who delivered her children, but why should she? They'd not looked upon her as men do at women. Nor had Caradoc, when he'd rescued her from Sarakos' bedchamber. Involuntarily she shuddered at the memory of Sarakos and his crone torturer.

My first time to lie with a man. She shuddered again. And to this day I must drink wine before I bed my husband, and that is shameful, for I love him as few women can ever have loved a man. Yet he knows, and he feels the loss. What can I do? Yatar has given us so much, we cannot complain that he holds back the final drops from the cup.

But if Caradoc had not come when he did! Involuntarily she nodded in satisfaction as she remembered the dead guards outside her room. Caradoc had killed four soldiers and taken her away through secret passages, out of this very castle.

"*Coronel* Caradoc," she called, using the new title of rank that Rick had conferred on him. "You have won a great victory. Tell us of it. As hostess I command it." And that's why he was nervous! He doesn't like to talk about himself, and of course he has to. "Footman! Fill *Coronel* Caradoc's cup, that he will not thirst as he tells us of his victory."

✛ ✛ ✛

He tells the story well, Tylara thought. But he tells more than he thinks.

The situation didn't sound good at all. The Westmen rode where they wanted to go, and their horses were so much faster than Drantos horses that they could seldom be brought to battle against their will— and they would not fight willingly unless they held an advantage.

"And so the Lord Mason conceived a plan," Caradoc said. "I regret that he is not here to tell of it."

Mason and Camithon stayed at the new army camp on the high

plains, while Caradoc and Geminius and a number of Roman supply officers came down to Dravan for supplies. There'd been no need for Wanax Ganton to come with Caradoc, but Octavia's presence had been an irresistible attraction.

"A wagon train," Caradoc said. "With a cavalry escort, to travel north and west, riding quickly as if hoping to avoid the Westmen. And certainly it was a clever ruse, for within two days the Westmen saw us and began to stalk us."

And that must have been unnerving, Tylara thought. To be followed by enemies you could not strike . . .

"At first they sought to draw the escort away from the wagons, to induce us to fight at a time and place of their choosing. Fortunately they did not succeed."

Not fortune, Tylara thought. Not fortune, but good planning. Most of the cavalrymen were either Romans or guardsmen; there would be few of the armed nobility of Drantos in *that* group, not if Mason had planned it. Yes, and Ganton knows that. Does he understand why?

"Arekor, the priest of Vothan who lived so long among them, said they do not like to fight at night. It is a matter of their gods and demons. Yet we did not know how much of this to believe, and we made camp more in the Roman manner than our own. But perhaps Arekor spoke truth, for although we heard their cries and saw their camp fires, we saw none of them at night."

He took another sip of wine. "Of course we had no real hopes they would attack a strong camp, and they did not. They waited until we had loaded the wagons and were well away from the camp, then struck at us to cut us off from it." He paused to let a steward refill his cup.

"Hundreds of them," Geminius said. He was a young man, and his speech was careful and precise in the Roman manner. A young lordling, higher in rank than his years deserved, Tylara thought. Yet the other soldiers thought him competent enough. "I confess I was near unnerved," Geminius continued. "By Lucifer's hooves! They came swiftly toward us, a veritable flood, and there stood Caradoc, the only calm man in the column! On they came, and still Caradoc did nothing! I had thought we waited too long."

"The Lord Mason had said 'Wait until you see the whites of their eyes,' and in truth we came near that," Caradoc said. "Then we threw off the covers from the wagons, and the archers and musketmen hidden inside them fired as if they were one man. The Lord Mason had said that first firing would have the greatest effect—"

"By the Lord he was right," Geminius said. "The slaughter among the horses was great. As great as when the Lord Mason used his star weapons at Pirion."

"You were at Pirion?" Wanax Ganton demanded. "With Publius?"

Octavia laughed, then busied herself with a napkin.

"Nay, Lord, with Legate Valerius and the Eighth Legion," Geminius said.

"Hah!" Ganton banged his flagon against the table. "I led the chivalry of Drantos that day!"

"Lord, I remember it. Was not your helm golden? Attended by a black-clad guardsman carrying a banner of the Fighting Man?"

"Aye!"

"And you rode next to a gold-bedecked barbarian riding a great black stallion and swinging the largest sword of my memory," the Roman said. "He was attended by the Great Banner of Tamaerthon."

"Aye," Ganton said. "I carried the banner of my house, not that of Drantos, for the Lord Rick was supreme that day. Ho, you do recall!"

Unlikely, Tylara thought. But the story has been told often enough, and what detail would he not have heard by now? My father is easily enough described—

Ganton's face fell. "My only battle," he said. "And I interrupt Caradoc telling of his victory. Forgive me, *Coronel.*"

Caradoc looked embarrassed.

They have had too much to drink, Tylara thought. I should end this night before one says too much.

"Come, finish your tale," Ganton said.

"There is little more to tell," Caradoc said. "As instructed, we fired at the horses. Westmen on foot are no match for Tamaerthan archers."

"Nor for Drantos warriors," Geminius added.

"Aye," Caradoc said. "And then we brought forward the wagon with the Great Gun. Pinir the son of the smith fired it with his own hand, and lo! it did not burst. It made great slaughter among the horses of the Westmen, for it was loaded with all manner of small stones, aye and lengths of chain."

What Caradoc called the Great Gun was what Rick called a "four-pounder." Tylara had three in the arsenal of Castle Dravan. More importantly, she had five larger guns capable of destroying siege towers. Dravan well defended had never been taken; held by a handful, it had stood against Sarakos until he brought up great siege engines. With the new guns even those would fail . . .

"And thus we defeated them," Caradoc said. "I fear it does not make a great tale."

"But a great victory," Ganton said. "Would I had been there."

"You will see more of battles than ever you want," Octavia said quietly. "And soon enough, I think."

"Lord, a great victory indeed," Geminius said. "And by Our Lord's death, more of a tale than Caradoc would have you know! The sound of the guns frightened our horses, and when the Great Gun was fired, many were in panic. Our victory was nearly defeat, for the Westmen began to circle and dart toward us, and there was naught to hold them save the Tamaerthan archers, for the *guns* are not quickly readied for another volley, and our own cavalry was useless! Aye, even Romans! My own units, I confess, veterans all, were in disarray.

"Then suddenly, through the noise of battle, all could hear Caradoc. He vaulted into the saddle and rode round, rallying Roman and Drantos horse alike. 'Follow me!' he shouted in a voice like thunder, and he led us through and behind the Westmen, thus holding them in play until the archers and pikemen and musketeers could finish their death work. In truth it is Caradoc's victory we celebrate here."

"Hah," Ganton said. "And what have you to say of this, *Coronel*?"

"Lord—"

"Come now, my lords," Tylara said. "In Tamaerthon it is the custom to boast of one's deeds. It is not so in Drantos. Which customs would you have him honor, my Lord of the North?"

Ganton took another deep drink of wine. "I will find bards to tell of his action, then," he said. "He should be rewarded. Are there no bards to sing of this?"

Octavia moved closer to Ganton. Tylara couldn't hear what she said. Suddenly Ganton shouted. "Aye! My lady, my lords, it has been greatly convenient to be here as a bheroman. I see, though, there are times when it is well to be Wanax." He stood. "Morrone! Morrone, where are you? Ho, Guards! The Wanax of Drantos requires his Companion! Find Lord Morrone!"

"Here, sire!" Morrone rushed into the hall. "Forgive me, I was napping in the corner—"

"Cease prattling and fetch me my sword!" Ganton shouted. "Quickly, quickly!"

"Aye, sire." Morrone ran to the far end of the hall and returned with a broadsword.

Ganton took it. "*Coronel* Caradoc, come forth! Kneel!"

"Aye, sire—"

"My lady, have I your consent?" Ganton shouted to Tylara.

"Aye, sire!"

"Then I, Ganton, Son of Loron, Wanax of Drantos, declare and proclaim Caradoc son of Cadaric worthy of the honors of chivalry." He struck Caradoc on each shoulder with the flat of the sword. "Arise, my lord. You shall have suitable income as befits your new station; and henceforth you shall be known as Lord Caradoc do Tamaerthon."

✢ ✢ ✢

The pen wrote well. A *space pen*, Rick had called it when he gave it to her, but he had not explained what that meant. But it was certainly easier to use than a gull quill.

> And so it was done. And I think well done, my husband. Caradoc has ever been a friend to this house, and I cannot believe that if Ganton gave him every honor within his gift he would change his loyalty. More, his interest runs with ours, as he is married to Gwen.

And a good thing, Tylara thought. Gwen must always be a temptation to Rick. She speaks his languages, and with her he can say what he will. Tylara looked to the mirror on the table. I think I am prettier than she. But—She looked to the bed and set her lips in a grim line. It is likely she is more skilled in the ways women attract men. Especially starmen. Yet men hold honor high. Surely Rick will not betray his friend and companion, his trusted henchman?

He has known other women since we were married. It must be. But he has been careful. There have been no stories, nothing whispered through the halls. Two women have claimed to carry Rick's bastards, but they have been proved to be liars. One could not have been in the same city with Rick when her child was conceived! And the other did not know of the strange surgery that prevails in his homeland.

She thought of Rick with another woman, and writhed. No matter how hard she tried, when she imagined Rick straining and groaning with another, the face beneath him was Gwen's. Enough! She lifted the pen again.

> But though Caradoc has won a victory, I think the war goes not well. The Westmen ride where they will, and we hold only castles and walled towns. There will be no crops throughout much of the high plains. The Roman scribes will tell you what now is required to feed the army and its horses. I cannot think those numbers will please you, nor will they please the peers of Drantos. The taxes of this war, added to what you require to keep your fields of madweed, would have ruined us if we had not the new plows. They may ruin us yet, though the first harvest in the Cumac has yielded more than we previously took in two. And the new forges and foundries produce wagons to carry the grain, so that we are able to send it to the high plains for the army. Yet I fear there will come a time when we have not wagons, horses, and grain in the same place at the same time.
>
> The Westmen are the death of the earth. Arekor, the priest of Vothan who lived among them, has told Caradoc—*Lord* Caradoc!—that they do this from policy. They burn and destroy, and pull down not only buildings and walls, but the very terraces, and stop up wells; for they live on so little that they can live in devastated lands when none of their enemies can. Thus do they keep the lands above the Westscarp in desert, and thus will they make desert of our lands above the Littlescarp if we cannot expel them or kill them.

She set the pen down and got up from the table. The next part would be very hard to write. A flagon of wine stood on a side table near her bed, and she filled a goblet.

I seldom drink wine, she thought. She looked at the empty bed. Except at night, before I go to my husband. Even now, even now, though he is gentle and kind and loves me. And though I love him

with all my heart, I know I pleasure him little that way, though he says
this is not so.

> My husband, as you desired, we held a Council of Chelm
> to consider defenses against the Westmen. Hilon the
> blacksmith of Clavton, who sits in my council—

She frowned and crossed through the last two words.

> —in our Council of Chelm, proposed that instead of
> supporting the army in the high plains, his town will buy the
> knowledge of how to make Guns, and pay to have the burghers
> taught in their use, and will buy firepowder.
>
> He spoke thus: "If we put Guns on the town wall, let the
> Westmen come to us. We will break their teeth. Much of that
> and they will cease to chew on us." You may imagine this was
> not greeted with joy by bheroman Traskon son of Trakon in
> whose lands Clavton lies.
>
> For it cannot be long before the towns find ways to buy
> these Guns, and then they will be as safe as Dravan, and how
> will their lords rule then? And now I think, nor town, nor
> Dravan is safe! For I had believed that with the Guns, Dravan
> would be safe from Siege towers, yet how are we safe from
> Guns which can batter down our very walls?
>
> My husband, great and momentous changes are upon us,
> and I no longer know what I must do to protect our children.
> I have often thought you know not enough of Drantos and
> Tamaerthon and this world of Tran to rule it. Yet if you do not,
> no one does, for only you know what has been unleashed upon
> us and what I will live to see.

She tapped the table with impatience, searching for the words to
tell him of her fear without sounding afraid. Finally she wrote again.

> For now you are my life as never before. Always I have
> loved you. Now I must needs obey you, for I know not what
> else I can do to preserve what is ours. And though I have not
> always understood, yet I have tried to make your work my

work, and your cause my cause; and now that must be so no matter how little I understand.

My fear is that I shall be asked to do that which I cannot do. But I am comforted, for you will never ask of me more than I can bear.

My lord, my life, my love, I am,

Tylara.

27

Rick cursed as he drank the bitter caffeine drink that for want of a better word he called tea.

His orderly watched the footman carry out the soiled breakfast dishes, then turned back as Rick cursed again. "My lord?" Jamiy asked.

"Nothing," Rick growled. "Leave me."

"Aye, Lord." The orderly hesitated. "You are to see Chancellor Yanulf this morning."

"And then Sergeant Major Elliot, and after that I have letters to dictate," Rick said. "Yeah, I know. Give me this much time." He held his fingers half an inch apart, indicating about ten minutes: the time it would take for a standard beeswax candle to burn down that far. Time measurement was not very accurate on Tran . . .

What the hell does Yanulf want, coming here from Edron without notice? I'll find out soon enough. Another goddamn day of work and another night alone. Why didn't I figure a reason for Gwen to stay—

Because, you damned fool, your wife would kill you. More likely kill Gwen, and it isn't just a figure of speech. Besides, it isn't Gwen you want, it's Tylara. Remember?

Yeah, and it really is. Only—

Only nothing, buster. Forget it! What's next? Your wife doesn't understand you? Tell that one often enough, and it'll be true. Or maybe that's what you want? You could do it. You have the guns. Leave Tylara, go to the University and shack up with Gwen. You could change the whole history of the planet that way. Of course, all this stuff you've

472

worked for goes down the tubes, but what the hell, a good lay is worth a lot, right?

Sure, with Isobel and Makail growing up to hate me. There'd also be the Caradoc problem.

"Hell," he said aloud. "It's not even tempting." He drained the cup of lukewarm bitter tea.

✣ ✣ ✣

Yanulf was attended by Apelles and two acolytes. The acolytes were dismissed at Rick's study door, but Apelles came in with the Chancellor. Yanulf looked older, as if he'd aged a year in the past few months, but his voice was as hearty as ever. He greeted Rick warmly, and Rick stood to clasp the priest's forearm before they sat at the conference table.

"And what brings you from the capital?" Rick asked.

"Not good news, I fear," Yanulf said.

"I didn't think it would be."

"This could be a matter for the Eqeta's Court," Yanulf said. "It would have been, had not Apelles sent the matter to me."

Rick frowned. "I'm not sure I understand."

"Technically, he has interfered with your justice," Yanulf said. "Yet I see not what else he could have done."

Rick warily eyed the two priests. "Why not tell me?" he demanded.

Apelles looked to Yanulf, then back at Rick. "It is a matter that I cannot resolve, Lord." He looked down at the table, then across at the maps, finally back to Rick. "A petition of right, on behalf of Nictoros, Priest of Yatar, was brought to me three ten-days ago. As is my duty, I sent forth writs inquiring into the matter, intending to lay it before you in open court." He paused again.

"And instead you wrote the Chancellor."

"No, Lord."

"You just said you wrote to Yanulf!"

"Aye, Lord, but I did not write to the chancellor. I referred the matter to Yanulf, Archpriest of Yatar, for it is a matter which touches the very honor of our god!"

Oh, Lord, Rick thought. What are we in for? The classic confrontation between church and state? Becket and Henry II, played out here? "Suppose you tell me about it."

Again Apelles looked to Yanulf, who nodded slightly. "Nictoros was born villein," Apelles said. "Within the lands of Bheroman Enipses. During the rebellion against Wanax Loron, Nictoros fled the land and took refuge with Galdaf, Priest of Yatar."

"Many fled in those times," Rick said. "And I think I see the problem. Enipses is a loyalist. Supported Ganton during the civil wars, supports Tylara and me now. The baron wants his villein back, and the church won't turn loose their priest. That's an easy one—"

"He was found to have both intelligence and a desire to serve Yatar," Apelles said, "and was made an acolyte, and in due time consecrated as Priest of Yatar. He later found favor with Bheroman Enipses, who appointed him to be priest in his own household."

Maybe it's not so simple, Rick thought.

"The war continued. Wanax Sarakos, aided by the starmen serving Colonel Parsons, invaded the land and drove Bheroman Enipses from his castle. Nictoros remained, as was his duty, and tended the caves beneath the castle. He fled only when the usurper placed there by Sarakos dismissed him."

"He fled to Dravan," Yanulf said. "And assisted me there. And learned from me. He learned much about The Time, and what must be done, and showed quick wit and understanding."

And you liked him, Rick thought. "I see." He tried to keep his voice noncommittal.

Apelles continued the story. "Then you, Lord, defeated Sarakos and brought the starmen to your obedience. When Bheroman Enipses returned, he dismissed Nictoros as priest of his household, saying that Nictoros should have accompanied him into exile rather than remaining within the castle. Nictoros departed, but you, Lord, were pleased to appoint him priest in the Eqeta's free town of Yirik, where there are also extensive caves and a large temple of Yatar."

Rick looked to Yanulf. "I don't recall the appointment. On your advice?"

"Yes. The order was signed by the Eqetessa. I did not agree with Bheroman Enipses, but certainly there was no need for dispute. Yirik was without a priest, and I had high regard for Nictoros' abilities." Yanulf fingered the medallion hanging from his golden chain. "It was a mistake," he said finally. "I should have sent Nictoros to a village beyond Enipses' domains. Perhaps even outside Chelm. But I did not. Continue, Apelles."

"Then, Lord, came your decree, requiring each bheroman to send laborers for the madweed. And other decrees, requiring grain to feed the madweed workers. These taxes fell heavily on Enipses, for he had lost many of his villeins during the wars, and thus last autumn much of his grain rotted unharvested before the rains destroyed it.

"Then came the Westmen, and still more taxes; but meantime The Time approaches, and Nictoros attempted to prepare as commanded by Yanulf."

Uh-oh. I see it now, Rick thought. And—

"Bheroman Enipses accused Nictoros of interfering with the collection of taxes; of taking grain belonging to the Wanax, which is a treason. But instead of applying to you for a writ to allow his constables inside Yirik, he waited with patience. This was rewarded, for Nictoros foolishly travelled beyond the town walls, and Enipses had men waiting, who brought Nictoros before the bheroman's court. He was found guilty; and sentence of death was passed. But, because the grain taken was placed in the caves of Yatar, and because Nictoros was a priest, the sentence was remitted to enslavement." Apelles shrugged. "He was sent here to labor in the fields of madweed. You may imagine my amazement when as I inspected the fields I was greeted in ways known only to the priesthood, and I was given a properly drafted petition of right."

That would be a surprise. The petition of right was a monopoly of the Yatar priesthood. It implored a ruler—bheroman, eqeta, even Wanax—to obey his own laws. It didn't have to be granted, but once it was, the matter was for the courts.

"I still don't understand. If you present me that petition, I'll certainly grant it. Let right be done. Then it's a matter for judges. Bheroman Enipses may not like it, but—" He stopped, because Yanulf was shaking his head. "What now?"

"If your judges examine the matter, they will find for Bheroman Enipses," Yanulf said. "Nictoros does not deny taking grain gathered for taxes and placing it in the caves. Nor would he return it when Enipses demanded it. Nor did the bheroman enter the caves, nay nor threaten to, but with great respect pronounced that what was done was done, and new grain must be gathered for the Wanax."

"But he arrested the priest," Rick said. "I see. But—if he's guilty, whatever possessed him to send in a petition of right?"

"Perhaps he believes he was right," Yanulf said. "Perhaps I believe he was right. But it is not law."

"Tear up the petition," Rick said. "I'll issue a pardon. Or you can draft one for the Wanax to sign."

"Would it were so simple," Yanulf said. "But it is not. The priests of Vothan know of this. They are asking Bheroman Enipses to dismiss all the priests of Yatar within his lands."

"In whose favor?" Rick asked.

"Perhaps they will not be replaced at all," Yanulf said. "Or perhaps by those who mouth the words of service to Yatar, but own allegiance to Bacreugh."

"Who the devil is Bacreugh?"

"Bacreugh is a priest of Yatar, from an order formerly known mainly in Tamaerthon. He is allied with Mac Bratach Bhreu. A kinsman, in fact."

"I see. Drumold's only real rival. But why is he followed in Drantos?"

"He preaches words comfortable to the nobility," Apelles said. "And he has made strong alliance with the priesthood of Vothan."

"More," Yanulf said. "You have been told of the vision of the Roman Bishop Polycarp?"

"Yes. Yatar and Jehovah are one. I wonder how the Jews will feel about that . . ."

"What are Jews?" Yanulf asked.

"Followers of Jehovah, but who believe the Christ has not yet come. They have strong dietary laws, and passionately believe there is only one God."

"There are no such in Drantos," Yanulf said.

"And now that I think of it, it's not likely there are any on Tran." Until now. How many of the mercs are Jewish? Bilofsky, I suppose. Lewin. Goodman. Schultz, only he's still down south. None of them seemed particularly devout, but you never know.

"The priesthood of Vothan laughs at Polycarp," Yanulf said. "And they do not favor the Roman alliance. Now through the followers of Bacreugh they seek control of the caves of Yatar. Bheroman Enipses may well yield those under his castle."

"Bacreugh and his order should be suppressed. And the priests of Vothan made humble," Apelles said.

Oh, no, you don't. You won't get me involved in religious persecutions. "I do not agree. But were it desirable, it would not be possible. Vothan has powerful friends." Including some of my mercs. They may not be believers, but they're superstitious enough. And a lot of the army is devoted to Vothan, or at least scared of him.

"You see now why this should not be seen in open court," Yanulf said. "And why young Apelles referred the matter to me."

"Sure. You're trying to undermine civil authority," Rick said.

"Nay, Lord!" Apelles said. "We are loyal."

I'm sure you think so. But if nothing else, you're inventing benefit of clergy, which apparently they don't have here. Still, the priesthood of Yatar, as organized by Yanulf, is the nearest thing to a literate civil service I have. They also have a monopoly on paper. I can't do without them.

"First," Rick said, "I hadn't known how serious Enipses' labor problem is. We'll have to do something about that."

"At harvest time there will be labor shortages everywhere," Yanulf said. "It has always been so."

Rick scribbled a note: Get Campbell working on a reaper.

"There is a machine," Rick said. "A way to harvest grain—grain! Where is the place for Hestia in this vision of Polycarp's?"

"As the mother of Christ," Yanulf said. "For as you know, the Christ was born of a virgin. Polycarp preaches a doctrine which he calls 'Immaculate Conception', under which Hestia took on the flesh of a mortal in order to bear a son to Yatar."

"And you believe this?"

Yanulf frowned. "I know not what to believe. One thing is certain, the prophecies of The Time are true. And they were revealed by Yatar himself. The Romans know much of The Time, and thus must once have known Yatar." He shrugged. "Perhaps Polycarp is correct, their Jehovah is Yatar. The names are not unalike."

"Fortunately we need not decide the matter today," Rick said. "For the problem at hand, I will remit some of Enipses' taxes. You will send a persuasive emissary to bear that pleasant news. Someone who will persuade Enipses that it would not be wise to make great changes in the governing of Yatar's caves. Someone to point out that neither Wanax Ganton nor I nor Eqetassa Tylara would favor Bacreugh's cause."

"That may be sufficient," Yanulf said.

"As to Nictoros, I will issue a pardon."

"Who will make up what you remit to Enipses, Lord?" Apelles asked.

"We'll have to work that out," Rick said. "Maybe you could see to it?"

"We will do that," Yanulf said.

Sure you will, Rick thought. And that'll fall on some poor schmuck who's irritated his local priest. But what the hell can I do?

I can get Campbell working on that reaper.

When dusk came, Jamiy brought in lamps. Rick sighed. They still hadn't managed good lamps. These burned a mixture of oil and naphtha, and gave better light than the older tapers, but the light was still too dim, and gave him a headache. One day, he thought, I'll need spectacles, and I won't have them. And then what? But this has got to be done.

Ganton had summoned the chivalry of Drantos to the high plains. Rick was horrified. He could see no use for that many undisciplined heavy cavalrymen. Useful or not, though, they had to be fed. Wagons, horses, grain, all had to be found and sent in a steady stream, and since the bheromen had contributed their share and more, a lot had to come from the free towns—who weren't anxious to provide it. Writs had to be prepared, spies sent to find new sources of wealth to tax, constables sent to harass the obstinate . . . He worked for two more hours.

"It is time, Lord."

Rick looked up from his paperwork to see Padraic.

"The night meal is prepared. You wished to be called," Padraic said. "The guards wait outside."

"Thanks. Come in, Padraic. There's wine over there. Pour some for both of us, and sit down." Rick carefully stacked the papers and parchments and leaned back in his chair. Far out to the west he saw moving lights in the semaphore tower, and wondered what message was coming in.

When Padraic brought the wine, he lifted his glass. "Cheers," he said, and laughed when his archer captain looked puzzled.

"An expression from my home world," Rick explained. "Tell me, how have the men taken the news of Lord Caradoc's promotion?"

"Well, Lord. It give hope to all, that one may rise high if one has talent and is willing."

And loyal. Let's not forget that one. "Yes. Well, here's to Lord Caradoc!" They touched glasses and Rick drained his, then held it out for a refill. "Tell me, Padraic, you were raised in Tamaerthon—what do you know of Bacreugh?"

There was a crash as Padraic dropped the pewter goblet. He bent quickly to pick it up and refill it.

Rick drew his colt and clicked off the safety. He held the pistol concealed below the table. "Sit down," he said. "I think we'd better talk."

"Aye, Lord. How did you find out?"

"I have ways." What the hell have I found out? "Now tell me about it."

"Lord, there is little to tell. My grandmother is sister to the mother of Mac Bratach Bhreu, and thus I am kin to Bacreugh. It was a kinsman who approached me."

"What did he offer?"

"He said that a friend to Bacreugh wished to speak with me, and that he would offer me honor and gold," Padraic said. "I told him that I have honor enough, and it may not be had for gold. Lord, what should I have done? For I cannot betray my kinsman, and indeed he *said* nothing of importance."

"What did he say?"

"Only that. Only that Bacreugh—he said a friend to Bacreugh, but I surmised that the friend would be Bacreugh himself—wished to speak with me, and it would be much to my interest to do so; that he would offer me honor and gold, and I need do little—but what I would be required to do he did not say."

Rick thumbed the Colt's safety on. "But you guessed?"

"No, Lord."

"Then why did you drop the goblet?"

"I had heard you can hear thoughts, Lord. I had not known it was true until now. For I was at that very moment wishing I knew what Bacreugh wished of me."

"You can do better," Rick said. "You must know they intended for you to kill me. Or let one of them get past you and do it."

"Nay, Lord, I do *not* know it. I know only that Bacreugh wished to make an offer—and that he is a kinsman, as was the man he sent to approach me."

"What other kinsmen have you within the Mounted Archers?"

"Only Caradoc, Lord."

"That's right, Caradoc is your kinsman—he is kin to Bacreugh, then."

"Aye, Lord. He is related much as I am."

"Did you tell him about this?"

Padraic laughed. "No, Lord. Lord Caradoc is—quick to defend his honor. I was his chosen under-captain. He might have seen an offer to me as an insult to him, a matter for blood. And I cannot think he would wish blood-feud with his own kin."

There was a furious knocking on the door. "Captain!" someone shouted. Rick recognized Elliot's voice.

"Come in, Sergeant Major."

Elliot was breathless. He held a paper in his hand. "Just decoded this from the semaphore, Captain. They've spotted a satellite over Castle Dravan!"

28

Elliot put the decoded message on Rick's desk. "Just as you told 'em, Cap'n. Right after the True Sun set and while the 'Stealer was low on the horizon, they saw a bright light moving across the sky."

"Direction?"

"Southwest to northeast."

"Has to be a satellite," Rick agreed.

"I checked the shrine," Elliot said. "Nothing on the radio, and there's been somebody there all the time."

"Hmm. They don't want to talk with us."

"Not yet, anyway."

"So the next question is, who is it? *Shalnuksis* or a human? They're a little early for *surinomaz*, and I'd think they'd know that. They're making observations they don't care to have us know about. Any ideas on that?"

"None I like."

"Me either," Rick said. He took a blank sheet of paper and began to write. REWARD THE OBSERVER. THEN COME AT ONCE. BRING CHILDREN. IMPERATIVE ARMAGH THOUGHT MAJOR AREA OF INTEREST.

He handed it to Elliot. "Get this coded and see that it goes off to Tylara."

Elliot glanced at the paper. "Maybe it'd be best for the kids to stay at Dravan."

"I thought of that, but—If they're here to drop bombs, I'd rather Tylara stayed at Dravan too. In the caves."

"Think she'd do it?"

"No." Rick took the message and crossed through the words BRING CHILDREN.

Elliot nodded agreement. "Not likely anything'll happen."

"Not this time," Rick said. "Not this time."

✢ ✢ ✢

The field stank of too many men and too many horses. Even in the headquarters tent which was carefully placed upwind of the main encampment, the smell was there, despite the moaning hot wind that blew down the Westscarp. Lordy, I want to go home, Art Mason thought.

The adjutant brought in a paper and handed it to Mason. Art examined it and whistled. "If we don't do something pretty soon," he said, "we're not going to have any army left."

"Surely you exaggerate," Ganton said.

"Hardly, sire," Camithon said. "One always loses more men to sickness than the enemy. We have been very fortunate—no. I will not say fortunate, for it is not fortune. Thanks to Major Mason, we have had fewer losses than any army in my memory."

"Morning report's pretty bad even so," Mason said. "Still too many down. Too many flies in camp. The Romans are all right, but I can't make the others dig the latrines deep enough. And this hot wind gets to them. We're losing troops to pure funk. Last night a trooper got up at midnight and ran out and started hacking down a tree, shoutin' that he hated it. Beat it up pretty good, too. Nobody in his company did a damned thing, except one guy yelled out 'Give it a whack for me, I hate it too.' That sounds funny, but it's not, not really. Yesterday we lost two archers to a knife fight."

"Many of the knights will depart also," Camithon said. "Their time of service will expire, unless we find ways to pay them."

"You mean that I summoned them against your advice," Ganton said. "Do not bother to deny it. You may even be right. Yet my father lost his throne though failure to keep peace with the great lords of Drantos. It is an error I shall not make."

"Reckon it can't hurt to have 'em here to keep an eye on 'em," Mason said. "And even with 'em here, we're spread pretty thin, keepin' patrols going everywhere. Reminds me of Vietnam, some."

"I know not that place," Camithon said.

"No sir, I don't reckon you would," Mason said. "Thing is, we won every damn battle in Vietnam. Troop for troop we had the enemy out-matched every which way. Only one problem. We lost the flippin' war."

"Some day you must tell me that story," Ganton said. "Meanwhile, we have the chivalry here, and some will remain even after their time is expired. Not all are more concerned for rights than for the safety of the realm."

"Been more like that we wouldn't have lost 'Nam," Mason said. "And I reckon we need your heavies. Light horse can't beat the Westmen. Knights can, if they stay together and fight together."

"And yet we plow sand," Ganton said. "The Westmen avoid us. They burn and destroy, and run away when we ride after them. Are they so much better than we, that they lose no men to sickness?"

Mason made an ugly sound, then shrugged. "They're used to living on short rations."

Ganton turned to the maps on the table. He used his dirk to trace westward along a river bed. "I would employ the bheromen and knights in some useful endeavor." He bent over the map. "The Westmen are said to have a great encampment here," he said. "Will they defend it if we attack?"

"We could ask that Arekor chap that lived with 'em," Mason said. "But it probably depends on what we attack with."

Camithon fingered the scar on his cheek and nodded. "Aye, though I do not like to say it. They fear Romans more than us. Romans and Tamaerthan archers."

"Perhaps we could make them fight us," Ganton said. "On terms we like."

"Wouldn't mind seeing how," Mason said.

"Star weapons," Ganton said. "Used against their horses in camp. They will come forth to fight if their horses die."

"Probably true," Mason said.

"You do not sound joyful," Camithon said.

"I keep remembering Vietnam," Mason said. "The French were there before us. They kept saying that if they could just make the enemy stand up and fight, they'd have it made. Eventually they did just that. At a place called Dien Bien Phu . . ."

✦ ✦ ✦

Camithon and Ganton listened as Mason told the story. Later, Ganton summoned a servant to bring wine, and they drank a toast to the brave legionaries and paras who died in the strongpoints with the strange names of Gabrielle and Isabelle and Beatrice.

"Did Lord Rick then name his daughter for that place?" Ganton asked.

Mason shrugged. "Don't know."

"There is more to this matter of forcing the enemy to fight than one may think," Camithon said. "Majesty, it is my counsel that we withdraw. The Westmen will follow, and when they have come far enough we can bring all of our strength against a part of theirs. With the aid of the *balloon* we can find their weak points."

"The *balloon* is worth much, truly," Ganton said. "Yet consider. It cannot move across the land like the—the *helicopters* Lord Rick had on his world. And any land the Westmen take they render worthless. If we abandon Lord Rick's lands, perhaps he will understand—but will Eqetassa Tylara? Tell me, Lord General, do *you* wish to explain this strategy to her?"

Camithon threw up his hands. "Shall we then risk all to avoid the wrath of one Tamaerthan—lady?"

"They are my people," Ganton said. "I am as sworn to defend them as they are to serve me. Is this not true?"

"Aye—"

"Then let us hear no more of withdrawal."

Camithon gently stroked his scar. "Then it is Your Majesty's wish that we attack the camp of the Westmen?"

"It is."

"I can but obey." Camithon looked to the map. Mason had put small parchment squares on it, each representing a unit of the Royal and Allied forces. Camithon had never seen such a thing before, but it made planning much easier. "If we are to move westward and attack, it were well to take all our forces," Camithon said. "All we can feed. And all the star weapons."

"Need some reserves to guard the supply route," Mason said. And the ammunition, for that matter. "But we'll want all the weapons."

"Let Westrook become the new supply center," Ganton said. "It is a strong place, and I doubt that Lord Murphy would leave it to his companion's widow if he were not certain of her abilities."

Mason nodded sourly. Her abilities my eye, he thought. I had a hell of a job gettin' Murphy out of there, and even then he wanted to leave the flippin' one-oh-six. Horse tradin', with *me*, over what weapons to leave in that castle, just like it was his home. Hell, I guess it is. Murph's found a home, and I doubt we'll see much of him if he lives to see the end of the Westmen.

"If Westrook is to be the supply center," Ganton continued, "then we must advance through *here*." He pointed on the map. "We will not want the Westmen to know what we are doing, yet we will wish to be certain that our wagons are not delayed at the river crossing." He looked thoughtful, then nodded. "The Romans are good engineers. Let the *Cohortes equitates* carry timbers and all other things needful for quick construction of bridges here, and here. Our forces can come by many routes. The Westmen will not divine our intent, and we need not be so concerned for supply."

"An excellent thought," Camithon said. He looked at the young king with new respect.

"And I think we will not raise the *balloon* until after the attack on the camp," Ganton continued.

"Sure help the artillery to have it up," Mason said. "For target spotting—"

"Yes," Ganton agreed. "And we shall do so. But think, it is too valuable to use as a lure, and when it is raised it will draw all the Westmen toward our main strength. Would it not be better to let them seek us as the star weapons fall among them?"

Camithon frowned. "If the *balloon* is needed, we can guard it with a small band—"

"No," Ganton said. "Think, my lord. A small band will fall to roving Westmen, and there are sure to be such. If we leave enough men to guard it, we should leave them all—else we divide our strength. That is what the French did at this place, Dien Bien Phu, and we have learned the cost to them."

Christ on a crutch, Mason thought. Maybe the kid understands this stuff better'n me. Hell, I'm no officer. I'm an NCO who got lucky.

Unconsciously Mason straightened as he turned to speak to the Wanax of Drantos.

29

The office was a penthouse on top of a two-story building, a veritable tower here. It was richly furnished, with thick carpets, elaborately carved furniture, and brilliant tapestries. Leaded glass windows looked out on green Tamaerthan hills to her left and a quiet quadrangle on her right. Gwen Tremaine had once seen *National Geographic* photographs of a European university rector's office, and she'd had her staff make as near a duplicate as they could.

The high-backed chair was large enough to swallow her completely, and since it faced the desk rather than a window, when she curled up in it she was utterly invisible from the outside. She tucked her feet up closer—

And if you regress any further, you'll be sucking your thumb, you twit! she told herself; but she didn't move from the chair.

Regression feels fine. Safe, even.

Hah. You can't run away from yourself, no matter how far you go.

Thanks a lot. But it isn't myself I'm running from. At least I can't see the sky. She reached forward to the desk and lifted the note from Larry Warner. Her hand hardly shook as she read it.

> Gwen: A couple of the lookouts on Ben Hakon report seeing a "walking star" not long after dusk last night. From the path it's got to be a satellite. I'm going into town about the reaper. Good luck.

We'll need luck, she thought. They're up there looking for progress,

486

and they'll find it. Then the bombs fall. Glory, why shouldn't I be afraid of the sky?

It's not the sky, it's who might be in that ship—

I'm not afraid of Les.

No? Then who stuffed the transceiver into a bale of *garta* cloth, and what do you expect will happen when he calls and you don't answer?

I don't know. Maybe he'll go away and leave us alone.

Oh, that's what you want? I thought you wanted Les!

Sometimes.

Often.

Often, she admitted. But mostly I don't want to hurt the University. Or Caradoc—

Or Rick?

Or Rick.

Because he's saving the world? Or because there's a chance, just a chance, that he might tell Tylara to go to hell and come shack up with you? Who do you want? Rick, Les, Caradoc—or all of them? At once or one at a time?

"Shut up!" Her hands found a Roman crystal pitcher. She hurled it against the desk. It caromed off a stack of papers and shattered against the wall. Then she sat still for what seemed a long time despite the work she had to do.

"My lady?"

Gwen looked up to see Marva. "Yes?"

"The Lord Campbell is here to speak with you." Marva eyed the wine spilled on the desk and the broken glass on the floor. "Shall I have that cleaned?"

"Yes, please."

Marva took a small bell from her sleeve. Two servant girls came in to mop up the floor as Marva tidied the desk and blotted wine from the papers.

"Do you like it here?" Gwen asked in English.

Marva hesitated. "Yes, my lady. It is"—she groped for the word—"useless to wish for what cannot be."

Whatever that is, Gwen thought. What might you wish for? Your husband again? Ben Murphy? Fortunately for me, you can't have either one.

Lafe Reznick's second widow had become nearly indispensable, a combination of housekeeper, lady in waiting, secretary, and den mother. The students saw her as nobility, the widow of a star lord, yet someone they could speak with. Much information came to Marva, but she gave little in return, except to Gwen.

"You may bring Lord Campbell now, if you please, my lady," Gwen said.

"Yes, my lady." Marva ushered the servants out.

Gwen patted her hair into place and tried to look calm as the red-haired engineering professor came into her office. "Yes, Bill? What can I do for you?"

"Steel," Campbell said. "I need a lot more, and I don't have it."

"For the reaper?"

"Yeah."

"Larry's gone into town about that—"

"He won't get anywhere. All the locals claim they've paid their taxes. They have, too. But Lord Rick wants a goddamn progress report every goddamn night! Now what am I going to do?"

"You're going to stop shouting at me and have some wine, to begin with."

Campbell started to say something, but caught himself. Then he grinned. "Yes, ma'am. What wine?"

"Oh—" She pulled the bell cord. Marva came in almost instantly. She was followed by one of the girls with a new pitcher and goblets.

"Good service," Campbell said. "Thanks, Marva, I can handle things now."

"Yes, my lord—" Marva indicated a place for the tray, waited until the girl had put it down, and waved her out. "Will there by anything more, my lady?"

"Thank you, no—"

"I will wait outside."

"Cold one, that," Campbell said when Marva had gone.

"You're not polite to her."

"The hell I'm not—"

"You're not," Gwen said. "You call her by her first name—"

"Just to be friendly. She speaks English—"

"But she is *not* an American, Bill. You and I can talk informally, and you think because you say it in English you can talk that way to

Marva, but you *can't*. Bill, Caradoc calls *me* 'my lady' most of the time. And have you noticed the way Rick speaks to Tylara?"

"Well, sure, but Tylara's one of the great ones—"

"Marva is *noble*," Gwen said. "To you it may seem a little silly that she's something special because your friend Lafe Reznick married her, but to her it's not." She threw up her hands. "Anyway, that's why she seems cold toward you. Call her 'my lady' once in a while. She'll warm up fast. Now what about your iron?"

"The Romans have iron."

"I'm aware of it."

"Can you get me some?"

"I'm also aware of what they'll want. Guns and gunpowder, and we don't have any to spare. But something just came in that may change things." Gwen flipped through soggy papers on her desk until she found the one she wanted. "Intelligence reports. The Romans will have a *big* harvest this year, and they're very low on slaves to bring it in. If you could have your reaper—"

"If I can produce something that works, the captain will send it west. No matter how good I am, there won't be enough equipment to send to the Romans. Not this year."

Gwen shuddered.

"What's the matter?"

"I can't trade them guns, and I can't promise them a reaper. There's only one thing I can send."

"Yeah." Bill Campbell went over to the window and looked out onto the University quadrangle. He spoke without turning back toward her. "They tell me the life of a Roman slave isn't so bad. No worse than peasants in Drantos."

"I'll keep telling myself that," Gwen said. "Maybe if I tell myself often enough, I'll believe it. Meanwhile—"

"Meanwhile I'll send some troopers out into the Pirate Lands," Campbell said. "Those people will drown or starve within the year anyway. Best to do it quick, before the so-called roads are too muddy. It's starting to rain again."

"That should help the crops," Gwen said. She smiled grimly to herself. Also, the clouds will hide the sky . . .

✣ ✣ ✣

Mad Bear woke to the sound of screaming horses, but he could not comprehend. Walking Eagle, chief of the Two Waters, had been generous when Mad Bear's band left him to return to their own Silver Wolves. His farewell gifts had included a barrel of the strong water the Green Lands folk made from grapes. It made men sleep sounder than beer or fermented mare's milk ever could, and Mad Bear had sat late drinking with Hinuta.

Another horse screamed in agony. Mad Bear leaped from his pallet. Then the *sky itself* screamed, and then there was a great sound, much like the sound the wizard-weapons made, and there was enough light to brighten the inside of the tent although the flaps were closed against the death bird. The captured slave woman squealed like a ranwang and burrowed under the hides.

Mad Bear ignored her and grasped his weapons. He saw clearly now. The wizards were attacking the camp. Attacking at *night*. Walking Eagle had said the wizards controlled demons. Did they then own the demons which made the night dangerous for the Horse People? They seemed to have no fear of them.

Well, the night will not be long. Suns climb the sky, and then we will have vengeance. He untied the tent flaps and went outside. Tents were burning, but the camp was lit brighter than burning tents could have made it. The sky screamed again, and there were more of the thunder sounds.

"UP! UP!" Mad Bear ran among his people. "To arms! Or will you allow the wizards to slaughter you like wolves bringing down a sick horse? Up, up!"

He was nearly trampled by a pain-maddened horse. It galloped past in panic, its mane on fire. Mad Bear leaped aside and fell, and again he heard the sky screaming. This time he saw it, a trail of fire across the night skies. It fell into the camp and there was more wizard thunder, with flame and smoke.

The shaman Tangra'al rushed from his tent and raved at the skies. He screamed the old legends, of *skyfire* and folk who rode across the sky in iron chariots. They were stories from Mad Bear's childhood, and he felt a tingle at his spine as he remembered; but he dashed at the shaman and struck him so that Tangra'al fell to the ground.

"They are only men!" Mad Bear screamed to his clan. "Those who fought at the Wagon Battle heard the wizard-thunder and felt their flame, but the wizards died as easily as any of the Green Lands folk! Arm yourselves!" He ran through the camp shouting; but inwardly he was afraid. The sky gods had made themselves enemies of the Horse People and had sent the wizards against them. Why? First the lands turned brown and the Horse People had to flee to the east. Now they faced enemies who held the thunder. Why?

But there was worse yet to come. Half a score of horses stampeded in panic and trampled his tent. Mad Bear knew that not all his warriors and few of his women had got out safely, and he cursed these foul enemies, wizards so evil they would turn the Horse People's mounts against them!

In time the wizard-thunder died away, and the Horse People were left to count their losses. From one trampled tent alone Mad Bear's band pulled out a warrior and three women, two of them slaves, who would not see dawn. Another warrior had been thrown from a horse and struck his head. He lay mewling like a baby, and he fouled himself. All across the great camp it was much the same, and the toll among the horses was worse.

But the sky brightened as the Father Sun approached. Soon the night watchers came in.

There would be a battle. Riders who had followed the retreat of the wizards brought words that made that certain. There were many who followed the wizards. Grey Archers, devils in women's skirts who could shoot as far and as straight as the Horse People. There were also many Riders of the Red-Cloak Chiefs, who fought as though one man's thoughts guided all the horses and men of their war band. It was no shame to the riders that they had not dared follow closely. Yet they had followed.

The wizards and their friends had all gathered in one place, less than half the morning's ride from the camp. It was a place the Horse People knew well, a valley of rolling hills. At its bottom snaked a wide stream no deeper than a stallion's knees, and there were no hydras in the muddy waters. And there the wizards had halted—

Do they challenge the Horse People? Mad Bear's heart rose within him, and he leaped upon his greatest stallion. "My people! Have we not said that those the gods will destroy are first driven from their senses? The sky gods are no friends to these wizards! The wizards await us, in a place we know well, in a place where we will triumph! We shall have the battle the Warrior desires, and this day we shall send many of the wizard-people to the Warrior's Lodge!

"For what do we face? Men of the Iron Houses, and this in a place we would have chosen! Have they not always been easy enough to kill?

"To arms! Fill the waterskins, and send for all the Horse People who camp through the plains and hills! Summon all the clans! All the clans shall fight as one this day, all the Horse People as brothers, for is this not the will of the Warrior? Come, come, we shall fill the Warrior's Lodge!"

30

Private Hal Roscoe shaded his eyes and stared down the valley in wonder. "Jesus Christ, Major, where'd they all come from?"

Mason waved him back into action without answering. Damn good question, Art thought. There must have been fifty thousand of the mothers, two or three times as many as Mason had expected, and they swarmed all across the valley of the Hooey River, on both sides and in the river itself, shooting as fast as they could, then closing in with lances and lariats and those goofy bronze swords. Anyone with a dead or hurt horse was a goner. Not even the mercs could cover him.

The whole operation had gone sour. "No battle plan survives contact with the enemy," Captain Galloway had told Mason; and Lord God was that true! Westmen had come boiling in from all directions, and despite everything the pieces of the Alliance army had got separated.

Now Mason's troops held the top of a hill only a little higher than the rest of the knolls that sprinkled the Hooey Valley. The visibility was lousy. Too much dust, and too many of those damned little hills. Mason cursed again as he scanned the valley with his binoculars. The Drantos ironhats were across the river on another hill, facing their own share of Westmen. And everything *flowed!* Caradoc's Mounted Archers had stayed with the mercs. Now they were out in front of Mason's troops, and the mercs didn't dare fire because the archers and the Westmen were all mixed together.

Vothan alone knew where the Romans had got off to. Mason

looked down the valley toward the balloon. They'd set it up in a strong place, where the Hooey Valley narrowed and flowed between much higher hills. He'd left Beazeley and a hundred guards to babysit it. The whole army of Drantos was between it and the Westmen. It ought to have been safe enough.

Ought to have been. The *balloon* was aloft, but the observers weren't paying any attention to Art Mason. Why hadn't they seen just how many Westmen there were? Every goddamn war, on every goddamn planet, the skyboys fight their own battle and let the grunts carry the can! Too damn late now. Art swept his *binoculars* along the limits of his vision. He couldn't see too far because of the damned low hills—but there was more dust rising in the west, which meant more Westmen.

Mason cursed. This could get sticky.

Across the river the mass of Westmen facing the Drantos knights thickened, churned, and split off a detachment. They cantered into the river, throwing up a cloud of spray and gravel.

"Murph!" Hell, I'm screaming, Mason thought. Scared spitless. Well, maybe I got a right to be. Wonder, if we buy it, will we go to Vothan's Hall? Or Heaven? Or someplace else, and would someplace else be better'n nowhere at all? "Murph! Put a couple rounds in the river!"

"Roger!"

The recoilless spewed flame. The first round was white phosphorous. Steam puffed up where the burning bits hit the water. Then a high explosive round took out nearly a score of Westmen. That slowed them enough to let some of the calivermen reload, and when the Westmen came on they were hit by a rolling volley, each man firing as soon as he heard the gun of the man next to him, fire rippling down the line with the one remaining four-pounder to punctuate the end of the volley.

It wasn't enough. There were too many Westmen trying to cross that river, and they could shoot even with the water up to the bellies of their horses. The arrow-hail came down again, and suddenly there weren't enough Mounted Archers to stop them. For the tenth time that morning Art wished the other four-pounder hadn't been abandoned with a broken carriage axle.

"Hey, Art!" Murphy called.

"Yeah?"

"Hell, I know we were supposed to make 'em mad enough to fight, but goddamn, this is *ridiculous!*"

Three of the troopers laughed, but it sounded a little hollow. Down below, the Westmen came on. A lot of the calivermen were down, and the rest were shaky. One platoon broke and ran. Caradoc, his red Roman cloak streaming out behind him, rode in to rally them. Some of his personal guards leaned from their saddles to collect guns. Then the whole crowd began to pull back, with the Westmen's arrows following them. Three men and a horse went down around the four-pounder, and the remaining gunners abandoned it to scramble higher up the hill.

By now the Mounted Archers had retreated far enough that the Guards and mercs would pretty soon have a clear field of fire. Mason sidestepped his horse and unlimbered his own H&K before he thought better and slung it again. Thinking like a corporal again, Art, he told himself, he rode around to check the position of the other mercs.

They were set up about as well as they could be. On the left flank, Walbrook had the mortar, with Bilofsky nearby with the light machine-gun. "Take care of that thing," Mason shouted. "That LMG may be all that's 'tween us and Vothan's hall!"

"Right-o!" Bilofsky answered. He grinned cheerfully. "Don't worry about a thing, Major."

Murphy and the one-oh-six were in the center of the line. There was a problem about the mortar and the one-oh-six. They'd used most of the ammo in the bombardment of the camp. Now there wasn't enough left to defend themselves. Maybe that's justice, Mason thought. Frig that. He used his *binoculars* to watch the situation develop. Now they had a clear shot.

"First Guards. On my command, IN VOLLEY—FIRE! Fire at will!" The platoon of guards let fly with their calivers. Meanwhile the other mercs blazed away with rifles. Most fired single shot. Somewhere a trooper had switched to rock and roll. He'd be out of ammo pretty soon.

They all fired low, as they'd been taught, and the volley emptied few saddles, but it did dismount a lot of Westmen. They leaped from their falling horses—and kept coming. Soon they were in among the dismounted archers, using spears and knives and a few swords, and small axes like tomahawks.

"God Almighty!" Private First Class Roscoe yelled. "Those are *mean* little mothers!"

"Kinda my sentiments too," Murphy said. "Art, we going to get out of this?"

"We can sure as hell try."

The LMG got in the act, bringing down nearly a hundred Westmen, and Art began to breathe a little easier. The mortar chugged away, lobbing WP and HE into the advance, and suddenly the Westmen didn't look so confident—but they were still coming. It wasn't going to be enough.

"Stand by to pull out!" Mason shouted in English, then switched to Tran dialect. "The First Guards will withdraw! Trumpeter, sound 'Boots and Saddles.' Rendezvous at Point Blue One." That was the mouth of the valley where Beazeley's squad was guarding the balloon and the reserve ammo. A strong place. Maybe not so easy to get out of, but easy to hold. Mason shook his head. Wish the captain was here. What would he do? Don't matter. What I'm going to do is get my shit together. Then we can make a stand or run like hell, depending. That's what the Drantos troops have done. Got a strong place across the valley where they can think things over. Wonder what they intend doing?

There were more arrows, and suddenly Bilofsky rolled over, staring at an arrow sticking out of his chest. The damned fool wasn't wearing armor! His number two, Private First Class Arkos Passavopolous, took over, but the belt ran out a long time before the Westmen did. Mason rode over. "Hey Ark! Get Bilofsky onto a horse!"

"No hurry about that, Major. Best I save the gun first."

"Shitfire. Okay, do it, fast!" Then his horse spooked, and while it was bucking another flight of arrows came in. The horse screamed and reared, and Art threw himself out of the saddle before it could fall on him. He went one way and the H&K went another, and now there was nothing left but the Colt. Mason held it in both hands and squeezed off rounds. One Westman down. Another, and another, but more were coming up, trampling over the dead and dying, lots more than he had rounds for the Colt, and Mason decided he hadn't really wanted to live forever. . . .

A great black horse loomed up behind the advancing Westmen, and a sword whirled and came down. A Westman tried to keep going with one arm off, and didn't make it. Another fell headless. The horse trampled two more, and then calivermen and Tamaerthan troopers were among the Westmen. The calivermen used bayonets with effect, and a few had reloaded and were able to fire. More of the Tamaerthans charged in, and the Westmen began to thin out. Then there weren't any at all.

Mason stood up as Caradoc rode up the hill. "Thanks."

Caradoc grinned and pointed with his bloody saber. Squads of troops moved off to deal with dismounted Westmen. The Archer captain waved again, and another trooper brought Mason a fresh mount, and now they had a few minutes breathing spell, but it was still going to be close.

Then he looked up and saw a new army of Westmen come over the ridge, and Art Mason wondered how many would make it to Point Blue One.

✣ ✣ ✣

There was no water on the hill where the fighting men of Drantos were gathered. Wanax Ganton had been about to drink when a young staff officer brought the news from Camithon. "The spring was filled with dirt and dung, Majesty. It will be long before it flows again."

Ganton thrust the plug into the mouth of the waterskin and handed it back to Morrone. So be it. "From this moment, the water is for the horses," he said. "Tell the captains."

"Aye, Majesty." The young officer hesitated, then set his lips. "Lord Camithon bids me say we have above two hundred men-at-arms killed, and another five hundred have been given to the care of the priests of Yatar."

"That many," Ganton mused. He straightened. "Tell Lord Camithon I will join him soon, and meantime he is to do as he thinks best. And tell all about the water."

"Aye, Majesty."

When the messenger had gone, Morrone whistled through pursed lips. "An eighth, more than an eighth of our strength lost, and now we are at bay, trapped upon a hill without water. What will we do?"

"I do not yet know," Ganton said. "First we will show ourselves to the soldiers. As we do, we will discover how it fares with them, and whether they will fight. And then we will take counsel of Lord Camithon. He has seen more battles than I have of years. Doubtless his advice will be good." And if not, I must yet listen. The Lord Rick has often told me that battles wander far from what we plan, and by Yatar this one has done so! Now we need harmony among the captains, and they must not believe I quarrel with Camithon.

He rode along the ridge with only his banner bearer and Morrone. Sometimes he stopped to hear a wounded man's message, or to praise a deed he had seen or been told of; and always he listened as he rode past. They cheered him yet, and he felt glad. They would follow him.

Across the valley the thunder of star weapons grew, then died. He climbed higher on the ridge and used the binoculars. There was no doubt of it. The Lord Mason was retreating, taking with him all the mounted archers and other Tamaerthan warriors as well as the starmen. Ganton was shocked at how few Tamaerthans remained.

Yet there were no instructions from the balloon. It floated high above the battle, but Ganton could not see the men within it. Had they been killed? Despite all his warnings, the forces of the Alliance had become separated, and the balloon left guarded only by a few. No one had desired it, but the Westmen had poured from behind every hill, across every ridge and through every valley, more Westmen than anyone believed possible, and bands of them had got between the host and the balloon.

Perhaps there would be no messages from the balloon.

He recognized Caradoc's scarlet Roman cloak, and saw figures in starman uniforms. Some lay still, lashed across saddles. The towering soldier they called "the Great Ark" rode a captured pony so small that his legs nearly touched the ground. Others had rigged poles out behind their horses and had lashed equipment onto them. They retreated in good order, fighting their way toward the balloon.

The valley below was a cauldron. Ganton swept his binoculars across the land again. The Westmen seemed divided in counsel. Some rode after Mason. Others milled about, shouting at each other.

And meantime there was nothing to do but wait, while the day grew warmer. Ganton cursed softly and once again looked toward the futile balloon. Where were the Romans? Were they gone as well?

✢ ✢ ✢

Mad Bear was trying to keep his horse from drinking the foul waters of the river when Hinuta rode up. He had a score of Silver

Wolves—and as well a hundred Two Rivers, and dozens more from other clans.

"Rejoice, Mad Bear, your deeds have been told throughout the Horse People, and many clans would follow you."

"Ah." Mad Bear looked again. There was one missing. "Where is Tenado, my son?"

"He turned his back on a dead Ironshirt," Hinuta said simply.

"Aiiiy." But this was no time for lament.

"I have brought the Ironshirt's hair. You may offer it to the gods," Hinuta said. He handed over a bloody bundle.

"You have my thanks," Mad Bear said. He looked around the valley. "The Ironshirts are worthy fighters. They die well."

"Many of them have not died at all," Hinuta said. "And many of the Red Cloaks have gone off down the river, where they hold the small hills near the trees."

"Ah."

"Let us gather our people and go join the battle against them. Tens of tens of tens would follow Mad Bear—"

"Nay." Mad Bear shook his head and pointed to the southern ridge covered with the horses and banners of Ironshirts. They had dismounted, and hid their horses behind their great shields. There were many of their archers as well. Ironshirt archers from the stone houses used a strange bow with metal parts to do the work of a man's strength. The bows would not shoot so often, but they ranged nearly as far as those of the Horse People below them.

"Those have not died either, and their chief of the golden hat rides among them. Kill him and the others will flee," Mad Bear said. He rode over to be near Hinuta. The loss of Tenado ate at his heart, but he could never show that. Instead he clapped Hinuta on the shoulder. "It is a great day!"

"A great day for the Warrior," Hinuta agreed. He eyed the encamped Ironshirts and grinned. "It was well that we stopped the spring on that hill. And if the Ironshirts will stay long—"

"Their horses will go mad. If the Horse People can fight as one, then we will send them all to the Warrior," Mad Bear completed. "Despite their wizard-fire." They both had seen the Mountain Walkers struck down by the wizards' thunder. "Go among the Horse People, and say that Mad Bear will lead them against the Ironshirts, as many as will follow."

Only the oath-bound warriors of his band *had* to obey; but many had heard of the deeds of Mad Bear, and many would come, would follow him. Soon there would be tens of tens of tens. Mad Bear would lead them toward the Ironshirts, then pretend to retreat. The Ironshirts would charge as they always did, and this battle would end.

And that would be well.

✢ ✢ ✢

They had to fight their way into Point Blue One. It took four rounds from the one-oh-six and a full belt from the LMG before the last of the Westmen were driven out. Mason shouted orders and the troops began setting up a perimeter, leaving Art to deal with what had been the headquarters area.

The balloon crew was dead. Flyboys and ground crew, all bristled with arrows, the airmen lying huddled in the bottom of their wicker basket. Near the wagon was Ski, big scar and all, with a dozen arrows just for him, and his scalp and ears cut away as well. The Tamaerthan and Drantos riggers had been hacked with swords, and the acolytes of Yatar literally dismembered. Art looked at the bloody scene and grimaced.

Just like the king said, Mason thought. A roving band. Something. Christ, who'd have thought they could get past all of us? Or that there'd be so many of the little mothers—

One of the piles of dead began to move. Mason had the safety off the .45 when Beazeley's bloody face popped out of the heap of bodies.

"I'll be dipped in shit! Welcome back, buddy," Mason said.

"Feel more welcome if you'd point a different way," Beazeley said.

"Guess you would." Mason didn't holster the weapon. "Know where the Romans went?"

"Last report they were over that way." He pointed off to the north. "But about then we had other things to worry about."

"When'd you duck?"

"I was about the last one," Beazeley said. "Figured there was no point in standing up, so I dove in, with my friend here in my mouth just in case . . ." He showed his pistol, then looked at the hacked and mutilated bodies of Ski and the priests and shuddered.

"Okay," Mason said. "Back to the line. Wait." He took out a flask. "Have a belt."

"Thanks. Ah, McCleve's finest. Must be a month old. Good stuff." He drank again.

Mason scanned the area with his binoculars. Over to his far right there was a lot of dust, and a sound that might have been Roman trumpets. Between them and the Drantos Ironhats a band of Westmen was crossing the low ridge, headed north and east. It looked as if they were trying to get behind the Romans.

"Holy shit!" Beazeley yelled.

Mason looked around. Another band of Westmen were coming across the ridge to his left.

Dien Bien Phu, hell, Mason thought. It looks more like Little Big Horn.

31

Ganton felt reassured when he had completed his inspection of the army. Camithon had arrayed the host well. The men were dismounted to rest the horses. Above every approach to the hill stood a band of crossbowmen protected by the shields of men at arms. Behind them were walking wounded to reload, and dismounted knights taking their ease. From this height a bolt could slay a Westman's horse before his own arrow could pierce armor, and a Westman on foot was no fair match for a Drantos warrior.

Ganton wasn't worried about a fair match. He wanted the Westmen dead, or at least driven from his land. If he could have slain them all with his Browning, he would have done so.

"Ha. And what of your love of battle?" Morrone said. "Glory for your bheromen. What of that?"

"I had not realized I was speaking aloud," Ganton said. "And there is precious little glory here . . ." He used his binoculars to look across the valley. Mason had retreated to where the balloon had been tethered and hauled it down. There was still no sign of the Romans. Had they taken a defensive position somewhere out of sight, or had they left the battle entirely? If they had run away, then Ganton's army would never leave this valley.

He moved on toward the end of the ridge, and now arrows fell more thickly around him. As he drew near to Camithon's banner, he saw why. The end of the ridge rose higher than any other part, but also jutted out toward the river like the prow of a ship. It was too steep to allow crossbowmen to perch on it, and the Westmen could ride in close enough to fire their arrows and receive only a few crossbow bolts in return.

Ganton dismounted. He had to scramble along the ridge to reach Camithon, who stood partially protected by guardsmen's shields.

"Majesty, this is no safe place for you!"

"It is no more dangerous for me than for you, my lord general. Now—what is your counsel?" When the Westmen first struck and the Drantos horses began to tire, Ganton had not objected when Camithon brought the troops up this hill and set them in a defensive perimeter. Doubtless the general had a plan in mind. Now, though, it was time to learn it. "We are safe and in good order for the moment, but we are not eagles to make our homes here."

Camithon grinned and waved the ancient battle-axe he had carried into every battle since his youth. "First, Majesty, let us get off this knife-edge." He led the way back along the ridge. "As to counsel, I would know better if I could see what you see."

"Ah," Ganton lifted his binoculars to hand them to Camithon. "First, though—" he said. He swept them along the river bank, then up to where Mason's banner stood with Caradoc's. A waving orange flag, invisible without the binoculars, caught his eye. "Ho! A signal! Fetch the scribes!"

A runner dashed down the ridge and returned with three young acolytes.

"I am Panilos, senior acolyte, Majesty," one said. He looked scarcely old enough to shave; the others were even younger.

"Take these, lad," Ganton said. He handed over his binoculars, noting that Panilos had no difficulty in using them. "Read me that signal from the Lord Mason."

"Aye, Majesty," the boy said. "Laran, make the signals. Wannilos, are you ready?"

One of the scribes held wax board and stylus. "Aye," he said. The other waved his flags while Panilos peered through the dust.

"R-O-M-A-N-S D-U-E N-O-R-T-H O-F H-E-R-E STOP," he called.

Panilos called off the message and Wannilos wrote it on the board, while the third acolyte acknowledged each word. They worked quickly, too fast for Ganton to follow. When they were done, Wannilos read it off.

"ROMANS DUE NORTH OF HERE. THE ROMANS HAVE TAKEN HEAVY LOSSES BUT ARE IN GOOD ORDER. WE HAVE LOST MORE THAN HALF THE ARCHERS. BALLOON DISABLED. STAR WEAPONS LOW ON MISSILES. SUGGEST WE WITHDRAW."

"If the Romans are due north of Lord Mason, they must be there," Ganton said. "Beyond those hills. There is enough dust there." He handed the binoculars to Camithon.

The old general held them gingerly. "Majesty, the Romans are not where I expected them to be. Now the Westmen will move to cut us off from the Romans. We must hasten to decide what to do. First, I will examine the battlefield. I wish to see the Romans."

The Roman position was north and east. Sight of them was cut off by trees as well as dust. From further south on the prow of the ridge they might be visible. Camithon took the binoculars and moved gingerly out along the knife-edge. Ganton wanted to call him back, but that would not be seemly. Instead he followed.

They had gone half the way when Camithon straightened and cried out. Ganton ran forward. Camithon was falling when Ganton reached him, and only then did he see the arrow sticking out of the general's left eye. Blood poured down over his scar. Ganton leaped to hold him, but the old man's dead weight was too much. They fell off the ridge and rolled down the hill.

"Rally!" Morrone screamed. He leaped down the hill to get below his king. "Guards! Shieldsmen!"

Other knights jumped down from the ridgetop to form a shieldwall. Behind them king and captain lay together on the ground.

Ganton heard none of this. With his ear practically against Camithon's lips, he strained to listen to the man who had been more to him than his father ever had.

"Make them stay together, lad. Use them well. And not too early—" The voice faded out.

"My Lord Protector. My friend," Ganton whispered.

The voice came from lips flecked with blood. "Lad—" Then only a final rattle.

Ganton raised the dead form and laid his general's head in his lap. He bent to kiss the bloody lips. Then he stood. A shower of arrows fell around them, and he realized it was his golden helm that drew the

Westmen. Had his vanity killed his oldest friend? "Bear him upslope with honor," Ganton said quietly.

Then he saw Camithon's fallen battle-axe. He pointed to it. "I will carry that," he said quietly. A knight handed it to him. Ganton slipped the thong about his wrist and whirled it until it blurred, remembering the hours Camithon had made him spend in the courtyard attacking wooden stakes.

There were shouts from above. Shouts and moving banners, with panic in some of the voices. "The Wanax has fallen," someone shouted.

Ganton scrambled furiously up the crumbling sides of the slope. It was steep, and his armor was heavy. The battle-axe hampered him, but he held it grimly. No one else would carry *that* axe, not today and not ever. Camithon had no son . . . no son of his body, Ganton corrected himself. He has son enough today.

They had rolled farther down the slope than he had thought, and the climb was exhausting. His chest heaved with the effort. Then two guards leaped down from the ridgetop. One extended his hand and pulled Ganton up. It wasn't dignified, but it helped him get up the slope.

"My horse!" he called to his orderly. "Bannerman! With me!" He spurred the horse to ride back along the ridge, hearing the cheers of his bheromen and knights as they saw the golden helm. "I am unhurt," he shouted. When he was certain there would be no panic, he returned to the southern tip of the ridge.

"Majesty, dismount," Morrone pleaded. "If you are hurt—" He didn't finish the sentence. He didn't have to. With Camithon dead, there was only one person the knights would follow.

Will they follow me? Ganton wondered. An untried youth, who has fought in one battle, one part of another; who has led them onto this hill of dusty death . . . what did Camithon intend? He had a plan, but I know it not.

And it matters not. It is my battle now, mine alone, and that is all I may consider now.

Some of the knights were standing by their horses. A few had mounted. Ganton rode toward them. "What means this, my lords? I have heard no trumpet!"

"We need no trumpet to tell us what to do."

It was difficult to know who spoke, but from the shield markings and scarf Ganton thought it must be Bheroman Hilaskos, an important lord who led many lances to battle.

"And what would you do, my lord?"

"Cut through the enemy!" Hilaskos said.

"And then?"

"And return to our homes."

"You would run away, then?" Ganton kept his voice low and calm, though it took a great effort to do that.

"No man calls me coward. But what honor is there to perch on a ridgetop until we die of thirst? The battle is lost, sire. It will not save my lands nor yet the realm for my lances to be lost with it."

"Your lances will not be lost, nor yet will you," Ganton said. "It is your Wanax who commands here. Dismount."

Hilaskos hesitated. "Dismount," Ganton said. "Or by Vothan I will take your head in sight of your knights. Dismount and kneel!"

One of Hilasko's squires came forward to hold his master's bridle. The baron hesitated a moment more, then got down from his horse. "Aye, sire," he said. He knelt. "I see we have gained a true Wanax this day."

The others dismounted, and Ganton rode again along the ridge. This time there were more cheers, and no dissenters.

"And what will we do now, sire?" Morrone asked when they were out of the others' earshot.

Ganton continued to scan the battlefield. "I do not know," he said.

✣ ✣ ✣

Art Mason watched the priest of Yatar place the guardsman's beret over his face and signal to the acolytes who were acting as stretcher-bearers. They picked up the dead man and carried him to the line of bodies already laid out just below the crest of the hill. A long line, too damned long, Art thought, and not all the guards' dead were in it.

And the priests had armed themselves with fallen guardsmen's daggers. For Westmen? Or for the wounded if they had to retreat? For the hundredth time Art wondered what Captain Galloway would do.

The situation looked sticky. There were only two qualified signalmen, and it would be a waste to send them up in the balloon even if they could get it repaired. The damned low hills would let the Westmen get close enough to shoot the balloon observers before the basket could rise out of range. Because of the hills there were thousands, tens of thousands of Westmen out there in a killing ground, but no way to kill them. Not enough ammunition, no clear fields of fire; they were down to four bombs for the mortar and no more than a dozen rounds for the 106.

Running low on ammunition, but not low on Westmen. Not at all.

He looked across at the Drantos forces again. They seemed intact, almost no losses, but they sat there on top of their damned hill. They'd acknowledged his message suggesting withdrawal, but they weren't doing anything about it. The Romans weren't acknowledging signals at all, which wasn't surprising; they were only visible for short intervals when the dust cleared. They'd only had one semaphore expert with them, and he was probably lost.

"So what do we do, Art?" Murphy asked quietly.

"Wait."

"For what?"

"I don't know, but you got a better idea? If we pull out—" He pointed to the low sunshade awnings the priests had erected to give shelter to the wounded.

"Yeah, I got that picture," Murphy said.

"Besides—"

"Yeah?"

"Hell, Ben, I don't think we *can* pull out." He pointed to the north. "A mess of 'em disappeared in that direction. More went east. Not enough to worry about, if that was all of 'em, but enough to ambush us good while we're trying to hold off pursuit."

"Well, we gotta do *something*."

"Yeah, maybe I'll think of it," Mason said. "Crap, Ben, you know I'm no mucking officer."

"Maybe not, buddy, but you're all we got now," Murphy said. He took a flask from his pocket. "Shot?"

"Yeah—no. Not just now." He lifted the binoculars again.

✣ ✣ ✣

Arrows fell around Ganton, but none got through his armor. Three knights held shields around him as he stood at the very tip of the ridge. From here he could see almost all of the battlefield.

The three groups of the Alliance formed a right isosceles triangle with the Romans at it apex. Across the valley, on the other side of the river, stood the Captain-General's banner with Lord Mason's.

Caradoc's stood close by them. Due east of Ganton and almost due north of Mason, the Romans held two more hilltops. He was separated from the Romans by a southward-jutting finger of the woody ridge that formed the north bound of the Hooey Valley.

I am the only one who sees all this, now that the balloon is gone, he thought. Knowledge is power, Lord Rick says. To know what the enemy does not know—what is it I know that they do not?

I know where all the Westmen are, and none of them can know this, for they are separated from each other by the low hills in the river valley. Even those on the tops of the knolls see only to the next hill.

And they were divided. The two largest groups face Lord Mason and the Romans, and those two groups are separated by the river. While below facing us—

Below were perhaps five thousand Westmen. A formidable number, but nothing for the host of Drantos to fear. Small groups of Westmen rode up and down their line, shouting to their comrades, and from time to time riders went toward the enormous bands facing the Romans.

If the Alliance forces were out of—*supporting distance*, as the starmen called it—so were the Westmen. And the Westmen had no wanax, no single commander.

"Stay here. They must believe that I will return," Ganton ordered the shieldmen. He moved back along the ridge to Morrone. "Send messengers," he said. "Water the horses. The host is to make ready to mount. I want no trumpets to sound until we are ready to ride. The squires and walking wounded will stay to protect the wounded and priests. The rest will prepare to charge. Go quickly now."

Morrone grinned like a wolf. "Aye, sire."

Ganton looked up at the vault of the sky. Father Yatar, give me clear sight. Is this right action?

There was no answer. Or was there? Far away he thought he saw an eagle circling above the valley. Almost he raised his binoculars, but then he let them dangle.

It is an eagle. It is an answer, he told himself. It is enough.

Morrone came up. "All is done as you ordered. Now let me aid you with your armor."

"Aye. Stay with my banner," Ganton said. "And if I fall, lead the host."

"Where, Majesty?"

"There." Ganton pointed southeast. "Through yonder band of Westmen. Ignore all the others. You and I will be at the left of the host. The others will form to our right. We break through that line, and ride eastward along the valley to there." He pointed again to where the finger of ridge and trees separating them from the Romans jutted down into the valley. "As soon as we have rounded that small hill, then charge northeast."

Morrone frowned. "Away from the Lord Mason?"

"Yes." He raised his voice to a shout. "Is all in readiness?"

A shout rippled down the line. "LONG LIVE WANAX GANTON!"

"MOUNT!" he ordered. He swung onto his charger. "Morrone, stay with me. I want nothing save my armor closer to my back than you!"

"With my life, Majesty!"

"Sound the trumpets!"

The wild notes of the cornets blared up the line. Kettledrums added to the din. The Westmen down below looked up, startled. Ganton whirled the ax above his head. "FOR DRANTOS. FOR CAMITHON AND DRANTOS!"

The line of heavy cavalry moved ponderously forward, until there was no sound but the thunder of hooves and the call of trumpets.

32

Mad Bear had once seen the side of a hill fall when the earth shook. Boulders the size of men had rolled toward him faster than a horse could trot, and dust went up until it seemed it must reach the Father's feet.

He remembered that now. There was dust in plenty, and it was as if the hill had fallen upon him—but now, each boulder was a man dressed all in iron, mounted on a horse so tall it seemed that a Horse People's stallion could pass under its belly, and those great horses wore iron!

The hill was alive with banners, and the earth shook to the thunder of hooves. Trumpet calls rent the air, trumpets and kettledrums and the triumphant shouts of the Ironshirts as their great lances came down.

Mad Bear had fought Ironshirts before, but always on an open plain. He had never imagined such a host of them coming directly toward him. He knew that he saw his death, his and all the Horse People who had stood with him. Somewhere downriver were more of the Horse People, but not enough had come, and now—

Now there was nothing save honor. The Warrior would see that Mad Bear could die as a man, and that was all he could hope for.

He wasted no time with words. The thunder of the charging Ironshirts was too much. No one would have heard him. Instead, he counted his arrows. A hand and one more. Not enough, not nearly enough. Well, that would have to do also. He would shoot his arrows and ride away. Perhaps the Ironshirts would scatter as they followed. He nocked an arrow to his bow and tried to aim at flesh, not iron.

✢ ✢ ✢

"For this was I born!" Ganton spurred his charger ahead. The line of Westmen had turned to face him, and they shot arrows as swiftly as they could. Here and there they struck home and a horse went down, causing others in the lines behind to swerve and stumble; but the host swept on inexorably.

"For this was I born!" he shouted again.

His lance took the first Westman in the throat, spitting him like a boar. Ganton let the lance dip and sweep behind so that his motion pulled it from the fallen enemy. He barely had time to raise it again before it struck home in a Westman pony. Ganton let it go and took the axe which hung by its thong from the saddle horn. As he swept past another enemy the axe swung to crash through a bear tooth and leather helmet and split the skull below it.

"Sire, let us pass!" Two guards rode alongside. "We have lances. Let us lead."

Almost he cursed them; then he thought again. If I fall, the day is lost. Morrone cannot do what must be done. And that is not right, battles and kingdoms should not stand and fall by one life, but today it is so. "You have my thanks," he shouted, and waved the Guards past. More drew alongside, and soon he was surrounded. Not by Guardsmen alone, he saw. Bheromen and knights, all eager to ride between him and danger.

If my father could have lived to see, he thought. And I live through this day, the throne is safe. Throne? Dynasty! Our children, mine and Octavia's, will hold this land forever!

Wanax and followers rode on until they were through the lines of Westmen.

"Trumpets," Ganton called. "Sound the rally. Bring the host toward me."

The trumpets sang as his bannermen raised high the Royal Banner of Drantos and the Fighting Man. Then a dozen Westmen galloped past. They lay flat to their horse's necks, their quivers empty. They were pursued by a score of Drantos horsemen thundering along behind the banner of Lord Epimenes. "Hold!" Ganton shouted. "HOLD!"

"The cowards flee!" the bheroman shouted.

They must hold, Ganton thought. He drew the Browning and fired toward Lord Epimenes' banner. There was no knowing where the bullet went, but the sound was heard even in the din of battle. "HOLD!" Ganton shouted again. "Lord Epimenes, stay with me! We have better work than tiring our horses in pursuit of empty quivers! Leave them for the esquires, for we have work worthy of bheromen and knights!"

Epimenes reined in. It wasn't clear whether he had been won over by Ganton's words or by the axe and pistol the Wanax carried, but the futile pursuit was stopped.

"Trumpets, sound the walk," Ganton shouted. In a more normal voice he spoke to the group around him. "We have broken through the first line. When we reach the top of yonder rise, we charge again. Morrone!"

"Sire!"

"Ride to the right flank, where Lord Enipses commands, and be certain that he follows where we lead." He pointed up the valley. "Lord Epimenes will remain to guard me. And return safely—"

"Aye, Majesty."

Ganton rose in his stirrups and grinned as he saw the heaps of dead Westmen behind them. A few Drantos knights lay among them, and more stood dismounted; but the host was an intact fighting force. He used the axe to point up the hill, and felt a lump in his breast as he thought how often Camithon had gestured with that axe. "Forward," he said.

The host swept north and east.

✛   ✛   ✛

"Major!" Hal Roscoe ran up shouting. "Here they come again!"

"Yeah, I see 'em," Mason said. He looked up and down his line and prepared to hold off yet another charge from the enemy.

If there'd been more ammo for the mortar—

It's no friggin' good. Mentally he counted magazines. Enough to get out of here, he thought. Hold 'em off until dark and go for it. We'll lose the wounded, and a lot of the equipment, but I don't see what else to do. We can't go after 'em, and these damn little hills give us too little clear field of fire for the rifles.

"Make ready to shoot!" he shouted. "Rolling volley from the left. Take aim! Fire!"

The calivermen fired and reloaded as fast as they could, and Mason used his own H&K to good effect. No point in acting like an officer now, he thought. I'm not all that good a one anyway, and there ain't that many orders to give—

"Cross the valley, Art!" Murphy yelled. "For God's sake, look!"

Mason stared across the river. "Holy crap! Look alive, troops! Looks like our little king's remembered us."

The Drantos heavies were coming down the hill. *All* of them. At least all that had horses. A few had drawn right up to the top of the ridge and set up a shield wall, but damn near the whole army of Drantos was riding down that hill.

The wild charge came down the mountain like a wall. From Mason's distance it looked like a huge wave that washed across the line of Westmen, leaving a wake of dead and dying behind it as the armored men simply rode the lighter horsemen down.

The front ranks were damned near solid with banners, and right out front on the left wing was the biggest banner of all, the Royal Standard of Drantos, and yeah, that was the golden helm that crazy kid fancied. They were coming straight toward Art Mason.

Then they swerved left, pivoting around the golden helmet.

"What now?" Murphy asked.

Mason frowned. "Don't know. But I'll bet you anything you like that kid knows what he's doing."

Murphy shaded his eyes and watched the last of the Drantos heavies vanish into the dust, then turned back to picking off advancing Westmen. "I sure hope you're right," he said.

✦ ✦ ✦

Julius Sulpicius, *primus pilus* of the Fourth Legion, rode up to Titus Frugi and saluted. "Those scouts we sent forward are late coming back," he said. He could have said that it was unlikely that they would return at all; but there was no need for that. One didn't work up to First Centurion of a legion by chattering at generals of Titus Frugi's years and experience.

Frugi cursed under his breath. That was the fourth scouting party he'd sent upriver. One had returned, unable to pierce the combination of Westmen and dust. The other three had not come back at all.

From time to time Titus Frugi had made out a gleam on the tip of a ridge far up the valley; a gleam and what seemed to be a banner. The sketch maps the *frumentarii* had made of the Hooey Valley showed that point as part of a defensible ridge, and Frugi wondered if the army of Drantos had taken refuge there.

Certainly the starmen and their Tamaerthan allies were holding another hilltop across the river.

"Third Cohort says the barbarians are thickening up toward the rear," Sulpicius added. His fifteen years of following the eagles gave him the right to say more, but with Titus Frugi that wasn't needed. His tone made the implied question clear enough: isn't it about time we get the hell out of here?

It was, but that didn't much appeal to Frugi. Withdrawing without orders would endanger an alliance that was all that stood between the Westmen and the Roman borders—if the legends were right, these Westmen had once come all the way to the gates of sacred Rome herself! No. Better to stand here, even if it cost the legion.

But—are we doing well? he wondered. We have taken positions here, and none will come past us, but what good do we do? From time to time the Westmen would try the Romans' mettle, but when they found they could not induce the Romans into futile wild charges they soon abandoned the sport. Now there were thousands—perhaps tens of thousands—of Westmen somewhere out in front of the legion, but they would not stay to receive a charge. Titus Frugi had fought many enemies in his service to Rome, but never one that he could not *find*! Yet between the dust and the hills that was precisely the difficulty; and if he thrashed about in that dust searching for the enemy, the horses would tire, and then he would indeed be lost.

Trumpets sounded at the forward outposts, and now the decurion and men he'd stationed out there as a screen were galloping back toward the main lines. More trumpets. "TO HORSE!" they sang, and if the centurions ordered that without asking Frugi's permission, the enemy was in sight! As he rode forward, the first of the Westmen came over the brow of the small hillock in front of the Roman lines.

The centurions knew their business. The *cohortes equitates* came forward with their shields and spears to protect the horse archers, while the cataphracti shot the Westmen down—

Shot them down, and the Westmen hardly resisted!

"This is no charge!" Titus Frugi shouted.

"Legate, you are right!" Sulpicius shouted. "They flee! But—what?"

Could it be a trick? No. The Westmen were clever, even devilishly clever, but they had not the discipline to sacrifice so many as a ruse. No, they fled an enemy behind them, fled in terror—

"Trumpet to arms!" Titus Frugi called. "Sound the 'Make ready.' The legion will advance! Fifth and Sixth cohorts to the wings to cut off enemy escape."

A cheer rang down the lines. Even the iron-disciplined Romans hated standing in place to be shot at.

"At the walk!"

The Roman line moved forward, down the slope and up the next, into the dust beyond. As they did, more Westmen poured out. The centurions hastily put men with shields and lances in the front ranks, spacing them so that the archers in the next rank could shoot between them. The *cohortes equitates* clung to the saddles of their mounted comrades; when the Westmen charged they moved expertly forward with spear and shield to catch the Westmen from below while the cataphracti threatened them from horseback. More Westmen died.

Then they were over the brow of the hill. The narrow valley below was a cauldron of dust and noise, trumpets of Drantos mingled with the screams of the Westmen and their horses. The Westmen were bunched together, trapped in the small valley so that they could not use their weapons, and with the Drantos force between them and the river, and the Romans coming in from behind, they could not run away.

The legion moved forward to crush Caesar's enemies.

✣ ✣ ✣

Ganton whirled the axe around his head, for now it was work for axes and swords. There was not room enough for a charge. None was really needed. The Westmen tried to flee, only to pile upon their fellows; then they turned to face the host of Drantos, but when an unarmored man with a bronze sword faced a steel-clad knight with longsword or axe, there could be only one outcome.

"They do not flee!" Morrone shouted. He hewed down another enemy.

Ganton was as blood-spattered as Morrone. His Browning was long since emptied, and he had no time to reload. Also, sometime during the charge he had lost his hatred of Westmen. Now he wanted only for the battle to end. *I know what Lord Rick must feel*, he thought. There can be enough killing, enough and more than enough. Yet we do what we must do. "It is the Romans," Ganton answered.

A Westman warrior broke through the leading ranks and dashed at Ganton, thrusting with a captured Drantos lance. The lance crashed against his upraised shield. The wooden shield cracked through the middle, but as it did it caught the Westman's lance. Ganton swung the axe to cut through the shaft, raised the axe and swung it again. His wrist had long ago tired, and the axe twisted as he struck so that only the flat smashed against the steel cap the warrior wore, but that was enough. The man went down, but there was another behind him, and Ganton's shield was gone. Desperately he tried to avoid the stroke—

Morrone charged forward and spitted the man with his sword.

Ganton waved acknowledgment. By now they had saved each other more times than either could remember.

"The Romans?" Morrone asked.

Ganton frowned. What was this question, and why should he answer questions at all? His head pounded with the sound of horns and drums, and he was exhausted. A council chamber with too many offering advice seemed an ideal place; but he knew he must keep his head.

What of the Romans? Ah. He remembered what he had said before the Westmen had attacked him. "They are ahead there," Ganton said. "I had hoped they would have sense enough to charge when we drove the Westmen toward them, and it seems they have. And could I but get to them—"

What would I do? I had a thought, and now it is gone, yet I think it was important. Could I get to the Romans—?

Ah. He stood in his stirrups. "Morrone!"

"Sire!"

"You command until I return. The Great Banner remains with you, and you speak with my voice. I must go to the Roman commander. Lord Epimenes!"

"Sire!"

"I give you command of my household. Join your men with mine and let us be off, for there are yet great things we may do if I can but speak with the Romans."

"Majesty! Command me!"

He must know how many will fall if we batter our way through that mass, Ganton thought. Yet he is eager to come. That is more brave than sensible. Aye, many of my bheromen are that way. Armored from head to foot and from ear to ear. But loyal, and today I need loyal men. Today they obey me as they would Lord Rick! For today I have given them the kind of battle they pray for through long winters, the battle they have dreamed of since first they couched a lance. Yatar—aye, Yatar and Christ!—grant that their loyalty continues.

He let himself be surrounded by guards and the knights who followed Epimenes. Then they lowered their lances and charged toward the Westmen. "For Drantos and Camithon!"

✣ ✣ ✣

The tribune Geminius rode up to Titus Frugi and saluted. "A party of Drantos nobility approaches, Legate. They have cut their way through the Westmen."

"Aid them."

"That is done, Legate."

Frugi nodded acknowledgment. Drantos warriors were not noted for their cooperation with others, but whoever was coming had risked much.

A headquarters optio rode in at the gallop. "Centurion says it's the banner of the Fighting Man!" he shouted.

"That's the Wanax himself!" Geminius exclaimed. "But why has he come? He has come without his royal banner!"

"I am aware of that," Frugi said impatiently. "Prepare to give him the proper honors and spare me your chatter. We will know soon enough why he has come."

That didn't stop the junior officers from making guesses, but at least it kept them from distracting him with them. Meanwhile, Sulpicius had reports from the cohort commanders.

Then the Drantos party rode in.

"Hail, Majesty!" Frugi called.

"Hail, Legate. We must speak, and quickly." The young Wanax gestured, and one of his squires leaped down to hold his horse as he dismounted.

Frugi noted the others in the royal party. Knights and bheromen, seasoned veterans all, carrying bloody weapons. They had come through much to get here—it was significant that veteran warriors would follow this boy king. Frugi wearily dismounted.

Ganton drew his dagger, knelt, and in the hard ground began to *draw a map* of the battle. It was not the best map Frugi had ever seen, but it would do. Aye, Titus Frugi thought. A map drawn by a lad who had never thought of maps as a weapon until the starmen came; it will do well enough indeed.

"We have nearly half the Westmen trapped between us," Ganton said. "As their ranks thin they will begin to escape; but we will kill enough, I think." He used his dagger to draw a circle around that combat area.

"The rest of the Westmen are here, across the river from us, encircling the Lord Mason. They face only star weapons, but so long as they do not attack the Lord Mason, they have little to fear because of the hills. There are not enough starmen to go seeking them."

Frugi nodded. "What know you of the *balloon*?"

"It does not rise," Ganton said. "I do not know why. But because it does not rise, the Lord Mason knows little of where the Westmen are. Yet they are here, and here, and—"

"I see," Titus Frugi said.

"The Lord Rick has taught me not to send all my forces into battle at once," Ganton said. "To hold what he calls *reserves*. I believe it is also the Roman way."

"Yes," Frugi said. He looked thoughtfully at the young Wanax. There were many more years behind the boy's eyes than there had been when they planned this battle.

"If you will divide your *reserves* into two parts, and send them here and here, then much can be accomplished," Ganton said. He drew lines on the map to indicate positions flanking the mass of Westmen facing Mason and Caradoc. "For in no more than a Roman *hour* the slaughter here will be finished, and the army of Drantos will be able to charge again. If we charge across the river, we will take the remaining Westmen from behind, driving them into sight of the starmen. Your *reserve* force will prevent them from escaping to the sides, and the star weapons will finish the task, I think."

"Unless the Westmen dislodge the starmen."

"No," Ganton said. "True, I have not spoken with the Lord Mason— but I do not need to do so. I know the Lord Mason and the Lord Caradoc. They will have a strong position. They will not be driven out by Westmen fleeing in panic."

"Umm," Frugi said. "Will your horses be able to make a second charge?"

"Aye. I have sent the—*support troops*—to the river for water. Our horses are well fed, thanks to Lord Rick and the Roman scribes who aid him."

He has indeed grown, Titus Frugi thought. And would be a formidable enemy to Caesar—

"For I have learned," Ganton said with a rush. "Neither I nor my knights, nor Lord Camithon himself, ever before dreamed how important it would be that a bushel of oats travel from a farmer's field to the belly of a war horse on the high plains. But I have learned. Aye, Legate, our horses are strong, and soon they will have water. They will charge truly."

Titus Frugi shaded his eyes and stared into the dusty valley below. The Wanax is right, he thought. An hour should see the end of that slaughter. Barbarians not fighting under one chief are not known for their readiness to come to the aid of fallen comrades. The reserve will not be needed to meet a rescue attempt. One cohort can hold the rear, and if this lad truly knows the position of the enemy we can yet have a decision this day.

"I suggest further that Drantos take the center," Ganton said.

"The chivalry of Drantos is best employed in a single striking mass; your legionaries are better at maneuver. And we will strike directly here—" He used the dagger to draw a thick arrow.

"You have tested the depth of the river, then?" Frugi asked.

"I have seen the Westmen crossing it," Ganton said. He held up his binoculars. "With these. At the crucial places the water comes to the bellies of the Westman ponies."

"Ah." Titus Frugi straightened from where he had bent over the map. The headquarters officers leaned forward eagerly. Frugi hesitated another moment, then asked, "What think you, Primus Pilus?"

"I think well of it, Legate," Julius Sulpicius answered.

"And there is no need to ask you, Tribune Geminius. Either you approve or you have adders under your breastplate. Very well. Tribunes, go and ready the cohorts. Wanax, how will you alert your own forces?"

"I will ride with you until we reach them," Ganton said. "If that is acceptable to you."

"More than acceptable." And I am glad enough to have you as Caesar's friend, for you would be a formidable enemy. Our military handbooks will need revision after this day, for they say that Drantos is a barbarian kingdom—and that is true no more.

33

Private First Class Passovopolous had just finished reporting the LMG back in action when Mason heard war-horns. They grew louder. A hundred Westmen rode at a gallop out of the dust across the river. Then, suddenly, the Royal Banner of Drantos burst from the dust-cloud behind the Westmen. In another moment, the opposite bank of the Hooey was alive with banners. "Murph!" Art shouted. "Use that one-oh-six! Targets of opportunity—"

"Rog!"

"Ark! Get ready with the LMG. Looks like they'll drive the bastards right out in front of us."

"Right," Passovopolous said.

"Reckon you were right," Murphy said. "Fire in the hole!" The one-oh-six roared, and a white phosphorus shell burst among a cluster of Westmen trying to organize at the river bank.

"Right about what?"

"Kid knew what he was doing."

"Yeah," Mason said. He sure did.

The LMG chattered, joined by the crackle of fire from H&K rifles; the Westmen's abortive attempt to rally at the river bank dissolved before it was fairly begun.

Then everything happened at once. The dust-cloud erupted warriors, Drantos knights and Roman cataphracts. They charged down the river bank and straight on into the shallow river, slowing for a moment there but building momentum again. By the time they had crossed the river, the Roman and Drantos forces had mixed, clumps of

Romans intermingled with the Drantos knights, both groups led by the mixed headquarters troops of both armies. It was hard to tell which crossed the river first: the golden helm of Wanax Ganton, or the scarlet cloak of Titus Frugi.

The Westmen made another attempt to rally, this time at the top of the knoll above the river bank, but a fresh group of Romans, both horsemen and *cohortes equitates* clinging to their bridles, appeared on their flank. The Roman infantry locked shields and advanced slowly while the cavalry sat their horses and shot down the Westmen. Meanwhile the combined force of Drantos knights and Roman lancers completed their river crossing. They dressed lines, and their officers rode up and down the line shouting. Then the wild war horns sounded, and Romans and knights alike spurred to a canter.

The Westman couldn't stand the combination of arrows from the flanks and lances from the front. Their line buckled, then dissolved. The Allied forces charged on, and the whole battle swept out of Mason's sight into a fold in the hills.

"They'll be coming over that hill pretty quick," Mason said. "No shooting at 'em on the ridge. Wait until they're just below us. That way we're sure of what we're shooting at." He sent a runner with the same message for Caradoc.

And now we wait, he thought. But this time we know what we're waiting for. It's all over but the mopping up.

✣ ✣ ✣

Mad Bear's surprise at getting across the river after the first charge of Ironshirts was beginning to wear off when the Ironshirts charged again. Even then he was not afraid. The Horse People could win against the Ironshirts, even Ironshirts with wizard allies.

"Stay with me!" he shouted. "We can yet win. The Ironshirts can be led into charge after charge until their horses tire, and then they are easy to kill. Stay with me!"

He was still shouting this when he saw Red Cloaks on both flanks of the Ironshirts, and more Red Cloaks at the mouth of the valley. Then he knew. The Father and the Warrior had indeed turned their backs on the Horse People.

The Red Cloaks came out of the dust behind their arrows and their terrible war horns, and Mad Bear knew that all the history of the Horse People would henceforth be divided by this day.

"To me!" he called. "If we cannot win, we can yet die as the Warrior expects! Let us all go up hill and kill the servants of the wizards!"

But few listened. The never-ending storm of Red Cloak arrows fell among the Horse People, and the Ironshirts hewed their way uphill. Their lances spitted the warriors, their great horses trampled the Horse People's mounts beneath their hooves, and their terrible iron swords and axes cut down even those who had found armor.

An arrow struck his horse in the neck, and as it reared two more took it in the chest. Two Ironshirts and three Red Cloaks cantered up the hill. They pointed at Mad Bear and spurred toward him. As they came they shouted something to him.

Mad Bear leaped upon a rock, bow in one hand and captured sword in another. He answered the shouts of his enemies with his own war cries. Then he nocked his last arrow and took careful aim at a Red Cloak. The man ducked behind a shield, and Mad Bear hastily changed his aim point to the chest of the nearest Ironshirt. At that range it went through the man's armor, and Mad Bear shouted in triumph, but then it was too late. His enemies came on. Something struck his head. He was vaguely aware that he had dropped his sword and was falling.

✧ ✧ ✧

Titus Frugi rode up to the spot he'd chosen for a command post, to find the starman Lord Walbrook already there. Then the Lord Mason came down the hill after the *cohortes equitates* relieved his guards.

The battle was over. There were still Westmen trapped in the valley or hiding among these low hills, but organized resistance had ended. Now it was enough to send out detachments, preferably with officers sensible enough to try capturing Westmen chiefs alive.

Westmen fought hard. At first very few surrendered, but now that they were cut off from the river, the need to water their horses would drive them to seek quarter. When they did surrender, it was always to warriors; they would commit suicide rather than be guarded by wizards or women.

"A good day's work," the Lord Mason said.

Titus Frugi nodded judiciously. "It has been done well," he said. "And proves the alliance has value to all."

Down below, the Tamaerthan archers were wading into the river to drag dead Westmen out to the bank. "That is well done," Titus Frugi said. "But it would be well to get the dead horses out also. Else the river will be too foul for drinking—"

Mason chuckled. "I'm afraid they're not thinking of sanitation, Legate. They're after Westman gold. Most of the Tamaerthan lads came on this campaign for loot."

"Ah. There is much to share," Titus Frugi said. "The legion has collected much gold, as have the Drantos warriors. How shall this be divided? We must speak of this with the Wanax."

"Yes, sir," Mason said.

"Meantime, your pardon—" Titus Frugi turned to greet Tribune Geminius.

"Hail, Legate," the tribune called. "There are still a few bands of Westmen on the ridge across the river. They left the dismounted ones behind to cover while the rest try to escape. Should we pursue?"

"No." He lowered his voice so that no one but Geminius could hear. "The legion is scattered. Many of our troops have left ranks to loot. Our horses are exhausted, and we would not pursue as an organized force. The cohorts I could send must remain to guard against a fresh attack. I tell you this because there is a chance—a small chance, but a chance—that you may yet be fit to command a legion."

"My thanks—"

Titus Frugi cut him off. "Meantime, stay here. The centurions know what must be done. It is the task of the officers to see that we face no fresh enemies until the legion is whole again. It is also our task to know what *not* to see."

"Yes, sir—should I then see to getting your tent erected?"

"How? By shouting orders to the headquarters troops? They would ignore you, Tribune, and quite rightly—what could you tell a ten-year veteran optio about caring for his commander?" Frugi chuckled again. "Dismount and relax, Tribune. And invite the star lords to come sit with us, for I see that Junio has found the wine, and the Wanax Ganton approaches."

✤ ✤ ✤

A young man who has learned much, Titus Frugi thought as the Wanax rode up with a dozen of his companions. Riders and horses alike showed the fatigue of a day's battle and two charges.

"Hail, Titus Frugi," Ganton called.

"Hail, Majesty. The day has gone well."

"Aye." Ganton dismounted and gestured to Morrone. For the first time since dawn, the golden helmet was removed.

Morrone took it from his Wanax with a gesture so graceful that the finest actors in Rome could not have bettered it. The young Wanax shook his head and tried to comb the snarls out of his dark hair with his fingers.

If there were a sculptor worthy of it, I would give him this as his subject, Frugi thought. He has won over his followers, aye and more than his followers—

Julius Sulpicius came up with a dozen other centurions. He saluted Titus Frugi, then turned to Ganton. The First Centurion looked to his fellows. All grinned.

I should halt this, Titus Frugi thought. But he saw the look that his *primus pilus* gave the foreign king, and knew it was already too late.

Sulpicius raised his arm in salute. *"Ave! Ave Ganton, Imperator!"* he shouted. "Hail, Imperator!"

The other centurions echoed the cry. After a moment the headquarters troops joined, then the other legionaries within earshot. In moments the cry rang through the Hooey Valley. "Hail, Ganton Imperator!"

I see, Titus Frugi thought. He remembered the first time Roman troops had saluted him thus. Imperator. Worthy to command Romans. It was not a title lightly given, even to Romans. He could not recall when a foreign chief was so honored.

If I join this cry, nothing will convince Publius Caesar that I did not order it. But if I do not—I will lose the trust of my legion.

I was prepared to sacrifice the legion to save the alliance. Now I can save both with words that cost no more than the good will of Publius Caesar—which I probably do not have anyway. And Ganton is worthy of all this day may bring.

Titus Frugi lifted his hand in salute. *"Ave!* Hail, Ganton Imperator!"

They cry was redoubled now. Drantos and Tamaerthan troops repeated it, not knowing what the ancient words meant, but understanding that this was honor to Wanax Ganton.

All joined in the cry. All but the Lord Mason.

"What's happening?" Mason demanded urgently. "What *is* this?"

Titus Frugi stared uncomprehendingly for a moment, then

understood. "Ah. *Imperator* is a title, Lord Mason. It can only be given by Roman soldiers to one who has led them in battle. Those hailed as Imperator are recognized as worthy to lead a Roman army."

"It doesn't mean, uh, like Wanax?"

"No. They do not hail him as Caesar. Only as *Imperator*."

"Yeah? And that's all this means?"

Titus Frugi sighed. "Certainly no one could be offered the purple who had not been hailed as Imperator."

"And if he marries Octavia . . ."

"*When*, my friend," Titus Frugi said. "As you well know. Nor can I think your Captain General Rick will be much surprised by this event—"

Mason shrugged.

It is hard to tell what the star lord thinks. But since I have no more of Publius' good will to lose this day—and I do know that Marselius Caesar thinks highly of his granddaughter—He turned to his tribunes. "Geminius."

"Sir?"

"When the messengers return to camp to bring up the supplies and the surgeons, you will go with them. Bring back a *corona aurea* for the Wanax Ganton. We will also need three *coronae civicae*, one each for the lords Mason and Caradoc, and one for the Lord Camithon's bier."

"Sir!"

"You are pleased, Tribune?"

"Aye, sir."

And so are Sulpicius and the centurions, Titus Frugi thought. Yet I wonder what will be the end of what we have begun this day . . .

⁘ ⁘ ⁘

Mad Bear woke in near-darkness. His head throbbed, and when he tried to lift his hands he found they were bound with cloth strips.

I am a prisoner. This is not the Lodge of the Warrior, nor is there so much pain that I have fallen into the hands of the demons. He sat up, and saw that he was in a dimly lit tent. A tent of the Horse People, not an Ironshirt tent.

At the door sat Arekor, the priest of the Warrior who had been a slave among the Red Rocks until he vanished in a raid on the Green Lands. Now Mad Bear was certain he had not died, for Arekor could never have earned so much honor as to guest with the Warrior—

"So, Centaur-lover. You have come to take revenge by taunting me?"

Arekor poured water into a cup and held it to Mad Bear's lips.

At first Mad Bear refused; but his thirst betrayed him. He took a sip, then drained the cup. Three times more Arekor held the full cup out. When he had drunk the last, Mad Bear said again, "Why do you taunt me?"

"No, Mad Bear. I have not come to taunt you. I have come from the chief of the Ironshirts, and what I speak you may hear without dishonor."

"I do not believe you."

"You will," Arekor said. "For I will cut you free and give you a warrior's knife, which you may turn on yourself if you believe you have been dishonored. It may even be that an Ironshirt warrior will fight you in a single combat, risking his life to let you end yours with honor. But first you must promise to hear me out, and not to attack me."

"Swear this is true!"

The priest swore such oaths that even Mad Bear was impressed. Not even a Green Lands priest who had submitted himself to slavery among the Red Rocks would use such oaths to strengthen a lie to a warrior of the Horse People—or if he could, then nothing among gods or men was as it had been, and Mad Bear could do what pleased him.

"What I will say can bring good to the Horse People," Arekor said.

"If this could be so—Give me the knife."

"Swear first."

Mad Bear swore by the Father and the Warrior. Arekor drew a short blade of Ironshirt make, and cut Mad Bear's bonds. Then he gave him the knife.

Mad Bear turned it over and over in his hands. The priest had spoken the truth—"Are there women or wizards within hearing of us?"

"I swear there are neither," Arekor said. "Only warriors."

Mad Bear tested the blade with his thumb. It was sharp, of good workmanship, quite good enough. No one would ever take that blade while he lived. "Now I will listen to your dream of bringing good to the Horse People."

The priest began to speak.

✣ ✣ ✣

Ganton reached for another sausage and felt the *corona aurea* begin to slip. He pushed it back into place with one hand and grabbed a sausage with the other. He could not remember ever having been so hungry.

The food was simple, but there was plenty of it. Once again he could admire Roman organization. The battle was done, and there were a myriad of details to attend to; but Roman optios saw to all that. For once the commanders could rest, with only the most important decisions brought to the command post.

The headquarters staff had set out a table overflowing with sausage and bread and jerked meat, and nearby a kettle of hot soup was just coming to the boil. There were also flagons of wine, well watered but of good flavor. The Romans hadn't asked if he wanted his wine watered; they had simply assumed that no commander on a battlefield would drink anything else. It was something to remember . . .

And not far away was the luxury of all luxuries: an optio supervised as Titus Frugi's servants erected a tent that would contain a canvas bath! Soon there would be hot water—

Perhaps, he thought, perhaps I will be able to clean my head without shaving it. He grinned to himself at the thought, trying to imagine what Octavia would say if he came to their wedding night as crop-haired as a slave.

That wedding would not be long coming. Then, married to Caesar's granddaughter, and proclaimed a leader of Romans—He could still feel the thrill of that moment. *Imperator!* The Romans had hailed him, soldiers and officers alike, and he could now appear before a Roman army wearing the *corona aurea*. And the army of Drantos was now loyal, the strength of the throne—With Octavia as his wife—what might not be accomplished?

PART SEVEN
SKY GOD

34

The moving light circled.

"That is it?" Tylara raised one hand and pointed. With the other she tightly held Rick's arm.

Rick nodded as he watched the ship hover above the bare hilltop. It was all too easy to remember the first time he'd seen one of the alien craft. That had been ten light years away, in Africa, and he hadn't believed in flying saucers.

This time, I *know* what it is, he thought. Does that make it easier? There are no Cubans coming to kill me. But I don't know who—or what—will be aboard, no more than I did then.

The instructions had been clear. Bring a work crew, all the *surinomaz* harvested so far, and no heavy weapons. The voice on the transceiver had been cold and mechanical, and had not encouraged conversation.

The moving lights came down with a rush. From the foot of the hill came a wail of terror and shouts that might have been prayers, then Elliot's curses. The ship settled to the hilltop. There was a long silence, broken only by a whine from somewhere within the craft.

"Can they see us without light?" Tylara asked in a whisper.

"Aye. And hear us as well."

She tightened her grip on his arm. "Will we see them?"

She's bearing up better than I did, Rick thought. "I don't know," Rick answered. "Nor do I know if this group will be human or *Shalnuksi*."

531

He hadn't wanted to bring her, but she'd been persuasive. If the purpose was to convince the *shalnuksis* that Armagh was the principal seat of Rick's holdings, they would expect his wife to be there; and if at the castle, then why not to meet the ship when it landed? "Would they think me afraid?" she asked. "Or that you would marry one who feared them?"

He'd had no answer to that. Perhaps it would help if she came. Perhaps not. He had no way of knowing how much they could find out from orbit. Certainly Armagh *appeared* to be an important place. At the moment the castle was crammed from rafters to cellars with household goods, supplies, animals, and people. There were courtiers and cooks, administrators and acolytes, scribes and scullerymaids, judges, journeymen, apprentices, and masters of nearly every trade; even two dozen of the Children of Vothan in training for domestic service, and several of their teachers.

There was nothing better than oil lamps and bonfires for light, but even so, Armagh ought to be visible from orbit. Every room and courtyard blazed as they celebrated the news of the great victory. The Westmen were driven from the land, and even now the Alliance army was escorting them northwards, out of Drantos, into the wild lands to the northwest, lands nominally part of Drantos but long ago claimed by Margilos on the one hand and the Five Kingdoms on the other. Let the High Rexja have both the disputed lands and the Westmen. Perhaps it would keep him too busy to annoy Drantos.

One problem down, another to go. The flying saucer didn't look like it was doing anything. Gingerly Rick detached Tylara's hand from his arm and walked toward the craft. "Hi!" he called. "Hello, the ship."

It could have been the ship that brought him to Tran. Certainly it was more like that than like the sleek craft that had rescued the mercenaries from their African hilltop. Even in the dim light of the Demon Star he could see that the hull showed stains, patches, and dents. There were bulges and flutings in random places on its surface. Les had once told them the ship that brought them to Tran was chartered; perhaps this one was also, or it might have been the same ship.

The whine muted and died, and the ship settled more heavily on its large circular landing feet. There were small crackling noises as it crushed the fragrant Tran shrubbery. A small square opened near the saucer's top, and the hillside was bathed in yellow light. Rick moved closer, carefully keeping his hands away from the .45 in its shoulder holster.

A rectangular hatchway opened into a gangway. The inside of the ship was bright with the yellow light the *Shalnuksis* seemed to favor. Rick could see crates and packages, a lot of them, many painted olive drab.

"Good evening, Captain Galloway." The voice boomed out unexpectedly, startling Rick. It was the same cold, impersonal voice he'd heard on the transceiver. It sounded like a recording, or perhaps like something synthesized on a computer. Its tones told him nothing about the person—or being—who spoke.

"Good evening," he said. He was surprised at how dry his mouth had gotten.

"You see we have brought you—supplies. Have you brought the— work crew—as instructed?"

"Yes."

"Excellent. Have them bring the *surinomaz*." The hatchway Rick was watching closed, and another, smaller doorway, leading into a much smaller compartment, opened about forty-five degrees around the base of the ship. "Captain, you will oblige us by remaining where you are, while others bring the *surinomaz*."

He felt rather than heard Tylara come up behind him. Then she took his arm. "We will stand here together," she said softly.

"A—noble sentiment," the impersonal voice said. "Very well. Instruct your crew to hurry. They are to carry no metal into the ship. Is that understood?"

"Right." He turned to face down the hill. "Elliot, get the stuff loaded in that open compartment. Make sure the troops leave all their metal behind. Daggers, armor, everything. Make it sharp."

"Sir! All right, you sons, move it." There was a cacophony of sounds from lower down the hill, then Elliot's voice rose above the chatter. "Move it *now*, or by Vothan you'll be in the madweed fields before the True Sun is high! Move!"

The clerks and apprentices scurried up the hill. They were led by Apelles, who looked like a man not entirely successful at trying to be brave. None of them had been armed, so it didn't take them long to shed all of their metal. Then they carried the semi-refined madweed into the small cargo compartment.

"It is not a large amount," Rick shouted. "The rogue star isn't close enough yet. Next year is supposed to be a better crop."

"We know," the ship answered.

Rick and Tylara watched as the cargo was loaded. Finally Apelles came out and signalled they were done.

"Now stand clear," the voice called. The compartment door closed. The whining noise rose in pitch.

"I had thought they had goods for us," Tylara said. "Will it rise now?"

"I don't know," Rick said. He turned away from the ship.

"Remain there, Captain. If you please." This time the voice sounded different.

Rick stood with Tylara for what seemed a long time. Then the first compartment door opened again. "Your men may now begin to unload. They will stay on this side of the ship, and they will not carry weapons. You will remain where you are."

"All right. Elliot, move 'em."

This time there was no argument from the work crew. The clerks and apprentices sweated and strained to get the boxes outside the ship. Others brought up mules and began to lash gear on their pack saddles.

Rick could see most of the cargo as it came out. A lot of it was ammunition. One crate was labelled "Armor, Body, Ballistic Nylon, Personal Protective." Another was unmistakably Johnny Walker Black, and two more bore Meyers Jamaica Rum labels. There was a case of Camel cigarettes.

Elliot came out grinning. He was holding a portable typewriter. "Carbon paper, too!" he shouted in triumph. "And a Carl Gustav recoilless."

"Just like Christmas," Rick answered with a grin. He didn't move from his place in the circle of light. "Tylara—they didn't say you have to stay here," he said softly.

"*They* did not," she answered.

"Hey, I love you."

"I think perhaps you do," she said. She squeezed his arm.

"Talisker Scotch!" Elliot shouted. "And Rennault fifty-year-old cognac! Can't say they don't pay for what they get!"

Oh, they pay, Rick thought. They understand about not binding the mouths of the kine that tread the grain. But they won't take us home, and they gave us damned little choice about coming here.

✢ ✢ ✢

The ship was unloaded, and most of the gear sent down the mountain on mules. The hatch closed, but the bright light from near the top of the ship continued to flood the hill with yellow light. Then the whine rose in pitch and became louder and louder. The ship seemed to lift slightly. It hung for a second, then rose swiftly and almost vertically into the dark sky.

"It is gone," Tylara whispered. "I had—you had told me. But until I saw—"

Rick laughed. "I know," he said. "Back on Earth *I* wouldn't have believed it." And I knew about airplanes, and radio, and—

"Rick." Tylara spoke quietly, but there was an urgent note in her voice. She tilted her head. "Look."

His eyes had not yet adjusted to the dark, and at first he couldn't see what had alarmed her. Then it became clear. There was a man standing beyond where the ship had been. He wore a Burberry raincoat and Irish tweed hat, and beside him stood a plain Samsonite suitcase. An instrument about the size of a small briefcase hung from a strap over his left shoulder. It glowed with faint lights from dials on its face.

The man waved. "Hello, Captain," he said.

It was Les.

✢ ✢ ✢

"He is but a man," Tylara whispered.

"Yes. He is the human pilot who brought us to Tran."

"You know him—then he is—"

"Yes. The father of Gwen's child. Tylara, do nothing. Say nothing, except to be polite. I don't know why he's here—but that box he's carrying can talk to the ship, and that ship could destroy this whole world."

"But if the box were destroyed?"

"Then those in the ship would do whatever they wish."

"I see." She released her grip on his arm and fell silent.

"Sergeant Elliot!" Rick shouted.

"Sir!"

"Clear the hill. Move everyone out, then come back for me."

"Sir."

"Sorry about the housekeeping," Rick said. He moved toward Les. "Welcome to Tran."

The pilot nodded. "It appears that you have come up in the world since last we met."

Cold, Rick thought. Cold and haughty, as if he is master here. I suppose he is. "Let me introduce you to my wife. Tylara do Tamaerthon. Countess of Chelm and Justiciar of Drantos." He used English and spoke rapidly despite Tylara's frowns.

"Making you what?" Les demanded.

"Eqeta—that's count—"

"I know the title."

"Eqeta of Chelm, and Captain-General of Drantos." No need to tell him about Tamaerthon at all. Or the Roman alliance. Let him find out for himself—or not find out, which would be better.

"Ah. But I forget my manners." The pilot turned to Tylara and extended his hand. After a moment she gave him hers, and he bowed and kissed her fingers. "I am honored to meet you, Lady Tylara," he said. His accent was not good, but the language was recognizably Tran local.

Usually Tylara was as resistant to male charms as a suit of armor, but she smiled warmly and thanked the starman. An act, Rick wondered? Or was she really impressed? Les was certainly handsome enough, and trying to be charming, but still—"How long will you be with us?" Rick asked.

"That depends," Les said. "I've come for my wife. Gwen must have told you I would come."

"She wasn't always sure she believed you," Rick said.

"Ah. Yeah, she had a right to her doubts," Les said. "That's over now. Where is she?"

"She didn't tell you?"

Les eyed Rick thoughtfully in the dim light. "So she told you she has a transceiver," he said. "And you want me to believe she's alive and it's working."

"She's all right, and the transceiver works to the best I know," Rick said. "I take it Gwen didn't answer you, then."

"No. Now where is she?"

"That sounds very much like a demand."

Les shrugged. "Take it any way you—no. Eqeta Galloway, I would count it a very great favor if you would conduct me to my wife."

"A couple of questions, first," Rick said. "As for example—do your employers know you're here?"

Les looked startled, then laughed. "I take it you mean, did I jump ship? No. My landing is—authorized, and the time I will stay on Tran is up to me."

And I can believe as much of that as I want to, Rick thought. But there's no point in standing here on a hilltop. "Welcome to Chelm. I trust you will do us the honor of being our guest."

"Thank you. But now that I've answered your question—where is my wife?"

Persistent chap, Rick thought. And maybe not quite as cool as he wants us to think—

"The Lady Gwen is well," Tylara said. "And your son is safe and well and under our protection."

The light was too dim for Rick to be certain, but he thought the pilot's face showed joy. His voice, though, remained unchanged. "My son. What did Gwen choose to name him?"

"Les," Tylara said.

Les turned to Tylara, but before he could say anything, she said. "The Lady Gwen is married to Lord Caradoc do Tamaerthon, a knight in my service. He is one of our most trusted captains, and my husband and I are very much in his debt."

"Married," Les said.

"Last autumn," Tylara said. "She believed that you were dead or had forsaken her."

"Well, I'm not, and I didn't," Les said. "And now I'd like to see her. If you please." His voice grew more stern. "Do you think I'd have come back to this—to Tran—for any other reason?"

Tylara shrugged. "I do not know the duties of those who serve the—Shalnuksis."

"So. You've told her everything," Les said.

"Shouldn't I?" Rick asked.

"I don't know." Les shrugged.

✣ ✣ ✣

"It's walk, ride, or wait all night until I can send for a sedan chair," Rick said.

Les laughed. "I'll ride, if the horse is tame."

"It's a mule," Rick said. "More surefooted for this mountain trail.

And it's certainly gentle enough. All right, Sergeant Major. Lead the way. Sergeant Frick will bring up the rear. And spread right out, gentlemen."

"Yes, sir," Elliot said. He rode on ahead, and Frick dropped back, so that Rick, Tylara, and Les rode alone.

"You have them well trained," Les said.

That didn't seem worth answering, and Rick said nothing. The trail was steep and frightening if you didn't trust the mules; the trick was to let the animals pick their own way and pace. Les seemed to be doing that.

They reached the bottom, and the trail widened. "All right," Les said. "Where is Gwen? And this—Caradoc."

"Lady Gwen is—in another part of the country," Rick said.

"And Lord Caradoc is a soldier," Tylara continued. "He is with the army in the west."

"Hah. Good battle, that," Les said.

"You watched?" Tylara asked. "But—" She fell silent.

"Saw some of it," Les said. "So. That's fortunate. Lord Caradoc is off to war, and Gwen is home alone. Good. If he stays out of my way, I won't go looking for him. No trouble at all, that way."

"He is her husband by Tran law," Rick said. And that sounds foolish.

"And I'm her husband by Earth law," Les said. "Does he have more right than me?"

You don't have any rights at all, Rick thought. You certainly didn't marry her. But it will be better to pretend.

"The case must be heard by the priests of Yatar," Tylara said. "Do you not understand? The Lord Caradoc is our captain. A knight sworn to our service—"

"And under our protection," Rick said reluctantly. Christ, this is going to be rough.

"I have no wish to shame the man," Les said. His words came slowly, as if forced. "Nor—nor do I bear him ill will."

The hell you don't, Rick thought.

"I do not wish to be disrespectful of your law," Les continued. "But I *will* see my wife."

"She is far from here," Tylara said. "The roads are poor, bandits are numerous, and our army has been sent against the Westmen. It will be no easy journey, and we would do the Lady Gwen an ill service to send you without proper escort—"

Les laughed, a short sharp sound. "An escort won't be needed," he said. "Tell me where to go, and I can call the ship."

35

There were only the three of them at Rick's conference table. Tylara sat at his right, and Sergeant Elliot on his left, leaving the long table nearly empty.

Like to have more, Rick thought. But who? Art. Larry Warner. Maybe one of them could think of something—

"If you're going to let her know, you'd best get the message out now," Elliot said.

Rick nodded. The semaphore line to the University wasn't finished. Messages had to go part way on horseback, and even with relay stations spaced Pony Express-style that took time. "I think we won't," he said. "What could I put in a message, even a coded one?"

Elliot gave him a significant look. So did Tylara.

Yeah, Rick thought: "Keep your pants on." I can just see me sending her *that* message. Hah.

"You learn anything from him?" Elliot asked.

"Not much we don't know," Rick said. "The council or whatever it is that governs the Confederation is still divided over what to do about Earth, and doesn't seem to know about Tran. Which means the *Shalnuksis* have a free hand, but we don't have to worry about the council sending the galactic navy. Not just yet, anyway."

He took Tylara's hand for a moment. She gave an answering half smile. He'd spent three hours trying to explain what he knew about the millennia-old Galactic Confederation and its human Janissaries, but she still didn't understand. That's all right, Rick thought. I don't either. And what the hell, Tylara has more experience unravelling plots than I do. Maybe she can understand a confederacy of a dozen or more star-faring races. According to Les, they haven't changed in five thousand years, mostly because of human slave soldiers.

It sounds nutty. It would sound nuttier if I didn't know the Turks used slave soldiers and administrators to run their empire. They called them Janissaries, and their empire stayed together for centuries.

"What about that Agzaral guy?" Elliot asked. "Is he on our side?"

"Don't know. Les won't say much about him. One thing's sure, he's playing a deep game," Rick said. "*He* knows about Tran, but his bosses don't. Yet he's a cop. Or something like a cop, anyway." Rick shrugged. "I don't even know how much Les knows. Maybe he'll tell us more."

"Yeah, if he lives long enough," Elliot said. "Christ, Cap'n, why'd it have to be *Caradoc* he's gonna put horns on? Nobody else is near that popular with the army. Even the mercs like him."

Tylara frowned. "Is it so certain that Lord Caradoc will be dishonored? Why do you think so ill of the Lady Gwen? Surely she knows what must be."

How do I answer that? Rick wondered. No way to tell her how I *know*. "Girls on Earth do not think as the women on Tran do. Les was her first love, and he will be insistent. Yet, you may be right. It may be that Lady Gwen will refuse his advances, at least until the case can be heard by a court."

"Fat bloody chance," Elliot muttered.

"You have knowledge?" Tylara asked.

"Some," Elliot said. "Look, I don't want to tell tales, but before she married Caradoc—"

"Yeah?" Rick demanded.

"Well, one night I heard shots from her room," Elliot said. "I came in to find Gwen breathing hard, Larry Warner with his hideout pistol, and Caradoc waving a bloody big knife. They straightened it all out, but—"

"But she is not a chaste woman," Tylara said.

"It's not that simple," Rick protested. "Different cultures, different—"

"I am more concerned with consequences," Tylara said coldly. "If the Lady Gwen cannot use proper judgement, then we must save her from her folly. And save the University, which is such a great part of what our children will inherit."

Damn all Tran dynasts, Rick thought. *But she's right.*

"My love, we both know Caradoc. He has always been quick to defend the right. Not his right alone. Ours as well. But my lord husband, my love, even now the Tamaerthan troops are returning. Caradoc will soon be here, and if he is wronged, if his wife has dishonored him, he must *act*! He will challenge Les."

"He'd probably lose," Elliot said. "I don't know what Les carries, but it's sure to be as effective as our pistols. Remember Art Masons' story? The walls of the ship shot him when he threatened one of the *Shalnuksis*."

"And Les and the others are human warriors," Rick finished. "Janissaries for the Galactic Confederacy." He laughed. "I don't want to believe that."

"Evidence is pretty convincing," Elliot said.

"Didn't say I *don't* believe it," Rick said.

Elliot laughed.

Tylara waited until there was silence. "It matters little whether Lord Caradoc wins or loses. He will insist upon his rights in this matter. He will insist that we come to his aid, or avenge him if he is killed."

"Army'll be on his side," Elliot said. "Hell, Cap'n, suppose Les kills Caradoc. You know damn well what you'd have to do."

"Yes." *Kill Les. Or be a lord who's broken faith with his followers. My name will stink from the Westscarp to Rome. Caradoc's relatives will want my blood—Padraic! My own bodyguard.*

"Do you see difficulties I do not?" Tylara asked. "We are two. We both have pistols. Les is only one. I saw no weapon upon him, but suppose he has? He can be killed. At this moment he is guest under our roof, but that need not be forever. *We* swore no permanent oath to him."

"You don't know what you're saying! You can't know what his ship will do," Rick said.

"There is no one in it," Tylara said. "I asked him. It could be a lie, but I do not think it was."

"Nor do I," Rick said.

"Then he controls the ship with that box. When we have killed him, we will take the box and use it," Tylara said.

"Won't work," Rick said. "There are—codes. One is obvious—he will not use English to speak with the ship. And smashing the box won't work, since we don't know what orders he gave the ship before he sent it up. He had plenty of time, after all."

"But what can a ship do?" Tylara demanded. "A ship with no master?"

"A lot," Rick said. "First, it will report to the next ship that comes. God knows what it'll tell them, but it can watch everything we do. It'll sit up there in the sky and watch us, and take pictures, and when the *Shalnuksis* come it'll tell them everything."

"And then comes *skyfire*," Tylara said thoughtfully.

"Unless we can work with Les to prevent it," Rick said. "One thing's sure. We won't learn anything from anybody else. Les is the *only* chance we have to talk the *Shalnuksis* out of bombing this place back to the Stone Age. Why would he try, except for Gwen? Yet, with his help, what we have built, the knowledge we will leave our children, might withstand even *skyfire*. The *Shalnuksis* might be induced to bomb the wrong places. But that's only if Les helps."

"And yet, all know what a debt we owe to Caradoc," Tylara said. "His honor is ours. You speak of what we will give our children. Do you wish to give them an inheritance of dishonor?"

Yatar, Jehovah, Christ, somebody, tell me how to answer that. Please.

Tylara sighed. "You have no answer. Nor have I. It seems that now we are both called upon to do more than we can do. Lord Elliot, have you advice?"

"No, Lady," Elliot said. "We need Caradoc, and we need Les. But it looks like one's going to kill the other, no matter what. Hell, it wouldn't settle anything if Gwen dropped dead! She's the only thing Les cares about—"

"There is his child," Tylara said thoughtfully. "If the lady Gwen were dead, there could be no quarrel—"

"Seems to me a man would be more likely to work for his wife than for a kid he's never seen," Elliot said.

"And we need Gwen if we're going to have a University," Rick said. "You are certain?"

"Yes, I'm certain, dammit! And do you think I owe Gwen any less than we owe Caradoc?"

"I see." Tylara sighed once more, than stood. "I will not swear to lay no hand on Les forever," she said. "But I will swear to let him take us safely to the University, and stand apart from his first meeting with the Lady Gwen." She gave a shaky smile. "I think if I did not swear this much, you would guard Les night and day with your *Colt* in your hand. Even against me."

No answer to that, either. "That's a good start." And—Gwen didn't get any messages from Les. Meaning what? Maybe her transceiver's busted, but maybe she isn't listening. Maybe she's in one of her moods—"He done me wrong and then run off and left me." When she's like that, she wants his *cojones* on a spear, and if she stays that way long enough for Caradoc to come back and make her realize that she's got to be sensible . . .

Maybe. It's a slim chance.

But everything else looks like no chance at all.

✢ ✢ ✢

This time the ship tilted slightly as it landed on a patch of softer ground. The whining sound grew louder and increased in pitch, and Les frantically manipulated dials on the box he carried. The ship righted itself.

Les inspected it critically, then seemed satisfied. "Okay, wait there," he said. Then he seemed to catch himself. He turned to Tylara. "With your permission, my lady, I'll go open a hatch."

He disappeared around the stern.

Tylara glanced at Rick, then stared at the ship. They stood together in the field, with only the Firestealer to give light. Tylara's lips were set in a grim line.

She's scared of *skyfire*, Rick thought. Well, so am I. The interesting part is that Les is nervous. These ships must be vulnerable. Not likely I'll learn how. Not likely the troops will see anything. But they might—

He had every merc with binoculars stationed around possible landing sites, and he'd been lucky. Elliot was out there watching this one.

After about ten minutes a hatch opened just in front of Rick and Tylara. A wide gangway lowered itself.

"Welcome aboard," the ship's voice said. It didn't sound anything like Les.

Tylara took Rick's hand. "Shall we go, my husband?"

He nodded, then grabbed her to kiss her. As he broke away he whispered, "Remember. Not only Les will hear everything we say while we are in that ship. Other—"

She smiled and nodded, and Rick wondered if she believed him. After all, she'd never seen a recording device, and describing one wasn't the same as showing it—

Nothing he could do about that.

They went inside. The compartment was nearly bare. Rick looked closely. There were stains on the deck in one corner. This was the same ship that had brought them to Tran, no doubt about that.

In one corner of the compartment there were two piles of Japanese *futons*. On top of one of the piles was a package wrapped in brightly printed paper and tied with a scarlet bow. Tylara stared at it. The paper was printed with replicas of famous miniature portraits.

"It is lovely," she said. "I have not seen—"

"Ah, my lady, it is a gift for you." This time Les used his own voice, rather than the impersonal computer-generated one he'd used earlier. "Now, please be seated—"

Rick pushed the two piles of *futons* together and flopped into one of them. Tylara gingerly sat beside him. She clutched the package tightly.

"Will you not open it?" Les asked.

"I—it is so beautiful—"

"Let me, sweetheart," Rick said. He took the package and carefully worked the bow so that it came off without damaging it. Tylara took it and held it experimentally to her hair. The ends of the package were sealed with Scotch tape. Rick took out his pocket knife and slit the tape so that he could remove the printed paper without tearing it. Tylara watched nervously.

"I should have brought more wrapping paper," Les said. "I think I have some picture books. You can have those."

"Thank you," Tylara said. She sounded sincere.

The box contained a bracelet and necklace of Navajo turquoise and silver, elaborately gaudy. Tylara gasped with pleasure. "Marvelous!" she exclaimed. She put on the bracelet and admired it on her arm. "There is nothing like it in all of Tamaerthon. Or Drantos."

That's for sure, Rick thought. But of course she'd like it.

They settled onto the *futons*. "Thank you," Tylara said.

A screen in the forward part of the compartment suddenly came to life. It showed Les in his command chair on the ship's semi-darkened bridge. "There's something for you, too, Colonel," Les said. "Under your cushions there—"

Rick felt under the pile and found a wooden box, not wrapped. Inside was a bottle of Talisker Scotch and four crystal glasses packed in Styrofoam worms. There was also a bottle of Campari.

"Have a drink with me?" Les asked. "Sorry I can't invite you up to the bridge. 'Thees starship ees going to Havana, Señor,' with those mini-grenades to make the point—well, the idea doesn't quite appeal to me."

"I don't suppose it would," Rick said. He tried to keep his voice calm. The grenades in his pockets suddenly seemed five times their size and weight.

"My lady might prefer Campari," Les said.

"Fat chance," Rick muttered. "She's had Scotch." He opened the Talisker and poured for himself and Tylara.

Les turned to the screen and lifted his own glass. "Cheers, then," he said.

"Cheers," Rick said. Tylara muttered something. They both drank.

Tylara grimaced slightly at the taste. Rick frowned a question at her.

"I recall the previous time," she said. "I was pleased with your strong—*whisky*. But—"

But you'd just been raped by Sarakos, Rick thought. And this reminds you. Yeah. I should have insisted you have Campari.

"Ready?" Les asked.

"Yes," Rick said.

A moment later they were pressed into the *futons*. The screen blurred, then showed the ground falling away. Tylara gasped and moved closer to him. The ship rose, and then they were high enough to see Castle Armagh with its blaze of bonfires. She shivered slightly.

"You ain't seen nothin' yet," Rick whispered. "We're no higher than—than the highest mountains." He'd almost mentioned Larry Warner and the balloon, but there was no point in telling the ship's recorders about *that*.

The ship began to move, and Armagh slipped off the edge of the screen. The Firestealer gave enough light to recognize the major terrain features. They were going west, following the main road to Castle Dravan.

Coincidence or design? Rick wondered. After all, when they first came to Tran they'd been set down not far from Dravan, and this was the main road west . . .

Tylara pointed and looked afraid. "The children," she whispered.

Yeah. Our kids are down there—He pointed and nodded. "Yes, I think you're right, that's where we established the orphanages," he said. "Not too far from where the ship first set us down. Les, are we sightseeing?"

"Maybe a little," Les said. "Do you mind?"

"Not at all. Except if you go much farther west I'd appreciate it if the ship isn't seen. Our army's out there somewhere. They just won a big battle with Westmen—those are nomads from the high plains above the big escarpment. The Westmen already think there was too much wizardry for it to have been a fair fight."

"So if they see the ship, they might think it's impossible to make an honorable peace, so they may as well die fighting?"

"Something like that, yeah."

"No problem," Les said.

The lights below shrank rapidly, and now there were clouds below them. After a few moments the screen changed, zooming in on the plains below. They passed the Littlescarp, and the scene on the screen changed rapidly, as if the camera were searching the high plains. Then it stabilized on camp fires, and zoomed in again.

Tylara stirred. "That is the host of Drantos," she said wonderingly. There was terror in her eyes. She started to speak, but Rick pulled her to him and kissed her.

She looked startled for a moment, then nodded understanding.

I know, my darling, Rick thought. There is our army, the most powerful force you've ever seen, down there below like toy soldiers, down there where it would be like child's play to throw *skyfire* at them. But don't say it, don't even think it too loud—

"How does Yatar rule those with such power?" she asked softly. "Or—*does* Yatar rule the sky-folk?"

Rick shook his head. "I don't know," he said softly. Not even if you translate the question into modern theology. Is there a God? Is there any reason for ethics? Does the universe care one lick whether people are decent or beastly to one another?

"He rules your heart, my love," Tylara whispered. "And that is enough for me."

The screen brightened, then changed to a map of the eastern part of the settled region of Tran. At least *this* settled region, Rick told himself. He'd never learned just how far west this continent was inhabited, or whether the other continent was inhabited at all.

The map stretched from Rome to the Westscarp, and as Rick watched, a numbered grid superimposed itself. "If you wouldn't mind," Les said. "It would be well to get on with our cargo collection."

That would be for the recorders. There'd be damned little cargo at the University, but Rick thought Les must have a way to deal with that. More interesting was how he carefully didn't mention Gwen in the hearing of the ship . . .

✤ ✤ ✤

The ship settled into the hills above the University. Les sent Rick and Tylara out, then joined them a few moments later. He was carrying his suitcase and the control box. The ship whined and rose into the dawning sky.

"Well, here we are," Les said. "What's down there?"

"My University," Rick said. "Gwen is the Rector."

Les whistled in exaggerated respect. "OH-ho. Well, we'd best get on with it. Looks like a long walk. Should have set the ship down closer."

Tylara chuckled. "Captain," she said, "one might almost doubt your love for the Lady Gwen. You complain of a few stadia we must walk. What of the tales of lovers who would swim boiling seas or walk ten thousand leagues to join their ladies?"

There was a pause long enough to worry Rick. Then Les laughed. "They may have had more difficult journeys," he said. "But none of them ever had a longer one."

36

The messenger from the Roman pickets brought word to Gwen Tremaine just as the True Sun rose. A skyship had been seen.

She put on a robe and covered her hair with a snood, and went to her office before she had tea.

"It was as you ordered, Lady," the decurion said. "We watched the hills, and we saw it descending, not so bright as a star. I have never seen its like before."

"Few have," Gwen said.

"The cohort now searches those hills for any gifts the skyfolk may have left. If we find any, we will bring them to the University. Have you more orders, Lady?"

"No. Thank you, Decurion." She opened a desk drawer and took out a bag of coins, and shook several into her hand. "Buy wine for your unit, and say they have done well."

"Thank you, Lady."

As the Roman left, Marva brought tea and biscuits.

"Join me," Gwen said. She indicated a chair. Marva sat and poured the tea.

"It is good news, Lady Gwen?"

"I don't know, Lady Marva. I truly don't know."

This is my life, Gwen thought. To be in this office, to govern this University. To teach these people, and watch as their lives improve. It is my life. She twisted her fingers together. This must endure. I've got to do something. Did it really land? And who?

549

Suddenly she stood, gulped her tea, and ran to her apartment on the floor below. *What should I wear? There's nothing here—*

By mid-morning she'd turned her closets into chaos, and brought both Marva and herself to tears.

Get hold of yourself, girl! Suppose it is *Les. Do you want him to see you like this? Send Marva for a stiff drink. Two, she deserves one for herself. And put on your regular working gown. It's the best you have except for the blue one Larry gave you, and that's too formal for daytime—*

And the children! If it's Les he'll want to see his son.

And if it's a Shalnuksi *executioner?*

It can't be—"Lady Marva?"

"Yes, my lady?"

"Have Nurse take the children to the Roman fortress. She's to keep them there until I send for them. You go with them."

"Is there—do you fear the sky-folk?" Marva asked. "But will they not be like—the others we have known?"

"I don't know," Gwen said. "And I'm afraid—"

"I will see to the children," Marva said. "Then I will return."

"No! Stay at the fortress—"

"My lady, not even the fortress will prevent us from *skyfire*. My husband told me that many times. But I can ask the commandant to send the children beyond the hills—"

"No, that's silly," Gwen said. "There will be no *skyfire*. All the same—do have Nurse take the children to the fortress."

✢ ✢ ✢

There was a knock at her office door.

"Come," she called.

Larry Warner came in. "First time ever," he said. "Nobody in your outer office. Why?"

"I sent—"

"Never mind. I know," Warner said. "The Romans sent word. They're on their way in now."

"Who?"

"Cap'n Galloway, Lady Tylara, and a starman."

"A star—*man*?"

"Yeah. All human. I described the *Shalnuksis* to the centurion, and he said it surely wasn't one of them."

"Larry, you shouldn't have described—"

"Oh, shove the secrecy up sideways! It's their planet, they have a right to know what's threatening it!" He gripped his hair with both hands.

"You'll be as bald as Telly Savalas if you go on doing that," she said. She giggled despite herself.

"Good to see you laugh," Warner said. "Now you keep your head and let me worry about mine." He drew his binoculars from beneath his professorial gown. "They ought to be just about at the town gates," he said. "Should be able to see 'em from your balcony there in a minute. Gwen—it's probably Les."

"I know."

"What'll you do?"

"That's what I don't know." She eyed him warily. "Are you about to give me advice?"

"No, ma'am." He winked at her. "You have to play this hand yourself, and I don't need to say it's important. Naw, all I was going to say is if you need somebody to watch your back, I'm available. I won't draw on the Captain for you, but short of that—"

"Larry, that's sweet of you."

He laughed. "Now that's just what a tough merc turned professor wants to be told," he said. "Sweet, for God's sake!"

✢ ✢ ✢

She'd sent Larry away, and was alone on her balcony as the party rode in: a dozen Romans, Rick and Tylara, and a third who sat his horse like a sack of potatoes.

He can't do everything.

He can blow your University right off the map.

They dismounted and entered the building. She went back into her office and stood near the desk. What can I say? What do I want to say? Why—

Too late for thought. There were sounds outside, then her door opened.

He came in alone. Over his arm he was carrying—

"Oh, no!"

She'd imagined this meeting for two years. She'd thought of being haughty. Imperious. Sexy and seductive, at least as much so as she could be. Tearful. Scornful. Cool, the University Rector.

She'd never imagined that she'd collapse in laughter. She threw back her head and roared, and had to lean against the desk for support.

He held his smile until she was finished. "Well, you *did* ask if I would buy you a grass skirt," he said. "So I got you the best I could find." Then his control gave way, and he began to laugh, and she joined him, and they kept each other howling. Whenever one would slow down, the other would point to the skirt and they began again, and . . .

And then he was close to her. She wasn't sure what happened next. She didn't think she'd moved toward him, but there she was, and his arms went round her, and their lips met.

"Les—"

He didn't answer. He didn't need to. He held her in an iron grip, but there were tears in his eyes, and suddenly everything was the way she'd dreamed it might be, back when she had good dreams.

The grass skirt fell to the floor.

✢ ✢ ✢

Rick's apartment was on the top floor of the University guest house, and the window looked out across the quadrangle to the town beyond.

In the traditional manner of Roman soldiers, the University cohorts spent much of their time building. The Roman camp was surrounded by coal-fired baths. A line of stone buildings was springing up next to it, while on the campus itself the Roman engineers had laid chalk lines to mark a new quadrangle.

The University was growing, but the sight could not cheer Rick. The axe would fall, and all too soon.

Meanwhile, he had a kingdom to administer. He hefted a stack of reports the Roman clerks had brought in. They had arrived by the Express Post that morning.

The most interesting was Art Mason's report.

"The Westmen are moving north as agreed. It won't be long before they're out of our territory altogether, and the only question will be whether they take on Margilos or the Five Kingdoms."

Tylara read over Rick's shoulder. She laughed haughtily. "If the Westmen attack Margilos, there will be fewer Westmen to reach the Five Kingdoms. They are as mad as the Westmen, those warriors of Margilos. And I think the Westmen know this."

"Good enough," Rick said. "So they'll go past Margilos and on into the Five. That ought to keep the High Rexja busy for long enough to get this Roman alliance firmed up. Once Ganton marries Octavia—"

"Um-hummm," Tylara said. "Did you arrange for the Romans to hail our Wanax as Imperator?"

"No, ma'am, he got that one on his own."

"You surprise me. True, I had not thought to arrange it, but when I heard, I believed you had. Perhaps Yatar does watch over us more thoroughly than we know."

Rick turned back to Mason's letter and read aloud. "Wanax Ganton proposes Ben Murphy as bheroman at Westrook. The Bheroman Harkon left a six-year-old kid, but Honeypie has just about adopted the kid, and she and Murph will be married as soon as he gets your consent, which I'd advise you to give. I think Murph can do a good job of holding the plains here. He likes it."

Murphy's first home, Rick thought. A long way from Belfast . . .

"A lot of the smallholders were killed by Westmen," the letter continued. "Some of the landless Tamaerthan troops like the weather up here, and they've petitioned to take over the ownerless farms. Murphy wants to let them do it, and it looks like a good deal to me, but of course it's part of Lady Tylara's county. If she approves, we can get started fast." Rick looked up at Tylara. "Well?"

"I consent," she said. "Should I not?"

"No. It's a good plan. Here's to Bheroman Murphy." He read the rest of Mason's report. "There is no longer a threat from the Westmen. Wanax Ganton has decided that his bheromen are able to escort them with Roman help, so we are returning to Dravan. The Tamaerthans who aren't staying up here want to get home, so Caradoc has taken them on ahead. You can use the semaphore to Dravan if you have other orders for them."

"They will not be long in Dravan," Tylara said. "Caradoc will not wait for orders. He will bring the Tamaerthan troops home—here! He will come here unless he is told not to come. And what reason could we give?"

"I don't know." Rick opened another pouch and took out still more reports. "Here's one for you," he said absently.

Tylara didn't answer. Rick looked up from his work. She was standing at the window. "He will learn soon enough," she said. She stared gloomily down at the campus and town. "He will learn, and this will all be destroyed."

"Perhaps not," Rick said. "Look, Les agreed to stay in the guest house. If Caradoc doesn't actually go looking for witnesses—"

"My husband, my love, you are not such a fool," Tylara said. "Caradoc's clansmen will learn. How could they not? Last night they visited the baths together. They were alone inside for time enough to grow three pair of antlers on Caradoc's forehead. You have sealed the town gates, and closed the semaphore, but it will do no good. He will learn."

"But what can I do?" Rick demanded.

"I do not know." Tylara sighed. "We need a miracle. Perhaps Yatar will send one." She stood a few moments longer at the window. Her hands were balled into fists. She drummed them against the window ledge. Then she came back to the desk, suddenly calm again. "Meanwhile, I must send a message to Dravan, and the semaphore office will not accept it without your approval." There was a brittle edge to her voice.

"Sweetheart, I didn't mean the restrictions to apply to *you*," Rick said.

She held her hard look for a moment, then smiled. "I know, my love. You have much to concern you. Still, I must see to our house, and quickly, so may I trouble you to put that in writing?"

"Sure." He sat at the desk and scribbled out an authorization. "I was hoping to keep anyone from telling Caradoc," he said. "Stupid, of course. But it does put off the evil day. And maybe the horse will learn to sing."

"Horse?"

"Old story," Rick said. "Very old. A thief was about to be executed. They did that in a particularly painful way in old Persia. Before they took him away, he told the Wanax that he could teach the Wanax's favorite horse to sing hymns, if the Wanax would give him a year.

"The Wanax took him up on it, and pretty soon, there was the thief down in the stables every day, grooming the horse and singing to it. His buddies told him he was crazy.

"'That may be,' the thief said. 'But I have a year, and who knows what will happen in that time? The king might die. The horse might die. I might die. And who knows, maybe the horse will learn to sing . . .'"

Tylara giggled, then nodded more soberly. "Yes. Time is always valuable," she said. "But I fear that time alone will not save us."

"So do I," Rick said. "But I don't know what else to do."

"You will do what you must," Tylara said. "That I have known all my life, and learned again from you. We do as we must."

✦ ✦ ✦

The four sat at Gwen's conference table: Rick and Tylara, Gwen and Les.

"It's just possible," Les said. He whistled, a long falling note. "Weee-ew. You're sure going for broke. Steel mills. Coke ovens. Printing presses. A full University. If the *Shalnuksis* find out—Rick, I don't know what they'll do if they find out."

"But you can help us hide all this," Gwen said.

"I can try," Les said. "And as I said, it's just possible, as long as Inspector Agzaral doesn't change sides, and he doesn't look like he's going to. Yeah, we've got a chance—"

"We," Gwen said. "You meant that, didn't you?"

"Yes, ma'am," Les said.

And that's clear enough, Rick thought. He's on our side as long as we're on his. And meanwhile Caradoc's coming back with the army.

He looked across the table to Tylara. She sat stiffly alert, cold, almost indifferent. Yet she was polite to Gwen when she spoke to her, and even encouraged Les to believe his attempts to be charming had succeeded.

Just what the hell game is she playing? Rick wondered. And what good does it do me to worry about it . . .

There were shouts outside, and they all rushed to the penthouse balcony. Far across town there was a pillar of black smoke. "Have the Romans organized fire departments?" Rick asked.

"Sure," Gwen said. "But they won't be needed there. That's the chimney in the coke oven. It catches fire every ten-day."

The office door opened, and Marva came in. "I do not wish to disturb you, my lady, but there is a message from the semaphore. It is marked urgent, and Lord Warner told me to bring it to Lord Rick immediately."

"Thank you," Rick said. He took the message paper. Tylara stood next to him and read as he did.

REGRET INFORM YOU LORD CARADOC DO
TAMAERTHON KILLED IN STREET RIOTS ONE MARCH
FROM DRAVAN. COURT OF INQUIRY HELD BY WANAX
RULES ACCIDENTAL DEATH BY FALLING. I AGREE
WITH THIS VERDICT. WANAX HAS PROCLAIMED
THREE DAYS OF MOURNING AND WILL PERSONALLY
COMMAND FUNERAL GAMES. WANAX HAS GRANTED
LIFE PENSION AND TITLE TO CARADOC'S CHILD.
AWAIT FURTHER INSTRUCTIONS.
MASON.

Rick stared uncomprehendingly at the paper. He felt Tylara's hand
on his arm.

"What is it?" Gwen asked.

"Bad news," Rick said. As he said it he felt waves of relief wash over
him. He was ashamed of that. Yet—"Bad news," he said again. "Lord
Caradoc is dead."

"Dead?"

"Yes," Tylara answered. "Your husband, my lady. He died in our
service, and whatever honors the Wanax has not granted I will give
from my purse. Husband, come, and leave the Lady Rector to her
grief." She turned and marched from the room.

Gwen looked from Rick to Les. The pilot opened his arms, an
almost imperceptible gesture, and she moved toward him.

Rick carefully closed the door as he left the room. We're saved
again, he thought. For a while, at least. A good man has died, but that
accident has saved more than Caradoc alive ever could. We have Les,
and with his help the *Shalnuksis* won't destroy everything. Knowledge
will survive.

When he reached the quadrangle, they'd put out the fire in the
coke oven.

BOOK II
STORMS OF VICTORY

PART ONE
SEARCHING

1

"Turn out the guard! Corporal of the Guard, Post Number Twelve!"

Rick Galloway turned toward the window and frowned. Sounds of shouting and running men floated up from the cobblestoned courtyard six stories below. "What in hell?" Rick muttered. Then he shrugged. "Guess I'll find out if I need to know. Okay, Art, what's next?"

"Next you get your armor on. Flak jacket first, then the mail."

"Christ, Mason! I'll roast. Look, I don't have to wear this tonight."

Art Mason spoke slowly and carefully. "Colonel, why do we have to go through this every week? You're not leaving this room without armor, not without you sending me to the brig first. Look, we've got that nice Kevlar jacket Les brought you. Only thing like it on this planet. And don't ask me who's going to shoot you. You know damn well the little king has that Browning."

"Ganton wouldn't shoot me." Rick held out his arms and let Mason help him into the Kevlar vest, then the fine chain mail shirt that covered it.

"I grant you that, Colonel. But I can think of some in his court who'd be glad to borrow that pistol. With or without Royal permission." Mason tugged on the straps. "And I grant you that Wanax Ganton needs you. The problem is, he knows he needs you. Kings don't like that. Neither do teenagers. We got a teenaged king, and if you know what he's going to do, you're doing better than me."

There were more shouts from below. "Sergeant of the Guard! Post Number Twelve. Officer of the Guard! Post Number Twelve."

"That sounds serious," Rick said.

"Yeah, maybe I better have a look." Mason glanced at his watch. "Better not. Can't let the troops think I don't trust them. Follow procedures—"

"Yeah. Follow procedures." Rick laughed, then went to the table and poured two glasses of wine. The table was massive, carved from a wood that had never grown on Earth. The goblets were gold, hammered with scenes of men riding centaurs and hunting strange beasts. Rick handed one to Mason. "Here's to proper procedures."

"Yeah." Mason sipped at his wine, then frowned as Rick drank his in a gulp. "Colonel, you drink too damned much."

"You sound like my wife. Are you my wife?"

"No, sir."

"I could say it's none of your business."

"No sir, you couldn't," Mason said. "Very much my business. Anything happens to you, and I'm supposed to be in command. Only you know damned well it won't work that way. Sergeant Major Elliot will choose your successor, and it may or may not be me."

"Well, nothing's going to happen to me tonight," Rick said. He poured another goblet of wine and sipped at it. "We were drinking to proper procedures. Ever think where we'd be if we'd followed procedures? What the hell *is* the procedure for meeting a flying saucer?"

"Yeah. Well, we managed all right," Mason said. "Bloody good thing it came along."

"Yeah. I guess."

"Guess, hell, Colonel. We were goners, and you know that better'n me." Mason swept his hand in a wide gesture to indicate the stone walls, tapestries, fireplace, and primitive furnishings of the room. "This may not be all we ever wanted, but it's sure as hell more'n the Cubans would have given us."

"Yeah, I know, Art, but . . ." Rick let his voice trail off as he heard more shouts from outside. "Think we ought to look?"

"No, sir," Mason said. "Fact is, that's your biggest problem. Colonel, I grant you we'd have been finished a dozen times without you, and not much gets done except it's in your name—but that doesn't mean you got to do it all yourself. Procedures. Make policy, approve procedures, and then let somebody else do the work. You're going to wear yourself out if you keep on the way you're going."

Rick sat at the massive table and fingered a stack of documents. An ornate dagger served as a paperweight. "Think I wouldn't like to? Only how in hell can I make policy on stuff we've never done before? None of us have any experience handling primitives. And Romans. And barbarians. And—"

"Well, yes, sir, but—"

"And not even the locals have any experience living with a rogue star coming. Just legends." Rick tossed off his goblet of wine and poured another. "Policy! Procedures! The whole goddamn planet's going to hell, and all they've got is a bunch of legends. Legends and us. And we don't know what we're doing."

Mason shrugged. "Colonel, for somebody who don't know what he's doing, you've done damned well. You must be doing something right, even if I do think you work too hard and drink too much."

"I'll—"

There was a loud knock at the door.

"Yeah?" Mason called. He took out a .45 automatic and glanced at the loads before returning it to its holster. "Who's there?"

The voice belonged to Rick's orderly. "The Star Lord Les wishes to speak with the Marshal of Drantos."

Mason looked at Rick. Rick shrugged, then nodded. Mason went to the door, looked through the peephole, then opened it.

The man who entered was shorter than Rick, about Mason's height. He didn't look much different from the other two. A starman, Rick thought. A real one. Not a cheap imitation like me. So how should a starman look? God knows his bosses look weird enough.

"Hello, Les. Wine?" Rick offered.

"Hello. Yes, small glass—and, Major Mason, if you don't mind—"

"Let him stay. He's my deputy," Rick protested.

"It's all right, Colonel. I better go check out that commotion in the courtyard. I'll be back to walk you to your meeting."

"Don't bother. Jamiy and the guards can do that."

Mason nodded. It wasn't hard to read his expression. Since Tylara's man Caradoc had been killed in street riots, there weren't as many locals Rick could trust to guard his back. Come to that, a lot of other things had changed for the worse.

"I'd rather you found out what the problem is down there."

"Okay." Mason threw half a salute and left without waiting for Rick to return it.

Rick poured wine and handed it to Les. They sat at the table and Rick lifted his goblet. "Cheers."

"Cheers."

They sat in silence. Finally Les spoke. "I'll be leaving in a day or so."

"Back to Earth?"

"Yes."

"I don't suppose I can talk you into taking us with you."

Les shook his head. "No. You wouldn't want me to." He wasn't smiling.

"Try me."

"You wouldn't. What would you do? Go to the authorities? Tell them you were kidnapped by a flying saucer and taken across light-years to another planet just so you could grow drugs?"

"Well, that would have the great merit of being true—"

"And the serious demerit that no one would believe you," Les said. "It would be worse if someone did. Either way you'd irritate the High Commission, make a deadly enemy of Inspector Agzaral, and spend the rest of your life dodging us. No, my friend, you do not want to be returned to Earth."

"What if—suppose we promise to lay low? Never tell what happened to us?"

"No," Les said.

"Yeah, well I suppose you can't believe us—"

"Even if I did, I couldn't hide the fact that I took you back to Earth. I could probably hide it from the Commission, but not from Agzaral. I don't know what he'd do about it, but I don't want to find out." Les sipped at his wine. "There's another reason. You may be safer on Tran."

"What? Come off it! This planet is coming apart! It's going to be fried by a rogue sun, the ice caps melt, coasts under water, migrations sparking wars everywhere, and your *Shalnuksi* friends are probably going to bomb the survivors back to the Stone Age anyway—and you say—"

"I say it may be safer than Earth," Les repeated. "Things happen so fast. Atom bombs. Space travel. Big colliding beam accelerators.

Huge lasers. Leave things alone and pretty soon Earth will have real space travel. There are factions on the Commission that don't want that."

"And they'd really bomb Earth?"

"I don't know. They could."

"You said Earth is the breeding ground for—for wild humans."

"Wild. Not like me," Les agreed. "Not slaves."

"Slave soldiers. Janissaries."

"I'm not a soldier," Les said. "But yes, that's as good a description as any."

"And you run the whole damned empire—"

"It's not an empire."

"Confederation. But humans run it. You have all the military power, but you're still slaves. It doesn't make sense."

"Put that way, maybe not. But you don't have to make sense of it. Lay off, Rick. Just lay off."

"Lay off. Look, I have to know. Are they going to bomb Earth? Us? Both?"

Les shook his head. "Rick, I don't know. I don't understand Federation politics. Agzaral may know what's going on. He claims to. But he hasn't told me."

"You haven't told me much, either," Rick said.

"I know. Look at it my way. It's all the *Shalnuksis* need, to find out Tran natives are discussing Federation politics! They'd sure know who told you."

"How will they find out?"

"The next time one of their ships comes here they'll see changes. More water mills. Your semaphore towers. They just might pick up some locals for questioning. One of your mercs. You, even. They're pretty lazy. They probably won't. But they could."

"Do they own this planet, then?"

"It's complicated," Les said. "The Commission has rules about dealing with primitives, but they don't seem to apply to this place. Most records of Tran have been lost. I expect the *Shalnuksis* paid plenty to lose them. There are rules, my friend, but who'll enforce them?"

"Agzaral?"

"Maybe. If it's to his interest."

"What is his interest?"

Les shrugged and held his glass out to be refilled. "I do not know. He doesn't tell me."

"But—"

"But I do as he says anyway," Les said. His voice fell and he grew more serious. "Agzaral's all I've got. I think he's doing his best to look out for humans. All humans, everywhere, and especially Earth. Think, hell. I don't think it, I *know* it. He's doing his best. Whether that's good enough is another story, but he is trying."

"Okay. But about the *Shalnuksis*—"

"They don't exactly own the planet, but you better act like they do. And if Tran looks like it's about to spring an industrial and scientific revolution, the Commission has some hard choices to make. They'd have to set up permanent surveillance, with an inspector. Like Agzaral's operation on Earth's Moon. That could be expensive. There'll be some to argue that it's cheaper and simpler to blast Tran back to the Early Iron Age."

"Like they did before—"

"Like the *Shalnuksis* did before," Les corrected. "Two or three times before. But that was their own work. If the Commission orders it, the bombardment will be a lot more thorough."

"Will they do that?"

Les shook his head. "Insufficient data. The *Shalnuksis* don't have as much influence in the Commission as they used to have. That's the good side. And there's Agzaral's plan."

"Whatever that is—"

Les nodded firmly. "Whatever that is. Because it's about all we've got."

✢ ✢ ✢

By the light of the Demon Star the dead sentry looked uglier than the run of corpses. Lord Morrone knew that there was no such thing as a handsome corpse; for all that he had not seen his eleventh name-day he had been in enough battles to learn that. Even so, the sentry was an unwholesome sight, his face dark, tongue protruding, and his clothes fouled and stinking. *It's not his look, it's what this foretells.*

Morrone and his guardsmen whirled, hands to swords, at the sound of footsteps.

"Belay that."

The voice was soft, but there was no mistaking it. "Lord Mason.

Well come. I feared it was another." Well come indeed, Morrone thought. Now work your star magic and discover who has done this—

"Who found him?"

"Guardsman Echaino. An accident. He came into this passage to relieve himself, found the sentry where you see him, and summoned the guard."

"Did you leave the corpse, Echaino?"

"No, my lord."

"Touch anything?"

Echaino shuddered. "No, my lord."

"Good man." Mason knelt by the body and took its wrist in his hand. He moved the dead arm back and forth. "Not dead long," he muttered. He poked at the body for a moment and stood. "How many men have you got with you?"

Morrone's lips tightened. That tone of command was not the proper way to address a Companion to the Wanax Ganton. Morrone let it pass. He had seen enough of the starmen and their peremptory ways. Strangely effective ways. There might yet be a reckoning over the place of the starmen in Drantos, but this was not the time for it.

"Twelve guardsmen and three of my own men-at-arms. You have brought nine. I fear we shall need more, if we are to search the Outer Bailey without making each searching party too small to defend itself."

Mason nodded. "Right." He turned to one of his men. "Lugh, take a message to Lieutenant Brionn. The ready platoon is to turn out in full kit and report to Lord Morrone at Hestia's Fountain. Tell them to move quietly, and tell anyone who sees them that this is a drill."

"Sir!" Lugh clicked his heels and hurried off. Morrone knew that Brionn would obey, for all that he was the son of a knight and his orders came to him by the son of a carpenter. A year ago Mason might have had to go himself to bring the platoon, but much had changed in that year. For the better or for the worse?

It couldn't matter. The urgent need was for a thorough search. That wouldn't be easy. Edron was the royal seat of Drantos, but it had never been planned as such. What had begun as a fortress tower had grown into a full castle, then into a city. The Outer Bailey was no open courtyard with few buildings set against the walls, but part of the city of Edron itself, walled off by the Wanax Ganton's great-grandfather to provide more quarters for his men-at-arms, servants, and (so the tales ran) mistresses. Except for one broad street leading from the Outer Gate to the Great North Gate of the castle itself, the Outer Bailey was as much a warren as any part of the city outside the walls.

In war the defenders would fire this area and retreat behind the flames to the castle. That was hardly the answer here, though Morrone was tempted. "What plot is afoot?" he asked.

Mason chuckled. "Must be fifty of them, wouldn't you say, my lord?"

"True enough." The royal wedding of Wanax Ganton and the Roman Lady Octavia Caesar had drawn lords, senators, merchants, barons, knights, soldiers, and wealthy magnates from a dozen lands, half of them at war or nearly so with each other.

"We'll be until the True Sun rises searching this lot," Mason said. "Who's out here?"

Morrone shrugged. "Am I a clerk? Those of rank who could not find room inside. Lords, retainers. Clergy. Great ones. Any might be the target of a plot." Or be plotters themselves. "Wanax Ganton will not care to have his guests turned out on his last night unwed. Nor, I think, will Caesar care for the complaints of his senators."

"Yeah. It's a problem. Got any suggestions?"

Morrone looked up at the sky, but Yatar Dayfather did not appear with an answer to his dilemma. Only the baleful glare of the Demon Star—which did give enough light to make the searching easier, for all that its growing power over the nights on Tran meant that the Time was coming nearer. . . .

"I think it would be well if I turned out the rest of my men-at-arms who are fit for duty," Morrone said. "Also—do you know who is quartered in this house?"

"Am I a clerk?" Mason said, but he was laughing, and turned to one of his Guardsmen, who produced a paper.

It was a list. Morrone took a mild pleasure in seeing that even starmen did not tax their memories with details more fit for clerks and scribes than for warriors.

"Nobody seems to be assigned to it," Mason concluded. "But the one to the left is for Councilor Daettan of Dirstvaal, who's Ambassador from Lord Gengrich. The one to the right is for the Lady Gwen, Lord Warner, and the rest of the University people. The one across the street is for Fabricius Maximus Valens, Marselius Caesar's ambassador, but he hasn't arrived yet. Too bad about that; I'd have liked to have seen these bastards take on some legionaries."

"Do you doubt the valor of the men of Drantos?"

"Not at all. It's just that if a legionary had been killed, we could have found more reliable troops for the searching parties without having to spread the word of what happened."

"Indeed." Lord Mason sounded sincere and spoke good sense, and there was no helping the starmen's fondness for the Romans. The other Rome on the starmen's home world—once our ancestors' home world, the starmen say!—had passed down much wisdom to the starmen, particularly in matters of war and statecraft. It was still just as well that Publius Caesar, the heir of Rome, saw the starmen as a new kind of "barbarian" and openly distrusted them; if starmen and Romans made an alliance only the gods could help Drantos.

"Okay, let's get at it," Mason said. "You take charge here. Post some guards. Maybe they killed that sentry to keep him from seeing something. Make sure there's men enough to see anything the sentry would. Then search this place as best you can."

"And you?"

"I'll wait for the duty squad, then somebody's got to tell Lord Rick and the king. Want that job?"

"No. No, the arrangement is satisfactory. Armsman Garrakos, take three companions and torches to search this house. The rest of you, move to surround it." Morrone shuddered. "I like it not, this skulking about in the dark. It makes me feel like an assassin. There can be no honor in it."

"Now there's something we can agree on," Mason said. "But there's not much more in letting the Wanax's guests be slaughtered on the night before his wedding. Steady up, my lord. I'll be back when I can come."

Morrone sent off a messenger for his men. "Now, Garrakos. Let us go see what we find."

The autumn night was chilly even though the wind had died, but Morrone felt himself sweating under his mail and arming doublet as he had not since the Battle of the Hooey River. "I like it not," he muttered to himself. "An evil omen. I like it not."

✛ ✛ ✛

Art Mason unbuttoned the flap of his shoulder holster and wished that the nearest tobacco wasn't ten light-years away. There was a kind of aromatic grass that grew in the High Cumac, and some of the troopers made it into cigarettes; Mason had tried it once. The stuff was probably related to madweed. It gave a mild high, nothing like enough to compensate for the awful taste.

Morrone was trying hard not to fidget or look nervous, but you could tell he wasn't too happy over the prospect of somebody's hired goons screwing up his friend's wedding. A lot of people on this planet believed in omens. The sentry was bad enough. If some high muckety-muck did get offed—

"Happened on my watch," Mason muttered. Not that all crime was his responsibility, but this was no burglar caught in the act by the sentry. Thin cord around the man's neck, dagger in just the right place. A professional job. "Damn professional," Mason muttered. "Green Berets?"

It was worth thinking about. Most of the Earth troops here on this screwy planet had some training in the dirty tricks department, and some of them had been Green Beret before the CIA hired them off to go mucking about in Africa.

All our troops are accounted for, Mason thought. But there's a dozen off with Gengrich. Gengrich's ambassador in yonder house. Says no starmen with him. None I recognized. But one could have been smuggled in—

Or, what the hell, there's no shortage of local talent good enough to do that job.

Wish it hadn't happened on my watch.

"Watch ho!" someone called. Mason heard the Outer Gate guards respond. There were sounds of horses and centaurs.

"Who is there?"

Mason couldn't make out the words of response, but one of the voices sounded familiar. The gate opened, and a smaller number of horses and centaurs came through the wall into the Outer Bailey.

A small mounted party guided by two guardsmen with torches appeared at the gate end of the street. Five armored men, a couple of unarmored ones, and a banner-bearer carrying the red raven banner of the Bheroman of Westrook.

By God, Mason thought. Ben Murphy. Grown pretty big for a private. Of course I was only a corporal when we came here.

Ben Murphy had defended Castle Westrook and its lands after the Westmen rode down out of the High Plains. When the Westmen killed Lord Harkon and most of his knights, the king had created Murphy a real honest-to-Yatar Drantos nobleman, so that on the local scale of rank he was senior to everybody else from Earth except the captain himself. . . .

"Hello, Art. How are things?"

"I'll be damned!"

"I hope not." The lead rider reined in, dismounted, and came over to Mason. It was Ben Murphy all right—no mistaking that big Irish nose or the way he walked. But until you got up close and saw the shoulder holster with the .45 in it, you couldn't tell him from your standard Drantos ironhat.

"Like I said, Art, how are things?"

"Could be worse, could be worse. Everybody and their Aunt Ermentrude's come to town for the wedding, so if you're looking for a billet in the castle—"

"No way. My—Lord Harkon's son Jan's—grandmother wants to look me over, see if I'm the right sort to be raising her daughter's son. She's the Dowager Eqetassa of Rhuinas, so what she wants she gets, and what she's got is everybody I brought with me billeted in her townhouse. The men-at-arms are stacked up like cordwood in the stables, but at least we've got a roof over our heads. I was afraid we'd have to camp outside the walls, along with the Romans. Did Publius really bring a whole legion to the wedding?"

"Two cohorts, under our old friend Titus Frugi."

"Oho. Little Caesar can't be too happy about that."

"No." Titus Frugi had commanded forces loyal to the old emperor. Now he was loyal to Marselius Caesar. Not necessarily to Marselius' son Publius. "No, I don't expect he is. Belay that. How are you getting along?"

"Not too bad, all things considered. The Tamaerthan archers who've settled the vacant farms pretty much make up for the people the Westmen killed. None of them have turned bandit, either."

"Lady Tylara will be happy to hear that. And how's Honeypie—I mean, Lady Dirdre?"

"We're going to be married, soon as I get back from the king's wedding. He's already given permission, but I want to swear fealty to him for Westrook and get an update on the charter before we make it legal. That way Dirdre inherits with no trouble if something happens to me on the way home."

"Yeah. Say, Ben, how many men do you have with you—here and outside the gate?"

"Six here, ten more outside. Why?"

"I got a problem and maybe you can help me solve it. Somebody killed a sentry just a few minutes ago."

"Blood feud?"

"Looked more like a professional job. Somebody's up to something, and I've got the reserve platoon of guards on the way. But I'd like some more reliable men on hand before they get here. If you help, I think I can persuade the captain and the Wanax that they owe you one, like maybe letting you billet some of your people in the castle."

"Sounds all right. Who's in charge?"

Mason jerked his head in Morrone's direction. Murphy frowned, raised his eyebrows, and lowered his voice. "Does he know what he's doing?"

"Close enough. He's got more guts and charm than brains, but he's not one of the real hard-core ironhats."

"Jesus, I hope not. Most of them were out for a short beer when God passed out the brains."

"Sure. Which is how you got your job."

Murphy grinned.

"Anyway. Bring in your men, and I'll pick my escort and go bring the captain up to speed."

Murphy grinned. "Escort? Come on, Art. You getting nervous in the service? I thought everybody knew by now that tackling an armed starman just gave Graves Registration some business."

"Some people are slow learners, and I'm pretty sure our killer isn't alone. Besides, I'm a great noble now, Lord Mason, Marshal of the Household to the Captain General of the Realm, Major of Guards, Scrubber of the Official Chamberpot of Chelm, and Yatar knows what else. I have to swank around. Hell, Ben, you should know that sort of stuff better than I do."

"Maybe a little. Oh well, it sure beats being stuck on a hill in Africa, with Cubans all around and the only way out a friggin' flying saucer."

"Damned straight."

2

Rick's party entered the long corridor leading to the Council chamber. There was a low whistle, then another group came down the stairs to his left. Rick's guards advanced slightly. The leading guards of the other group fell in behind. This group moved down the corridor.

Rick waited. After a moment Tylara came in. Silently she fell in beside him. When she was exactly even with him, they followed the forward guards, while the others merged behind them.

"You are well, my husband?" Tylara said formally.

"I am well. And you?"

"Very well, thank you."

Are you well? Very well. What in God's name has happened to us? Rick wondered. How long has it been? Weeks. Months.

He could remember when the sight of her was enough to make his heart leap. God, she's beautiful, she's still beautiful, and I love her still, but we meet in corridors with guards and witnesses, we speak in formalities, we haven't been alone in weeks.

When? How did it happen?

After the last campaign. After Les came. After Caradoc was killed in a street riot. Could that be it? Was she in love with Caradoc? Her bodyguard, her captain, her rescuer? She knew him long before she knew me.

No! She had plenty of opportunities with Caradoc, before we met, after we met. She never showed that kind of interest in him. Or anyone else. We were in love, and now we are not in love, and I don't understand it.

"I understand the Wanax will not join us tonight," Tylara said.

"Eh? But the summons to Council—"

"Was withdrawn," Tylara said. "We meet with the Eqeta of the Riverland." She smiled at his puzzled look. "It is an ancient convention. No decisions can be taken if the Wanax is not present. Thus Wanax Ganton chooses to be represented by the Eqeta of the Riverland. Who is of course Ganton."

"Oh. Something of that sort was done on Earth. Perhaps it's as well. I don't know what to recommend anyway."

"Doubtless you will think of something," Tylara said.

And she says that as if she believes it. As if she still believes in me. But she won't sleep with me, won't even see me alone. Now we go in there, and Gwen will be there.

Gwen. Could that be it? Tylara always was afraid of Gwen Tremaine. Could she know about that one time—nonsense. No way. It happened long before—before she started acting funny. And no one knows, except Gwen, and she sure won't tell.

Jamiy, Rick's orderly and chief of guards, rapped on the Council room door. In response to the challenge from inside he answered, "The Lord Rick, Eqeta of Chelm, Captain General of the Host of Drantos, Lord of Star Lords."

Rick glanced at Tylara. She winked.

So she still has a sense of humor. And knows I do. So what in God's Name is wrong?

✦ ✦ ✦

Gwen Tremaine finished her presentation and waited while the young man at the head of the long table stared at the map on the whitewashed wall. Finally he spoke.

"Then is there no hope for us, or at least no more than there was before the starmen came? Have they in fact shed so much blood only to put us in greater peril of *skyfire* than we were before?"

Rick frowned. Who'd been talking to the king? Ganton had every damn reason in the world to be grateful to Rick Galloway and his troops, and why was he taking that tone? Rick was about to speak when Tylara laid her hand lightly on his arm. "She speaks. Let her," Tylara whispered.

Feminism? Not hardly. Or does she hope Gwen will stumble? Damn. I used to understand Tylara. Not now.

The others waited expectantly as Gwen paused to marshal her thoughts.

She had painted a grim picture of the future. The dwarf sun that everyone on Tran called the Demon Star was approaching. At perigee it would add more than ten percent to the planet's illuminance. That didn't sound like much, but it was enough. Ice caps would melt. Weather and climate would change, and all for the worse.

And now it was happening. The seas were rising, and the southern zones of this hemisphere were hot. Drought there. Rain here. Floods everywhere. Tribes, whole nations and populations fled northward. . . .

Rick saw that Tylara wasn't the only one staring at Gwen Tremaine. She'd told them the worst. Now the entire Inner Council waited for her to give them some shred of hope.

Yanulf, Highpriest of Yatar and Chancellor of Drantos, sat impassively. Nothing Gwen had said would surprise him. The Yatar hierarchy had preserved the legends of previous visits of the rogue star. They knew what the Time would bring, and wanted only to prepare for it. So long as the ice caves were filled with grain and other food, Yanulf would be happy.

Sergeant Major Elliot. Career soldier, U.S. Army, on loan to the CIA for an African adventure. Now a long way from home. Trustworthy, Rick thought. So long as I don't screw up. But his loyalty's to the outfit, not to any individual. And if push came to shove, as many of the mercs would take his orders as they would mine.

Warrant Officer Larry Warner. They called him Professor when he was a private. Now he was Chancellor of the University, and a good job he was doing. Gwen as Rector, Warner as Chancellor, and they were teaching the locals everything from the calculus to how to make paper and soap. With luck, knowledge would be spread so wide this time that nothing the damn Demon Star could do would stop it.

Lucius, in theory no more than Marselius Caesar's freedman. Lucius had been tutor to Marselius' son Publius, and every Roman senator had heard the old scholar referred to as Caesar's oldest friend. A delegation of senators had been sent as the formal representatives of Rome. Perhaps some of them believed Caesar read their dispatches with as much attention as he gave Lucius. Perhaps.

And the others. All waiting, like the young king, for Gwen to say what good would come from this alliance with the starmen.

Gwen swallowed and brushed back into place a few blond curls that had escaped from her wimple. In her Gown of Office she looked remarkably like an old-fashioned nun—a misleading impression if there ever was one—

And that was no safe thought, not with Tylara sitting right beside him!

"Your—my Lord Count," Gwen began. "I know you speak in anger and grief for those of your subjects you will not be able to save from the Time. Yet in truth much has already been done that will make this Time different from all those before."

Sure, Rick thought. Different. Provided that Les was reading Agzaral right, and Agzaral knew what he was doing, and the crazy-quilt union of races that governed this end of the galaxy didn't decide to take matters into its own hands. And a lot of other ifs. We can't talk about any of that here.

"Tell of this," Yanulf said.

"Blunt bastard," Rick whispered. Tylara touched his hand with dagger-sharp nails.

"The servants of Yatar have ever foretold of the Time," Yanulf said. "Often have we been ignored. It is well that as this Time approaches all believe us. But how else will the Time be different from the past? What has been done?"

"Much for this Realm," Gwen said. "The starmen's weapons and knowledge of war have saved this Realm. Not once only. The Lord Rick has cast down in succession Sarakos the Usurper, Flaminius Caesar the Dotard, and the Westmen. Drantos itself survives because of them."

Yeah, Rick thought, but what have we done for them lately?

"And there is more. There is knowledge," Gwen said. "They have taught the servants of Yatar the skills to heal the sick and wounded."

Yanulf nodded sagely. He hadn't known of the small devils that lived in septic conditions, which could be killed by boiling and ritual cleanliness. The knowledge made the priest healers enormously more effective.

At a cost, Rick thought. Yatar heals, Vothan the Chooser of the Slain takes fewer guests to his hall. The Vothan cult has no great reason to love us—

"And with the balloon they have made accurate maps where there were none before, maps that even the Romans envy. Iron plows turn the earth deeper, increasing yields, so that there is more to store in the Caves of the Preserver. There is paper, for records, so that the knowledge of the Time will be preserved, and the Wanax can know all that is known about his Realm. With the new healing knowledge, fewer wounds fester and fewer mothers die in childbirth, so that the number of His Majesty's subjects increases.

"My lord, the starmen are not gods. They do not claim the powers of gods. Yet they have much power, and all that they have has been freely used in the service of the Wanax and the Realm of Drantos. Much has been done. There will be more."

Someone shouted in the courtyard below. Ganton glanced at the window, then back at Rick.

"You speak well," Ganton said. "I am certain that the Wanax knows of his indebtedness to the Star Lords. Yet he also has obligations to his barons. And to all his subjects."

Rick looked to Tylara and got an answering nod. So that's it. The bheromen always did resent us. Ganton's father lost his throne when the barons deserted him. Ganton won't make that mistake. Meaning that we'd better be more careful than I thought.

"I know this," Gwen was saying. "I have told you what I know. Now the Captain General should speak."

Damn Gwen, Rick thought. She could have given me a little warning.

As he took the pointer from Gwen, he caught a whiff of her perfume. It was the same herbal essence she'd been wearing the day— no time to think of that. He glanced nervously at Tylara.

Begin with what they know. No matter that Gwen just told them. Tell them again. If enough of us tell them often enough, maybe they'll believe it. Maybe *I'll* believe it.

Tran was a planet in a triple-star system, consisting of the True Sun, the more distant Firestealer, and the Demon Star. Every six hundred Terran years—the Tran year was 1.7 of those—the Demon Star's eccentric orbit carried it close enough to Tran to affect the climate. For the two years of closest approach there would be few crops harvested.

But. As the Demon Star approached, the warmer weather did some good. In the years before closest approach crops were better, growing seasons longer. There was another effect. The increased sunlight made the plant the locals called madweed grow very well indeed—and madweed was much in demand as a recreational drug in interstellar trade. "Tran Natural" commanded an excellent price, and the *Shalnuksi* merchant adventurers had a monopoly on it, so long as they could get kidnapped human soldiers to collect it for them.

And they've been doing that for three thousand years I know of, and Gwen says more like five. The *Shalnuksis* had brought in Achaean Bronze Age warriors. Romans from the time of Septimius Serverus, and again from the Byzantine period. Franks. Celts. Scythians. Cultures mixed together, and none allowed to develop, because as soon as Tran threatened to become civilized the *Shalnuksis* bombed them back into a new Dark Age.

Not this time. Damn all, not this time! They can destroy technology, but we'll spread something more powerful than technology. We'll teach the scientific method. They can't bomb that out! Only we have to live through the next few years.

That wouldn't be easy. If anything, it was going to be worse than Gwen's lecture indicated—and that was worse than any of them except Yanulf had expected.

The rising seas would swallow most of the coastal cities, adding their people to the hordes of refugees already heading north. Storms and tsunamis like the one that had already mangled Rustengo's waterfront would scour the coastal areas. Tylara's homeland of Tamaerthon would become a rocky island. Rome would be reduced to the highlands, which could only support a fraction of its people. The Romans were well organized, but no organization could make a single ton of grain feed a thousand people for two years.

What Tran needed was the miracle of the loaves and the fishes. How fast did fish grow here? Weather changes would stir the water. Nutrients should upwell from the sea bottom. Ocean plant life would bloom. How long before the fish population rose significantly, and could anyone take advantage of that? Another task for the University.

"I see two choices," Rick began. "Both involve the Five Kingdoms. Drantos is inland. There will be flooding, but not so bad as in the coastal regions. Still, we will have famine, and there will be refugees from the south. Hordes of them, some well armed and desperate. We will need armies to hold them out lest they eat everything we have.

"Famine and border war will weaken our army. The High Rexja of the Five Kingdoms has already invaded Drantos and nearly unseated our Wanax Ganton. Had his son Sarakos been more concerned with rule than destruction, Drantos might today be one of the Six Kingdoms."

Ganton frowned. "I think I would not care to remind the Wanax Ganton of too many painful matters."

Rick shrugged. "Yet these things must be said. The High Rexja has not given up his claim to Drantos. In the early years of the Time his lands will have better crops as ours have worse. We stand as his defense against the refugees—"

"Give them safe passage to the north," Tylara said.

"If we could. But they would have to be fed and transported at a time when we will have little food for our own men and horses. I do not think it possible." Rick spread his hands. "Eventually Toris or his ministers will realize that Drantos is his for the taking, and come south with an army."

"Star weapons," Ganton said.

"Star weapons," Rick agreed. "But never enough. I have fewer than a score of starmen. We will never have more. I have little enough ammunition for our weapons. We can get more of that, but to do so we must continue to grow and harvest the madweed. That takes great effort—"

"More than you know," Yanulf said. "Slaves and convicts to grow the crops. Cavalry to guard the slaves so they do not run away."

As I would, if I could. Growing and harvesting that stuff is the worst work in the world.

"Soldiers to watch the guards, men and wagons to bring in the food for slaves and their guards and soldiers. And those who grow the food and bring it must themselves be fed."

He's learned well. "Precisely," Rick said. "But we have no choice regarding madweed. If the—great Star Lords—do not get the madweed they want, not only will they cease to bring us tools and ammunition, they may well throw *skyfire* in their anger."

"So we are told," Yanulf said. "A tale I believe. We have temple records, and everyone has heard how dangerous it is to deal with the demon gods who come with the Demon Star."

"You say, then, that they will grow stronger as Drantos grows weaker," Ganton said.

"Yes."

"And two choices."

"Yes. Either we invade the Five Kingdoms now, or we make peace with them now."

"It is not time to talk of war," Yanulf said. "The Time approaches. We must have peace."

"Yet an alliance of Rome and Drantos might take the Five," Ganton said. "If Drantos will grow weaker during the Time, will not Rome be harmed more? With lowland fields flooded—will not many Romans need shelter, here and wherever we can find food for them?"

"It would be well to have that choice," Lucius said. "My Lord Marshal, you have said there are two choices, but you have not said which you favor."

"Peace," Rick said. "The gods themselves conspire to bring death and destruction. Should we add more?"

"Well said." Yanulf nodded approval. "Well said."

And Lord knows if we do march into the Five we'll leave enough devastation in our wake. Tran armies live off the land, and discipline means they only rape the women.

The north is the right place to be at the height of the Time. And it's better to trade than fight. Trade iron, warhorses, maybe eventually gunpowder, for food. Teach the High Rexja how to set up his own University and send a cadre of people to help. Try to turn the High Rexja into an ally, instead of an enemy to be fended off or destroyed. . . .

"Can we make peace?" Ganton demanded.

"We can send a reliable commission to try."

"Nothing else?" said the Wanax/Count.

"At this time, no," Rick replied. "We do not wish to appear too eager. That would make the High Rexja suspect that we were weak or fearful."

"Since we are neither, why should the Wanax not wish to put forward his own claim to the High Throne?" said Ganton. "His grandfather's sister was wife to Toris, and because of this Sarakos put forward his claim to the throne of Drantos. Why should not such a claim travel north as well as south?"

"Because making it would mean yet another war," growled Yanulf. "The Time approaches, with the gods only know what perils and horrors yet unrevealed, and this Council would advise the Wanax to throw away blood and treasure on a petty dynastic quarrel!"

"If it gives us the land that it seems we shall most surely need, how can it be petty?" said Ganton.

"We might lose," Yanulf said. "If we can gain what we need in peace, can any cause be great enough to be worth yet another war? We must certainly send an army south to deal with those fleeing toward the city-states. We are certain to hear more from the Westmen. Will we advise His Majesty to the folly of new wars when the old ones may not yet be done?"

"That may be wisdom," Ganton said. "What say our Roman allies?"

"I do not think that the High Rexja will give us more than a pittance, without our paying a price greater than we can afford."

"Greater than another war?" muttered Yanulf.

"More than likely," said Lucius. "Toris may have given no further offense, but neither has he made peace. If he sincerely wished it, he could have had it anytime during the past year."

Ganton looked thoughtful. "True. If an offer had been made we— the Wanax would have put it before the Council. None was made, yet we have no further quarrel with the High Rexja."

"As I thought." Lucius spread his hands. "Then it seems most likely that the High Rexja only wishes to choose his own time for avenging Sarakos. Why should the Wanax wait for the blow to fall, rather than unsheathing his own sword and ending the menace of the Five Kingdoms at a blow?"

Not at a blow. And what's your game, anyway? Rick wondered. One guess: peace between the High Rexja and Drantos might turn into an alliance. Would turn into an alliance, if Rick gave the Five Kingdoms any star wisdom, let alone a University. That was an alliance that could turn against Rome—and for all that Lucius was trustworthy enough to be sitting on the Inner Council, he was still friend and counselor to Marselius Caesar.

Marselius was growing old, his son Publius was a good soldier but had more than his share of enemies. Ganton had been hailed by a Roman legion as "Imperator"—worthy to command Romans—and was about to marry Caesar's granddaughter.

An alliance with the Five Kingdoms could tempt the Wanax of Drantos to the purple, unleashing another civil war on Rome with the

Time closer than ever. A war between Toris and Drantos, on the other hand, could keep Rome's two most formidable rivals chewing on each other for long enough to let Marselius put things in order. Perhaps long enough for Marselius to retire in favor of Publius.

You knew Lucius wouldn't give disinterested advice. Disinterested be damned, is it good?

Rick turned that question over in his mind as the debate went around the table. Lucius was pro-war. Yanulf of course was against it. So were Gwen and Warner, although the Professor seemed rather lukewarm for peace. Why? Warner liked his post at the University. What else did he want?

Another question they never raised in ROTC classes on leadership, and one with no answer for now.

Elliot was in favor of war, as long as they first settled accounts with Gengrich and the rest of the mutineers who were still in the south. Rick had the feeling that Elliot didn't much care whether that settlement left Gengrich and his men alive or not. The Sergeant Major was loyal to Rick and his plans and knew Gengrich's ten men might make a difference in carrying them out. He was also too good an NCO to be very happy about depending on men who'd already mutinied once. In his books they couldn't be trusted not to do it again.

Tylara was blunt. "It will take more than one defeat to make Toris give up the idea of taking our lands. Every High King for two centuries has known that Drantos and Chelm were once a sixth Kingdom, and dreamed of making it one again."

"Toris is old and by all reports feeble," said Yanulf. "Will such a man do more than dream? Will he not rather concern himself with assuring the peaceful succession of his last surviving son, Prince Akkilas?"

"He will best assure that by taking Drantos and avenging Sarakos," said Tylara. "His eqetas and bheromen will not swallow their defeat forever. If Akkilas comes to the High Throne as the conqueror of Drantos, his way will be easy. If not, the warriors of the Five Kingdoms may turn to one who will give them that victory. There is Prince Strymon, heir to Ta-Meltemos, and he is only the most formidable out of several captains."

"War now. Peace now," Ganton said. "Can we win if we strike now? How much aid will Rome give us?"

He's forgotten the myth about being Count of the North or whatever.
That's the king talking, and a nervous one at that. And what the hell's
keeping Art?

"I can convey a request to Caesar," Lucius said smoothly. "But I
cannot make promises—"

"Convenient enough," Tylara said.

"But what shall we do?" Ganton demanded.

"Send commissioners to Toris," Rick said. "And others to Rome.
After tomorrow it should be more difficult for Caesar to refuse a
request from our Wanax."

"He cannot honor a request for soldiers he does not have," Yanulf
said. "Rome must look to the south. As must we."

And that's for sure. Plenty of danger of there. Not only the hordes
of refugees. There were also rumors of a fanatical religious leader, who
was welding the horde into a crusade against the new idea of Christ as
the Son of Yatar. Rick hoped the rumors were just that; religious
warfare was one ingredient the Tran stew didn't need.

"There is another thing," Warner said.

"Yes?"

"By all reports, the Westmen are marching north as they agreed,
after the Wanax's great victory at the Hooey River."

"True enough," Rick said.

"I'd guess they'll bounce off Margilos and head right into the Five
Kingdoms. Toris can probably beat them, but I bet it'll take a year to
drive them out."

"A year in which the Five do not become stronger," Tylara said
thoughtfully. "This is welcome news. We have, then, a year—"

There was a knock at the door.

Elliot got up with a frown. He came back to stand next to Rick.
"Beg pardon, Colonel. Art Mason's outside. Wants to talk to you.
Seems like there's trouble in the Outer Castle."

"What kind of trouble?"

"Assassins. One sentry's dead already. He's alerted the ready platoon
and Ben Murphy's on hand with a bunch of his men."

"Good. Who'd he leave in command?"

"Morrone."

"Oh, crap."

"Yeah."

"I better go look. We're not going to decide anything here anyway."

And Tylara won't care where I am. God, what happened to us?

3

"Okay, Art, what is it?"

"Damfino. Look, Colonel, I wouldn't have called you but you said I should if I didn't know what's going on—"

"And?"

"And I don't. There's a dead sentry. Professional job of killing him. Too damn professional to be a blood feud. But we've looked, and we can't find one damn thing."

"Looked. Looked where?"

"Well, you know, all around out there. It's the Outer Bailey, it's a warren. Nobody ever found anybody in that place. Look, you wanted me to tell you what's happening. I did. Now get back to your meeting. I can handle it."

"Sure you can, but I'm damned sick of meetings. Let's go look."

"Well—I guess I got enough troops."

Rick laughed. "Art, if we don't have enough firepower between us to handle anything this bunch of primitives can throw at us—"

"Primitives."

Okay, so I don't talk that way usually. So I'm getting sick of some of the Mickey Mouse crap. "Let's go look."

✢ ✢ ✢

"Whose quarters?" Rick demanded.

"Nobody yet," Mason said. "Not this house. But over there is Daettan of Dirstvaal, and over there is the place Gwen and Warner share—"

585

"Eh?"

"Gwen and Warner. And some of the other University people."

"Who's in there now?"

"Hell, Colonel, I don't know. Their people I suppose—"

"Let's go check."

"Eh?"

"Call it a hunch." *Call it that Tylara's acting funny, and she's scared of Gwen, but I'm damned if I'll tell you that.* "Let's look."

"Okay. Lugh."

"Sir."

"Take some troops around back of that house. Lord Rick and I are going to search it."

Lugh's eyes widened slightly, then he grinned. "Sir."

"Don't think anybody but us could get away with looking into *her* place," Mason said.

"Rog. Maybe not even us. But here goes." Rick waited until Lugh and his Guardsmen had deployed around the house. "Okay."

Mason banged on the door. "Open in the name of the Guard."

He waited and banged again. "Nobody home."

Rick lowered his voice. "Bullshit. She's got half a dozen servants. So does Warner. Somebody's in there to unbolt the door."

Mason whistled, low. "Sumbitch. Goddamn, Cap'n, you're right. So what do we do?"

"Knock one more time and act like we're going away."

"Right—" Mason pounded once more. "Nobody home," he said loudly. "Let's go—"

They walked around the corner of the vacant house. The dead sentry still lay there, now covered with some guardsman's cloak. "Sir?" Mason said.

"First. Get five mercs back to the Council room, and nobody leaves there until I get back. Nobody. Alert your guardsmen and have them take over the corridors, but when I get back to that chamber I want Elliot and the troops with rounds chambered."

Mason nodded slowly. "You sure—"

"Who gives a shit about sure? Better to be ready and not need it—"

"Sir."

"And who the hell did you send down here to take charge? Not Morrone—"

Mason looked pained. "No, sir. Murphy held the fort until I could get Henderson. He's in back—"

"Right. Get him over here and get on your way."

Rick watched Mason go around the house. *It's probably all bat turds. But suppose it's not?*

"Colonel?"

"Right. Henderson, go get me one of the Daughters of Yatar. In full robes. A short one."

"Sir?" Corporal Henderson frowned. "Uh, Colonel—"

Rick consulted the papers Mason had left him and pointed. "Down there. That house. There ought to be a dozen of them. I just want one. Get a couple of footmen while you're at it. And don't forget, a short Daughter of Yatar, in robes."

"Sir? Yes, sir." Henderson bolted off. Rick chuckled to himself.

✣ ✣ ✣

"Okay, here's the drill," Rick said. "My Lady Iris walks behind the troops. Lady Gwen copied her robes of office from the Daughters of Yatar. In this light nobody's going to know it's not Gwen come back from Council. You two footmen, go up, bang on the door, and shout to open in the name of the Lady Rector. Then get the hell out of the way."

The footmen glanced at him nervously. Then they looked at the squad of determined guardsmen and star lords, and looked resigned.

"If anything happens"—he turned to Lady Iris—"anything at all, forget your dignity and get the hell behind somebody and stay there."

"Certainly. I take it you do not mind if I pray?"

Rick looked at her closely and laughed. "For all of us, if it please your ladyship. Okay, troops. Let's do it. And remember. We want live ones."

The footmen went to the door and knocked. "Open for the Lady Rector."

For a moment nothing happened, then a light flared inside the house. Shutters above the door opened, and a torch was thrust out. A muffled voice shouted, "My lady!" and the shutters closed again.

So. There is someone in there. He waited until he heard the door unbolted. It seemed to take forever, then it opened. He dashed forward and threw himself against it. "Inside! Move!" he shouted. He felt the door slam into whoever had opened it.

That one's out of action. He left him for the followers and dashed to the next room. Rick heard motion and whirled. Someone had been standing at the doorway and had swung a bludgeon at him. "Stand!" The man raised the club.

Rick lowered his aim point and fired at the groin. The .45 flared in the dark, and the man doubled over. *That's two. How many?* He moved on through the room. The last room was the kitchen, and it was empty.

Behind him his troops poured into the house. "Gotcha!" Henderson shouted.

That's that one. Rick found the stairs. *They'll be alerted and ready. I should wait for troops. Or burn the place and be done with it. We've got two, and both will live long enough to answer questions.*

And you're a track star.

This is stupid. He darted up the stairs. At the top he continued, but kept low, diving across the floor to hit and roll. Two figures loomed behind him.

Rick fired once between them. "Move and get your testicles shot off."

Everything froze for a moment. Henderson and the others were running up the stairs. Then one of the men turned—

Rick moved without thought, diving into the man, knocking his outstretched arm up. Three gunshots thundered in the enclosed space. Henderson and his troops came fast. There was another shot, and one of the guardsmen fell. Henderson threw Rick's opponent against the wall. Someone swung a club and the other enemy went down.

A torchbearer climbed the stairs. Long before he got to the top Rick looked at his prisoner, nodded, and said, "Private Rand, I believe—"

✢ ✢ ✢

"You can talk to me, or the royal executioners. Just one thing. Once I turn you over to them, I can't get you back."

"Hell, Captain, I'll talk to you. Just give me a second to catch my breath."

Harvey Rand didn't look much like a Star Lord. He was bearded like most Tran nobles. His clothes were the remnants of Tran finery, but they had seen much better days.

Rick fingered the Walther PPK they'd taken from him. It was clean and well greased. "How much ammo does Gengrich have left?"

"Not a lot, but he don't tell me—"

"Mason, maybe you better alert the executioner."

"Captain, dammit, I'll tell you what I know!" Rand shouted. "You don't want me to make things up—"

"Don't," Mason said.

"So what were you doing here?" Rick demanded.

Rand looked resigned. "Trying to—look, it was a snatch job. Kidnap the lady that runs the University."

"Gwen Tremaine. Why?"

"Look, can I have a drink?"

"Sure." Rick gestured to Mason. "And have a seat." He indicated the bench beside the oak table. "Just remember, my office is a hell of a lot more comfortable than where they'll take you if I get tired of listening. Now what's all this about?"

"Arnie wants to come in."

"Good. We want him. What's that got to do with Gwen Tremaine?"

"What do we come in as?" Rand asked. "Not just us. Our friends. Wives. Relatives. There's a lot of us."

"And Gwen?" Rick kept his voice deceptively calm.

"Bargaining chip. Figured if we had her you'd listen while we talked status."

Rick's orderly came in with a pitcher of wine and goblets. Rick poured three. Mason shook his head and stood in the corner. "I'll pass."

"Christ, Art, you don't have to worry about me," Rand said.

"It's Major Mason."

"Well smell—yes, sir. Major Mason."

"And don't play games, Rand." Art Mason sounded tired. "Bargaining chips are fine, but who did you mean to bargain with?"

Rand looked scared.

"Thought so. Colonel, they want to grow goddamn madweed and sell it direct."

"Cut out the middlemen, so to speak," Rick said. "That true, Rand?"

Rand gulped wine. "Yes, sir."

"What made you think it would work?"

"We—"

"Who?" Mason demanded. "One of my troops?"

"I don't know—"

"Bull shit. You've got a spy in the University. Right in Lady Gwen's office, probably," Mason said. "That's one of mine, and I want the son of a bitch dead. If I can't have him I'll take your balls to make a purse out of."

"Dammit Major, I don't know! Gengrich knows, but I don't."

"And he sent you—"

"No."

Mason started to say something, but Rick gestured him to silence. "What do you mean, 'no'?"

"Gengrich don't know nothing about this."

"I think you'd better explain."

"I'm trying to! Look, we're all in the same racket, right? Only you're doing better than the rest of us. But we're all in the same damn boat."

"On the same planet," Rick said. "So?"

"Captain, we never deserted from you. After Parsons ran you off, we ducked out on him. By the time you were back in charge we had things going down south. Now you get stuff from that flying saucer, and we get dick. Dammit, that ain't fair."

Mason snorted.

"Well, okay, Ar—Major. You ducked out with Captain Galloway. Smart move. We cut cards on that. Remember?"

"Damn all. He's right, Colonel. I forgot. Rand was one of them that volunteered to go with you, only Elliot wouldn't let but one go."

"Okay. How does that change things? Who the hell are you working for?"

"Some locals. Daettan of Dirstvaal."

"Gengrich's ambassador."

"Well, yeah, only—look, Colonel, there's a lot of them. Locals. They're scared. They figured if they had Gwen, they'd have a chance. We could trade her to Gengrich. Or you. Or something."

"In other words," Mason said, "Gengrich is running out of ammo, has a lot of locals mixed in with his troops, and ain't got a pot to piss in."

"Pretty close," Rand said.

"And he didn't approve this operation."

"Christ no! But he does want to talk."

"Right. Mason, take over. I'd better get back to the meeting."

"What do I do with this one?"

"Dammit—Major—I got a name and you know it. Look, okay, it was a fool stunt and we lost, but I got a right to hire out. Don't I? What the hell am I supposed to do in this stinking place?"

Good question. "Just talk to him, Art. Hang in there, Rand. We'll think of something."

Rick left the office. A dozen guardsmen fell in around him as he went down the corridor to the Council chamber.

✤ ✤ ✤

Clavell and Beazeley stood outside the Council chamber door. Both held battle rifles. A dozen guardsmen with drawn swords were with them.

"Alert's over," Rick said. "We got them. Remember Rand?"

"Harv Rand," Clavell said. "Yeah, he was in my squad back in Africa. Good man with a garotte."

"Too good for one of our sentries." Rick spoke in English too rapidly for any local to understand. "Anyway, we got him. And the others. You can stand down."

"Yes, sir."

Inside the chamber things looked about the same—except that Elliot, Warner, and Gwen all had pistols lying on the table. Ganton's Browning was still in its holster, but the strap was undone.

Rick glanced at Tylara. No weapon in sight. But her right hand was in her left sleeve. . . .

Larry Warner was reading from a long document. After a moment it was obvious what it was. The official history of the coming of the starmen.

"Alert's over," Rick said.

"You say no more than that?" Ganton demanded.

"No more to say, my Lord Count. Some thieves attempted to rob the house assigned to the Lady Gwen. They have been captured. Two guardsmen were killed, and one wounded." *That'll do for now.* "If you'll continue, my lord?" Rick gestured to Warner.

"Yes, sir."

Warner read with animation. In ten minutes he had killed Sarakos in a village boobytrapped with a ton of gunpowder, married off Rick and Tylara, delivered their daughter Isobel, and was starting on Marselius Caesar's rebellion.

Not really rebellion. After our raids into Marselius' prefecture he could either revolt or let Flaminius the Dotard kill him. Not much choice there.

"So Marselius Caesar, Tamaerthon, and the Realm of Drantos became allies against Flaminius. Their host marched into the Dotard's land and fought a great battle against the Romans under the Legate Titus Licinius Frugi. The Romans fought gallantly, but to no avail against the star weapons, the balloon, and the valor of the men of Drantos and Tamaerthon. A wise captain, Titus Licinius Frugi yielded to save his men, and thus ended the Roman civil war."

Ganton smiled. "I see that Lord Rick follows the custom of Drantos, and does not boast of his deeds. The tale of that battle passes over his capturing Titus Frugi with his own hands."

"It is enough that you know, your—my Lord Count."

After the Roman alliance came Bishop Polycarp's vision. One night he had dreamed that Yatar came to him and proclaimed that Christ was His Only Begotten Son, borne of Hestia, who had taken the form of a mortal woman. So the followers of Yatar and the followers of Christ should be as brothers to one another.

For some people on both sides the vision came as a blessing; there was a real "ecumenical movement" growing up on both sides. For others it was like throwing a hand grenade into the middle of a cocktail party. There were the rumors about that madman in the south, and the priests of Vothan hadn't been heard from yet. Rick didn't like to think about what the priests would have to say.

The rest of the story was mostly the campaign against the Westmen, ending in Ganton's great victory at the Hooey River and the withdrawal of the Westmen to the north. After that came a note on Caradoc's death in a riot, another on the betrothal of Ganton to Octavia Caesar (who'd come to Drantos as a hostage but would remain as a queen), and a wish that Yatar and Christ His Son might bless all who read these words.

Rick led a round of applause.

Warner had the grace to blush. "Thank you, my lords and ladies. Does this mean I can put the scribes on to making copies?"

Ganton nodded. "Speaking for the Wanax, I say yes. I am sure he will want as many of the wedding guests as possible to carry away this wisdom when they depart."

How many of them would call it wisdom and how many would call it heresy, God (any or all, take your pick) only knew, but they had to start somewhere. In fact, Rick wondered if that might not be a good, if unofficial, motto for the House of Galloway—"You have to start somewhere."

✢ ✢ ✢

Lucius dipped his gullfeather pen in the ink and continued writing. No doubt the young men learning to write now would find the new iron-tipped pens child's play, but he was too old a dog to learn new tricks.

Also a rather weary one, with little hope of getting a decent night's sleep before the wedding. The Demon Star was already sinking toward the hills beyond the Roman camp, the wedding would begin shortly after noon, and yet this letter to Marselius had to be completed before he could rest.

> The Lord Rick told the Council that thieves invaded the University. They could be no ordinary thieves. My agent with the Guardsmen tells me that one of these thieves had a star weapon, and spoke in a strange language with the Lord Rick. The man was of the party sent by the Star Lord Gengrich. We may be safe in assuming this was no ordinary robbery attempt. I could speculate on the real purpose, but my guesses will be no better than yours.

> Could there be opportunity here? It may be that Lord Gengrich would welcome new allies. Certainly we could use assistance in recovering the lost southern provinces, and Gengrich is there.

> It was the Wanax's wish that Lady Octavia be told of the night's events at once. He grew angry at the suggestion that she might not bear the news well, saying that it was to insult his bride and Caesar's House to suggest she lacked the courage to hear bad news.

> It fell to me to be the news-bringer. Lady Cyra, chief among Octavia's new Drantos attendants, attempted to bar my path until I had given her the message, which I was strictly instructed to bring only to Octavia's ears. When Octavia did appear, Lady Cyra refused to depart, and only force could have moved her.

When I gave the news to Octavia, Lady Cyra screamed aloud and flew into a great passion, crying that it was an evil omen for the Wanax's marriage. Lady Octavia flew into as great a rage as I have ever seen in her, and said that Lady Cyra was a fool. It was a very good omen, that those loyal to the throne of Drantos could so easily defeat an attack by one of its enemies. She would pray to Christ and his Father Yatar that the throne should face no worse enemies in the years to come.

She then asked if the dead Guardsmen had wives or children. When told that one had a daughter of three and a second child to be born in mid-winter, she swore before Yatar, Christ, Hestia, and all the saints to provide the daughter with a dowry when she came of age and to stand godmother to the unborn child.

This silenced Lady Cyra, a feat I had thought impossible. With her present I could not linger, but I assure you that I have never in my life felt so proud of Octavia.

I do not know if Lady Cyra is naturally lacking in good sense or seeks to wield power over the Lady Octavia. I also do not know if such a desire is her own, or given to her by her husband Bheroman Kilantis. He is a leader among those lords who swore oath to Sarakos and were afterward pardoned. Not a few of those are less than pleased with the Roman alliance; they fear that a Wanax of Drantos with legions at his command may seek to rule without the consent of his nobles and knights, in the manner of a Caesar. The fear is all the greater, because Ganton's father Loron did exactly that, and so brought much suffering to Drantos.

And it is time you bring this letter to a close, Lucius! You are telling Caesar things that he already knows. Next, you will be telling him that his son Publius does not much care to have Titus Frugi commanding the cohorts charged with his safety at the wedding. . . .

Lucius spread sand on the parchment, shook it off, rolled the parchment into a wooden cylinder, and sealed it. Then he stamped the still-soft wax with his signet and rang for a messenger.

4

Archbishop Polycarp wore his pearl-studded mitre and his robes of cloth-of-gold. Highpriest Yanulf wore his robes of blue *garta* cloth and carried his great silver staff set with Father's Eyes. To Apelles, neither priest appeared half as splendid as the royal couple kneeling before them.

The Wanax Ganton wore his finest robes under a cloak of ermine and the Great Crown of Drantos. Its rubies and amber threw back the light from the hundreds of candles blazing around the altar, until it seemed that the Wanax wore a crown of flame.

Lady Octavia was dressed more in the Roman style, with a mantle of cream-colored *garta* trimmed with gold over a bronze-hued gown of the finest linen trimmed with pearls. She also wore a veil hanging from a circlet of silver flowers, in the manner of the women of the skyfolk. At the end of the ceremony, the Wanax would lift that veil to kiss his bride.

Apelles knew this and many more details of the royal wedding, down to the very undergarments the Wanaxxae would be wearing on this day. As Yanulf's right hand, he had been set to more labors than Hercules in the matter of the wedding.

Once he had ventured to ask, "I know that the Lord Publius Caesar has no living wife and that his sister is not well enough to make such a long journey so late in the year. Yet could not much of what has fallen to me have been done as well by the Eqetassa of Chelm or the Lady Cyra?"

"Lady Tylara will be chief among the bride's attendants at the wedding," Yanulf had replied. "Until then, her duties as Justiciar of Drantos and mistress of the Captain General's household will prevent her from doing as much as I am sure she would wish to do.

"As for Lady Cyra, she too has much to occupy her in the Lady Octavia's household. Also, she knows little of Roman customs and might give offense without meaning it."

It was then and remained now Apelles' opinion that Lady Cyra knew a great deal about Roman customs and was utterly opposed to seeing any of them introduced into the Court of Drantos. The Chancellor's tone of voice had spoken whole scrolls about the unwisdom of saying this aloud.

At least his labors had obtained for Apelles a good place in the hall, into which half the Realm seemed to have crowded and in which half the Realm had certainly sought places. The only people closer to the altar than the row in which Apelles stood were the attendants of the bride and groom and the guardsmen double-ranked across the hall between the altar and the guests. *A long way for a swineherd to come.*

Incense rose in a cloud. So did Polycarp's thin voice.

"Dearly beloved, we are gathered here today in the sight of Yatar Dayfather, Christ His Son, Holy Hestia the Mother of Christ, and this noble congregation, to join this man and this woman in Holy Matrimony, which is an honorable estate—"

Apelles felt someone prodding him in the ribs. The dignity of the occasion kept him from prodding back. Instead he turned his head as far as he could, to see Eyan son of Fnor, the guardsman assigned him as a messenger. At least that was Yanulf's tale; after seeing how many other "messengers" were scattered through the crowd, Apelles suspected they were really there to keep watch on those guests out of sight or reach of the Guards before the altar.

"What of Vothan?" Eyan muttered. "I like not this casting out of the Warlord."

"What casting out?" said Apelles. "It is written, that when the Christ was upon Earth, he said, 'I come to bring not peace, but a sword.' Who else would say that, but Vothan? It is also written that he was hung upon a cross and seemed to die, yet rose again wiser than before. Is that not also said of Vothan?"

"They also call the Christ 'Prince of Peace,' " said Eyan.

"Has this ever kept the Romans from fighting?" replied Apelles. "Or made them fight less fiercely when they marched against us?" Eyan shook his head with a wry grin.

"Even the starmen are Christians," Apelles went on. "And do they not enjoy the blessings of Vothan?"

"The starmen are Christians?" Eyan frowned.

"Yes, and from his first day in our land the Lord Rick has always honored Yatar and Vothan as well as Christ."

"That is true," said Eyan slowly. He seemed to want to say more, but Apelles saw the looks their whispered conversation was beginning to draw. He waved the Guardsman to silence.

Very likely he had awakened as many doubts in the man as he'd laid to rest. Not just in Eyan. *I am no warrior, but it would be a harsh world indeed if brave men had no hope of guesting with One-eye Vothan after dying in battle.*

Polycarp droned on. "—but reverently, discreetly, soberly, and in the fear of Yatar and Christ, duly considering the causes for which matrimony was ordained.

"First, it was ordained for the increase of mankind, according to the will of Yatar and Christ, and that children might be brought up in the fear and nurture of Them, and to the praise of Their Holy names. . . ."

✢ ✢ ✢

Tylara shifted restlessly.

"Thirdly, it was ordained for the mutual society, help, and comfort, that the one ought to have of the other, both in prosperity and adversity.

"Into which holy estate, these two persons present come now to be joined. . . ."

If the Lady Gwen had not been standing close beside her, Tylara would have shut her eyes. *That is as it should be. As it was. And I have forfeited the love of the gods, and worse, of my husband.*

I have betrayed them all. Yet what could I have done?

The thoughts raced through her head in well-worn grooves, raced endlessly. Caradoc. Loyal to Tylara and her house. Married to the faithless Gwen. And Gwen's true husband returning from the stars, returning with a star ship and *skyfire*. With the means to lay waste all Rick had built.

What could I do?

Kill the Star Lord Les? And as he died his ship would send *skyfire*. So said Rick. And she had seen the ship. It could do all Rick said, and more.

Kill the Lady Gwen? *I owe her nothing. Yet the University is more than nothing. It may be the only inheritance I can leave my children. So say the legends of the Time. So says Rick.*

But Caradoc and Les must not meet.

It had been simple enough. Coded orders to the Children of the Eighth House of Vothan. And waiting, which was worse than any battle, wait and wait and—

And comes the news, of a riot and a horse that stumbled, and her protector and rescuer—

Rescue. Sarakos had read her aright, curse him; in the end she would have broken, begging to please him if that would earn her a swifter end. . . . Until Caradoc came, and with Yanulf led her through the caves of Yatar, and away.

And now he was dead. Of an accident. And none knew. My husband probably does not even suspect; he does not think like a Tran lord.

None but me. And it will be me the gods judge. Not my instruments. Yatar forgive the Children. They acted for me. They know no better.

If anyone learns. Blood feud with those most loyal to our house. And no matter. I have brought cold and ruin to our marriage. And what right have I to "mutual society, comfort, and help," in the eyes of the gods or anyone else?

She did not close her eyes, but she kept them fixed on the rush-strewn floor, fearful of what she might see if she looked up.

⚜ ⚜ ⚜

"Octavia Marselia Caesar, wilt thou have this man to thy wedded husband, to live together according to the laws of Yatar and Christ in the holy estate of matrimony? Wilt thou love him, comfort him, honor, obey, and keep him, in sickness and health; and forsaking all others, keep thee only unto him, so long as ye both shall live?"

"I will."

Publius' frown deepened. He had been frowning ever since Yanulf began to speak. It was infuriating that a Roman archbishop should have such a pitiful excuse for a voice while a barbarian priest could thunder like a centurion drilling an entire cohort. Now this damned promise by Octavia to *obey* her husband!

The barbarians must have put that in their new marriage ceremony on purpose, to cut away his own authority over his daughter. Matters should have been left so that in any dispute between Drantos and Rome, Caesar's house could invoke the *patria potestas* it held over Drantos' Queen.

They would have been left that way, too, if someone among the barbarians hadn't as good as read Publius' mind and added that little word! Or was it someone among the barbarians?

Frugi. Yes! That contemplative smile must hide treachery; that gilded legate's breastplate hides a heart gone over to the barbarians. Who else could it be, but the man who had allowed the Fourth Legion to hail a barbarian king as "Imperator"?

Frugi. You command here. Once in Rome it will be different.

And yet. He is loyal to my father, and he is a good general. Rome has need of generals. Flaminius the Dotard killed his best commanders—and now his bones wash down the Tiber.

And I have no heir. None but Octavia. She will have need of generals no less than I.

So. Live, Titus Frugi. And I will watch you, and send you where I have need.

Publius smiled thinly, hoping that a time would come when he could tell Lucius about this moment. His old tutor had always urged him to think before he spoke, and often doubted that he would ever learn.

⁜ ⁜ ⁜

"Forasmuch as Ganton son of Loron, Wanax of Drantos, and Octavia Marselia Caesar have consented together in holy wedlock, and have witnessed the same before Yatar, Christ, and this noble company, and thereto have given and pledged their troth to each other—"

Gwen Tremaine felt her eyes ready to overflow.

Stop it, you twit. Do you want Tylara to see you crying?

I always cry at weddings.

How many have you attended?

Well, there was Beth Allison's, there's this one, and both of my own.

You call marrying Les a wedding?

You want to argue with Yanulf? Or Les?

The voice was silent. Gwen blinked, thinking that maybe she wasn't going to cry after all but glad that here on Tran there was no mascara to run if she did. Drantos women used no makeup, although they did use perfume. They were better off than the Roman ladies, who used cosmetics McCleve had said were mostly lead-based. *A good thing Octavia seems to be adopting the Drantos custom, but then at nine Tran or fifteen Earth years old she hardly needed makeup.*

Octavia and Ganton made a handsome young couple, no doubt about it. *Octavia would never be beautiful. But she's tall! With that red hair and those legs everyone notices her. And she may not be through growing!* Ganton looked almost too hefty in his royal robes, but Gwen had seen him working out in the courtyard with that battle-axe of his; she knew all that bulk was iron-hard muscle.

The tears threatened again as Gwen thought of Octavia's luck— from hostage to queen in a single year, and from a dynastic match to a love match. She'd been more or less handed to Ganton like a suckling pig on a platter, but she'd found she could love him, and now she would have him by her side every day and night.

Gwen had picked her own husband, got on board a flying saucer because she loved him, and now she was going to have him with her about a month out of every two Earth years.

Not fair, dammit! So who said the Universe is fair? Or cares?

"—I pronounce that they be man and wife together, in the name of Yatar Dayfather, Christ His Son, and the Blessed Hestia Mother of Christ. Amen."

The tears overflowed. Gwen didn't fight them, because she saw that Tylara was crying too.

✛ ✛ ✛

The wedding party flowed out to the sound of drums and trumpets. A Guards captain shouted importantly.

"Gunners! Salute!"

Goddamn twenty-one-gun salute. Sure wish I had that much gunpowder at Westrook. I got a feeling I'll need it.

The cannon drowned out the thump of the Guards' boots and the thud of their musket butts as they formed a double line from the cathedral door to the waiting carriage.

Ben Murphy waited, hand on the hilt of his sword, until the man beside him started to move toward the aisle formed by the Guards.

Lord Enipses. I think. I sure better start learning all the names and faces and estates. Another part of good manners I never thought of. But bad manners can sure get you killed. And I always thought being a landlord was easy.

It looked as if half the high muckety-mucks in the kingdom were coming to stand between the Guards. Not just the Drantos nobles, but Romans too, Publius and Titus Frugi, to start with. Mercs. The Captain, Elliot, Art Mason, and the rest. Except for the guys with scoped rifles up in the towers.

Ganton and Octavia reached the top of the great stone stairway. Rick nodded to Elliot.

"Wedding party—draw—swords!"

Murphy drew, pulling the draw slightly to keep from ramming the sword's point between Hilaskos' teeth. What sounded like a whole battery of guns went off. Murphy could smell powder smoke. Then people were cheering, Ganton was lifting the veil from Octavia's face and kissing her a lot more enthusiastically than ceremony required, and the newlyweds were marching down the stairs under the arch of swords.

Murphy kept eyes front but knew when Ganton and Octavia reached the courtyard gateway and the crowd out in the capital streets saw them. Even Elliot couldn't have out-shouted that cheering. Then each pair in the arch in turn sheathed their swords, as Yanulf and Polycarp came down the aisle. It looked as if Yanulf were supporting the Archbishop, but both of them were smiling and looked as if they'd just married off favorite children. Murphy found himself reaching for rosary beads he hadn't worn since he was a boy as he went through a Hail Mary he hadn't said more than a couple of times since.

Maybe old Polycarp had really had a vision from Somebody Upstairs. Even if there wasn't anybody upstairs to send visions, it made sense if Rome and Drantos were going to be allies.

It's got to be better than Ulster. Lord God. Anything is.

✣ ✣ ✣

The Roman buccinae bellowed, the drums rolled, and the Praetorian cohort just ahead of Art Mason stepped off. He looked back along his mounted Guardsmen formed up in a column of fours. *Sharp troops. Maybe not up to what the Romans can do, but sharp enough considering they were plowboys a year ago.*

"Pass in review!"

The crowd cheered as the Praetorians came out onto the field. It sounded just like a football crowd back home—and come to think of it, they'd have called this real good football weather, back home. With a little imagination Mason could think he was in the grandstand, watching the Sailors take the field for the kickoff.

Make that a lot of imagination. The sky was the wrong shade of blue; the hills beyond the Edre were the wrong colors, the smell on the wind was roast meat, gunpowder, wood smoke, and unwashed people, and the music wasn't any brass band that ever showed up at a football game.

The signal gun bellowed. Thank God they were just using a little one-pounder and weren't firing the bombards anymore. They must have used up half the gunpowder in Drantos in salutes.

Art Mason raised his sword and swept it forward in command. "Drantos!" He gave a touch with his spurs and the horse moved into a swift trot. The Praetorians were taking their own sweet time, as if they wanted to tell all the barbarians that nobody made them move faster than they wanted to. For a minute Art was afraid he'd have to order the Guards down to a walk. But then the Praetorians were clear. The bright tapestries of the reviewing stand were coming up on the right.

His sword went up, trumpets blared, and the platoon sergeants shouted, "First Guards, eyes—right!"

Mason's sword dipped in the royal salute, until the point was aimed at the ground. As the Guards trotted past the reviewing stand, he wished he'd seen more movies with cavalry parades. *Guess those Hollywood budgets didn't run to enough trained horses. Or riders . . .*

There was the little king, in armor now with that gold helmet he favored. They'd never let him give it up even if he wanted to; after the Hooey River everyone thought it was lucky. Same thing with that battle-axe of old Camithon's.

Octavia—she looked like she was walking on air, with a smile too big for her face. Publius was grim, Titus Frugi was smiling, and they weren't looking at each other even though they stood side by side. The captain looked worried, but on a big day like this he always did. Lady Tylara—she looked like she'd been crying. . . .

And no guesses. Mason had gone as far as he could with guessing. *Maybe too far. Damn all.*

A coded message. In a code none of Mason's clerks could read. None of Apelles' people either. And none of the captain's. What in hell was Lady Tylara doing, sending a message the captain couldn't read?

Lady Tylara at the University to Castle Dravan—and just in time for somebody to reach that town where Caradoc was killed. In a damn funny riot.

I don't much believe in that riot.

And now what? Tell the captain he's maybe married to Lady Macbeth? Shut up and soldier!

They were coming up to the corner of the reviewing field. Kitchen lads and girls were running from the roasting pits to the Guardsmen's tables. They all stopped to cheer, and Mason acknowledged.

"Left wheel!"

The Guards pivoted expertly, from column of fours to company order, each quartet of horses turning as if they were tied together.

A damned good outfit, and the Second Guards were shaping up almost as well. Their cadre had missed the Hooey River and nobody was letting them forget it, so they were training the Second Guards as if they were going to have to win the next big fight singlehanded.

A good outfit. *I'm married to the outfit.*

Maybe it's time for more than that. We're not going home. No way. Tran or no place, and damn I'm getting lonesome.

And suppose you find one like the Lady Tylara?

There's something to be said for being single.

✢ ✢ ✢

Tylara stood at the edge of the bed. Her fur-lined chamber robe covered her from her throat to the floor. Rick remembered better times, when she'd worn a sheer *garta* cloth nightgown. Of course the weather was warmer then, and she'd had three goblets of good wine, but—

She smiled lightly. "My husband. You have not properly celebrated the Wanax's wedding." She held out a wine goblet.

He tried to smile in return as he took the goblet and touched hers with it. "Thank you."

"You are troubled."

"Some. Mostly trying to decide what to do with Harvey Rand."

"Rand. The Star Lord in the attempt on the Lady Gwen."

"Him. I think I have a solution, but as Justiciar of Drantos any case involving a nobleman could end in your court."

"Yes, if he demands."

At least you don't question that he's noble. I'd hate for that question to come up. "We can't just hang him."

"To be sure. It would be work for the headsman."

"Not that either. He's got friends."

"I had thought he might," she said.

"And there's Gengrich. I need every soldier I can get. Thing is, if you have enough problems they can solve each other."

She looked at him quizzically.

He grinned. "I thought it might work this way. Harvey gets fined the blood price for the dead sentry, and double that for not thinking ahead. Since he hasn't got anything but his uniform, I'll pay the fines. Then he owes me." Rick drank half the wine. "Good stuff."

"What will you demand in repayment?"

"Well, I thought a Tran year in the madweed plantation garrison. Nobody wants that job, but it has to be done. Even Rand's friends can see that."

"He will also be a long way from the men of Eqeta Rudhrig." Her smile had faded.

"Exactly. So when Gengrich comes in, he'll want to bargain. Rand can be another chip I hold. If Gengrich wants his title recognized he'll have to assume responsibility for Rand. Pay his fines." Rick shrugged. "There's even some justice in it. Madweed guard duty's nothing soft."

Tylara stepped back a pace. "A wise solution, my lord. You have learned the laws and ways of the great lords very well indeed."

"Yeah, I thought—hey, what's wrong?"

"What makes you think there is something wrong?"

"I don't know, you just seem—"

"There is nothing wrong, my lord."

Rick got up and went to her. He put his arms around her and tried to draw her to him. After a moment he went back to the bed. "Sure. Nothing wrong."

She snuffed the last candle and lay down with her back to him.

Now what? Another nightmare about Sarakos? She was all right for a minute there. Did I put my foot in it about the laws? Or what?

"Tylara, what have I done *now*?"

"Nothing. Good night, my lord."

Something about Gwen? I should put a medal on Rand for trying to snatch Gwen?

He lay in the dark and tried to sort memories, of Tylara and Gwen, and finally he got up and found the pitcher of wine his orderly had left for him.

✣ ✣ ✣

"My lord husband!" Octavia put down the hair brush but did not giggle, as much as she wanted to. She knew that Ganton did not like women who giggled.

"Yes, my lady?"

"I have won my wager with the Lady Gwen."

Ganton frowned. "A wager?"

"Yes. I fear you might think it unseemly, but—"

"We both owe the Lady Gwen much. Even if it is unseemly, I will hold my tongue."

"Your word of honor?"

"By Yatar, Christ, the honor of the throne of Drantos, my love for you, and my feet which are beginning to freeze, I swear to do no harm to the Lady Gwen by word or deed."

"Very well. She wagered that you would wear your Browning when first you came to my bed."

Even in the candlelight she could see Ganton's face turning red. Then he threw back his head and howled with laughter. When he could speak again, he shrugged.

"The Lady Gwen has a most unwomanly mind. I think I am well enough armed."

"So it would seem. But any weapon must be well wielded."

"It shall be, and at close quarters."

"Then let the contest begin!"

5

The narrow streets of the Outer Castle were better lit than usual tonight, although not like last night. Then there'd been bonfires on every corner, candles in every window, and torches in the hands of half the revelers staggering from drink to drink. *Big send off for the royal wedding. Not so big for me, on my last night here.*

One house was brighter-lit than most. Les stopped below an open window. Voices were singing in English.

> *What shall we do with the Wanax Ganton?*
> *What shall we do with the Wanax Ganton?*
> *What shall we do with the Wanax Ganton,*
> *Early in the morning?*
>
> *Give him a ladder as a wedding present.*
> *Give him a ladder as a wedding present.*
> *Give him a ladder as a wedding present,*
> *Early in the morning.*

The Earth mercenaries, of course. With Jack Beazeley's song about Ganton's wedding. Beazeley had been more than a little nervous when he got a royal command to sing it for Ganton. By the time he got to the verse that went, "Wrap their kid in a purple diaper," Ganton had been laughing so hard he had to call for wine when he got his breath back.

Four Guardsmen saluted at the door to Gwen's house and passed him inside; two more escorted him up the stairs. As he knocked on the door to the private chambers, Les was beginning to wonder if they were going to tuck him into bed. Then he heard Gwen's voice.

"Come on in. I've given Lady Marva the night off."

Les swept Gwen into his arms. It was quite awhile before he could say anything that wasn't muffled in her hair. Eventually he broke away and poured wine. "Have you heard about the Great Council meeting?"

She nodded. "Larry Warner was by earlier and told me all about it. They're up to letting a woman be Rector of the University, but not up to letting her represent it on the Great Council."

Les' wine cup paused on its way to his lips.

Gwen frowned. "Les, are you jealous of Larry Warner?"

Les emptied the cup and he set it down with a steady hand. "You wouldn't be flattered if I said I was. I wouldn't be telling the truth, either. I may let myself be jealous someday, when I can be a full-time husband, but now, when I'm on Tran once a year if I'm lucky . . .

"Sorry. You must have been thinking about that even more than I. Here." He put an arm around her and let her cry on his shoulder. When she stopped, he kissed her. "You've just made my point for me. When I'm fifty light-years away and you need a shoulder to cry on, why not Larry Warner's? It's a damned sight safer than Captain Galloway's."

"Ugh."

"My sentiments exactly. I don't know if Tylara's a good friend, but she's a bad enemy. You know she's been trying to pump me about the Galactic Confederation, outside of the Inner Council?"

"No, but I'm not surprised. She is one shrewd lady."

"My opinion is you could put her down in a howling wilderness, and inside of five years she'd be running the place. She might have to convince the local headman that he needed a raven-haired concubine, but that wouldn't stop her."

"She'd probably create a vacancy among the concubines. What did you tell her?"

"Not much. I'm not convinced she's given up trying to hijack my ship. Rick has already told her more than I would." He shrugged. "Not that I know much to tell. That's Agzaral's department."

"If you're not careful she'll learn more than you know."

"Yeah. Look, maybe I don't think enough about local politics. Somebody tried to kidnap you last night."

"No, that was thieves—"

"No. Not thieves. One of them was from Earth. One of Gengrich's people. Galloway has him in a cell. Gwen, Gengrich, or somebody close to him, wanted you."

Her eyes seemed twice as large as usual. "Why?"

"Because you're such a damned good university administrator? Hey, it's all right. I don't know why. The Earth guy says it was so they'd have a better bargaining position with Rick. Me, I think they wanted your transceiver as much as anything. So they could bargain directly with the *Shalnuksis*."

"Oh. But—Gengrich couldn't have hoped to get away with that."

"They aren't sure he had anything to do with it. Right now Galloway suspects the captain of the ambassador's guards, Aidhos do Viz. They don't have any evidence that would justify arresting a diplomat, but they're pretty sure he was in on it. He'd be high in Lord Gengrich's favor if he got you, and if he failed Lord Gengrich could disavow him."

"Gengrich is going to be dangerous, if he commands loyalty like that."

"Captain Galloway thinks so too."

"All right. And they asked you not to tell me. Right?"

"Right."

"Thanks for not listening to them."

"I did listen to them, for a while. Then—well, everybody talks about Lady Tylara's pride, but they don't know you the way I do." He kissed her.

She held him until he broke away. "Look, we have to talk," he said.

She held him. "So talk."

He broke away and went to the door to look outside. The four Guardsmen were at the end of the hall. "My lord?"

"Nothing. Stay on watch."

"Les, what—"

"Want to be sure no one's listening."

"The Guards don't understand English—"

"It isn't the Guards I'm worried about." He lowered his voice almost to a whisper. "Look, I think I've worked out a plan. I can take you back. You and the kids. To Earth."

She ran toward him, then stopped at his look.

"There's a catch. I could never see you again. But I could set you up. Not so rich that people would notice, but comfortable. Gold—"

"Gold. You trying to buy your way out?"

"No! I mean—"

"What do you mean?"

"It's just something I thought of. I couldn't hide you from Agzaral, but I think I could talk him into letting you alone."

"But I'd never see you again."

"Probably not."

"So. I go to Earth and hide, live on your money and not see you. And do what? What would I be? Les, even a kept woman gets to see her lover once in a while." Then she laughed. "Besides, if you're going to send me back to Earth, I want more than gold."

"What?"

"Do you know they have a complete Ptolemy's *Life of Alexander the Great* here on Tran?"

"You mean Arrian's?"

"No, Ptolemy's. The one written by Alexander's own best general and half-brother after he was King of Egypt. Arrian probably used it, but on Earth it's been lost for centuries. Octavia gave Ganton a copy as a wedding present. There are a thousand other pieces of classical literature I could sell for a fortune. Do you know I spent a whole afternoon reading a Latin translation of Aeschylus' *The Myrmidons*? Mary Renault got it almost exactly right in *The Mask of Apollo*, when Nikeratos puts it on at Delphi."

"Now I know you're crazy."

"Why? Who would know? I'm sure classical scholars and universities would put a fine smokescreen against any awkward questions."

"Maybe. Maybe not. If it wasn't fine enough—Agzaral wouldn't hesitate to send agents to Earth to kill you and the children. Kill you and disintegrate your bodies, so nobody would find anything suspicious in the kids' DNA."

"He wouldn't!"

"Maybe he wouldn't. Maybe. But somebody would. Gwen, I don't know what they're going to do about Earth, but if your people learn about the Confederation it could—Look, one faction wants to destroy Earth now.

"Even if nothing happened to Earth, the secret of Tran would be out. Then the *Shalnuksis* would have to cover their tracks. Gwen, they have a weapon that could make the True Sun go nova."

"Good God. You're—no, you're not joking. Anyway, it doesn't matter. I'm not going back."

Thank the Light. "Why not?"

"Because I'd rather have you once every couple of years than never, you goose."

She came to his arms and he held her tightly.

Tran's your home, and you're important here. But maybe I am part of it.

"Just come back. Please."

"I'll always come back."

The nightmares were still close, but they knew what would drive them away, for a while. Dreams and nightmares alternated through the long Tran night.

✢ ✢ ✢

Gwen woke to find an empty bed and a pillow wet with tears she was quite sure weren't all hers.

I've lived through plenty of mornings without you. What's one more?

She slipped out of bed and stepped into the outer chamber. Marva was asleep in her bed and the children in theirs, with the maids on their pallets.

Gwen clapped her hands. "Up, up, everyone. Rise and shine."

6

The mist was closing in and the track underfoot was even worse than Gengrich remembered it. Well, he hadn't approached Castle Zyphron this way since early summer, before the Westmen invasion up north, and there'd been a hell of a lot of rain since then. No wonder the track had potholes you could damned near bathe in!

Alex Boyd, riding beside him, frowned at the hills slowly disappearing behind the grey wall of mist. "Arnie, if I remember right the track runs along the side of one of those hills. There's woods upslope, enough to hide a whole battalion."

"Ambushes?"

"Could be."

"What about riding downhill, off the track?"

"You could swing it in good weather. I've done it myself, riding light. With the grass wet, the ground soft, and the horses tired—no way."

It seemed like a good idea when they started off in the morning, on the last day's march homeward. Why not approach Castle Zyphron from the west, to smoke out any bandits who might have thought there was safety in a place the Lord of Zyphron would never think of looking? They'd certainly chased enough of them out of other places; the city council of Valus would be happy as a grig with the heads they'd sent in.

It had seemed like a good idea at the time. Now that the autumn rains had started the notion didn't look so good. Progress came a yard at a time, even when they dismounted and led the horses through the worst of it. Now it was mid-afternoon, visibility was going to hell, they were still seven klicks from the castle, and there wasn't a dry campground in sight. No dry wood, either.

They'd better move on and try to make it home tonight, or there were going to be seven hundred men thoroughly pissed off at one Lord Gengrich do Zyphron, former Corporal, U.S.A. Come to think of it, he was fairly pissed off at himself. *This stuff is worse than the 'Nam highlands. Should have expected it.* "Alex."

"Yeah?"

"The men won't like sleeping out in the wet this close to home. Take Clayton and Green and a double load of ammo and fifty men and ride up ahead. Picket the road every couple of hundred meters. If that smokes out an ambush, we can come up and bail you out. If it doesn't, we can push on through."

Boyd nodded slowly. "If you say so—"

"What's buggin' you, Alex? The ammo?"

"Yeah. I don't mind shooting it off, but risking its being captured . . ."

"Got any better ideas?" Boyd shook his head. "Then move it. We sure don't want to be out here in the dark."

"Aaaa-men, brother."

Gengrich watched as Boyd rode off to round up the other two mercs for his fire team and pick a half-company of locals. He spat into a clump of sheepdog bush beside the track. *Never knew what officers did. Until I had to be one.*

Christ, for a nickel I'd give it up. Except that doesn't work either. Bad enough taking care of two thousand people, but damn all it's worse being alone. Goddamn crummy planet.

A snatch of song ran through his mind. Something he'd seen on an arts channel movie. "And it is a pleasant thing, to be a pirate king."

Flipping bullshit it is!

At least the harvests hadn't been too bad, which had bought him a little time to play what was now really his only card. He didn't know what good would come of sending an embassy north to Ganton's wedding, but old Daettan had a reputation for being a pretty smart bargainer.

No harm asking. Maybe the captain will take us all back. Only what happens if he wants just the mercs and none of the locals? What in hell do I do then?

When Alex's patrol rode through Gengrich ordered the others to dismount and lead. "Save the horses." There were grumbles, and some arguments. One of his NCOs shouted and he heard blows.

No flipping discipline, and what do I do about that? Pirate king my ass.

✣ ✣ ✣

It was just enough darker to notice when Gengrich heard the shots. Six that sounded like one of the H&Ks and another that sounded like a .45. That meant trouble unless it was Green firing; he had a bad rep for being trigger-happy.

"Red alert!"

Gengrich heard the order relayed as he swung up into his saddle. If it was Green wasting ammo again, he'd just made a real good down payment on being the first merc to really smoke for screwing up—

"Bandits!" somebody shouted, invisible in the mist ahead. Then two more bursts and a lot of wordless yelling, some of it not even sounding human.

Gengrich felt his hands quiver the way they always did when he knew a firefight was coming. It never bothered him once he was doing some personal shooting, but sitting and watching or even worse listening always got to him.

"First and Fourth Companies, mount up! Second and Third Companies, take the flanks and advance for dismounted action!" Please God the horseholders knew their business and all the bandits were up front and not lurking down here ready to grab the mounts.

Gengrich drew his sword and dug in his spurs. Gravel flew as he came level with the captain of Fourth Company. As the mounted column got into motion, it made enough noise to alert any bandits for miles around. Not enough to drown out more bursts of firing up ahead. Gengrich concentrated on controlling his horse with one hand. He could now manage a horse if he kept his mind on it, although he suspected that most of the born-in-the-saddle types among the locals still sniggered at him behind his back.

He was so busy with his mount that he didn't notice the battle noises getting louder. Suddenly they were all around him, and he saw

Alex Boyd down on one knee behind his dead horse, one arm dangling useless, firing his pistol with the other hand.

Gengrich opened his mouth to shout to Boyd. Before he could take a deep breath not just the battle noises but the battle itself was all around him. A stand of scrub oak spewed ragged figures in all directions. The captain of the Fourth Company flipped backward out of his saddle, his face mashed into jam by a flail. Someone leaped into the emptied saddle and started to turn the mount's head, then screamed even louder and fell under its hooves as Boyd shot him in the belly.

Two other bandits closed in on Gengrich. He slashed down at the head of the one in the lead. The man's long dagger gashed his boot as the sword came down. The man tried to slash again as he reeled back, his skull split open, then crumpled. The other bandit let out a scream that turned Gengrich's stomach and leaped like a frog, left hand gripping the bow of the saddle and the right the horse's reins. As Gengrich realized the bandit was a woman, she brought the knife in her right hand around toward the horse's neck. His swordcut only gashed her shoulder, but it broke her grip in time to save the horse. He made another wild slash at her and felt it hit something, but didn't see what happened to her after that. The bandits who'd run past him came running back, and after them some reinforcements from the First Company.

The bandits didn't wait around for the full four companies to come up; they scattered with what they'd managed to grab or strip from the dead. Gengrich was just starting to think of casualty reports when he heard four evenly spaced rifle shots from back where the horses of the dismounted companies were being held. He was turning his mount when he heard a horse's scream, another shot, then silence. He waited while the silence dragged on, then sighed. Whatever it was back there, it wasn't a full-scale attack on the rear.

What the bandits up in front had done was bad enough. Joe Green was going to have to be trigger-happy with his left hand; somebody had hacked off the first two joints of his right index finger. Alex Boyd would be out of action for a while with a broken arm; that was a mace. Twelve of the locals were dead and about twenty had reported wounded, which meant probably twice as many needing the medics. The local habit of proving your guts by not reporting wounded wasn't quite as bad as it was before Gengrich trained the medics in antisepsis; now you could prove your guts by letting boiling water be dumped on your wounds. You still got a lot of people walking around with legitimate Purple Hearts and never saying a frigging word!

The bandits left fourteen bodies behind, and any of them who lit out with a bad wound was probably going to die, but they'd also made off with a dozen weapons and five horses. No star weapons or ammo, thank God; Gengrich still knew that Alex Boyd had come too damned close to being a prophet instead of just a casualty.

A scribe was getting the figures down on a wooden tablet when Private Alan MacAllister rode up the track. "That's wrong," he said, pointing at the figures.

"Yeah?"

"I got five more back there. They tried to come through the horses. I think they were in a hurry."

"They probably were. We weren't exactly running a resort up here."

"I know. Like I said, I got five more back there."

No time to send somebody for a body count, and no need either. MacAllister was about the surliest merc in the whole outfit and always had been. He was also the best and coolest shot Gengrich had ever known, and was real sticky about an accurate count of his kills.

So that meant nineteen bandits in return for a dozen locals down plus two starmen and twenty-odd locals hurt. With the loot they'd snagged, the bandits might be calling it a victory.

Victory. Right. Who was that guy who said, "Give me another victory like this and I'm dog meat"?

✦ ✦ ✦

The rising wind whipped the flames of the torches on the gate towers but the light rain wasn't enough to put them out. Helmets and shield bosses glistened as the sentries presented arms. Gengrich returned their salutes and rode on through the smelly darkness of the gate itself into the courtyard of Castle Zyphron.

Behind him rode the mercs, the wounded with the medics and stretcher-bearers, and his own personal bodyguard. The rest of the column would probably already be settling down in New Zyphron, which was their fancy name for the walled camp at the foot of the hill.

At least they'd take care of their horses and armor before they went looking for wine and an audience. He'd made it a rule from the first, that a man who neglected his mount joined the infantry and a man who neglected his armor or weapons joined the bandits. He'd had to fight twice, once against six men, before he made that rule stick, but that was the last bit of trouble.

Frank Guilford came up, saluted, and went off to triage the wounded without waiting for a reply. After him came the seneschal, Master Arranthos. *Master Arranthos. Damfino master of what. Some city guild until politics got him. He sure don't talk about it.*

"Master Khemos thinks that the south gate must be braced, at least, to see the winter through."

"Can't he finish the repairs?"

"The foundation on the left side needs work. The ground will be too wet for safe digging until the frosts come."

After that it would be too hard, of course. A sweet set of choices—override a master mason, start work and risk Khemos quitting or people getting killed; block off the castle's escape hatch to mounted men for the rest of the winter; or do nothing and watch the gate fall on somebody's head in the first blizzard.

"Give Master Khemos my compliments and tell him to brace the gate." *Read that in a novel once. Sure comes in handy.*

This far south a light-infantry army that didn't need forage for cavalry or a siege train could campaign damned near all year 'round, but that wouldn't be a menace to Castle Zyphron. They couldn't be in real hot water before spring, and then if they did have to get out in a hurry it'd be for good and damned sure they wouldn't be riding!

"Yes, my lord. The Lord Holloway says he expects the forge to be fit for the making of—guns—in another ten days. He asks whether you wish iron or bronze guns."

Now that was almost good news! Siggie Holloway was just as good a blacksmith as he said he was, and ready to bust his tail in the bargain. Once they'd decided that their gunpowder was good enough to use in guns, he'd rounded up the people and the tools without anybody having to ride herd on him.

Bronze or iron was still a question. Iron they had, but nobody on Tran seemed to know how to cast it, except maybe the Romans. They'd have to use guns hammered together out of wrought-iron bars; they'd be heavy mothers and likely to blow up in your face if you gave 'em a dirty look.

Bronze could be cast, and that meant lighter, stronger guns that wouldn't rust. But both bronze and the bronzesmiths would have to be imported from Rustengo. *Who in hell do we know in Rustengo besides Mort Schultz? Have to ask around. Guess we'll have to make peace with Schultzy. But not just yet.*

"Iron, I think. We have the men with the art of working it, and it is easier to come by. We'll need a lot."

Arranthos gave Gengrich's H&K a pointed look. "The star weapons seem to wield great power, though they are small."

Why try to bluff? "That is true. They are also made with starmetals that may not exist on this world, and with magic that none of the starmen know, not even the Lord Rick."

Arranthos looked thoughtful. "Very well. Lady Helena asks that you see her as soon as your duties permit. Your son Dan has been sick with the lung-fever these past three days. Lord Guilford does not hold out much hope."

"Oh, Christ."

Gengrich briefly closed his eyes and tried not to sway in the saddle. It was all just too damned much. Dan was such a likable baby, with his mother's blond hair and his father's dark eyes, and Helena had gone through hell having him. She was so proud, too, because Erika had a girl, then miscarried so that she couldn't have any more. . . .

Pneumonia didn't care whether you liked somebody or not. All it cared about was whether there were any drugs to fight it off. There weren't and there weren't going to be any, and that was that, although Frank had done some pretty good work with home remedies picked up from the local mid-wives.

"Forgive me, my lord, that I brought—"

"Oh, it's not your fault. Tell Lady Helena I'll be with her as soon as I've prayed to Hestia." *And washed up, but I can't get them to understand about that.*

"Yes, my lord."

Gengrich dismounted and strode off toward the shrine of Hestia without noticing if his squires caught his horse. Please, God or Hestia, or Somebody, don't let Dan die. What did he do to anybody?

Maybe Hestia would answer.

And maybe Elliot would fly down from the sky in a balloon with a case of penicillin and a case of Lone Star beer.

✣ ✣ ✣

Dan died just before True Sun-rise the next morning. The last thing on Tran or any other world Gengrich wanted to do was stay in the sickroom looking at his son's body. But Helena was crying so hard he didn't want to leave her alone.

Hell, even Erika was crying. Maybe that meant he wouldn't have woman troubles with Erika crowing over her rival's losing Dan. . . .

By late morning Helena was cried out. Gengrich staggered into his chamber and collapsed on the bed. He didn't bother taking off his boots, but he did grab a jug of Guilford's Private Stock. It was about eighty proof and tasted even worse than Gengrich felt.

He'd thought one drink would be enough to send him off, but he was on his third when he heard a knock at the door.

"Go to hell."

"It is Lord Severianus, Lord Gengrich."

"He can go to hell too."

"My lord," came a more educated voice. "I fear this is worth disturbing you. When you have heard me, then if you wish I will go to hell."

Gengrich groaned. "Let him in."

Marcus Julius Vinicianus strode in. He'd been a drunk ever since Flaminius exiled him ten years ago for some satirical verses on Caesar's inability to make up his mind. The booze had left his nose, eyes, and cheeks permanently red and given him a potbelly, but he still walked and carried himself like a drill sergeant.

"All right. What is it?"

"Forgive me for breaking in on your grief. May Christ and all His Saints keep your son, and send you and Lady Helena—"

"I can hear condolences some other time. What else?"

"Some news from the north. I fear we have misjudged one of the men we thought we could most trust, and much evil may come of—"

"Marcus, if you want your neck wrung like a chicken, just go on trying to be polite. Spit it out."

Uninvited, Vinicianus poured himself a cupful of whiskey and drank. "Captain Aidhos do Vis assisted by the starman Harvey Rand made an attempt to carry off the Lady Gwen Tremaine and bring her south to you."

"Christ! Why?"

"He thought she would be of value, to force the Star Lord Les to help you speak to the skyfolk. Or perhaps she could help you do that herself. Either way, you would be able to trade madweed for star weapons and tools. For medicines. Aidhos no doubt expected that you would be grateful for this, and give him honor and wealth."

"Jesus Christ." *What have they got me into?* "That's what he tried. What happened?"

"Four of his men were killed or captured, including the starman Rand."

He's no loss.

"Two confessed under torture and were executed. No one seems to know what happened to Rand. Lord Rick spoke harshly to Master Daettan in Council and accused him of bringing thieves to a royal wedding."

"Thieves?"

"Yes. Except for the Inner Council of Drantos, all are being told that the men were only thieves. Nor had Captain Aidhos been arrested at the time the message left Edron."

That could have long since changed, of course. But if Aidhos was going to be let go to protect the captain's cover story . . . "Marcus. Do you have any reliable informants in Vis?"

"Need you ask?"

"Not really." Vinicianus had informants everywhere. *Including in my household, I expect. But he's useful.* "Have them learn all they can about Aidhos' friends and kin. I do not want to be at feud with half of Vis for taking Aidhos' head, but if I can do so safely, I will have it."

"To what end?"

"As a present for the Lord Rick."

"It will take more than that to make peace with him."

"What makes you think I want to make peace with Lord Rick?"

"I predict that we will have no choice by spring."

"When I want predictions, I'll hire a soothsayer."

"Very well. You know better than I, whether the 'magic' of the star weapons will last beyond this winter without being renewed."

There wasn't anything to say to that. "Sure, I'd like to make peace. I'll be his ally if he'll have us. All of us, everybody who follows me. Anyway, we can't wait until spring."

"We agree, then."

Damn nice of you. "So. You look into Vis and I'll send somebody to talk to Schultz in Rustengo."

"An alliance with Rustengo will anger the Prophet Phrados."

"Tell Phrados to kiss my arse."

"Impractical. How does one compel the master of a hundred thousand soldiers?"

"The man who says he has a hundred thousand soldiers."

"Yes. It is not quite the same thing. But he certainly has a large host, and we have no spies in it."

"So I'll keep it a secret that I'm talking to Schultz. For God's sake, leave me alone!"

"As you wish."

"Stop." The liquor and the exhaustion were hitting now; Gengrich felt as if his arms and eyelids were weighted with lead. "Sometimes I don't know what I'd do without you, Marcus."

"Today you would go to bed with your boots on," said Vinicianus, expertly heaving Gengrich's legs onto the bed and starting to unlace the boots. A snore was the only reply. He pulled the boots off and piled furs over the sleeping Star Lord.

"Sleep, my friend, and God give you peace if men cannot."

7

Master of Foot Mortimer Schultz stood up in the sternsheets of the boat. The boat swung to port as the helmsman put the tiller over to avoid the submerged ruins of a wall. Schultz spread his legs to balance against the sudden motion. They glided into open water. Two crewmen furled the sail and hoisted the leeboard. A moment later they slid aground on a muddy bottom that had once been a hillside above a fishing village east of Rustengo.

"Well done," Schultz said. The helmsman grunted something that might have been "thanks." The sailors of Rustengo were a close-mouthed lot at best, and the helmsman no doubt suspected the Master Schultz knew little of ships. He was right; before Schultz joined the Army to escape going to rabbinical school his only acquaintance with ships had been the Staten Island Ferry.

Schultz's four guards splashed ashore and took up positions where they could cover the hillside with their crossbows. Schultz followed them, then called back to the crew, "If we have not returned by darkness or if anyone attacks the boat, you must bear word to the house of Mahros."

"Master—"

"I don't doubt your courage. But if we meet danger today, it will come from more men than the three of you could fight, were each of you an Achilles."

"As you wish, Master Schultz." For the helmsman, that was an oration. As Schultz led the guards up the hill the crew were already breaking out poles to push the boat back into water deep enough for safe anchorage.

Not that he expected trouble, even if the Prophet Phrados was a *gonef* of the worst sort and his envoy no better. Four guards hand-picked from the Bronzesmith's Cohort would make easy and silent assassination impossible. *He can't kill me without the City finding out. Is that enough? Hell, I'm engaged to the daughter of the Master of Bronzesmiths. That has to be enough.*

Not even Phrados would be mad enough to start a new war with the city Guilds.

Up the hill, over the crest, and down the other side. The point man had out his brush-cutter, a big curved wooden stick like a boomerang with a cold-worked bronze edge riveted to the inside. It was getting a workout. This path had got pretty nearly overgrown during the summer, now that the tidal wave and the rising sea had swallowed the village below it. The vegetation was dying back with the coming of autumn, but enough fleecevine and hydras bane was left to occasionally give Schultz the feeling he was back in the Mekong Delta.

The path dipped sharply fifty yards beyond the crest. *Ha. Used to be level here.* The whole hillside was sliding down into the sea. *Quake or undermined by water? No matter. This is our last trip here.*

He slipped on a patch of mud and caught himself with the rifle butt. Once again Schultz thanked the Lord that Gengrich and Warner had managed to snag H&Ks for everybody when they led the mutiny. M-16s would never have stood up to this kind of punishment and skimpy maintenance. He patted the plastic butt for luck.

The old path now wound down to the water's edge and vanished. A new path branched off to the left, following the new shoreline to a sprawling building of logs and driftwood with a thatched roof. A crudely lettered sign over the door told the world that this was "Charon's Rest."

A while back the river running down through this little valley was something you could wade across on a summer day. Then the earthquakes and tidal wave dumped a hill across its mouth; the rising sea did the rest. The valley was flooded a good eight or nine klicks back into the hill. Between the end of the valley and the next good road to the north was a lot of rugged hills and more bandits than anything short of a century would care to tackle, although Gengrich was supposed to be getting on top of those bastards.

Right now, though, anyone coming along the coast road had to pay the owner of Charon's Rest for a ferry across the valley. If it was too late for the traveler to reach Rustengo before the gates closed, a traveler could also pay stiff prices for bad food, worse wine, and vermin-ridden beds. Before the rising sea washed Charon's Rest away, its owner was going to be a rich man—if an earthquake didn't dump the whole thing into the water.

The sign's rusty chains squealed in the rising wind as Schultz led his men in through the door. The owner's wife greeted him.

"Your friend has already arrived. He is in the back room."

Schultz handed her two Roman silvers and five Rustengo brasses. She bit one of the silvers, then nodded. "He is alone there. Another man came with him, to tend their horses."

That pretty much ruled out treachery. "What does he look like?"

"He dresses like a merchant from just north of the Sunlands, but he does not look like one. More like a soldier. He also speaks with the tongue of an educated man of the north."

"Thanks."

A lot of people running around these days weren't what they looked like—and that included Anna Schultz's son Mortimer. *Northerner. Could be. Wonder if he knows what's happening up there?*

Schultz nodded to the guards. "Follow me."

✢ ✢ ✢

Matthias, Highpriest of Vothan, watched the starman enter. He was no taller than most men of this world, but his strange green and brown tunic and trousers made him look otherwise. He also carried both a large and a small star weapon.

Two Rustengan soldiers followed him into the room. One stood by the door, holding his crossbow so that it was ready to shoot without appearing so to an inexperienced eye. That pleased Matthias. It suggested that the starman was accepting him as the merchant he said he was.

Best not to accept things too calmly, however. "I asked that we meet alone, Master Schultz."

"We will, once my men have searched this room for spies. Would you trust the owner to hold his tongue? Either gold or less gentle means might give our secrets to God knows who."

So Schultz believed there was only one god. That meant he was a Christian like the other starmen. A pity. It would have been agreeable to learn that he lived apart even from Lord Gengrich because he worshipped other gods, even if they were not the true ones. Something might have been made of such a quarrel.

The Rustengans knew their business. After the search one pronounced the room "clean" and went outside to stand by the door. The other vanished, to return shortly with sausages, cheese, and wine, then join his comrade. Schultz closed the door and poured out the wine.

"To prosperity for all honest traders."

Matthias doubted there was such a thing, but it was a toast the man he pretended to be could not have refused. He drank, then picked up a sausage and cut a piece of cheese with his knife.

Schultz ate no sausages, only cheese, and mixed his wine with water from a strange flattened metal jug at his waist. Their talk wandered over many matters—whether there was any profit to be found in the rebuilding of Rustengo's walls, how many guards a caravan needed to be safe from bandits, what were the best (or at least the safest) inns for outland merchants, and much else.

Matthias felt that it fouled his tongue to speak of such matters. He also knew that he had done as much in the service of Vothan, and would do worse in the service of Issardos, High Chancellor of the Five Kingdoms. "How tender a conscience can we allow ourselves, when we fight men who seem to have no conscience at all?" was the Chancellor's question, and many nights of fasting and meditating at Vothan's shrine had given Matthias no clear answer.

At last matters turned to rebuilding certain temples of Yatar fallen or damaged in the earthquake. "Some say it is wasted effort, with the Time so close and other needs so pressing," said Schultz. "Others say that it is never a waste, to honor the gods. Even some of the Christians say that they wish to help honor the Father of Christ, although what they would say if their own churches had not largely escaped I do not know."

"Then the vision of Archbishop—?"

"Polycarp."

"That vision, it has won converts in Rustengo?"

"Does this surprise you?"

"No, since I know that the followers of Christ and the followers of Yatar have long been at peace with each other in Rustengo. Yet I warn you, this will not please the Prophet Phrados."

For a moment Matthias was in fear that the Star Lord would draw his weapon. It would be godless treachery, but if the Star Lords thought themselves so close to the gods that they need not fear them . . . ?

The moment passed, but the unfamiliar and unwelcome taste of fear did not leave Matthias' mouth. He drank more wine, glad to find his hand steady.

"I thank you for your warning," said Schultz. "It is not unknown, that the Prophet Phrados seeks to defend the honor of the gods by smiting those who believe in Polycarp's visions. I return the favor by giving my own warning. Rustengo has ruled itself in such matters even when it was under the Empire of Rome. It will do no less now. Anyone who seeks to dictate the City's religions had best bring an army with him."

"The Prophet has just that."

"He is *said* to have just that, my friend. Surely you have heard of enough ghost armies to believe only what you see."

"I have. The Prophet marches with a host the like of which no living man has seen. With my own eyes I have seen ten thousand men swearing themselves into his service. I have counted thrice that many already sworn. More come each day."

"Rustengo has ships, men, and walls enough to defend herself against any who seek to break the Great Peace."

"Ships and men, perhaps, but walls?"

"What has fallen can be raised again."

Matthias shrugged. "May Yatar watch over Rustengo, and Vothan strengthen the arms of its defenders."

The wine was surprisingly good. Matthias drained the last and set down his cup. "It is said that the men of Lord Gengrich also follow the new way of Polycarp's vision. Or so I was told in the camps of Phrados."

Schultz's expression told nothing. "I have no great quarrel with the Lord Gengrich, but I cannot say that I am much in his confidence either. The Star Lords themselves are worshippers of Christ, but like all wise men they honor His Father and the Warlord as well. I do not know what gods Gengrich's men worship. I am told that all who will obey his orders are welcome in his service."

"Even outlaws and bandits?"

"Outlaws, very likely. Bandits, I much doubt it. I know that he has fought bandits side by side with the soldiers of half the city-states and a good many of the mercenary bands. Most speak well of him, although they also say he is a hard man in bargaining for pay and a dangerous man to cheat."

"He will hire himself to anyone?"

"I have not heard that he refused any offer, unless he was already in another's service or the pay was too low."

Those were the words from Schultz's lips. What Matthias heard in his mind was, "Why don't you come right out and say what would be Phrados' price for Lord Gengrich's men?"

Once again Matthias reminded himself that a merchant would not show a nobleman's anger. "It may be to Lord Gengrich's—profit, to have made no alliance with those whom the Prophet calls enemies."

"I am sure that the Lord Gengrich will hear that message. As to what he may do afterward . . ." The shrug was not only a dismissal of the matter, it was very nearly a dismissal of Matthias.

Matthias did not rise in anger, but swore that the next time he spoke to Master Schultz the Star Lord would learn to respect one who served Vothan and was also kin to the Crown of Ta-Lataos! Aloud, he said only, "Shall we order more wine?" and nearly sighed with relief when Schultz shook his head.

✦ ✦ ✦

Schultz huddled amidships, back against the straining mast, trying to stay under his oilcloth cloak. Every so often the boat stuck her nose in deep enough to throw spray, and his boots were already wet from what was sloshing around in the bottom. They'd have to start bailing pretty soon, and it was getting dark. . . .

They were sailing across what used to be swamp. Now it was open water with a few treetops. Fewer of those every day.

The helmsman shouted. Schultz saw a wavering glow in the twilight about a klick off to starboard. That must be the new lighthouse, and it was a lot brighter than the last time he'd seen it. They must have got the reflectors installed. Last time he'd passed, the light from the fish-oil lamps was so dim that a good-sized ship would damned near run aground before anybody aboard saw the light.

The helmsman shouted again and the boat heeled as she came

about. Schultz threw one arm around the mast and held on. He'd a lot rather have an arm around Diana, but he'd have that in another hour, now that they were on course for the harbor.

Schultz smiled as he thought of Diana waiting in her white robe with her blond hair unbound and flowing down over her shoulders. She'd lead him to the bath, of course. Funny how the Rustengans weren't hung up on the virginity of their daughters. Guess it came from having been under the Romans without ever really turning Christian. Roman baths and willing girls made up for a lot of things, like having to deal with that wacko ambassador from the Prophet who called himself a trader.

What *was* that *momser's* game, anyway? With Rustengo, it was pretty clear. If the city did anything against the Prophet Phrados, they'd be in trouble—as much trouble as the Prophet's army could make for them.

That could be a lot. The city's walls really weren't in too great shape; a general who didn't care about casualties could probably storm the city outright. The Rustengans couldn't march out and fight in the open either, not if the other side had any good cavalry. From what Schultz knew about the Sunlands and the rest of where the refugees came from, the Prophet wouldn't have any now, but if he got some of the better local mercenary outfits on his side . . .

Maybe that was why he wanted Gengrich. Arnie had some fair to middling cavalry of his own. More dragoons than cavalry, but not bad. He also had a lot of contracts with other mounted mercenary outfits.

Mort, you better get up north to Castle Zyphron and lay all this on Gengrich, before that Prophet gonef *sends him an offer he can't refuse.*

It would be a lot harder to make peace with the Captain if Gengrich signed up with somebody fighting the Captain's new religion. *Arnie has to know that. If he doesn't—*

If he doesn't, we're both finished.

Damn the Prophet anyway! Going north meant leaving Diana. It meant leaving the shop right when things were about to click on moveable type—and *that* would guarantee him red-carpet treatment from the Captain. For him and anybody he wanted to bring along. It meant leaving his century, right when they were beginning to shape up. . . .

Arnie, you're going to owe me one. Hope you figure that out.

✣   ✣   ✣

It was so dark under the trees that Matthias didn't see the sentries' lanterns until a moment before they challenged him.

"Who is there?"

"The True Servant."

"Thank Vothan! We were beginning to worry, my lord. Is all well?"

Matthias dismounted without answering, and took a bowl of hot soup from a man-at-arms. Tonight's march would be no easy task, but there was no other way to get safely into the hills by daybreak. Bandits would not trouble eighty armed men. At least no small band of them would, and Lord Gengrich and his allies had left few large ones.

A good war captain, Gengrich, by all appearances. Could he be turned against his Captain General? Then the Five Kingdoms could crush the starmen and their allies one by one. But it must be done quickly, before everyone was overtaken by the Time.

The cult of Yatar had its records of the Time. So did the Priests of Vothan, although they did not boast of them. In the Time, the lands of the Five Kingdoms would grow strong—and the hordes from the south would come. So said the records.

As the men-at-arms began beating out the campfire, the horses suddenly neighed in a ragged chorus. The air grew still. Matthias felt a moment of dizziness. Then the ground quivered. It felt as if he stood on the back of a large animal.

"Forget the campfire!" he shouted. "Lead the horses out of the trees!"

By the time they were out of the trees, the campfire was only a dim glow in the distance. A hasty count showed that all the men and horses were safe. Anyone coming on the remains of the camp would think bandits had struck.

Matthias swung into the saddle and led the way northward. His head held confusion. When the very earth under men's feet betrayed them, was this a time to do the will of men who seemed to worship nothing but their own magic, and led others to do the same?

And if their magic is a gift from the gods?

He rode on without answers. The trail led steeply uphill, and it took all his skill and attention to keep his seat.

No more earth shocks came, but when they reached the open hills, it was snowing.

INTERLUDE: LUNA

The man Rick Galloway knew as Inspector Agzaral studied the telltales on the device clipped to the underside of his desk and smiled to himself. For the next hour anyone listening would hear only meaningless pleasantries. When the office door opened he rose and went more than halfway to greet the woman who entered. He raised her hand to his lips, an act that would have astonished both humans and nonhumans who knew him. It would not have surprised those who knew of his relationship with Jehna Sae Leern, but there had been no such person of any race in forty Terran years.

"You haven't changed much," she said. She glanced at his desk.

"We can talk," he said. "Or—"

"Later." She smiled.

"How was the Council meeting?"

"To anyone but us, entirely routine."

"So. There was pressure on anyone to declare their position on the future of Earth."

"Nothing overt."

"No faction believes it has won, then."

Jehna smiled. "You can see the sun by daylight. And yet, I sensed that some were waiting. To pounce, to change sides—I don't know. Is there anything in those decanters?"

Agzaral chose a Waterford decanter and two Scandinavian glasses in the shape of dragons. "A new sherry. I think you'll find it drinkable."

"I'd rather have whiskey." They raised their glasses. Jehna tossed hers back stiff-wristed. "Free stars."

Agzaral glanced at the telltales on his desk. "Free stars! Are you mad?"

"I think not. If I read the meeting right, we may have opportunities. Better than in the past five hundred years."

"A long time."

"I mean it. At least three of the Five Families might be glad to see Earth humans burst into space on their own. It's all on the tape. Listen, then tell me."

"I'll listen. But why might they want that?"

"Ennui. Look at it through their eyes. A lifetime of centuries with everything the same at the end as at the beginning. They don't even have to work at it. You and I do it for them."

"War as a cure for boredom. Interesting. But the Ader'at'eel are beyond that."

"Are they? Listen to the tapes and say that again. I don't say they want war. They're just bored, and not too concerned about the Confederation. Did you ever see a film made on Earth called *La Dolce Vita?* It may be a disease of ruling families of every race. Everywhere."

"Are the Ehk'mai among the Three Families who feel this way?"

"Ah. I think you do understand."

"Perhaps. Have they prepared to take advantage of the instabilities—Hah. Put wild humans in space and none of us can know what will happen."

"Isn't that what we want? The only really predictable thing is stasis. Anyway, I don't know what the Ehk'mai have planned." She grinned. "You expect me to know a lot. Courier First-Rank isn't even the highest human rank in the service of the Ehk'mai."

"But can you find out?"

"I have some access to both humans and Ader'at'eel at the proper level. Is it wise to ask such questions?"

"We have to know. It will be dangerous to ask?"

"Of course, and since when have you become protective?"

"Merely concerned with timing. One wishes to choose the most profitable moment to go—'in harm's way' is the phrase an Earth sailor once used."

Jehna smiled. "K'yar, you are not deceiving me, let alone yourself. You are worried—for me, and for what the Ader'at'eel might be plotting."

Agzaral sipped his sherry. "That may be." He looked thoughtful, then decisive. "At all events, this is not the proper time for you to go in harm's way. You wouldn't learn enough. The time will come, and now I think sooner than we expected."

"You sound almost—pleased."

"Does this surprise you?"

"Somewhat. You have always been the perfect cynic. Now you seem to be welcoming a situation that could force you to choose sides."

"You are surprised that I can see the sun by daylight?"

"It isn't that clear to me."

"Perhaps it will be clearer once you have seen a film I have for you."

"A film?" She raised one eyebrow. "From Earth?"

"Not that kind. You would not believe how Terran erotica has deteriorated in the last few years. Most would nauseate anyone but sadists, and bore them."

"You intrigue me!"

"I'd be a poor host if I didn't." He turned off the scrambler and rose. "Come. The caviar is Persian, but the smoked salmon is Fortnum's best. There's an extra side of it for you."

‡ ‡ ‡

The film had been shot against a green-sprayed wall of lunar rock. Les was holding up a photograph as he talked.

"Gwen isn't the only one who bounces back when she's knocked down. Take Jack Beazeley. His hobby is folk singing, and he's missed having a guitar. So he learned to play the lyre, and rescored a lot of songs for it. Then he sat down with an instrument-maker and described a twelve-string guitar. You see the results. I don't think any Earth folk singer would recognize it, let alone be able to play it, but I've heard Beazeley give a two-hour concert on it. Next time I'll bring a tape of his less ribald compositions."

Les stopped smiling. "I think the *Shalnuksis* badly underestimated what they turned loose on Tran. There've been a few duds like Parsons, but most of Rick's people are turning out to be the sort you don't want mad at you. And they've been turned loose on a planet that was settled with fairly tough people to start with—people who've been systematically selected for survival qualities by a hostile environment and periodic doses of A-bombs.

"If I were one of the *Shalnuksis*, I'd be frightened, but I'm not one of those sons of bitches. I'm proud to be human and proud to be Gwen's chosen mate. I'll always be proud of these things, whatever happens to me or to Tran."

The screen went blank. Jehna picked up a forkful of sachertorte, then put it down.

"So that's Les."

"An interesting specimen, isn't he? Not particularly discreet, but—"

"I'd like to meet him."

"To see if he's irresistible?"

"Jealous, K'yar?"

"Envious, rather. Les—I believe the phrase is 'has to beat women off with a club.' "

"In that case I'd rather meet Gwen. He's obviously found *her* irresistible." Jehna finished the torte and rubbed her stomach. "I shall have to fast halfway to Aderat to lose the weight your hospitality has put on me."

"If you find yourself a trifle full—"

"Satisfying one appetite doesn't satisfy all of them, my friend. You knew that once. Have you forgotten?"

He rose and stood behind her, his hands on her shoulders, and took her neck in his teeth. When she gasped he put his hands on her hips. "No, I haven't forgotten."

"I see you haven't."

She slipped out of her robe and he saw that she still swam and sunbathed nude; the long limbs were as brown and supple as ever. He moved against her. They both knew that they were in danger, and as usual this was exciting her.

Danger was too constant a companion to excite him but he didn't object to its effect on Jehna. He would not forget their interlude in Seoul in 1950, the last time he and Jehna went Earthside together. . . .

As desire replaced thought, Agzaral could not help wondering whether Les had stumbled on an important truth. Had the *Shalnuksis* conjured up a danger to the whole Confederation?

INTERLUDE
✠✠✠
GWEN TREMAINE'S DIARY

25/Mists/Ganton 2—Routine University business all day—inspecting the firewood and coal supplies and sending for more, reading reports, sitting on a court of inquiry on two legionaries found drunk in the women's quarters, etc., etc., *ad nauseam*.

Day only redeemed at the end by dinner with Larry Warner. He's got a positively courtly manner now, and a slight potbelly that he's fighting by working out with the Romans every morning. He's also obviously still interested in me, but not pushing it.

Just as well. The loneliness hasn't hit yet, but it will, after the child comes.

Should I have told Les about the child? He was frank enough with me about the kidnap attempt. I just don't know how much he will tell me. He says he doesn't want me to worry. If he keeps enough secrets about the Galactics I won't have to worry, I'll be dead! I don't know, but at least there won't be any question about whose kid this one is!

So far no morning sickness, so I haven't had to tell anyone but Marva and Sergeant McCleve. He's going to be really handy to have around if I have another hard time; he's reinvented obstetrical forceps. That could do almost as much for a population boom as antisepsis.

Back to the dinner. Larry read me a letter from Lance Clavell, our new Ambassador Extraordinary, Plenipotentiary, etc., to the island city-state of Nikeis. It sounds like a cross between Venice and

Mont-St. Michel. Better than Venice. High ground. Won't sink. Or get flooded in the Time. I'd sure like to see their arsenal. Larry heard they can work on a dozen ships at a time.

For the record, Nikeis is governed by a Council of Guilds and merchant houses. Sounds like Venice again. They've got a figurehead Eqeta and some theoretical allegiance to Drantos, but I notice Drantos doesn't collect taxes there! And the last time their Eqeta defied the Council they got a new one. The old one and his heirs went off a cliff as a special sacrifice for good weather. . . .

The Nikeians import most of their food, but they do grow some in terraces. Larry got figures for yields so high we don't really believe them. If it's true, we want to know how they do it. They use fertilizer, mostly from guano deposits on the Glacier Coast. We've asked Clavell to negotiate for a shipload for the University experimental farms. Larry Warner says he wants to see Marva's face when she learns she has to find storage for ten tons of seagull dung!

Clavell says that his assistant and chief of staff Clarence Harrison is "getting enough action for a whole platoon." It seems Nikeis was once saved by an admiral who also had lost his left hand. Not many people believe Lord Harrison is really this character come back, but a lot of people think he has mana.

There's a rumor that Gengrich had Captain Aidhos do Vis executed for "dishonoring" the Embassy to Ganton's wedding. I said, "Good riddance to bad rubbish" before I could stop myself, which made Larry give me a really odd look. I'd completely forgotten I'm not supposed to know that Aidhos was trying to kidnap me. I will not kick all overprotective men in the shins. I will not kick all overprotective men in the shins. I will not kick all overprotective men in the shins. . . .

Anyway, Larry said Aidhos probably deserved what he got, but he hoped the man didn't have any family who'd think they were now at blood-feud with Gengrich. From what I've heard of Gengrich he'd check that. How could he have lived this long and not known that much about local customs?

Larry knew Arnold Gengrich in Africa. After he talked about him for a while I said Gengrich sounded like an intelligent street gang leader. That got me another funny look, then Larry said that's just what Arnie used to be. Sounds like he'll fit right in, if Rick can talk him into coming back.

We ended the dinner when the candles began to gutter and smoke. Larry says he's trying to invent a clean-burning candle, and I promised to remember anything I could about candlemaking to help him. Oh, if we only had a couple of copies of *The Way Things Work*. *The Foxfire Book* would be even better.

PART TWO
DISCOVERIES

8

Mason squinted against the glare of the sun from snow-covered hills. Then he raised his hand against the icy wind. "First and Second Platoons, form a mounted perimeter around the farm. Third and Fourth Platoons, prepare for dismounted action. Platoon leaders, this is a battle warning."

Mason pounded his numb hands together as the order passed back along the column. Tran cold-weather clothing was pretty damned good for a medieval society, and the Guards and starmen got the best. Mason had better: a polystyrene leotard and vapor-barrier aluminized cloth over that. Put that under furs and you'd be warm in a blizzard.

The perimeter platoons moved out at a walk. They churned up fresh snow that fell back like sprays of tiny jewels. *Come on, come on. Let's get this over with.*

He kept hoping he was wrong about this old manor farm. *Maybe nobody's here. Or they bugged out already. They had time since the scouts found this place.*

A manor not on the registry, with no clear ownership. Land not only not cultivated but gone to thorns. Nothing else like that within a day's ride from Castle Dravan. No manor lord, it had to be directly held by the Eqeta. Or the Eqetassa . . .

Let's hope they bugged out. It could get sticky if they're still here.

"What the hell is this place, Major?" Jack Beazeley had no real trouble saying "sir" to Art Mason, for all they'd been friends before Mason's commission. He'd say "sir," but he'd still ask questions.

"Jack, I damn well don't know. I got a hunch—"

Beazeley waved to indicate the Guardsmen surrounding the place. "Sir, you got more than a hunch. Just how much trouble do you expect? Sir."

"None at all, or maybe a lot."

"A lot. Lot as in mercs with ammo?"

"Huh? Naw. Not that. Locals, but damn good locals."

"Okay, as long as I know what to expect."

"I'll go in first."

"Like hell."

"Corporal, I'll go in first."

Beazeley shrugged. "Yes, sir."

The perimeter was formed, two lines of Guardsmen. One line faced in, the other outward. More troops held positions as reserves. Musketeers unslung their weapons while their loaders drove in the rests and nervously counted the charges on their bandoliers.

"We're set to take on a whole damn army," Beazeley said.

"Yeah. And it won't be that." He rose in his stirrups. "Sergeant Bisso!"

"Sir."

"Stay out here. You're in charge. Anything happens, report to the colonel. Take live prisoners if you can. That may not be easy."

"Sir."

Bisso was a sergeant when I was a corporal. Don't seem to bother him a lot, but anything he knows, Elliot's going to know. Just as well, I guess.

Mason dismounted, drew his .45, and checked the loads. Then he signaled to Beazeley.

"Jack, follow me. Anybody in there knows we've come loaded for bear. If it's what I think, they're going to fight. I want prisoners. Live ones. Just remember that."

Beazeley tilted his head to one side. "Yes, sir."

✢ ✢ ✢

The farmhouse showed signs of recent repairs, rough but sturdy. The only unusual thing was an image of Vothan One Eye painted on the door.

"Another orphanage of the Children of Vothan?" Beazeley asked.

"That's what it says."

"But why out there?"

"Good question. Now shut up." Mason rapped on the door with the butt of his .45.

Silence.

Mason knocked again. After a moment there was a click, and movement behind Vothan's eye.

"Who seeks entry to the House of the Wolf?" The voice was unfettered.

"Open in the Name of the War Leader of Drantos."

"There is plague in this house, my lord."

Mason and Beazeley exchanged looks. "All the more reason to open the door. I bring starhealing and medics."

"My lord, we—"

"Open in the name of the Wanax and the Captain General of Drantos!"

Silence.

"Prepare to batter down the door."

Beazeley handed his M-16 to an orderly and took out a grenade. "Blow it in?"

"If it needs it."

"Right. Here goes." Beazeley tied a string to the grenade pin and wedged it against the door. "Stand back."

They heard the sound of bolts being thrown back. Beazeley retrieved the grenade and his rifle and moved to cover the door as it opened slowly to reveal an unshaven man in peasant dress.

"I am Bartolf, my lord. A sick child and I are the only ones in this house. The plague took the ones who did not run away to seek better healing than I can give. The gods grant they find it."

"Indeed. Now if you will show me through the house."

"My lord, I beg you, do not expose yourself—"

"Now, Bartolf." Mason shouldered his way through the door. "Stick with me, Jack."

"Sir."

Bartolf led them off to the right along a low hallway lit by a pair of rush dips. There wasn't enough dust to show footprints.

"Damn fast plague," Beazeley muttered.

"Yeah."

"The boy is in here," Bartolf said, gesturing toward a curtained door. Beazeley tapped the opposite wall with a rifle butt. The wall was solid. Beazeley backed against it as Bartolf raised the curtain.

Inside was a row of pallets. A blanket-shrouded figure tossed and moaned on one of them. Bartolf led the way in. Mason raised his pistol and slipped through the door sideways. *It may be just what it looks like. But I might as well give Jack a clear field of fire.*

The moaning stopped and the blanket fell away. The small figure on the pallet held a crossbow. Mason ducked and fired. The .45 slug showered plaster over the pallet as the crossbow bolt ripped through the hood of his coat. A club smashed across his mailed shoulders and sent him sprawling onto the pallet.

Who? Bartolf was in the doorway, but there was someone else in the room and no time to think about that. The boy flung the crossbow away and pulled a dagger from under the pillow. Mason ignored the new man behind him. *Leave him for Jack!* Art dove toward the boy feet first. His boots smashed against the kid's elbow sending the knife flying across the room.

Art kicked at the boy's head and turned on Bartolf.

Bartolf threw up his hands. "My lord—"

Whatever he was going to say didn't matter. Mason chopped at the older man's throat, and when Bartolf raised both hands to ward off the blow Mason came down hard on both insteps. Bartolf grunted and Mason slammed him against the doorpost, kicked at a kneecap, and turned back toward the boy on the pallet.

Bartolf's fall left the doorway clear. Beazeley came through. The third man leaped at him with a short sword. The blade hacked deep into the jacket Beazeley had wrapped around his left arm. Beazeley feinted high to bring the man's arms up, then drove four stiffened fingers into his attacker's solar plexus with a blow that lifted the man from the floor.

That's one. As Mason turned the boy leaped toward him. He held the dagger. Any inhibitions Mason had about cold-cocking children vanished. He stepped sideways and slammed the blade of his right hand into the base of the boy's neck. As the child thrashed, Mason braced two fingers under the boy's chin, and dug into the carotid arteries. He held on as the boy's other hand flailed against him. In fifteen seconds the boy slumped. Mason held the grip another ten seconds and then drew his Colt.

The only other person on his feet was Jack Beazeley.

Mason shook for a second while his mind accepted the fact that it was over. "Thanks, Jack."

"Any time. Now, what the hell was that all about?"

"Later. Right now, you go out and give Bisso—" The sergeant and five Guardsmen burst into the room.

"We heard shots. No action outside, and I've got the First Platoon in tight around the house, so—"

"No need, Bisso. There were two sick people instead of one. Wrap 'em up like mummies. Jack, you come with me."

✢ ✢ ✢

Mason and Beazeley sat at a table in what must have once been the manor's bedroom. "Jesus." Mason waved to indicate the pile of objects on the table. "All that stuff."

There was a lot. Noose. Garrote. Bastinado. Fishskin buskins for climbing. Masks and scarves and hoods. Daggers. Crossbows, and the quarrel the boy had shot at Mason. There were also a dozen clay pots with lead stoppers. The crossbow quarrel and all the dagger points were stained with a dull green oil. "Want to bet those are poisoned?" Mason asked.

"Don't have to bet. I've smelled hydras bane before. Art, what in the hell is this place?"

"I'm still not sure, but—Jack, you ever hear of Ninjas?"

"Jap assassins. Every now and then some merc claims to have ninja training. Never met one who knew anything. But yeah, I heard of them. Supposed to be able to walk up walls and turn invisible."

"I think that's what this place is. A training ground for the Tran equivalent."

"Humph. That kid can't be more than twelve. And all this gear is kid-sized. Apprentices? Maybe it makes sense."

"They're more than apprentices. Look how much trouble I had taking that one. A lot of good troopers got killed in 'Nam by kids no older than him."

"Yeah, I'll buy that, but Jesus, Art—Major—teeny-bopper ninjas? Whose?"

"Who do you think?"

"I don't get paid to think. But since you ask, let's see. Not the Romans. Not Ganton, he's not old enough. This place has been going since before he got crowned. Not the captain. He doesn't think that way. So who?"

"This is a House of Vothan. Who founded them?"

"Goddamn! Major, you think the captain knows?"

"I *know* he doesn't know. Next question. Do we tell him?"

"Why not? So his wife keeps a herd of trained juvie assassins. So what?"

"So one of them offed Caradoc."

Beazeley whistled. "Shee-it. You sure? Sir?"

"Wasn't until we took this place. Sure now."

"Okay. I guess I believe. Now what do we do?"

"We tell people. Start with Bisso and Elliot. That's enough so that if the mean little kids come after us somebody's left to tell the captain."

Mason fingered a wine jug. "I sure want a drink, but—"

"Right. I wouldn't touch nothing from this place. Okay, we spread the word. What do we do with Bartolf and the others?"

"Good question. This place belongs to the Lady Tylara. Who's our boss, sort of. Makes them hers. But damn all, she's got no right keeping a herd of private killers."

"So what do we do?" Beazeley demanded.

"Turn them loose. I'll swear not to harm them or this house, if they swear to harm only the proclaimed enemies of the Crown of Drantos. If they go with that, we can leave them alone. I'll make that Bartolf write a report for our great Lady Eqetassa, explaining what we know, and what we made them promise. That ought to make her go easy on everybody."

"You hope. Sure it won't hit the fan anyway? Sir?"

"Hell, it probably will. Most of the kids got clean away. And there's fresh snow. We sure as hell can't track them. Look, we take this lot back under guard or we turn them loose under oath. I don't think of any other choices."

"So do we tell the captain?"

"Shit. Ask Yatar. Ask Christ. Ask Ghu, but for Christ's sake don't ask me—"

"Still your job." Beazeley chuckled. "Major, I'm sure glad *I'm* not an officer."

✠ ✠ ✠

The room was small and had earthen walls. The only entrance was hidden behind the coal bin, but tubes ran to all the rooms in the House of Vothan. Chai listened to Mason and Beazeley and smiled. He hadn't understood all of what they said, because they often spoke in star language; but when they called in Bartolf and the boy called Bennok they had to explain again.

So, he thought. The starmen are not going to burn out the Children root and branch. They were not going to reveal what they had learned to their soldiers. They had not even slain any of those who attacked them.

Yatar be thanked we shed no starman's blood.

The prayer came easily, and brought a wry grin. He had not always been called "Chai," and he had once been a consecrated priest of Yatar. That was before the infernal starmen with their new wisdom caught him stealing temple revenues. A change of names and tasks seemed preferable to an appointment with the Eqetassa's hangman.

Chai pulled a piece of sausage from inside his robe and munched it cautiously. It might have to last him for several days until the starmen led their Guards away.

Let it be soon. Chai had long practice in hiding, but being able to endure it was not the same as enjoying it. For many reasons it would be best if the Guards departed swiftly. The Lord Mason had found that four of the children's rooms had been empty far longer than the others, but he hadn't understood. Now it was too late. The four who went south would surely complete their mission. . . .

Still, one must be sent to warn the Lady Tylara that this house had been found. When the messenger and the four who went south returned, all the Children of the Wolf could move to the other house, the house on the Littlescarp that no one would ever find. Then let Mason rage.

Oaths? What were oaths to those destined for Vothan's Hall, chosen by Vothan the Chooser to do His will in this world?

Gengrich looked up at the grey sky. The villagers standing in front of him would probably think he was praying to Yatar for the wisdom to give fair judgement. Actually he was trying to guess if it was going to rain before he reached home.

The sky said nothing about either rain or judgement. He could wait on the rain, but the judgement had to be given now. The villagers had given up half a day's work to bear witness before their lord; they would resent no judgement almost as much as a bad judgement.

Here goes nothing.

"I have heard all the witnesses from the villages of Fallen Eagle and Oak Creek. I have prayed to Yatar for guidance. Now I, Lord Gengrich do Zyphron, do give this as my judgement in the matter of the strayed cow of Oak Creek.

"I judge that the cow was indeed found unlawfully in the pastures of Fallen Eagle. I also judge that the cow strayed because of negligence by the herdboy, Bemis son of Nestor."

The faces of the Oak Creek people looked as grim as the sky. "I also find that the herdboy was trying to herd the cow back home when the men of Fallen Eagle came upon him. Therefore they had no cause to beat him so that he has been unfit for work these past ten days. They also had no cause to hurry the cow along so that she miscarried of a heifer calf."

"That old screw would've miscarried if we'n tapped her w' a feather!" shouted someone from Fallen Eagle. "Everybody knows that!"

"That cow was as healthy as yer big wind, Kuris!" came an equally loud reply from the Oak Creek side.

Now voices were raised on both sides, and a few fists. It would be knives and flails next. Gengrich signaled to Boyd, who shouted: "Silence for the Lord's judgement!" and signaled to the guards. The thump of pike-butts striking the ground brought results.

"I therefore find that the offense of Fallen Eagle is the greater, and they owe a fine of four silvers plus two silvers toward the cost of healing the herdboy. I have also learned that this is the cow's third miscarriage. I will therefore buy her from the village of Oak Creek for eight silvers, that she may be slaughtered and provide a feast for both villages. If at that feast they will also swear peace with each other, I shall send bread and wine from my cellars."

Gengrich studied the crowd and was relieved to see long faces turn to smiles. A few villagers from Fallen Eagle still looked sullen, and a few of the Oak Creekers made rude gestures, but it looked as if the feud had been headed off.

"I thank you for your loyalty in bringing this matter before me. Yatar grant you warm beds this winter and good crops and sleek beasts next year."

Fat bloody chance, he added to himself. Aloud, he called for his horse.

They were riding past the stumps of the oak trees that had given Oak Creek its name when Boyd pulled close to him. "Arnie, how'd you know about the cow's miscarrying? She looked like it to me, but you're a city boy. No offense meant."

"I'm a city boy who knows how to use spies. One of Vinicianus' people went in disguised as a traveling shoemaker. He kept his ears open and his mouth shut until he got home."

"Oho."

The bridge over the creek had fallen during the last bunch of earthquakes, but it hadn't rained for a couple of days. They forded with the water no higher than the bellies of the horses, and were checking their gear on the far side when four men in Gengrich's colors rode up leading one of his warhorses.

"Lord Gengrich! A message from the Lord Vinicianus. He begs you to return at once to the castle. He has sent a fresh mount."

The horse was Buster, Gengrich's favorite. If Vinicianus had risked sending *him* out, it must be something worse than a flooded privy. Still, he was supposed to hear cases in three more villages. . . .

"What is it?"

The messenger lowered his voice. "He says it is an important message from the north."

"Very well. Alex, take fifteen men and ride on to the other three villages. Hear the witnesses—"

"Me? I'm no feudal judge!"

"You're the best they'll get today, buddy. Or do you want to spend half the winter patrolling their fields for barnburners and cattle thieves?"

"You put it that way, no. Okay, hear the witnesses, and then—?"

"Tell each of them to send a man to Castle Zyphron. I'll give my judgement tomorrow."

Gengrich waited until Boyd had picked his men. *Alex has his problems. But he takes orders and you don't have to watch him every minute. It's worth a few bribes to husbands and fathers.*

✢ ✢ ✢

Bloody tears ran from the staring eyes of the man in the bed. The fingers of his bandaged hands all ended at the first joint. His cheeks and nose were blackened ruins, stinking with infection and decay.

His moans rose to a gasping scream as Guilford unwrapped the bandages from one foot. Gengrich turned away, his stomach twitching. The foot was black halfway to the heel. The toes dangled in shreds of flesh, and the smell was beyond anything Arnie Gengrich could have imagined.

He forced himself not to be sick as Guilford snipped away the dead flesh, amputated the ruined toes, doused everything with antiseptics and ointments, and put on fresh bandages. When Guilford started on the other foot, Gengrich bolted for the door. As he went out he heard the screams turn into words.

"Evil—bandits—thought she sent them—didn't know—killed—killed . . ."

Gengrich stopped. "Eh?"

Guilford shook his head. "No point in you staying, Arnie. That's more sense than he's made in the last couple hours. Go on, before I have to tend you too!"

Gengrich nodded and stumbled through the door.

He stood on the castle wall and drew in deep lungfuls of damp chilly air. He watched the carpenters at work on the south gate. The castle had come off pretty well in the last quakes. Not like Rustengo. The big port city was supposed to be one-third in ruins now, with a lot of the rest ready to fall down if you sneezed hard.

He wondered if that would take some of the wind out of Schultzy's sails. Last time Mort had come for a visit he'd acted like a royal ambassador. Maybe he did have clout in Rustengo; he'd always been good at looking out for himself. Lucky too, and Gengrich had learned that luck counts for a lot.

Time, Mort. For you and me. We got anything the captain wants, time to produce it. We ain't either one of us going to hold on down here much longer.

"Arnie?"

Guilford was standing behind him. "Yeah, Frank?"

"I gave him a knockout dose of babble juice. If he's lucky, he won't wake up."

"That bad?"

"That bad. If I was a real M.D. with the whole nine yards I still couldn't save his hands or feet. As it is, the gangrene's spreading, he's got hemorraghic fever, and he's developing pneumonia. I'm surprised he got far enough for our patrols to pick him up."

"He's from up north?"

"Far as I can tell. From what he said before he went out of his head, he was some kind of clerk at Castle Dravan. Something made him think he and a couple of his friends were in danger. They cooked up a story about a dying mother and rode off in the middle of a snowstorm. They figured nobody would try to track them. If they didn't come back at all, everybody would think the storm got them.

"It did get one of them, and that's where—Karl, I think his name is—started the frostbite. Bandits killed another one south of Vis. Karl was going on sheer guts when he ran into one of our patrols."

Guilford rummaged in his bag and pulled out an oiled-leather packet sealed with wax. "He had this sewn into the lining of his coat. I thought you ought to see it first."

Gengrich drew a knife and slit the leather pouch open. A folded piece of parchment dropped out. He caught it and started reading.

"Jesus H. Christ!"

"Last time I called him, I got put on hold—" Guilford stopped at the look on Gengrich's face. "Trouble?"

"Yeah, but—Frank, you really didn't read this?"

"You had to cut it open, didn't you? Is it hot?"

"Too hot to talk about here. It's trouble, but maybe not for us. I need to talk with friend Marcus."

✛ ✛ ✛

The long-expected rain was turning to wet snow. Gengrich hoped Alex and his men would make it home safely. Meanwhile he was fighting the chill with a roaring fire and a jug of Guilford's homebrew.

Marcus Julius Vinicianus sat across the table from him. He turned the parchment over and over in his fingers. He hadn't taken a drink since he began to read. Finally he shook his head. "I find it hard to believe that Lady Tylara would employ assassins to kill the man who saved her from Sarakos."

"Not just Caradoc. They suspect she offed Dughuilas. She set up somebody else, too."

"And I am probably looking at him?"

"Got any better candidates?"

"No. You hold your people together as an organized force. Without you to control them your Earthmen would fight. Your local recruits would be divided and many would desert. By spring the Lord Rick could set any terms he liked for taking your surviving men back under his rule."

"Just what I was thinking." Arnold Gengrich drained his cup and refilled. "Which means I have to stay alive. That's a real interesting proposition, seeing as how I also have to let these thugs try to assassinate me."

Vinicianus looked down into his cup. "Does the wine speak, or did I hear you say you must allow an attempt on your life?"

"You heard me right."

"Then—may I say that I honor your courage, but your judgement . . . ?"

"Is okay. Look, Marcus. This is something that can blow the captain's alliance up north to little bits. If he stands by his wife, he's at blood feud with Caradoc's clan. If he dumps her, he's not Count of Chelm anymore. No land of his own. That'll make it hard for Ganton to keep him on as Captain General. And old Drumold will take his archers home. What's he got left?"

"Anarchy. And the Time drawing closer. The priests of Yatar will not be pleased either."

"*Nobody's* gonna be happy if this gets out. The worst of it is we don't *know* anything. All we have is this paper, and it's not signed by anybody. No proof she did it."

"But you believe—"

"I don't believe in coincidences. Not big ones. If Caradoc hadn't went west, things would have come apart."

"I reached the same conclusion. Caradoc's death was very convenient. Too convenient. What has this to do with letting them attempt your life?"

"Hard evidence. We let 'em try and catch one in the act. Give the kid to the captain for a present."

The Roman looked thoughtful. "That would work. But you must catch your rabbit before you make a stew. You leave yourself as bait for assassins whose numbers and skills may be greater than we know."

"Give me a better idea and I'll take it."

"Stay guarded."

"How? I have to ride circuit to give judgement. And I can't live with guards under the bed. Marcus, I am damned if I'll sit on my ass in this room all winter!"

"I sympathize. But I would not trade places with you. Given the Lady Tylara's reputation I would suppose she would not employ any but the most competent assassins.

"So. You seek evidence of the plot in order to trade with the Lord Rick. What else do you offer him?"

Gengrich shook his head to try to clear out the wine fumes. "I don't get you."

"I think we should be able to aid Lord Rick as well as threaten him. Threats alone might not move him, but if we have both carrot and stick . . ."

"With luck I'll have the stick. What's the carrot?"

"The craftsmen of Rustengo. The Lord Rick's University designs many new and useful devices, but there are few craftsmen in Tamaerthon or Drantos to make them. The Romans would gladly help, but Lord Rick does not altogether trust Romans."

"Smart man."

Marcus gave a tight smile. "The Lord Schultz has influence among the Guilds of Rustengo, if he is telling the truth."

"He's probably exaggerating, but Schultzy's no B.S. artist. If he says he can swing the Guilds, at the least they listen to him."

"Excellent. Then let us offer to guard all those Rustengan craftsmen who wish to seek new homes in the north. I imagine that many would have already done so, except for the winter storms at sea and the bandits on land. We can do nothing about the weather or the lack of ships. We have already done much about the bandits, and allied with the Lord Rick we can do more."

"That makes sense. Hell, Marcus, he might go better than that. To get a couple of thousand craftsmen for the University's shops he might even spring for enough ammo to fight Phrados' whole damned army!" Gengrich lurched to his feet, picked up the jug of homebrew with one hand and gripped Marcus' shoulder with the other. "Friend Marcus, let's drink a toast. To you and me never being enemies!"

⊹⇒ 10 ⇐⊹

"Present—*arms*!"

Twenty soldiers banged pike-butts on the stone floor. Two officers drew swords. A herald dressed in a moth-eaten scarlet robe strode forward.

"Who comes before Arnold son of Maximilian, Lord Gengrich, Lord of Zyphron?"

Schultz nodded to his own herald. The boy hitched up his robe, which was too long for him and made of plain blue cloth, though without moth holes. Then he stepped forward and shouted, while Schultz prayed his voice wouldn't break: "Master of Foot Mortimer Schultz of Rustengo, speaking for the Great Guilds of the Free City of Rustengo."

"Bear you proof of this?"

"I do."

The boy's voice had been steady. Now his hands were too as he pulled Schultz's credentials out of his purse and handed them to the other herald. Schultz made a mental note to praise the boy for doing so well his first time as a herald. The job should have been filled by somebody more experienced, but the Great Guilds hadn't been able to agree on whom. So it went to young Dylos, who was some sort of cousin umpteen-times removed to Diana. He'd lost most of his family in the last quake, and landed on Schultz's doorstep with nothing but the clothes on his back. He couldn't just be turned away, so it was good to know he might really earn his keep.

In fact, the Great Guilds hadn't been able to agree on damned near anything other than sending this embassy. Schultz hoped Vinicianus' spies weren't as good as they were supposed to be, otherwise Gengrich would know too damned much about what a poor hand old Schultzy held.

The other herald turned toward the dais where Gengrich sat. "By my own honor and that of my office, by Yatar and Vothan, I swear that these are the true seals of the Great Guilds of the Free City of Rustengo."

Gengrich took the parchment. "Then I greet you, Master Schultz. How does the Free City?"

"Well enough." That was actually pretty close to the truth. The Rustengans were a tough lot, and were already pulling themselves together even before the last of the quake's thousand dead were dug out and buried. If the walls hadn't been so badly damaged that the city couldn't be made defensible before spring came and with it Phrados' army—

"We honor the men of Rustengo, and join you in mourning your dead. Yet if matters are well in the Free City, what do the Great Guilds ask of us? And why do they send an ambassador who will not submit to having his weapons peacebonded?"

Dylos' mouth dropped open. Schultz put a hand on his shoulder before he could say anything. "Lord Gengrich, two strong men may yet find themselves still stronger by joining forces. That could be the case with the Free City and the Lord of Zyphron."

"Indeed."

"As to why I refused to submit to peacebonding—I do not wish to insult your valiant men, but I could not be sure they had their orders in this matter from you. If it was indeed your wish that this be done . . ."

Schultz let his voice trail off and fixed Gengrich with a look. *I can play cockamamie games too.*

It was an old argument in this area: did a Master of Foot of a Free city rank as a noble with the right to be received in formal audience bearing an unbonded weapon? Or did he rank as a merchant, whose weapons had to be bonded?

It didn't make much personal difference to Schultz. He still had his holdout gun and boot knife. It was obviously important to Gengrich. His people wouldn't let him back down.

It would also stick in the craw of the Great Guilds if they had to put up with contempt from an ally. In fact, they might refuse the alliance. But if Schultz flat out refused the peacebonding, the alliance might never even be offered.

The thought of Diana being crushed in the next quake or turned over to Phrados' men settled Schultz's mind. "Lord Gengrich, to honor custom I shall submit to the peacebonding of my sword. You have but to give the order in my presence, and I will say no more."

Gengrich nodded graciously. "I see that the Great Guilds have chosen their ambassador wisely. To honor him and that wisdom, I will peacebond Master Schultz's sword with my own hands."

Schultz relaxed. That was an honor often shown to men who were noble in their home countries but not here—Romans of equestrian rank, for example.

Gengrich stepped down from the dais. One of his guards handed him a yard-long leather thong. He wound it several times around the hilt and guard of Schultz's short sword, then began an elaborate knot. As he tied it he bent down until his mouth was next to Schultz's ear.

"Schultzy?" The whispered question was in English.

Schultz nodded.

"Don't say anything. Don't give up your holdout gun, but don't let anybody see it. How are things in Rustengo, really? Not so bad?"

Schultz nodded again.

"Not so bad that you're beggars?"

A third nod.

"I didn't think you would be. Well, I don't think I'm going to be asking for anything you can't give." He tightened the knot. "Someone with my signet ring will come around to your quarters about a candle after sunset. Follow him. Don't take anybody with you—"

Schultz shook his head.

"Okay, take your herald. But that's all. Understand? Otherwise no deal!"

A nod. Gengrich finished the knot and straightened up. "Let this peacebonding be a sign of the strong peace between Zyphron and the Free City in days to come. Long live the Free City!"

The cheering was ragged, but with a couple of drums thrown in there was enough noise to hide Schultz's sigh of relief. He'd made it to first base without giving up anything important. Now Arnie wanted to talk for real.

Schultz backed away from the dais. *I could turn, but it doesn't cost anything to be polite. But I'm sure going to be in armor when Arnie's messenger comes with that ring.*

✛ ✛ ✛

Gengrich sighed contentedly as the bathmaid poured another bucket of hot water into the tub.

"I think it's time to start warming the oil."

"I've already warmed it, my lord. Then I wrapped it in a hot towel."

"Good, Risha. You're learning your work very fast."

The girl blushed and looked down. She was the shy kind, never speaking unless you spoke to her first. Probably that busted nose and the scars on her chin and her left ear made her think she was ugly. She had a real nice figure, though, and with that head of blond hair—well, if he hadn't valued peace with his women, Gengrich would have asked her to shuck off her gown and hop in the tub with him.

It was a Japanese-style tub, one of the little comforts he'd insisted on introducing to Castle Zyphron. Originally it had been founded as a Roman camp, back when this was part of the Roman provinces, but that was so long ago that you'd need a steam shovel to dig out the Roman baths. The tub leaked a couple of gallons every bath, but it still beat standing bare-assed in a stone-cold room and taking a sponge bath—

Someone was shouting outside the bathroom door, then Gengrich heard running feet. Fists pounded on the door.

"Lord Gengrich! Lord Gengrich!"

"The lord is at his bath—" began one of the guards at the door.

"Fire in the kitchen!" someone shouted.

"Damn!" said Gengrich. He stood up, sending water sloshing over the rim of the tub. A fire in the kitchen could be dangerous, with all the grease and oil ready to go up. Even if it didn't spread, it could fill the whole place with smoke and force everybody outside on a miserable cold wet night—

"One of you go down and help fight the fire," he said to the guards. "The other stay here, but leave the door open in case we have to leave in a hurry. Risha, you'd better go too."

"Thank you, Lord, but with you here there is no danger."

Gengrich grinned, not quite sure if he'd been flattered or insulted. Better warn her not to try any remark like that on Alex Boyd. . . .

One of the guards ran off to join the fire-fighting. The other wedged the door ajar with the lid of an oil pot and stood facing the opening. Risha went over to the hearth and picked up a cloth-wrapped bundle. Gengrich heard more shouting in the distance and sniffed for smoke.

Running feet echoed in the hallway. A man wearing a sodden cloak peered around the door. "Lord Gengrich! There's a fire at the south gate! The scaffolding—ah!" He broke off with a gasp. Then he clutched at the back of his neck and fell.

As he hit the floor Gengrich saw Risha's blue eyes blaze open. The look on her face turned her from a pretty teenager to a demon.

"Look out! The girl!" Gengrich shouted.

His warning was too late for the guard. Risha flung the oil pot straight at his head. Gengrich heard the crunch of bone, then the guard was down on top of the worker, writhing and clawing at eyes blinded by hot oil.

Risha reached under her gown and came out with a knife that looked two feet long.

He was already climbing out of the tub as she reached him. She stabbed upward toward his groin. Gengrich twisted and the thrust missed its target, but his violent movements upset the tub. It went over with a crash, and sent a wave of oily water across the floor. The water reached the hearth; the fire hissed, spat, and poured out a cloud of choking smoke.

Risha lost her footing on the suddenly slippery floor and went down. Gengrich stood and turned to run. She rolled and bounced to her feet like a trained athlete. She slashed at his leg and the knife left a thin line of red.

"Ho, guards! Assassins! To your lord!" Then, as Risha dashed between him and his sword he shouted again. "Help!"

The knife flicked across Gengrich's left arm, leaving more red—and now he felt more pain in his leg than a light cut like that should have left. Poison on the knife? God, what a hell of a way to go, cut to bits by a teenaged girl!

"Goddamn you!" He struck at her and missed, feinted to the left, then kicked as she turned. She was fast but not fast enough to escape entirely. His bare foot whacked solidly against her left arm.

He feinted again, and stepped on a broken piece of oil pot. *God dammit!* He felt himself going over, and dived into a roll toward the girl. She slashed at his thigh, but that brought her knife hand in reach of his left. He grabbed the wrist, squeezing and twisting and heaving all in one motion. She let herself rise, then came down with her heel just missing his groin. He clamped his legs together on her foot without letting go of her hand, then rolled. She went down, but her thick pad of hair saved her skull.

"Give up, damn you!"

She didn't answer. Her left arm wasn't working. She clawed at his eyes with her right hand. "Enough," Gengrich shouted. He locked the fingers of his free hand into her hair and smashed her head against the floor. She moaned but still struggled. He smashed her head down again. Then a third time, for luck and hate.

She was still breathing. He took a deep breath and resisted the impulse to stamp on her throat.

✣   ✣   ✣

Schultz turned the corner behind the guide and cursed the cold and damp. He was sneezing before they reached the end of the corridor. *Damn and blast.* Colds were no fun on a planet ten light-years from nasal spray and Kleenex!

Maybe it would have helped if he hadn't worn armor. He could feel the chill of his mail shirt even through the arming doublet. Now a couple of extra layers of wool might have done a nice job—

"Look out!" The shout made the guide draw his sword and sprint down the hall toward a half-open door on the left side. He'd covered maybe ten feet when the shadow of a beam seemed to turn solid and stick a knife in him.

At least that was the way it looked to Schultz. "Dylos, stay behind me—!"

"Ho, guards! Assassins! To your lord!" Smoke poured out of the door. "Help!"

The solid shadow came at Schultz with a knife in its hand.

Schultz's nine-millimeter Star was in his hand before his attacker got to knife range. He squeezed off three rounds before he took time to wonder why the man looked so small. Schultz fired once more as he fell. *That's one.* He turned warily.

A crossbow twanged from farther down the corridor and a quarrel sprouted from Dylos' chest. Lord, why hadn't the kid worn armor?

Schultz fired twice into the darkness and was rewarded by a scream and the sound of a falling body. *Six rounds. Two left.* He wished for his nine-millimeter H&K with its fifteen rounds, and groped his way into the alcove.

Small fingers with an iron grip clamped around his wrist. At the same time a knife thrust toward his thigh. It struck the tail of Schultz's mail shirt. He heard a high-pitched curse and the grip on his gun hand tightened.

The attacker was small enough to lift from the floor. Schultz picked him up by the groin and threw him against the stone wall. The grip relaxed and he brought the Star to bear, thought better of it, and smashed the barrel into the attacker's throat. *Not too hard. Not to break anything.* Then he brought the butt of the weapon down on top of the assassin's head.

Suddenly the hall was filled with guards. They eyed his pistol warily.

"Schultzy?"

"I'm okay, Alex. I heard Arnie call from in there. Tell these jokers I'm not an assassin."

"Oh, shit. Joe, stay here and square it. You can see what Schultzy caught." Boyd ran on down the corridor.

"What did you catch?" Green asked. He lifted the hood from the nearest attacker. "Christ, he can't be more than twelve."

"Twelve or fifty, he damn near killed me," Schultz said.

The other two were maybe a year older. One was a girl. Both were dead or dying.

"Good shooting," Green said.

"Yeah. Sure."

"Like Cui Nol." Green turned to the guards and pointed at the younger boy. "Tie him up good. If he dies I'll kill the man who killed him. If he gets away I'll go after families."

"Rough," Schultz said in English.

"Arnie's been after a live one. We owe you, Schultzy."

"A fat lot of good that's going to do Dylos," was the answer Schultz wanted to give. He swallowed it. Instead he bent over the dying boy. The crossbow was only a little one, the kind used for small game, but the quarrel had gone deep into Dylos' unprotected chest.

"You did well, Dylos. Your family will be proud."

"No family, Mas—No family. Only you. So—didn't want to dishonor—you. Herald's honor too. Can't—distrust men by—wearing—"

Blood trickled from the corner of Dylos' mouth and his eyes rolled up in his head. The hand Schultz was holding twitched a couple of times, then went limp.

Schultz was still holding that hand when Boyd came up beside him. "There's another of them in there with Gengrich. Girl about fifteen. She's alive. Good figure, too."

Alex always did have woman problems. That was just too bad for the girl; nobody forced her to make a living sticking knives into people.

"How's Arnie?"

"The girl nicked him a couple of times with a poisoned knife. Frank's in there with him now. Says it doesn't look serious.

"It looks like the girl was the primary," Boyd went on. "These three were back-up and guard. They came up the wall on a rope with a hook on the end. Set fires in the kitchen and the south gate with volcano-bush resin in cubes, then used the confusion to make their move."

Schultz wasn't sure whether he was hearing things or Boyd had gone crazy. "Alex, they're kids! Just what the hell is going on around here?"

"Schultzy, we'll tell you as soon as we know ourselves."

✢ ✢ ✢

Gengrich winced as Frank Guilford pulled the last strip of bandage off his left arm. "Can you make a fist?" the medic asked. Gengrich winced again but succeeded.

"Good."

"What about delayed effects?"

"Not with hydras bane sap in this dosage. You'll have scars, but you got off real light."

Gengrich hoped Frank knew what he was talking about. His arm and thigh looked and felt as if a red-hot poker had been laid along them.

"It's the oil," Frank said. "That sap dissolves in oil. Your fancy bubble bath saved your ass, or anyway your leg."

Gengrich sipped from a cup of hot wine and gritted his teeth as

Guilford cleaned the wound and applied a freshly boiled bandage. Finally the medic was done.

"You won't be wrestling anybody for a couple of weeks, and I'd go easy on the wine. Now I'll go make up more babble juice."

"I still say wring the little bastards dry without any juice," said Alex Boyd. "Give me the girl."

"For Chrissake let's not start that again," Gengrich shouted. "I want them alive. Not just to talk, alive to take to the captain, dammit."

"I won't kill her," Alex said. "She might wish I did."

"Maybe you would," Guilford said. "Alex, you didn't get a good look at that girl when I was treating her. I don't know what happened, but she's been to hell and come back. I'd bet you'd lose interest before she said a word—"

"Now listen, you goddamned—" began Boyd.

"Can it, both of you," said Gengrich wearily. It was an old quarrel between Guilford and Boyd. "You got anything else to say, Frank?"

"No, sir."

"Okay. Dismissed."

Guilford went out. Gengrich ignored medical advice and poured himself more wine. Over the rim of the cup he saw Schultz and Vinicianus trying to pretend they hadn't heard Guilford and Boyd shouting at each other.

At least it was a change from trying to pretend they didn't see each other. Vinicianus didn't want Schultz in this little council of war. *And bull shit. Schultzy saved my ass. He can sure as hell find out what he saved it from.*

Vinicianus still looked daggers at Schultz when he thought Gengrich didn't see.

"Okay. We've got the goods on the Lady Tylara and her mean little kids. But damn all, the only way the captain's going to believe this is to talk to those kids. I mean it, Alex, we got to keep them alive. That means no rough stuff, and no 'killed while trying to escape.' "

"That could mean asking people to get killed to save those little bastards."

"So what? Give 'em a hero's funeral. But keep those kids, because that's our only ticket into Galloway's service. And don't you forget it. We are agreed, aren't we? We go north as soon as the captain will let us?"

"Yeah, sure," Boyd said.

"What's in it for the Guilds?" Schultz demanded.

"Safe passage north. We'll escort as many craftsmen as will come. And negotiate with Galloway for you."

Schultz thought for a moment. "We can live with that."

"Right. Face it, the captain had three times the balls and twice the brains Parsons thought he did. Now we've got us an ace in the hole, 'cause the captain's lady has screwed up but good. Here's to Lady Luck, also known as Tylara do Tamaerthon, Eqetassa of Chelm and Mrs. Rick Galloway."

They drank the toast. By the time Schultz went over to the fireplace to heat more wine, they'd roughed out a text of the letter that would go north.

"I'll write it myself in Tex-Mex. Larry Warner knows that and I don't think anybody else does. Certainly none of the locals. Larry's got his head screwed on the right way; he'll see that it gets to the captain. Marcus, your people can get a letter into the University without too much trouble, I suppose?"

Vinicianus smiled thinly. He had stayed soberer than usual when the wine was flowing freely; Gengrich could recall his taking only two cups. Was having a rival going to cure his boozing?

"If they cannot, then I have spent much gold to very little purpose."

Over the second batch of wine they roughed out a treaty between the Lord of Zyphron and the Free City of Rustengo and any allies that either party wanted to include.

"Your people and Rustengo," Vinicianus said. "But not the Roman provinces."

"Which are?"

"The boundaries are not agreed. But if you include as your allies people Marselius Caesar thinks are his subjects, it can do no good and may do much harm."

"Leave 'em out," Gengrich said. "Don't cost much. We don't control much of the old Roman territory anyway. The thing is—" He hiccoughed and drank again. "The thing is, find out what people want and push where it gives. And maybe you'll get lucky. We just did."

╪══ 11 ══╪

". . . problemas formidables por el capitan. Yo creo que el capitan es un hombre muy sensible, y el capitan esto tambien comprende. Es imposible que el capitan no vide una ruta que no me permitera la silencia sobre la muerta de los caballeros Cara—y Duig—. Usted sabe ques los fueron.

Su amigo
Arnold G

Larry Warner laid the second page of Gengrich's letter on top of the first. This was the third time he'd read it. The initial shock had worn off, but his hands weren't any steadier. *Problemas formidables indeed. For the captain, the University, and everybody else.* He didn't need much help from either his imagination or the chilly room for his hands to shake.

At least he could do something about the chill.

"Hamar!"

The boy's head popped around the door. "Yes, Lord Warner?"

"More wood for the fire, and a pot of McCleve's Best."

"At once, my lord."

He didn't really want to get drunk. *Can we trust Arnie?* He tried to remember what he knew about Gengrich. Not a lot. Good man in a fight. Medium on leadership. Talked us into running away from Parsons, but couldn't hold the group together. Not officer material. *Hah. Maybe not, but he's sure got an officer's problems now!*

And so do I. What the hell do I do with this thing? Who do I tell?

The candle on Warner's desk burned steadily, without guttering or flaring. Funny how something as simple as twisting three strands to make a wick could make such a big difference. It had all been trial and error, too; he couldn't have explained exactly what difference it made to save his life. Didn't matter. University-made candles brought a hell of a profit, and would until the local chandlers figured out the secret. *They will, too. That's one bit of knowledge we don't have to try to spread.*

Warner realized he was holding the two sheets inches from the candle. A little closer to the steady flame, and this particular hot potato would be ashes. *And what the hell good would that do? If Arnie can write a letter in Tex-Mex to me he can write one in English to the Captain. Or in local to any damn body he feels like.*

One thing sure. It's no bluff. Gengrich named too many people, places, and dates to be making this up.

Warner put the letter down and looked up at the sooty ceiling. He knew he probably had what Gwen called his "Why me, God?" expression on his face. That was certainly how he felt.

Speaking of Gwen—what about telling her? Warner got up and began to pace the length of the room. *It's her fault. In a way. Marrying Caradoc, then running straight back to Les when he showed up.*

She'd screwed up, and got a damned good man killed. That would always lie between her and Warner now. He'd be polite to her, no problem with that, but nothing else, and she'd notice it. She'd start to worry, then maybe start to prod, and if she didn't get answers would they be able to work together? The captain was going to have a few things to say to both of them if they mucked up the University.

A knock on the door.

"Come in, Hamar."

The boy set the pot of homebrew on the desk, piled the armful of logs on the fire, then came back to fill Warner's cup. It was silver, commissioned from a Roman soldier who'd been apprenticed to a silversmith before he joined the legions. Lovely work, with centaurs and horses chasing each other around the rim. Probably cost a thousand or more back home.

Back on Earth, you mean. Tran's home now, Tran or nothing. *And Tran's not so bad. Consider the bracing climate, the quaint customs of the natives, the chance to sample genuine medieval living, the spice of danger to keep you from going soft, the headaches caused by women who can't keep their pants on . . .*

Warner swigged down his wine. Oh well, there was always one thing to do with a hot potato: pass it up the chain of command. That meant Elliot. Let the sergeant major worry about it. Let *him* tell the captain.

"Here's to the chain of command!"

✛ ✛ ✛

Mason pulled his chair out and turned it so that he could sit with his feet toward the fire.

Elliot handed around cups of herb tea well laced with McCleve's Best. "Not bad stuff, Professor," Elliot said. "I expect the major can use a bit more of that."

"Damn straight. The passes are full of snow. They say this is a mild winter." Mason drained half the cup. "Hate to see a bad one. Now what's all this about?"

"In a minute," Warner said. He refilled the cups.

"Where's Gwen?" Mason asked a couple of swallows later.

"Interviewing her new—guess you'd call it office manager," said Warner. "Not a secretary—that means a scribe to the locals, and that's not work for a noblewoman. This girl's a granddaughter of old Camithon."

"Is she good-looking?" asked Mason.

"What's the matter, Major?" said Elliot. "Another suit fall through?"

"Top, it never got off the ground in the first place," Mason said. "What I really need is a professional matchmaker. Or better yet, a Polaroid camera."

"You'd have to be careful taking pictures," said Warner. "Somebody could decide the camera was stealing their souls."

Elliot laughed. "The Ay-rabs believe that. Least the Yemeni did. Hadn't heard they think that here."

"Neither have I," said Warner. "But an awful lot of the locals still believe that what was good enough for great-grandma is good enough, period. Hell, talk to some of the local chandlers about my new candle wicks. I figured they'd copy them just for the money, but naw, they waiting for a sign from Yatar—"

"Okay, you got good candles. And I didn't ride through half the snow on Tran to hear about them. Spit it out, Professor."

Warner sighed. "Yeah." He pulled out the two sheets of parchment covered with tight handwriting. "It's in Tex-Mex, so you'll have to trust my translation."

"I can read that lingo too, Professor," Elliot said.

"I guess Arnie didn't know that."

"Arnold Gengrich doesn't know anywhere near as much as he thinks he does," Elliot said.

"So one of you read it to me."

"I'll do it." As Warner finished each sheet he passed it to Elliot.

Art Mason got up and poured another cup of tea. "Read that way to you, Top?"

"Yes, sir."

Yes, sir. Elliot's all of a sudden glad he's not in charge. Mason turned to Warner. "Think he's bluffing, Professor?"

"No, sir."

"He's not. I found out a few things on my own." He looked significantly at Elliot, who nodded. "No bluff, and he's got all the proof he needs."

"Does the captain know yet?" Elliot asked.

"Not yet. Unless Larry sent in a report—"

"Not me," Warner protested.

"We have to tell him."

"Yes, Sergeant Major, we have to tell him."

"Major, we ought to have told him the instant you found that damned Wolf House."

"Maybe. Warner, who else did you talk to about this?"

"Nobody."

Mason raised one eyebrow. "Not even Gwen?"

"No, sir. I figured this one was too big for me to handle."

"You figured right," Elliot said. "You go on keeping your mouth shut around Gwen and I'll begin to think you're as smart as you say you are."

Art Mason paced the length of the room. "Okay. Larry, you're coming to Edron with us. Find yourself a good reason. The captain will be there if we leave now. You know Gengrich better than the rest of us. How much time do you reckon we have?"

"Awhile. Until spring, I'd guess. Arnie knows we can't march in the winter. He wants to come back, not mess us up."

"It could mess things pretty good if we say 'Come back, all is forgiven,' " Elliot said. "He set up on his own. Did a good job, too. Bring him back and he gets a lot more firepower. Do we trust him with it?"

"Don't know, Sergeant Major. But what are our choices? Suggestions, Top?"

A long silence. "None, sir."

"Okay. Another thing. No semaphore messages on this. None. If any more code clerks desert, the system comes apart."

"Yes, sir," Elliot agreed.

"Anything more? No?" Art held out his cup. "How about a refill, Professor. Leave out the tea."

✢ ✢ ✢

They were a long way from Earth and military formalities, but Warner, Elliot, and Mason stood at attention in front of Rick Galloway's desk. Rick laid the parchment sheets aside and regarded them coldly.

"Okay. You aren't the first to hide something from the Old Man. I don't need excuses or apologies. What I need is answers. Mason."

"Sir."

"You say the House of the Wolf was abandoned just after you went in there. They didn't care dick about the oath you made them take. Right?"

"Looks that way, Colonel."

"Any chance of finding the Children?"

"No sir. The trail's cold and there's been new snow. I put Beazeley and the Intelligence people on it, and that's about all I can do without turning out enough manpower to make people curious."

"So they could have gone anywhere. Including south."

"Yes, sir," Elliot said. "Which means Gengrich may have more to worry about than he knows."

"Holy—we can't alert him," Warner blurted. "Least I don't know how. The semaphore system—"

"I thought of that," Rick said. "But thanks for bringing it up. You three made one good move there. None of this goes onto the semaphore. Elliot, we've got to restructure that system. Beef it up. I want it tougher, and more secure. And under *our* exclusive control."

"Yes, sir. I'll get on it."

"There's maybe one way to find them," Mason said. He fell silent.

"Spit it out."

"If we knew where to look."

"Oh." Rick thought about that. "She would know, wouldn't she?"

"It's a safe bet, sir."

Art looks relieved. Why? Because I'm taking it so well. Oscar time, Galloway. "The question is, do I let her know that we know?"

"Nobody can decide *that* but you," Warner said. Elliot glared at him.

"May I say something, sir?" Mason asked.

"Yes."

"Like I told Beazeley, Lady Tylara has a short fuse but she isn't crazy. It's why I didn't stake out the place and round up the Children when I had a chance. I don't know what she's planning—"

"But you think it might be useful."

"Yes, sir. Exactly."

"I'm sure she'd appreciate the compliment."

"There's something else," Elliot said.

"Yeah, Top?"

"You already know it, Colonel. We put too much effort in this and the story'll leak out. God knows what happens then, but it won't be good."

"Blood feud. Not just Lady Tylara, but her father and his whole clan," Larry Warner added. "Against Caradoc's people. That sets a good part of the University garrison into civil war."

"So we have to see it doesn't get out," Rick said. "That's priority one. What can we do if it leaks out anyway?"

Art Mason shook his head. "Colonel, you know as well as me. Lady Tylara would have to disown her little assassins, and turn them over alive to Caradoc's relatives. Or put their heads on pikes."

Which she won't do. If she gave the orders, she'll protect the kids who carried them out. I think. I sure as hell can't assume she won't. Jesus Christ, no wonder she won't sleep with me! "And even that won't work."

"Probably not," Warner said. "It's too big for blood money. This was—was—"

"Cold-blooded betrayal of a loyal subordinate," Rick finished for him. "Yes, Mr. Warner, I'm aware of that." *And I shouldn't talk to him like that.*

"There's another problem, Colonel," Mason said. "Caradoc commanded the Mounted Archers. Some of our most loyal troops. If they find out—"

"Who watches our backs," Rick finished. "Thank you for reminding me. We don't have any choices. So. Assuming we can keep secrets—"

Elliot drew himself up to say something.

"And we can, it boils down to Gengrich. How smart is he? Mr. Warner?"

"Colonel, I thought about that all the way here. I'd say plenty smart enough." He spoke in a rush. "He'll have given himself insurance. Told some people. Too many for us to off. Not enough that it'll get out if we cooperate with him."

"Sure of that?"

"Pretty sure, sir."

"Elliot?"

"Yeah, he'd try to do it that way."

"Can he bring it off?"

Elliot hesitated. "Yes, sir. I think so."

"So. Gengrich wants full pardons for his people, and confirmation of his field promotions. Can we live with that?"

"No problems with the pardons," Elliot said. Mason nodded agreement. "Promotions may be stickier."

"They're also more likely to be negotiable," Warner said. "You can be sure that Arnie asks for more than he thinks he'll get."

"We can promote our own people," Rick said. "Rank inflation. Everybody moves up a couple of notches." *And it helps that we've got about a dozen organizations and everybody has different ranks in each.* "All of Gengrich's mercs will be Star Lords."

"Which will mean one hell of a lot more here than down there," Mason said.

"Will it?" Rick asked. "We live better, but we've also got discipline. Elliot, what kind of problems is Gengrich bringing?"

"Boyd's the biggest one. Lot of ability, but he chases. Chases anything, married or not."

"He'll keep it in his pants here," Rick said. "See to it."

"Sir."

"That's settled, then. Next question. Gwen. How much does she know?"

"I said I didn't tell her, Colonel—"

"I know what you said, Mr. Warner. Are you sure that's the only way she has of finding out?"

"The letter was sealed."

"And in Tex-Mex," Elliot said.

"Gwen knows Latin," Rick said.

"Oh, shit, of course she does."

"So how sealed?" Rick asked.

"Looked good to me. Sewed up and sealed in leather, Arnie's high-school class ring stamped in wax all over it. Colonel, I'd bet a lot nobody opened that before me."

"We are betting a lot. If she knows and we don't know it—damn, I'm almost tempted to tell her myself."

"Might not be a bad idea," Warner said. "This might be a strain—"

"Three can keep a secret if two are dead," Mason said. "Colonel, there's enough know this now. It's sure to get out, no matter what we do. The longer that takes, the better. Long enough and it's just another rumor."

"Okay. We don't tell her." *You don't. Maybe I will. Be a good reason to go see her.* "Anything else?"

"No, sir."

"Good. Dismissed."

Rick waited until the others had left. *Les always thought Gwen would marry me. I suppose he thought I'd be civilized about things when he came back.* He lifted the wine cup, and stared at it a moment. Then he threw the wine into the fire.

INTERLUDE:
GWEN TREMAINE'S
DIARY

—the first day I felt like being up and around since Caradoc's birth. I still don't have enough milk to nurse him, but he's thriving on what the wet nurses give him, and otherwise he didn't give me much trouble. That's one hard delivery and two fairly easy ones. Maybe I'm getting the knack. If I'm going to be Fertile Myrtle on a planet with medieval obstetrics and gynecology, I'd better.

The name won't fool anybody into thinking the boy is Caradoc's, at least anybody who can count. It doesn't matter that much. It would have if I'd remarried and gotten pregnant barely two months after Caradoc was killed. Funny how charitable people are now that my long-lost Earth soldier husband is back from the dead.

The weather is mild enough to make you think spring really will come before you're old and grey. One thing about being pregnant in the winter: it makes the cabin-fever even less endurable. But it does look like the winter will end.

Larry Warner came by for lunch. He's still as wound up as he was before he went up to Edron. What does he know that he's not telling me? I tried to find out, but he started talking about the guano shipment from the Nikeian islands. . . .

Damn whoever or whatever made Larry so nervous around me! It's spoiled my only real open friendship on this damned planet.

It doesn't help that Marva has accepted Campbell. They're going to be married when Rick comes through on his way south, so we'll have plenty of high-ranking witnesses and sponsors. Marva's going to keep working, at least until the kids start coming, but now she'll pass things on to Campbell that maybe he shouldn't know. One more problem.

I thought Lady Siobhan would be able to take Marva's place, but now it looks like Art Mason has staked a claim. He writes to her, and the last time he was here he started giving her English lessons. Of course he'll probably let her go on working. The University is one of the safest places around. But she's only seventeen. Who'll have her loyalty—the University or her husband? Foo. Another confidante lost. She'll be the next thing to Rick's spy here.

Rick. I asked Larry how he and Tylara are, and got the oddest look. Not surprise, exactly; but—I wish I knew what Rick is thinking. Last time I was there, he and Tylara weren't what you'd call chummy. Suppose—No. I cannot think about that. I simply cannot.

Les, I miss you. Don't sideswipe a black hole or anything stupid like that.

PART THREE
PROPHETS

12

It was spring at Castle Armagh. Spring meant there was no more ice. The roads were slow because of mud. In a normal year that would get better as summer came on, but Rick wasn't betting on it.

"We can march tomorrow," Art Mason reported. "Nobody likes it, but we can do it."

"Then we will. Plan on an early start." Rick inspected the field gear laid out on his work table. In addition to armor and weapons, there was elaborate sleeping gear, and a hot-draft stove that burned twigs and pine needles and could boil water for tea in minutes. "Sure a lot of stuff to carry around."

"Only we don't have to carry it," Art Mason said.

"Yeah. Makes me feel a little funny. We don't let the troopers take this much gear."

"Rank Hath Its Privileges. Colonel, there's not a man in the army would begrudge you a few comforts."

"You sure?"

"Yes, sir. I'm sure."

"Okay. Hoped you'd say that. Jesus, Art, I'm tired of campaigning."

"So skip this one—"

"Can't. Too many complications. Religious war. Gengrich. The Rustengo artisans. Roman allies. The religious merger. Just too many balls to juggle."

Mason sighed. "I read it that way, too, sir. This one needs you."

There was a knock at the door.

"Who?" Mason asked.

"Tylara."

Rick raised an eyebrow. "Come."

There was no one with her. She was dressed in a long gown of *garta* cloth dyed an off-red. *Doesn't really flatter her,* Rick thought. *But it's sure expensive.* She was also wearing a malachite necklace Rick had given her.

"My Lord Mason," Tylara said.

"Good day, my lady. I was just leaving." Mason ducked out and closed the door on the way.

"You come unescorted. Is that wise?"

She laughed. "It is safe enough. Who would harm us in our own castle?"

You'd know that better than me. "What brings you—"

"You leave tomorrow."

"Yeah."

"There was a time when that would have been more than enough reason to see—for us to see each other."

"I suppose that's true," Rick said.

"As you say." Tylara smiled. "But my reasons are not entirely frivolous." She took a small packet from her sleeve.

"For me?" Rick unwrapped the cloth and unrolled a long pair of woolen knitted stockings. The Chelm crest-of-arms was worked into it, and the wool was extremely fine. "Should fit, too. Thank you. This must have taken a long time."

"I had some help." Tylara smiled again.

Help. Right. Always there when you need it. He felt the stockings. *Poisoned thorn in the toe? Don't be ridiculous.* He stuffed the socks into the pouch on the leg of his coveralls. "Thanks, then."

She frowned puzzlement. "Rick, I—"

"Dammit, where the hell did Mason go?" He brushed past her with relief to go to the hall, then stopped. *No! She came to make friends, why am I so suspicious?* But when he turned back, she was already leaving through the other door.

✠ ✠ ✠

"Hey! Get your ass out of the saddle and lead that horse!"

Apelles drew himself upright into a dignified pose. Who—

"Hey! I'm talking to you! You in the blue bedgown! You and your servant get down and lead your horses. Nobody rides across this bridge, not Caesar himself."

The commands had come from a Roman centurion who stood at the near end of the floating bridge across the Dnaster River. Apelles pressed his knees into his mount's flanks. The road was muddy and he wasn't a very good rider. The horse moved forward at a walk.

"Halt or be stopped!" The Roman raised an arm; several archers who'd been lounging on the bank rose to their feet.

"Are you mad?" Apelles halted and slid out of the saddle. There was no one to hold his horse or stirrup, and he very nearly fell. The mud was deep over the tops of his sandals.

"Centurion, I am Apelles, Priest of Yatar and Nuncio of—"

"Apelles?" said the centurion. His tone changed. "I'll be damned!"

"I hope not, Quintus," said Apelles, much relieved. Quintus Pollio of the Eleventh Legion had been captain of the Roman fire department at the University. His was the first familiar face Apelles had seen in days.

"That's as Christ and St. Michael—and Vothan—will have it," said Quintus cheerfully. "But none of them will save me if I let you or anybody else ride across the bridge. Take a good look at it, friend Apelles, and see if you don't agree with me."

Apelles tossed his mount's reins to his freedman and followed Quintus down the bank to inspect the bridge. The plank roadway was less than two yards across and there were gaps a hand's breadth wide between the planks, which rose and fell as the boats under them jerked and bobbed on their anchor cables in the swift current of the Dnaster. "Uh—friend Quintus, is it safe to cross at all?"

"Walking. If you're careful," Quintus said. "We only lost three parties today. The ferryman downstream picked up two. Hydras got one."

"Hydras."

"Actually that was yesterday. I think we got all the big ones. Bent sword points into hooks, and—"

"There's a ferry? I'll take it."

"Not a chance. Wagons only. Everybody else goes by the bridge."

"Archbishop Polycarp is expecting me by nightfall—"

"Ho. Why didn't you say so?" Quintus said. "You walk. I'll see your horse gets across."

"The blessings of Yatar on you," Apelles said with feeling.

✢ ✢ ✢

Apelles reached the other bank ready to kneel and kiss the muddy ground. The bridge had swayed every bit as much as he'd feared. Two corpses had floated under it while he was crossing. *There can't be any hydras left. No big ones, anyway.*

Apelles' spirits revived when he was mounted again. In his own village of Nial's Mercy, only three men outside the household of Bheroman Rhegmur had horses. *Even on this slow-gaited dun hack, I'm the equal of a knight. Well, almost.*

In fact he had far more power than any knight, and more than most bheromen. As assistant to the Chancellor of Drantos, Apelles could send warrants and writs the length of the kingdom. His pen and inkwell held life and death for mere knights.

✢ ✢ ✢

Apelles had never seen an army in the field. He had expected the host's camp to be one vast city of soldiers. Instead he found over a dozen smaller camps. Each squatted on its hilltop or in its valley, some completely undefended, others behind ditches or rough walls of sharpened logs. None showed the elaborate work he had heard that the Romans put into building a camp.

"Where?" his freedman asked.

"Palomas, you talk too much. I should never have set you free."

"We are lost, then."

It was true enough. He knew only that Polycarp's tent lay in Caesar's camp. Where was that?

"We should have asked the centurion," Palomas said.

"Yes, of course, and be silent or I will billet you with the kitchen apprentices."

"That may be better than we'll have tonight."

"Ask those women."

The two women carried buckets and sacks of washing. Palomas rode forward. *He rides better than I do. He has never said how he was enslaved.*

"Ho, goodwives," Palomas said. "Can you tell us how to find Caesar's camp?"

One of the women looked him up and down and then gave him a gap-toothed grin. "Don't think you'll find much pleasure there, my friend. Publius the Satyr keeps it all for himself. We can show you a better time—"

"Chara, that one's a priest," said the other woman.

Chara shrugged. "He's no bishop or highpriest. Stay with us, friend. Chara of Glinz has a name—"

"There are no soldiers quartered in Vis, then," Apelles said.

"Only officers," Chara said. "How did you know?"

"You tempt me, fine lady that you are," Apelles said. "But I must find the tent of Bishop Polycarp by dark. Can you direct us?" He clinked copper coins.

"Ah," said Chara. "See that hill off to the west?" She flung out one large red hand. "Caesar's camp is just beyond it."

Apelles followed the gesture with his eyes. "Thank you." He tossed her two coppers.

Her look told him he'd paid her too much.

✢ ✢ ✢

The candles on Archbishop Polycarp's camp table neither guttered nor smoked. Their flames seemed as steady as Polycarp's gaze.

"The centurion refused to allow you to ride, and denied you the ferry?" Polycarp demanded.

"Yes, my lord."

"He will regret that."

"My lord, it is no matter—"

"You are Nuncio from the Highpriest of Yatar. You are deputy of the Chancellor of Rome's most powerful ally. Caesar's officers must learn respect."

My office demands dignity. I do not. But in a moment he will give orders—"I learned much, my lord. Do you know that the merchants of Vis had bought hydra flesh? Not merely the fishermen, who use it as bait?"

Polycarp had stood. Now he sat again. "There is famine in Vis, then."

"It seems."

"I will speak to Caesar's supply officers. Vis is an important city. We cannot—you are certain of this?"

"Aye, my lord."

Polycarp smiled. "I think my colleague of the Temple of Yatar has chosen his servants well." The smile faded. "Or I would, had I not yesterday received a letter from the Highpriest Yanulf. He speaks of the young woman called Maev."

How in the Name of Yatar did he learn that? "Yes, my lord?"

"What is your relationship with this woman?"

"We—we are betrothed by handfasting, before the shrine of Hestia Christ's Mother."

"Ah. Your superior feared much worse."

Hah. Maev would never have let me within a stade of her bed without—

"Are you aware that when the Instrument of Union is signed, married priests will not be eligible for the higher offices within the united faith?"

"I am." Yanulf himself had told him Polycarp insisted on that provision. "It is not our intention to marry. At least not yet."

"Indeed." Polycarp turned away for a moment, and Apelles thought he heard muttered prayers. Then he turned back, and Apelles would rather have faced a hydra than the archbishop, for all that his voice was still calm.

"Apelles, you give every appearance of being guilty of what in a priest is an even worse sin than lust. You are ambitious. You wish to rise in the service of God and do your duty to Him, yet you will not do your duty to others who have claims on you. And do not insult me by saying your duty to God comes before all others. To honor Maev and the child she may bear you is also a duty set you by God."

It was told of Polycarp that in his youth he had been a zealous persecutor of the worshippers of Yatar, able to ferret out any secrets and strip away any lies or disguises.

"My lord," Apelles said, and to his surprise his voice was steady, "it was the thought of a child that made us swear before Hestia. We neither of us wished Maev's child to bear the name bastard."

"Then—she is carrying your child?"

"She was not when we parted."

"Christ has blessed you, then. There is still time to pray for guidance and perhaps even to find it."

"Guidance?" Apelles was not feigning bewilderment.

"Toward what you truly wish, for yourself and for Maev."

"Even if I truly wish to become a highpriest rather than to marry her?"

Polycarp frowned. "Were you listening when I spoke of the sin of ambition in a priest?"

"I was, but I did not hear you say what it is to be ambitious. Is it ambitious to wish to serve God where one may do it best? And if one has it in oneself to make a good highpriest or bishop, does one serve God best in a lower position?"

"It is vanity to think one has that ability."

"Is it vanity to think that one *may* have that ability? And if I do, should I deny God any service I may give Him?"

"It is—" began Polycarp. Then the archbishop laughed softly. "Stop, my son. I believe you could talk the Devil into giving up hell without a contract."

"Forgive me, my lord. I meant no disrespect—"

"I saw none. Yanulf was right. You sometimes do not think before you act, but you will not wittingly harm anyone. It is well to know that the Chancellor of Drantos is a good judge of men."

"My lord, I am grateful—for your mercy and for Yanulf's trust in me."

"God has found good servants in far worse than you. There is one further matter before I dismiss you. Have you made a testament in Maev's favor?"

"I did not think—"

"Do so before the battle."

"Yet I have heard that Phrados is no captain. Certainly no match for either Ganton or Publius."

"God will give us victory over this servant of the Devil, but He does not promise who shall be alive to enjoy it. Find parchment and pen. I will witness what you write."

Apelles' hands were steady enough as he wrote out his will, but afterward he felt very ready to pray. He and Polycarp had just knelt when they heard the sound of Roman horns and Tamaerthan drums. A large force of cavalry was moving out.

A messenger dashed in. "My Lord Archbishop! Lord Gengrich's men and the Rustengans have been sighted. The Tamaerthan Hussars and a cohort of the Fourth are going south to escort them."

"Yatar and Christ be praised! Let us continue our prayers."

✢ ✢ ✢

Matthias stifled a sneeze. The incense and herbs in the braziers were losing their fight against the smells of the camp. Unwashed humanity. Campfires—too few for such a host, because too many draft animals had died to allow for large wood-gathering parties. Cooking meat. Kitchen middens. And over it all, the reek of rotting human corpses. Eight of them hung in chains on a gibbet high above the camp where all could see them.

Best pay attention to Phrados or I'll be the ninth.

"—has gone too far north without giving me his allegiance. Therefore he will not give it. Therefore he has betrayed the gods and must die."

"Let Gengrich die," shouted the twelve Defenders standing six on either side of Phrados.

"Let Gengrich die," shouted everyone in the room. "Let Gengrich die. Let—"

"Cease!" shouted a Defender, crashing the butt of his spear against the floor. Phrados rose from his stool and advanced on the men standing before him. Although he was half a head shorter than the least of them, none of them met his eyes as he walked along their line.

"Tyras," Phrados said, stopping before the tall headman of a southern town whose earthquake-shattered ruins must already be yielding to the forest. "You did not shout as loudly as the others."

"I feel as strongly as you or they, Prophet." He licked his lips. "Yet—forgive me—"

"I will not forgive you if you seem to hide your thoughts. I may forgive those thoughts." Phrados raised a hand; four Defenders raised spears or swords.

Tyras swallowed again, then the words poured out. "Should we not wait to see how Gengrich is received by the other starmen? If they give him only a traitor's welcome, he may yet be forced to turn to us with all his men."

"You would stay the smiting of a traitor to the gods?"

"I would not be so quick to condemn the Lord Gengrich as a traitor to gods he was not born to worship, Prophet. I think—"

"You have thought too much, Tyras, and known too little of God's truth. Gengrich has been condemned. So have you."

Before Tyras could take another breath, a hand signal brought four of the Defenders around him. Two grasped his hands and held them behind his back, while a third cut his throat. As his body thudded to the floor, the last Defender thrust his spear into Tyras' chest. The smell of blood joined the other smells in the room.

From first to last, Phrados had not raised his voice above a conversational tone.

"So perish traitors to the gods," shouted Matthias.

"So perish traitors to the gods," the others shouted. One or two voices sounded unsteady to Matthias; he did not dare look to see who the waverers might be. When Phrados dismissed them, Matthias walked as steadily as the others, and never looked back.

The Prophet is mad. Tyras was not the first condemned to death on a whim, but he was the first of Phrados' old followers from the south. *Sooner or later we will all die.*

Prayer and meditation had once been Matthias' answer to all doubts, but it had been many days since they did any good.

By the time Matthias passed the scaffolding, Tyras' body had joined the other eight.

13

Alex Boyd lowered his binoculars. "Here they come. Still think it's just scouts?"

"We'd be seeing the infantry if the main body'd come up," Gengrich said.

"Pretty heavy for scouts," Boyd said. "Some of those patrols we sent out last night, they might have found the infantry but not got a message back."

"You're a pessimist, Alex."

"Yeah. I'm also still alive."

Exactly what that proved Gengrich wasn't sure, but he was willing to admit it proved something. All of the mercs who'd started north from Castle Zyphron were still alive, but over two hundred of the local troops and several hundred dependents weren't. They'd have lost more if the Rustengan infantry hadn't been pretty much out of the fighting. The Rustengans had medics to spare and space in their wagons for the sick and wounded, and as long as their own people didn't need it they were generous.

The Rustengans had lived close enough to the Romans to get Roman notions of camp sanitation, which meant no plagues and not too many fevers. *We still lost too many,* Gengrich thought. *Old folks and kids dead of fever. People who lost their draft animals and couldn't keep up. And we can't slow down, not with Phrados and his horde dogging us.*

They would have lost a lot more if Gengrich hadn't used

ammunition at a prodigal rate. *No point in saving it. When we reach Captain Galloway we get new supplies. We don't reach him, we're dead.*

"More coming," Boyd said.

"Yeah." Gengrich lifted his binoculars. Two groups of cavalry, both about eight hundred strong. The leading group was a mob, but the second group kept good formation behind blue and silver banners. Most of its lancers wore broad-brimmed helmets and back-and-breasts instead of fur jackets or leather jerkins.

"That second looks like some city's regulars," said Boyd.

"Yeah. Alan!"

An arm waved from a stand of scrub oak in the center of the position. The oaks looked natural enough among the native chaparral, but they'd never evolved on this planet. *Lord knows how those trees got here. Acorns scattered by the* Shalnuksis? *Planted by some pig farmer a thousand years ago?*

"When that second outfit gets in range, start with the banner-bearers!"

Another wave. MacAllister was perched where he could see without being seen and snipe in all directions, with a hundred rounds to snipe with. That was one-sixth of the remaining ammo and some people weren't too happy about that, but nuts to that; if they wanted a bigger ammo allowance let 'em learn how to use it like Alan—

"Heads up!" said Boyd. He signaled to the horse-holders to bring their mounts forward. By the time they'd mounted the first outfit was in good shooting range. MacAllister squeezed off six rounds, picking off six horses at intervals in the first line. Gengrich waved his thanks, then signaled to the other mercs. By the time they'd each used up their six, there were more gaps than horses in the first line. The second and third lines bunched up just beyond bowshot. They were ragged enough that you really couldn't call them lines anymore.

The whole second outfit was still coming on too. The orderly formations were just at the rear of the first mob, and didn't so much cut off the mob's retreat as push it forward. By the time the archers had a good target the second outfit had turned the first one into a kind of shield.

"Anybody from that front outfit lives through this, he's going to be mighty pissed at the guys behind," Gengrich said.

Boyd nodded agreement. "Yeah, but let's make sure we're around to be invited to the party."

He's got a point. Gengrich's archers were no longer very well equipped to take on massed cavalry. The caltrops were long gone, the stakes running short, and today there hadn't been time to drive them anyway. *Better get the archers in with the pike squares.* A lot of the archers had started off the march on horseback and turned into infantry when their mounts died. If they got cut to pieces in their first fight as infantry, they wouldn't have any morale worth mentioning by the time they joined up with the captain.

"First Company, rally on the oaks! Second and Third Company, rally to the pikes on the left and right!" One nice thing about fighting on a medieval planet: most of your men could be in range of your voice when you had to give an order in a hurry. Of course there was a legend of a battle lost because some lord had a cold, but better than busted or jammed radios any day!

The archers were moving now. The enemy didn't have any horse archers in range, so Gengrich's archers had it all their way. They could move by platoons and stop to shoot every few yards. Arrows fell into the leading enemy formation. *Can't call it a formation. Just a mob. They'd break if that second outfit wasn't pushing them on.*

"Snipers, take out officers in the second group. Leave that first outfit to the archers," Gengrich shouted. He heard the orders passed down the line. Banners began to fall. There were still twelve hundred and more horsemen coming at him.

The mercs were coming in toward the oaks. They fired as they ran. Joe Green was fumbling a fresh magazine into place as he moved; had the son of a bitch shot himself dry already? The archers on the left were almost safe behind the pikes; the oaks hid what was going on to the right. More banners were in range now. MacAllister took out three, *wham, wham, wham,* three shots, and Gengrich and Boyd threw in four rounds apiece before putting their heads down and their spurs in. When he reached his new position among the oak trees he could spare time to see how much time they'd bought.

Maybe enough. The Rustengan infantry had moved into position. The Rustengan militiamen were hungry and they weren't used to fighting in the open. On the other hand, they'd fight. They were all that stood between their families and Phrados.

MacAllister shot off half a magazine right over Gengrich's head and suddenly there were a lot fewer banners out front. It didn't help enough. That first outfit was still taking most of the fire, and they were going down but they weren't breaking. Maybe it was guts, maybe it was fear of Phrados or the guys behind them. . . .

A couple of hundred men and horses down now; Gengrich tried to shut his eyes and ears against how they looked and sounded. Horses wouldn't step on corpses or wounded, but there was plenty of bare ground and that second outfit looked to be good riders even if their mounts were a little thin-flanked.

A wave of mounted men from both attacking groups broke over a platoon of archers; Gengrich saw men using their bows like clubs as they went down. Beyond the horsemen he saw the pikes dipping. Arrows soared from inside the pikes.

A second wave, mostly from the second outfit. This time it broke against a platoon of archers helped by star weapons. More arrows flew from the oaks. The southern bow wasn't the Tamaerthan longbow, but at a hundred yards it would punch through any armor these characters were wearing.

The survivors of the platoon moved toward the oaks. They hadn't broken; they still had their bows and some of them had stopped to pick up enemy swords and helmets. Gengrich counted them; he'd passed twenty when he saw one carrying an H&K and two more with a limping figure between them.

"Larry!"

Joe Green sprinted out from the trees. He'd covered half the distance to his buddy Larry Brentano when the third wave came up the slope. Green went to one knee, snapped up his rifle, and let fly on full rock and roll. Gengrich, Boyd, and MacAllister slammed rounds into the cavalry as if there was no tomorrow and no shortages.

There were just too many men and horses. Even some of the riderless mounts were part of the mass that poured over Green before it melted away under the arrows and bullets. Gengrich used every obscenity he knew, then gaped as the last few archers picked their way through the shambles, still carrying Brentano.

"I good as tripped over my own feet, Arnie," he said. "Busted an ankle, twisted my wrist. Did Joe . . . ? Oh hell," as Gengrich's expression answered him.

And still more of the blue-bannered bastards! Gengrich cursed the bad luck that had disabled their last onager three days back. The massed cavalry would have been a sweet target for a barrel holding ten pounds of black powder and ten pounds more of scrap iron and small stones.

"Hey, Corp!" shouted MacAllister. "Somebody new's joined the fight!" From his perch in the tree he was the only one who could see over the heads of the attackers.

"Let 'em come," Gengrich shouted. "There's enough party for everybody." For about one more attack, that is, and after that we'll be out of bullets and damned low on arrows, and thank God Erika and Helena and Chrissie are back behind the Rustengans and Schultzy's Diana is looking after them—

"Hey! That's a Tamaerthan banner! Our friends have arrived!"

Gengrich slung his rifle with steady hands; this was one fight where he'd been too busy to get the shakes. Then he breathed a silent prayer of thanks.

✢ ✢ ✢

Gengrich and his men were spectators for the rest of the battle. A few minutes after the Tamaerthans hit the enemy from the rear, a cohort of Romans rode through the Rustengan line and took them in front. After that Gengrich's men were in more danger of being trampled by their allies' horses than of being overrun by their enemies.

Gengrich and Boyd watched the Romans mopping up the last of the blue banners.

"They do fight," Alex Boyd said. "Wonder why?"

"Phrados has those Defender goon squads in their homes?" Gengrich mused.

"Or they got no homes at all. Yeah."

"Listen," Gengrich said. "M-16s I'd swear."

"Schultzy's got an H&K .308—"

"Yeah. Captain Galloway sent those troops." Gengrich wanted to shout.

"Maybe it's himself."

"Either way, he cares. We don't forget that."

The fight was nearly over, but knots of enemy fought on. They were badly outclassed, caught between Roman legionaries with their horse archery and Rick Galloway-trained Tamaerthans. When the survivors finally broke and rode for their lives, they left more than a thousand behind.

✠ ✠ ✠

"Okay, Alex, what's the butcher's bill?"

"Green KIA. Brentano will be out of action for a week anyway. Thirty-four locals KIA. Twenty-seven wounded, and three missing."

"Not as bad as it might be."

"Nope. And this chap wants to see you."

Boyd indicated a young Tamaerthan nobleman cantering toward him. If the guy had been astride a choppered Harley and wearing a leather jacket instead of a mail coat, he'd have been a dead ringer for Panzer Klewicki, back on the Southwest Side. Was Panzer still riding, or had he busted his neck?

And did it matter, if you were never going to find out? For a moment Gengrich felt desperately homesick for Earth.

"Lord Gengrich?" The Tamaerthan reined in.

"The same. Who do I have the honor of thanking for his timely arrival?"

"Teuthras, son of Kevin, of Clan Mac Clallan. Coronel of the first Tamaerthan Hussars and cousin to Tylara, Eqetassa of Chelm," he added.

"We are grateful. I do not doubt that we would have prevailed in the end, but with your help we have smitten our enemies far harder."

"Indeed. They were a worthy foe. Have all of Phrados' men fought so well?"

"These were the best. Although I do not know if all of the others had orders to press home their attack."

"We can talk more of this later. I have orders from the Lord Captain General to welcome your return to his service. He has sent the Lords Bisso and Beazeley with new strength for your star weapons, firepowder bombs, medicines, and strong waters.

"We hoped we would be able to join you and give your weapons their new strength before this battle. However, when we reached you the enemy was already attacking. It seemed better not to wait. The Lord Rick often quotes an old commander of his, the High Rexja Napolyon—'Ask me for anything but time.' "

So the captain was claiming to have served under Napoleon was he? When bigger and better whoppers are told . . . Anyway, that explained the other star weapons. Wonder how many rounds the captain sent, and what orders he gave Bisso about issuing them?

All around the battle was dying down. Most of the Romans had ridden off in pursuit. A lot of the Tamaerthans had dismounted, to loot the bodies and if necessary make sure the bodies were properly dead. They'd posted about half a squadron of sentries, though, and they were bringing the loot to a central collecting point. The captain had done a good job with these people, which was really no surprise but nice to see all the same.

For the first time in longer than he wanted to think about, Gengrich felt safe.

They were bringing in Joe Green's body tied over a mule. As they did, Schultzy rode up, with blood on his Rustengan armor. He gave Boyd a sour look as he dismounted; Gengrich wondered if Alex had been sniffing around Diana again. Better ask, but not here. Right now Gengrich wanted to say goodbye to Joe Green. Joe hadn't been any Audie Murphy, but wasting ammo was his only real vice. Otherwise he'd been reliable and hardworking and sensible, never making any trouble. *Damn all. Another hour—*

Gengrich walked up to the mule carrying Green's body. A man in peasant clothing stood on the far side, another at its head. A couple of boys were playing kickball with a bound-up leather jerkin whose owner would never need it again.

"Bring the body to Lord Brentano, fellows. He and Lord Green were comrades."

"Yes, my lord—"

"Look out, Lord Gengrich!"

The high-pitched shout had Gengrich jumping back from the mule before the man on the far side came in under its belly and out with a knife in his hand. The blade leaped up, seeking a path under Gengrich's armor and into his belly. As the blade rose, one of the boys suddenly flung the kickball. It hit the man in the head, making the knife thrust miss.

The man at the mule's head had also drawn a knife, but now the mule was rearing. It threw him off balance. By the time he was steady on his feet, Gengrich had his Colt out. He shot the man in the chest as the first man closed for another stab. The boy ran up to the mule, vaulted over it with his hands on Joe Green, and slammed his bare feet into the back of the first man's head. The blow knocked the man sprawling. The thongs holding the body broke, and body and boy together tumbled down on top of the man. Gengrich stamped hard on the man's wrist. The knife dropped to the ground.

Now two more men were running toward Gengrich, and a third was unlimbering a crossbow. Teuthras spurred toward the archer, sword swinging down, and flew out of the saddle with a quarrel sticking out of his chest. His fall wasn't all bad; it gave Boyd and Schultz a clear field of fire at the other two. Who hit which man first was never clear and didn't matter anyway; both went down.

This left the archer, who was ten feet from a stray horse and already on the move, reloading and recocking his bow as he ran. Too many people around him for gunplay, too, and none of the dumb bastards were lifting a finger to stop him!

"Grab that man, you—!" yelled Boyd.

The other boy caught up with the fleeing man as he reached the horse. The crossbow twanged and a quarrel tore into the boy's belly, but he already had his arms around the man's thigh. Then his teeth sank into the leg, through leather and into flesh. The man screamed and beat at the boy. For a moment his head was clearly silhouetted— and a moment was all MacAllister ever needed for a clear shot at longer ranges than this. The man's head snapped back and he fell off his horse on top of the boy.

"Medics!" yelled Schultz.

Gengrich said nothing. He really wanted to go off somewhere and have that case of the shakes. He knew he ought to see how Teuthras was—although any man who was sitting up already and swearing like that couldn't be too badly hurt.

What he was going to do was ask a couple of pointed questions of a young lady named Monira. Brushing off Boyd's hands and several other people asking questions, he strode toward his horse.

⁜ ⁜ ⁜

"The one by the mule was Alanis, from what you say. The other was Cyra."

Was there a moment's hesitation in the level voice, or a flicker in the steady blue eyes? Gengrich thought he detected both. And did that mean the disguised girl who'd taken out the crossbowman at the cost of her own life was somebody Monira didn't know? From another House of the Wolf?

The idea that more of these pint-sized assassins were running around loose made Gengrich ill. Should he dose Monira with more babble juice?

No point. It would be Captain Galloway's problem soon enough. But there was one question Gengrich had to ask.

"Why did—your friends save me?"

For a moment it looked as if Monira was really going to smile. But she only shrugged. "It was our duty, now that it serves Lady Tylara that you be alive. We swore an oath."

We swore an oath. And because they'd sworn an oath, some of those kids had come all the way south to take him out, and others had come south after them to hide among his men, watching him without being detected ever since last winter. How many were there? He knew he'd never get an answer to that question.

At least there was one question he didn't need answered. What would have happened to him if they'd decided it was their duty to keep trying to kill him? He knew that too well.

He started to say, "Thank you, Monira." The words stuck in his throat. He had to get out of here, out of this dark smelly wagon where Monira and Euris sat half-naked in moldy straw with about as much expression as a couple of goddamned temple statues!

Gengrich was twenty yards from the wagon and bumping into Schultz before he knew where he was. Schultz grabbed his arm.

"Good Lord, Arnie. You look like your own ghost." He lowered his voice. "Find what you were after?"

"Yeah. I guess."

"You look like you could use a drink. Here." He held up a flask and pulled out the cork. "McCleve's Best Panther Piss. I traded Jack Beazeley for a couple of jugs."

"Thanks. Ah. Good stuff. How's Teuthras?"

"Frank says he's got a couple of cracked ribs and a concussion. He got those falling off his horse. The crossbow just gouged the skin over his ribs. Frank's disinfected it already." Schultz grinned. "The guy nearly took Frank's head off when he said he might miss the big battle. Said that was to call him as weak as a woman." The grin faded. "I didn't tell him the 'boy' who avenged him was a girl."

"How—?"

"She asked for the knife. We let the other one use it. Mind if I have that back?"

"Be my guest."

Schultz gulped from the flask, then stoppered it. "Arnie, do you suppose you could lean on Alex to stay away from Diana, before I have to? If I don't, her family will take a hand."

"I told Vinicianus—"

"Screw your Roamin' Roman. Diana says the last couple of times Boyd dropped around, Vinicianus was with him. Didn't lift a finger to stop his hassling her, either."

"Schultzy, if you're trying to make trouble—"

"Arnie, Horny Alex's already doing that, with your Roman advisor backing him up. I'm trying to stop trouble."

Gengrich reached for the flask again. "I'd better talk to both of them."

"Yeah, you do that."

Gengrich drank. Maybe it hadn't been such a good idea, to play Schultzy and Vinicianus off against each other for the job of—oh, call it grand vizier. If Vinicianus was putting Boyd up to something that could get him shot—not that Alex ever needed much putting up where women were concerned. . . .

Not my problem anymore. The prodigal's home and Daddy, you take over!

14

"Welcome, Lady Tylara. Did you have a good journey?"

Tylara stopped at the threshold of the rector's private chambers and let Lady Siobhan take her cloak. It was the first time she'd visited the University since Les' return; had Gwen added any more luxuries and would it say anything if she had?

I must not *go about looking upon Lady Gwen as an enemy whose strengths and weaknesses I must spy out. She is no fool; if I do this she will know and tell Rick. And if by some strange working of fate she is in truth not my mortal enemy . . .*

A strange working of fate that would be, indeed, unless my husband is not as other men are.

Tylara forced a smile, before the silence grew too long. "Well enough. At this season it is no great hardship to travel any distance. I confess I will not be unhappy to live to see the days when Tran has the—*freeways*—of Earth."

And that is to admit a weakness, and to Gwen! Must I seem a witling?

"Let's hope we all live that long. Would you like some tea, or would you prefer wine? I have some sherry I've been saving for an occasion, and I think this is one. It's a dark, sweet wine, stronger than ordinary vintages."

"Thank you, my Lady Rector. I will have a glass."

One glass of anything should not weaken my wits or lower my guard, unless the gods have already seen fit to do it.

"Lady Siobhan. Two glasses of the Bristol Cream—oh, and bring that letter you received yesterday from Lord Mason." The girl went to a carved cupboard by the window and pulled out an Earth bottle and two Roman glasses.

"She reads English very well now," Gwen continued. "I wish I had half her talent for languages."

Do you need that, when you have—other talents? No, that is not just. None of the men she seems to attract can be wound around her finger by no more than a whore's arts.

That is why it is so hard not to fear her. Bedsport is one thing. A true meeting of minds is far more. And since Rick and I have not had either since mid-winter . . .

"Thank you, Lady Siobhan." The sherry was indeed stronger than common wine. Tylara sipped cautiously, not sure she cared for the sweetness. "Is Lord Mason well?"

"Oh yes, my lady. Or at least, he was when he penned the letter, some twelve days ago. I pray that nothing has happened to him in that time."

The look on Siobhan's face was unmistakable. So Lord Mason's suit is succeeding, is it? Well, both could do far worse, she one of the greatest of the Star Lords and a good man for a husband, he a granddaughter of faithful old Camithon for a wife. And my husband—

For a moment Tylara could not complete the thought. Then she forced her wits onward, like forcing a skittish horse across a swift-flowing stream.

My husband will be happy. Did he not say once, "Art Mason's got to limit himself to officer-class ladies from now on. No more barmaids. In fact, he really ought to get married."

And am I so lost to loyalty and good sense that I wish my husband to be unhappy? Especially in a matter so nearly concerning one of his most trusted men, to whom I owe no small debt myself?

"Pour yourself a glass, Siobhan, and sit down," said Gwen. "Let's not stand too much on ceremony."

"Thank you, my lady." The girl didn't take the drink, but sat down, unfolded three pieces of paper, and began to read.

"To my dear Lady Siobhan, greetings and hopes that you are as well as I am.

"By the time you read this, we may have fought the great battle against the horde of the Prophet Phrados. Certainly it will be fought sooner rather than later. They have eaten the country bare behind them, and have no way to go but forward. Nor can they move east into the Roman Provinces, not without leaving us free to strike at their flank and rear.

"Publius Caesar seems to doubt this last. He has kept three of his six legions in the Provinces, together with several cohorts of garrison troops and some thousands of militia. To do him justice, he may fear rebels or bandits as well as Phrados, and does not wish to admit it. In his position, I suspect I would do much the same."

Hah. He fears unfriendly eyes will read his message. Unfriendly, or a stranger. Who in Caesar's camp knows English? A starman hired from the south, one of the deserters? It could be. And Gengrich.

Will Lord Gengrich be truly loyal? He has been pardoned, but will he do treason anew? And if he is, what does that say about my husband's notions of how to deal with traitors?

And mine?

As before, the answer was silence.

Siobhan went on. "However, we have enough here to do the business. Two legions of cavalry, one of pikemen, the Tamaerthons, the Drantos knights and infantry, Gengrich's men, and contingents of infantry from Rustengo, Vis, and a baker's dozen of other towns and small cities, plus the—my lady, what is—?"

"The artillery. That's the large firepowder weapons."

"The artillery, the star weapons, the balloon, and a few tricks the Captain General undoubtedly has up his sleeve. That's forty thousand men and a lot of weapons most of the horde has never even faced of, let alone faced. They have a hundred and twenty thousand, or so we've heard from the last batch of scouts, but only about a quarter of that is much more than an armed mob. . . ."

As Siobhan continued, Tylara more and more ceased to listen. Instead she tried to imagine her husband's face as he planned the battle. As hard as she tried, she could imagine nothing except the cold mask that he had worn since mid-winter. Aye, worn even those few times they shared a bed, as though only his body touched hers, while his mind was somewhere else, with someone else. . . .

What else could he be hiding behind that mask, other than such a shift of allegiance? If by some mischance the secret of the Children of

Vothan had been discovered, surely he would have had the wits to see that this was a matter they could discuss as equals. They had a common interest in seeing that their plans and the future of their children were protected from the consequences of Gwen Tremaine's not being a chaste woman—or at least being chaste only by the customs of an Earth she would never see again.

If Rick had been silent for so long, there could be only one reason—that what was dividing him from her was a matter on which no words would make the slightest difference. There could be only one such matter.

Am I helpless in the face of this change of allegiance?

Perhaps not. But I must move cautiously. If Rick has hidden his heart so well for so long, it could be that he is now as skilled in dissimulation as any Tran lord. Skilled in our ways of intrigue. How otherwise could he have devised so wise an end to the problem of Lord Rand? The man who saved me would not have been so wise.

If wise as Tran lords, than—as ruthless? It has been known, to use the children by the first wife as hostages to secure acquiescence in a second. As long as the second is fertile. Which, Yatar help me, Gwen certainly must be. . . .

Has my husband finally succeeded in frightening me?

The gods have mercy, yes.

She shivered.

"Lady Tylara, are you cold? Here, Siobhan. Pull the shutters and make up some tea."

Even worse, I must endure this intriguer's hiding her triumph behind a mask of graciousness!

✣ ✣ ✣

The bonfires at either end of the bridge and the torches held by the sentries showed the last wagons more than halfway across. The floor of the bridge was sagging to within a foot of the water, but with the extra boats tied in place a few days ago the bridge was holding.

Rick still didn't uncross his fingers until the last wagon had rumbled off the bridge onto the north bank of the Dnaster. He turned, to see Drumold looking at him with what seemed suspiciously like a smile.

"Ye have the air of a man who is hoping that a man ye have to trust really knows what he's doing."

"Is it that obvious?"

"To one who knows ye well enough, Rick, I canna say that you are any great hand at hidin' your thoughts."

I am better than you think, my friend, Rick mused, *or you and I would not be standing on this hillside, having this amicable discussion.*

"Well, I'm not surprised that Lord Holloway knows his business. He's almost as good an engineer as Lord Campbell. I was surprised how many suggestions he made. He wasn't the only one of Gengrich's men who did more than I expected."

"Mayhap Gengrich knows that his fate is now linked to yours, and would rather stand than fall."

"Likely enough. He never was stupid." *Maybe, just maybe Gengrich would be smart enough to play it straight from now on, and the secret he held would never come out.*

That's hoping the horse will learn to sing with a vengeance, and is there going to be anything left of your marriage even if Gengrich keeps his big bazoo shut for all time to come?

Don't work yourself into a stew over that, or Drumold will notice enough to ask questions you'd rather not answer.

The torches were now moving onto the bridge. Some of the sentries were kneeling, tools in hand, while others held the torches.

"We're going to dismantle the bridge into four sections tonight. Tomorrow night we tow it downriver and reassemble it under the walls of Vis. It would be too hard to defend where it is. Also, if we fight where I expect to and we do need to retreat, we'll have a shorter and more easily defended route to the bridge."

"Best not mention that to Publius Caesar."

"What kind of fool—?"

"Can you no tell a jest when ye hear one?"

"Sorry." *Got the windup. Shouldn't show that, to Drumold or anyone else.* "Has Publius said anything new that he shouldn't have?"

"Not since the last Council of War." At the last council Publius had brusquely suggested that all the contingents of cities and towns claimed by Rome should fight under Roman command or not at all. He'd at least had the sense to leave it as a suggestion, but tempers had been frayed all the same.

"Publius cannot control his tongue." Drumold looked thoughtful. "Yet he might do us no small favor if ye asked him fairly. I have read over the muster roll of Gengrich's men. He has some twelve-score men of the Clan Mac Brayne and the Red Mac Beans among those who follow him."

"I'm afraid that doesn't mean as much to me as it should, Drumold."

"No shame to ye, Rick. Ye have so much wisdom in war that did I not know ye well, I would be among those who called you wizard. Ye have less knowledge of the clans of Tamaerthon, and indeed who outside the hills does not?

"It is only that the Mac Braynes and the Red Mac Beans have been at feud with Mac Clallan Muir since my grandfather bore the title. It little matters who gave first offense, and indeed it may well have been my grandfather. His temper made him enemies from the cradle to the burial mound. Very surely, though, the two clans he outlawed shed much blood in reply. They are now at feud not only with me and mine but with the Mac Bretachs and so many others it would be past dawn before I'd numbered them all. . . ."

"I'll take your word for it. I gather you'd rather not have the two clans anywhere near the rest of the Tamaerthons?"

"Not unless ye want them shot at from both the front and the back."

"Good God no! So where should we put them? Gengrich won't be too happy with losing them altogether."

"Aye. Yet if he's no fool, he'll know ye canna leave him with such an army loyal only to him. What matters it if his men start leaving before or after the battle, so long as they go to good service? If Publius would offer to enlist them as auxiliaries, with the hope of earning Roman citizenship in time, would Gengrich not think he was being honored? And if Publius will no offer, can we not ask Titus Frugi—?"

"Don't get within a mile of Frugi without Publius' permission! Frugi's the senior legate. He has to be Publius' second-in-command. But you may have noticed that Publius keeps a whole Praetorian cohort around his tent, to make sure Frugi doesn't succeed to the command. . . ."

"If Publius doesn't stop looking for assassins under the tiles of his tent, he may well find one where he's not looking for it."

"You know that. I know that. Publius doesn't know it." God, was there no end to intrigues, plots, and double-crosses? Probably not, and now he couldn't even hope to find a refuge from them at home. Quite the contrary. Rick found himself looking forward to the coming battle.

It would be a horrible business, pretty much a straightforward killing contest, but it would be simple.

"My lords?" A slightly diffident voice spoke from behind Rick. He turned to see Apelles, Yanulf's young assistant. "Yes, Apelles?"

"Archbishop Polycarp sent me. He will hold a united service of worship in half a glass, in his tent. He would be honored if you would attend."

And insulted if we didn't. Not to mention all the rumors that would fly around that Lord Rick's heart really wasn't in this union of the two religions and that he was a secret worshipper of Christ or Vothan or Ronald McDonald . . . !

I'm a politician. I kiss babies, eat blintzes, and go to masses. And if need be, put on Indian feather bonnets and get adopted into tribes. Right. "Thank you, Apelles. We shall be present. Where have you been assigned for the battle?"

"With the vanguard of the Drantos cavalry, Lord Rick. I am to send the healers where they are needed and to write down the dead and the hurt."

A combination medic and staff officer, but he'd be in the thick of the fighting even if it went well. If it didn't—well, there was something to be said for the fatalistic notion that Vothan One-eye would have a man he wanted, however far he had to seek or however young or old the man might be. Come to think of it, Apelles wasn't all that young— getting on for twenty-four Earth years, and Rick hadn't been much older than that when he signed up with the CIA for what turned out to be a trip to a really "unknown destination."

Rick Galloway, you are getting too old too fast, and you know the reason.

God dammit, Tylara. WHY?

15

"The horse will be divided into two equal parts. One will advance on the left. The other will advance on the right. The foot will advance in the center. The honor of the gods will be avenged."

"For the honor of the gods!" shouted the Defenders standing three deep around Phrados the Prophet.

"For the honor of the gods!" shouted all the captains sitting on their horses in a wider circle around the Defenders.

Highpriest Matthias shouted as loudly as any. It would not be within reason for the Defenders to drag him off his horse and cut his throat now, in the very presence of the enemy—but many things Phrados had ordered in these past few days were not within reason. Tyras now had plenty of company in whatever land a madman's victims went to after death.

Even those who had grown used to capricious murders had been shaken by the slaughter of the women and children of Myreis. Over a thousand of them butchered in a single night after Phrados learned of their men's surrender to the skyfolk.

Clearly Phrados had intended that his soldiers fear him and the Defenders more than the enemy and his magical weapons. Had the Prophet accomplished this? Matthias doubted it, but it was a measure of how much fear Phrados had sown that Matthias dared not speak to anyone about these doubts.

He also doubted that the fear would much outlast the Defenders. If they perished in the battle, whether it was won or lost, not one in ten of the host would thereafter blindly obey Phrados. From such a situation, a man prepared to counsel the captains, as nobleman, warrior, and priest, might draw much to the advantage of both himself and his masters.

But that was pricing the unborn calf. Matthias made a gesture of aversion with his armored gauntlet and gathered up the reins. He wanted to lead his men into position on the right, as soon as Phrados finished giving more precise orders for the battle.

Now the bearers of the Prophet's litter were coming forward. Matthias realized with dismay that no more precise orders would be given. He wondered if the other captains were also dismayed, but those whose faces were visible under their helmets might as well have been wearing masks.

Prophet or no Prophet, it was tempting the gods to make such scanty plans for a battle on which so much depended. The skyfolk and their allies were outnumbered three to one, but even their foot was better than most of the Prophet's. Two-thirds of their horse were the armored knights of Drantos and Tamaerthon or the still more formidable legions of Rome. With or without star weapons the Prophet faced a formidable foe—

And there would be star weapons. The tales of their work in the battles against the Rustengans and Lord Gengrich had lost nothing in the telling, but it seemed to Matthias that the star weapons were indeed formidable. Would they be less formidable if one did not gather one's men in great masses and hurl them at the starmen?

No matter. Such a stratagem was not within the power of the Prophet's host. It had too many captains, too many who did not know their work, and none Phrados would trust to fight except under his eye.

Also, even if a captain did move his men to find a place where the star weapons were weak, would he not be seen at once by the balloon? There it was, hanging in the sky over the hill at the rear of the starmen's host. Smoke trailed from the basket under it. From this distance Matthias could not see the men in the basket, but he knew from the stories of last year's battles that they would be there.

Was the balloon a living creature from Earth? There were no tales of such things in the time when men first came to Tran, but that was long ago. The art of taming balloons might not have been known then.

Or was it a creation of magic? Or—and these tales persisted, though they seemed altogether improbable to Matthias—was it a mere machine, like a wagon or a ship? Could anyone master the art of making balloons and thereafter gaze down upon his enemies with an all-seeing eye?

Perhaps they would find out today, if the gods smiled on the Prophet in spite of his folly. Meanwhile, there were ways to lessen that folly. If he could move his men to the left instead of the right, there would be captains willing to listen to him once out of the hearing of the Defenders. He could do something to make sure that the village on the High Road was held, that the High Road itself was held where it left the forest, and that no one advanced down the High Road into what would surely be ambushes.

Beyond that, he could offer even his best friends among the host of Phrados nothing but his prayers.

✛ ✛ ✛

The vanguard of the knights of Drantos had beaten off their third attack by the enemy's horse when the Roman tribune rode past Apelles. The priest looked to see that the bandage he'd just finished putting on a man-at-arms' leg wasn't too tight, then watched the tribune. He made a very fine sight in his molded and silvered armor, with his escort of twenty almost equally splendid soldiers of the Praetorian Guard.

The tribune rode up to the banner of Rudhrig, Eqeta of Harms, and saluted in the Roman manner.

"Hail, Lord Rudhrig. Publius Caesar hails your victory and the valor of your knights, and bids you withdraw your knights to the slope of the hill just above the edge of the forest and there await further orders."

Even from where he stood, Apelles could see the Eqeta's face change color. "The knights of Drantos do not give up ground they have held thrice over. We will await our orders here."

"Publius Caesar commands—"

"Publius Caesar can command you to come and babble to us of dishonoring ourselves. He cannot command us, unless he comes himself."

"An order brought by a tribune of Caesar is—"

"A fart in a wine cup, as far as it concerns me. Now, tribune, will you take that message to Publius Caesar or not? It matters little to me."

What the tribune might have said in reply was lost in the blare of enemy horns signalling a new attack. Apelles saw the tribune's face twist with conflicting desires—return to Caesar or stay and prove that he would not at least turn his back on a foe.

"They come!" one of the acolytes gibbered. "The enemy comes, and we will be abandoned!"

"Calm," Apelles said, although he felt little enough calm himself. "Not all of them come. They are not clever enough to attack all at once. We defeated them before. We will again. The honor of the bheromen of Drantos protects us. They will not leave us." Or at least they will not leave their dead and wounded. "Now. You neglect the cleansing. Let us wash our hands together, and say together the prayers of exorcism."

When Apelles looked up again he saw that the Roman tribune had joined in the counter stroke. The swiftness of the enemy attack had left him small choice.

"I think they have no one captain in command," Apelles said to a knight as he poured—*disinfectant*—into a deep thigh wound. The leg was broken and would have to be set.

The knight grunted in pain. "This captain seems clever enough. He has pressed home his attack—"

And that he has, Apelles thought.

The enemy horse archers swept around the Drantos left and reached the scrub on the fringes of the forest. For about as long as it would have taken Apelles to drink a cup of poor wine, the ground to the rear of the Drantos vanguard was beaten by enemy arrows. Some fell close to the wounded, and several mules and packhorses went down.

Then the Tamaerthan archers appeared at the edge of the forest. A trumpet sounded. They were too far for Apelles to hear their commander, but in his mind he heard the cry anyway. "Let the grey gulls fly!"

Three hundred arrows arched toward the Prophet's men. Then three hundred more, and in a breath another flight. The horse archers went down. A brave few spurred toward the forest, but no more than a score came close enough to loose their own arrows. Then they too were shot out of their saddles.

The rest of the enemy withdrew. Before they could escape, horse archers and lancers alike were shattered by a Drantos charge. Eqeta and tribune rode boot to boot into the enemy's ranks.

Once the road to the rear was open, the tribune and his surviving Praetorians took it. The Eqeta led his men back past Apelles, dropping off five more dead and fifteen more wounded on the way. Apelles ordered one of the acolytes to divide the wounded into the gravely and the lightly hurt, and a scribe to record the names of the dead.

It was a good thing that so far there were fewer than two hundred wounded, and many of those were tended by their squires or servants. Apelles could have used three times as many acolytes and twice as many scribes.

I am an *administrator*, not a healer, he thought. Neither Yanulf nor Polycarp disputed that, but still he was sent to take his turn in the field hospitals. *They say it is a lesson in humility. It is certainly that.* When he was in his office, surrounded by files and papers with a dozen clerks on call, he was a man of consequence. Here the knights were all too ready to forget that Yatar had made him a priest, and to remember that he had been born a swineherd.

Yet it does no harm to learn the arts of healing, and an administrator *must know something of war.*

Few of the wounded this time needed more than a cleaning of their wounds and a bandage. Apelles had time to gaze around him, and notice that the mass of foot in the enemy's center had grown larger. It also had a vanguard of men in armor, or at least helmets and breastplates, and armed with shields and swords or spears.

It seemed to Apelles that there was wisdom in Publius Caesar's orders. Certainly the eight hundred lances of the vanguard had done well, slaying or unhorsing half again their own numbers. Yet if the enemy chose to support their next attack with some of that mass of foot, would the knights find it as easy to clear their retreat? Apelles did not call himself a man of war, but he knew that heavy cavalry could not easily retreat through a forest and that eight hundred lances were far too many for Drantos to lose.

Not to mention the wounded and dead, whom he could not abandon to an enemy who took no prisoners.

Apelles was just beginning work on an arrow sunk three fingers into a knight's left buttock when horns and hoofbeats made him rise and stare. For a moment he thought it was another attack, but these horns were the deep-toned Roman ones and the horsemen riding up were Roman Praetorians. Roman Praetorians, a whole cohort of them—and in the middle a familiar small figure in gilded armor, with a deep red cloak flowing back from his shoulders.

Publius Caesar had come to give his orders in person.

Apelles signaled to the apprentices to busy themselves in their work. It would not do for them to stare. He himself moved closer, so that he would miss nothing. *If healing is part of my training, so is this.*

"After the Hooey River I thought you well-born witlings knew how to fight," Publius roared. "Titus Frugi even doubted that you were barbarians. Now I know that he was wrong, and you remain barbarians who know nothing except how to die with honor."

"Who is the barbarian?" replied the Eqeta. "Those who know how to die with honor, or those who have never heard of honor at all?"

The quarrel went on from there. No doubt it helped that five hundred Praetorians were enough to quell any ideas of laying hands on Publius but not enough to give Publius ideas of forcing the knights to move.

"You would not obey my order when I sent it to you," Publius finished. "Now I *bring* it to you, at a time when I and my Praetorians could as well be fighting our common foe. You said you would obey me. Whether you live or die, you will not seem very honorable if you do otherwise. Now—I command you and the vanguard of Drantos to withdraw to a position I will choose for you."

Lord Rudhrig's hesitation lasted only a moment, although it seemed like half a glass to Apelles. Then he nodded, and with a wave of his hand sent messengers riding down the line to carry the order to retreat.

✣ ✣ ✣

"Here." Apelles indicated a ditch that would be the outermost boundary of his new field hospital at the rear of what everyone was calling the Great Redoubt. Acolytes came to erect the tent, with its solid roof for shade, and its thin netting that gave ventilation but prevented flies and borers from entering. More star lore, but it seemed to work. *Something* worked. Exclude the small devils that hid in dirt from entering the body, and more often then not wounds healed. And certainly flies and borers and carvers carried dirt on their feet. . . .

"I have never heard anyone speak so to an Eqeta." Fnarg was senior acolyte. His father had been a silversmith and town councilor.

"Nor I," Apelles said. "And if we are wise we will not remember that *we* ever heard such."

Apelles knew that Publius Caesar was right, but his heart was with the knights of Drantos. Perhaps they had not chosen the wisest way of proving their honor, yet what honor was there in calling them "barbarians" to their very faces?

Moreover, was the Roman kind of obedience really what he wished to see in Drantos? Publius had ordered eight hundred lances of Drantos knights led by one of the five greatest nobles of the Realm as if they were spitboys or sweepers. Not even the bheroman of Apelles' native village would have dared order his father about so—at least where it was a matter of knowledge of swine and where they had the right to feed.

As with Maev, Apelles found he was not quite sure if what he'd thought he wanted was in truth his real desire. He was no more sure when the knights finally rode past the Great Redoubt.

As they did, horns and drums signaled another enemy attack.

✣ ✣ ✣

Rick watched helplessly as the cavalry rearguard, two cohorts of the Fourth Legion, dissolved under the massed enemy cavalry. If they'd had room to maneuver or arrows to shoot, they might have made a fight of it. Backed against the forest they couldn't maneuver, and they'd emptied their quivers covering the retreat of the Drantos ironhats. The Tamaerthan archers in the forest and the star weapons in the Great Redoubt had plenty of ammo, but no clear targets.

A couple of centuries of the *cohortes equitates* came pelting down the hill, but all they could do was drag a few wounded out from the fringes of the battle. That was one legion that was going to have a blood debt to settle today. Rick only hoped they weren't too weakened or shaken to take it when they had a chance.

When the cavalry action petered out, Rick saw that the enemy was now across his line of retreat up the hill. Ganton needed him as a Captain General, the Tamaerthans and the city-state infantry needed him as a CO. Neither needed him as a casualty.

"Let's move, Top!" he called to Elliot.

"Sir." Elliot waved commands.

Twenty Guardsmen moved ahead. Rick had long since got used to that: the elite troopers weren't about to let him lead the way into combat. They rode across the leading skirmishers of the Prophet's army. Lances dipped, and rose dripping red. Sabers flashed. Rick, Elliot, and the fifty Guards of his headquarters troop rode through the enemy foot at a gallop.

When they were past they saw the cavalry.

"Damn all!" Elliot shouted. He raised his Ingram. "Going to take shooting to get through those."

"Right as usual," Rick said. *And we're getting low on ammo. Should be more in the Redoubt.* He smiled to himself. *The Great Redoubt. Like Borodino. Ring it with artillery. Fill it with star weapons. And wait. The Prophet would send his troops charging toward it, to be cut down in thousands.*

Good battle plan, Rick thought. *Good enough? What the hell is a track star doing in a place like this?*

Elliot's Ingram sounded like tearing paper as he fired off a full clip into the lancers blocking their path.

*Trouble with those things. Easy to shoot up too much ammo for too little effect. And we're getting low on nine-millimeter Parabellum—*He raised his automatic and shot an approaching cavalryman out of the saddle. *How casually you do that. Having fun, Galloway?*

Then they were past. A dozen Guardsmen wheeled behind Rick to cover his retreat. He turned to urge them to follow him, but saw they were needed. The enemy cavalry wasn't retreating at all. *Fanatics. They all fight like fanatics. I guess the rumors are true, the Prophet holds all their families hostage.*

Another fifty yards. He spurred his horse forward. The Guards shouted behind him. "Cover them!" Rick shouted to Elliot.

"Roger." Elliot wheeled and rammed a new clip into the Ingram.

Rick came to the ditch and abatis of the Redoubt. Larry Brentano waved, something like a salute.

"Help Elliot," Rick ordered.

Brentano waved again and ran to the edge. After a moment his H&K chattered. Then Elliot rode in followed by the rest of the Guards.

"Who'd we lose?" Rick demanded.

"None," Elliot said proudly. "Two wounded." He pointed to the hospital area at the rear. "Get 'em up there, Sarkas."

"Sir." The Guards lieutenant shouted his own orders.

"Colonel!" Brentano shouted. He pointed downhill.

The Prophet's army was moving forward in one vast wave of infantry.

"You taking command now?" Brentano asked.

"Right. Just give me a moment to have a drink." He reached for the wineskin attached to his saddle and tried to look casual as the Prophet's drums and horns sounded again and again.

✣ ✣ ✣

Rick hitched one leg up to sit casually atop his horse as he watched the enemy boil forward. Somebody had finally got them organized. As organized as that outfit would ever be. "Forty thousand?" he asked Elliot. He tried to keep his voice calm and casual.

"Maybe that many," Elliot said. "Maybe even a few more. How close you going to let them get?"

"Not much more," Rick said. He signaled to his signalmen. "Trumpeter, sound the General Alert, then All Units."

The notes sang out.

Gunners stood to their guns.

"Sound Fire on Command," Rick said. He reached out to his signalman and took the red and white striped flag, raised it high, and waited as the enemy infantry moved forward. When they reached the clump of brush he'd mentally selected he brought the flag sharply down.

The Redoubt erupted in fire. Bombards, musketeers, all the mercs, including the mortars and the crew with the Carl Gustav. The mortars were right on target: Rick saw whole squads fall in the center of the enemy ranks. Meanwhile twenty-pound stone balls from the bombards cut lanes from front to as far as Rick could see into the enemy formation.

The one-oh-six blazed again. White phosphorus exploded just at the enemy first rank. Men screamed in horror and ran trailing smoke.

"That ought to stop them," Elliot said.

"Yeah, it ought to, Sarge," Brentano said. "But it don't look like it did." He raised his H&K and fired slowly and deliberately. "And I don't reckon we're going to stop them."

✣ ✣ ✣

"Fire in the hole!"

The one-oh-six roared, and more of the Prophet's army died.

Not enough. Rick raised his own H&K and fired carefully and deliberately. Men fell.

"They just keep coming," Elliot said. "Goddamn, Colonel, I could sure use troops like that."

"Yeah." With any competent leadership those men could take any army on Tran. Fortunately they didn't have competent leadership.

"Defenders," Elliot muttered. He pointed to a formation at extreme range. "Six thousand, I hear. That's the damned secret. Everybody in that army knows them defenders will kill anyone who runs. And go back and mop up the village he came from to boot." Elliot rose in his saddle. "Ernikos! Keep them musketeers loading properly. That last volley was ragged."

"Aye my lord!" came the reply.

"They're going to get in here," Elliot said. "Dismount?"

"No. We'll need to fall back."

Elliot looked at him quizzically but said nothing.

"I remember a Korean vet," Rick said. "He said watching men try to put out a fire by jumping into it will give you the willies if you let yourself think about it."

"Right," Elliot said cheerfully. "So don't think about it."

"Sure." But it took a very experienced soldier not to think about what would happen if that kind of man reached you. Most of the locals weren't that experienced.

What the hell, Rick Galloway? Are you that experienced yourself?

"Sappers," Elliot said. He pointed. "Masked by the first wave. I thought their infantry wasn't supposed to get here. Good planning."

The leading infantry had taken the casualties. Now, behind them, were several compact formations of men who carried brushwood fascines and axes.

"They'll sure as hell get in here, Colonel," Elliot said. "We got maybe five minutes. No more. And I better see to my gunners."

"Right."

Elliot rode off. The Guards officers were chanting orders as the Guards musketeers loaded in unison. "Bite your cartridge. Spit. Ram. Return ramrod . . ."

The Artillerymen were struggling to lower the aim points of the bombards. They'd never been intended to be depressed that low. Then from the center of the Redoubt the LMG opened up. Private First Class Arkos Passovopolous had it, with Gardner as his number-two; it was in good hands. Ben Murphy would have been even better, but he had to ride with the Drantos ironhats if he wanted to hold onto Westrook.

For a couple of minutes the battlefield was almost silent, except for the mortar and recoilless rounds falling into the sappers and the boss gunner, Pinir son of the smith, roaring at his men. Then the sappers hit the ditch and the abatis, and what they lacked in skill they made up for in numbers. The logs of the abatis seemed to dissolve like the cohorts of the Fourth Legion, and suddenly the whole southern end of the Great Redoubt was open to the enemy.

"Fall back in order!" Rick shouted. There wasn't a trumpet command for that. He backed his horse away from the oncoming enemy. At intervals he fired his H&K. *Set an example. About all you can do.*

"Get First Pikes up to the northern end of the Redoubt," Rick shouted to a staff officer. The man rode off and another took his place next to Rick. "Vis infantry to connect with First Pikes. Move them north, and have them connect First Pikes to the Tamaerthan archers. And keep the archers supplied."

"Aye my lord."

And did you understand? I should write orders, but there's no time. Not with the enemy fifty yards away and closing.

He fired again and again. Then trumpets sounded behind him. He stood in his stirrups, then turned back with relief. First Pikes hadn't failed him.

"Close on First Pikes! Retreat behind the pikes!" He sent messengers down both sides to repeat the orders.

Elliot rode up. "They're keeping better order than I'd have thought," he said. He gestured to indicate the Guards musketeers, who had loaded while retreating and now turned to deliver another terrible volley at point-blank range.

The battle dissolved in confusion. For a while it seemed that the Redoubt was full of people with every kind of weapon or none at all, trying to run in three directions at once. Rick's Guardsmen had to draw their swords and hack their way through the enemy's skirmishers, then prod their way through the retreating musketeers and gunners.

Gunners drew swords and prepared to die by their bombards.

Rick rode down the line of gunners. "Retreat! Fall back behind the pikes! We'll take the guns again, and you'll use them again! Fall back!"

They did, although they wouldn't have if anyone but Rick had ordered it.

Close one, that. Even my middle-class gunners get the ironhat mentality. Never retreat. Never budge. . . .

A mob of half-naked men, heads shaved, wielding long knives, poured over the LMG's pit. Rick mentally awarded the Great Ark and Gardner posthumous Medals of Honor; they'd stayed on the gun long enough to take a big bite out of the enemy.

Then the mob stopped, churned, and went abruptly into reverse as the Great Ark erupted out of the pit. He held the LMG under his arm and swept it back and forth until the belt was gone. Then he tossed it to Gardner, drew a short sword with one hand and a long-handled mace with the other, and waded into the enemy.

From the speed of their retreat, it looked as if they'd finally found something that scared them more than the Defenders.

Gardner and Passovopolous fell back. Halfway to the pikes, Gardner went down with an arrow in his leg. The Great Ark picked up his number-two, machine-gun and all, slung the whole load over his shoulder, and kept on going.

Rick mentally erased the "posthumous" from the Medals of Honor and added an unlimited line of credit at Madame Echenia's for the Great Ark and a case of McCleve's Best for Gardner. They'd probably enjoy that more than the medals.

Everyone cheered as the Great Ark carried his load into the ranks of the First Pikes. Then they cheered again as Lord Rick rode up. Rick waved his binoculars to acknowledge the cheers, but it took an effort to hold his hand steady as he did. "No battle plan ever survives contact with the enemy," but this one had been a little too short-lived for his peace of mind.

Or had it? The enemy had spent his energy and most of his ammunition. He held much of the Great Redoubt, but it was a pit of carnage, worthless to the enemy—and they'd made no progress against the pikes at all.

"Mortars," Rick called. "Make them regret being in the Redoubt."

"Roger," someone shouted. A pair of mortar bombs fell among the enemy. Dead and living men were tossed about. The one-oh-six added white phosphorus. The interior of the Redoubt was a scene from the Inferno.

"City infantry's holding."

Rick turned to see Elliot on his right. The sergeant major looked as calm as he did on parade.

"And the Guards." Elliot raised his hand and brought it sharply down. A volley crashed out from among the pikemen. More of the Prophet's troops fell.

The city infantry on the left were indeed holding, but the enemy was doing no more than skirmishing with cavalry there. The allies' own cavalry was out of danger too, both the Drantos knights and the two mounted legions, the Eighth and the chewed-up Fourth.

The trouble was that the enemy's infantry had pushed so far forward and was massed so solidly that Rick's cavalry didn't really have room to charge. Rick had hoped the enemy would jam themselves between the river and the forest like a cork in a bottle; what he hadn't expected was that they'd do it so fast they immobilized most of his own cavalry. Now the two armies were like two porcupines facing each other in a sewer pipe, neither able to back up without giving the other an advantage.

"Damn Rudhrig," Rick said. "If he'd stayed a bit farther back—"

"Sure," Elliot said.

No point in if. "The key is those Defenders," Rick said. "Eliminate them and the Prophet's whole army comes apart." *I hope.*

16

Art Mason looked at the map and nodded. "No question, Colonel. Them Defenders are the key. Get them out of the way and all that infantry will run like blazes. They're only holding on because they got no place to go."

"Good. Glad you agree. Top?"

"Looks that way to me, too," Elliot said.

Mason stood and swept the area with his binoculars. The Prophet's infantry must have taken at least fifteen-percent casualties; in places the ditch was solid with bodies, some of them still moving. They'd all run if they could.

"So what do we have to hit the Defenders with?" Colonel Galloway asked.

Mason thought fast. *Good question.* "Well, we can't use the Romans. Or Drantos heavies, for that matter. The only way in there would be the High Road."

The Colonel nodded. "Bottleneck. We hold it with minimum forces, but that works both ways. We'll never get through their blocking force. Unless we can lure them off?"

Mason shook his head. "Tried. Didn't work. Whoever's holding that area knows what he's doing and has steady troops."

"Damnedest thing," Elliot mused. "How did a madman like the Prophet get first-class troops?"

Who cares?

"It's messed up from here to the Lynos River," the colonel said. "But south of there is Herdsman's Ford."

714

"Herdsman's Ford. Right!" Art said. "Wide enough to send cavalry across in column of squadrons. If—" He frowned.

"I think we can do it," the colonel said. "If we can clear off that blocking force on their side of the river and push a couple of thousand horse across we can sure give the Defenders something to worry about. Now who do I send?"

"Reckon I know," Mason said. "I'll round up volunteers. What can I have?"

"The Carl Gustav for one thing."

"Right, I'll need that. And enough more firepower to clear the river guards. Say a squadron of Guards. Two troops anyway. And for the main body—Colonel, can we borrow some Romans?"

"Doubt they'd follow you, Major," Elliot said. "Or that we can get Publius to lend them."

"Not without being here until the True Sun comes up," the colonel agreed. "They used to teach us that 'unity of command' was a major principle of war. Hah."

"Worse down there," Elliot said. He waved toward the enemy.

And that's for damned sure. Now, who can the colonel order directly? Hah. "Sir, what about Gengrich's troops?"

"Nowhere near enough," Galloway said. "They're not very reliable just now, either. Need rest and training. No, Art, there's only the one group we can send. Drumold's Tamaerthan chivalry. There's close to three thousand of them."

"It's also the whole nobility of Tamaerthon," Elliot said.

"Objection, Sergeant Major?"

"No objection, Colonel. Just reminding you. Sir."

"Thank you. It's a chance we'll have to take. Mason, I'll give you a written order to Drumold. Take your Guards, and our people, and get moving."

✠ ✠ ✠

Ganton made a point of studying the messages from the balloon, then scanning the battlefield with his binoculars, before turning back to the Imperial headquarters staff. "The enemy does not know what to do," he said. "While they argue, we should strike."

"How do you know they are confused?" Publius demanded. "If your knights had withdrawn when ordered we would have no doubts about this battle."

"We have none now," Ganton said. "Yet certainly I have cause to be displeased with my knights and barons." As perhaps you have to be displeased with the Fourth Legion. The legion that hailed me as worthy to lead Romans.

It had been a heady moment, there after the battle of the Hooey River, when the Roman soldiers hailed him as *Imperator*. Worthy to command Romans, but not a Roman. I am no threat to Publius Caesar, but can he believe that? Ganton stole a glance at Titus Frugi, who was pointedly studying the battle.

"Patience is a Roman virtue that I wish my barons would learn. Ever do we seek to ride to the battle and trample our enemies beneath the hooves of our horses. Sometimes that is the best way. Often it is not."

"It would seem, Titus Frugi, that my son-in-law has learned much."

"Thank you, Caesar," Ganton said. "Would you care to instruct me further today?"

Publius looked at him sharply, but Ganton showed no expression at all. *It's true. I have much to learn. More from Titus Frugi than from Publius, but—*

"The High Road," Publius said finally. "It is the key to this battle." He gestured, and a headquarters optio came forward with maps pinned to a board. "The balloon reports that five thousand horse and nearly that many foot hold the High Road. They have been blocked by the Tamaerthan archers."

This time Publius did wince. It wasn't hard to know why. Tamaerthan archers and pikemen, aided by no more than two starmen, had defeated a Roman legion and sacked a Roman town. That was years ago, but it was not easily forgotten.

Ganton pretended to study the maps, but in fact he had memorized the terrain. He had found that Romans were not so well trained as he in that art. They didn't have to be. They always had maps.

"Bad ground for cavalry," Ganton said. He indicated the area along the High Road. "Narrow. Best for foot."

"Agreed." Titus Frugi pointed to the massed troops milling around the Great Redoubt. "You see that Lord Rick sends the chivalry of Tamaerthon toward the river ford. It is easy to guess his plan."

"And there is a rider coming to tell us anyway," Ganton said. "I do not doubt that, even though the Lord Rick commands Tamaerthon independent of me."

"You have a plan, Frugi," Publius said.

"Yes, Caesar. Send the foot to menace the High Road. I will keep the survivors of the Fourth, and the *cohortes equitates*, to support Wanax Ganton. The Seventeenth will stay between your command, ready to move either way, and we will see who first can advance."

"A good plan," Publius said. "I agree."

"Thank you, Caesar," Ganton said. *And you too, Titus Frugi. I reward my friends, and you are a true friend.*

✤ ✤ ✤

Three arrows thrummed past Matthias. Two of them found targets, one in a centaur's belly and a second in the thigh of one of his guards. The man reeled in his saddle but said nothing. The centaur screamed until its rider dismounted and cut its throat.

"Retreat," Matthias ordered. "Fall back. Carefully, carefully." He rode up and down the line, making certain that this was a retreat and no rout. Whatever the skills of the Tamaerthan hillsmen, whatever Ganton of Drantos had learned, the Romans at least would know the value of the High Road, and must have troops poised to take advantage of any disorder here.

I could lose this battle in an hour, and Phrados the False Prophet does not even know. A fool. He looked to the sky for a sign from Vothan. *Am I to be chosen today? Or have you more work for me?*

They withdrew out of bowshot from the forest. For the third time they had ridden up the High Road to test its defenses, and for the third time the Tamaerthan archers had warned them against going too far.

"It's hopeless." The mercenary captain spoke in a low voice so that only Matthias could hear. "We need infantry to clear out those woods." He pointed to more than three hundred bodies, men, centaurs, and horses, that littered the road and its ditches. "Cavalry will never get through alone. We need infantry."

"We have none, Captain Marikos. The Prophet, praise his holy name, has ordered the foot he sent here to stand fast and protect the road."

"If they'd attack, they could keep the damned kilties busy enough—"

"But they cannot attack. They have orders from the Prophet himself. Praise to the gods."

Marikos looked at Matthias quizzically. "As you say. You could ask for a change in orders. Or more infantry."

"I have sent messengers to ask that," Matthias said.

"But they have not returned," Captain Marikos said.

"Yes—"

"Killed by the Defenders as deserters."

Matthias frowned. "I would hope not—"

"You know they were. The Defenders are mad, and the Prophet as well. A child could have won this battle, but instead of a child we had Phrados."

"That is blasphemy—"

Marikos waved airily. "My troops are closer than yours. But you're no believer. You never have been. You're an orthodox priest of Vothan."

"Why do you say that?"

"I have eyes. I see where you look for signs. And what you wear under your armor. I've heard how your servants address you. Honorable, I'm surprised the Defenders didn't find out."

As am I, perhaps. "I see. And what now?"

"We save what we can. I've got men watching behind us. When the Defenders are engaged—and they will be, today or tomorrow—I'm taking my troops out of here."

"Where will you go?"

"Anywhere. North. I've heard Prince Strymon can use good soldiers. I've got two thousand cavalry."

"And their families?"

"Already alerted. Unlike yours, my messengers really were deserters. They got through. And one returned. He saw your messengers killed by the Defenders. No message you sent the Prophet ever got to him."

"How do you propose to get past our own foot soldiers, who stand between you and freedom precisely to keep you from running away?"

"That's my business."

"I see. And what do you want of me?"

"Nothing. Stay out of my way. But since you've been a friend, I'll give you warning. Three blasts of the trumpets followed by two more. If you hear that, save yourself, and your men. If you can."

"Thank you." *What more can I do? It would be folly to warn Phrados. There are no Defenders here, and Marikos is surrounded by his officers and loyal men. It was the act of a friend to warn me. Now I must think how to make use of that warning.*

A cloud of dust rose from the hill beyond the narrow area of the road. A sizable enemy force was approaching. He turned to see that the commander of foot soldiers had seen it also and was placing his men.

✛ ✛ ✛

The horseman spurred straight at Art Mason. He wielded a heavy battle-axe and was screaming praises to the gods. Mason shot him twice with his .45 Colt, and even then had to dodge the axe. One of the Guardsmen brought his own axe solidly onto the man's head, and another seized his horse.

"No ransom for these fanatics," the Guard sergeant said contemptuously. "But some of them have good horses."

"Yeah, sure. Now let's ride." He signaled Teuthras to advance with the light cavalry.

Amazingly, the enemy melted away into the cultivated land west of the river.

"From that last chap I'd have thought they'd fight like tigers," Mason said aloud.

"My lord?" his orderly prompted.

"Nothing."

The enemy light cavalry retreated, with Teuthras and the Hussars in pursuit. Mason was about to signal recall when he saw that Teuthras had halted his pursuit, set pickets to watch to see that the enemy didn't return without warning, and was coming back.

Well done, Mason thought. More locals learning to think ahead. Not long ago they'd have chased that enemy cavalry forever.

"Messenger from the balloon," his orderly called.

"Right."

The man had ridden hard. Both he and his horse were lathered. He held out a square of paper.

"Thank you. Orderly! Wine for the messenger. A groom to walk his horse."

"At once, Lord."

Art read the message aloud as Teuthras rode up.

WARNING TO BATTLE GROUP DRUMOLD; ENEMY CAVALRY PRESENT ON WEST BANK OF RIVER CLOSE TO HERDSMAN'S FORD.

Teuthras grinned. It probably would have hurt too much to laugh;

he was riding in a sort of corset of bandages to keep his cracked ribs in place. The priests had wanted him to stay in bed, but nothing short of a direct command from Yatar could have kept him out of this battle.

"Was it not Lord Rick's intention, that the men in the balloon should see what others could not and give warning? If all they can tell us is what we have seen for ourselves . . ."

"Yeah, that can happen. But remember Pirion. The balloon saved our asses there."

"I do. I also remember the Hooey River."

So did Mason, and so did the captain. That was why the balloon was so far back, so its anchor and ground crew wouldn't be overrun. The Westmen had done that, killing not only the ground crew but the aeronauts. It took a long time to train those crews, not just technicians for the balloon but competent observers.

All very well, but it would be nice to have more information. And who was antsy about being an officer? Yeah. A corporal who got promoted over his head, and too late to think about that now.

The rest of the Tamaerthan arrived at a fast walk. Drumold was in sight, and so was his son Balquhain, in that tent-sized green cloak he'd adopted in order to be recognized in battle.

Just as important, so was the Carl Gustav recoilless and its crew. Time to get the troops deployed.

✤ ✤ ✤

"Stand by to fire," Mason said.

Rudolf Frick grinned like a wolf. He knelt, and Doug McQuade knelt behind and to his left. Three Guards brought ammunition from the pack mules.

Mason stood in his stirrups and looked up and down the river line. The Tamaerthan chivalry were arrayed three deep, lances erect, armor gleaming.

They looked more impressive than they were. Tamaerthon was mountainous land, poor horse country at best. Its real strength was in its infantry, especially longbowmen, and now the disciplined pike formations Colonel Galloway had trained. And none of that made any difference. The nobility of Tamaerthon wore armor and tried to make believe they were as good as the Drantos ironhats.

"All I got," Art muttered to himself.

After it crossed Herdsman's Ford the road led through a draw between two low but steep-sided hills. The enemy cavalry commander had bunched up his forces there. He'd also put archers on the hilltops, and in front of the archers was a line of infantry forming a shield wall. It wasn't a very solid shield wall, but it would be good enough to shake up Tamaerthan cavalry.

Well, first things first. That enemy cavalry force made a beautiful target. Hadn't those idiots ever heard of star weapons? "Six for effect, Rudy. Concentrate on the cavalry. Fire when ready."

"Yo!" Frick took aim.

"Stand clear behind!" McQuade shouted and rammed a load into the small shoulder-fired recoilless.

"Fire in the hole!" The Carl Gustav roared, and flame belched from both ends of the recoilless. The shell slammed right into the middle of the enemy horsemen, twenty yards to the right of the CO's banner. The second shell took out the banner.

By the time the fourth shell was on the way, the first rank of the enemy cavalry had broken. They turned on the troops behind, so that the entire force was in disarray. Mason turned to his trumpeter. "Sound the charge."

He was only just in time. The sight of enemy backs was too much for the Tamaerthan heavies, and not even Drumold and Balquhain could hold them. They'd already begun to move when the trumpets sounded. In seconds they were waist-deep in the water.

Two upstream cavalrymen suddenly screamed as translucent tentacles reached up and around them. The men slashed wildly with their swords as their horses bolted in panic. The other cavalry spurred onward. Some emerged with half a dozen foot-long hydras clinging to the horses. Their comrades smashed at them with sword flats. The hydras dropped off and were trampled.

Now the heavies were in extreme archery range of the troops on the hilltop. They hadn't lost a man crossing, but now Mason saw three fall. Then two more horses were down.

Frick slammed four more rounds into the retreating enemy cavalry, then turned to harass the shield wall on the hill to his left. Three rounds, and the first of the infantry threw down their weapons and ran. By the fifth round they were all running, and carrying the archers with them.

Teuthras was just crossing the river. He saw the hill cleared and led his light cavalry across the rear of the charging heavies and up the left side hill. It was tough going on the steep hillock but there was no opposition and soon he'd outflanked the enemy cavalry in the draw below.

On his own initiative, too, Mason thought. We got ourselves some decent officers, by God!

The Tamaerthan heavies lowered their lances and charged home into the enemy cavalry in the gap. The enemy was already in retreat. Now it became a headlong rout. The infantry on the right-hand hill threw down their weapons and knelt. Some held up charms, of Yatar and Vothan, as tokens of surrender. A quarter of an hour after the first round was fired there wasn't an armed enemy to be seen.

Drumold and Balquhain held up their banners, waited until their troops had rallied and were in formation, and led the way into the gap.

And that tears it, Mason thought. We're well beyond any intelligence I've got. There was supposed to be one hell of a lot of enemy here. So far it's been easy. Too damned easy.

✣ ✣ ✣

Drumold's banner had reached the head of the draw when Mason saw it stop. Art spurred his horse ahead along the column, but the rough ground on either side of the road slowed him. As he came in sight of more open ground the Defenders began their move, but between them and the Tamaerthans was a solid mass of cavalry coming on at a trot.

Drumold stood in his stirrups. "Spread out! Get in line!"

"That's where they were," Mason muttered. "Frick! Follow me! Guards, rally here!" He turned to scramble up the left side hill. "Get up here and set up! Your target is the oncoming cavalry. Fire at will!"

We're in time, he thought. Just. But they sure act like nothing can stop them—

Skin-clad figures seemed to sprout like mushrooms from the scrub to Mason's left. He shot one, hacked through a spear-wielding arm with his sword. He caught a flicker of motion out of the corner of his eye, then a sling stone smashed into his helmet. He saw blood-red fireworks against a black sky and barely had time for one thought as he toppled out of the saddle.

Maybe that enemy commander was right in thinking he couldn't be stopped.

✢ ✢ ✢

Ganton focused the binoculars, and the banner on the hill by Herdsman's Ford sprang into clear sight. Lord Rick's plan had worked well so far; the Tamaerthans were in the rear of the Defenders and in no small strength.

Yet the Defenders had cavalry aiding them. Together might not the enemy's strength be too much for Drumold and Lord Mason? It very well might be, and then whether the battle was won or lost, Tamaerthon would be a long time recovering from the loss of its knights and archers.

I owe Titus Frugi much, and that is good and sufficient reason not to shame him without cause. I owe the Tamaerthans more—my very throne, indeed. But is that cause enough to risk shaming Titus Frugi, to say nothing of quarreling with my wife's father?

Only Yatar or His Son could be certain. I only know this: I will not have it said that the Wanax Ganton of Drantos was like his father, without honor. That he let the chivalry of Tamaerthon be cut to pieces when his aid could have saved them.

"Morrone!"

"Majesty?"

"Sound the trumpets and advance the banner of the Fighting Man. We ride to aid the Tamaerthans!"

If Morrone's grin had been any wider it would have met at the back of his head. "As you command."

"Oh, and send a messenger to Lord Rick."

"And one to Publius?"

"To Publius, of course. But send the one to Lord Rick first."

✢ ✢ ✢

The Drantos heavy cavalry took up all the space between the hill and the forest, so the Romans had to follow them. Rick saw that Ganton was taking his time, too. The heavies moved at a walk until they were on level ground, and even a little farther, until they were on ground that wasn't littered with bodies from the earlier attacks.

Then the knights of Drantos shook out their lines, and even from the top of the Great Redoubt Rick could see Ganton's golden helmet take its place in front. They worked up to a trot, and at a trot they rolled across the rear of Phrados' host, straight toward the Defenders and the cavalry around the Tamaerthans.

That solved one of Rick's biggest headaches, and without his having to say a word. Just as well, because Publius must be about ready to have a stroke. He might not risk insulting his son-in-law, but his son-in-law's captain general?

And isn't that thinking a lot like a medieval politician—like your wife, in fact?

A moment later he saw the Romans move out. The Praetorian Eagle led the way, but the Fourth was close up behind it, and the Eighth brought up the rear in a really beautiful formation.

A messenger rode off, with a signal for the balloon to send: TO TAMAERTHAN ARCHERS ON HIGH ROAD; PREPARE TO ADVANCE DOWN HIGH ROAD IN SUPPORT OF SEVENTEENTH LEGION WHEN SEVENTEENTH ADVANCES.

If Publius had the brains God promised little white mice, he'd move his own pikemen and foot archers out of cover to stiffen up the cavalry cordon he would soon have drawn around the enemy's infantry. Then the Tamaerthan archers could leave their cover and stiffen the Seventeenth, and the enemy's whole center would be surrounded—Tamaerthan and Romans on two sides and the river on the third.

Close off the Redoubt and they'll be surrounded—provided of course, that I can retake the Great Redoubt. Time to fight again.

Rick sent off another messenger to the heavy weapons, then rode down to First Pikes and stood in his stirrups. "First Pikes, Guardsmen, gunners! Follow me! Let's clean these vermin out of our house."

He drew his sword to signal the advance. Suddenly the men to either side dropped their pikes and bows and ran forward to grab his bridle, his stirrups, even his horse's tail. Shouts rose.

"Go back, Lord Rick!"

"Stay back, Lord Rick!"

"We won't advance until you're safe, Lord Rick!"

Then: "Lord Rick to the rear!"

—and everybody picked up on that and shouted it until Rick's head ached.

Elliot rode up grinning like an idiot. "Captain, looks like you're outvoted. They think you're their good luck charm. Maybe you are."

"Elliot—"

"Think about it, Colonel. They'll follow you, all right. But if you buy it, this outfit's finished, and we all know it. For Christ's sake, sir! You don't have to prove anything."

I don't have to prove anything? "All right, Sergeant Major. Carry on."

"Sir!" Elliot rode out in front of the pikemen, fired a burst into the air from the Ingram, and shouted, "Okay, you crazy bastards! Do you want to live forever?"

Cheers rose, pikes followed, and the counterattack charged down the hill. Mortar and recoilless rounds fell among the enemy. In the center of the line rose two giant figures, the Great Ark swathed in ammo belts and Gunner Pinir with a barrel of powder under one arm and a rammer over his shoulder.

The enemy troops in the Redoubt stood for a moment. Then someone raised a shout. "The Defenders! The Defenders are running away."

It was true enough. Ganton's chivalry had struck the Defenders in flank even as they were closing on the Tamaerthan knights, and the Defenders dissolved into uncoordinated groups. Some stood and fought like demons. More turned and ran as they realized their gods had forsaken them.

"They run! The Defenders run!" The shout rang through the Redoubt.

First Pikes came at a steady lope, pikes aligned into a forest of advancing points, in step as if on parade. A few of the bombard gunners ran ahead of the pikemen to beat the last of the Prophet's men from their guns, then wrestled the bombards back into action. Three were actually firing at the retreating enemy when the Seventeenth Legion marched out of the forest followed by Tamaerthan archers.

✛ ✛ ✛

Art Mason woke to a thundering head and a sharp pain in his leg. He tried to sit, but was restrained. It was a struggle to open his eyes. Somewhere nearby a man was screaming. Many men.

The first thing he saw was the smiling face of Yanulf's sidekick, Apelles.

"Praise Yatar the healer," Apelles said. He turned and shouted to an apprentice. "Carry the word to the Lord Rick."

"At once."

So the Colonel's alive too. We're getting too old for this. He listened, and heard distant sounds of guns, but not nearly enough.

"Can you count the fingers I hold up before you?" Apelles asked urgently.

"Fingers? Four. No." He tried to shake his head and that hurt. "Two."

"Good." He wiped Mason's face with a wet cloth. "The Lord McCleve has been summoned."

"To hell with McCleve. Who's winning?" Mason demanded.

"All is well."

"Talk, damn your eyes!"

"You should rest—very well." Apelles wiped Mason's forehead again and held a cup of water to his lips. "Drink. Then I will talk."

The water was bitter.

"Where to begin?"

"The goddamn cavalry was about to grind up my troops!"

"Ah. The captain of that cavalry had arrayed his men without telling Phrados. Phrados thought he was deserting. He ordered the Defenders to attack."

"When the Defenders advanced, Lord Balquhain held his forces and waited until the Defenders had finished their work. Then he charged."

"Good man." Mason tried to grin, but it hurt.

"Then our gracious Wanax Ganton most honorably led the host of Drantos against the Defenders! He smote them to the ground! They never rose again!

"Publius Caesar, envious of our king's glory, led his legions against the enemy's center, and the Lord Rick retook the Great Redoubt and the Guns.

"The day is ours."

The day is ours. His head buzzed. There had been something in that water. He closed his eyes to sleep, and a smile drifted to his lips. *Survived again.*

✛ ✛ ✛

The Prophet's tent stood. The interior was stripped bare. The great wheeled altar lay on its side. Holes gaped where there had once been bronze handles and silver fittings.

Matthias turned away. He handed his torch to a guard and mounted.

Captain Pharikos rode up. "It's like this everywhere, sir." He shrugged. "At least one thing's for the best. If they don't find Phrados' body, anyone can claim to be him. If Drantos has to fight a new Phrados every year, they'll get a bellyful of fighting. If we send all those Prophets silver and arms—"

"Peace. The gods have judged Phrados. It is not for us to question their judgement."

Matthias knew that he had spoken sharply, but not why. He turned his horse away and waved his band forward out of the camp.

Screams echoed behind him. Screams of both men and women. Matthias was glad of his two hundred armed and mounted men. *Men I can trust. There are few enough honest men left here.*

It was not until the camp was several stades behind that Matthias thought of his harsh words to Captain Pharikos. *The strategy is sound. It would rob the starmen of much of the profit of today's victory.*

He rode on in silence. *No. To harass the starmen with false Prophets will strengthen their alliance with the city-states. The men who would rise in that alliance will not be those of the old blood who honor the old ways. Mercenary captains, merchants. New men who will multiply like lamils in the breeding time.*

And that is what I must tell Issardos, yea, and the high Rexja Toris himself.

He would not speak of the judgment of the gods to any but Vothan.

17

Gwen dismissed her servant, then helped Siobhan lift Art Mason's injured leg onto the carved ironwood table.

"And Publius Caesar took back not one word of what he said to the knights of Drantos?" asked Siobhan.

Art Mason grunted as she loosened the binding holding the poultices Apelles had applied from ankle to mid-thigh. "Not that I heard, but then he'd hardly do it in public. Maybe to Ganton, in private—"

Siobhan bristled. "Then the knights of Drantos have known great insult, with no redress. Will the Wanax let matters rest there?"

Mason and Gwen Tremaine exchanged smiles. Earthmen against locals, but also discreet age against hotheaded youth. Getting any kind of smile from Art—and from Sergeant Major Elliot, Larry Warner, and Rick—was lifting Gwen's spirits more than she would have believed possible. Whatever had been making all four of them look through her, then shy away from any explanation, the victory over Phrados' host and the end of the southern war had helped a lot.

Helped, but hadn't ended it. *What do they know, and why won't they tell me?*

Siobhan saw their conspiratorial glances and laughed softly. Gwen smiled to herself. Mason was going to have his hands full with that young lady after they were married—and that seemed certain now. There was no mistaking Siobhan's reaction when she heard that Mason had been wounded, or when she saw his troops bring him through the

728

University gate on a horse litter. *Chalk up another arranged marriage that's turning into a love match. Hah. Les intended that for Rick and me.*

"Publius Caesar drips insults like a hydra feeds. It doesn't mean all that much," Mason said. "I think we're just going to have to live with it."

Siobhan frowned.

"Ganton will probably give Rudhrig an important post next time," Mason said. "I just hope Rudhrig's learned enough that a lot of good men don't get killed for his damned honor. Anyway, that'll have to do. Ganton has a few other things on his mind." He grinned. "Like becoming a father."

"It's official then?" said Gwen. "Octavia's pregnant?"

Siobhan looked intently at the fire.

"The priests say so," Mason said. "I hear the formal announcement goes out over the semaphore in a couple of days. When the Roman bishops say the signs are right."

"Hallelujah!" said Gwen. *I hope I sound surprised.* She thought of the letter Octavia had written to her ten days ago.

"A good thing," Siobhan said. She sniffed. "Lady Prygisia has told the entire court that our queen is barren. And some listened, too."

"This should help," Art said.

"I'd think so." Gwen brushed back a wisp of hair. "The great ladies of Drantos weren't too pleased that our Wanax went to Rome to find a queen." *Poor Octavia. Hardly any friends at all, so when Ganton isn't home she broods.* "This will put a stop to that particular gossip anyway."

"Especially if it's a boy," Siobhan said. Then she giggled.

It was Art Mason's turn to look at the fire.

✦ ✦ ✦

Siobhan had finished with Art's leg and was trimming his hair.

Art Mason reached up to take the scissors from her, and looked at them closely. "Steel?"

"Sort of," Gwen said. "Something between a good-tempered iron and real steel. The University makes them. Actually we were looking for better ways to make swords and bayonets, but one of our apprentices made scissors, and now we make a good profit selling them."

"Much to the annoyance of the Guild of Smiths," Siobhan said.

"Yes. I've been thinking of some way to license our inventions. Patents. Something—"

"Far as the captain is concerned you can give it away," Mason said. "Spread the knowledge—"

"Yes, but if we can't afford to do the research, how will we have knowledge to spread?" Gwen demanded.

"Hmm. Budget time again?" Art grinned.

"How did you know? But seriously, we need to get along with the locals, but we need to reward our people for doing good work, too."

"Right. I'll bring it up next staff meeting." Mason took a folded sheet from his pocket and made a note with a ballpoint pen. "Sure wish your husband would bring us proper notebooks."

"Daytimers, adjusted for the Tran calendar! Art, not to change the subject, but did any of the Defenders escape?"

"Not many. Once the Prophet's people saw they could surrender to us without being killed, a lot of the infantry—ours and theirs—settled their scores with the goon squad. It wasn't pretty. A lot of the Prophet's main body got away though. Ten, twelve thousand, maybe more."

"Hah. I wondered why Publius accepted Rick and Yanulf's terms on the disputed lands."

"Hadn't thought of it, but I guess Rome would have a problem with that many of the Prophet's people running around. 'Tween them and the just honest-to-Yatar bandits, it'd need at least two legions to tame that area. And they ain't got any legions to spare."

"Not if they want to resettle their old Southern Provinces." Gwen looked thoughtful. "That's going to be a powder keg pretty soon."

"Yeah, until everybody starves."

"Starves, or gets killed by refugees from the far south." Gwen shuddered. "And next year things get really bad."

"The city-states are what really worried the colonel," Mason said. "Not too much off the top, where—"

"My lord?" Siobhan asked.

"Nothing. Joke that doesn't translate."

"My lord, why was the Lord Rick so concerned about the city-states? Are they not loyal to the alliance?"

"They are now." Mason reached out to touch Siobhan's hand. "But they're short of troops, and sure don't have enough cavalry to spare to police the disputed lands. Only somebody's got to hold that territory to keep the refugees from streaming through."

Gwen smiled to herself. Siobhan was hanging on every word Art said. *But she's really interested, too. She'd better be. We'd all better be.*

"Anyway," Art said, "that's how Morrone wound up as Protector of the Southern Marches. Gives him the same rank as an Eqeta, and he gets a little army of his own with everybody chipping in to pay for it." Mason laughed. "Damnedest little army you ever saw. He's got hill tribes, some of those outlaw Tamaerthans Gengrich brought north, a lot of younger sons, a bunch of mercenary cavalry from Phrados' horde, and Vothan only knows what else."

"Even so, I should think the Lord Morrone would be pleased," Siobhan said.

"Oh, he's happy as a grig. The only man who even raised an eyebrow was Eqeta Rudhrig. He said that Lord Morrone's great and undoubted gifts seemed to fit him better for a place closer to the throne."

Siobhan smiled. "Does he wish the Protectorship for himself, or does he think Morrone less than fit?"

Hah. She's pretty when she smiles. And that's a sensible question. Mason could do a lot worse.

"Damned if I know. His Lordship of Harms is like Publius these days. He's got it in for the whole world, so you don't know how much he really means. On the other hand—I like Morrone, but I've never seen him with an independent command."

Gwen nodded. *And maybe Ganton is being bought off from doing something about the Roman insults to his knights—Rudhrig's knights— by a Roman gift to his Companion.*

The thought disturbed Gwen. Was Ganton letting the Romans bribe him? One compromise didn't make a pattern, but—She remembered King Stephen of England. *He couldn't say no to anyone. And brought on one of the worst civil wars in English history. A king who will blow this way and that is bad news.* "Can Morrone do the job?"

Mason shrugged. "Personally, I don't think he's much of a diplomat, but it'll be a year before he'll be out of the saddle for two days running. By then we'll have him fixed up with somebody like Apelles. Or maybe that oddball Vinicianus."

"I see." The haircut was nearly done. Gwen stood. "If you will excuse me, I have work. Ring for anything you like. I will be in my study."

She climbed the spiral staircase to her loft. It was the only spiral staircase on Tran, and she had had it and the little study built during the nesting stage of her last pregnancy. Being a noblewoman with a lavish supply of cheap labor had its advantages. *Of course it spirals the wrong way. How did I know you want to hamper a swordsman by putting his right side against the core of the stairs? Oh, well. Nobody else knew, either. Except Rick. And I have my pistol.*

The window of the studio was only an arrow slit, but it gave her a good view of the west wall of the University and the cemetery beyond it. There were a lot of new monuments there; the bodies of the dead at Vis had been burned or buried where they fell, but the Romans who'd returned had been busily carving monuments to the comrades who hadn't.

They bought us time. They deserve their monuments.

A shift of the wind brought a cloud of stone dust from where the Roman masons were building the new workers' quarters and a block of shops. Mortimer Schultz had his eye on that block as just the right place for Tran's first printing press.

The clink and rattle of masons peaked, then gave way to the shouts of drill sergeants. The University's immigrant craftsmen were getting their basic training. Elliot wanted to train them all with the Tamaerthan longbow. Gwen couldn't convince him it took years to train a competent longbowman, especially since Elliot had learned to use one well enough to win prizes.

There was another problem. The Tamaerthans wouldn't much care for foreigners learning their national weapon.

If it isn't one thing, it's another. Which would cause the more trouble, trying to teach foreigners to use the Tamaerthan longbow, or teaching them musketry? Either way some of the Tamaerthan clans would be unhappy.

But we have to do something. Suppose the Romans abandon us? This place can't be defended. And it damned well is going to be!

First things first. She'd need both archery and target ranges. Gunpowder. Carronades. How did that Kipling poem go? No, said the cannoneer, shooting from the wall. Iron, cold iron shall be master of you all.

Damned right, provided I get all that brush cut away from around the walls. Fields of fire—

First I'm a medieval politician, now a medieval general. Next?

Whatever. Tran is changing us as fast as we're changing Tran, and neither of us is going to recognize what we were before Rick Galloway came here with that flying saucer full of mercs.

INTERLUDE
D'JORR

The viewer on the polished wood table was as plain as everything else in the chamber, but it was of high quality. The Guides of the Way of the Warrior did not live luxuriously, but they lived well.

Right now it showed Les' head silhouetted against the main screen on the bridge.

"You will note that his screen is off," Agzaral said.

The robed man seated behind the table nodded. "His third visit to Tran, did you say? Then why does your pilot wish to conceal his location from you?" A faint smile came to his lips. "Agzaral, I think you have not told me everything."

Agzaral returned the smile. "Everything of importance. Watch his report."

Les' image continued unemotionally. "Captain Galloway continues to work toward raising a professional standing army loyal to its commissioned officers, in place of a medieval host loyal to feudal lords. He has to move slowly, for many obvious reasons, not the least of which is to keep the support of the Wanax Ganton.

"Ganton feels much more secure on his throne now that he has a male heir, but he always remembers that his father lost his crown by ignoring the advice and the interests of his nobles, and he's determined not to make that mistake. As a practical matter he hasn't much choice. Any of his nobility who get sufficiently annoyed can always side with the High Rexja Toris when the war with the Five Kingdoms begins.

"Meanwhile, Captain Galloway does what he can with the Mounted Archers and the Guards. This is not much, because the Mounted

Archers ultimately follow him because he is War Leader of Tamaerthon, and the Guards because he is Great Captain General of the Realm of Drantos. Were he to lose either post, he might have some difficulty commanding the allegiance of anyone not sworn to him as Eqeta of Chelm."

Agzaral's companion chuckled. "Not entirely unlike Council politics, my friend."

"Precisely. It is one reason I find Tran such a fascinating place." Agzaral adjusted the gain on the viewer.

"War with the Five Kingdoms is inevitable. In my opinion it will come next year. The High Rexja has recovered from the Sarakos war, and commands considerable resources. He has a popular and damned competent leader in Crown Prince Strymon of Ta-Meltemos. Strymon's armies turned back the Westmen quite effectively. There are still a lot of Westmen, but I doubt they can make much trouble for a couple of years."

"Victory feeds victory," Agzaral said. "The High Rexja has a leader and a proven army. He will certainly use it."

"The weapons I delivered on this trip could be decisive, but Galloway won't trust many locals with modern weapons."

"Wise of him," Agzaral's companion said.

"He hasn't got enough mercenaries, and now they're growing *surinomaz* in several places besides the fields around Armagh. That all has to be defended, along with the stockpiled food and the bricks of processed *surinomaz*."

The robed man frowned. "I think that is not all Captain Galloway may care to defend."

"Perhaps not," Agzaral replied.

"—more decisive will be the role of the two northern city-states, Nikeis and Margilos. Nikeis will surely be neutral. Most of their trade depends on peace with the Five Kingdoms. So does their mainland rice crop.

"Margilos will probably stay neutral, but may ask a high price. They haven't forgotten that the Drantos-Roman alliance drove the Westmen north and forced the Margilans to fight a sharp campaign against them. They bear no love for the Five Kingdoms and never have, but Drantos has most recently offended them."

"Who will win this war?" Wilno asked.

"I don't know. For all our sakes, it had better be Captain Galloway."

"You cannot give him greater resources?"

"Not more than I have already sent. His problem is that he casts his nets very wide indeed. He is not content merely to secure a small area and grow *surinomaz*. He seeks to spread civilization across much of the planet."

"This Galloway is not a typical mercenary soldier."

"Obviously."

Agzaral and his companion watched in silence until Les finished with technical details of the status of his ship, and a polite farewell. The screen went grey and the robed man turned to Agzaral.

"He is being rather discreet."

"I imagine there had been some developments which he did not wish the *Shalnuksis* to know about at this point. I can hardly imagine anyone of Les' intelligence trusting their judgement. Can you?"

The other man smiled faintly. "Hardly. But I can hardly imagine anyone of your intelligence not trusting a classmate with the information needed to carry out his assignment. Yet it has happened. So perhaps Les—"

"Wilno, what makes you think I am not trusting you with necessary intelligence?"

"What makes you think I've forgotten the time you wanted me to make a diversion while you reprogrammed the mess computer? I might have been thrown out of the Academy for that!"

"True. But you were not, and you must remember why?"

"Indeed, you retrieved that situation in your inimitable manner. As you always do. But this time you will be light-years away during the crucial moments of whatever it is you want me to do."

Wilno was smiling, but Agzaral was not deceived. Wilno was trying to keep the atmosphere pleasant out of old friendship, not out of weakness.

He would have to put the full details of the Tran situation in the hands of someone not already part of his plans. This was a moment he'd known for some time would come; he could not regret too much that it had come so soon.

"It is important, what I am asking of you."

"I suspected as much. You aren't the sort to spend your leave traveling a hundred and seventy light-years on four different ships over a trivial matter."

"It is also secret."

"If it involves the *Shalnuksis*, how could it be otherwise?"

"Very well. What I want you to do is serve as weapons officer aboard the *Shalnuksi* ship they will send against Tran when they believe they will obtain no more *surinomaz*. It may be a crucial task."

"As usual, the Council knows nothing of this?"

"As usual, some know and some do not. Wilno, we are both committed. The future of our species is no small matter."

"No. But why do you believe we are crucial to that?"

"Because we are." He handed Wilno a plastic envelope. "Put this in water for a minute, then play the disk inside. It will tell you most of what you need to know. If you need any protection for your viewer—"

His companion laughed. "Thank you, but there is no need for your skills. Confederate Intelligence pays little attention to the Houses of the Guides. If we were annoyed we would not be so useful."

The controlled anger in Wilno's voice and the eager way he reached for the envelope gave Agzaral more hope. He let none of it show on his face as he walked to the door of Wilno's chamber.

÷ ÷ ÷

The red dwarf sun of D'Jorr was touching the peaks of the mountains on the horizon. The valley below the viewing gallery was already in shadow, but sun still blazed from the snow near the summit of the great triangular peak across the valley. A dancing plume of snow trailed from the summit like a feather from a war helmet.

Higher still, a vapor trail crept across the sky, with a golden glint at its head. Human or Confederate? At this distance it was impossible to tell. Agzaral decided to have his eyes examined soon. He would not again need the keen sight of his youth, but he would need every year left to him. It would be as well to lose none of them getting new eyes.

Probably Confederate, he decided. Few humans came to these mountains, which ranked above the Himalayas for both height and splendor, except the Guides and some hardy climbers. Both came on the ground. On the other hand, the flying city of Nesha was barely an hour's flight beyond the horizon. Doubtless there would be some Galactics aboard it who had never seen the mountains and would now be taking the chance to fly over.

"A beautiful view," said a soft voice behind Agzaral.

He turned to see Wilno. The Guide had taken off his red robe and boots and wore only undertunic, kilt, and sandals. His expression was unreadable.

"Very. Earth's Himalayas and Chrin's Giants are almost as splendid."

"I have never seen either. Nor do I really need to, after seeing these. I fell in love with this view when I was only a lay servant. I think I would have stayed on in the House even if I had never risen higher, if only to look at the mountains at sunrise and sunset.

"Let us go to my quarters."

When they were alone, Wilno's smile broadened, until it was an old familiar grin. Agzaral had seen that look when Wilno took a choice assignment from a rival.

"I would judge that you find the mission worthy of your attention?" Agzaral asked.

"You'd have to shoot me to keep me off it now."

"Our *Shalnuksi* friends may yet save me that trouble."

Wilno shrugged. "Then I die in battle. Better than dying here as Chief Guide, and a damned sight better than dying in some Slave hospital or by my own hand!"

Agzaral could find no reply to that. He knew even better than Wilno the toll suicide took among the Slaves of the Confederation. However light his chains, a slave was still not a master, even of himself.

"Questions before we settle details," Wilno said. "I think I understand why you don't want Les for the job. Even a *Shalnuksis* might be suspicious of his presence on the bomb ship. Also—I can see circumstances under which our interest lies alongside the *Shalnuksis*. You may wish Tran bombed."

"Reluctantly."

"I would be as reluctant as you. Let us not think of such unpleasant things."

"And your other question?"

"Is there any chance that our grey-skinned friends will be able to come up with someone for the job themselves?"

"A small chance. If their Intelligence somehow concludes that the secret has leaked out, they may override the Council of Merchants."

"Why don't I believe you've told me everything?"

"I have told you all I know. Wilno, I am doing all I can. All that anyone in my position can do."

"And you fear it is not enough."

Agzaral spread his hands. "There may be ways to obtain more resources."

"My friend, it is no great matter to deceive the *Shalnuksis*, but robbing them is something else entirely."

Agzaral smiled.

Wilno shrugged. "Since I have known you, Agzaral, I have had many complaints, but boredom has never been one of them."

PART FOUR

THE ROYAL SACRIFICE

Gwen Tremaine's Diary

Almost summery weather today, even by the standards of Iowa. By the standards of Tran, it's a blistering heat wave. I'd try introducing the bikini or at least the sunback dress, but who's going to spend money on clothes useful maybe ten years out of every six centuries?

Lunch with Larry Warner, who turns out to be riding off on the mission to Margilos with Rick and a whole bunch of the other rough-and-tough types. I asked him why, when the Margilans are supposed to be hostile and the rule is "No University People in Combat."

He said the Margilans have promised the mission safe-conduct, and by all reports they have an ironbound sense of honor that won't let them do anything to guests who don't insult them. I asked him if he knew all the things Margilans consider insults, and he decided he'd better keep his mouth shut. As if he could.

Apparently having the Westmen dumped on them was more of a fight than the Margilans liked, and they want to find out if this was part of some new policy toward them, or just the fortunes of war. So maybe the Margilans aren't so dangerous, but then there are stray bands of Westmen. Larry says the expedition will be armed to the teeth. I hope so. We need Rick. For that matter I need Larry.

Even if the risk was a lot greater, Larry says it would be worth it to visit Margilos. Apparently they have some very unusual methods of gold-mining, plus hot springs where they can dump the gold if the city is in any danger. Also, they can do things with centaurs nobody else can, like teaching them to use simple weapons.

After the second cup of wine I realized that I was going to miss Larry a lot. So I kissed him goodbye. He turned red and didn't kiss me back, but he didn't back away either. I have the feeling that Larry is settling into kind of a brotherly attitude toward me, which is better than nothing. Besides, suppose he was just as indispensable to Rick's plans but a real slimeball like Alex Boyd? Boyd's going to Margilos, and if the Margilans want to string that one up for messing with their women I hope somebody invites me!

Later—A letter from Octavia, sent from Benevenutum. The visit to show Publius his grandson Adrian was a great success. Maybe that will mellow Publius. I know Rick hopes so.

Rick. What's wrong with him? The servants tell stories. He hasn't been alone with Tylara for a year. A year. Rick's a normal man, he must hate that. And don't get ideas, Tremaine. . . .

Of course the Roman matrons are tongue-clucking the way the Drantos ladies used to, only it's "Octavia's barbarian husband" instead of "the Wanax's Roman wife." At least Octavia has learned to laugh at the old biddies.

Old. None of them are really old. This place ages people. It hasn't done that to me yet. Has it?

Publius is quite the proud grandfather. I wouldn't have thought he had it in him. I guess knowing his line won't die out makes a big difference to him. Even if it does have to be passed on through his daughter. Note: Be even more careful with Catwin than with Les and Caradoc. As long as Caradoc's only legitimate child is alive, that family has got an obligation to help you, or at least not help your enemies.

Still Later—Mortimer Schultz dropped in. He says Diana is doing fine; Campbell expects the kid any day now. Mostly he wanted to talk about printing presses. I admit I groaned when he started off, because he's kind of obsessed with getting moveable type introduced before the *skyfire* falls, but this idea made a lot of sense.

He thinks we should make up several portable presses, with all the metal parts bronze so they won't rust, and train a couple of dozen acolytes of Yatar as printers. Then we store the presses in the Caves of the Preserver along with everything else we want to keep safe from the bombs. When the fallout's gone and it's safe to come out, we can start on printed books. The *Shalnuksis* won't be back for a long time. . . .

I suspect there are a few holes in that plan, and it probably gives the priests of Yatar a monopoly on printing. Does that matter? Schultz is right, moveable type is one thing that's *got* to survive the Time, however we manage it. I asked him for an estimate on labor and materials, and I'll write to Yanulf as soon as I get it.

And now Rick is gone to Margilos, Larry with him, and Les is God knows where, and Caradoc's dead. When will Rick be back? And when he comes back—enough. Back to work.

Elliot reined in close and spoke low. "Colonel, something's got Sam spooky." He indicated the older of the two centaurs the Margilans had given him as goodwill gifts.

Larry Warner eyed the sling hung round Sam's neck. "Still don't know if I want to trust those things with weapons."

"My problem, Professor," Elliot said.

It could be bigger than that, Rick thought. Most of the Guards felt the same way Warner did. But no doubt about it, Elliot was proud of Sam and wasn't going to part with him. And we trust dogs with teeth, don't we?

Sam wrinkled his nose and swung his greying head from side to side. His hands clenched into fists. Pete, the younger centaur, wasn't sniffing the air but Sam's nervous excitement had made him skittish.

"Badger-bear? Cat?" said Rick.

"This isn't cat country. Or wasn't last year."

"Yeah. A lot of the wild herds have come north. If the cats have followed them . . ."

The greatcats were larger than mountain lions and would attack a mounted man if they were hungry enough. "Okay. I don't want to stop, this close to Westrook."

"Sir!"

Rick lifted his canteen. Nearly empty. Well, it wasn't far to Westrook, and there were streams. He shifted in the saddle. Twenty-five miles a day in armor. But tonight he'd be in Murphy's castle, with bath—hot water! And maybe Murphy had some Preparation H left—

Sam screamed and reached for his sling. He plucked a stone out of the cloth bag hung below the sling. Pete threw up his head, and waved his arms. He backed away to give his mentor and friend room to use his sling.

"Sam! Hold!" Elliot shouted.

Dust rose at the crest of the next hill. Half a dozen leather-armored men on scrubby ponies rode into view.

"Westmen!" one Guardsman screamed. Another nocked an arrow and started to draw before his sergeant stopped him.

"Skirmishers left and right!" Elliot commanded. "Colonel? How you want to handle this?"

"Hold what you've got," Rick said. He pointed. The Westmen hadn't moved from their hilltop, and no more came to join them. The Westmen held at the hilltop until it was clear that everyone had seen them. Then they came down at a fast walk. Just beyond longbow shot they stopped and waited again.

"Odd enough," Elliot said. He lifted his binoculars.

"You know it." *And thank God there aren't more of them.* In the previous Time six hundred years before, a Westman army washed clear across Drantos and almost to the gates of Rome itself.

"The one in front's got his hands out. And Colonel, none of them have drawn weapons."

"I see that," Rick said.

"Big wads of turf on their lances, too. I got no experience with Westmen, but these sure don't look hostile."

Mason rode up. "Cap'n, I think they want to parley."

"Looks like it."

"But what about?" Elliot demanded.

"I don't know, but it can't hurt to find out," Rick said.

Mason frowned. "Okay, Captain. Not you. I'll go talk to them—"

Three more horsemen rode over the crest of the hill. They were mounted on full-sized horses and wore Drantos clothing and armor. The leader carried a Westman bow, and reined in to speak briefly with the Westmen before he rode on toward the column.

Curiouser and curiouser, thought Rick.

"Those are Murphy's troops," Mason said. "He got Westmen for allies?"

"Sure like to ask him a couple of questions," Elliot said.

Me too.

The three men rode up to Rick. "Lord Murphy bids you welcome to his lands and hopes you will avail yourselves of the hospitality of Westrook."

"Now just a goddamn minute—" began Art Mason. Rick raised a hand.

"Perhaps you would be kind enough to tell us who you are? And of your friends there."

"I am Etro, son of Panar, headman of Irakla, steward to Lord Murphy. This has been my reward, for fighting well when the Westmen came to Irakla in the year of the Wanax Ganton's great victory on the—"

"Who the hell are those Westmen?" Rick didn't realize that he'd shouted, but Etro looked stunned and Sam reached for another stone for his sling.

Elliot gentled the centaur. Etro stammered, "My Lord Eqeta, they are not enemies! These are warriors sworn to the Chief Mad Bear. Mad Bear found enemies among his own people and fled here."

The Guardsmen who weren't looking at each other in confusion were glaring at Etro.

A strange enough story, Rick thought. A Westman chief seeking sanctuary? Or alliance? There's more to learn about Tran than I thought. Or Ben Murphy's a damned fool. Or both.

Only one way to find out. Rick waved the column forward.

✣ ✣ ✣

Mad Bear stood a bowlegged five and a half feet tall. His skin was the color of the leather trousers and tunic he wore, and his head was bald except for a single grey-shot scalplock. Bone and gold wire ornaments dripped from both tunic and belt, and a Drantos-style dagger rode on his right hip in a gilded horsehide sheath.

He looked as if he could have been dropped into the front rank of one of Genghis Khan's armies with nobody the wiser.

Rick couldn't help wishing that when Mad Bear was putting on all his finery for the Great Chief of the Stone Houses, it had also occurred to him to bathe. Or else that this meeting was taking place outdoors with Mad Bear downwind, instead of in Ben Murphy's study. At least Westrook's thick stone walls kept out the worst of the heat. *I could use a bath myself.*

Mad Bear was speaking through an interpreter. Rick recognized the Margilan priest of Vothan. He'd been a slave among the Westmen for ten years until Ben Murphy rescued him during the Hooey River campaign. Since then he'd served as a combination of chaplain, administrative assistant, and translator to Murphy. *Ben reports everything, but I could sure use that man back at Armagh. Oh, well.*

"So it came to New-Grass Time," Mad Bear was saying. "Once more I was hailed as chief of all the Silver Wolves. So by the gods and the laws I could do nothing but what I did, when the warrior Chintua slew a man of the tent of Walking Stone. He slew the man honorably, for the man had said Chintua was not father of his sons, and then struck the first blow.

"Yet Walking Stone would not come forth to avenge his tentman. Instead he sent a hand of men against Chintua by night and slew him, then carried away his body so that his kin could not honor it. Chintua's spirit and body alike died that night.

"I went to Walking Stone and demanded that he face me, or be known evermore as a man without honor or shame. Walking Stone said that he and those chiefs who had sworn to him were now the judges of honor among the Horse People. They judged that there was no honor in such as Chintua, and that such men as Chintua were no better than weakling foals, to be cast out lest they breed more weaklings.

"I could not believe that any of the chiefs had sworn to follow such a man. Yet it was so. I will not name them, for they may still return to the way of honor. But there were so many that I was fortunate to pass alive from the tent of Walking Stone.

"Walking Stone could not fall without warning on the Silver Wolves as he had fallen on Chintua, but yet we could not stay close to him. If we moved swiftly, the gods might yet grant us a life with our kin and our herds, and without shame. So we rode to the Green Lands, and sent messengers to the Great Chief of Westrook. He gave us honor in our need, as he had given it in our defeat."

Mad Bear sat down cross-legged on the floor, arms folded on his chest.

"Great Chief, eh, Ben?" Elliot said.

Murphy shrugged and turned to Rick. "Mad Bear brought the message himself, Captain, him and six others with turf on their spears.

"He swore a whole bunch of oaths that he'd keep the peace. I called up enough of the ban to keep them out of mischief, and gave them a campsite and some food. The crops were real good last year."

And the surplus should have gone to the Caves of the Preserver, but let's not get into *that* now. "Have they behaved themselves?"

"Far as I can tell. There've been a couple complaints of missing sheep, but a little silver took care of that. I sent a report, but I reckon you were on the road out of Margilos by then. So I had to sort of make do."

Make do. And it's always easier to get forgiveness than permission. Rick was certain that despite Murphy's elaborate politeness, Ben had decided to make alliance with Mad Bear no matter what Rick Galloway might want.

Typical Drantos nobleman. But dammit he reports to me. . . .

"All right, Sergeant. How many warriors does he have?"

Mad Bear clearly understood the question. He made rapid gestures with his hands. Rick noticed that he had a long scar across the knuckles of the left one.

Baldy, the interpreter, nodded. "He says—call it three hundred and fifty. He speaks the truth, for I have seen the camp and counted that many but no more."

"Okay. I suppose something can be worked out, if he's telling the truth about wanting—"

Mad Bear glared and his hands twitched. Then he snarled something Rick hardly needed interpreted, and went on with a speech that made Baldy turn pale under his tan. The priest could barely keep up with the flood of words.

"He says that he has already taken all the oaths before all the gods that a warrior may honor. If the Great Chief of the Stone Houses doubts him, then let the Chief Murphy take those oaths. Better, let the Great Chief take those oaths himself—or if he is too much the coward to bear the fire, the sun, or the wind, let him come against Mad Bear with a warrior's steel. Mad Bear will meet him with no more weapons than his knife and his honor, and let the gods judge who lies."

Suddenly Rick was glad of the .45 in his shoulder holster. "I meant no offense. Tell him that. Offer him whatever is customary."

Mad Bear spoke again. This time he seemed less angry. The priest translated. "I hope the Great Chief of the Stone Houses is wise enough to see how much he may win by friendship toward the Silver Wolves. Sooner or later, Walking Stone will drive other clans to do as we have done. If they may hope for friendship among the Stone Houses, they will come in peace.

"If they cannot do this, then they may yet follow Walking Stone's banners when he marches again. We fought well when our horses were thin. Think how we shall fight when our horses are fat." He sat down again.

Murphy shrugged. "It's pretty much as he says, Captain. The grazing is getting a lot better out to the northwest. If Walking Stone can unite all the Westmen, they'll really be a handful. From what Mad Bear says, they weren't exactly driven out of the Five Kingdoms. Walking Stone and some other big chiefs ordered a retreat, and made the order stick."

It made sense to provide a way out for the chiefs and the clans who didn't want to follow this self-proclaimed Genghis Khan. *But do we want any Westmen allies at all? Mad Bear came south because Walking Stone had the sense and the muscle to try sitting on blood feud. What will the chiefs say when they find out they've got less freedom to follow their old customs in the south?*

He wants an answer. Think fast, Galloway.

Mad Bear grinned. "I know that there may yet be a blood price we owe you, for the last time we came. I will ask the gods. If they say so, my warriors and I will swear to ride with you against your enemies in the north. We know they dream of avenging their defeat upon you. The prisoners we took said as much. If the gods will it, we will shed our blood in battle at your side."

That sounded a lot like an offer of alliance—gods permitting. "Will the other chiefs do the same?"

"I can bind no other chief. Each must call upon the gods himself. Yet surely if the Silver Wolves are bidden to swear oaths of friendship with the Chiefs of the Stone Houses, it will be a sign to others."

Which, freely translated, hinted that Mad Bear might twist a few arms.

Ben Murphy looked expectant. So did Baldy. Mad Bear had no expression at all.

I'd hate to play poker with him. Man for man the Westmen were the best light cavalry on Tran. They weren't all that bad in bunches, either, if they could get behind a single chief. *Damn Ben Murphy and damn Mad Bear. I want a bath and Preparation H, not decisions—*

"Surely Mad Bear must seek the will of his gods. No man of honor could do less." *And just hope that doesn't mean human sacrifice or I'm for it with the Yatar people. But I think they just sacrifice horses.* "If the gods wish that the Silver Wolves ride with us against our common enemies, they will be greeted with honor. If that is not the will of the gods, the Silver Wolves may depart in peace."

Mad Bear grinned widely as Baldy finished the translation. So did the other two. Rick wished he felt as relieved as they did. He'd committed not only himself but the whole alliance to friendship with rebels against Walking Stone. *Serves me right for praying for a chance to make a decision without having to consult everyone and his fifth cousin's steward.*

Rick recalled a Chinese proverb. "Be careful what you wish for. You may get it."

✢ ✢ ✢

The anticlimactic council of war took place after the dinner Murphy hosted on the roof of the keep of Westrook. Murphy had had a table, benches, and several kegs of beer lugged up, then dismissed the servants and sat down at the foot of the table. Rick took the head and Bisso, Elliot, Warner, and Mason ranged themselves along the sides.

Rick had drunk too much beer and eaten too much beef and venison. He felt a little groggy, and knew only part of it was a proper meal after too many days in the saddle. The rest was trying to forget what he might have let his friends and allies in for, and particularly what Tylara might say: *You've allied with Westmen and traitors to boot.*

It was that way every time they tried to talk. Within seconds she had found something to resent. Or he had. It was easier to avoid each other. *It can't go on like this. The kids aren't old enough to know what's happening, but I think they feel it, and I know that damn clanswoman nanny of hers hates my guts.*

When I get home we're going to have it out. I tell her what I know, and she tells me why.

Clouds hid both the Firestealer and the Demon Sun, but Murphy had laid out lanterns, and the bonfire in the courtyard added more light. Rick glanced over the battlements at the dancing figures around the fire. It was amazing how much noise two drums, a lyre, and a set of pipes could make.

Alex Boyd reeled through a patch of firelight, a woman on each arm. Tonight all the unattached females of Westrook seemed to be making themselves available. *Alex shouldn't have to take "no" for an answer tonight, and that's one less damn thing to worry about. It sure wouldn't hurt if somebody's husband or father did pound on Volunteer Boyd good and hard.* Rick blearily realized that the others were waiting for him to speak.

"All right. We've got Westmen whether we like them or not. Like fleas. Murphy, what do the people around here think?"

"Well, some think the only good Westman is a dead one. Sir. But they don't all feel that way. Mad Bear did his oath-swearing in front of a couple dozen village headmen and knights. Baldy did the interpreting. They trust him, you know. I taught him a lot of 'star medicine' and he's delivered a lot of babies who wouldn't have made it."

"So they're willing to let things ride as long as the Westmen behave?"

"That's about it, sir. They will behave, too, while Mad Bear's running things."

"Okay. Next question. Suppose he dies. Or suppose his gods tell him not to make an alliance with us. What then?"

Murphy shrugged. "If Mad Bear dies, the Silver Wolves elect another chief, and we start over again."

"The new chief wouldn't be bound by Mad Bear's oaths?"

"No, but he wouldn't start a fight unless he was real dumb. Any new chief has to be an experienced warrior, and I don't think any of them are stupid enough to fight star weapons or a castle."

"And if the gods don't come through?"

"Captain, your guess is as good as mine. One thing, though—I'm not going to force him and his people back to Walking Stone. We couldn't if we wanted to, and they'd fight to the death if we ever tried."

"Murphy—" Elliot began ominously.

Rick shook his head. "I wasn't thinking of doing anything of the kind, Sergeant. Being a bheroman doesn't give you the right to assume your CO's an idiot."

"Yes, sir."

"Still, we can't keep him and his people around here forever. Not enough good grazing land, for one thing. Besides, some hot-headed warrior or a villager with a grudge would make trouble sooner or later."

Warner frowned. "Captain, I don't know what your lady would say to giving away Chelm land—"

You certainly do, but thanks for being polite. "Depends on what land."

"Way down south. I went through there when I ran away from Parsons. That area's going to get pretty warm, but there are springs. The land's too rocky for farming but not for grazing. A bunch of hills, but nothing those little scrubs the Westmen ride couldn't handle."

"I know that area—is there Earth grass there? Horses can't eat Tran scrub—"

"Westmen horses can," Elliot said. "Have to have some grain too, but they make out."

"Genetic drift?"

Elliot shrugged. "Don't know, sir. But it's for sure Westmen ponies can live awhile on Tran plants."

"There's Earth grass anyway," Warner said.

Probably scattered broadside by the *Shalnuksis* a thousand years and more ago. They seemed to do that: bring in Earth plants and animals and turn them loose. It made a goofy ecology, but there's always *some* kind of ecology. "That's near the city-states," Rick mused. "What the hell, if the city-states can't handle three hundred Westmen, what are they good for?"

The other laughed. A servant filled their glasses again.

It's still alienating Chelm land. Poor land, but Chelm land. I'll have to get Tylara to buy off on that. Anything else and there'd be trouble with the bheromen and knights. Not to mention Companion Morrone; his claim to Chelm was just as good or bad as ever, and now he had an experienced little army of his own. Making him a Marcher lord had made him tougher but not a whole lot smarter. He'd listen to an appeal from any bheromen who claimed the Eqeta was violating his oaths. *Another reason Tylara and I have to talk, if we didn't have enough already.*

"Okay, I can agree. In principle, anyway." Rick shrugged. "We have to settle Mad Bear and his people somewhere safe." Don't even think the word "reservation," and maybe you can avoid what usually happens when a nomadic people runs into a sedentary one. *If civilization survives and spreads on Tran, the Westmen are doomed; but maybe we can give them a more dignified end than the American Indians got.*

And maybe Tylara will get down on her knees and beg your—

"Excuse me, Captain." A servant stood at the head of the stairs. Murphy went to him and came back with a sealed message paper. Rick broke the seal.

"Christ!"

"Sir?" Elliot prompted.

Rick read the message aloud.

SUTMARG REGION INVADED BY HOST OF TA-MELTEMOS UNDER PRINCE STRYMON. HOST OF DRANTOS ASSEMBLING TO MEET IT. HAVE SUMMONED THE BAN IN THE NORTH. UNIDENTIFIED HORSEMEN IN THE HIGH CUMAC MAY BE SCOUTS FOR SECOND HOST OF HIGH REXJA. WANAX RETURNING FROM BENEVENUTUM. I LEAD THE VANGUARD OF DRANTOS NORTH TO MEET STRYMON. WITH RESPECT SUGGEST YOU REMAIN IN WEST TO MEET INVASION THERE.

MORRONE,

PROTECTOR OF THE SOUTHERN MARCHES

ACTING CAPTAIN GENERAL

TYLARA DO TAMAERTHON, EQETASSA OF CHELM

JUSTICIAR OF DRANTOS

✢ ✢ ✢

"Has that little bastard gone crazy?" Mason said.

"No. At least not yet," Rick amended. "With both me and Ganton away from Edron and Armagh, he's the highest-ranking officer around. He's sure got the authority to summon the host and lead it north." Rick thought for a moment. "Fact is, I think he's right. Strymon moves fast. Give him half a chance and he'll be through the Sutmarg and into the south in no time. If Morrone moves fast enough he may be able to bottle him up long enough for us to get the Romans into the picture."

"If they'll help," Mason said quietly.

"Yeah." *They have to.* "Sergeant Major."

"Sir."

"There's a hell of a lot we need to know. What's Strymon got? How did he get into the Sutmarg without any kind of fight?"

"Maybe—"

"Maybe. Exactly. Everything's a maybe. We need information. Now."

"I'll get patrols out."

"Send enough that they can leave messenger relays. I want to know things fast. This is a good time to try that new heliograph system."

"Sure," Elliot said. "I'll send back to Armagh to have a team meet us north of here."

"Right. We're going to have to make a visit to Armagh ourselves, but it's best to get them started. Murphy."

"Yes, sir—"

Rick stood up. His head felt clearer. "Murphy, Westrook is now the Captain General's temporary GHQ. I want the semaphore manned around the clock. Ban and arriere-ban, and full patrols north and east. Look for these 'mysterious horsemen.' They may be garbled reports of your Westmen, and they may be some of Strymon's light cavalry. Find out. Send steady troops. We need live witnesses, not dead heroes."

"Sir! Uh— Cap'n?"

"Yeah?"

"Ban and arriere-ban, and I've got nobody to plow and plant."

"Christ, Murphy, you think he don't know that?" Elliot demanded.

"It's all right, Top. Murphy, I don't expect you to keep everybody mobilized all summer, but it can't hurt to muster them and see what they've got."

"Yes, sir."

"I have to get back to Dravan. This place is too far west for a main base. When you get organized here, send me what you can spare. I'll have to leave that up to you."

"I'll have a lot after we get the crops planted," Murphy said. "Not much I can send you until then."

"Yeah, I know that. Next. If the gods tell Mad Bear he can join us, send him as escort for some of our hussars. If he doesn't join up, you'll have to escort him out of our territory. South. Be polite when you tell him, but he joins us or he goes."

"Yes, sir."

"Bisso, Warner, you take five troopers and half the Guards back to Edron. Make sure that you take Sniper MacAllister and at least one more of Gengrich's men. Not Boyd, he stays here."

Elliot looked pained.

"Okay, I know you rely on Bisso, but it can't be helped."

"Yes, sir."

"Warner, when you get to Edron, assess the strategic situation. Consult Gwen. You're authorized to evacuate the University and escort what you can to Edron. Use the Guards, and if you can get any of

Drumold's people to help, do it. Bisso, you're field commander. Warner calls the shots, but you're in charge outside the walls. You'll also be Acting Provost of the University."

Rick watched Larry Warner for signs of resentment, but saw none. *Maybe he's learning.*

"Yes, sir." Bisso didn't look too happy.

Rick suppressed a grin. Independent command was always a nice dream until it turned into a real hot potato. *And it's time we promoted some more NCOs to officer status.*

Of course they already were, as far as the locals were concerned. Star Lords. Brave wise men from the sky. Hah.

"Do the University people fight?" Warner asked.

"Not unless you have to, but it's likely you'll have to," Rick said. "You know the situation better than me, but I'd guess some of the minor clans are going to see this as a great opportunity."

"I hate to abandon the place—"

"Warner, the University is its people. Buildings are easy to come by. Trained personnel aren't. And Gwen's not replaceable at all." *There, I've said it.*

No one argued with him.

"And me, Colonel?" Art Mason asked.

"Stand by. We'll all be going to Dravan as soon as possible, and after that somebody'll have to collect the ammo from the dump at Armagh. And see to the *surinomaz.*"

"That's you or me, Colonel," Mason said.

"Yeah." Rick thought of the long ride to Dravan, and even farther to Armagh, and shuddered.

"Anything else?" Mason asked.

"Not that I think of." For the moment he needed to hit the latrine. As he headed for the stairs, he heard Warner tell Murphy, "Hey, Ben, it just hit me. Once we've won, we give Mad Bear land in the Five Kingdoms."

Bloody hell, he thought. They all have such complete confidence in me. Yeah, and sooner or later my luck will run out, and what then?

What now? Everything's hanging on a thread, and Tylara acts like she's afraid of me. That's a mess that can still wreck everything.

What's a hero? A track star with no place to run. That's me, all right.

19

The wind moaned across the hilltop and the corpses swung from the long gallows erected there. Some of the corpses still had faces—faces as grey as the sky overhead. Tylara shivered. The wind seemed to blow through her, and the corpses seemed to beckon her to join them.

Wait a little, my friends. The gods will give their judgment soon enough. Do not do what I have done. Do not think that you know better than the gods.

"The one in chains is Carlga the Smith," her guide said. "He tried to send warning of Lord Ajacias' treachery, but was caught and tortured for the name of the message-bearer. He died rather than betray the man."

And Carlga's son rode in the Guards. He would have a bleak homecoming.

"He will be avenged," Tylara said, the same way she might have said, "It is raining." The Christians spoke of leaving vengeance to God, but there were some things honorable men could not entrust to God or Vothan. One was to leave Ajacias unhanged and his sty of a castle standing.

Tylara's resolution faltered. If she submitted to the judgment of the gods, she might not live to see the Wanax's punishment of the traitor.

That might be the only pleasure life still held for her. Yet the blood guilt on her would grow no less, and the gods' judgment was certain. If not on her, where would it fall? Perhaps on Drantos. Perhaps it had begun when Ajacias turned traitor and allowed Prince Strymon to cross the border.

No. The blood guilt was hers and hers alone, as surely as if she had thrust the knife into Caradoc with her own hand. She alone must answer for it.

"Have them taken down and buried with reverence," she said. "Now let us rejoin Lord Morrone."

Her Tamaerthan archers drew around her. She turned and rode back down the hill.

✣ ✣ ✣

Morrone had ridden ahead to scout when Tylara reached the campfire. She was eating porridge and sausage when he returned.

His grin was wide. "Either the tales that put Strymon's host at above ten thousand are lies, or else he has divided his forces most unwisely. Our scouts have found no more than three thousand of his horse and a thousand foot. They are drawn up on the flank of Piro's Hill. I will order our men to eat, then advance straight to battle."

That was wisdom, if four thousand was truly Strymon's whole strength. Seven thousand against four. A thousand of the seven were Tamaerthan archers. It promised victory. But—

"Might Strymon have hidden part of his host to tempt you into just such action, my lord? Or perhaps he can hold until *reinforcements* can be summoned?"

Morrone shrugged without altering his grin in the slightest. "If he can hide more than three thousand men, Strymon is a wizard greater than any starman. My scouts turn over every fallen leaf. As for his calling up his—*reserves*, the faster we strike, the less time he will have to do so."

Tylara did not share Morrone's confidence in the irregular light-infantry levies he'd brought from the south. They were certainly loyal to their lord, tough, enduring—and as good at looting inns and farms as they were at fighting. Tylara would have had more confidence in half as many Guards or Mounted Archers, but the Guards were with Rick and Ganton.

Moreover, Morrone resented the least criticism of his faithful levies. Did their loyalty flatter him out of all judgment? Tylara only knew that she had twice come close to quarrels with him over the levies' poor discipline. A third on the day of battle would only hand Strymon the gift of a divided enemy. Morrone did her as much courtesy as she could expect by listening to her at all in matters of war.

"I await your orders, Lord Morrone."

"I would order you to keep yourself safe, but I know what you would say to that." Tylara forced a smile. "Your archers are on our left side. That is good. Bring them forward to extreme bowshot and harass the enemy's infantry until my knights are set to charge, then guard our left flank. If Strymon does launch an attack from that direction, I can trust you to keep your head and not see fifty men as a five thousand."

"Thank you, my lord."

Morrone waved to his squire and vaulted into the saddle without touching the stirrups. Another wave of his hand, and he was off at a brisk trot, followed by the cheers of everyone around the campfire.

Tylara cheered with them for a moment, then turned away. *He can win the hearts of fighting men. Yet can he win battles as well as the husband I have betrayed? Or does he crave a victory of his own? Crave it so greatly that he sees nothing that he does not wish to see? And if that is so, and I accept the gods' judgment, who will be left to lead the host of Drantos until the Wanax rides north?*

No. These are only more excuses. I have sworn to submit to the gods. I broke my oath to Caradoc; I will not break this one.

✢ ✢ ✢

The host of Drantos closed with the enemy as the True Sun touched low hills at the horizon. There was not enough time or light to lure the enemy from his chosen position, nor to maneuver behind him. The attack must go straight in, and the gods grant victory to boldness.

She led her archers forward and halted them a full three hundred and fifty paces from the enemy's infantry. Her arm swept up, then down.

"Let the gulls fly!"

The Tamaerthan arrows did their terrible work against the enemy's shielded warriors. Arrows flew in flights, half shot high to fall against those who raised their shields, half lower to strike those who held steady. Infantrymen fell. Some turned to run.

Rick always said that frontal attacks on a prepared enemy were wasteful, yet perhaps Vothan will favor us today. Now, Lord Morrone! A charge of chivalry has won more than one battle for Drantos.

Morrone's forward battle came into sight. The sky was the color of old lead. The True Sun was half out of sight when the Drantos vanguard broke through the enemy's screen of light cavalry. More trumpets sounded, and the Drantos horse parted, turning to either side to chase Strymon's skirmishers from the field.

The main body of Drantos heavy cavalry moved forward.

The Tamaerthan archers could no longer help for fear of striking their own men, but that did not matter. The enemy infantry broke and ran. The way lay open for a single grand charge to sweep through the fleeing infantry and crush the knights who stood behind them. The day might be won in an hour.

Grant that it be so. Tylara did not know to whom she prayed, and turned her mount toward the several stades of hills and scrub oak that she and her archers watched over. There were enemies there, but in no great force, certainly not enough to break through a thousand Tamaerthan archers who could shoot a man out of his saddle at four hundred paces.

The horns signaled for the charge; Tylara turned in her saddle to watch it. The steel-clad knights rode in a solid formation, banners in line as on parade. As they lowered their lances they looked fit enough to carry all before them. The trumpets signaled the trot. Then the charge.

The steel lance points reached the fleeing enemy foot-soldiers— and suddenly half of Morrone's line was in chaos, horses screaming and falling, knights toppling from the saddle. The enemy foot turned from fleeing rabble into deadly foes. They ran in among the horses to slash with long knives and thrust with short spears.

Pits. Morrone's right had been lured into a chain of pits dug in front of Strymon's shield wall. Those knights would be lucky to save their lives, let alone carry their charge home. But the left was still intact— and now Strymon's horse were wheeling, to fall on Morrone's left with equal numbers and the advantage of the higher ground.

No, superior numbers. Over the crest of Piro's Hill came a solid line of horse, light and heavy mingled together but coming on at a good pace, with the Great Banner of Ta Meltemos in its chariot in the middle of the line.

Trumpets sang, and the Drantos left slowed, then reformed to receive charges from two directions. Morrone was not such a fool as to hope for victory now. He galloped up and down the line like a maniac. Tylara could not hear, but she could imagine what he was saying.

He might yet save much of the host.

If Morrone could stand off the first charge until his right untangled itself from the pits, he might yet manage an orderly retreat. Then superior numbers would tell—

"Ho! Archers! Look to your front! Let the grey gulls fly!"

The cry went up and down the Tamaerthan line and Tylara whirled. Light cavalry were pouring out of the scrubby oak forest. Some of the horsemen were already falling to arrows but more took their place every moment. Tylara's mind had room for only two thoughts:

I have seen a good captain routed by a great one.

The gods have given their judgment. Now—how best to submit?

It seemed wisest to stay where she was and let the enemy come to her. Soon her archers would retreat before the press of Strymon's cavalry; then if she rode forward only a few paces she would be beyond the protection of her own troops. *So be it. The guilt is mine alone. I will take none of them with me.*

Some of the enemy cavalry were horse archers. Their light bows could not match the range of a Tamaerthan longbow, but that was no handicap for Strymon's archers. They used the cover of the scrub oaks to slip close. *They can shoot from horseback, or lying on the ground, while my archers must stand.* Tamaerthans fell, and arrows whistled around Tylara. *If my horse is killed—*

"Lady, time for ye to be out of here," an archer captain said. He gripped her bridle and turned her mount away from the line.

"Thank you, but it is better that I stay."

"Lady, ye'll be goin', if I have to—"

Tylara never knew what the archer captain would have done. An arrow pierced his face and he fell, his fingers still clutching the bridle. Tylara's horse shied and reared.

With perfect clarity she saw herself draw her light battle-axe and strike with the flat of it until the dead man's hand slipped from the bridle. She urged her horse forward, and the animal leaped over the captain's body. Other archers ran toward her and she drove her spurs in hard. Her gelding bolted past the approaching archers and through the fighting line.

Tylara whirled the axe as she rode. Tamaerthan oaths and Drantos cheers came to her lips. The hail of arrows from both sides slackened as the Tamaerthans held their fire and the enemy used the pause to rally. A mass of horsemen took shape ahead of her. She settled into the saddle and rode straight at them.

Two arrows hit her horse in the flank. He reared, screaming. She kept her seat but the battle-axe slipped out of her hand and hung by the thong around her wrist. A horseman rode down on her, and she saw the gods' judgment coming toward her in the steel tip of his lance.

"For Caradoc! Vothan!"

The lance tip drove into her horse's chest. The gelding stumbled and she tried to throw herself clear. Too late. The stirrup leather was wound around her leg and her horse was falling. The gelding rolled over her and the eye of her battle-axe struck her on the forehead. *I've failed*, she thought, and the blackness took her.

‡ ‡ ‡

Apelles had put his field hospital near good water, on a rise with a good view of the battlefield. He would have preferred a site that his handful of men could defend. He didn't fear the enemy so much as Morrone's southern levies once their lord was too busy fighting to watch them.

He cheered with the rest as the host of Drantos drove forward. After that he had a fine view of the defeat, and the horror of Lady Tylara's fall.

Light horse from behind the hill swept around to surround the Tamaerthan archers. The clansmen drew into a square. The light cavalry charged once and were driven back by flights of arrows, then withdrew to beyond bowshot, where they stood watchful. The Tamaerthans were no longer a danger to Strymon's main battle. Apelles wondered if they could withdraw, of if they would stand, never to leave the field unless Prince Strymon granted them quarter.

On the right Morrone's levies were scattering. The Drantos knights formed into groups and began a more orderly retreat. Apelles hoped they would win free, but they were not his concern. He had known what he must do from the moment he saw Lady Tylara ride into the ranks of the enemy.

Her futile charge had not greatly surprised him. Thrice since the host of Drantos rode north he had seen Lady Tylara when she thought no one was watching. Each time, her eyes seemed those of one who had gazed into the Christians' Hell.

If Lady Tylara had found what she sought, he could at least bring out word of her death, so that her kin would hear it from a friend. If she yet lived—she might think herself in Hell while still in this world. No one should have to face that alone.

"Culin!"

"Yes, Father Apelles?" That was not yet the accepted title for priests of the Dayfather, but the boy could not be broken of using it.

"I am going to go down and surrender to the enemy."

"You cannot—"

". . . to assure honorable treatment of our wounded prisoners. You will bear a message to Yanulf. Ask him to care for Maev and our daughter."

"Fa—you cannot command me to do that. It would be turning my back on the enemy." He looked indignantly at Apelles.

Apelles noticed that Culin's eyes were now on a level with his. Soon he would be taller, if he lived. Apelles remembered the scrawny, gawky boy he'd found at a House of Vothan and taken as his servant a year ago. Now Culin could read and write, his clothes would not have disgraced a yeoman's son, and he had his whole life before him.

He would not lose that life, if Apelles had aught to say about it.

"Culin. If you do not go to Yanulf, he will think I have gone mad. That would take honor from me. And from you as well. Besides, if Yanulf thinks I have gone mad, will he care for Maev and our daughter? Would you have them begging their bread, with the Time approaching?"

"No, Father."

"And you have sworn obedience. Was that a false oath?"

"No, Father."

"Then be off. I will wager you a meal in a good inn that we shall see each other again."

"How shall I pay if I lose?"

"By selling the horse you will need to steal to reach Yanulf."

Culin's mouth opened, but no sound came out. Then he knelt, kissed Apelles' hand, and ran off.

Apelles watched him go, glad that he had no running to do, in search of a horse or anything else. His knees seemed to lack the strength they'd had this morning. His mouth was dry, and his breath came quickly as if he'd been running.

Now he might never have to choose between his family and a bishopric in the united faiths. Certainly he would have liked to see

Maev again. Or discuss the Act of Union with old Polycarp. It would be pleasant to sleep in his own bed in his own chambers once again, and drink a cup of the good wine he could never have afforded as a swineherd's son. . . .

None of that mattered. His god had called him to Lady Tylara. He strode down the slope and never looked back.

PART FIVE
AFFAIRS OF HONOR

✦═ 20 ═✦

Rick reined in at the top of the small hill. Castle Armagh was visible ahead. He dismounted. Time to walk the horses. Ten minutes every hour. Every movement was an effort, and he felt as if someone had been standing on his back.

Only ten more miles, he thought. We've made good time from Dravan in the last week. Ten more miles. Fifteen minutes in a car. An hour in a four-wheeler with no roads. Half a day's ride for us. Silently he cursed the *Shalnuksis* and all their works. *But if they hadn't taken you off that hill, where would you be, Galloway?*

Dead, I expect. But I wouldn't be responsible for saving civilization for a whole planet.

✦ ✦ ✦

Fields of young wheat filled the valley between the road and the hills. It looked like they'd have a good crop, enough to feed the region, with a lot left over to be stored in the Caves. *If we can keep Strymon's army from trampling it. Or burning it. Or burn it ourselves, only I won't do that. Sure, we'll have plenty for a couple more years. But then the Time will come, and the* Shalnuksis . . .

Rick couldn't see the fields on the other side of the hills, but he knew what they held. Tangles of *surinomaz*—madweed, as the locals called it—tended by convicts and slaves under the watchful eyes of armed guards. *I wouldn't blame the slaves for running. Cultivating madweed's hard work. Dangerous, too. But if we don't grown the stuff, we'll have nothing for the* Shalnuksis, *and they'll bomb the planet just to*

keep it in the Stone Age. And if I tell myself that often enough, maybe I'll
believe it's all right to be a slave master. Maybe.

✣ ✣ ✣

As they approached Castle Armagh the gates opened and four blue-
robed priests of Yatar rode out. When they were closer, Rick saw that
their leader was Yanulf.

What's he doing here? Rick wondered. His place is at Edron. Or
with the Wanax. There's not much here but mercs and madweed, and
those are my job, not his.

"Hail, Lord Rick."

"Hail."

Yanulf gestured, and the junior priests and apprentice who'd ridden
out with him drew away. "I would speak with you alone," Yanulf said.

Rick waved his guards back and rode on with Yanulf. "Bad news?"

"The worst," Yanulf said.

Worst. "Tylara's dead."

"No, my lord. Captured by Prince Strymon. Morrone lost half his
force, and both he and the Eqetassa were taken."

"But she's alive."

"Yes, when last we heard. But there is more you should know."

Rick studied Yanulf's expressionless face. "If she's being
mistreated—" He shuddered. Yanulf would remember what Tylara had
suffered from Sarakos as well as Rick did. Better.

"It is not that. My lord, she rode out through the lines of her
archers, and alone charged the enemy cavalry."

"That doesn't make sense—"

"She is the leader of a clan of Tamaerthon. Could she believe she
has lost the favor of God?"

Rick glanced at his watch and reined in. "Time to walk," he said.

"My lord—"

"Give me a minute." He dismounted carefully and walked ahead.

Lost the favor of God. Yeah, and her husband, too. And all her
husband's friends. And—

Damnation, she tried to talk to me. Why didn't I give her the
chance?

"Who brought the news?"

"The boy Culin. When Apelles saw the Lady Tylara captured, he sent
his servant to me, and followed his lady into the camp of the enemy."

"Good man. I owe him. I suppose he's getting messages out through the priests of Yatar in Strymon's army?"

"Of course. Those who serve Yatar know that the Time approaches, and who their true friends are."

Rick glanced at the front of Yanulf's robe, where a pectoral cross lay over the circled thunderbolt of Yatar. "How do you feel about the unified faith?"

"Some accept, some do not. Those who accept help as best they can."

"Strymon permits the new faith in his camp?"

"A quarter and more of his soldiers have accepted it. How could he not?"

"Oh. Thanks. I didn't know you'd made that many converts." He walked on a few paces, then turned. "If the priests can get messages out, I can get one in."

Yanulf nodded. "It can be done."

"Thank you." *And what in hell will I say to her?* He laughed bitterly. *"Come home, all is forgiven." Now how the hell do I say that in a message that half the priesthood's going to read?*

"What will you do?" Yanulf asked.

"Get the hell up there and see how many of Ganton's people will help me get her out."

"Calm. I know you wish to act, but think first. Prince Strymon has a reputation for honor, and surely will not demand excessive ransom. If you attempt a rescue, she may be killed. I am no soldier, but most battles hastily begun are easily lost."

Rick was silent for a long moment. "All right. I'll get the stuff I came here for and go back to Dravan. By then we'll know more. If that—If you can send messages into Strymon's camp, send him this one. If he harms her in any way, by spring a year from now there won't be a living thing left in his kingdom."

"I will send the message, but I doubt it will be believed."

"Tell him anyway."

✣ ✣ ✣

Gwen and Siobhan acknowledged the sentry's salute and turned down the hall toward Octavia's chambers. Voices reached them before Gwen was close enough to knock at the door of the royal apartment. *If Octavia ever finds herself at the head of a legion, she'll have no trouble making herself heard. That's for sure.* She motioned Siobhan behind her and stepped close to the door.

"—abandon Edron, which has never fallen save by starvation or treachery? We have provisions for at least two winters. If you know of traitors among us, tell me now lest I suspect you of being one of them!"

Octavia's command was answered by an incoherent chorus of protestations. *She must have half the ladies of the court in there. This sounds interesting.* Gwen glanced back down the hall. The sentry was out of sight. She waited, one hand poised to knock.

"... much of Morrone's host escaped Piro's Hill and will soon fight again. The Wanax will take the field against Strymon with the knights Morrone couldn't muster. Tamaerthan pikemen will join him. Tamaerthan pikes and archers alone once defeated a Roman legion! And then there are the star weapons— God knows how many *guns* we can field against Strymon. It is the host of Ta-Meltemos that should be thinking of fleeing to safety! Not us."

"But, Your Majesty—you cannot—"

"Your son, Prince Adrian—" This round of protestations was slightly more coherent.

"No. I am the daughter and the granddaughter of soldiers, who held their posts where God and Caesar sent them. Can I do less? What honor does it bring them or your Wanax if I teach my son to flee at the first sign of danger?

"I cannot. I will not. Enough of this nonsense. I will hear no more." Octavia's tone held all the finality of the headsman's axe.

"That's our cue." Gwen took Siobhan's hand and led her down the hall away from the sentry. They turned the corner and flattened themselves against the wall as ladies-in-waiting bustled out of Octavia's apartment. *Not this way, ladies. You're already annoyed that Octavia booted a couple of you out of your rooms for me when we evacuated the University. You don't need to know that I've heard the queen dressing you down like raw recruits.*

Gwen waited until the ladies had left the corridor, then motioned to Siobhan to follow her back down the hall. She knocked at Octavia's door and a maid admitted them. Octavia was sitting on a window bench, pretending to knit. Gwen had taught her Earthstyle knitting, and the queen was quite good at it—when her hands weren't shaking.

Octavia turned a pale face to Gwen as the Earthwoman entered. "I expected you earlier. Did you hear those mewling biddies? Do they think they can find any place that's safer than Edron? Strymon will never get this far. Ganton will see to that."

Octavia's smile was strained. Gwen realized that the girl was as scared as any of her ladies. *She's just hiding it better. Goes with being Queen, I guess.* Gwen smiled. "Forgive me. I don't doubt the Wanax will make short shrift of Strymon."

"I'm glad to hear you believe that. But . . . I'm frightened. We will surely win, but at what price? We've already lost four thousand good men slain or taken, and Lady Tylara and Lord Morrone are prisoners."

What price indeed. If I had the answer to that question, I'd be Yatar or some other Higher Authority. As it is—"I'm scared too Octavia. But we'll just have to do the best we can. One thing, you might admit to your ladies that you're worried about your husband. Most of them are probably scared for their men too."

"Thank you, Gwen. Will you—will you give me advice and counsel? Yanulf returns today. When he rides north with the host, you'll be the only one I can talk to."

"Of course." Gwen realized she was thinking of the power that position would give her. *What's worse is that I don't despise myself for it. Is this what they mean when they talk about doing well by doing good?*

A faint knock sent Octavia's maid to the door. "The Lord Chancellor of the University, Lord Warner, craves audience with the Wanaxxae Octavia and the Lady Gwen."

"Come."

Octavia and Gwen sat side by side to receive Larry Warner's graceful bow. *He's becoming quite the courtier. I wonder how many ladies he's courted into bed?*

"Your Majesty. My report on the University's contribution to our coming victory. With your permission?"

Octavia laughed. "Lord Rick has made it *very* clear that the University is no part of either Drantos or Rome. You need make no report to me."

"Well, Majesty—" Warner was obviously amused. "That's true, but I am supposed to report to Gwen, and besides, I've brought some troops to add to the defenses of Edron."

"Ah. Proceed, then." Octavia smiled. "You may speak to Gwen or to me, as is most appropriate." Then she laughed.

"Yes, ma'am," Warner drawled. "All the essential records and equipment from the University are safe in Edron now. The Romans withdrew most of their University cohort to support the defense of the south, but since most of the threat is from the south, that's not as bad as it sounds. Still, it left us with not much more than Rustengans and other craftsmen too old or too young to go to war, and some random Tamaerthans from the major clans."

"All the clans?" Gwen asked.

"Most of them."

Gwen nodded in satisfaction. "Good. Then any clansmen who attack the University will be at blood feud with their own relatives."

"Right. Anyway, the Roman tribune wanted to take the whole cohort, but Lucius convinced him he'd better leave some of them with us. So he and his centurions rolled dice to see who'd get to leave. I think he used his own dice, because he got to go himself."

"Larry, what's the bottom line?" Gwen asked in English.

"Yes, ma'am. Well, the University is defended by the Tamaerthan clansmen, the worst half of the Roman cohort, the city militia, and God Almighty. I've brought a token century of Romans, a company of Tamaerthan archers, all the University craftsmen who think they're militia and volunteered to travel, and the First Balloon Squadron, commanded by Your Servant Warrant Officer Warner."

"Balloon? Larry—"

"Well, I admit it'd do more good out west, but it'd take forever to get it there."

"The Wanax wishes each to fight whatever enemy is closest," Octavia said. "I think you will soon find many of them close enough."

"Yeah—Yes, Majesty. I'm afraid you're right."

"That's good strategy. It's even better politics," Gwen said. "Fighting the enemy where he is has got to be better than just defending your own land. Drantos has no national army. Rome sends troops where they're needed."

"Maybe the ironhats will learn and maybe they won't," Warner said. "Anyway, we're here, and I no sooner got here than we were ordered to join Ganton's army. We move out tonight. What am I getting into?"

"I don't know how many troops the enemy has," Gwen said. "But I can tell you what the Wanax's forces are." She looked to Octavia and got a tiny nod of approval. "With your people—and I expect he can use your aeronauts—he ought to have nearly ten thousand, plus the field guns, and seven mercs with rifles. Eight, counting you."

"No Romans," Warner said.

"Caesar will send aid," Octavia said.

"Majesty," Warner said gently, "I am certain that Marselius Caesar would like to send aid. I also know that even a single cohort is valuable to him at this moment. The turmoil in the south grows worse each ten-day, and as the weather improves and the Demon grows closer, Rome will need even more legions to hold the southern borders."

"They disbanded two legions after the last southern campaign," Gwen said.

"Sure," Warner said. "And they'll probably call them up again, but it sure won't be until they've got crops planted. Otherwise, what'll they eat this fall?"

And it takes time to assemble militiamen, Gwen thought.

"Whatever the Romans can do, they won't be sending any legions tonight," Warner said. "And that's when we march. Your Majesty, my lady. This is farewell, until we come back with Prince Strymon's head."

"God be with you," said Octavia.

Gwen fumbled for words. "Come back safe" didn't sound right, but what—? "Good hunting," she said grinning.

Warner embraced her and kissed her on the forehead, in a less brotherly fashion than usual. Gwen felt Octavia's eyes on her and blushed. She was still blushing when the door closed behind Warner.

"Lady Gwen," said Octavia, carefully looking at her knitting.

"Yes, Your Majesty?"

"Is Lord Warner your—lover? He has a reputation—"

"Almost as bad as Lord Morrone's?"

"I wasn't going to insult him, but . . ."

That came close to confirming the rumor that Morrone was jealous of Octavia's being both wife *and* confidante of his friend Ganton. It also suggested that Octavia's watching her father be the Don Juan of Rome had given her a distaste for unchastity in others.

If I want to be Octavia's friend and confidante, does this mean I have to keep my pants on except when Les visits?

Probably. And now the sixty-four silver question: Can I do it?

Maybe. If Rick's not interested. Meanwhile, I can tell Octavia the truth. . . .

"Lord Warner is not my lover and never has been. If Caradoc had not offered first, I might have married Lord Warner, as we have much—much in common. But I have been faithful to Lord Les, and pray only that Yatar, Christ, and all the Holy Archangels bring him safely back to me at the end of his travels."

That last part, at least, was the truth and nothing else.

✢ ✢ ✢

"Please be seated, my lords. Wine?"

Murphy and Bheroman Traskon sat down at the big table in Rick's conference room at Castle Dravan. Rick noted that Murphy sat down as quickly as Traskon. The first time he'd addressed a group of nobles that included Murphy, Ben had glanced behind him to see who was being spoken to. Now Murphy wore the title as easily as his Tran clothing.

Rick sat at the head of the table. The noon sun lighted the white plastered walls covered with maps drawn in charcoal. Murphy kept glancing at them.

"They're current as far as I know," Rick said. "After lunch you can help update them."

"Main thing is we haven't found any new threats."

"Good."

"On the other hand, everybody agrees on the twelve thousand we know about." Murphy pointed to the arrow indicating a detachment of Strymon's army marching toward Dravan.

"We can hold those." Rick kept his voice even, and turned to Traskon. "My Lord Bheroman."

"My Lord Captain General," Traskon said. "My knights and I await your orders. I have assembled the ban and arriere-ban to hold our lands, and my knights are ready to ride. Tell us how we may avenge the dishonor to our Lady Eqetassa."

"Thank you. I expected no less." Rick swallowed hard, as he always did when he thought of Tylara in Strymon's hands. *Tylara might have been Traskon's stepmother, if Sarakos hadn't thrown his father off Castle Dravan's battlements. And I'd never have met her. Would that be better? No. But—Traskon wants something. What?*

Murphy cleared his throat. "My Lord Captain General, it has come to my ears that you plan to arm the villagers, that they may defend themselves as they did against the Westmen."

"Yeah, Sergeant?"

"Captain, they say you're going to give them guns—nothing big, maybe, but *guns!*"

"So have I heard also," said Traskon. "When the Westmen came, Hilon the blacksmith of Clavton, a town in my lands, proposed that the town buy guns to defend itself. I asked then, and I ask now, how can we be sure that villages and towns so armed will defend themselves only against our common enemies, and not their lawful lords? How shall a bheroman do his duty, if his towns can refuse theirs? It also seemed to me—and forgive me, my lord, if this grieves you—but the Lady Eqetassa seemed willing to hear me."

Damn right. Tylara isn't about to arm towns against the nobility. And now what? Rick laughed aloud.

"My lord?" Ben Murphy asked.

"Nothing. Your pardon." *And one thing's for damn sure, Ben Murphy's gone native. The great-grandson of a man hanged for shooting a landlord's rent collector is trying to keep people from shooting his rent collectors!* Rick spoke quickly in English. "Found out being boss man isn't all that easy, right, Sergeant?"

"Sir!"

And now for my stuffiest shirt. "My lords, I will never arm rebels. Moreover, our guns are too few for me to allocate them to the villages. That is true also for our firepowder."

"Thank you, my Lord Captain General," said Traskon. "And—may I say that our thoughts are with you, in your grief for the Lady Eqetassa?"

"Thank you." Rick forced a smile. "It could be worse. She's alive, so we should see her again once the ransom's paid. She'll probably throw a pot at me for spending so much."

The two noblemen laughed dutifully and bowed themselves out. Rick sat motionless until the door closed. Then he got up and poured himself a cup of the wine the others had refused.

I didn't talk to her for a year, and now she's a prisoner. That has to be a nightmare all by itself.

It was hard to think like the Tamaerthan nobility, but couldn't she think that was punishment enough? He had no way of knowing. *She thinks every bad thing that's happened in the last year is her fault. Everything from crop failures in the south to Morrone's defeat.*

The only good thing about the situation was Apelles. *I'm glad he went with her. He's no psychiatrist, but he's smart, and she listens to priests. If anybody but me can talk her out of the crazy notion that she's got the world on her shoulders, it'll be him.*

And meanwhile he had eight thousand men to command and twelve thousand enemies to face, and despite his assurances to Murphy and Traskon he was pretty sure the enemy's strength was growing. He went to the map and stared at it. It had cost good men to fill in the information there, but now he knew that Strymon held all the roads north into the Five Kingdoms, and could bring down reinforcements as needed.

The only thing to slow them down would be the remnants of Morrone's force, and the sheer logistics of marching an army in the spring when there wasn't much grass and granaries would be empty. A quart of wheat a day for each man. A bushel for each horse. It all added up to a *lot* of transport, and the transport horses had to eat, too.

If that damned Ajacias had kept all the grain supplies in his goddam castle, Strymon wouldn't have—

If wishes were horses, beggars could ride.

"Jamiy!"

His orderly opened the door.

"Officers' Call in one hour."

✣ ✣ ✣

The Death Wind Bringer hung low on the horizon, bloated until it looked more than ever like the evil eye. Around it the stars were coming out, as Mad Bear walked out of the Silver Wolves' camp toward the vigil hill.

He walked slowly, according to custom, but his thoughts ran on ahead of his feet. The sacrifice was ready at the hilltop.

It had never before occurred to him that he should defy the gods. Yet now he thought he would aid the Stone House Chiefs no matter how the sacrifice went. The thought was frightening.

If he didn't stay with the Stone House Chiefs, there would be no home for the Silver Wolves. Without a home, they would perish, Walking Stone's work would be done for him, his enemies would lose heart, and all this without costing the dung-weaned son of a diseased mare a single warrior!

This was the truth, but not all of it. The rest of the truth was that

Mad Bear had begun to see that the sky-wizards themselves might be the sign from the gods. If they were indeed wizards. Mad Bear had begun to doubt even this. Certainly they had wizardry at their command, but they bled and died like men—and when they died, they died like warriors.

It seemed true, what he'd thought first in the tent where he awoke a prisoner of the wizards. Nothing among gods or men would ever be the same again, and a wise man would do what his own wisdom told him to do, not wait for signs that the gods might have already given.

Mad Bear knew that he himself would not live to see all that would come of the rule of the wizard-warriors. Still, he might get sons who would, and *their* sons might stand beside the wizard-warriors as blood brothers and fight among the very stars.

He would have to be content with drinking his death toast from Walking Stone's skull.

The path began to climb the hill. Mad Bear slowed further and raised his spear to the Child of Fire. He would keep the vigil according to custom, give judgment likewise, and make the horse sacrifice afterward.

He would make the horse sacrifice alone, though, with no one aiding. If by some chance he *had* angered the gods, let their punishment fall on him alone.

21

Tylara awoke with a headache that felt as if Great Guns were being fired inside her skull. Dull knives stabbed her in the ribs every time she breathed. Her left wrist and right ankle throbbed so hard she was glad she was in bed with no reason to move them.

It wasn't much of a bed—she felt straw under her and smelled damp fleeces piled over her—but it was a bed, inside some building with whitewashed plaster walls around her and a thatched roof overhead. The knowledge that she was safe in a bed, out of the weather and perhaps in the hands of friends, made her groan in a way the pain could never have done.

She had given herself into the hands of the gods as a sacrifice, to turn away their vengeance from her husband and children, from Chelm and Tamaerthon and Drantos. She should not be alive. She *could* not be alive unless the gods had rejected her sacrifice.

What she felt now was worse than the pain of her wounds, although she had not endured such pain since she bore Isobel. It was despair, which she had not felt since she crouched in Sarakos' bedchamber, wondering who would come next, Sarakos or the crone with the whip?

The despair was not so much for herself, although she knew that if the gods had not allowed her to offer her own life in return for Caradoc's they would demand something worse. The despair was for those innocent men and women who would now be dragged down with her into the gods only knew what pit of demons.

Except that in a pit of demons, one could at least be sure that one

778

was already dead, and that matters could grow no worse. Tylara knew that her husband's punishment, her children's, Ganton's—all would begin like hers, while they were still alive to taste the worst of it.

Pride still forced her to cram her right fist into her mouth to stifle another groan. A moment later she saw faces looming over the bed. A woman and two men. One of the men was armed, while the other looked vaguely familiar. She knew she ought to know him, but she could not remember his name. The woman washed her face and neck, and the man held a cup of cool water that tasted of wine and herbs to her lips. They did things to her wrist, ankle, and head that both hurt and soothed at the same time.

She was still trying to put a name to the man when her eyes grew too heavy to be worth the trouble to keep open, and she let them fall shut.

✣ ✣ ✣

The second time Tylara awoke, the pain in her head was only muskets firing, not Great Guns. She realized that her ankle was twisted and swollen, that her wrist and at least two ribs were probably broken, and that her stomach was dreadfully empty.

The idea of food still made her gag. The sound and movement brought her three attendants to her bedside again. This time she recognized the one who'd seemed familiar. It was Apelles. He had washed his face and found a clean robe somewhere. He smiled as he lifted her wrist to study the bindings.

"Greetings, my Lady Eqetassa. I rejoice to see you awake. It is a good sign."

Tylara tried to turn her head. This set the muskets to firing volleys, but she saw that the opposite wall was now hung with a tapestry of dragons hurling *skyfire*. The floor was a finger's-length deep in fresh rushes, and the damp fleeces piled over her had given way to dry furs.

Tylara wasn't sure that her healing was a matter for rejoicing. It seemed not unlikely that she would save everyone a great deal of trouble by dying. She also knew that she was most unlikely to die of these wounds even if she refused further care—and if she did that, they would doubtless only treat her as a madwoman and take her fate even further out of her own hands.

Her thoughts must have shown on her face. Apelles frowned, then gestured toward the door. The woman and the armed man went out.

Tylara caught a glimpse of the ragged and mud-smeared surcoat he wore over his short mail coat. It had once been white and green—the colors of Ta-Meltemos.

"Apelles," Tylara said when they were alone, "who is the prisoner here—that soldier of Prince Strymon or—?"

Apelles did not met her eyes. This time she had the strength to weep, but pride kept her eyes dry.

"Morrone led a final charge when he saw the archers breaking," Apelles said. He still couldn't meet her eyes, and busied himself washing her hands and feet. "He caught Strymon's knights unready. They thought the battle already won. The host of Drantos drove many of the Meltemes from the field."

"Then we won?" Tylara asked wonderingly.

"No. Strymon rallied his forces and held Morrone's charge. Drantos was already defeated when he challenged Morrone to single combat. Bards will sing of that fight for a thousand years! Morrone fought most valiantly, but he was unhorsed, then stunned. Then our knights who remained on the field yielded on the customary terms of ransom. The Fourth Pikes also yielded, on terms of life and limb."

"And—the Tamaerthan archers? Morrone's levies?"

"Most of the levies did not wait on the outcome of the charge, but fled the field. The Tamaerthans—they advanced—they advanced—"

"They advanced too far trying to save me, and could not make a safe retreat?"

"A good ten-score did, my lady."

Ten-score, out of more than eight hundred. Once again she had led the clansmen to slaughter, as she had done against Sarakos. Would they have been able to escape and go on stinging at Strymon if she hadn't dragged them after her?

Only the gods could know the answer to that. What she knew was that her people had already suffered part of the punishment she had hoped to turn away by her sacrifice. She had betrayed them as she had betrayed Caradoc, and their blood was on her hands as surely as his was.

Worse, she had blundered. Rick had defeated a Roman legion with nothing more than Tamaerthan pikes and archers! *If I had used them properly, we might yet have saved the day for Morrone.*

She made an animal noise in the back of her throat, tried to swallow, and found that an iron band seemed to have tightened about her neck. Then Apelles was beside her, a surprisingly strong hand gripping her right wrist.

"My lady. It is not quite unknown—what you tried to do. I do not know why you passed such a judgment on yourself. I do not wish to know, unless you choose freely to tell me. Although you might do well to speak of it to Yanulf, if it lays such a burden on you and for some reason you cannot speak of it to your lord and husband."

Tylara's eyes filled with silent tears.

"I can say this. You fear that the gods have judged you unfit as a sacrifice, and have some further punishment—"

"Isn't a lost battle, thousands dead or taken, and all of Drantos open to Prince Strymon punishment in the eyes of any god or man?"

Apelles' face told her that she'd cried loudly enough to be heard outside the chamber. She went on more quietly. "Apelles, don't treat me like a child."

His face now told her that he would not give her the comfort of losing his temper. Then he smiled.

"My lady, I am only a consecrated priest of Yatar, so I am not as sure of His will and that of Christ His Son as you seem to be. I suppose it is possible that horrors beyond belief await you and yours because you were not a fit sacrifice.

"Yet I think it likely that whatever your sin, it was not one for which Yatar asks the lives of you and your people. Few sins are as great as that! And beware of assuming that the judgments of the gods are always so simple that men may easily understand them."

"Small comfort—"

"Hear me out. My lady, I know that will be small comfort to you. What you would consider a true comfort, my oaths as a priest of Yatar forbid me to offer, even if common sense did not. Will you swear by Yatar, Vothan, Hestia, and your own honor to lay no hands upon yourself nor to contrive that others aid you in so doing? If you will not, I must lay this matter before Prince Strymon."

Tylara now realized why Apelles had gripped her good hand before beginning to speak. If it had been free, she would certainly have thrown something at him. With steel in her hand . . .

Yet whether or not he was right—and perhaps the will of the gods *was* harder to guess than it had seemed to her when she rode toward the enemy—he had certainly bound her as tightly as a babe swaddled in a cradle. She had to live. Her only choice was whether she lived with her secret still hers, or with her shame brought before a mortal enemy.

"By Yatar, by Vothan, By Hestia, and by the lives of Mikail my son and Isobel my daughter, I swear to do myself no harm while I—enjoy Prince Strymon's hospitality."

"Yatar and Christ bless you, my lady."

Tylara could not quite keep from smiling. "I think we have spent time enough guessing what the gods may wish. Would it be possible to bring me a meal? I did not swear not to tear your arm out of its socket and start gnawing on it if I am not fed!"

"Prince Strymon has ordered that you and Lord Morrone be fed from his own table. I shall bring something immediately."

"I thank you, Apelles."

The priest was out the door and the woman and the guard were coming back through it before Tylara realized that she hadn't asked about Lord Morrone. Well, Morrone's skull was thick enough. *He'd few enough wits to begin. I hope no more were knocked out of his head.*

✢ ✢ ✢

Her meal was meat broth thickened with barley and a small piece of bread. Apelles cheerfully ignored her demands for three times as much, but at least allowed her to feed herself. As she ate the guard unshuttered the room's one window. Tylara saw a manure pile, a pigsty, and beyond it the True Sun setting. Apelles brought her a larger cup of the same sleeping draught—a silver cup with Prince Strymon's stylized megaron device on it—and from somewhere a thin brown and white cat appeared and curled up at the foot of the bed. She drank the sleeping draught thirstily and stretched out under the furs.

As she did, she realized that since her talk with Apelles she had been behaving as if the gods would allow her to put both Caradoc's death and the battle behind her. Those debts were still unpaid, and now she had new ones to the kin of the archers who'd died trying to save her.

That was at least one good reason for staying alive. Another was to learn about Prince Strymon's camp, his host, perhaps even his plans. There should be a way to send word to her husband and Wanax Ganton.

Have the gods judged that my punishment is to leave me alive to undo the damage I have done?

✢ ✢ ✢

The motion of Tylara's litter changed as the bearers broke step to cross the wooden bridge over the stream known as Sigbard's Run. Tylara parted the side curtains and looked out. The water level was lower and the current was slower than seven days ago when she was first carried out of the farmhouse they'd given her.

This was no surprise; there'd been no rain for twelve days, and the mud that had held up the baggage trains of both sides was now gone except in low-lying spots. In the hills, the survivors of her Tamaerthans and Morrone's levies would no longer be eating cold food and sleeping fitfully in sodden rags. They would be preparing to ambush the Melteman patrols, loot Melteman supply wagons, drive off cattle and even horses, and slit the throats of unwary Melteman sentries.

They'd done plenty of that already using the weather for cover. *Tamaerthan clansmen and southern outlaws. It wasn't so long ago that Drantos considered all of Tamaerthon as no more than a home for bandits. But it is no wonder that I get black looks from Strymon's officers. They must have lost much to our raiders.*

Rick had once called it "guerrilla warfare." Chivalry and peasantry alike had harassed Sarakos and Parsons. Now it would be Strymon's turn. Doubtless there would be a reckoning for this, but until then Tylara could take comfort both in her own returning health and strength and in the knowledge that her people were helping Rick win this war.

She had no doubt at all that he would win. *The gods do not hate him. He had no part in my sin. And only the gods could best him.*

It was barely a hundred paces from the bridge to the wealthy peasant's house that had been turned into quarters for her. Strymon had offered her hospitality in Bheroman Ajacias' castle, but the idea of accepting so much as a crust of bread from that traitor revolted her.

That would be reason enough, but she also suspected that Ajacias was more the ally of Prince Teodoros, Strymon's younger brother, than Prince Strymon. Strymon deserved his reputation for honor and chivalry. She was not so certain of his brother, and she feared the men around Prince Teodoros. She was particularly concerned about a burly Vothanite archpriest who spoke like a king's councilor and moved like a warrior. The little she'd heard him say showed that he knew far too much about Drantos, Tamaerthon, and even Rick's star warriors.

The litter bearers had brought her nearly to the house when half a score of riders reined in. The helmeted axemen surrounded a tall bareheaded man in silvered mail. His fair hair seemed to glow in the light of the rising True Sun. He wore a surcoat of Nikeian red, and an amber-hilted sword of state. Jewels flashed at his ear lobes. Tylara smiled; Prince Strymon could not be called vain about his good looks, be he did not exactly try to hide them either!

Tylara's smile faded when he dismounted. Prince Strymon's face was as friendly as a battle-helm.

"Welcome, my lord," Tylara said. "I bid you enter, but will you give me a moment?"

He nodded curtly and paced while Apelles helped Tylara inside to a settee and arranged a bright silk coverlet over her legs. When the bearers left, he stormed in unasked. "Leave us," he commanded Apelles.

"Your Highness," Tylara protested. "Apelles is a consecrated priest of Yatar. His oaths—"

"I know the oaths of a priest of Yatar. I also know that his master is Yanulf, Chancellor of Drantos, and that half the priests of Yatar follow him no matter what land they serve in."

Tylara bristled. "Do you doubt my honor?"

Strymon returned an encouraging ghost of his usual smile. "No more, my lady Eqetassa, than I doubt your beauty or the sharpness of your tongue. Do you doubt my wits? I wish to speak to you alone."

Tylara sighed. "Apelles, if you please—"

"Certainly, my lady. I will wait outside."

Apelles went out; two of Strymon's guards brought honeycakes, fine bronze cups set with seashells, a jug of water and another of wine. Another brought a small folding table fitted with ivory and silver. Strymon on campaign seemed half a Roman. He carried the luxuries of a Praetor, but he also fortified his camps, sent out scouts, paid attention to sanitation—and mixed his wine half with water.

Strymon did that now and filled their cups. Tylara sipped at hers. The brown and white cat who had adopted Tylara jumped up on the settee. Strymon absently broke off a piece of honeycake and gave it to the cat, who took it and jumped to the floor.

"My lady. I cannot imagine that you do not know that the survivors of your—of the Host of Drantos—continue to fight in the hills around us. Supplies and messengers are not safe unless they are escorted by five-score and more armed riders. Men have been sent gullfeathered to Vothan's House without ever seeing an enemy. Others have gone to sleep three under a blanket, and in the morning the one in the middle has awakened to find his comrades lying with their throats cut."

Tylara recalled hearing Rick speak of such a trick used on Earth, by warriors who swam into battle in the country called Vietnam. "Surely you do not complain that my people are teaching yours the folly of sleeping on watch? When they have done their work, you will have a smaller host, but most assuredly a better one."

"This is not a matter for jesting. I want it stopped!"

"That is easily done. Release us and return to your own lands. Do that and we will harry you no more."

"There could be a blood price for such obstinacy. Not your blood alone, either."

"Threats, Highness? Against your prisoners? I take it you are not satisfied with the songs the bards will sing of your combat with Morrone. You wish them to sing of your dishonor as well."

"Lady—"

"Your Highness, your can do nothing to me, or Lord Morrone, that will win you the smallest victory over the men in the hills. What you can do is make certain of war to the knife. You believe you have won a victory because you bested a foolish King's Companion and a woman. Wait until you face not the chivalry of Drantos, but Romans, Tamaerthan pikes and archers who have bested Romans, Great Guns and muskets—and star weapons. Wait until you face the Wanax Ganton who is your equal, and my Lord Rick who is the master of us all! When you have bested *them* you may proclaim victory."

"Enough!"

Tylara smiled. "Forgive me, Your Highness. I do not doubt your courage. I only warn you that if any harm comes to me, my Lord Rick will defeat your armies, and turn loose the clanless ones of Tamaerthon to pick Ta-Meltemos to bare bones, and this is as certain as anything mortal man can know."

"Your lord or the Wanax Ganton might not place so small a value on the lives and limbs of those I hold. Are you sure that you can speak for them?"

"Hah. Who can speak for a Wanax? But do you think I have

married a fool, or that I have lived with him these years and borne him his children, and yet do not know him? For him may I speak; and I tell you, he knows terrible things, and in his anger he will use them against all of you. You have doubtless heard that he and his men are not of this world. I tell you that is true, and I tell you beware harming what little he holds of value here lest he let this entire world go to its doom."

Strymon looked thoughtful. He took a paper from his glove, glanced at it, then returned it. "My lady, many have marched against me. None have returned. I stand on your land, not you on mine—"

Tylara laughed. "Forgive me, Highness. Again I do not doubt your skills. Yet ask yourself this. Sarakos with the aid of the traitor Parsons was able to conquer Drantos, yet he could not hold it. Three days after Lord Rick killed Parsons he drove the host of the Five Kingdoms from our land. What can my husband do now that he has gathered his strength? I tell you that you do not know what you face.

"Consider the star weapons, the least of which can strike down a man four stadia away. There is another, named for a king from another world, and with that Lord Rick can tear a castle gate to splinters from twice bowshot. How long can your castles stand against that?"

"That will depend, I suppose, on whether there are more gates than this—Carl Gustav—has bombs."

Tylara's bowels went cold. Strymon knew the very name of the star weapon! What else might he know? And from what source?

For a moment she toyed with the idea of attempting Strymon's life herself. *Ridiculous. It is dishonor, and what he knows, his brother knows.* "That is one of my husband's weapons. He has more. Many more," Tylara said. "Your spies have told you truly, that the star weapons are like bows—useless when there are no more arrows. It is even true that we do not have so many arrows as you have castles. We do have quite enough to batter down any castle unfortunate enough to shelter you or any of your family. And surely you have heard—no. I have said enough. But consider all these things, before you lift a hand against any of your prisoners." She laughed. "My Tamaerthans in the hills will be flattered that you have found them so great a menace that you contemplate dishonor."

Tylara sipped wine and watched as Strymon poured more for himself.

He took his time doing it, and when he turned, his face was

expressionless. Then he smiled. "I knew it would not work. Matthias thought it worth trying. My lady, I contemplated nothing dishonorable, but could I have persuaded you I did, you might have given orders to your men." He shrugged. "I owed the attempt to my soldiers."

Tylara began a smile, then wondered. Would this work against Morrone? But there was nothing she could do about that, at least not while Strymon was watching. Tylara sipped more wine and reached for a honeycake. She had not quite touched the plate when Strymon laid a hand on her wrist.

"A moment, my lady. Where is the cat?"

"You gave her a piece of cake, the shameless little beggar! I have not seen her since."

"Nor have I." Strymon put the plate of cakes on a bench out of Tylara's reach, looked around the room, then knelt down and looked under the settee. A moment later she heard a muttered oath, and he straightened up, holding the cat in both hands.

The cat hung limp, eyes closed and bloody foam dripping from her mouth.

22

Strymon stared at the dead cat in horror. "Guards! To your prince!"

The door crashed open and five of Strymon's guards tried to come through a door that would have been snug for two. They regrouped and entered, Apelles behind them. One of the guards raised his axe and stared around the room for the threat to his prince.

"Hold! Guard this lady!" Strymon gestured and the guard lowered his weapon. Two of the guards took positions at the head and foot of the settee. Two others ranged themselves on either side of the door.

"Send for Gythras," Strymon snapped. The fifth guard saluted and ran from the room. Apelles knelt to examine the dead cat.

Tylara watched Strymon pace furiously up and down the room. *He must be innocent. No man is that good an actor. Besides, he knows my death would not drive my archers from the hills. I am in danger, certainly, but not from him.*

The fifth guard returned with a blue-robed priest of Yatar. "Ah, Gythras." Strymon gestured toward Apelles and the cat. "Find out what killed it."

Gythras knelt beside Apelles. The two healers poked at the cat and exchanged a few muttered words. Then Gythras rose and sniffed at one of the remaining honeycakes.

"Goat's-ear root, most probably, Your Highness. Its flavor is musky, but sweet enough to blend well with honey."

"Indeed," said Strymon. Gythras picked up the dead cat and the plate of honeycakes and went out. Strymon nodded to his guards. They left, taking Apelles with them. The prince closed the door, pulled the bench close to the settee, and sat down.

"My lady. I ask you to believe that I would not dishonor myself by an act such as this."

"I never doubted that," Tylara said. "But I think less honorable men have power over one of your cooks."

Strymon smiled grimly. "The cooks will be questioned." He opened the door and spoke to one of his guards. "Put all the camp cooks under guard. Bring the Master of the Kitchen to my tent and wait for me there."

"Your Highness." The man saluted and left.

"And until the cooks are questioned, you'd prefer that I not ask questions that you cannot honorably answer? Very well, Your Highness," Tylara said. "But I urge you to take some thought for your own safety. Do we know whether the poison was meant for me or for you?"

Strymon's expression softened, and Tylara smiled back. *No man, prince or not, can entirely resist hearing that a fair woman prefers him alive.*

"Both of us, I think. Last night I made no secret that I would visit you this morning."

Tylara nodded slowly. "Your Highness, if it is in your power, will you return my star weapon to me? The next attempt on my life will probably come with steel. I am a bedridden woman with only one hand fit for use, but with the star weapon in that hand I may give a good account of myself. Its—magic, let us call it"—he lifted one eyebrow at that, and she answered with a grin—"its magic is too weak for me to harm anyone outside this chamber. I could hardly injure your guards, let alone your host, and as for fighting my way out of the camp—I could sooner fly to Castle Dravan by waving my arms!"

"You ask much."

"You risk much. If I am killed, you will never be free of suspicions."

"True." He thought for a moment longer. "Very well. You may have your star weapon. With my thanks for the opportunity to examine it."

Of course Strymon would have taken the Colt apart. *And ten crowns says it'll come back with seven cartridges instead of eight. Ah, well. Rick always said it would not be very long before everyone knew the secret of firepowder weapons, and victory would go to whoever made the best use of what everyone had!*

Tylara spoke with elaborate casualness. "I trust you did so with due care."

Strymon tilted his head in an ironic little nod. "I am as you see intact. . . . Would you convey to Lord Rick my request that such a star weapon form part of your ransom?"

"Yes, I can convey that request. But only Lord Rick can grant it."

"Of course."

"By Yatar and Vothan, Your Highness, I swear that none but your enemies shall face the magic of the star weapon as long as I am in your camp."

Strymon raised Tylara's hand to his lips. There was a knock at the door. Strymon dropped her hand and stood, one hand on the hilt of his sword.

"Come." The door opened and Apelles came in.

"My lady, I—" he began.

"It's all right, Apelles. His Highness will grant us a few minutes so that you may tend my wounds." She smiled up at Strymon. "He will bring my star weapon to me after I have dined."

"My lady." Strymon nodded and left, and Apelles began to loosen the bandages on her leg.

"Tell me, Apelles. How soon will I be able to walk again?"

"At least seven days, my lady. Perhaps sooner, but I doubt it."

Tylara sighed. She might need the Colt as more than just a symbol of Strymon's honorable intentions.

✣ ✣ ✣

The lamp hanging by the door had long since burned dry. Tylara's searching eyes found only darkness, yet she was sure she'd heard a sound, either from above or from outside the door.

The sounds came again. Above *and* outside. Tylara drew the Colt from under the furs and snapped off the safety. A round was already in the chamber. She had only six others. Yatar grant that she should need no more.

The sound from above now sounded like the scampering of rats. Then she smelled smoke. Had someone fired the roof thatch?

A moment later—

"Fire! Fire! Guards, save Lady Tylara!"

The sounds outside turned into stamping feet and fists pounding on the door. Then—

"No, Lady Tylara! Treachery, treachery, treach—!" Apelles shouted from outside.

She could not let herself think of what might have happened to cut him off. She had the Colt raised and aimed as the door flew open and two men in the colors of Strymon's guards plunged through.

She shot the first man in the stomach and he slammed backward into the second to knock him off his feet. Outside the door a third man was gathering himself to leap over the two fallen ones, when yet another man seemed to fall from the sky onto him. The last man left on his feet was unslinging a short bow when Tylara shot him in the face.

Apelles staggered into the room. Blood streamed down one arm but he held a knife in his good hand, and swore terrible oaths in most unpriestly language. A dozen and more of Strymon's host ran up to the door. Apelles examined each before letting him in, but even so the room was suddenly full of people. Tylara snapped the safety on the Colt. Her hand was shaking so badly she was afraid she might fire by accident.

She did not stop shaking until Prince Strymon appeared in a sleeping robe with a sword belted on over it. Gythras was behind him, followed by two servants laden with bottles and instruments. From overhead the crackling of flames gave way to the hiss of water, and Tylara smelled steam instead of smoke.

The three would-be murderers who could walk were led away. As Gythras examined Tylara, Strymon kneeled over the two she'd shot. He frowned at the man with the belly wound, then went over to the one shot in the head.

"All the gods be merciful! I did not think . . ."

Two of the guards held up the dead man. He looked as Rick had told her to expect—a bloody hole in front, and the back of his head nearly blown away, so that blood and brains oozed down onto his clothes.

Gythras turned away from his examination to stare. So did Apelles. Then Apelles took a stumbling step forward and toppled to the floor. Gythras turned to him, and muttered imprecations about priests who thought they were knights and didn't have the sense to admit they were wounded.

When Gythras had finished, litters were brought for both Tylara and Apelles. Gythras mixed a sleeping draught and handed it to her. As the bearers carried her out of the house, she fell asleep—but it was a sleep troubled by nightmares, in which Prince Strymon kept turning into the High Rexja Toris, into one of the *Shalnuksis*, and worst of all, into the Wanax Sarakos!

It was the last that made her wake screaming and stay awake until just before the rising of the True Sun.

✦ ✦ ✦

When Tylara awoke, the walls around her were canvas without windows and the door was a hanging now tied half-back. It revealed a patch of trampled bare ground with Strymon's guards standing practically shoulder to shoulder. Beyond them she could see another tent striped in Strymon's colors.

It was clear that she had been moved into the royal compound. She might not be as safe here as Strymon hoped; not unless Prince Teodoros and his people had been moved out of the compound. Still, this was more evidence of Prince Strymon's concern.

Gythras arrived with a speed that suggested he had been waiting outside for her to awake. He and a priestess of Hestia examined Tylara from head to toe.

"By the mercy of Yatar, she is unharmed," Gythras said.

"I thank my Lady Hestia—"

It seemed to Tylara as if they were trying to reassure themselves as much as her. Well, they had some right in the matter; their fate would not be pleasant if she died, and her waking screaming must have been heard from one end of the camp to the other.

They took their time, and when they left, Price Strymon himself entered. His hair was uncombed and he had not shaved. There was both soot and blood under his nails.

He drew a stool close enough to the bed so that he didn't need to speak above a whisper, and sat without asking her leave. After a moment he got up again and untied the hanging to close the tent door.

"Your priest Apelles lives," Strymon began. "He has a long and deep cut in his shoulder and arm, and has lost much blood. He has already told Gythras how to drive out the fester-devils from water, wounds, and bandages, and his wounds seem the better for it. He will still be writing letters left-handed for a time, though—unless his wounds fester after all."

"That is with Yatar and Hestia, is it not?" said Tylara. She sensed an uneasiness in Strymon that went beyond the danger to his honor.

"It is, if Apelles and the other healers who have dealt with your wounded have been told the truth by the starmen. It is said that in casting out the fester-devils as Apelles taught us, we let in other and worse devils."

No need to ask who said that. She shrugged. "It is the way he treats me. Do you see me infested with devils?"

"No— My lady, why would you allow your enemies to learn this great secret? If this is true, many soldiers will live who should have died. My soldiers."

"My Lord Rick has commanded that this wisdom—and much other that he knows—be given freely to all on this world," Tylara said proudly. "He says that knowledge is not to be hoarded as a miser hoards gold, but spread to the winds."

"I—see," Strymon said. "Now, my lady, are you well enough to discuss serious matters?"

"I am quite well. Haven't the healers told you?"

Strymon reddened. "Forgive me, but in the night we heard you screaming—louder than the wretches we were questioning about the attempt on your life. Gythras would not tell me, but it seems to me—"

"It was a nightmare, Your Highness. An old nightmare, from a time I thought I had put behind me—"

The wide grey eyes were suddenly as cold and hard as the stones of Castle Dravan. "Then the tales of how Sarakos dishonored you are no tales." It was not a question.

Tylara swallowed twice before she could say, "No. But he is dead and food for worms."

"Worms that fed on Sarakos' corpse probably died of it." His face twisted. "I have never been wholly easy in my mind, over refusing to serve under Sarakos. Had I been there, I might have prevented—My lady, I can only beg your pardon. I gave too much thought to defending my own honor, and not to how I might defend that of others."

"You could not have known that Sarakos would be a fool as well as a brute—" she began, but Strymon raised his hand to stop her.

"I cast nothing on the High Rexja, but his eldest son always behaved like one begotten in a kitchen-midden. I cannot in honor say that I should not have known better."

"Your own honor is pure as fire, Strymon. That makes you less than the best judge of those who have none."

Unbidden and surprising, but not unwelcome, an old thought entered Tylara's mind. How would matters have gone, if Strymon had been willing to march against Drantos as a captain under Sarakos?

Rather ill for Drantos, she suspected; the horse and foot of Ta-Meltemos would have given Sarakos a third again his strength, apart from Strymon's skill. The contest in the field would have been foreordained. Yet without Sarakos free to indulge his bloodlust and treachery, might not more of the men of Drantos have seen surrender as an honorable alternative?

And her own fate—what of that? She might not be a widow at all, for Strymon would never have done to her Lamil as Sarakos did, cutting his throat like a pig while a dozen men held him. Strymon would have faced Lamil in single combat, almost certainly defeated him, but left him alive if he was prepared to yield at all.

If by some chance Lamil had died—Strymon would hardly have slaughtered the men of Castle Dravan. That would have left Bheroman Trakon alive to press his suit. Or perhaps Strymon himself would have courted her. His first wife had died bearing him a daughter, the year before the war began. She could see herself captured a little at a time by his charm, his grace, his good looks, his concern for her honor as well as his own. . . .

And then what would have happened to the starmen, if she had not been in need of an ally to destroy Sarakos and regain Chelm, and if Sarakos had not been in need of someone like Colonel Parsons to put down the guerrillas in Drantos?

Were the gods as capricious as that, in sending fates to men and women? And if they were that capricious, how could anyone be sure what they demanded?

Another question for Yanulf—and now she realized that Strymon had begun an account of the night's events, while she was lost in dreams of how things might have been.

"—was able to buy men, but not men brave enough to simply storm into your room and shed your blood with their own hands. Had they done that, some would surely have died from the star weapon, but the rest would have killed you.

"As it was, they conceived an elaborate scheme and divided

themselves into three parties, all disguised as my guards. One party set fire to the roof. The second would rescue you from the fire, and when they were safely out of the house the third would dash up and stab you. Even with all these foolish complications, they might have done their work if it had not been for Apelles. He saw that the second party were not the new watch of guards, but impostors, and gave the alarm. The man who wounded him also knocked down the ladder in the struggle. One man fell from the ladder and the other man was trapped and burned to death on the roof."

Tylara could not keep back a smile. Her would-be murderers seemed to have been a pack of prize fools. Had Yatar addled the murderers' wits to save her?

"Have you—is there anything you may tell me of who hired those men?"

"Matthias, priest of Vothan, fled the camp before True Sunrise," said Strymon. "Several of his men went with him. They passed the northernmost of our outposts before the alarm, and told the officer of the guard that they were on urgent business for the High Rexja."

"I suppose that can be called the truth," said Tylara. "Fleeing from the headsman is certainly best done in haste."

Strymon's smile was forced. "My lady, how much do you know of Ta-Meltemos?"

She shrugged. "We hear stories—"

"Yes, yes. Stories you are too polite to repeat. They are true. My fathers seems in good health, and has a sweet and forgiving nature. But—" Strymon swallowed hard. "He cannot find his way from bedroom to throne room without a guide, and lately we do not even dare have him appear on state occasions."

"I had heard," Tylara said gently.

"The last time, he rose from the throne to question the High Marshal of Ta-Boreas about sweets and children's toys."

"Then you govern the land."

"I confess I do not. I have always been a soldier. You must understand, until recent years Wanax Palamon was as good a king as ever ruled our land. It was only when he—changed that Toris took new advisors, and the first wars between Drantos and the Five Kingdoms began."

"Your brother—"

"Was much younger then. Lady, Ta-Meltemos is ruled by Chancellor Rauros. He was sent to us by Issardos, and found much favor with my father during his declining years. Now he is sometimes—Lady this is not easily said. There are times when Palamon recognizes no one but Rauros. Not even his sons."

"It cannot be easy, living in such a court. I see now why you and your brother would prefer the field. In your place I would do the same. Prince Strymon, do you believe that Rauros knows of this plot against your honor?"

Strymon pressed his lips into a thin line. "I do not know. But I will know."

"How?"

"Yes. That is the question, is it not? The only men I can trust are soldiers with no more skills at intrigue than I have."

You need a woman. I will find you one. But for now—"There are priests of Yatar whose loyalty is to honor and the gods. They might serve you well."

"Priests of this new religion?"

"It is not *new*, Highness. It is the religion of the starmen. We—New Christians—honor all the commandments of Yatar. We also recognize His Son, the Christ."

"I must think on this."

"Of course. For now, we must think again who is behind this plot. The High Rexja—"

"Again, I do not know. I can say nothing against the High Rexja. Nor can Teodoros."

"You asked him?"

"Yes, my lady. My brother says he doesn't know anything about plots." Strymon shrugged elaborately. "I would be surprised if he did. It is not in his nature."

"Issardos," Tylara said carefully.

Strymon nodded. "It would not surprise me if Chancellor Issardos had a hand in this. It would insure war to the death between Ta-Meltemos and Drantos. If half what you say of Lord Rick's abilities is true—and Matthias has, it seems, seen Lord Rick in battle—then I might well die in such a war. That would leave Teodoros on my throne."

"As Issardos' puppet," Tylara said softly.

Strymon sighed. "I love my brother, but—yes. I can trust Teodoros, but without me to guide him, he would be no match for Issardos. I doubt Issardos would care if Teodoros ruled over ruins and beggars, so long as he could not disturb the peace of the Five Kingdoms."

"Issardos is a fool," said Tylara. "The Time will disturb everyone's peace, and the skyfolk will do worse."

"Perhaps a fool, but a dangerous one." He straightened and squared his shoulders. "You will sleep and wake surrounded by my guards, and eat and drink nothing that has not been tasted first." Strymon raised his voice. "The baker who prepared the honeycakes and those who sought your life last night have an appointment with the headsman. Their bodies will be cast into the middens and their heads borne through the camp by heralds crying out 'Here be hardy traitors, who sought the lives of the Crown's prisoners.' "

Strymon looked around the tent, then lowered his voice to a true whisper. "That should discourage the faint-hearted. With Matthias gone the stouter spirits have no leader. If these measures are not enough, I swear by Yatar, Vothan, and Hestia that I will release you without a ransom and send you to your husband.

"Yet I would not do that before we have talked further. I have thought on what you said yesterday, and I have listened to my own priests of Yatar tell about the Time. It seems it has never been easy for the Five Kingdoms."

"This my husband says."

Strymon fell silent. Then he turned and paced the length of the tent. For a moment he stared at the tapestry of dragons spitting *skyfire* onto a melting city. Then he took a deep breath and turned to Tylara. "My lady, there may be ways to bring peace to the Realms of Drantos and Ta-Meltemos."

Tylara caught her breath. She was not wholly surprised. *But I thought it would take much longer.* Inwardly she thanked Matthias and Issardos for making her work easier.

Now I know why the gods spared me. Am I fit for this task? Dayfather, Warrior, Mother, you have given me back my life. Now give me strength and wisdom to use it in your service.

23

Rick Galloway looked at the map on the camp table in front of him. An inkwell, a dagger, and a pair of gloves held down the corners and kept the hot wind off the Westscarp from blowing the map as well as the dust all over his tent.

If maps had faces, Rick decided, this one would be wearing a sullen frown. He remembered telling his "General Staff" classes that you should always look at a map when you couldn't think of what to do next. The map would almost certainly tell you something.

The problem was that the map wouldn't always tell you anything you didn't already know. The map in front of him was a case in point. The blue pins showed the twelve thousand men of his Army of Chelm exactly where they'd been the day before, and the day before that, and the day before *that*. Same thing with the red pins for the twenty-odd thousand men in the High Rexja's Army of the West.

It wasn't the odds that bothered him. Two to one wouldn't be enough against star weapons and Tamaerthan archers. Some of the enemy captains were veterans of Sarakos' campaign, of course; they would have seen the archers and the weapons in action, and might have worked out tactics to make them less effective. Still, tactics wouldn't hold troops together if the one-oh-six started dropping WP into their formations from five stadia away. Black magic did a lot to wreck morale—at least the first time around. Rick was pretty sure that if he was willing to use up most of his ammo, he could keep the Army of the West from fighting again, at least for another six months.

The problem was, the High Rexja's captains had learned something even more important than how to meet star weapons—they'd learned scouting. Maybe they'd always known something—a lot of their cavalry was light stuff, mounted on centaurs or scrubby little hacks like Scots border horses. Those ponies could scatter across country and live on forage where heavy cavalry mounts would starve.

Certainly they'd learned a lot from a year of fighting the Westmen. The ones who'd survived were light cavalry of a quality that Rick had hoped he wouldn't see on the other side for quite a while. A dumb hope, he now realized—nobody but Yatar could make sure that your enemies would always learn slower than your friends, and Yatar seemed to be sitting this one out.

So he couldn't hope to take Captain General Ailas by surprise and defeat him in detail. Ailas would get word in time and pull his three "divisions" together. Or maybe he would hold with two and send one around Rick's rear. He might even just stay where he was, with his army divided into three for better grazing and water supplies, and wait for Rick to move—forward or back, it didn't matter. As long as Rick and his men were here in the west while the main army of the Five Kingdoms crunched into Drantos farther east, cutting it off from Rome, Ailas was helping win the war for his king without killing a single enemy!

It didn't help that only half of Rick's army was cavalry, and their mounts weren't in the best shape. The rains had stopped and now the streams were drying up. Before long Rick might have to move his army just to stay near water.

What I need is the Tamaerthans. Pikes and archers. Then I could move them up, and to hell with Ailas. He can attack good pikemen with heavy cavalry and get his lunch, or he can hang back and let the archers have at him. Either way—

None of it mattered though, because he didn't have the archers and pikemen. Ganton did. *And I hope to God he uses them better than Morrone did.*

I've got to get up there where the real action is. This is nothing but a holding operation.

As for here, he'd have to do something soon enough or withdraw without a fight, and that would lose him his reputation for invincibility. When that went, a lot of men would go with it, some because they wouldn't follow a leader who wasn't lucky, but a lot more because they didn't want to abandon their lands and would swear fealty to Toris to keep them.

Tylara wouldn't like that. *Wouldn't she ever.* If they ever sat down and had it out over what she'd done with her junior-grade ninjas, she'd be able to claim that he'd betrayed his own men and her just as badly. Stalemate—and from there Rick could see things going in a lot of different directions, most of them labeled "from bad to worse."

He looked at the map again. Lost reputation or not, he'd better put the army on the move before it *had* to move to stay near water. Then there'd be too good a chance of Ailas cutting him off from water and doing to at least a part of his army what Saladin did to the Crusaders at the Horns of Hattin.

The key to the campaign was that damned light cavalry. Ailas had been using it to scout in front of his army. Suppose he had to watch his rear? "Damn right," Rick said aloud. "Now who do I send?"

There weren't many candidates. The striking force had to be all cavalry, and there was a good chance it wouldn't be coming back soon. That ruled out leading them himself, but the leader would have to know modern tactics and weapons. Somebody who would be obeyed by both mercs and Tran soldiers, and knew the territory well enough to make a small force do the work of a big one.

Exactly one man matched that description.

"Jamiy!"

His orderly appeared and saluted with a click of heels. (Rick wondered how much of his income from bribes Jamiy spent on new boots that would click properly.)

"My compliments to Lord Murphy, and I'd be pleased to see him at once."

"Sir!"

✢ ✢ ✢

"—stays dry for another couple of days, the water in Dead Gunkel Lake will be down enough for us to march along here." Ben Murphy traced a line on the map with a forefinger.

"That's pretty close to Ailas' Second Division, isn't it?"

"There's a couple-three klicks of scrub and thicket just above the shore, between the lake and the camp. Even bandits don't go there very much. It's full of patches of quicksand and something that must be a wild cousin of madweed. Stinks like it, thorns like it, and it makes you crazy if you put the sap in booze."

"They could still get wind of your movement, and put an ambush at Gorgon Pass to cut you off."

"Not if we have a couple of heavy weapons along. Blast 'em out with a mortar or the Carl Gustav, and pick 'em off with one of the LMG's as they run." He frowned. "Mortar'd be better, I think. We don't have to have it in line of sight, now that I've taught some of the local kids flag signals."

"Sergeant Murphy, what the hell makes you think you're going to have any heavy weapons at all?"

"Captain, I've been thinking it over. I know there's a risk of losing them. but if I don't get some of the big magic, my people might start wondering if they're being sent on a suicide run. I may not be able to get them out of the camp, let alone keep them from running away if it hits the fan. And look, we can do a lot more damage with some heavy firepower. I think you want to stomp the bastards, not just tickle them!"

"What you really mean, Sergeant Lord Murphy, is that you *won't* order your people out without heavy-weapons support."

"Yeah, I guess so."

Sure. And now what? I don't need a crisis just now.

Jamiy's blank expression matched Murphy's. Rick hoped no one could ever pry this story out of him. It would make a story to tell, all right, one of the starmen bargaining with the Lord Rick. Shades of Parsons' and Gengrich's mutinies!

Not really, though. This wasn't an officer dealing with an insubordinate NCO, it was the Captain General of Drantos dealing with a bheroman who owed it to his people not to put them in needless danger. Murphy couldn't really do much else. *But I bet the SOB. is having fun.*

"Okay, Lord Murphy. You can't have the Carl Gustav anyway, and I'd rather give you some rifle grenades than an LMG. You shouldn't have to face a massed attack. We're damned sure going to have to if it comes to the crunch."

"Captain, if you give me an LMG I think I can beef up my force with Mad Bear's Westmen. They're used to raiding, and if they think they have some really big wizards on their side . . . Besides, I think they're not too happy sitting around camp half the time."

True enough. Despite Mad Bear's oaths, his three hundred warriors weren't really pulling their weight in the campaign, because nobody except Ben and a couple of his men-at-arms knew how to handle them. Not many in the army trusted them, either. There'd been a few nasty incidents—not too many, considering that a lot of men in the camp had lost homes and kin to the Westmen, but enough to worry about.

"I'm going to have to be sticky about the LMG, Lord Murphy. What about some rockets?"

The bargaining went on long enough for Rick to send Jamiy for more wine. They compromised: a section of First Rockets with twenty-five rounds, and Second Engineer's portable ballista with twenty bombs, but no LMG. Ben would take two hundred and twenty-five Westmen warriors; the rest would stay in camp to protect the women, children, and remounts.

"That's five hundred men, near enough," Rick said.

"Yes, sir—"

"It's enough. During the Civil War Ben Grierson covered Grant's advance on Vicksburg with not many more, and he had to face a lot better men than Ailas has."

"That right? Yes, sir. I'll try. There is one more thing—"

"Yeah?"

Murphy poured himself more wine. "I want your permission to swear blood-brotherhood with Mad Bear."

"Holy hell—why?"

"Captain, the thing is, if I'm blood-brother to Mad Bear he can never fight against you again unless I release him from his oath to me. Or you release me from mine to you."

Better not ask what else Murphy might feel released him from his oath to his Captain General. "You've got a point. Go on."

"It'll also help in picking the men to go, 'cause they'll all want to, and I may have to order some to stay behind. They'll take it better if I'm sworn to Mad Bear. Besides, I may have to order night marches. Mad Bear doesn't worry about demons as much as he used to, but a lot of his people do. If I've sworn never knowingly to put a warrior in the path of demons . . ."

"Okay, okay. Swear anything you think you can keep without having to rebel, only tell me about it afterward. Fair enough?"

"Sure thing, Captain."

After Murphy left, Rick considered the new lesson he'd just learned. It wasn't the stupid mercs who were dangerous. There were some who thought modern weapons could let them live as petty kings, but they weren't the problem. It was the smart ones, like Gengrich and Murphy. The ones who knew how to give loyalty as well as take it.

The ones who knew how to be feudal lords.

✦ ✦ ✦

Ben Murphy scrambled out of the warm, muddy stream. Rough-barked branches and sharp blades of grass scraped and pricked his bare skin. *Hell of a skinny-dipping party. Not a girl in sight. And Dirdre wouldn't like it if there was.* It was funny how possessive she was now that they were hitched. Even funnier was the fact that he didn't mind. Dirdre was a damned fine woman, even if she probably wouldn't ever forget Lafe Reznick. Reznick had been one hell of a good man. One of the happiest days of Ben's life at Westrook was the day they dedicated the shrine to Lafe, so that all the young men could come ask his spirit to bless their weapons and give them courage in war—

"Come, brother-to-be." Mad Bear's voice broke into his thoughts. "It is time to run."

They loped up the north side of the little valley. Ben gritted his teeth as the stones and scrub punished his bare feet, but pushed himself as hard as he could. He didn't want Mad Bear to have to hold back for him.

By the time they reached level ground, Ben had worked up enough of a sweat to satisfy any reasonable god. *Wouldn't old Father McCarthy have a fit if he heard that!*

He stumbled and nearly fell as a root snagged his left foot. He didn't need Mad Bear's warning cough to remind him that falling on his face now would bode very badly for their blood-brotherhood. Murphy emptied his mind and settled down to the run.

The Firestealer silvered the water of the stream behind them and gave enough light for Murphy to find a path through the scrub. Night birds called, but Murphy couldn't hear anything but his heartbeat, his pounding feet, and the rasp of his breath. *Benjamin Murphy, you're too damned old for these barbarian rituals.* It was too late now. Murphy realized that he'd been heading toward this oath and tomorrow's raid ever since the day Mad Bear and his tribe rode into Westrook.

It was the wives and kids that had done it. Murphy couldn't send them back with their men to be slaughtered by Walking Stone. He couldn't do that, any more than he could have said, "Sure, and I'll be glad to blow up a store full of grandmothers and children, as long as some of them are Protestants," when the two Provo gunmen came to reason with him.

He was three-quarters through the run. Another half-klick, then jump over the bonfire and enjoy the applause. Sure. *I never was much for jumping. Hope I can get over it without losing something Dirdre might miss.*

Closer up, the fire was less intimidating. It was burning in a little hollow, and the light reflected from the sides of the hollow made it look bigger than it was. Murphy flexed his knees as he reached the raised lip of the hollow. *Holy Geronimo! Here goes—*He sailed over the fire and landed on his feet. But the grass was slippery and the hill sloped away under him. He overbalanced and went down on hands and knees in front of two dozen Westmen.

Mad Bear landed on his feet beside him, but the tribesmen were already hissing and muttering. *Not too swift, Murphy. Now what? Ah.* He remembered one of the Captain's history lectures. He pulled up a clod of earth and grass with each hand, and held them high as he got to his feet.

"I hold this land I have taken with both hands," he shouted. "None of the High King's dogs will drive me from it. With my brother-to-be, I will whip them all back to their kennels." From the corner of his eye he saw Mad Bear grin. The hisses and mutters died away.

They drank water from the same cup, and sipped fermented mare's milk mixed with blood from the same bowl. They ate from the same piece of break sprinkled with salt. It was lousy bread, but Murphy didn't care. The ritual had called for him to fast from the setting of the Father Sun, and now he was hungry enough to eat a lamil raw.

Murphy took out his knife. *Mad Bear's knife, actually. Arekor gave it to him while he was a prisoner.* He held it high, then laid its blade against his wrist. A moment later he handed the blade to Mad Bear, who did the same. They pressed the cuts together while someone started beating a drum. Someone else piled more branches on the fire, and Mad Bear began to chant.

"Father Sun, Father Horse, Father Grass, see us."

"They see us," responded Murphy.

"We have crossed the water."

"This we have done."

"We have shed our sweat in the running."

"This we have done."

They recited how they had jumped over the fire, drunk water and milk, eaten bread, and mingled their blood. Finally Mad Bear shouted, "Are we not brothers?"

"We are brothers!" Murphy yelled, and the Westmen joined in. "They are brothers!" A young boy handed Murphy another bowl of fermented mare's milk. *Even without blood in it, it'll never replace Tullamore Dew. But at least this time I don't have to hold my nose.*

Elliot was playing the part of Murphy's kinsman. He came forward with Murphy's coveralls and rifle. Elliot wasn't going on the raid; Jack Beazeley, newly promoted to corporal, would be the senior man. *Jack's a good guy. If it comes to a fight, he's got his head screwed on with the nose to the front.*

Elliot handed Murphy his M-16. He slung it, sat down, and started in on a bowlful of raw horsemeat and wild-grass stew the youngster handed him. *The Savoy Grill this ain't. But we won't leave camp until just before True Sun-set tomorrow, and I'll probably be too busy to sit down and eat during the day.*

✤ ✤ ✤

"Colonel—"

"Dammit, Art, I'm going. I don't give a damn what they say about Prince Strymon's honor; he's got my wife and I'm going to go get her back."

"And just how are you going to do that?"

Rick laughed. "Good question, but look, I'm not doing a damn bit of good here. You can handle this situation as well as I can. Wait until Murphy draws off some of that cavalry, and keep the pressure on to take up the slack. This is a holding operation. We can't win the war out here."

"No, but we can sure lose it here, Colonel."

"Can, but won't. The worst that happens is you withdraw to Dravan. You can do that. *I* can't, without everybody thinking I've lost my touch."

Mason looked thoughtful. "You know, that just about makes sense."

"I'll tell you something else that makes sense. I know how to handle Tamaerthan pikes and archers. Ganton doesn't, but he's got them."

"Yeah. Okay, I buy that. But damn all, Colonel, those ironhats won't obey me—"

"Sure they will, for all you have to do. Look, we sent all the big cheese types off to Ganton. All you've got to deal with are some minor barons and city fathers. They'll *want* somebody to tell them what to do. If you can't do that as chairman of a council of war, I've promoted the wrong man."

"Maybe you—"

"And don't give me that crap. Look, Art, all we're doing here is keeping Ailas from coming into Drantos by the back door, and at the same time making him keep his army here instead of going over to join Strymon's force headed for Edron. He wins just by existing, but so do we! And don't tell me you can't do that as well as I can, because I don't want to hear it."

"Colonel—"

"Art, I'm taking a couple of squadrons and getting the hell out of here, and you're going to shut up and soldier."

24

The Wanax Ganton reined in at the foot of the gallows. He looked up as a gust of wind rattled the dangling chains. *Ajacias will be hanged here. I think I shall build a new gallows for him. Then his ghost will not trouble the good men he killed here.*

Of course the Christians said that a man like Ajacias would go to Hell and suffer torments from the Devil until the end of time. It pleased Ganton to imagine Ajacias spending eternity in the hands of a being like the Roman *quaestionarii. But does that mean I may take no vengeance on the wretched traitor myself? I shall have to ask Octavia or Archbishop Polycarp.*

The Demon Star silhouetted horsemen on the crest of the hill. Lord Enipses and Lord Hilaskos were forming up patrols. Each led a hundred lances, charged above all things with the Wanax's safety. With Strymon's camp only fifty stadia away and his scouts perhaps no farther than the other side of the hill, a century of lances was none too few.

A voice called the challenge and Lord Drumold replied. Someone else observed loudly that if a certain misbegotten son of a she-goat was late serving the Wanax's dinner, in the morning he'd find himself serving the Wanax's hounds.

Ganton called a squire to hold his horse and dismounted. He wanted to set a good example for those of his knights whose pride in their shiny-bright armor kept them in the saddle, never mind how their preoccupation with their looks wearied their horses. Hadn't the bheromen and knights of the Wanax of Frankia lost a great battle to the Wanax of Angeland by doing just that? Lord Rick had told him such a story, and his tales of battle rang true, even when he himself had not been in the field. To be sure, Lord Rick spoke of battles as though he had been in all of them. *To have been in so many he would have to be three hundred years old. No matter. Those are fine stories for a winter night, and they give soldiers courage and trust in our captain general.*

The Lord Rick is as wise in war as if he really had been a soldier for centuries, and so far he has freely given his wisdom to the Realm of Drantos. Yatar, Vothan, and Christ grant that he continue.

Food and Lord Drumold arrived at the same time. Ganton and Drumold drew a little apart and ate their sausage, bread, and cheese in silence. It was a cold meal. Ganton had forbidden fires with the enemy this close, at least until the Second Division arrived tomorrow and the army was complete.

"Mergil," Ganton called softly.

"My lord?"

"Go to the duty commander and have him send two squadrons of Hussars to patrol the roads between the First Division and the Second."

"Ye suspect my son may have forgotten?" Drumold asked.

Ganton listened for any tone of resentment but heard none. "Well, my lord, with the enemy so close in front, perhaps my lords Balquhain and Teuthras have not given thought to the rear. We are all still learning the new ways of war. But I am Wanax, and if any important thing is left undone, it will be on my head."

"Aye," Drumold muttered. "We all learn from my daughter's husband." He went back to his sausages and cheese.

And I thank Yatar for this alliance. We need the clansmen in this war. "Not that Strymon can place any great force between Balquhain and Teuthras," Ganton said. "Our scouts will warn us if Strymon sends out a troop of any size."

Drumold grunted.

"But it does not take any large force of cavalry to ravage our supplies. We will need all our firepowder, and fodder for the horses—"

"Aye, lad—Majesty," Drumold said. He chuckled. "And I too have commanded on nights before battles. 'Tis no easy thing."

They heard the staff officer ride away to carry Ganton's orders to the Hussars, then moments later the sound of galloping hoofbeats reached them from the far side of the hill. Ganton stood and lifted his battle-axe. Drumold continued with his sausages.

"Who is there?" the sentry demanded.

"Messenger from Lord Balquhain, for the Wanax Ganton!"

Indistinct mumbling, then several horses moved on at a trot. Ganton laid down his axe and sat again on his saddle as the messenger reached him.

"Majesty, Majesty! A message for you. An urgent message! I am bidden—"

"You are bidden to stop stammering and give me the message. The sooner the better." Out of the corner of his eye, Ganton saw Drumold trying not to smile.

"Yes, Majesty. Prince Strymon has released the Eqetassa Tylara do Tamaerthon and enough of our captive knights to form an escort of honor. They have met with our scouts. Lord Balquhain will furnish them with fresh mounts and send them to you guarded by a squadron of his Hussars."

Drumold opened his mouth and dropped a piece of cheese. The Wanax smiled to himself and turned away. *Give him a moment to compose himself. He has known for some time that his daughter was alive, and we heard from the priests of Yatar that she is well, but who can know? And there is the evil rumor that Tylara went alone to charge Strymon's cavalry at Piro's Hill. That must be a lie, but it also must have given her father many sleepless nights.*

"My Lord Mac Clallan Muir. Will you ride with me to greet the Eqetassa?" Drumold's face gave Ganton his answer.

"Was there any word of Lord Morrone?" It was said he'd survived the battle, but wounds and captivity might have done for him.

"I am bidden to tell you that the Lord Morrone is alive and well and giving honorable service to the Realm." The messenger looked at Drumold, then at Ganton. "Your Majesty, this was for your ears only—"

Drumold swore and Ganton glared. "Pray cease insulting Lord Drumold. Or have you some reason to suggest that his son should not trust him?"

The messenger gulped. "Pardon, Majesty. Lord Balquhain says further that the Eqetassa brings an urgent message from Prince Strymon, heir to the Wanax of Ta-Meltemos."

"Indeed." Ganton spoke to keep his mouth from gaping open in a manner quite unfitting to a Wanax. What could his enemy want? "Then it is all the more important that we bring the Lady Eqetassa safely home." He took a deep breath and squared his shoulders. "

"Squires! To horse!"

✣ ✣ ✣

Ganton, Drumold, Balquhain, and Tylara huddled near the tiny fire. A score of bodyguards stood just beyond earshot, and the others patrolled farther out.

"Peace," Ganton said. "On what terms?"

"Aid in surviving the Time," Tylara said. "Alliance against invaders, and a promise of aid after the Demon has withdrawn from our skies."

"And in return?" Ganton prompted.

"Ta-Meltemos withdraws from Drantos. Majesty, Prince Strymon may even lend his personal aid to Drantos. He has no love for Chancellor Issardos and his agent Matthias."

"You speak of Prince Strymon's promises. He is not Wanax of Ta-Meltemos. Not *yet*."

Tylara forced a smile. "Majesty, Prince Strymon betrays neither Wanax nor father. The stories we have heard are true. Wanax Palamon has the mind of a child."

Ganton shivered. "Yatar grant me death before that. It seems that we must meet, Prince Strymon and I, and soon. The loss of Prince Strymon's army will do great harm to Toris."

"Losing Strymon as a general will do even more," Balquhain said.

"That is so. Now tell me, Lady Tylara, why was Morrone not released?"

Tylara sipped hot tea and brandy. "He did not wish it, Majesty. Lord Morrone said that my own release might be managed without offending the High Rexja's captains or exposing Strymon's suit for peace with Drantos. But Lord Morrone could not honorably accept his own unransomed release without that of all the other prisoners. That would surely give the enemy more than a hint of our plans."

"Arrh. We could do wi' a bit less honor an' a bit more common sense." Drumold spat into the fire.

Ganton's face was unreadable. Tylara decided it didn't much matter whether she knew what he was thinking. *One thing's certain. There's very little of the boy about our Wanax.* She found that thought oddly comforting.

"I continued to talk with Strymon," Tylara said. "He fears no man, but he truly fears the Time."

"As he should," Ganton said.

"As he should. Then we received word that the vanguard of Toris' great host was on the march to join us. We had also heard that the Host of Drantos was on its way north. Prince Strymon feared that battle was inevitable, and once our forces were engaged, peace might be impossible.

"Then Morrone escaped."

"Escaped?" Ganton asked. "Surely he had given his parole—"

"It seems he had not. It had never been asked. From the moment they lifted him from where he fell he had been treated as guest, not prisoner—"

Balquhain chuckled. "An easy mistake."

"So where is Morrone?" Ganton demanded.

"I know only the plan he told me," Tylara said. "He intended to gather as many of his southern forces as he could, and any clansmen who might follow him, and go north to harass Toris and delay his march."

Ganton smiled for the first time. "There are places north of the Sutmarg where fifty archers can stand off an army for a whole day. Perhaps we should send reinforcements."

"Aye," Tylara said. *And I did that once, in the war against Sarakos. Long ago.*

"Indeed," said Balquhain. "But how should we make our way back across the Sutmarg, if the rains come again and the rivers rise?"

Tylara looked at her brother with new respect. He would not have asked that question two years ago. *My lord husband, you will have more and stranger monuments than you can imagine.*

"All the better, for neither the enemy's host nor Morrone's men will be able to cross the Sutmarg," Ganton said. "We shall have all the time we need to parley with Strymon, and prepare a warm reception for the enemy when they *do* cross."

"And it were me of the older days, I'd not be returning at all without a victory to dim the memory o' Piro's Hill," Drumold said.

"So Morrone has ridden north, then?" Ganton asked.

"Three days ago. His escape delayed my release. Prince Strymon was not pleased to have a wolf free behind him. But then the prince realized that if we waited any longer, Toris might send south a band of horse too strong for my escort. We rode out of the camp as the Demon Sun was rising."

"And Apelles? Yanulf will ask after him," Ganton said.

"He is in no danger now that Matthias and his minions have fled. He stayed to tend the sick and wounded."

"And to send us information as he can," Drumold said. " 'Twas how we knew ye'd not been harmed."

"Then we must act swiftly," Ganton said. "Before Toris merges his army with Strymon's."

"Majesty, there is more you must know—"

"My lady, it will wait until morning. Your rest cannot." Ganton stood. "Lord Enipses!"

"Majesty!"

"Take your lances and join the scouts. Our patrols must be able to fight an enemy as well as to find him. For the next three days you must prevent any enemy spies from leaving our realm alive. This is most important."

"Majesty."

"Lord Hilaskos, you will ride north with me tomorrow to view the battlefield my rangers have chosen. We must be able to fight either, neither, or both of the foreign hosts in the land of Drantos. That will mean bringing up the Great Guns as well as the Musketeers—yes, Lord Enipses?"

"Surely, Your Majesty will not ride north with less than the entire host? At least let me come with you."

"I have given you your task. Do you refuse it?"

"No, Majesty."

"Good."

"And what of treachery?" Balquhain asked quietly. "I have never met the man who could deceive my sister, but there is always the first time."

✦ ✦ ✦

Drumold glared at his son, but his frown showed his concern.

"I know I was not deceived," Tylara said. "In any event I will go with Your Majesty."

"That you will *not*," Ganton said. "I will be surrounded by the best fighting men of Drantos and Tamaerthon. Nothing that can catch us can beat us. Now, peace. Unless there is more—discussion?"

No one spoke. Whatever doubts remained, no one would give them tongue in front of a Wanax who had clearly made up his mind.

Ganton called his staff officers to arrange foraging parties and other details of battle. Tylara drew her cloak more tightly about her.

Drumold stood. "You're exhausted, lass. Come."

She remembered her father leading her from the tiny council fire to a tent that seemed miles away. She remembered his laying her on a bed as if she were a child, and pulling furs over her until at last she stopped shivering. She remembered swallowing most of a cup of hot wine. Then she remembered nothing more.

✛ ✛ ✛

The True Sun had risen and nearly set again when Tylara awoke to see her father sitting beside her bed. His eyes were red with lack of sleep, and for the first time she saw how much of the grey in his beard had turned to white.

She smiled. "Thank you, Father."

He smiled back. "And what good would I be, lass, if I couldna help ye in a time of need? The gods willing, I'll be ready to hand for many a year yet." He handed her a bowl of porridge and watched as if determined to force it into her by sheer will. When she had emptied the bowl, Drumold took it from her, stood up, and went outside briefly. When he returned, the smile was gone.

"This is the Wanax's own tent, so I much doubt there'd be any ears about that shouldna be. Still, best to be sure. . . ."

The frown deepened. "Daughter, there have been rumors of what ye did near the end of the battle. Or rather, rumors of what ye wouldna do, which is to let yourself be saved to fight another day. I ask ye for the truth."

Tylara wanted to weep with sheer relief, to learn that her father had guessed so little of the truth, and that little something she could talk about freely. A moment later she was weeping in her father's arms.

When she was done, he found a cloth to wipe her face and pulled a stool close to the bed. "I willna say that a lost battle is nothing. But no orders of yours began that battle. 'Twas Morrone, who never did know the value of the clansmen. I am thinking that the Wanax will have aye to say to him on that."

"But, Father, I obeyed him."

"I should hope ye did! Would ye be like Dughuilas, always disputing orders until someone sent him to dispute wi' Vothan?"

Tylara shuddered, but Drumold did not notice. "I'd disown ye, an' ye did that! Daughter, I've gone myself where you went the day of Piro's Hill. Aye. Long before you were born, I led the clansmen against Roman slave raiders. I led them back too, but many fewer than I led out.

"I thought the gods had turned from me, and long I stood on the great cliff looking down at the sea. But I could no hear the gods' voices clear, only my own shame, and it seemed a coward's deed, to run away from only that.

"So I walked away from the cliff, and when next I led the clansmen forth, the Romans bled a much as we. That was when I fought side by side with your mother's kin, and how ye came to be."

"But—"

"Hush. Your luck's better than mine. I had to wait half a year to know my luck had turned. Ye charmed the very man who took ye prisoner, until now he's thinking after giving away his whole victory!"

"It may be a false promise."

"Hah. Your brother said it. Who last fooled you? Lass, lass, you must no think less of yourself than you are worth. Modesty is no virtue for those who lead good men to war."

25

The wide valley was green with maize not yet high enough to form ears. Tents stood at each end, green and white at the north, blue and gold to the south. As the True Sun stood high overhead, a single trumpet sounded in the southern camp, to be answered by one from the north.

Ganton mounted carefully. *Vaulting into the saddle is all very well, but this is no time to break a leg. Or be in pain.*

Drumold was helped to his saddle by Balquhain.

"I like this not," Hilaskos said. He glared at Drumold.

Ganton ignored him. He signaled to his squire to raise the banner of the Fighting Man and ride ahead. Ganton and Drumold followed.

"Be careful of the corn," Ganton said.

Drumold nodded. "Aye. An' this goes not well—"

If this doesn't go well, there won't be anything standing here, or in a dozen other valleys.

A party of three rode toward them from the other end of the valley.

"We're out o' range o' *their* bows," Drumold said.

And the center is beyond range of both. But Drumold has a point. I wonder what orders he has given those clansmen of his? "By Yatar, he's brought Apelles!"

"So 'tis no trick," Drumold said. "Or Strymon's the greatest fool in nine kingdoms."

Ganton's squire reached the tiny flag the scouts had set twenty paces short of the field's center. He halted, and Ganton rode on ahead. Drumold waited with the squire.

"Hail, Prince Strymon."

"Hail, Wanax Ganton."

He dresses well. Ganton smiled grimly. His own armor was still stained with dust from the trail, and the golden helmet tied to his saddle had dents from battle. Despite the protests of his bodyguards he'd left his axe and carried a jewel-hilted sword of state, not really fit for war, but otherwise he looked very much the commander of an army.

If Strymon wore armor, it was concealed under his green and white surcoat and scarlet silk cape. His sword was hilted in amber, and he wore gold rings on fingers and ears.

No helm or shield. Ganton relaxed. He unslung a flask from his saddle horn. "Wine, my lord?" He poured into the goblet that hung from his saddle, drank, and turned the goblet over to show it was empty.

Strymon grinned. "With pleasure, Majesty." They came closer together. Strymon accepted the flask, drank deeply, and returned it. "Excellent wine. I should have my vintners speak to yours."

"Thank you."

Strymon's grin faded. "If the Time leaves any grapes at all in our lands. Your pardon, Majesty, but we have little time this day. The High Rexja's army approaches, and much of his vanguard will be in my camp by tomorrow night."

Ganton shrugged. "Highness—your army is in my lands, not mine in yours."

"Yes. I received my orders, and I obeyed them—"

"Whose orders?"

"Yes. You know, then. Orders signed by Wanax Palamon, but never written—never *understood* by him."

"In a word, orders from Toris."

"Or Issardos." Strymon shrugged. "Does it matter? The question now is, can we come to terms we can both accept? I confess, Majesty, that I have always been a simple soldier. I am not accustomed to thinking like the Wanax of Ta-Meltemos. War has been my profession. Now I must think of my people."

"I see you have brought Apelles."

"Yes. He has much experience at—what he calls *administration*. I have learned much from him. Majesty, I know his true loyalty is not to me."

"Nor to me," Ganton said. "Apelles serves Yanulf, who may be my chancellor, but who is first and always Highpriest of Yatar. You could have chosen a worse advisor."

Strymon shrugged. "Except for military officers, there is no one in my camp I can trust not to give first loyalty to Chancellor Rauros or his master Issardos."

"Highness, if you wish the services of Apelles for the future, I am certain Yanulf will give his consent." *He'd better!* "This is an odd moment. We each have an army. We each believe we would win victory were we to fight."

"And we would each lose no matter who has won," Strymon said. "Were it not for the Time, it would be—interesting to see whether your *guns* could make the difference. I tell you this, no army of mine is going to ride down this valley against nine of those monsters."

Ganton grinned wryly. "Your scouts are better than I had thought. But we have eleven."

"Nine. One has lost a wheel, and another was overturned in a river last night."

Yatar, Christ, and Vothan! "I—see. Thank you, my lord. Battle between us might be more—interesting—than either of us would like. But your army must leave my Realm!"

"Of course. That will not be as easy to accomplish as I would like." Strymon's voice dropped even lower. "Majesty, less than half my troops are of Ta-Meltemos."

"Issardos again."

"Yes. I see now that he schemes to make the High Rexja into a Great King of Kings, and I have been his catspaw. Majesty, all of the chivalry of Ta-Meltemos will follow me north, but the rest probably will not."

A problem I cannot solve for you, my friend. "Where will you go?"

"To the Green Palace, to send Rauros packing! I see my duty is to take the throne, in fact if not in name."

"A hard decision."

"Not so hard. My father will not know the difference."

"I grieve for you." *My father knew he had been cast out. You're lucky, my friend.* "Now to terms. You will withdraw your army. Ta-Meltemos will give no more aid to the Five Kingdoms in war against Drantos, and will send aid to Drantos in war against anyone *but* the Five Kingdoms."

Strymon considered. "I can agree to this. In return, you seek no reparations for damages done in this campaign, and you will share your knowledge of the Time with us."

"That is easier to agree to than you think," Ganton said. "Even if we all stand together, few enough will survive the Time and the *skyfire* that follows."

"Those stories are true, then?"

"You will learn." Ganton raised his voice. "Apelles."

"Majesty?"

"Prince Strymon, may he approach?"

"Certainly. Apelles, if you please."

Apelles rode up to join them. "Majesty. Highness."

"Apelles, from the moment that Prince Strymon's army marches northward and out of Drantos, you will share with him all your knowledge of the Time, and of our preparations for it, saving only what you may know of our recent troop movements."

"All." Apelles tilted his head to one side. "All?"

"All. Including the sky box that talks, and the great sky-ship you have seen. All."

"I gather I am not to go home so soon as I thought," Apelles said dryly.

"I am certain that Yanulf will consent," Ganton said.

Apelles grinned. "So am I. Majesty, I must send letters—"

"Of course. We will send apprentices and a priest to aid you, as befits your new station." *And Yanulf will make you a bishop at least, or he's going to find it harder to collect his tithes.*

"May I offer advice, Majesty?" Apelles said.

"Why do you think you're here? Speak!"

"I do not care for the reports I receive from the Green Palace," Apelles said.

"What do you know of my father that I do not?" Strymon demanded.

"Only that Rauros grows more bold. Highness, think upon what might happen if a messenger brings a Royal Writ under the Great Seal, accusing you of treason. Or accusing Wanax Ganton of atrocities and demanding that his lands be laid waste. Or—"

"I see. I must return at once."

"Highness, you cannot," Apelles said. "Without you, your army will put this land to the sword."

"Then what must be done?"

"Send Prince Teodoros. At once."

The lady Tylara does not think much of Teodoros. How can I say this?

"Apelles, my brother is loyal, but he—"

"Is no statesman," Apelles said. "True. He will need good advice, which we must be at pains to send often. But I see no other way."

Strymon looked thoughtful. "It may be enough. I suppose you can suggest an advisor to accompany him?"

"Prakes, Priest of Yatar," Apelles said.

"Um. I would have thought him young, but yes, he has my brother's respect if any churchman does. A convert to the new faith, I believe—"

I would wager half a kingdom he is a convert, Ganton thought. "Highness, I see we must move swiftly. Shall we bring witnesses to our agreement?"

"I am ready. Yon squire is Bheroman Tarmon do Karimos. I am afraid I cannot trust many more of my officers to know our terms."

"Bring him then. I will summon Drumold, and we five will be witness enough."

‡ ‡ ‡

"You are mad!" Bheroman Darkon pounded on the council table. "Withdraw? Nonsense. We lost time while you were enthralled by that highland witch, but we can still thrust to the walls of Edron in a ten-day!"

Strymon stared at the map on the table, then lifted his eyes to scan the faces of the dozen lords and officers around him. He thought most approved of Darkon's speech. "Perhaps, if the weather holds," Strymon said. "And what then?"

"Then we will have won!"

"We will have won nothing. Edron will not fall to threats. Let me remind you, my Lord Darkon, it is they, not we, who have the *guns.*"

At least two barons muttered approval.

"Then we must destroy them in the field. Kill or capture that boy king of theirs. That will certainly bring us victory."

"It is easy enough to speak of destruction, and I do not doubt we could hurt Ganton badly. But my lords, the trick is to avoid being destroyed ourselves. You've heard the reports of our scouts. Before he left us so strangely, Matthias told us what *guns* and star weapons can do. Ganton seeks no battle. He will choose a strong position and make us come to him. My lords, I doubt no one's courage, but this is no way to make war."

"If you hadn't stopped here," Darkon said.

"My lord," Strymon said gently, "I was ordered to remain here to await the High Rexja's army."

"So we serve fools—or—" Darkon caught himself.

Pity. Had he said "coward" I could have killed him with honor. "I will not hear that said of our high king," Strymon said. "Nor yet of me, and I would *be* a fool to remain here facing the host of Drantos on its own terms. Captain Ninas, how long will the fodder last?"

"Highness, no more than a ten-day. Even now we feed the horses but seven pecks of the eight they need."

Bheroman Abados grunted. "And meanwhile Ganton's tame wolf Morrone rages through *my* lands. Whatever the rest of you do, I want permission to take my forces home and put a stop to that."

"Granted," Strymon said.

Some of the others glared.

"My lords, many of your homes are far from here. Think upon the Time."

"Legends," someone said.

"It is legend that the seas rise? That the rains come late, then beat the crops into the ground? The Demon Sun is no legend." Strymon shrugged. "I do not know what the other kingdoms will do, but Ta-Meltemos cannot afford war with men when the very gods war with one another across our lands!"

"You seek peace without the High Rexja's permission!" someone shouted. "Treason!"

"The High Rexja is not *yet* Great King," Strymon said. "And who here wants him to be? My lords, do you all wish to be slaves to Issardos?"

"By Vothan, it *is* treason!" Darkon shouted. "Guards! Treason, treason!"

"My lord, I think you do not wish to shout so loud, lest *my* guards believe you threaten me," Strymon said carefully.

Darkon dashed to the tent doorway. "Soldiers! Hear me! Prince Strymon abandons the High Rexja!"

A dozen troops in the green and white of Ta-Meltemos charged forward with drawn swords. Strymon held up his hand. "Let him speak," he said.

Darkon opened his mouth to shout, and saw that everyone within earshot wore green and white. "I see." He turned to Strymon. "Will you let me address the troops in assembly, then?"

Strymon grinned. "Certainly, my lord. As soon as we are across the border."

INTERLUDE
LUNA

Agzaral sat across the table from the three *Shalnuksis*. "My thanks, Excellencies, for setting the cabin temperature for human comfort."

"You are welcome," Karreeel answered.

Agzaral had dealt with *Shalnuksis* long enough to recognize the tone. They wanted something. It would take some time to find out what. *Shalnuksis* were long-lived and had a great deal more patience than humans.

They had arrayed themselves in their traditional pattern. Karreeel, the only one Agzaral had much experience of, sat in the middle chair. That meant the others outranked him. The *Shalnuksis* to his left wore the silver-blue tunic of the Council of Merchants. Badges of civic achievement decorated his collar. Agzaral knew nothing else about him except that his name was Lyaaarin.

The third *Shalnuksis* was Tsirovv, one of the nine members of the committee known as the Sentinels of Governance. *Shalnuksi* government was complex, with a multiplicity of officers and officials, and a Grand Council that was in theory supreme. The Sentinels were something between Ephors and ombudsmen, and were supposed to represent the best of *Shalnuksi* business ethics.

Agzaral smiled to himself. The best in business ethics did not prevent the Sentinel from coming to Luna to negotiate what was, after all, if not a criminal activity, then certainly one the *Shalnuksis* did not care to have come to the attention of the Confederation and its Council.

Tsirovv was nearing the end of a long career, begun in the year

822

Louis XIV of France died. He was one of the few living *Shalnuksis* with a reputation for statesmanship. His presence on this unexpected delegation to Luna could mean anything. *The matter is more important than I had thought.*

Agzaral's smile was exaggerated. *Shalnuksis* did not easily read human expressions; best to make them unambiguous. "Excellencies, how may I serve you?"

Karreeel made some entries in the portable computer on the table in front of him and inclined his head toward the Councilor. The Councilor contracted his nasal slit, the *Shalnuksi* equivalent of a frown.

"Do you wish to claim that the additional heavy weapons and ammunition were procured and shipped to Tran by the Slave Les without your knowledge?"

"Should I? Excellencies, my time is yours, but surely you have not come all this way to discuss trivia. I sent Captain Galloway most of the equipment he requested, including ammunition, toilet paper, a product known as 'Preparation H,' and cartons of a particular brand of cigarette. I believe you have an inventory. If not, I can provide one. Are you suggesting I have overcharged you?"

"Do not be hasty," Karreeel said. He exchanged looks left and right. "We must be certain you are in control of what can be—a delicate situation."

Delicate. If the Council officially hears of what you're doing, "delicate" won't begin to describe the situation. For you or for me. "Excellencies, many matters demand my attention, but be assured that I am fully aware of Tran and what happens there. As witness the fact that I have, here on Luna, more and better *surinomaz* than you have seen in your lifetimes."

"Ah." The three exchanged looks again. "We knew we had made a good choice in you, Inspector."

"Thank you. You have arrived just in time. I was about to send the *surinomaz* to the usual place. Now you may collect it and save us all trouble."

"Thank you. That is however not why we have come."

"Indeed. Excellencies, I forget my manners. Will you have refreshment? I have a well-stocked bar, and the kitchen staff has been informed of your arrival. Luna is not the Capital, to be sure, but I think our provinces are not entirely barren. There is an ethanol-based drink known as 'Grand Marnier' which I think you might enjoy."

"Perhaps a sip," Karreeel said. "After our talk."

"As you wish, Excellencies."

"Inspector, I believe you are often invited to attend meetings of the High Commission."

"I have been, Excellencies. Not since I was sent to Luna, of course."

"You have agents there." Tsirovv spoke for the first time.

Agzaral kept his smile tiny and ambiguous. "Excellencies, I have many friends in many places."

"We know the ways of Important Slaves," Tsirovv said. He looked again at Karreeel.

"Inspector, we have also heard disturbing rumors of the actions of the Council," Karreeel said.

Time to get down to cases. "Yes, Excellencies?"

"Actions that may affect our trade."

"Ah. Excellencies, are you not aware that no one of my rank is ever truly alone?" He looked exaggeratedly at the walls.

The three exchanged glances again. "We trust your—discretion," Tsirovv said. "We will speak if you will."

"How may I serve you?"

Karreeel flared his nasal slits, and the color of his eyes changed to a deeper shade of blue. "Inspector, we are told that the Council is contemplating decisions regarding the development of Earth. Meanwhile, they have become much more strict about contact with humans. We have heard there was a motion to bombard Earth."

"Tabled by a large majority," Agzaral said.

"But the suggestion was made. Inspector, how many in the Council know of the existence of Tran?"

And now we have come to the point. "More than one. Not all."

"That is not a satisfactory answer."

"It is all the answer I have, Excellencies. I have given no information to the Council. I know that at least one group of the Ader'at'eel is thoroughly aware of Tran, but they seem as determined to keep that a secret as we are."

This time the silence was long. Agzaral had long wondered whether the *Shalnuksis* were telepathic. If so they were unique. *On the other hand, it may be equipment. Transceivers in their heads. That never worked for humans although it should have.*

"We thank you," Karreeel said.

Agzaral bowed to acknowledge the compliment. *Threw you, didn't it? You're not in a position to take on the Ader'at'eel. That would take a bigger coalition than you'll ever build.*

"What is the Council likely to do about Tarn?" Karreeel asked.

"Excellencies, I do not know."

"We wish you to find out. We will not be ungrateful."

"It will not be easy. It takes—resources—to keep my friends in the Capital."

"We know this," Tsirovv said.

"I believe we may be able to help," Karreeel said.

"Excellencies, I shall endeavor to give satisfaction." *You cannot possibly have read Wodehouse.* "Now shall I send for refreshments?"

PART SIX
CHURCH AND STATE

26

Castle Fasolt rose proudly from a low hill at the border between Drantos and the Five Kingdoms. Ganton reined in at the top of the path it guarded, and looked down at it with his binoculars. Details were easy to see in the midmorning sun. The ground around the castle had been cleared and plowed for a Roman mile. The gates were closed, and the only road up the hill was blocked with stakes and barbs.

"I see no streams," Lord Enipses said. "Perhaps thirst will force Ajacias—"

"There are both cisterns and a spring," Ganton said. "I've been there."

"Ah. Majesty, may I?"

"Certainly." Ganton didn't like parting with his binoculars for even a moment, but the request was reasonable. He put the strap over Enipses' head before letting go of them. The University craftsmen were making single tubes they called *telescopes* that worked much as the binoculars, but the images were never as clear. Some of them even turned things upside down!

Ganton waited until Enipses had finished his examination and he had retrieved his star gift. "Well?"

"It will be no easy task," Enipses said reluctantly. "Even with the Great Guns."

Only one of the field pieces was really suitable as a siege cannon. The others could not fire heavy enough balls far enough to be useful against walls. Ganton had been told this often enough that he believed it, although he still did not understand why. Artillery remained a black art practiced by wizards, mostly the sons of craftsmen. *I should have paid more attention to those classes at the University. I know this now. Why didn't I then?*

"Still, we must take it," Ganton said. "We cannot leave open this gate to Drantos."

"Majesty," Enipses said, "without disrespect—can we not take that castle in the same way that we drove Prince Strymon's armies from Drantos?"

"What do you know of this?" Ganton demanded.

"Majesty, it is common knowledge! The Lady Tylara—somehow enchanted Prince Strymon. The Highpriest Apelles brought him to the knowledge of the New Christ and Your Majesty showed him that his invasion of our lands was a sin. Everyone knows this."

"Everyone knows this. I see." *Not only do they not give me credit for victory, I have the least part of this matter. Lord Rick once said there is no limit to what you can accomplish if you do not demand credit for it. I see I am learning this lesson better than I wanted to.* "Does everyone also know how we are going to rest tonight in that castle?"

"No, Majesty, but I am certain you do."

Yatar's Teeth. Ganton lifted the binoculars to study Castle Fasolt again. *A third or more of those I see on the walls wear green and white.* Ganton smiled. "Perhaps I do, my lord. Only perhaps."

✢ ✢ ✢

Rain beat down on the encampment. The Guards had erected enough shelter to keep the royal campfire burning, but it didn't keep out all the rain.

"Perhaps," Enipses muttered.

Ganton laughed. "Not even kings have their own way all the time. At least we have a fire."

"And they have the castle."

"When I invited you to take Lord Morrone's place as Companion during his absence, it did not occur to me that you would adopt his manners. May I have more wine, please?"

"At once, Majesty." Enipses poured from the pewter flagon heating near the fire.

Someone shouted from the distance. "Stand! Who is there?"

"Balquhain do Tamaerthon and guests."

"Stand and be recognized!"

Enipses jumped to his feet. "Guards—"

"That was Balquhain," Ganton said. "Didn't you recognize his voice?"

"Yes, sire—"

"And he would not come here without reason. Sit down before you insult him."

✢ ✢ ✢

"Guests, you said." Ganton looked at the cloaked figures around his campfire. "Guests. Prince Strymon, what are you doing here?"

Strymon laughed. "Majesty, I am a fugitive."

"You?"

"My choices were to flee or continue a civil war within my own army." He glanced nervously at the others around the fire.

"I think it matters little who hears us and who doesn't," Ganton said. "Still—" He sighed. "Lord Enipses, if you please, I would be alone with Prince Strymon and Lord Balquhain."

"Majesty—"

"And Apelles, of course." Ganton poured wine while Enipses led the others out of the shelter. "Now, Highness, if you are comfortable—"

Strymon sat on the log nearest the fire. "Majesty. The vanguard of the High Rexja arrived as my rear guard crossed the border. Matthias led the Royal bodyguard. He carried a direct commission from Toris relieving me of command, and ordering my arrest for high treason."

"I—see." Ganton sat heavily on the log across the fire from Strymon.

"I had sent home most of the Melteme troops as escort for my brother. Only my personal Guard remained. They were sufficient to prevent Matthias carrying out his order immediately, but he and Bheromen Darkon then appealed to the soldiers from the other kingdoms. The host of Ta-Boreas rallied around Darkon, and the others were ready to follow."

"Highness, could you not have sent for your Meltemes?" Balquhain asked.

"Perhaps, my lord, but it seemed better to let them ride on. I would rather see my brother secure in the Green Palace than have more of my Meltemes killed in a hopeless civil war."

"Then I confess, Highness, I do not know how you got here alive," Ganton said.

"My Lord Father Apelles," Strymon said. "He did what I never could have. As Darkon and Matthias sought to rally the troops against me, and I saw to arming myself, Apelles rode up and down the lines of the army shouting to all the New Christians. 'Brothers! Will you fight your Brothers? Will you take arms against the Nuncio of Archbishop Polycarp and Highpriest Yanulf?'"

Ganton looked quizzically at Apelles. Apelles' face retreated deeper into the cowl of his robe.

"Great Yatar," Balquhain muttered.

"His speech was—heard, then," Ganton said.

"The army dissolved. Some came to me. Some threw their weapons down. Many rallied around my Lord Father Apelles, to stand between him and any who would do him harm."

"Apelles—"

"With apologies, sire, he deserves his titles," Strymon said.

Ganton gulped. "My Lord Father Apelles—"

"Majesty?"

"I think we will speak later. I also think Highpriest Yanulf will have something to say."

"I make no doubt of it," Apelles said. "But Majesty—I could think of nothing else to do. And soon Bheroman Darkon approached Prince Strymon, to offer him safe conduct from the camp—"

"He ordered me out," Strymon said. "And I was glad to go."

"How much of your army came with you?" Ganton asked.

"Perhaps one part in ten. At least that many more simply went home."

"He has lost a quarter of his strength, then."

"Of Prince Strymon's own soldiers, Majesty," Apelles said. "And one part in ten of those who came with Matthias have seen the True Light. They await Your Majesty's inspection at the perimeter of this camp. Lord Drumold is with them."

Lord Rick always said there are better ways to conquer than battles and war. I should have believed him. "My Lord Father Apelles, you have done well indeed. Prince Strymon, who will command their army now?"

"They have sent for Prince Akkilas."

"The heir himself? Sarakos' brother?"

"I think the army would follow no one else."

"He is said to be hotheaded," Ganton said. "Is this why his father has kept him from command?"

"Hah. High Rexja Toris sent the boy to me to learn the art of war. I think he has listened to too many of the tales of the prowess of his name hero. After a month I sent him back to Teveron to organize reinforcements and supplies. He is intelligent enough, but young and impetuous. It is dangerous to trust such a one with soldiers who will follow without question."

Something to remember. Lord Rick would do much with this knowledge. Perhaps I can as well. "Well. In any case, Highness, welcome to my hospitality, such as it is."

Strymon laughed. "Why, Majesty, I thank you, but will you allow me to offer you mine? I know of a much dryer place we can sleep tonight."

✛ ✛ ✛

The stamping feet of Guardsmen sword dancers and the drone of pipes made the Great Hall of Lord Ajacias' Castle Fasolt as noisy as a battlefield. The Wanax Ganton watched from the High Table. Prince Strymon sat at his right, and the Lord Highpriest Apelles at his left. Stewards filled their wine cups as fast as they were emptied.

Ganton remembered the last time he had sat at this table in this hall. *Well over a year ago. I received a letter from Octavia. I think it was then I knew we'd marry.*

On Lord Rick's advice he had honored Lord Ajacias with a royal visit. It had been intended to uncover any plots Ajacias might contemplate, and strip him of the gold he needed to carry them out.

Perhaps the High Rexja Toris sent more gold. Perhaps Ajacias was a greater fool than anyone could imagine. For whatever reason, this was one plan of Lord Rick's that hadn't succeeded. Ajacias had gone on plotting until he admitted Prince Strymon's army into Drantos.

Thanks to Prince Strymon, the traitor cannot be hanged. It was a bitter thought. Before Strymon would order his men to eject Ajacias and open the castle gates, he made Ganton swear to exile Ajacias.

In his place I could do no less. But the Lady Tylara is not pleased, and I think Lord Rick will be no more so. Yet what choice had I? It would take half a year to reduce this castle. My people are better employed growing food for the Time.

Ganton gulped wine, then grinned. *Only five companions chose to go with Ajacias. He will live without gold, without friends, in a foreign court. He may yet wish he had been hanged.*

At that last banquet the Lady Cara, Ajacias' daughter and heir, had partnered the Wanax at dinner. Now she was in the custody of Lady Tylara. Morrone had been King's Companion and carved the stag. Now he led a ragged band of *guerrillas* Yatar alone knew where. And Lord Rick had watched from his own table, instead of commanding the Army of Chelm somewhere in the west.

The shaggy head of Master Gunner Pinir loomed through the candle smoke. Prince Strymon stood and raised his wine cup. "Ho, Pinir son of the smith!"

Pinir made his way around the dancers and approached the table. He looked like a full-grown war horse passing through a herd of yearlings. Even when he knelt, his eyes were on a level with Ganton's.

"Your Majesty, Your Highness. I am at your service."

"Indeed, and good service it has been. A full day of instructing me in the mysteries of the Great Guns. You have my thanks."

"Highness, you are most welcome."

Strymon laughed. "Matthias has left me little enough, but you deserve more than thanks."

Strymon rose, and his chair went over backward with a clatter. He took a ring from his finger and gave it to Pinir. "Wear this, in token of my gratitude."

Pinir stood and took the ring. It would barely pass the first joint of his smallest finger. "With your Majesty's permission . . . ?"

"Oh, have it, have it." Ganton waved his hand. "But I ask you, Prince Strymon, why do you presume to reward *my* master gunner?"

"Is it so great a presumption?"

"Great enough that I must demand satisfaction."

Strymon laughed. "Indeed, we never broke lances against each other. I rather regret that."

"I am as sorry as you. But I think that is a pleasure we need not be denied. One course with the lance, then on foot with my axe against whatever you choose?"

"My sword, I think. Ah, what a grand spectacle it will be! We can have three knights from each host as judges, with Chancellor Yanulf to cast a deciding vote if need be. We—"

"You will not have Yanulf, Highpriest of Yatar and Co-Vicar of Christ on Tran, to judge this foolish combat," came a voice from behind Ganton. Strymon tried to turn around, caught his feet on his fallen chair, and fell on top of it. Ganton jumped, knocking over his wine cup. The wine dripped from the table onto his robes.

"I will not judge this combat. If you are determined on this folly, I shall stand in the middle of the lists, and you will have to ride me down!"

Ganton felt about six years old. Without turning around he said, "My Lord Chancellor, you presume rather greatly."

"You may have that office." Yanulf snatched the chain of office from his neck, threw it on the table, and stalked away.

"My Lord—Father Apelles, reason with him!" Ganton said. "Tell him I—tell him any damned thing you like, but give him back this chain!"

"Sire." Apelles took the chain and followed Yanulf toward the back of the hall.

"He'll do it," Strymon said. He tried to get up and fell against the table. "Majesty, I think we had best postpone this tourney."

"I have pondered the matter, and I agree," Ganton said. He looked up. The first eyes he met were Pinir's. The gunner was still kneeling, with the ring in his hand. His face was the color of dirty chalk.

Ganton hiccoughed. "Master Gunner, I think you will have tales to tell. Tell them well. You are dismissed."

"Majesty—"

"Go!" He looked down and smiled. "Send Prince Strymon's body servants to carry him to his chamber. And when you tell this tale, be sure you say that Wanax Ganton walked to *his* chambers on his own legs!"

✢ ✢ ✢

"Enter," came Yanulf's voice through the heavy oak door.

Tylara took a deep breath and opened the door. Rusty hinges screamed like demons; her carefully gathered composure weakened. She walked into Yanulf's chamber and pushed the door shut behind her.

Yanulf sprinkled sand on the letter he'd been writing and capped his inkwell. "Greetings, my lady. How can I serve you?" A second look at her face and he rose, pushing a stool toward her. She sat down heavily.

"How fares the Lady Cara?" Yanulf asked. His tone was casual. "We are grateful to you for taking her as your ward."

"You may be," said Tylara, amused in spite of herself. "She is not. She has refused everything this 'hill-robber's daughter' has offered her. Besides, she giggles. I beg you not to speak of this to anyone else," she added. "My brother would be furious, and my father might not hold him back."

"I see." Yanulf pursed his lips. "I think I shall propose that the Lady Cara marry a loyal knight whose lands lie far from the Sutmarg. Perhaps you know of one."

"No." Tylara knew she'd answered too abruptly. "I am glad to see that you wear the chain of the Lord Chancellor."

Yanulf smiled. "Men will be boys. But I doubt you came to me to inspect my attire."

Tylara's mouth was dry. She shook her head.

"I thought not. Daughter, I know that matters have not been easy between you and your lord. You have come to talk to me. Speak."

"It—I—Apelles—Yanulf, I am dishonored in the eyes of the gods. Caradoc's blood is on my hands."

Her words came slowly at first, then faster. "The Lady Gwen had married Caradoc, truly married him before all the clans, yet she could not resist her—former husband—when he returned from the stars. She lay with him. She was not even discreet. Caradoc would learn of it, and when he did, all that my husband had built, all that we had planned, would be lost. In the Name of Yatar, what could I do? The instrument lay in my hands. Father Yanulf, I swear, I had not planned that the Children of Vothan be used that way!"

The candles on Yanulf's table had burned to stubs before she finished.

"Come, my child." She knelt with her head on his knees. Yanulf laid his hand on her shoulder and cleared his throat. "I have no easy answers. Nor do I think you expect one. Indeed, I think you decided there was no answer save your own death. Is that not so?"

Tylara shuddered. "Yes, Father."

"Is that still your belief?"

"As Yatar is my witness, I do not know. I am alive when I expected to be dead. I may even have done some good for my people."

"It is plain to all that you have done much good for your people."

"If you say so. Truly, I do not know. I don't even know whether my life offends the gods."

"Apelles said that you swore—"

"Not to lay hands on myself while I was in Prince Strymon's custody? That is so, and I kept my oath. Now I am free again."

Tylara stared into the fire. Yanulf's silence stretched on for minutes. *I can't look at him. My fate will be written in his face.*

"Penance."

"What?"

"Penance. A rite of the Christians. One confesses one's sins to a priest, who is sworn never to reveal what he hears. The priest then orders one to perform certain—charitable works."

"What—what sort of works?"

"Prayers, pilgrimages, offerings . . . as he may discover through his own prayer and meditation. One performs them, and thereby is freed of one's guilt, in the eyes of man and the eyes of God."

"In God's—Yatar's eyes."

"Yes. Tylara, your fear is not for yourself. What you fear is the wrath of God against your husband and your children. It was fear for others that drove you to ride against the enemy. If you were as evil as you seem to think, you would be thinking only of yourself. You are not a monster, and neither God nor man will call you such if you open your heart to them."

All the tears Tylara had been holding back flowed in a rush. "But how can my husband forgive me? I never told him what I did. And now he seeks heirs by another."

"What makes you think this?"

"He is cold. He is never alone with me."

Yanulf wiped her eyes. "Tylara, have you never thought that he has discovered your secret? And that he is cold because he believes you do not trust him?"

"I—No."

"I would be amazed if he had not. As to seeking heirs by another, there is little I do not hear, and I have never heard that."

"Never?"

"Not one word."

"Then what must I do?"

"Tell him everything."

"After the best part of two years?"

"Yes. It is only your pride that fills you with doubts. The Christians show great wisdom when they call pride one of the Seven Deadly Sins. Where is the sense in thinking the worst of your husband when you will not speak to him? Can speaking to him be so much harder than speaking to me?"

"You have learned much of the Christians' ways. Father Yanulf, have you yourself been baptized?"

"Child, I have told you nothing tonight that is not written in books."

"This—penance. Can it be offered to those who have not been baptized as Christians?"

"Christians or New Christians? The Faith of the New Christ holds confession and penance as sacraments."

"Then can you—"

"You have already made your confession."

"Then what is my penance?"

"Child, it is my turn to confess. This is new enough to me that I must meditate and pray. I know this much. You must make amends."

"I have stood as godmother to Caradoc's child—"

"Not to Caradoc. To the Children of Vothan. You have robbed them of their innocence."

Tylara turned away from him. Tears streamed unchecked. "I had—I had not wanted to. They were lost, and—" She waited, hoping that Yanulf would interrupt, but he said nothing. "They were lost, and I used them for my own ends! Father Yanulf, what must I do?"

"You must see that they learn new trades. Trades of honor. You cannot restore their innocence. What you can do is give them, not pride, but faith in themselves."

"Trades of honor? They know no skills but death—Wait! Father—those who know the skills of assassins can also protect! What better dog to guard sheep than a wolf? Would that fulfill this penance?"

"Lady Tylara, what are you thinking of?"

"Prince Teodoros. I do not believe he will long be alive in the Green Palace. Unless—"

Yanulf was silent for a moment. He fingered the Great Seal of Drantos on its chain. "You still command the Children?"

"Yes, Father."

"Then—I lay it upon you. A portion of your penance shall be to send those Children to protect Prince Teodoros. Go. Go quickly. And go with God."

27

Ben Murphy dipped his pen into the ink horn.

Task Force Murphy War Diary. Mission Day Twenty-three. Position seventeen kilometers WSW of Shora's Rift, northern portion of the Sutmarg.

Day's march fourteen kilometers. Day's casualties one dead (sunstroke), one MIA, six horses disabled and abandoned. Strength seven officers, four hundred sixty-eight men. Twenty-nine WIA, twelve fit to fight. Five hundred thirteen horses. Ammunition remaining: twenty-two percent for star weapons, forty percent for rockets, fifty percent for arrows. Recovery of arrows is running well ahead of estimate.

Comments: Looks like we've outrun all of the High Rexja's western army. Estimate three regiments were chasing us. I make that "Mission accomplished" for drawing off their cavalry. The problem is we've run into the rear of Prince Strymon's army, and they're between us and Drantos.

So far we're all right. We have good water and there are meadows of Earth grasses scattered through the Tran scrub. Between that and the oats we've captured we have fodder.

I plan to rest up the horses for a couple of days. Once everybody's fit to move I'll decide whether to raid Strymon's rear or head south and join up with Ganton.

Morale solid. Minimum tension between our people and the Westmen. I still try to keep Westmen and Drantos fighters in separate

840

units because of language problems, but pretty much everybody on either side trusts the other now. They've been saving each other's asses a couple a times a day for nearly three weeks.

"Sarge?"

Murphy looked up to see Hal Roscoe dismounting. "Yeah?"

"Scouts just rode in. There's a big supply convoy laagered up about six klicks ahead."

"Fortified?"

"Just a wagon circle. Some VIP's banner over the CP."

"Whose?"

"Damfino."

"Yeah." Most of his rangers were former poachers, and wouldn't. And the Westmen scouts sure didn't know heraldry.

"Want to go after it, Sarge?"

"Does the bear shit in the woods? Tell 'em 'Well done' and I'll be along in a few minutes." ·

"Okay, Sarge." Roscoe remounted and rode off.

"Lucky break," Murphy wrote. "VIP banner means food. Remounts, and maybe some decent loot. We'll take this thing just after the True Sun sets. The Demon will give us enough light."

✢ ✢ ✢

The Father Sun had set, and the Child was only a crimson smear in the east. The baleful eye of the Death-Wind Bringer cast a red glow over the clearing. All was deep shadow near the woods where Mad Bear's people waited.

The wizards' firesticks—the *rockets*—soared up from behind the line of Horse People and arched across the sky. Two, three, four of them plunged down onto the enemy camp.

Mad Bear saw warriors making gestures against evil spirits. Others struggled to control jittery horses. He himself no longer feared the wizards' firesticks, any more than he feared fighting at night. Clearly the wizards' magic was stronger than that of the night demons. Therefore it must be stronger than that of the men in the camp, who had not dared to move by night.

Only one fire sprang up where the rockets fell, but it was enough to show horses and oxen milling in panic. Mad Bear grinned and drew his sword to await the signal from his chief and blood-brother.

Murphy's trumpet sounded and was followed by a long, shrill blast on his iron whistle. Mad Bear rammed his heels into his mount's flanks. The pony leaped forward like a maddened ranwang. Mad Bear swept his sword down the way he had seen Chief Murphy do it, then reined his horse aside to let the archers sweep past.

The archers were a hundred paces ahead of Mad Bear when they came within bowshot of the wagons. A few arrows arched out to meet them. Two of Mad Bear's warriors fell from their saddles.

There were two Horse People for every archer in the wagon circle, and the Westmen's arrows carried farther and struck harder. Soon the screams of men joined the screams of the horses, and fewer arrows flew from the wagon circles.

Mad Bear rode up to the line of archers. There was movement in the enemy's camp. Torches glowed, and armored men mounted their horses. A squire handed a banner to one of the knights. The banner bore the same device as the one that had flown over the tent. *Ah. The chief of the camp would do battle with us. Father, Thunderer, grant that he may be fodder for my lance.*

Mad Bear sheathed his sword. It was an iron sword, a gift from his blood-brother, and in more skilled hands no doubt it would be a match for the armor of any Ironshirt. It was well to have an iron sword, and to learn the Ironshirt way of war, but the Horse People had trained with the lance from the day they had been set in the saddle. It would always be Mad Bear's first choice. Mad Bear's steel lance head had been passed down through five generations.

The enemy horsemen rode out in fours. Some of the archers began shooting at them. Mad Bear shouted. "The camp. Leave the horsemen to us!" Without the Ironshirts to defend it, the camp would certainly fall, and it was the camp they wanted. That was another thing Mad Bear had learned from Murphy. Do not swerve from your target. Do not be deceived by the prospect of easier prey.

The archers turned back toward the camp and advanced slowly, followed by the dismounted troops who would storm the wagons.

The enemy horsemen massed for a charge. Mad Bear led a hand of hands of lancers to meet them. Enemy horns sounded. Mad Bear's hand of hands faced no less than five times their strength. "The darkness must be our friend," he shouted to his band. "When they come close, run away, and lead them far from here!"

He urged his pony forward. One Ironshirt rode far ahead of the others. Mad Bear whirled his pony to the right, as if to avoid the man. His enemy followed, but his heavier mount was not as agile as Mad Bear's pony. As he turned, Mad Bear whirled back and thrust his lance into the man's throat. His fall twisted the lance from Mad Bear's hands.

To his left a man in silver armor slew two of Mad Bear's people. Mad Bear pivoted toward him, but a dozen enemies came between. Mad Bear drew his sword and shouted at them. He waited until they were close enough to hear his insults, then spun away. He kept his pony at a slow gallop and stayed just far enough ahead to lure them farther away from the camp.

When he'd led them far enough he turned to his right, riding past the older warriors who waited in the darkness at the edge of the woods. Then he gave them no more thought, and wheeled back toward the camp.

Most of the Ironshirts had halted at the edge of the firelit circle, but two had ridden farther on. One was the man in the silver armor who had slain Mad Bear's kinsmen. Mad Bear felt the blood lust rising in him. Such feelings were always dangerous. The Horse People had long ago learned that it was better to tire your enemy, and kill him in your own time, than to fight him when he had his full strength.

The silver-armored Ironshirt shouted and rode toward Mad Bear. He was followed by another, a mere boy, who carried a banner. *A chief*, Mad Bear thought.

Mad Bear dashed toward his enemy, then halted three lance lengths away and wheeled to his left. He dashed forward ten lengths and stopped again, to let the chief hear his laughter.

The Ironshirt shouted curses. Mad Bear could not understand them all, but he heard the Ironshirt word for "honor." He grinned and rose in his stirrups. "You have no honor!" he shouted.

The Ironshirt chief cursed louder and spurred his horse toward Mad Bear. Mad Bear grinned again. He had learned that phrase from Murphy. *And my brother wondered why I wanted to know that!*

Mad Bear let his pony dance across the field, staying always three lengths ahead of his enemy. The Child had risen enough now to show the lather on the flanks of his enemy's horse. *A little more*, Mad Bear thought. *Just a little farther.*

"Coward!" the Ironshirt screamed, and reined in. He looked back, and saw that he had been led far from the battle. His banner-bearer was fifty lengths away.

Now!

Mad Bear galloped up behind and to the left, and struck with his sword. His blow landed on the Ironshirt's shield. Mad Bear galloped past and wheeled twenty lengths beyond his enemy. The banner-bearer was coming up fast. Two Ironshirts together would always be a match for one warrior of the Horse People. This must be done quickly.

Mad Bear rode forward, and suddenly the man spurred his horse at him. It was a better horse than Mad Bear had ever seen. Lathered and snorting, it yet dashed forward at the chief's command. The Ironshirt lance came down and thrust deep into the throat of Mad Bear's pony.

As the Ironshirt let go the lance to draw his sword, Mad Bear leaped leftward over his dying mount's neck and rolled to break the fall, then dived over his fallen pony and rolled on his back to thrust his sword upward deep into the belly of his enemy's mount.

The horse screamed and reared. The Ironshirt chief kicked free of the stirrups and leaped backward over the horse's rump to land on his feet. Mad Bear tore out a handful of turf and threw it at the Ironshirt's visor. Then he dashed to his left and rolled to kick the man's legs from under him, then stood and pushed him down. As the ironshirt thrashed, Mad Bear tried to drive his dagger through the eyeslits of the visor. The Ironshirt smashed at his head with his steel gauntlet, and sparks flew in Mad Bear's vision. He leaped to his feet and jumped backward. The Ironshirt rose to his knees and lifted his sword to slash at Mad Bear, then got to his feet as Mad Bear leaped back. Mad Bear circled toward the fallen horse, and the man turned to face him. When Mad Bear struggled to pull his sword from the horse, the Ironshirt retrieved his shield.

The banner-bearer rode down on them. He had dropped the banner and held a sword. As he rode past, Mad Bear dove to the ground, then leaped up before the dismounted Ironshirt could strike. The banner-bearer halted and turned. His Ironshirt master shouted commands that Mad Bear could not understand.

Where are my clansmen? Mad Bear turned to run away. As he did, a mounted starman rode up. The starman shouted, and the banner-bearer turned toward him. The small star weapon they called the "Ingram" made it sounds of tearing cloth.

The Ironshirt chief's chest turned from silver to red. He crashed to the ground and lay still. The banner-bearer tried to raise his sword to strike, but he had no strength, and toppled from the saddle. Mad Bear dashed forward to grasp the horse's bridle to secure it for the star warrior.

The starman shouted something and rode away. Mad Bear turned back toward the camp. The circle of archers had grown tighter around it.

Mad Bear turned to his dead horse and took off saddle and bridle, then cut loose the feathers and claws woven into the top of the mane.

✣ ✣ ✣

It had been a tougher fight than Murphy wanted. *Sure were a lot of guards for one goddamn wagon train. And not all that much loot, either. Glad we had the Westmen, instead of Drantos ironhats, or we'd never have beat that many heavies.*

Murphy sent a scout platoon to chase the enemy survivors farther from the camp. *And that's funny too. One minute they fought like tigers, then all of a sudden they couldn't run fast enough.* He didn't expect to catch the survivors. Hell, he didn't *want* to catch them, just keep them from regrouping to launch a counterattack.

Murphy went with the detail guarding all the prisoners who could walk. It was the only way to make sure the Westmen didn't cut their throats. Westmen didn't believe in prisoners, and they believed even less in leaving live enemies behind them.

The camp and the wounded were left to what might loosely be called the mercy of the Westmen. The only way the Drantos men could stop them if they wanted to cut throats was by a fight. If it came to that, Murphy would rather lose sleep over dead prisoners than over a task force that chewed itself to bits in enemy territory.

Besides, we got no doctors. Anybody hurt bad enough he can't walk and unpopular enough his friends won't carry him isn't going to make it anyway.

He stood watch until the prisoners built a camp outside the wagon ring. They been stripped of their weapons, and footgear, despite

Murphy's best efforts, most of their valuables as well. *I cannot make these damn fools understand that it's better to carry oats than gold.*

Murphy heard snatches of bawdy songs coming from the wagons. Somebody had found the wine. He sent two sergeants to be sure the duty platoons stayed sober, and prayed there wasn't an enemy reaction force anywhere near. *Bit different when* we're *the Viet Cong. . . .*

Discipline was holding pretty well, though. Probably everybody had filched one choice piece of loot to hold out from the general division of the spoils, but that was nothing new. What mattered was that the horses and the wagons were in good shape.

A man-at-arms met Murphy as he rode up to the wagons.

"My lord. Arekor wishes you to speak to Mad Bear and Lord Roscoe before they slay each other. He says it is a matter of honor."

"Oh, shit. Okay, I'm coming."

✢ ✢ ✢

Murphy found the three men standing beside a camp bed in the former CP tent. On the bed lay the body of a tall blond man of about twenty-five. He'd been shot at least five times in the chest with a nine-millimeter weapon. *Ingram. Roscoe's kill. So?* "What's the problem?"

Mad Bear promptly burst into a torrent of words, so fast that Murphy couldn't understand more than one in four. Arekor tried to translate, then gave up and started again after Mad Bear ran down.

"He says that the Lord Roscoe insults him by giving him Prince Akkilas' head when he did little to—"

"What the hell—? Hal, is this Prince Akkilas, Sarakos' kid brother? Really?"

"Sarge, he wore steel armor with silver inlays. Toris's griffin defaced on his shield, and on the camp banner. He's got a birthmark on his left ear, and wears a silver griffin earring. Who the hell else could he be?"

"Holy Mother of God," said Murphy softly. "No wonder the prisoners are acting spooked. That's why they all ran, once the banner was down! Jenri, go get me a couple of the prisoner officers."

"Sir." His orderly went out.

"Now, assuming that's who we've got—"

"It is," Roscoe said. "Believe it."

"I do. Which still doesn't answer the question. Why the hell do you want to give Mad Bear a head he thinks you should have?"

"Mad Bear did most of the work. He'd got him off his horse, and in another minute he'd have killed him. I just speeded things up. Hell, Sarge, I was trying to be friendly!"

"Yeah," said Murphy. They all looked at him. "Gimme a goddamn minute, will you?"

Mad Bear muttered something Murphy didn't understand.

"Arekor, be real careful when you say this to Mad Bear. Tell him Lord Roscoe offered the head to Mad Bear as brother to his chief. Tell him that Lord Roscoe did not understand that this is not the custom of the Horse People. Roscoe, you nod like anything, you hear me?"

"Yes, *sir*!"

Arekor spoke rapidly. Mad Bear glared, then looked at Murphy, back at Roscoe, then at Murphy again. He grinned and spoke.

Arekor translated. "He says he has been with you long enough to know something of the ways of starmen, and it will not be necessary for you to swear this is true."

"Good. Now somebody send for some of that goddamn wine. And some of that mare piss my brother drinks."

His orderly came in with two of the prisoners. Murphy pointed to the body. "Is this Akkilas Son of Toris?" he demanded. He waited a moment. "I see. Take them out. Fellows, we got ourselves either an opportunity or one hell of a problem."

✢ ✢ ✢

When the others had left, Murphy poured drinks for himself and Corporal Roscoe. "It all comes down to this," Murphy said. "Kings don't like people killing kings and princes unless they do it themselves. I'm going to buck this one up the chain of command."

"How in hell are you going to do that when we can't even get home?" Roscoe demanded.

"For starters, we take off this guy's head and pickle it. Keep the shield and banner, too. Then we give the whole goddamn mess to the first senior officer we find, and hope like hell that turns out to be Captain Galloway."

"I'll buy that one," Roscoe said. "But it ain't likely. Ganton's army is a hell of a lot closer."

"Yeah, I know," Murphy said. "I've just been studying the best way to join up with him. Of course it'd help if we knew exactly where he was."

"You could send the Westmen out looking."

"Could, but won't. We all came in together, and we'll go out together." Murphy unrolled a map. "Look, the last we heard, Ganton was just south of Castle Fasolt. It ain't likely he's moved too far away. Tomorrow we'll go looking for him."

"About time. Even with the stuff we took tonight, we're gettin' low on everything. Especially horses. And your buddies have used up a lot of those ponies of theirs, too." Roscoe scratched his head. "Sarge, you gotta teach me more about getting along with those touchy little suckers."

"Hah. When I learn, I'll tell you. I know one thing. You and Mad Bear did a hell of a night's work. You could get a goddamned knighthood out of this. You realize that with Akkilas dead, Ganton's the nearest male heir to the High Throne?"

"No shit? But I thought it wasn't exactly hereditary—"

"Yeah, yeah, I know. That's so if the blood heir's an idiot they can pick somebody competent to hold things together. So who's a better candidate than our Wanax, especially with his Roman connections? And he's got the captain on his side, too."

"You mean, Ganton could be High Rexja because we zapped Akkilas?"

"May gunkels eat my underwear if I kid you."

"Shit." It was nearly a prayer. Roscoe shook his head.

"I wondered where Akkilas was," Murphy said.

"Eh? Yeah, I keep forgetting you've gone native, Sarge."

"Ah, cut the crap—"

"Well, maybe I didn't mean it quite like it sounds. You think like the captain does. Like these people do. Me, I just go where they tell me. You're a goddamn officer, even if I don't have to say 'sir' every two minutes."

"Yeah, sure. Thanks. Anyway. I did wonder where they were keeping Akkilas."

"Now we know," Roscoe said. "Where they thought he was safe. Guy sure had more *cojones* than brains."

"So it goes." Murphy looked at the body. "He had *some* smarts as well as guts. He got those troops mounted and riding out damned fast, and was ready to take the mounted archers in the flank. He could have done some real damage if Mad Bear hadn't held them up till I threw in the cavalry reserve."

He shook his head. "Hal, sometimes I have nightmares about the greyskins cutting off our ammo right when somebody has really learned how to fight us. Combined-arms army, gunpowder and guns, professional soldiers, logistics, the whole bag. You ever heard the definition of the Second Law of Thermodynamics?"

"Can't say I have."

" 'You can't win, you can't break even, and you can't get out of the game.' Sometimes this whole mess seems like that. Not that it isn't better than being dead, but still . . ."

"Sarge, you've been listening to the captain too much and drinking too little. Mind if I break out some of Akkilas' private stock?"

"Go ahead."

✢ ✢ ✢

Mad Bear walked until the fires around the camp faded in the light of the rising Child. He took bow, quiver, sword, and dagger, for this was not a true vigil in which a man had to trust to the protection of the gods. Some of the camp's Ironshirts might have had the courage to lie in wait in the darkness. He did not care to be easy prey for them.

At last he reached a grassy hummock, drove his sword into the ground so that it might drink the strength of the earth, and sat cross-legged beside it. It was as well that this was no vigil, because for once in his life Mad Bear did not even know what to ask the gods, let alone what answer he wished to hear.

By all the laws and customs in war Mad Bear had ever known, the kill of Prince Akkilas belonged to the warrior Roscoe. Yet it seemed his dearest wish to give it to Mad Bear, for all that this was taking honor not only from himself but from his sons.

Perhaps he had no sons? Some warriors took vows to lie apart from women until they had accomplished some great deed or sworn vengeance. They accepted the danger that their line might die with them, if they died before fulfilling their vow. Certainly not all the wizard-warriors were like that. His blood-brother had been married twice, as well as having concubines in between.

Roscoe might be such a man—if such oaths were known among the wizard-warriors. Mad Bear did not know, nor did he have much hope of learning soon. The gods had sent the wizard-warriors and made them—or at least some of them, for now—friends of the Silver

Wolves. That was enough. A warrior who had sworn to aid these—whatever they might be—whether the gods said yea or nay—well, he had small claim on the gods for easy answers to hard questions.

Mad Bear decided that the gods had given him enough and more than he had any right to. He had his life, his wits, his eyes, ears, and tongue. If he lost none of these, he might in time know all that he needed to know of the wizard-warriors.

The wizard-warriors were like a great storm, blowing *mekar* seeds across the land. They blew some men to victory, others to defeat. Tonight they had blown him to victory.

Mad Bear laid a captured sword on the earth beside his own, raised his arms to the sky, and began to sing his victory song.

28

Chief Captain Volauf entered the tent as Matthias was pulling on his gauntlets.

"Good day, my lord. You are awake early."

"I have been at my prayers, that Vothan may grant us his favor."

In truth Matthias had barely slept. Many things could happen in battle, and Vothan One-eye was notoriously fickle, even toward those who defended his honor. He had always been so. Yet the cause of the High Rexja had prospered under the House of Vothan.

That was not all. This mad new religion, this fusion of the ravings of Roman scholars and the worst of the preachings of the House of Yatar, had driven many of the priests of Yatar to alliance with Vothan. Matthias had seen that happen in the Five, and even in Drantos. If they did no more than send information, they served. When the Ottarn bridge gave way and carried off three pack mules, Matthias had learned almost as soon as Ganton.

"Captain, have you new reports?"

"Only one, Honorable. In addition to Morrone's band in the north, we have heard that a small band of raiders has come from the west. My scout officer believes it is the remains of a force sent to harass Captain General Ailas."

"Ah." Ailas held Ganton's western army in check. Poised to threaten the High Road past Dravan, Ailas was doing greater service by existing than most generals could give by a victory. "Nothing more on Morrone?"

"No, Honorable. Our supply trains now require heavier escorts, but Morrone's raiders are more an annoyance than a real threat."

"Good. When we have won this battle we will deal with him."

"Otherwise, Honorable, all remains as it was last night. We have twice Ganton's strength. Our light horse is spread across his rear. A mixed blessing, Honorable. We cut into his supply, and we can turn any retreat into rout, but the knowledge that we have forces behind him will make his men fight all the harder."

Matthias smiled grimly. "They do not know how much strength we have behind them. I had rather have my enemies looking over their shoulders. And now that one of the greatest of their star weapons lies at the bottom of the Ottarn to amuse the hydras, they have even more to fear."

"I have never faced the magic of guns before," Volauf said.

"I have. In the south. Captain, guns need firepowder. That is not made by magic, and without firepowder the guns are as useless as unstrung bows or empty quivers."

I also have friends who went with the traitor Strymon, but that is no concern of yours, Captain Volauf.

"Your pardon, Honorable, but it is my duty to ask. Are you certain we should begin this battle before Prince Akkilas comes to lead the host?"

"It is your duty to ask. A moment." Matthias went to the chest that stood at the foot of his bed, and took out a parchment. He unrolled it. "You see the Seal of Issardos. See this."

Volauf read. "I see. He shows great confidence in you."

"You mean that he shows less in the prince. Captain, we carry Prince Akkilas' banner before us, and we give our orders in his name. The bards will say that he won this battle. You and I will know different."

"You and I," Volauf said. "And Chancellor Issardos."

"Yes, of course. You will not be forgotten, Captain Volauf."

"I thank you, Honorable."

Matthias waved his hand in dismissal. "Is my horse ready?"

"Yes, Honorable."

"I will be there presently."

✢ ✢ ✢

Ganton was watching the Second Division move into position when the messenger reached him.

"Majesty, a bheroman of Toris' host has ridden close to our front and challenges you to single combat."

"Indeed," Ganton said. "And who might he be?"

"Majesty, he gives his name as Roald of Caemoran. He says that you are no true Wanax if you refuse him battle to hide behind wizards' magic."

"Indeed," Ganton said in a tone that made the messenger flinch. "Lord Hilaskos, have my squires bring my warhorse to Prince Strymon's banner." He put spurs to his palfrey. After a moment he swallowed his rage and reined in the horse, so that his guards would not have to tire their own mounts to keep up with him. The fate of Drantos today might rest on how many fresh horses the host could command at the end of the battle.

When Ganton reached Strymon's banner he reined in and used his binoculars to inspect the area between the two armies. An armored man on a bay gelding walked his horse in a large circle. The red and white of his shield matched the pennon on his lance. Every time he completed a circle he shouted, "I am Roald of Caemoran. I call the Wanax Ganton of Drantos to honorable single combat. If he comes not, I denounce him as no true Wanax, but a coward who hides behind godless wizardry!"

Ganton listened to this three times while waiting for his warhorse to arrive. Finally he pulled out his battle-axe, his only weapon, and wrapped the thong around his wrist.

"Your Majesty!" exclaimed Strymon. "You are not going down there as you are, with neither armor nor weapons nor warhorse, to fight a full-armed—"

Ganton whipped the battle-axe up and in a circle over his head. "This is enough weapon for any man."

"Your—" Strymon lowered his voice. "Ganton, my friend, it is not well done to call a Wanax and ally a fool, but—"

"The more reason, then, for not doing it. I know what I am about, and I do not think Roald of Caemoran does."

"At least let me take the challenge as your champion!"

"No. It is not you that Roald calls a coward who hides behind wizards."

"My friend, you have told me that when one becomes Wanax, one can no longer act as one wishes. I believe this. Are you not being foolish, to endanger the day in this way?"

"I thought on this as I rode here," Ganton said. "The Lord Rick is not here. We lost a star weapon when the bridge collapsed. The clouds are low, so that the balloon will not be useful. The army knows that we have little enough of wizardry today, and we face forces larger than our own. I think it can do no harm to show our men that their Wanax has not forgotten the old ways."

"Then be careful, my friend."

"I will. Be ready to avenge me if I fall." He turned to his staff officers. "You will follow Prince Strymon as you would me."

"Sire—"

"Silence. You have your orders." He kicked his horse to a walk.

"Go with—Yatar and Christ," Strymon said.

As Ganton rode down the hill, he shifted his Browning so that he could draw it with his left hand, and clicked off the safety.

✛ ✛ ✛

Tylara could not hear the conversation between Ganton and Strymon, but she could see Ganton ride out to accept the challenge.

He is no foolish knight, yet he acts like one. This is not the act of the Wanax I saw in council. Her heart turned to lead. For a moment all the assurances of Apelles and Yanulf seemed vain lies. Not given the sacrifice they demanded, the gods *were* striking at those about her, starting with the Wanax, whom they had just afflicted with madness. . . .

The moment passed swiftly. *He is in range of my best archers. No. Half our knights would ride away if it appeared that the Wanax had so little honor. I cannot even avenge him that way.*

She watched with dread as Ganton rode down the hill.

When Ganton rode out into the circle Roald had trampled, the bheroman shouted and spurred his horse to a canter.

His horse is tired, she thought. *And Ganton has a fresh mount.*

The Wanax rode directly toward Roald. Roald's lance came down. The bheroman spurred his horse into a lumbering gallop. Three lengths before they met, Ganton swerved sharply to his left. Roald's lance tried to sweep in a circle to follow, but Ganton was already out of reach of the point. Then he turned to his right and rode directly at Roald.

Ganton passed just behind the bheroman, and as he did he swept his axe in a backhand blow at Roald's neck. As Roald crumpled and fell, Ganton rode back toward his own lines without looking back.

There was a moment of silence, then the deafening cheers of the army.

✣ ✣ ✣

The ridge was low, but high enough to overlook the battlefield below. When Tylara rode up to Ganton's banner, she saw that the staff had placed a low trestle table there for Ganton's maps.

She was the last to arrive. The most senior officers were seated at the table. Other staff officers stood behind them. At the foot of the table Apelles looked uncomfortable in robes hastily altered to show his new station. Drumold indicated a place to his right, where she could look across the maps to the battlefield.

It had taken years of Rick's instruction, but she was now familiar enough with maps that she needed only a cursory glance at the field below to see what was represented on them. Still she took her time with her binoculars, looking at the field and then back to the map.

The army was divided into three Divisions. Each Division had horse, foot, and guns, and was a small army complete in itself. Ganton had heard Rick say that was the way armies were organized on his home world. Tylara wondered if that would be so appropriate here, but the Wanax was proud of what he had done. She looked beyond the host of Drantos to the enemy.

"Griffin," she said almost to herself.

"Yes," Ganton said. He nodded to acknowledge her arrival. "They raised the banner of Prince Akkilas an hour ago. Your pardon, Lady, if I do not begin again. I do not think we have much more time."

He pointed again to the map. "It is called *echelon*," he said. "Each Division supports the others."

Tylara remembered Rick's lectures on the formation. A Wanax of the Germans, one later called Great, had used it. Each of the three Divisions could attack or defend, and each guarded the flanks of another. There was no way an enemy could crush one Division without fighting at least one other. No way that the host could be defeated in *detail*.

Ganton had also held back what Rick called *reserves*. They stood behind the Second Division: the starmen and their weapons, more guns, the Tamaerthan chivalry, Nikeian city militia who fought with great axes, and the handful of Romans who had come with Larry Warner from the University.

The balloon was nowhere in sight, and Tylara guessed that the clouds were too low for it to be useful. The air felt heavy and smelled of coming rain.

"Are there to be no Romans?" Hilaskos asked.

"No, my lord. Our Roman allies do us good service in keeping safe our southern borders. How long has it been that the host of Drantos can be sent north without a care for south and east? If we cannot defend one of our borders without crying for Legions, we are poor allies indeed."

"What is the signal for the advance?" Rudhrig asked.

"We will not advance," Ganton said.

Rudhrig growled. "I feared as much."

"My lords," Ganton said. "We have no need for battle at all. We stand at the very border of our lands. We are well supplied. Our enemy is deep in Ta-Meltemos, a land turning more hostile to him each day. Lord Morrone harasses his rear—"

"We've taken our share of that," Rudhrig said. "Your pardon, Majesty."

"When you have matters to say in Council, say them," Ganton said. "I did not call you here to be silent. I am as aware as you that half a thousand of enemy horse are in our rear. They are pursued by the local levies and our Mounted Archers, and I do not think they will be a threat for long. Certainly they are not as great a danger to us as Lord Morrone is to Akkilas."

Rick always said defense is stronger, but it seldom wins decisions, Tylara thought. I hope that Ganton is right today, but I have doubts. She raised her binoculars to study the enemy.

Their heavy cavalry alone outnumbered Ganton's entire army. The enemy had dismounted well beyond range of bowshot. They stood or sat on the ground, waiting, and did not seem to be impatient. Small blocks of infantry, mostly crossbowmen, filled gaps between the blocks of enemy cavalry. The enemy line stretched beyond Ganton's on both the left and right. On the Drantos right were four stadia of swampy lowland, then the Ottarn River. Any of Akkilas' cavalry who waded through the swamps would not be in good formation to receive a charge from the reserves at the top of the hill.

The Drantos left rested against a bluff. Tamaerthan archers and Drantos levies held its top, and in any event the sides were too steep for cavalry.

If we must defend, it is a good place for it. Still, I wish he had kept the pikes and archers together. Rick always does. And where are you, my husband? I think we need you.

And if we do not, then Ganton will soon prove that he can win battles without the War Leader of Drantos. How long before Ganton takes that post for himself? Or gives it to another?

Horns sounded across the quiet field. The enemy soldiers stood. Cavalrymen began to mount.

"My Lord Father Apelles," Ganton said. "But—please be brief."

Apelles looked out at the bustle of activity below, then stood and raised his hand in blessing. "Go with Yatar and Christ His Son."

"Thank you. Now to your posts, my lords. My lady. Go with Yatar and Christ." Ganton raised his hand high and brought it down sharply. The Great Guns roared.

Before Tylara reached her Hussars, the battlefield was dimmed with smoke.

✛   ✛   ✛

As the third charge retreated, Volauf rode up to Matthias. He plucked an arrow from his saddle and another from the gambeson covering his mail.

"Are you wounded?" Matthias asked.

"I have felt worse from bees. No, Honorable, the Chooser has not yet called me to his Hall."

"He has called more than I like." A thousand and more of the host lay in heaps between the three great battles of the enemy. They were hidden by the sharp-smelling smoke that covered the low area.

"Or I, honorable. This formation of theirs is damnable. We advance against one group, and the others fly on our flanks, or shoot us down with arrows. And always there are the *guns.*"

"At least we know this much. The guns are not wizard weapons. They are only machines. You saw it as I did. They are served by men, who fill them with firepowder and stones, and bring torches to make them shoot. Kill those men and the guns are as useless as any other weapon."

Volauf frowned in thought. "Honorable, I believe you. But what of the star weapons?"

"I believe they are the same," Matthias said. "Nothing but more powerful guns. They need—arrows, stones, firepowder as guns do, and they must be wielded by men."

"But what can we do? Honorable, I believe the men will charge once more if I lead them. I cannot guarantee you twice."

"Wait. Refresh yourself, and see that your officers are ready. I will not send you forth again without a plan."

✛ ✛ ✛

"All is ready, Honorable," Volauf said. "Have you commands?"

"I believe so. Captain, what makes archers cease shooting?"

"They cease when they have used all their arrows. Or when the enemy is amongst them."

"Nothing else?"

"Ah! When friend and foe are so mixed that they cannot be sure who they will hit."

"Exactly so. The guns and star weapons must be much the same. Captain Volauf, ride to those captains of horse and foot you trust most. Say that if they will follow me even to Vothan's Hall, we may yet bring home victory to the High Rexja!"

"The Council of Captains—"

"Demons fly away with the Council of Captains! This must be done quickly or not at all!"

✛ ✛ ✛

Larry Warner and his aeronauts were held in reserve at the command post. The balloon was useless, and now smoke lay so heavy across the battlefield that it was rare to get a semaphore message through. No one had any orders for him, so he watched the battle.

Larry had a bad feeling about the enemy charge the minute he saw it was led by that crazy with the Vothanite robes over his armor. The guy might be crazy, but he had guts, and his men stayed with him.

The charge came right at the corner of the Third Division.

Smart, Warner thought. The corner of a square is always the weakest point.

The archer and musketeers in reserve in the center of the square ran to support the corner, but before they could arrive the enemy cavalry struck home. The cavalry were followed by infantry, then more cavalry, and it looked to Warner as if the entire enemy army was ready to pour into that one area.

The corner broke. Pikemen tried to close around the point with breaking ranks. Warner mentally crossed his fingers; that was the

Fourth Pikes, who'd been a little shaky ever since they'd been forced to surrender at Piro's Hill.

The pikemen held for a moment. Then the sheer weight of the enemy's numbers tore two holes in the line. Cavalry and infantry poured through. Third Division's archers tried to loft their arrows over the pikemen and into the enemy cavalry, but they were harassed by arrows from horse archers.

The musketeers formed ranks. Warner held his breath. If there was any way to get a message to the musketry captain—

The muskets ripple-fired, more than a hundred going off so fast they sounded like one enormously loud and long shot. Enemy cavalry and friendly pikemen took the bullets in about equal proportion.

The ranks of the pikemen bulged inward. More pikemen turned and ran away, running the Tamaerthan archers and upsetting their aim or just getting in their way. The Tamaerthan officers screamed curses, and some of the pikemen stopped to try to hold with the archers, but not enough.

The pike wall was broken. More enemy cavalry poured into the gap. By now the entire corner and half the sides of Third Division was crumbling. Light cavalry charged through the gaps and laid about with saber and lance.

And now somebody on the other side had seen what was happening, and was bringing up the goddamned infantry! Warner thought up two interesting new punishments for the son of a bitch who'd lost the LMG and prayed Bisso would let the mortar open up. They'd been waiting for a good target, because they only had fifteen rounds and some of those not too good. That infantry would be a mortarman's dream, though.

By the time the infantry got into safe mortar range, the Third Division was no longer a square but a slightly ragged rectangle. Where the enemy had hit first was an almighty brawl, with everybody hacking and poking at each other for dear life.

The CO of the Division—Eqeta Rudhrig, Warner remembered— seemed to have his act together. He was pulling cavalry over to stiffen the pikemen who'd lost their nerve and help the archers and musketeers who couldn't shoot without hitting friends. They were slinging their bows and muskets and wading into the fight with cold steel, and maybe they would be enough.

Maybe not, too, because more enemy cavalry was working around the Division's right flank, where it didn't have any support. Time to commit the reserves, Ganton old buddy old pal, and where the hell was that mortar . . . ?

The eighty-one millimeter coughed. Smoke sprouted just short of the advancing infantry. A second round landed right in the middle of them. Three more rounds did the same. Warner breathed easier. The infantry and more cavalry were pushing into the gap between the Third and Second Divisions, where they could also be hit by the Second. That was Teuthras', and with a little help from the mortars he could—

"Oh. *shit!*"

The fifth round from the mortar was a short. It didn't touch the enemy, but it landed right in the middle of a battery of four-pounders. From the amount of smoke, it must have touched off some of the ammo.

Warner snapped off the safety on his G-3 and chambered a round. He wasn't completely sure who he was going to be shooting at. Probably Toris' people, but no way you could get around the fact that all of a sudden the battle had got a whole lot hairier, and if somebody started looking for scapegoats, the starmen were going to be well up toward the head of the line. . . .

✛ ✛ ✛

Rudhrig, Eqeta of Harms, saw the corner of his Division crumbling. He shouted for archers and musketeers from the *reserve* in the center of the square. Then he remembered to send messengers as well. The starmen's way of war called for armies so large and battlefields so noisy that a captain's voice could not always reach those who must hear it.

Some of the musketeers and more of the archers didn't wait for orders. They hurried toward the corner of the square where the enemy charge had struck. Rudhrig waved to his house knights, urging them to one side so that his foot could shoot freely.

It was unknightly that his best men should be reduced to guarding the flanks of the sons of Drantos peasants and Tamaerthan hill-bandits. Yet there was no other way to keep the enemy from crushing his division. Saddles fell empty swiftly, but two men took the place of each fallen rider.

Rudhrig shouted. "Raise high the White Hawk, Guy! Let them know whom they face!"

His son grinned and raised the great banner of Harms with both hands, then waved it back and forth. Rudhrig prayed that Guy would have no more dangerous work this day. When Sarakos' host had marched into Drantos, the Eqeta of Harms had had three sons. When it marched out, he had only one.

The guns hurled stones into the enemy's ranks. Men toppled, headless. Horses screamed. An angry din grew behind Rudhrig as the musketeers joined the shooting. More enemies fell.

Pikemen fell too. Rudhrig looked for the enemy's archers and cursed. The musketeers were hitting their own comrades as well as the enemy! Gaps appeared in the pike ranks as men fell. Enemy shortswordsmen swarmed into the gaps, slashing and stabbing. The gaps grew wider as Fourth Pikes gave way.

"Death or glory!" A high-pitched young voice gave the battle-cry of the Eqetas of Harms. Rudhrig's bowels turned to ice. The White Hawk swept down the hill. Guy held the banner-staff in one hand and his sword in the other. "Men of Harms! To me!"

The boy reached the fleeing pikemen just as the enemy horsemen poured through the gap in Fourth Pike's line. Guy laid about him with his sword, trying to rally the foot soldiers. Then he vanished among the enemy.

Rudhrig had no breath left to give orders or even to curse. He needed none. His men surged as one toward the enemy. Riflemen ran, holding their empty weapons like clubs. Archers ran, slinging their bows and drawing swords. The Eqeta's house knights charged toward the White Hawk banner before their lord could put spurs to his horse.

Three horsemen rose from the ground at Rudhrig's feet. His lance flung one out of the saddle and broke. Rudhrig carved the second man's shield with a blow from his sword, then slashed the man's face. The third enemy rained stout blows on Rudhrig's shield and mail. A knifeman slipped closer.

Two archers ran up to Rudhrig's side. One clubbed the knifeman with his bow, and the other slashed at the last horseman's mount. The horse reared, giving Rudhrig an easy target. He ended the fight with a sword cut to the man's neck.

"My thanks!" Rudhrig gasped, and charged down the hill.

The archers and riflemen had closed with the enemy before the knights reached them. The fleeing pikemen were thick enough to block a horse, but men on foot could slip through. Now the archers forced the pikemen back into ranks at the point of their swords. The riflemen ran to either flank. The White Hawk was nowhere in sight.

Dayfather, grant me Guy's life, and you may have anything you ask of me.

More enemy horse rode toward the Eqeta, but this time his knights were there to meet them. Two knights and six of the enemy went down. Tamaerthans ran in to slit the enemy's throats almost as fast as they fell.

Rudhrig saw the enemy foot pressing up into the gap between the remnants of his Third Division and the Second Division to his left. The guns fired faster, flailing the enemy with stones that cut great swathes through the ranks. His pikemen reformed their ranks. Riflemen and archers joined them, and the enemy cavalry gained no more ground. Rudhrig shouted for a messenger. If the Wanax threw his reserves against the enemy's horse and foot—

Three archers and a musketeer ran out of the press, carrying a limp figure. The banner of the White Hawk was still in his hand. Rudhrig suddenly lacked the breath even for a prayer.

The limp figure raised its head and shook off the hands that tried to hold him down. Rudhrig found himself at his son's side. "Guy—my boy! How is it—"

"I'm not hurt, Father. Please tell these sons of swineherds to stop stepping on my hands!" His voice held both indignation and affection. "I'm sorry the White Hawk's been muddied."

"They could have used it to wipe Toris' arse!" Knightly language be damned, Rudhrig thought. Thank Yatar, my son is safe. "Guy, you must take a message to the Wanax Ganton."

"Father, I *won't* be sent away like a disobedient—"

The Great Gun of the starmen opened fire. Rudhrig counted five shots from the—the *mortar.* There was a crashing explosion, and a great cloud of white smoke poured up beyond the enemy. Rudhrig scrambled into the saddle.

The smoke cleared and he saw that the barrels of firepowder must have exploded. Had the starmen's mortar by chance struck at friends? Certainly something had destroyed two of the guns. The ground was littered with the bodies of the men who had tended the guns.

Three of the guns remained, and the men who served them were still alive. Limping, black-faced, half-clothed, they took their places. Rudhrig remembered what he had heard of the fight at the Great Redoubt: how the gunners had charged with Lord Rick himself to take their weapons back from the enemy.

Courage comes in many forms. As does honor. And there were things not even knights or Eqeta could face undaunted.

✧ ✧ ✧

Ganton saw the enemy thrusting into the gap between the battered Third Division and Teuthras' Second. A messenger rode off to Lord Drumold to bring up the Tamaerthan horse. Then Ganton spurred toward the gap.

Hilaskos and the Guards had just caught up with him when the starmen's mortar opened fire. The first four rounds gave Ganton hope the enemy attack would never reach the guns. The fifth round dashed that hope. When the smoke cleared, two of the five guns were overturned, and many of the gunners lay on the ground. Ganton cursed.

"Guards, halt! First Squad go tell the starmen—" *Tell them what? Not to kill our own people?* "Tell them to be careful. I am going to rally the gunners." He sent a messenger to Lord Clavell and his Nikeian axemen: rally at once at the banner of the Fighting Man.

"Where will that be, Majesty?" asked the messenger.

"Among the guns," said Ganton, pointing downhill. The messenger swallowed but his Wanax's glare froze any argument on his lips. He rode off as Bheroman Hilaskos raised the Fighting Man and the royal party trotted downhill.

They reached the rear of the guns just as the enemy's foot recovered their courage and came on. The Guards musketeers fired from the saddle, a ragged volley that still couldn't miss a target the size of the oncoming foot. Their wine-colored tunics identified them as spearmen of Ta-Kartos.

The enemy surged forward, the Guards dismounted to reload, use their bows, or hold horses. Master Gunner Pinir ran about, using a rammer to prod reluctant gunners back to their duties. The gunners seemed more afraid of him than of the enemy.

From behind the enemy's foot horse archers began shooting. With the short northern bows, few of their arrows reached hostile targets. A good many struck their own foot. The attack wavered again, then wavered still more as the musketeers of the Second Division opened fire.

Ganton's horse was spent. He dismounted. Moments later he was in the middle of another battle. Enemies were all around him. He drew his sword and lashed out. *Lord Rick would never approve. I am no more than a common foot soldier. And who commands now?* He tried to hack his way to the rear so that he could return to the command post. There was nothing to be done here.

Hilaskos fought beside him, holding the Fighting Man. A spearman ran at him and thrust him in the thigh. Hilaskos brought the banner pole down on the attacker's head. A Guardsman cut the spearman down, just as Hilaskos staggered, then fell. A squire ran forward to lift the banner. "Hold it high! You are a knight as of this moment!" Ganton shouted.

More enemies, with swords and ironbound clubs for close work. Ganton's sword broke on the head of a club but his Guards were all about him, throwing their shields in front of him until they made a wall. Ganton drew his Browning and fired between the Guards' shields. Five of the enemy went down. Others heard the thunder of the star weapon and held back.

More of the host of Drantos rallied to the Fighting Man, until his friends were causing as much confusion as enemies. Rudhrig brought up the last of his cavalry reserves. They began their advance into the gap, not in a solid line but picking their way forward in twos and threes. With swords and lances they cleared the rear of the guns of enemies, then formed into two columns. One to the left, one to the right, they passed through the guns and into the enemy's foot.

The Ta-Kartos spearmen were neither armed nor trained as well as Lord Rick's pike regiments; they could not stand against cavalry and did not. They would have fled, except for their own horse pressing hard against their rear. So most of them died where they stood. Those who did not die under Drantos steel died from the arrows and bullets of both Divisions; the archers and musketeers of the Third had rallied.

At last there was nothing in front of Ganton and the guns save dead men or wounded that the cavalry were finishing off with lance-thrusts from the saddle. Rudhrig had his knights well in hand; Ganton had no fear of their charging too far. When he'd seen Hilaskos bandaged and carried off the field, he remounted and ordered the Nikeian axemen to the right of the Third Division. Their long-handled axes would do well against either horse or foot, as long as the Fourth Pikes did not give up the fight.

The Guards reformed their shield wall. Some time before the low clouds had broken into misty rain. One after another the guns fell silent. Ganton had time to pull out the arrows stuck in his gambeson. None had penetrated the mail beneath. He reloaded the Browning.

The rain would silence guns and muskets alike. Thick smoke from the firepowder lay across the entire battle area. Archers could not see a hundred paces into the gloom, and had no targets.

The battle would be won by whoever could bring home a charge, infantry or cavalry. There could be no strategy, and in this smoke weapons that struck at a distance were useless.

Vothan favors the side with the greatest numbers. Ganton had heard that as a child. Today it might be true.

The enemy trumpets sounded again.

29

Tylara watched the battle until the rain and smoke closed in. Then there was nothing to see.

Balquhain rode up. "Mac Clallan Muir sent me to ask if you know who commands this army."

"It is certainly not me." She pointed down the hill into the smoke. "The Wanax Ganton rode that way with the Banner of the Fighting Man half an hour ago. I have not seen him since."

"I think our father knows this."

"So do I. Why did he send you here?"

Balquhain shook his head. "You always did know him better than me. But I think he wants you to take command of the army."

"Take command—"

"Tylara, you are Eqetassa of Chelm and Justiciar of Drantos. The Wanax has vanished. Someone must command—"

"Brother, the knights will not obey me. I am Eqetassa, not Eqeta—"

"Drantos knights would obey you more than me, or Mac Clallan Muir."

Yatar, is this part of my penance?

"Father says we must do something or the battle is lost."

Tylara peered into the smoke. The sounds of battle flowed up the hill. Screaming horses and men, the clash of swords and shields, and other sounds she did not recognize. None of them told her what was happening. Just as the weather closed in completely she had seen

866

Akkilas' forces rally and attack once more. She had no guess as to their progress, but many of them had moved against the weakened Third Division. *Without orders the other Divisions will not move. They cannot support each other if they cannot see. We may yet be defeated* in detail. *Rick says that is nearly always how battles are lost or won.*

"He may be right. Do you wish me to command?"

"Mac Clallan Muir does."

"Then ride to Prince Strymon. Offer to take command of his Division, or to serve him in any other way, and beg him to come here and take command of this army."

"Tylara—"

"You wanted orders, Balquhain. You have them."

"You always did get your way. Yes, Sister. As to my squadrons—"

"Send them to me. Tell them to obey me. I have work for them."

"May I ask what?"

"Balkie, none of us do any good here, and in this rain the guns cannot defend our right flank. I am afraid the enemy will come through there. I will take the clansmen to stopple that hole."

Balquhain grinned. "Hurrah for Tilly! I'll tell Father." He turned his horse, then stopped and looked back. "Tylara—"

"Get out of here!"

"Yes, my lady."

⊹ ⊹ ⊹

The sounds of battle came over the hill. Rick stopped for a moment to listen. "That way!" he shouted. He spurred his horse forward.

"Colonel," MacAllister shouted. "It ain't going to do nobody any good to get there with dead horses!"

"Sh—" Rick caught himself. "Right, Corporal." He reined his horse to a walk. "Who's got the best mount?"

"You do," MacAllister said. "Colonel, we're *all* wore out, and you got to know it."

Which didn't help a bit. Somewhere ahead was a battle. Rick looked at the sheaf of semaphore messages he had received. Tylara's ransom. Tylara's release. Strymon an ally. Castle Fasolt taken. And now a battle in the Ottarn Valley, only that wasn't in any message. "What in hell is going on?" he said aloud.

"Beats me, Colonel," MacAllister said. "I just know it's time to walk the horses."

"Oh, shit. All right, Corporal." As Rick dismounted he wished for a Honda Tricycle.

✢ ✢ ✢

Tylara waited impatiently for Balquhain's squadrons. The rain was falling more heavily. It washed away the smoke from the guns, but still she could not see into the valley below. There were no more sounds of gunfire anywhere, but the other noises of battle were undiminished.

Where are the starmen? More important, where was the king?

Hoofbeats. Drumold rode up through the rain. "I've brought the clansmen, Daughter. Your brother said you had need for us."

"That may be. Certainly we do no good here." She pointed to her right. "There is a gap yonder between the Third Division and the village. Guns were to protect it, but in this rain they cannot fire."

"Does the enemy advance there, then?"

"Father, I don't know. I only know that we do no good waiting here, and if Akkilas brings his cavalry through there we are lost."

"What is the ground there?"

"Solid down the slope. Then mud."

Drumold grinned. "So they come from mud to face us on solid ground?"

Before she could answer, two of her cavalrymen rode up the slope. They reined up and the older one said, "We have heard horsemen in the swamplands."

"How many?"

"We cannot tell. The noises of battle are too great. But horsemen are advancing."

"Well done," Drumold said. "My lady, should we not go to meet them?"

"Father—"

"Lass, I am Mac Clallan Muir, but you are Justiciar of Drantos. I wait your command."

She wheeled her horse and beckoned to her light cavalrymen. "Follow me." She led the way down the slope.

✢ ✢ ✢

The sounds of battle grew louder. *To hell with the horses.* Rick remounted and spurred his mount into a trot. As the slope grew steeper the beast dropped back into a walk. Rick cursed. *One consolation. A walk's easier on my arse than a trot. And thank God Agzaral sent the Preparation H.*

A banner showed in the gloom. Green and white, a stylized megaron device—"Ta-meltemos?" He took the sheaf of semaphore messages from his belt pouch and read again. There was no ambiguity.

STRYMON OF TA-MELTEMOS JOINED TO HOST OF DRANTOS AS ALLY

First time I've ever worried that somebody cracked the semaphore code. "Let's go."

"Who is there?" someone challenged.

"Eqeta Rick, Captain General of Drantos." *And I ought to have your arse for letting me get this close.* "Take me to the Wanax."

An officer rode up hastily. A dozen Guards scrambled after him. The officer stared. "My lord. Your pardon. You were not expected."

"I sent the message by semaphore."

"We have received no semaphore messages for two days. Prince Akkilas' cavalry destroyed the station south of Castle Fasolt."

"All right. I'm here now. Where is the Wanax?"

The Guard officer turned away, then stammered, "My Lord Rick, we do not know."

"What? How in hell can his Guards not know where he is?"

"My Lord, he told us to wait, and rode down into the battle."

"Does he live?"

"We have not heard."

Oh shit. "Who is in charge here?"

"Prince Strymon, my lord."

"Take me to him." *Holy shit.*

✛ ✛ ✛

Rick clasped hands with Prince Strymon.

"My lord," Strymon began. "I—I am pleased to meet you, and apologize for any trouble I may have caused your lady—"

"We haven't a lot of time, Highness," Rick said. "I've already heard that Lady Tylara is safe. Now what's going on here?"

"I wish I knew."

"Jesus Christ. You're in command!"

"My lord, a quarter-hour ago I was summoned by Lord Balquhain to assume command of the army. It took nearly that long to give Lord Balquhain command of my Division and come here. I arrived to find that the Wanax Ganton is there—" He pointed downslope into the rain and smoke. "I am told that the Third Division is in trouble, but I do not yet know what that means, or what to do about it."

"Christ on a crutch. Look, can you at least tell me where the Third Division is?"

"At once." Strymon produced a map from inside his surcoat. He unrolled it. Rain spattered and the ink began to smear.

Rick took the map and tried to orient it. *The enemy is that way. Ah. Here's the ridge we're on.* He turned the map so that it faced the same direction as the terrain. "Third Division. This one?"

"Yes," Strymon said.

"And the other Divisions? What's in them?"

Strymon shrugged. "Everything. Pikes, horses, archers—"

"I see." *Damn kid took my lesson in Napoleonic organization too bloody seriously.* "But First and Second are intact?"

"First certainly is. I believe Second is as well."

"Reserves." Rick pointed. By now the rain had half-washed away the marks on the parchment. "Tamaerthans here."

"No longer," Strymon said. "They were brought around to secure our right flank. Your lady and her father lead them."

"Good." *Okay. Right flank secure. Maybe. No need to ask what's happened to the guns. In this rain we'll be lucky if they get off a round every hour.* "Highness, you had First Division?"

"Yes."

"Any action?"

"We were charged by cavalry earlier this morning. The guns dealt with most of it. I took few losses."

"Have you ever commanded pikemen?"

"Not until this morning."

Yeah. But as a distinguished ally, you had to have a suitable command. Holding the left flank. "Your orders were to hold?"

"Yes. I would have preferred a more active role."

"You'll get it." He rose in his stirrups. "Ark!"

Passovopolous rode a mule. Nothing else would carry him for long. "Sir!"

"Take the weapons squad down there." He pointed off to his right.

"Go that way and down hill until you get to the village. Get through it and set up the weapons with a good field of fire."

"Colonel—"

"I know, I know, you can't see a damn thing. Just do the best you can. You go set up and wait. You're the anvil. Someone find me a fresh horse. I have to go get the hammer."

✢ ✢ ✢

It took five minutes for the staff officers to find Teuthras and bring him to the rear of the Second Division. Rick kept glancing at his watch. *Tylara, Tylara. Are you safe? Where are you, my love?* It would do no good to go riding after her. The battle had to be won. *I heard she rode right into the enemy lines at Piro's Hill. Bull shit. She's not like that. So why do people tell me that?*

"My Lord Rick," Teuthras shouted. "Welcome."

"Thanks. My lord, what is happening with your Division?"

"Little. We heard sounds of fighting in the Third, but we have had little of the battle for an hour."

"What are you doing to support Third?"

"What can we do? I have sent cavalry to stand ready in case we are ordered to attack, but—"

"I see." *Shit fire. For years I tried to get them to obey orders and not just go charging off to the thickest fighting. Now we'd have been better off if they'd never learned any discipline.* "Thank you. My lord, I intend to send First Division across your front, then pivot and move down toward the Ottarn. We will sweep the enemy before us into the star weapons I have placed near the river village."

Teuthras grinned widely. "How can we help?"

"Second Division will be vital. As we cross your front, the enemy's cavalry to the northeast will fall on First Division's rear. When they do, you must move forward to counterattack and cover us."

"Ah! Gladly."

"I will also want your pikemen in the vanguard of that counterattack. It may be that I will assume personal command of those pikemen."

Teuthras frowned. "I would hate to lose them."

So you would. You know more about pikemen than any of the other Division commanders. "Belay that. I'll leave you First Division's pikes," Rick said. "What you must do is use the pikes as a walking wall to shield the rear of First Division's sweep."

Teuthras looked thoughtful, then grinned. "Aye!" He looked up into the sky and blinked away the raindrops from his eyes. "Alas, we cannot support them properly with archers. But then the enemy cannot attack the pikes with archers, either. Lord Rick—where is the Wanax?"

Beats the shit out of me. "Rallying Third Division."

"Ah. That's Ganton. In the thick of the fighting." Teuthras grinned widely. "I had not heard you would be here, but well come, my lord. Well come."

⁜ ⁜ ⁜

Balquhain's shout of welcome left no doubt of its warmth. "You have come to take command!"

"More or less. I left Prince Strymon in charge at headquarters."

"Have you seen Tylara?"

"No, dammit! And I can't go looking for her until I get things moving."

"Aye. What must I do?"

Good man. Rick held out the rain-spattered parchment. The ink had long ago blurred to meaningless smears. He pointed to the top left blob. "We are here. We're going to take your cavalry straight east, across Second Division's front, then pivot on Second and sweep down toward the river. Lord Passovopolous and the weapons squad are set up there."

Balquhain frowned. "My lord—will the others not come through the gap I have left and attack the others from behind?"

"I was getting to that. You're making the sweep with the cavalry. As you advance, leave the pikes behind. Teuthras will add his pikemen to yours. I'm leaving two Star Lords with rifles. That's more than enough to hold this line."

Balquhain considered that for a moment. "Especially in this confusion. Akkilas cannot know more about this battle than we do. Good. Another question, my lord. We attack from one side, and drive the enemy toward the river, but what is to prevent them from running east?"

"Nothing. I want them to. My lord, we aren't trying to win any great victory here. Once those troops start running in this rain and mud it will take a ten-day to make a fighting force out of them again. By then the rest of the Drantos chivalry will be here."

"I see." Balquhain grinned. "And by then *you* will be in command."

✤ ✤ ✤

Balquhain's trumpets sounded. His cavalrymen moved out in good formation at a slow walk. Pikemen marched to beat of drums to close across the front the cavalry had vacated. Archers stood behind the pikemen. Most had unstrung their bows to dry the bowstrings inside their clothing.

At first there was no opposition. The rain fell harder. *A hundred yards visibility. If that.* Rick looked around to be sure that a full score of staff officers, mostly young squires from the great houses, were following him. They didn't look happy to be left out of the fighting, although Rick had told them that communications would be the most important weapon Drantos had. He sent one officer out to the left side. "Just see what's happening, and be sure the formation's holding," Rick said. "And when you see the enemy, ride like hell back here. Don't get in the fighting."

"Yes, sir." The squire didn't look happy, but Rick thought he'd do it.

The right flankers reached the edge of Second Division. "Here's where it gets tricky," Rick muttered. He sent another messenger to the left flank. "Tell them to start the sweep." As the boy galloped away, he sent a third rider to the right.

"Slower, damn you!" Rick shouted at the troops in front of him. "Wait for the men on your left!" He turned to his messenger pool. "Ride down the line shouting that."

The trouble with great turning maneuvers was that the troops at the pivot had to stay in position while those at the end covered a large arc. Since everyone wanted to get it over with, there was a tendency for those nearest the pivot to move too fast. This could leave gaps in the line. Worse, the whole front might bow backward.

The first squire Rick had sent to the left galloped back. "Enemy in sight. Light cavalry ahead and to the left."

"Which way was that?"

The boy thought for a moment, then pointed.

"Good. Now go tell Lord Balquhain please to send a company of the reserves to watch them. Watch and nothing else."

They continued at a fast walk. Rick peered ahead into the rain. Suddenly a man on his left shouted. "There they are!"

They were dead ahead, a ragged line of heavy cavalrymen. They were nearly flank on to Rick. The far end of the enemy line was visible in the gloom. "Trumpeter! Sound the trot. Have at 'em!"

The enemy commander tried to rally his troops, but it was too late. Caught in the flank, fifty men of the enemy right faced a thousand of Rick's heavies. Before Rick's cavalrymen could reach the enemy's right flank it dissolved as first individuals, then whole squads turned to ride away into the rain. Within minutes there wasn't an enemy to be seen. "Sound the walk," Rick said. "And get the goddamn line dressed again."

✢ ✢ ✢

"It's the waiting I hate," Drumold said.

"Yes." Tylara cupped her hand behind her ear and listened. Definitely closer, she thought. There were at least a hundred men out in the swamp. *Probably many more. It would be foolish to send only a hundred.*

"I'm thinking we may be too many here," Drumold said.

Tylara shrugged. "We can only guess."

"Aye. I know." Drumold pointed off to his left front. "And that way the ground is solid enough, if it's needed that we join the main battle. I think you've chosen well." He hunched his shoulders and drew his cloak closer around him.

He looks old today.

A rider came up behind her. "My lady! Lord Rick has come!"

"Rick!" *Prayers are answered, then.* "Where is he?"

"My lady, he asked after you, then took command. He goes to bring the First Division down to the aid of Third."

"I see." Tylara closed her eyes and brought up a mental picture of the battlefront. She could see First Division sweep around Second, move down and to the right—"Where are his star warriors?"

"They were sent to hold yonder village."

Tylara frowned. Why would Rick do that? She brought up her mental picture again. *Ah. To be certain the enemy does not get past us.* "Well done, kinsman. Now, if you will, go find Lord Rick and tell him where we are and in what strength. Tell him also that Mac Clallan Muir and the Eqetassa of Chelm await his commands."

✢ ✢ ✢

Rick rode up to Balquhain and drew his horse to a walk. "The tricky part's done," he said.

They'd run into three more enemy formations. Two had run. The third had a more able commander. He rallied his soldiers into something like a charge, but couldn't get them into a useful formation. They'd struck in driblets rather than all at once, and were driven away like the others.

Rick pointed ahead. "Now all we have to do is go forward. Teuthras can guard our rear. Our left is vulnerable, but not if we keep the reserves out there. The important thing is not to use up the reserves chasing shadows."

A messenger rode up. "Lord Teuthras says the pikes are now in line."

"Good. Now go up and report to Prince Strymon. Tell him where we are, and where the pikes are, and anything else you know."

"Yes, sir—" The boy rode away.

"He'll be thinking this a strange kind of war," Balquhain said. "All riding and no fighting."

"I'll be glad enough if we've done all the fighting we're going to do." *We haven't, though. When we start closing this box—*

Another messenger came up. *Ha. That's the boy I sent looking for Rudhrig.* "Report, lad!"

"Lord Rick! I bring commands from the Wanax."

Well I will be go to hell. "Uh, what would His Royal Majesty like us to do?"

"He said to greet you welcome in his name, and say that you should come to his aid."

"Thank you."

"Generous of him," Balquhain muttered.

"I expect he's in trouble," Rick said quietly. He raised his voice. "Where is the king?"

"He said to say: 'I stand where the banner of Third Division stood as the day began. There are enemies a hundred paces away.' "

Aha. "That would be near the center of the old square. Lord Balquhain, I think we must shift to our right."

"I agree."

On a parade ground I'd just say 'Right Oblique, March.' This is going to be a bit tougher. Rick called his messengers together.

✤ ✤ ✤

"Enemy in sight!" The shout went up from a dozen men at once as the rain slacked off.

"Well, my lord, we have found the fighting you wanted," Rick said.

Balquhain grinned. They had reached what had been the corner of Third Division. Now it was covered with enemies, thousands dead but many thousands more still alive and fighting. None faced Rick's force.

"Sound the charge," Balquhain ordered.

"Damn right! Go like hell." *Nothing like surprise.* "Messenger, ask Lord Teuthras to send any cavalry he can spare. Have them come directly here." He drew his sword and rose in his stirrups as the trumpeters sounded the charge.

✣ ✣ ✣

Tylara heard the trumpets sound charge just as the rain stopped. "To your horses!" Drumold shouted. "Ah, lass, now I truly believe your husband is here."

Ha! I had not planned for our first meeting to be on a battlefield, but now I think it is well.

Minutes later enemy cavalry galloped into view. They veered off at the sight of the Tamaerthan chivalry.

"Should we not charge?" Drumold asked.

"I think not yet." *Rick, where are you?* "I think there will be more, soon, and it is best we wait."

The enemy was out of sight in moments. Then, suddenly, Tylara heard the sound of star weapons to her right. "The—*light machine-gun!* Lord Rick must have brought another."

Drumold raised the nasal bar of his helmet and grinned. "Whoever was thrashing about in yon swamp will have good company I'm thinking. I doubt we've aught to fear from that place now."

Tylara smiled agreement. Few captains could get men to go forward through retreating comrades. None could make them do it against star weapons. "It means, I think, that we are free to do whatever we think best," Tylara said.

The rain had stopped, but she still couldn't see much. Far ahead and to her left were the pickets marking the rear of Third Division's area. Off to the right was the village, and somewhere beyond it were Rick's starmen.

More trumpets sounded far to the left. *That must be Rick. It must be! Who else could win the day two hours after he came to the battle?* She turned to Drumold and grinned. "Is it no time that the clansmen had their wish? Yonder trumpets signal the charge. Shall we no obey?"

Drumold drew his sword and stood in his stirrups. "Aye, Lass. Forward!"

Tylara spurred her horse to a trot. Soon enough the thin mud of the slope changed to the deeper mud of the valley. The Tamaerthan forces angled off to their left, trying to stay on more solid ground. They had gone a quarter mile when Tylara remembered to send messengers, to Strymon, and to Rick and Ganton if they could find them.

The rain began again as they passed the corner of Third Division's old square. Now the wind came up from behind her. *A good sign. It drives the rain into the enemy's face, not ours.* The sounds of battle were louder.

She turned to one of her officers. "Go and find Lord Rudhrig. Be sure he knows that we are here. I would no care to be charged by his horsemen."

"There, lass." Drumold pointed.

A gust of wind blew away smoke and rain for seconds. The enemy was ahead.

"We can no do a proper charge in this mud," Drumold said. "But we can try." He stood in his stirrups. "Charge!"

Someone behind shouted "Mac Clallan Muir!" A thousand more took up the cry. Kettledrums and horns sounded. The clansmen spurred forward.

✤ ✤ ✤

Matthias cursed the rain. Victory lay less than a hundred paces ahead, where Ganton stood in his golden helmet beneath the banner of the Fighting Man. They had only to kill Ganton and the war was over. Akkilas would have no difficulty persuading the barons of Drantos that this was no time for an infant Wanax.

Men fell all around him, but he was untouched. "Forward! Forward to victory!"

The spearmen of Ta-Kartos advanced. They struck the shield wall of Ganton's bodyguards, and the battle held there. Whenever a man fell on either side, another replaced him. The rain cleared for a moment. Matthias looked around for more forces to throw into the attack. He had waved a new group of infantry forward when he heard horns.

Drantos horns. "What call is that?" he demanded of an acolyte.

"Honorable, it is their charge."

Matthias cursed. "They have brought up the others at last." Where were the blocking forces he had set to watch the enemy's middlemost battle? No matter. Clearly they had been driven away without even sounding an alarm. "Captain Volauf! Press forward here! I go to meet this new attack."

"As you will, Honorable."

His spirit is broken, I think. Better to leave him here than to let him run away. Matthias signaled to his personal guards. Many of them were veterans of the southern wars. There were only two hundred, but they were all he had left. "Follow me! Find the enemy commander and slay him." *It is all we can do. It may be enough.*

Matthias mounted. He thought it would not be easy to get through his own troops, dead and living, but he found the Drantos forces were much closer than he had expected.

The day is lost. Why has Vothan given victory to our enemies? The wind blew into a real storm, but through the gusts of driving rain he caught sight of the banners ahead. The leaders of this new attack.

Could we yet win? We still have more strength than Ganton. Kill these leaders and this attack comes to naught. Then I can return to kill Ganton. We have not lost yet. "Forward!" He galloped toward the banners, and rejoiced to hear the hoofbeats of his men following close behind.

The fury of his charge carried him through the first of the enemy's line. "Ignore those!" he shouted to his followers. "Ride for their banners! Kill the leaders."

Now he was close enough to see the banners clearly, and he rejoiced. The War Lord of Drantos led here! His death would harm the Drantos cause nearly as much as Ganton's.

Matthias's horse was tiring. A dozen of his followers came level with him, then passed him. They dashed on toward the banners.

✦ ✦ ✦

Tylara's light cavalry dashed ahead of Drumold's heavy chivalry. The surprise was total. Much of the enemy cavalry was dismounted, and their infantry faced Tylara's left. In the distance she could see the shield wall of Ganton's Guards, and behind that his banners. She rose in her stirrups to look back at Drumold, and pointed toward the Fighting Man with her axe.

She couldn't hear his acknowledgment, but he waved to his left and his heavy cavalrymen struck the Ta-Kartos spearmen from behind.

Tylara nodded in satisfaction and waved her own men ahead, toward where she had last heard Rick's trumpets. *They must be his. And I will go to him.*

The Tamaerthan Hussars swept through the disorganized enemy. None fought, except to defend their own persons, and as soon as they were not threatened they ran away. A whole block of cavalry led by a great banner crossed just behind Tylara. Infantrymen clung to the horsemen's stirrups. All fled to the east. Others ran behind them, some calling to their comrades to hold up.

"We have won!" Tylara shouted. "Victory! For Yatar and Christ!" Rain swept across the field. She could see nothing, but ahead she heard the sounds of fighting, swords against shields. Then the rapid fire of a battle rifle. Pistol shots.

"Rick!" she waved toward the sounds and spurred her horse on. She slapped him gently on the neck. "On! On my wonder!" *If you live through this day, I will see you have apples every day forever.* "Drantos! For Yatar, Christ, and Drantos!"

There were cavalrymen ahead. A solid formation, in line—

"Drantos!" she cried again.

They answered. "Drantos!"

More rifle fire to the right, and now three pistols shots, rapidly.

✦ ✦ ✦

Rick took out a flask of brandy and drank a hefty shot.

Done, he thought. The enemy ahead couldn't run away fast enough. First Division's charge carried right through the enemy lines, such as they were. Anyone who didn't run away could be left to Teuthras' cleanup squads.

Now to find Tylara. Oh. And the king. He waved the troops forward at a walk. "Save the horses," he called. "Pass it on."

The line was stretched too thin, but that couldn't matter. The only opposition was from disoriented enemies who couldn't see that the way east was clear and thought they had to fight to escape. It didn't take long to kill them or chase them off.

The wind came up from the southwest and turned the squall into a real rainstorm. Gusts drove cold rain into Rick's face. Rick wiped his eyes. "I won't be sorry for a fire tonight."

"Me either, Cap'n." MacAllister rode alongside. "Any chance there's more in that flask, sir?"

I don't really encourage— "Sure." Rick took out the flask and handed it over. "You didn't get much action today."

"All I want, Captain."

"Me too—" Rick lifted his helmet and listened. "What in hell is that?"

"Cavalry—" MacAllister unslung his H&K battle rifle. "Coming right at us, I'd say."

"Who in hell?" Now he could see the galloping horsemen. Rick stood in his stirrups. "Drantos!" he called.

"Holy shit!" MacAllister shouted. "They sure ain't ours!" He shouldered the weapon and fired, slowly and deliberately. The oncoming cavalrymen dropped one by one. Still they charged onward. "Jesus Christ, Cap'n, it's *us* they want!"

Rick shifted his sword to his left hand and drew his Colt. He thumbed off the safety. *Wish I'd kept a rifle for myself. Never was much good with this—*

MacAllister fired the rest of his clip. The oncoming enemy was no more than ten yards away now. One group dashed at Balquhain. Henchmen rallied to him.

Rick's first round took the lead man full in the chest. He wheeled to his right to avoid the second, then shot the man as he came closer. He wanted to use a two-handed grip, but he didn't dare let go of the sword in his left hand, and there was no time to sheathe it.

He fired three times, rapidly, and prayed that MacAllister would be able to reload in time. Then he was surrounded by enemies, and his pistol was empty.

He managed to thrust the Colt back in its holster and shift his sword to his right hand. As he did, his orderly spurred forward to take his place on his left. "Your shield!" Jamiy shouted.

Before Rick could take it, another horseman was on him. Rick parried the sword thrust and the man swept past. Rick had no chance to see what happened to him.

Ahead were half a dozen more of the enemy. The one in the center wore the robes of a priest of Vothan over mail, and carried a sword. He was screaming curses.

Rick looked around for MacAllister but couldn't see him. He heard more riders coming up fast from his right front. *Looks like this is it.*

"For Yatar and Christ!"

What? Who says that?

A rider in flowing cape appeared out of the rain beyond the enemy cavalry. The rider's cape and long black hair streamed in the wind. A woman. She whirled an axe over her head, and screamed war cries. *My God, a Valkyrie!*

The priest of Vothan turned to look. He stared, then slumped in his saddle. His sword fell forgotten as he turned to face the oncoming apparition. "Father Vothan! I come!"

Good God, it's Tylara!

She rode past the mailed priest and struck at him with her axe. It knocked his helmet askew and he fell. His companions halted. One dismounted, and with the aid of another lifted the priest so that he lay across the saddle of his horse. They led him away.

Two of Balquhain's henchmen rode after him, but the priest's companions turned to fight.

"Let be!" Balquhain shouted. "There's few enough with that courage."

Tylara reined up alongside Rick. "My husband. I have come."

Rick drew a deep breath. "So I see. What kept you?" He stood in his stirrups to look around the battlefield. The last of the enemy were riding away to his left. Behind him MacAllister was getting to his feet beside his fallen horse. "But just in time. Well come." Rick sheathed his sword and drew the Colt. "Do you have any ammunition?"

"Why—yes."

"Then why the hell didn't you use it instead of that goddamn axe?" He leaned closer and touched her hair. "And for Christ's sake, you're not even wearing a helmet!"

She gripped his hand and held it against her cheek. "Forgive me, my lord. My husband. I did not think—"

"Yeah. Neither one of us has done much thinking for a while." He squeezed her hand and let go, then leaned back and whacked her horse on the rump. "Race you back to Ganton's tent!"

She steadied her mount and grinned back at him. They spurred their horses and galloped together into the storm.

the Frigid Lands

NIKEIS

T H E   E M P I R E

TAR KARTOS

ROMA

GARIOCH

TAMAERTHON

N

Roman
Provinces

Roman Battle

CROPLANDS

RESERVES

LEGIONS (PUBLIUS)

FOOT (MARSELIUS)

LEGION

CHIVALRY

MILITARY ROAD

SECONDARY ROAD

dirt track

ORCHARD

SWAMP

FOREST

The Battle with the Westmen

BATTLE OF VIS

Lynos River

Balloon

Gengrich

City Levies

Galloway Pikes

Ganton

8 Publius

Pikes

Great Redoubt

17

Defenders

Herdsman's Ford

Drumold/ Mason

Phrados

Rudhrig

To Vis

High Road

Village

Matthais

Defenders

Phrados's Camp

Farm

Dnaster River

N
E
W
S

T-Tamaerthan troops
R-Roman troops
D-Drantos troops
C-City troops
(black or white) - infantry troops
cavalry troops
trees
hill
cannons in place

BATTLE OF THE OTTARN

Ottarn River

Swamp

Ford

Village

Rudhrig

3rd Division

Teuthras

2nd Division

Strymon

1st Division

Ganton

Reserves (incl. Starmen)

Allied Camp

High Road

Village

① Marthais's attack
② Ti-kantos attack
③ Tyfara's charge
④ Rick's charge

⌃ hill
cannons
swamp
▲ village